Peter V. Brett is the international bestselling author of *The Painted Man* and *The Desert Spear*. Raised on a steady diet of fantasy novels, comic books and Dungeons & Dragons, Brett has been writing fantasy stories for as long as he can remember. He received a Bachelor of Arts degree in English literature and art history from the University at Buffalo in 1995, and then spent more than a decade in pharmaceutical publishing before returning to his bliss. He lives in Brooklyn.

www.petervbrett.com
Twitter @pvbrett
http://www.facebook.com/petervbrett

D0278833

By the same author

The Painted Man
The Desert Spear
The Daylight War

Short Stories

The Great Bazaar and Brayan's Gold

PETER V. BRETT

THE DAYLIGHT WAR

HARPER
Voyager

Harper*Voyager*
HarperCollins*Publishers*
77–85 Fulham Palace Road,
Hammersmith, London W6 8JB

www.harpercollins.co.uk

This paperback edition 2013

1

First published in Great Britain
by Harper*Voyager* 2013

A catalogue record for this book
is available from the British Library

ISBN: 978 0 00 727620 2

Typeset in Sabon by Palimpsest Book Production Ltd, Falkirk, Stirlingshire

Printed and bound in Great Britain by
Clays Ltd, St Ives plc

Map by Andrew Ashton

MIX
Paper from
responsible sources
FSC
www.fsc.org   **FSC® C007454**

For my parents, John and Dolores, who still read together on the couch at night.

Acknowledgements

Increasingly paranoid as I get older, I played this book closer to the cuff than any in the past. I let only a handful of people peek at the work in progress, and am eternally grateful for their thoughts and input. Thanks most of all to my agent, Joshua, as well as Myke, Lauren, and Dani, my editors, Tricia and Emma, my assistants, Meg and Rebecca, copyeditor Laura, and the international publishers and translators who have worked so tirelessly to bring my stories to other parts of the world. Special thanks to all my readers, especially those who have taken the time to get in touch. Your letters, comments, tweets, posts, online reviews, fan contest entries, and the like have been a needed bedrock of support and circle of succour as I ascend Demon Cycle Mountain. Thanks for climbing with me.

Contents

Prologue: *Inevera*   1

Chapter 1: Arlen   37

Chapter 2: Promise   57

Chapter 3: The Oatingers   69

Chapter 4: Second Coming   90

Chapter 5: Tender Hayes   128

Chapter 6: The Earring   152

Chapter 7: Training   157

Chapter 8: *Sharum* Do Not Bend   198

Chapter 9: Ahmann   235

Chapter 10: Kenevah's Concern   258

Chapter 11: Last Meal   276

Chapter 12: The Hundred   302

Chapter 13: Playing the Crowd   329

Chapter 14: The *Song of Waning*   347

Chapter 15: The Paper Women   389

Chapter 16: Where *Khaffit* Cannot Follow   407

Chapter 17: *Zahven*   434

Chapter 18: Strained Meeting   450

Chapter 19: Spit and Wind   488

Chapter 20: A Single Witness   510

Chapter 21: Auras   542

Chapter 22: New Moon   573

Chapter 23: Trap   600

Chapter 24: Attrition   634

Chapter 25: Lost Circle   653

Chapter 26: *Sharum'ting*   663

Chapter 27: Waning   701

Chapter 28: Early Harvest   721

Chapter 29: Eunuch   737

Chapter 30: My True Friend   759

Chapter 31: Alive   770

Chapter 32: *Domin Sharum*   778

Krasian Dictionary   792

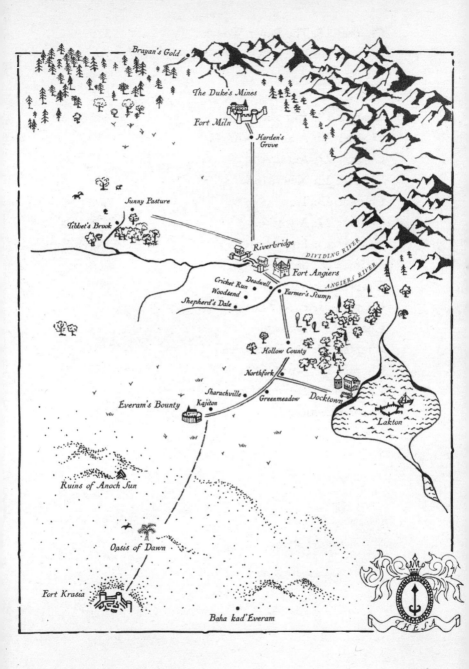

PROLOGUE

Inevera

300 AR

Inevera and her brother Soli sat in the sunlight. Each held the frame of a basket between their bare feet, nimbly turning it as their fingers worked the weave. This late in the day, there was only a tiny sliver of shade in their small kiosk. Their mother, Manvah, sat there, working her own basket. The pile of tough date palm fronds at the centre of the ring they formed shrank steadily as they worked.

Inevera was nine years old. Soli was almost twice that, but still young to be wearing the robes of a full *dal'Sharum*, the black cloth still deep with fresh dye. He had earned them barely a week ago, and sat on a mat to ensure the ever-present dust of the Great Bazaar did not cling to them. His robe was cinched loosely on top, revealing a smooth, muscular chest glistening with sweat.

He fanned himself with a frond. 'Everam's balls, these robes are hot. I wish I could still go out in just a bido.'

'You may have the shade if you wish it, Sharum,' Manvah said.

Soli tsked and shook his head. 'Is that what you expected? That I would come back in black and start ordering you around like . . .'

Manvah chuckled. 'Just making certain you remain my sweet boy.'

'Only to you and my dear little sister,' Soli clarified, reaching out to tousle Inevera's hair. She slapped his arm away, but she was smiling as she did it. There was always smiling when Soli was about. 'With everyone else, I am mean as a sand demon.'

'Bah,' Manvah said, waving the thought away, but Inevera wondered. She'd seen what he did to the two Majah boys who teased her in the bazaar when they were younger, and the weak did not survive in the night.

Inevera finished her basket, adding it to one of the many stacks. She counted quickly. 'Three more, and we'll have Dama Baden's order complete.'

'Maybe Cashiv will invite me to the Waxing Party when he picks them up,' Soli said. Cashiv was Dama Baden's *kai'Sharum* and Soli's *ajin'pal*, the warrior who had been tethered to him and fought by his side on his first night in the Maze. It was said there was no greater bond two men could share.

Manvah snorted. 'If he does, Dama Baden will have you carrying one oiled and naked, celebrating the Waxing by offering a full moon of your own to his lecherous old hangers-on.'

Soli laughed. 'I hear it's not the old ones you need to worry about. Most of them just look. It's the younger ones that carry vials of oil in their belts.'

He sighed. 'Still, Gerraz served at Dama Baden's last spear party and said the *dama* gave him two hundred draki. That's worth a sore backside.'

'Don't let your father hear you say that,' Manvah warned. Soli's eyes flicked to the curtained chamber at the back of the kiosk where their father slept.

'He's going to find out his son is *push'ting* sooner or later,' Soli said. 'I won't marry some poor girl just to keep him from finding out.'

'Why not?' Manvah asked. 'She could weave with us, and

2

would it be so terrible to seed her a few times and give me grandchildren?'

Soli made a face. 'You'll need to wait on Inevera for that.' He looked at her. '*Hannu Pash* tomorrow, dear sister. Perhaps the *dama'ting* will find you a husband!'

'Don't change the subject!' Manvah slapped at him with a palm frond. 'You'll face what's between the Maze walls, but not what's between a woman's thighs?'

Soli grimaced. 'At least in the Maze I am surrounded by strong, sweating men. And who knows? Perhaps one of the *push'ting dama* will fancy me. The powerful ones like Baden make their favourite *Sharum* into personal guards who only have to fight on Waning! Imagine, only three nights a month in the Maze!'

'Still three nights too many,' Manvah muttered.

Inevera was confused. 'Is the Maze not a holy place? An honour?'

Manvah grunted and went back to her weaving. Soli looked at her a long time, his eyes distant. The easy smile melted from his face.

'The Maze is holy death,' her brother said at last. 'A man who dies there is guaranteed Heaven, but I am not so eager to meet Everam just yet.'

'I'm sorry,' Inevera said.

Soli shook himself, and the smile returned in an instant. 'Best not concern yourself with such things, little sister. The Maze is not a burden for you to bear.'

'Every woman in Krasia bears that burden, my son,' Manvah said, 'whether we fight beside you or not.'

Just then there was a groan and a rustling behind the curtain in the back of the kiosk. A moment later Kasaad emerged. Inevera's father didn't even look at Manvah as he nudged her out of the shade with his boot to take the coveted spot for himself. He threw a pair of pillows to the ground and lounged upon them, already tipping back a tiny cup of couzi. Immediately

3

he poured another, squinting in the light. As always, his eyes passed over Inevera as if she didn't exist, settling quickly on her brother.

'Soli! Put that basket down! You are *Sharum* now, and should not be working your hands like a *khaffit*!'

'Father, we have an order due shortly,' Soli said. 'Cashiv . . .'

'Pfagh!' Kasaad said, waving his hand dismissively. 'I don't care what that oiled and scented *push'ting* wants! Put that basket down and get up before someone sees you sullying your new blacks. Bad enough we must waste our day in the filthy bazaar.'

'It's like he has no idea where money comes from,' Soli grumbled, too low for Kasaad to hear. He didn't stop weaving.

'Or the food on his table.' Manvah rolled her eyes. She sighed. 'Best do as he says.'

'If I am *Sharum* now, I can do what I want. Who is he to tell me I cannot weave palm, if that gives me peace?' As Soli spoke, his hands moved even faster, fingers a blur as he wove the fronds. He was close to the end of a basket, and he meant to finish it. Inevera looked on in wonder. Soli could weave almost as fast as Manvah.

'He is your father,' Manvah said, 'and if you don't do as he says, we'll all regret it.'

She turned to Kasaad, her voice sweetening. 'You and Soli need only stay till the *dama* call the gloaming, husband.'

Kasaad's face soured, and he threw back another cup. 'How did I so offend Everam, that I, the great Kasaad asu Kasaad am'Damaj am'Kaji, who has sent *alagai* beyond count to the abyss, should be lowered to guarding a pile of baskets?' He swept a hand towards the stacks of their work with a look of disgust. 'I should be mustering for *alagai'sharak* and the night's glory!'

'Drinking with the other *Sharum*, he means,' Soli murmured to Inevera. 'The units that muster early go to the centre of the Maze, where the fighting is fierce. The longer he lounges, the less his chance of actually having to face an *alagai* while he's drunk as camel piss on couzi.'

Couzi. Inevera hated the drink. Fermented grain flavoured with cinnamon, it was sold in tiny clay bottles and sipped from even tinier cups. Just sniffing an emptied bottle burned Inevera's nostrils and left her dizzy. There was no hint of cinnamon in the scent. It was said the taste only became clear after three cups, but after three cups of couzi, whose word could be trusted? It was known to lend itself to exaggeration and delusions of grandeur.

'Soli!' Kasaad snapped. 'Leave the work to the women and come drink with me! We will toast the deaths of the four *alagai* you slew last night!'

'You would think I did the whole unit's work myself,' Soli grumbled. His fingers moved even faster. 'I do not drink couzi, Father,' he called. 'The Evejah forbids it.'

Kasaad snorted, tipping back another cup. 'Manvah! Prepare your *sharik* son some tea, then!' He tipped the couzi bottle to his cup again, but this time only a few drops fell. 'And bring me another couzi.'

'Everam give me patience,' Manvah muttered. 'That was the last bottle, husband,' she called.

'Then go and buy more,' Kasaad snapped.

Inevera could hear her mother's teeth grind. 'Half the tents in the bazaar are already closed, husband, and we must finish these baskets before Cashiv arrives.'

Kasaad waved a hand in disgust. 'Who cares if that worthless *push'ting* has to wait?'

Soli drew a sharp breath, and Inevera saw a smear of blood on his hand, cut from the sharp edge of a palm frond. He gritted his teeth and wove on.

'Forgive me, honoured husband, but Dama Baden's factor will not wait,' Manvah said, continuing her own weave. 'If Cashiv arrives and the order isn't ready, he will go down the lane and buy his baskets from Krisha again. Without this order, we won't have money to pay our war tax, much less buy more couzi.'

'What?!' Kasaad shouted. 'What have you been doing with my money? I bring home a hundred draki a week!'

'Half of which goes right back to the *dama* in war tax,' Manvah said, 'and you always take twenty more for your pockets. The rest goes to keep you in couzi and couscous, and it isn't enough by far, especially when you bring home half a dozen thirsty *Sharum* every Sabbath. Couzi is expensive, husband. The *dama* cut the thumbs from *khaffit* caught selling it, and they add the risk to the price.'

Kasaad spat. '*Khaffit* would sell the sun if they could pull it from the sky. Now run and buy some to help ease my wait for that half-man.'

Soli finished his basket, rising and slamming it down atop his pile. 'I'll go, Mother. Chabin will have some, and he never closes before gloaming is sung.'

Manvah's eyes tightened, but she did not take them from her weaving. She, too, had begun weaving faster, and now her hands were a blur. 'I don't like you leaving when we have a month's work sitting out in the open.'

'No one will rob us with Father right there,' Soli said, but as he looked to his father, trying to lick a last drop from the couzi bottle, he sighed. 'I will be so swift you won't even know I've gone.'

'Back to work, Inevera,' Manvah snapped as Soli ran off. Inevera looked down, realizing only then that she had stopped weaving as she watched the events unfold. Quickly she resumed.

Inevera would not dare look right at him, but she could not help watching her father out of the corner of her eye. He was eyeing Manvah as she turned the basket with her nimble feet. Her black robes had risen as she worked, exposing her bare ankles and calves.

Kasaad put one hand to his crotch, rubbing. 'Come here, wife, I would . . .'

'I. Am. Working!' Manvah took a palm branch from the pile, breaking fronds from it with sharp snaps.

Kasaad seemed genuinely confused at her reaction. 'Why would you refuse your husband, barely an hour before he goes into the night?'

'Because I've been breaking my back over these baskets for weeks,' Manvah said. 'Because it's late and the lane's gone quiet. And because we've got a full stock out with no one to guard it but a horny drunk!'

Kasaad barked a laugh. 'Guard it from who?'

'Who, indeed?' a voice asked, and all turned to see Krisha stepping around the counter and into the kiosk.

Krisha was a big woman. Not fat – few in the Desert Spear enjoyed that luxury – but a warrior's daughter, thickly set with a heavy stride and callused hands. Like all *dal'ting*, she wore the same head-to-toe black cloth as Manvah. She was a weaver as well, one of Manvah's principal rivals in the Kaji tribe – less skilled, but more ambitious.

She was followed into the tent by four other women in *dal'ting* black. Two were her sister-wives, their faces covered in black. The others were her daughters, unmarried, their faces bare. From the looks of them, this drove away more potential husbands than it invited. None of the women was small, and they spread like jackals stalking a hare.

'You're working late,' Krisha noted. 'Most of the pavilions have tied their flaps.'

Manvah shrugged, not taking her eyes off her weaving. 'The call to curfew isn't for the better of an hour.'

'Cashiv always comes at the end of the day before Dama Baden's Waxing Party, does he not?' Krisha said.

Manvah did not look up. 'My clients do not concern you, Krisha.'

'They do when you use your *push'ting* son to steal them from me,' Krisha said, her voice low and dangerous. Her daughters moved to Inevera, separating her from her mother. Her sister-wives moved deeper into the kiosk towards Kasaad.

Manvah looked up at this. 'I stole nothing. Cashiv came to

me, saying your baskets fell apart when filled. Blame your weavers and not me for the loss of business.'

Krisha nodded, picking up the basket Inevera had just added to the pile. 'You and your daughter do fine work,' she noted, tracing a finger along the weave. Then she threw the basket to the ground, stomping down hard on it with her sandalled foot.

'Woman, you dare?!' Kasaad shouted in shocked disbelief. He leapt to his feet, or tried to, wobbling unsteadily. He glanced for his spear and shield, but they were back in the tent.

While he was finding his wits, Krisha's sister-wives moved in unison. Short rattan staves wrapped in black cloth fell into their hands from out of voluminous sleeves. One of the women grabbed Kasaad by the shoulders, turning him into the other's thrust to his stomach, holding him to make sure he took the full brunt. Kasaad grunted in pain, the wind knocked from him, and the woman followed up the blow with a full swing to the groin. Kasaad's grunt became a shriek.

Inevera gave a cry and leapt to her feet, but Krisha's daughters grabbed her roughly. Manvah moved to rise as well, but Krisha's heavy kick to the face knocked her back to the ground. She gave a great wail, but it was late and there was no answering cry.

Krisha looked down at the basket on the floor. It had resisted her stomp, returning to its original shape. Inevera smiled until the woman leapt on top of it, jumping three times until the basket collapsed.

Across the kiosk, Krisha's sister-wives continued to beat Kasaad. 'He shrieks like a woman,' one laughed, again striking him between the legs.

'And he fights even worse!' the other cried. They let go of his shoulders, and Kasaad collapsed to the floor, gasping, his face a mix of pain and humiliation. The women left him and went to work kicking over the stacks and smashing baskets with their rattan staves.

Inevera tried to pull free, but the young women only tightened

8

their grips. 'Be still, or we will break your fingers so you can weave no more!' Inevera stopped struggling, but her eyes narrowed and she shifted slightly, readying herself to stomp hard on the instep of the one closest to her. She glanced at Manvah, but her mother shook her head.

Kasaad coughed blood, pushing himself up onto his elbows. 'Harlots! When the *dama* hear of this . . .!'

Krisha cut him off with a cackling laugh. 'The *dama*? Will you go to them, Kasaad son of Kasaad, and tell them you were drunk on couzi and beaten by women? You won't even tell your *ajin'pal* as he buggers you tonight!'

Kasaad struggled to rise, but one of the women gave him a quick kick to the stomach, and he was knocked onto his back. He did not stir.

'Pfagh!' the woman cried. 'He's pissed himself like an infant!' They all laughed.

'That gives me an idea!' Krisha cried, going over to a scattered pile of baskets and hiking up her robes. 'Why get ourselves in a sweat breaking these abysmal baskets when we can just soil them instead?' She squatted and let her water flow, swinging her hips from side to side so the stream hit as many baskets as possible. The other women laughed, hiking their robes to do likewise.

'Poor Manvah!' Krisha mocked. 'Two males in the family, and not a man among them. Your husband is worse than a *khaffit*, and your *push'ting* son is too busy sucking cock to even be here.'

'Not quite.' Inevera turned in time to see Soli's thick hand close on the wrist of one of the young women holding her. The woman shrieked in pain as Soli yanked up with a cruel twist, then kicked out, sending her sister sprawling.

'Shut it,' he told the screaming woman, shoving her back. 'Touch my sister again and I'll sever your wrist instead of just twisting it.'

'We shall see, *push'ting*,' Krisha said. Her sister-wives had

9

straightened their robes and were advancing on Soli, staves at the ready. Krisha flicked her wrist, and her own club fell into her hand.

Inevera gasped, but Soli, unarmed, approached them without fear. The first woman struck at him, but Soli was quicker, slipping to the side of the blow and catching the woman's arm. There was a snap, and she fell screaming to the ground, her staff now in Soli's hand. The other woman came at him, and he parried one blow from her staff before striking her hard across the face. His movements were smooth and practised, like a dance. Inevera had watched him practise *sharusahk* when he came home from *Hannu Pash* on Wanings. The woman hit the ground, and Inevera saw her lower her veil to cough out a great wad of blood.

Soli dropped his staff as Krisha came at him, simply catching her weapon in his bare hand and stopping it cold. He seized her by the collar with the other, turning her around and bending her over a pile of baskets. He slammed her head down for good measure and reached down for the hem of her robes, yanking them up to her waist.

'Please,' Krisha wailed. 'Do as you will to me, but spare my daughters their virginity!'

'Pfagh!' Soli spat, his face a mask of disgust. 'I would as soon fuck a camel as you!'

'Oh, come, *push'ting*,' she sneered, wiggling her hips at him. 'Pretend I'm a man and have my ass.'

Soli took Krisha's rattan staff and began whipping her with it. His voice was deep, and carried over the sound of the wood cracking loudly on her bare flesh and her howls of pain. 'A man need not be *push'ting* to avoid sticking his cock in a dung-heap. And as for your daughters, I would do nothing that might delay them marrying some poor *khaffit* and finally putting veils on their ugly faces.'

He took his hand off her neck, but continued whipping, guiding her and the other women out of their kiosk with sharp blows. Krisha's daughters helped support her sister-wives as the five women stumbled off down the lane.

Manvah got to her feet and dusted herself off. She ignored Kasaad, going over to Inevera. 'Are you all right?' Inevera nodded.

'Check the stock,' Manvah said. 'They didn't have much time. See if we can salvage . . .'

'Too late,' Soli said, pointing down the lane. Three *Sharum* approached, their black robes sleeveless, with breastplates of black steel hammered to enhance already perfectly muscled chests. Black silk bands were tied around their bulging biceps and they wore studded leather bracers at their wrists. Bright golden shields were strapped to their backs, and they carried their short spears casually, sauntering with the easy grace of stalking wolves.

Manvah grabbed a small pitcher of water and dumped it on Kasaad, who groaned and half rose to his feet.

'Inside, quickly!' Manvah snapped, kicking him hard to get him moving. Kasaad grunted, but he managed to crawl into the tent and out of sight.

'How do I look?' Soli brushed and tugged at his robes, opening the front further.

It was a ridiculous question. No man she had ever seen was half so beautiful as her brother. 'Fine,' Inevera whispered back.

'Soli, my sweet *ajin'pal*!' Cashiv called. He was twenty-five, a *kai'Sharum*, and easily the handsomest of the three, his beard close-cropped with scented oil and his skin a perfect sun-brown. His breastplate was adorned with the sunburst of Dama Baden – no doubt in real gold – and the centre of his turban was adorned with a large turquoise. 'I'd hoped to find you here when we came to pick up the night's . . .' He drew close enough to see the chaos in their kiosk, 'order. Oh, dear. Did a herd of camels pass through your tent?' He sniffed. 'Pissing as they went?' He took the white silk night veil resting loose around his neck and lifted it over his nose. His compatriots did likewise.

'We had some . . . trouble,' Soli said. 'My fault, for stepping away for a few minutes.'

'That is a terrible shame.' Cashiv went over to Soli, taking no note of Inevera whatsoever. He reached out a finger, running it over Soli's muscled chest where a bit of blood had spattered. He rubbed the blood thoughtfully between his thumb and forefinger. 'It seems as though you returned in time to handle things, though.'

'That particular herd of camels is unlikely to come back,' Soli agreed.

'Their work is done, though,' Cashiv said sadly. 'We'll have to buy our baskets from Krisha again.'

'Please,' Soli said, laying a hand on Cashiv's arm, 'we need this order. Not all the stock was ruined. Might we sell you half, at least?'

Cashiv looked down at the hand on his arm and smiled. He waved dismissively at the clutter of baskets. 'Pfagh! If one's been pissed on, they all have. I will not take such tainted goods to my master. Dump a bucket on them and sell them to *khaffit*.'

He moved in closer, putting his hand back on Soli's chest. 'But if it's money you need, perhaps you can earn it carrying baskets at the party tomorrow instead of selling them.' He slid his fingers up under Soli's loosened robe to caress his shoulder. 'You could return home with the price of the baskets three times over, if you . . . carry well.'

Soli smiled. 'Baskets are my business, Cashiv. No one carries better.'

Cashiv laughed. 'We'll be by tomorrow morning to collect you for the party.'

'Meet me in the training grounds,' Soli said. Cashiv nodded, and he and his fellows sauntered off down the lane towards Krisha's kiosk.

Manvah laid a hand on Soli's shoulder. 'Sorry you had to do that, my son.'

Soli shrugged. 'Some days you're the cock, and some days you're the bum. I just hate that Krisha won.'

Manvah lifted her veil just enough to spit on the ground. 'Krisha won nothing. She has no baskets to sell.'

'How can you know that?' Soli asked.

Manvah chuckled. 'I set vermin in her storage tent a week ago.'

After helping restore the kiosk, Soli escorted them back to the small adobe building where they kept their rooms just as the *dama* sang the gloaming from the minarets of Sharik Hora. They had salvaged most of the baskets, but several needed repair. Manvah had a large bundle of palm fronds on her back.

'I'll need to hurry to make muster,' Soli said. Inevera and Manvah threw their arms around him, kissing him before he turned and ran into the darkening city.

Inside, they unsealed the warded trapdoor in their apartment and headed down into the Undercity for the night.

Each building in Krasia had at least one level deep below the ground, these linking to passageways leading to the Undercity proper, a vast honeycomb of tunnels and caverns that ran for miles. It was there the women, children, and *khaffit* took refuge each night while the men fought *alagai'sharak*. Great blocks of cut stone denied demons a clear path from Nie's abyss, and they were carved with powerful wards to keep those that had risen elsewhere at bay.

The Undercity was an impregnable refuge, designed not only to shelter the city's masses, but to be a city in and of itself should the unthinkable happen and the Desert Spear fall to the *alagai*. There were sleeping quarters for every family, schools, palaces, houses of worship, and more.

Inevera and her mother had only a small basement in the Undercity, with sleeping pallets, a cold room for food, and a tiny chamber with a deep pit for necessaries.

Manvah lit a lamp, and they sat at the table, eating a cold dinner. When the dishes were clear, she set out the palm fronds. Inevera moved to help.

Manvah shook her head. 'To bed with you. You have a big day tomorrow. I won't have you red-eyed and sluggish when the *dama'ting* question you.'

Inevera looked at the long line of girls and their mothers before her, each awaiting their turn in the *dama'ting* pavilion. The Brides of Everam had decreed that when the *dama* sang the dawn on spring equinox, all girls in their ninth year were to be presented for *Hannu Pash*, to learn the life's path Everam had laid out for them. *Hannu Pash* could take years for a boy, but for girls it was accomplished in a single foretelling by the *dama'ting*.

Most were simply deemed fertile and given their first head-scarf, but a few would walk away from the pavilion betrothed, or given a new vocation. Others, mostly the poor and illiterate, were purchased from their fathers and trained in pillow dancing, then sent to the great harem to service Krasia's warriors as *jiwah'Sharum*. It was their honour to bear new warriors to replace those who died battling demons in *alagai'sharak* each night.

Inevera had woken filled with excitement, donning her tan dress and brushing out her thick black hair. It fell in natural waves and shone like silk, but today was the last day the world would ever see it. She would enter the *dama'ting* pavilion a girl, but leave a young woman whose hair would be for her future husband alone. She would be stripped of her tan dress and emerge in proper blacks.

'It may be equinox, but the moon is in full,' Manvah said. 'That is a good omen, at least.'

'Perhaps a *Damaji* will take me into his harem,' Inevera said.

'I could live in a palace, with a dower so great you would never need to weave again.'

'Never able to go out in the sun again,' Manvah said, too low to be heard by those around them, 'or speak to anyone but your sister-wives, waiting on the pleasure of a man old enough to be your great-grandfather.' She shook her head. 'At least our tax is paid and you have two men to speak for you, so there's little chance you'll be sold into the great harem. And even that would be a better fate than to be found barren and cast out as *nie'ting*.'

Nie'ting. Inevera shuddered at the thought. Those found infertile would never be allowed to don the black, left in tans their entire life like *khaffit*, faces uncovered in shame.

'Perhaps I'll be chosen to be *dama'ting*,' Inevera said.

Manvah shook her head. 'You won't be. They never choose anyone.'

'Grandmother says a girl was chosen the year she was tested,' Inevera said.

'That was fifty years ago, if it was a day,' Manvah said, 'and Everam bless her, your father's honoured mother is prone to . . . exaggeration.'

'Then where do all the *nie'dama'ting* come from?' Inevera wondered, referring to the *dama'ting* apprentices, their faces bare, but in the white of betrothal to Everam.

'Some say Everam Himself gets his Brides with child, and the *nie'dama'ting* are their daughters,' Manvah said. Inevera looked at her, raising an eyebrow as she wondered if her mother was joking.

Manvah shrugged. 'It's as good an explanation as any. I can tell you none of the other mothers in the market has ever seen a girl chosen, or recognized one by her face.'

'Mother! Sister!' A wide smile broke out on Inevera's face as she saw Soli approaching, Cashiv at his back. Her brother's blacks were still dusty from the Maze, and his shield, slung over one shoulder, had fresh dents. Cashiv was as pristine as ever.

Inevera ran and embraced Soli. He laughed, picking her up with one arm and swinging her through the air. Inevera shrieked in delight, not afraid for a moment. Nothing could frighten her when Soli was near. He set her down gentle as a feather and went to embrace their mother.

'What are you doing here?' Manvah asked. 'I thought you would already be on your way to Dama Baden's palace.'

'I am,' Soli said, 'but I couldn't let my sister go to her *Hannu Pash* without wishing her all the blessings in Ala.' He reached out, tousling Inevera's hair. She swatted at his hand, but as ever, he was too quick and snatched it back in time.

'Do you think Father will come to bless me as well?' Inevera asked.

'Ah . . .' Soli hesitated. 'So far as I know, Father is still sleeping in the back of the kiosk. He never made it to muster last night, and I told the drillmaster he had a belly fever . . . again.' Soli shrugged helplessly, and Inevera lowered her eyes, not wanting him to see her disappointment.

Soli stooped low, lifting her chin with a gentle finger so their eyes met. 'I know Father wants every blessing for you that I do, even if he has difficulty showing it.'

Inevera nodded. 'I know.' She threw her arms around Soli's neck one last time before he left. 'Thank you.'

Cashiv looked at Inevera as if noticing her for the first time. He smiled his handsome smile and bowed. 'Blessings to you, Inevera vah Kasaad, as you become a woman. I wish you a good husband and many sons, all as handsome as your brother.'

Inevera smiled and felt her cheeks flush as the warriors sauntered off.

At last, the line began to move. The day wore on slowly as they stood in the hot sun, the girls and their mothers admitted one at a time. Some were inside for mere minutes – others, nearly an hour. All left wearing black, most looking both chastened and relieved. Some of the girls stared hard at nothing, rubbing their arms absently as their mothers steered them home.

As they drew close to the head of the line, Inevera's mother tightened her grip on the girl's shoulders, nails digging hard even through her dress.

'Keep your eyes down and your tongue still save when spoken to,' Manvah hissed. 'Never answer a question with a question, and never disagree. Say it with me: "Yes, Dama'ting."'

'Yes, Dama'ting,' Inevera repeated.

'Keep that answer fixed in your mind,' Manvah said. 'Offend a *dama'ting* and you offend fate itself.'

'Yes, Mother.' Inevera swallowed deeply, feeling her insides clench. What went on in the pavilion? Hadn't her mother gone through the same ritual? What was she so afraid of?

A *nie'dama'ting* opened the tent flap, and the girl who had gone in before Inevera emerged. She wore a headscarf now, but it was tan, as was the dress she still wore. Her mother gentled her shoulders, murmuring comfort as they stumbled along, but both were weeping.

The *nie'dama'ting* regarded the scene serenely, then turned to Inevera and her mother. She was perhaps thirteen, tall with a sturdy build, harsh cheekbones, and a hooked nose that made her look like a raptor. 'I am Melan.' She motioned for them to enter. 'Dama'ting Qeva will see you now.'

Inevera took a deep breath as she and her mother removed their shoes, drew wards in the air, and passed into the *dama'ting* pavilion.

The sun filtered through the rising canvas roof, filling the great tent with bright light. Everything was white, from the tent walls to the painted furniture and the thick canvas flooring.

It made the blood all the more startling. There were great splashes of red and brown marring the floor of the entranceway, as well as a thick trail of muddy red footprints heading through partitions to the right and left.

'That is *Sharum* blood,' a voice said, and Inevera jumped, noticing for the first time the Bride of Everam standing right before them, her white robes blending almost perfectly with the background. 'From the injured brought in at dawn from *alagai'sharak*. Each day, the canvas floor is cut away and burned atop the minarets of Sharik Hora during the call to prayer.'

As if on cue, Inevera heard the cries of pain surrounding her. On the other side of the thick partitions, men were in agony. She imagined her father – or worse, Soli – among them, and winced at every shriek and groan.

'Everam take me now!' a man cried desperately. 'I will not live a cripple!'

'Step carefully,' Dama'ting Qeva warned. 'The soles of your feet are not worthy to touch the blood honoured warriors have spilled for your sake.'

Inevera and her mother eased their way around the stained canvas to come before the *dama'ting*. Clad from head to toe in white silk with only her eyes and hands uncovered, Qeva was tall and thick of frame like Melan, but with a woman's curves.

'What is your name, girl?' The Bride of Everam's voice was deep and hard.

'Inevera vah Kasaad am'Damaj am'Kaji, Dama'ting,' Inevera said, bowing deeply. 'Named after the First Wife of Kaji.' Manvah's nails dug into her shoulder at the addition, and she gasped involuntarily. The *dama'ting* seemed not to notice.

'No doubt you think that makes you special.' Qeva snorted. 'If Krasia had a warrior for every worthless girl who has borne that name, Sharak Ka would be over.'

'Yes, Dama'ting,' Inevera said, bowing again as her mother's nails eased back.

'You're a pretty one,' the *dama'ting* noted.

Inevera bowed. 'Thank you, Dama'ting.'

'The harems can always use a pretty girl, if she's not put to good use already,' Qeva said, looking at Manvah. 'Who is your husband and what is your profession?'

'Dal'Sharum Kasaad, Dama'ting,' Manvah said, bowing. 'And I am a palm weaver.'

'First Wife?' Qeva asked.

'I am his only wife, Dama'ting,' Manvah said.

'Men think they take on wives as they prosper, Manvah of the Kaji,' Qeva said, 'but the reverse is true. Have you tried to secure sister-wives, as prescribed in the Evejah, to help with your weaving and bear him more children?'

'Yes, Dama'ting. Many times.' Manvah gritted her teeth. 'Their fathers . . . would not approve the match.'

The Bride of Everam grunted. The answer said much about Kasaad. 'Is the girl educated?'

Manvah nodded. 'Yes, Dama'ting. Inevera is my apprentice. She is most skilled at weaving, and I have taught her to do sums and keep ledgers. She has read the Evejah once for each of the seven pillars of Heaven.'

The *dama'ting*'s eyes were unreadable. 'Follow me.' She turned away, heading deeper into the pavilion. She gave no mind to the blood on the floor, her flowing silk robes gliding easily over it. Not a drop clung to them. It would not dare.

Melan followed, the *nie'dama'ting* stepping nimbly around the blood, and Inevera and her mother trailed after. The pavilion was a maze of white cloth walls, with many turns that were upon them before Inevera even knew they were there. There was no blood on the floor here, and even the cries of the injured *Sharum* grew muffled. Around one bend, the walls and ceiling shifted suddenly from white to black. It was like stepping from day into night. After turning another bend, it became so dark that her mother, in her black *dal'ting* robes, was nearly invisible, and even the white-clad *dama'ting* and her apprentice became only ghostly images.

Qeva stopped suddenly, and Melan moved around her to pull open a trapdoor Inevera hadn't even noticed. Inside she could only just make out the stone staircase leading down into a deeper dark. The cut stone was cold on her bare feet, and when Melan pulled the trap shut behind them, the blackness became complete. They descended slowly, Inevera terrified she might trip and take the Bride of Everam tumbling down the steps with her.

The stairs were mercifully short, though Inevera did indeed stumble in surprise when she came to the landing. She caught herself quickly, and no one seemed to notice.

A red light appeared in Qeva's hand, casting an evil glow that allowed them to see one another, but did little to abate the oppressive darkness around them. The *dama'ting* led them down a row of dark cells cut into the living rock. Wards were carved into the walls on both sides.

'Wait here with Melan,' Qeva told Manvah, and bade Inevera to enter one of the cells. She winced as the heavy door closed behind them.

There was a stone pedestal in one corner of the room, and the *dama'ting* deposited the glowing object there. It looked like a lump of coal carved with glowing wards, but even Inevera knew better. It was *alagai hora*.

Demon bone.

Qeva turned back to her, and Inevera caught the flash of a curved blade in the woman's hand. In the red light, it appeared to be covered in blood.

Inevera shrieked and backpedalled, but the cell was tiny, and she soon fetched up against the stone wall. The *dama'ting* lifted the blade right up to Inevera's nose, and her eyes crossed trying to see it.

'You fear the blade?' the *dama'ting* asked.

'Yes, Dama'ting,' Inevera said automatically, her voice cracking.

'Close your eyes,' Qeva commanded. Inevera shook with fear, but she did as she was bade, her heart thumping loudly in her chest as she waited for the blade to pierce her flesh.

But the blow never came. 'Picture a palm tree, weaver's daughter,' Qeva said. Inevera didn't wholly understand, but she nodded. It was an easy image to form, as she climbed palm trees every day, nimbly shimmying up the trunk to harvest fronds for weaving.

'Does a palm fear the wind?' the *dama'ting* asked.

'No, Dama'ting,' Inevera said.

'What does it do?'

'It bends, Dama'ting,' Inevera said.

'The Evejah teaches us that fear and pain are only wind, Inevera, daughter of Manvah. Let it blow past you.'

'Yes, Dama'ting,' Inevera said.

'Repeat it three times,' Qeva commanded.

'Fear and pain are only wind,' Inevera said, drawing a deep breath. 'Fear and pain are only wind. Fear and pain are only wind.'

'Open your eyes and kneel,' Qeva said. When Inevera complied, she added, 'Hold out your arm.' The limb Inevera lifted seemed detached from her, but it held steady. The Bride of Everam pulled up Inevera's sleeve and sliced her forearm, drawing a bright line of blood.

Inevera drew a sharp breath, but she did not flinch away or cry out. *Fear and pain are only wind.*

The *dama'ting* lifted her veil slightly and licked the knife, tasting Inevera's blood. She sheathed it at her waist and then reached out with a strong hand to squeeze the cut, dripping blood onto a handful of black, warded dice.

Inevera gritted her teeth. *Fear and pain are only wind.*

When the blood struck them, the dice began to glow, and Inevera realized they, too, were *alagai hora*. Her blood was touching the bones of demons. The thought was horrifying.

The *dama'ting* took a step back, chanting quietly as she shook the dice, their glow increasing with every passing moment.

'Everam, giver of light and life, I beseech you, give this lowly servant knowledge of what is to come. Tell me of Inevera, daughter of Kasaad, of the Kaji line of Damaj.'

With that, she cast the dice to the floor in front of Inevera. Their light exploded in a flash that caused her to blink, then reduced to a dull throb as the glowing symbols on the floor laid bare the fronds that wove her fate.

The *dama'ting* said nothing. Her eyes narrowed, staring at the symbols for a long time. Inevera could not say exactly how long it was, but she wobbled as the muscles of her legs, unaccustomed to kneeling so long, began to give way.

Qeva looked up at the movement. 'Sit back on your heels and keep still!' She got to her feet, circling the tiny cell to inspect the pattern of the dice from every angle. Slowly the glow began to fade, but still the *dama'ting* pondered.

Palm in the wind or not, Inevera began to grow very nervous. Her muscles screamed in strain, and her anxiety doubled with every passing second. What did the Bride of Everam see? Was she to be taken from her mother and sold to a harem? Was she barren?

At last, Qeva looked at Inevera. 'Touch the dice in any way, and it will mean your life.' With that, she left the room, grunting commands. There was a sound of hurried footsteps as Melan ran off.

A moment later Manvah entered the cell, stepping around the dice carefully to kneel behind Inevera. 'What happened?' she whispered.

Inevera shook her head. 'I don't know. The *dama'ting* stared at the dice as if unsure what they meant.'

'Or she didn't like what they told her,' Manvah muttered.

'What happens now?' Inevera asked, her face going cold.

'They are summoning Damaji'ting Kenevah,' Manvah said, drawing a shocked gasp from Inevera. 'It is she who will speak the final word. Pray now.'

Inevera shuddered as she lowered her head. She was frightened enough of the *dama'ting*. The thought of their leader coming to inspect her . . .

Please, Everam, she begged, *let me be fertile and bear sons for the Kaji. My family could not bear the shame if I were* nie'ting. *Grant me this one wish, and I will give myself to you forever.*

They knelt in the dim red light a long time, praying.

'Mother?' Inevera asked.

'Yes?' her mother said.

Inevera swallowed the lump in her throat. 'Will you still love me if I'm barren?' Her voice cracked at the end. She hadn't meant to cry, but found herself blinking away tears.

A moment later Manvah had folded her in her arms. 'You are my daughter. I would love you if you put out the sun.'

After an interminable wait, Qeva returned, another Bride of Everam at her back – this one older and thinner, with a sharp look. She wore *dama'ting* white, but her veil and headwrap were black silk. Damaji'ting Kenevah, the most powerful woman in all Krasia.

The *Damaji'ting* glanced at the huddling women, and they quickly separated and wiped their eyes, returning to their knees. She said nothing, moving to the dice. For long minutes, she studied the pattern.

At last, Kenevah grunted. 'Take her.'

Inevera gasped as Qeva strode up, grabbing her arm and hauling her to her feet. She looked frantically at her mother and saw Manvah's eyes wide with fear. 'Mother!'

Manvah fell to her belly, clutching at the hem of Qeva's white robe as the *dama'ting* pulled her away. 'Please, Dama'ting,' she begged. 'My daughter—'

'Your daughter is no longer your concern,' Kenevah cut her off, and Qeva kicked to snap the robe from Manvah's grasp. 'She belongs to Everam now.'

'There must be some mistake,' Inevera said numbly as Qeva guided her along the road with a firm grasp on her arm. It felt more like she was being escorted to a whipping post than a palace. Damaji'ting Kenevah and Melan, the *nie'dama'ting* apprentice, walked with them.

'The dice do not make mistakes,' Kenevah said. 'And you should be rejoicing. You, the daughter of a basket weaver and a *Sharum* of no particular note, will be betrothed to Everam. Can you not see the great honour paid to your family this day?'

'Then why wasn't I allowed to say goodbye to them? To my mother, even?' *Never answer a question with a question*, Manvah had said, but Inevera was past caring.

'Best to make a clean break,' Kenevah said. 'They are beneath you now. Irrelevant. You will not be permitted to see them during your training, and by the time you are ready to test for the white, you will no longer even wish to.'

Inevera had no response to such a ridiculous statement. Not want to see her mother again? Her brother? Unthinkable. She would even miss her father, though in all likelihood Kasaad would never notice she was gone.

The Kaji Dama'ting Palace soon came into sight. Equal to those of even the greatest *Damaji*, the Dama'ting Palace had a twenty-foot-tall wardwall, proof against daylight enemies as well as *alagai*. Over the top of the wall she could see the tall spires and great dome of the palace, but Inevera had never seen inside the walls. None but the *dama'ting* and their apprentices ever passed its great gates. No men, not even the Andrah himself, could set foot on its hallowed grounds.

That was what Inevera had been told, at least, but as the gates – which had seemed to open of their own accord – closed behind them, she could see a pair of muscular men pushing them shut. They were clad only in white bidos and sandals, and their hair and bodies glistened with oil. Each wore golden shackles on his ankles and wrists, but there were no chains Inevera could see.

'I thought no men were allowed in the palace,' Inevera said, 'to protect *dama'ting* chastity.'

The Brides of Everam barked a laugh as though this were a great joke. Even Melan chuckled.

'You are half right,' Kenevah said. 'The eunuchs are without stones, and thus not men in the Eyes of Everam.'

'So they are . . . *push'ting*?' Inevera asked.

Kenevah cackled. 'Stoneless they may be, but their spears work well enough to do a true man's work.'

Inevera gave a pained smile as they climbed the wide marble steps, polished a pristine glistening white. She held her arms in close, attempting to be as small and unobtrusive as possible as the great doors were opened by more handsome, muscular slaves in golden shackles. They bowed, and Qeva ran a finger under one's chin.

'It has been a trying day, Khavel. Come to my chambers in an hour with heated stones and scented oil to stroke the tension away.' The slave bowed deeply, saying nothing.

'They are not allowed to speak?' Inevera asked.

'Not able,' Kenevah said. 'Their tongues were cut out with their stones and they know no letters. They can never tell of the wonders they see in the Dama'ting Palace.'

Indeed, the palace was filled with luxury and opulence beyond anything Inevera had ever imagined. Everything from the columns and high dome to the floors, walls, and stairs was cut from flawless white marble, polished to a bright shine. Thick woven carpets, amazingly soft beneath her bare feet, ran along the halls, filling them with bright colour. Tapestries hung on the walls – masterworks of artistry bringing the tales of the Evejah to life. Beautiful glazed pottery stood on marble pedestals, along with items of crystal, gold, and polished silver; from delicate sculpture and filigree to heavy chalices and bowls. In the bazaar, such items would have been under close guard – any one of them could sell for enough to keep a family in staples for a decade – but who in all Krasia would dare steal from the *dama'ting*?

Other Brides passed them in the halls, some alone, others in chattering groups. All wore the same flowing white silk, hooded and veiled – even inside with no men to see. They stopped and bowed deeply as Kenevah passed, and though they tried to hide it, each gave Inevera a curious and not altogether welcoming appraisal.

More than one of the passing Brides was great with child. It was shocking to see *dama'ting* in such a condition, especially if the only men allowed near them were gelded, but Inevera kept her surprise beneath a haggler's mask. Kenevah's patience might be tested by such a question, and if she was to live here, the answer would become apparent soon enough.

There were seven wings to the palace, one for every pillar in Heaven, with the central wing pointing toward Anoch Sun, the final resting place of Kaji. This was the *Damaji'ting*'s personal wing, and Inevera was escorted into the First Bride's opulent receiving chamber. Qeva and Melan were instructed to wait outside.

'Sit,' the *Damaji'ting* said, gesturing to the velvet couches set before a polished wood desk. Inevera sat timidly, feeling tiny and insignificant in the massive office. Kenevah sat behind the desk, steepling her fingers and staring at Inevera, who wilted under the harsh gaze.

'Qeva tells me you know of your namesake,' Kenevah said grimly, and Inevera could not tell if she was being mocked. 'Tell me what you know of her.'

'Inevera was the daughter of Damaj, Kaji's closest friend and counsellor,' Inevera said. 'It is said in the Evejah that she was so beautiful, Kaji fell in love with her at first sight, claiming it was Everam's will that she be first among his wives.'

Kenevah snorted. 'The Damajah was more than that, girl. Much more. As she lay in the pillows with Kaji she whispered wisdom into his ear, bringing him to untold heights of power. It is said she spoke with Everam's voice, which is why the name is synonymous with Everam's will.

'Inevera was also the first *dama'ting*,' Kenevah went on. 'She

26

brought us healing, and poison, and *hora* magic. She wove Kaji's Cloak of Unsight, and etched the wards of his mighty spear and crown.'

Kenevah looked up at Inevera. 'And she will come again, when Sharak Ka is nigh, to find the next Deliverer.'

Inevera gasped, but Kenevah gave her only a tolerant look. 'I have seen a hundred girls with your name gasp so, girl, but not one has produced a Deliverer. How many are there in the Damaj clan alone? Twenty?'

Inevera nodded, and Kenevah grunted. From inside her desk she produced a heavy book with a worn leather spine. Once it had been illuminated in gold leaf, but only bare flecks remained.

'The Evejah'ting,' Kenevah said. 'You will read it.'

Inevera bowed. 'Of course, Damaji'ting, though I have read the sacred text many times before.'

Kenevah shook her head. 'You read the Evejah, Kaji's version, and that altered to suit the *dama*'s purposes over the years. But the Evejah is only half the story. The Evejah'ting, its companion book, was penned by the Damajah herself and contains her personal wisdom and account of Kaji's rise. You will memorize every page.'

Inevera took the book. Its pages were impossibly thin and soft, but the Evejah'ting was as thick as the Evejah that Manvah had taught her to read. She brought the book close to her chest, as if to protect it from thieves.

The *Damaji'ting* presented her with a thick black velvet pouch. There was a clatter inside as Inevera took it.

'Your *hora* pouch,' Kenevah said.

Inevera blanched. 'There are demon bones inside?'

Kenevah shook her head. 'It will be months at least before you are sufficiently disciplined to even touch true *hora*, and likely years more before you are allowed entry to the Chamber of Shadows to carve your dice.'

Inevera undid the drawstrings and emptied the contents of

the pouch into her hand. There were seven clay dice, each with a different number of sides. All were lacquered black like demon bone, with symbols engraved in red on every side.

'The dice can reveal to you all the mysteries of the world if you can learn to read them truly,' Kenevah said. 'These are a reminder of what you aspire to, and a model to study. Much of the Evejah'ting is devoted to their understanding.'

Inevera slipped the dice back into the bag and drew it closed, putting it safely in her pocket.

'They will resent you,' Kenevah said.

'Who will, Damaji'ting?' Inevera asked.

'Everyone,' Kenevah said. 'Betrothed and Bride alike. There is not a woman here who will welcome you.'

'Why?' Inevera asked.

'Because your mother was not *dama'ting*. You were not born to the white,' Kenevah said. 'It has been two generations since the dice have called a girl. You will have to work twice as hard as the others, if you wish to earn your veil. Your sisters have been training since birth.'

Inevera digested the news. Outside the palace, everyone knew the *dama'ting* were chaste. Everyone, it seemed, except the *dama'ting* themselves.

'They will resent you,' Kenevah went on, 'but they will also fear you. If you are wise, you can use this.'

'Fear?' Inevera asked. 'Why in Everam's name would they fear me?'

'Because the last girl called by the dice sits before you now as *Damaji'ting*,' Kenevah said. 'It has always been so, since the time of Kaji. The dice indicate you may succeed me.'

'I will be *Damaji'ting*?' Inevera asked, incredulous.

'*May*,' Kenevah reiterated. 'If you live long enough. The others will watch you, and judge. Some of your sisters in training may try to curry your favour, and others will seek to dominate you. You must be stronger than them.'

'I—' Inevera began.

'But you must not appear *too* strong,' Kenevah cut in, 'or the *dama'ting* will have you quietly killed before you take your veil, and let the dice choose another.'

Inevera felt her blood run cold.

'Everything you know is about to change, girl,' Kenevah said, 'but I think you will find in the end that the Dama'ting Palace is not so different from the Great Bazaar.'

Inevera cocked her head, unsure if the woman was joking or not, but Kenevah ignored her, ringing a golden bell on her desk. Qeva and Melan entered the chamber. 'Take her to the Vault.'

Qeva took Inevera's arm again, half guiding, half dragging her from the couch.

'Melan, you will instruct her in the ways of the Betrothed,' Kenevah said. 'For the next twelve Wanings, her failures will be your own.'

Melan grimaced, but she bowed deeply. 'Yes, Grandmother.'

The Vault was not in any of the seven wings of the palace. It was set below, in the underpalace.

Like almost every other great structure in the Desert Spear, the Palace of the Dama'ting had as many levels below as above. The underpalace was colder in both temperature and décor than the structure above. There was no hint of the paint, gilding, and polish of the palace proper. Away from the sun, the Undercity was no place for garish displays of luxury. No place to be too comfortable.

But the underpalace still offered more splendour than the few adobe rooms Inevera and her family called home. The soaring ceilings, great columns, and archways gave even the bare stone grandeur, and the wards carved into their faces were works of art. Even away from the sun it was comfortably warm, with soft rugs running along the stone floors, wards stitched into the edges. If *alagai* somehow entered this most sacred of places, the Brides of Everam were secure.

Dama'ting patrolled the halls, occasionally passing them by. These nodded at Qeva and walked past, but Inevera could feel their eyes boring into her as they went.

They descended a stairwell, continuing through several more passages. The air grew warmer, and moist. Carpets vanished, and the marble floor became tiled and slick with condensation. A burly *dama'ting* stood watch over a portal, staring openly at Inevera as a cat stares at a mouse. Inevera shuddered as they passed into a wide chamber with dozens of pegs along the walls. Most held a robe and a long strip of white silk. Up ahead, Inevera could hear the sound of laughter and splashing.

'Take off your dress and leave it on the floor to be burned,' Qeva said.

Inevera quickly removed her tan dress and bido – a wide strip of cloth that kept the ever-present sand and dust of the bazaar from her nethers. Manvah wore one of black, and had taught Inevera to tie it in a quick, efficient knot.

Melan undressed, and Inevera saw that under her robe and silk pants she, too, wore a bido, but one far more intricate, woven many times over from a strip of silk less than an inch wide. Her head was wrapped in silk as well, covering her hair, ears, and neck. Her face remained bare.

Melan untied a small knot at her chin and began undoing her headwrap. Her hands moved with quick, practised efficiency, reversing what Inevera could see was an intensely complicated weave. As she worked, her hands twisted continually to wrap the silk neatly about them, keeping it taut.

Inevera was shocked to see that the girl's head was shaved bare, olive skin smooth and shiny like polished stone.

The headwrap ended in the tight braid of silk that ran down Melan's spine. The girl's hands continued their dance behind her head, undoing dozens of crossings in the silk until two separate strands reached her bido. Still the acolyte's hands worked.

It's all one piece, Inevera realized, staring in awe as Melan slowly unwove her bido. The air of a dance only increased as Melan began to step over the uncrossing strands, her bare feet tamping a steady rhythm. The silk crossed her thighs and between her legs dozens of times, layering weaves one atop another.

Inevera had made enough baskets to know good weaving when she saw it, and this was a masterwork. Something so intricately woven could be worn all day and never come loose, and someone unskilled would likely make a botch of it and never get the weave undone.

'The woven bido is like the web of flesh that safeguards your virginity,' Qeva said, tossing Inevera a great roll of thin white silk. 'You will wear it at all times, save for ablutions and necessaries, done here in the lowest chamber of the Vault. You will not leave the Vault under any circumstances without it, and you will be punished if it is woven improperly. Melan will teach you the weave. It should be simple enough for a basket weaver's daughter to master.'

Melan snorted at that, and Inevera swallowed hard and tried not to stare at the girl's bald head as she came over. She was a few years Inevera's senior, and very pretty without her headwrap. She held out her hands, each wrapped in at least ten feet of silk. Inevera mimicked her, and they stepped over the strip of silk between their hands, bringing it to rest across their buttocks.

'The first weave is called Everam's Guardian,' Melan said, pulling the silk taut and crossing it over her sex. 'It crosses seven times, one for each pillar in Heaven.' Inevera copied her, and managed to keep up for some time before Qeva cut in.

'There is a twist in the silk, begin again,' the *dama'ting* said.

Inevera nodded, and both girls undid the weave and started afresh. Inevera knitted her brows, doing her best to mimic the weave perfectly. Kenevah had said Melan would bear the weight of her mistakes, and she did not want the girl punished for her clumsy hands. She managed to keep up all the way to the head-wrap before the *dama'ting* broke in.

'Not so tight,' Qeva said. 'You're tying a bido, not trying to keep a *Sharum*'s broken skull together. Do it again.'

Melan gave Inevera a look of annoyance that made her face flush, but again they reversed course, undoing their bidos entirely before beginning anew.

By the third repetition, Inevera had the feel of the weave. Its flow came naturally to her, and soon she and Melan stood in identical silk bidos.

Qeva clapped her hands. 'There might be something to you after all, girl. It took Melan months to master the bido weave, and she was one of the quicker studies. Isn't that so, Melan?'

'As the *dama'ting* says.' Melan gave a stiff bow, and Inevera got the sense that Qeva was taunting her.

'Into the bath with you,' Qeva said. 'The day grows long and the kitchens will soon open.'

Inevera's stomach rumbled at the mention of food. It had been many hours since she had eaten.

'You'll eat soon enough.' Qeva smiled. 'Once you and the other girls finish serving supper and scrubbing out the crockery.'

She gave a laugh and pointed towards the source of the steam and splashing sounds. Melan undid her bido quickly and headed that way. Inevera took longer, trying not to tangle the silk, then followed, her bare feet slapping the tile.

The passage opened up into a great pool, its water hot and the air thick with steam. There were dozens of girls inside, all of them as bald as Melan. Some were Inevera's age, but many were older, some grown almost fully to womanhood. All stood washing in the stone bath, or lounged on the slick stone steps at its edges, shaving and paring nails.

Inevera thought of the bucket of warm water she and her mother shared to wash. Their ration let them change it only sparingly. She waded out in wonder, the hot water caressing her thighs, running her fingertips through the surface as if through silk in the market.

Everyone looked up as they entered. The loungers sat up like hissing snakes, every eye in the misty room focused on the two girls. They moved in swiftly, surrounding them.

Inevera turned back, but the way was already closed, the ring of girls tightening, barring any escape and blocking them from outside view.

'This is her?' one girl asked.

'The one the dice called?' asked another. The questioners were lost in the steam as the girls began to circle, eyeing Inevera from every angle in much the same way Qeva had studied her dice.

Melan nodded, and the ring tightened further. Inevera felt crushed under the weight of their collective stare.

'Melan, what . . .?' Inevera reached out, her heart pounding.

Melan caught her wrist, twisting and pulling hard. Inevera fell towards her, and Melan caught a fistful of her thick hair, using the momentum of her fall to push her head under the water.

There was a burble, then all she could hear was the rushing of water. Inevera reflexively inhaled water and choked, but she could not cough underwater, and her insides spasmed as she resisted the urge to breathe in. The hot water burned her face and she struggled violently, but Melan kept her hold and Inevera was helpless against it. She thrashed as her lungs began to burn, but like Soli in the kiosk, Melan was using *sharusahk*, her movements swift and precise. Inevera could do nothing to resist.

Melan was shouting something at her, but the sound was muffled by the water, and Inevera couldn't make out any of it. She realized then that she was going to drown. It seemed so absurd. Inevera had never stood in water past her knees. Water was precious in the Desert Spear, both currency and merchandise in the bazaar. *Gold shines, but water is divine*, the saying went.

Only the wealthiest of Krasia's citizens could even afford to drown.

She was losing hope when Melan gave a jerk and pulled her upright with a splash. Inevera's hair was plastered to her face, and she coughed, gasping breaths of thick, steamy air.

'—just walk in here,' Melan was shouting, 'speaking to the *Damaji'ting* like she was your pillow friend, and learning the bido weave in three tries!'

'Three tries?' a girl asked.

'We should kill her just for that,' another added.

'Thinks she's better than us,' a third said.

Inevera glanced around desperately through her matted hair, but the other girls watched impassively, their eyes dead. None of them looked like she might lift a finger to help.

'Melan, please, I—' Inevera sputtered, but Melan tightened her grip and thrust Inevera back under the water. She managed to hold her breath, but that soon ran out, and she was thrashing wildly again by the time Melan let her up to gasp another breath.

'Do not speak to me,' Melan said. 'I may be bound to you for one year, but we are not friends. You think you can come in and take Kenevah's place overnight? Over my mother? Over *me*? I am Kenevah's blood! You are just a . . . bad throw.'

She produced a sharp knife from somewhere, and Inevera flinched in terror as Melan slashed it through her hair, cutting off thick locks. 'You are nothing.' She flipped the knife in her fingers, catching the blade and handing it hilt-first to the next girl who approached.

'You are nothing,' the girl echoed, grabbing another lock of Inevera's hair and slicing it off.

Each girl came forward and took the knife, cutting at Inevera's hair until all that remained was a ragged and uneven shadow, patched and bloody. 'You are nothing,' they said in turn.

By the time the last of the girls drew back, Inevera was on her knees in the water, limp and weeping. Again and again she broke out coughing, the convulsions tearing hot fire through her throat. It was as if there was some last bit of water in her lungs they were determined to expel.

Kenevah was right. The Dama'ting Palace and the Great Bazaar weren't so different after all, but here there was no Soli to defend her.

Inevera thought about Manvah, and her final words about Krisha. If she could not match *sharusahk* with Melan and the other girls, she would deal as her mother had done. She would keep her eyes down and do as she was told. Work hard. Listen. Learn.

And then, when no one was looking, she would find Melan's storage tent and put vermin in it.

1

Arlen

333 AR Summer
30 Dawns Before New Moon

Renna kissed Arlen again. A gentle breeze swept across the thin sheen of sweat on their bodies, cooling them as they panted on the hot night.

'Been wonderin' if you were tattooed under that cloth nappy,' she said, nestling in next to him and putting her head on his bare chest, listening to his heart.

Arlen laughed and put his arm around her. 'It's called a bido. And even *my* obsession has limits.'

Renna lifted her head, putting her lips to his ear. 'Maybe you just need a Warder you trust. It's a wife's duty to take good care of what's in her husband's bido. I could paint you with blackstem . . .'

Arlen swallowed, and she could see his skin flush. 'The wards would distort even as you drew them.'

Renna laughed, wrapping him in her arms and dropping her head back to his chest.

'Wonder sometimes if I'm cracked,' she said.

'How's that?' Arlen asked.

'Like I'm still sitting in Selia Barren's spinning room, staring off into space. Everything since has been like a dream. Wonder if my mind just took me to a sunny place and left me there.'

'You've a poor imagination if this is your sunny place,' Arlen said.

'Why?' Renna asked. 'I'm rid of Harl and that corespawned farm, stronger than I ever imagined, and dancing in the naked night.' She swept a hand around her. 'Everything's awash in colour and glow.' She looked at him. 'And I'm with Arlen Bales. How could my sunny place be anywhere else?'

Renna bit her lip as the words rushed to them. Words she had thought to herself many times, but never dared say aloud. Part of her hesitation was fear of Arlen's reaction, but much of it was her own doubt. All the Tanner sisters had been willing to run to the bed of the first decent man they met, but had any of them ever been in love?

Renna had thought she loved Arlen when they were children, but she only knew him from afar, and understood now that much of what she cherished had been her imagination of what he was like in close, rather than the boy himself.

Renna had convinced herself that she loved Cobie Fisher this past spring, but she saw the lie of that now. Cobie hadn't been a bad sort, but if any other man had come to Harl's farm, Renna knew she would likely have seduced him, too. Anything to get away, because anywhere was better than that farm, and any man in creation was better than her da.

But Renna was done lying. And done biting her tongue.

'Love you, Arlen Bales,' she said.

Her courage fled as the words left her lips and she held her breath, but there was no hesitation as Arlen tightened his arms around her. 'Love you, Renna Tanner.'

She exhaled, and all the fear and doubt left her.

Charged as she was with magic, Renna found no sleep as they lay, but she would not have wished for any. Warm and safe, she wondered almost idly how she and Arlen could have been fighting a demon prince and its servants on this very spot a few hours before. It seemed a different world. A different life. For a short time, they had escaped.

But as the sweat dried and the glow of passion faded, the real world began to creep back into focus, terrible and frightening. They were surrounded by the bodies of dead corelings, black ichor splattered all over the clearing. One, the shapeshifting demon, still wore her form, its head neatly severed and leaking ichor. Not far off, Twilight Dancer still lay with his legs in splints after nearly being killed by a mimic demon.

'Going to need to heal Dancer again before he can walk,' Arlen said. 'Even then, it might be another night or two before he's at full strength.'

Renna looked around the clearing. 'Don't like the idea of staying here another night.'

'Me neither,' Arlen said. 'Corelings will be drawn here tomorrow like worms to a rain puddle. I have a safehold nearby with a cart big enough to carry Dancer. I can fetch it and be back not long past sunrise.'

'Still have to wait for nightfall,' Renna said.

Arlen tilted his head at her. 'Why?'

'Horse weighs more'n your da's house,' Renna said. 'How we gonna get him in the cart without night strength? Who'll pull the thing, for that matter?'

Arlen looked at her, and even through the wards tattooed all over his face, his expression told all. 'Stop that,' she snapped.

'What?' Arlen asked.

'Deciding whether or not to lie to me,' Renna said. 'We're promised now, and there oughtn't be lies 'tween man and wife.'

Arlen looked at her in surprise, then shook his head. 'Wan't gonna lie, exactly. Just tryin' to decide if it's time to talk about it.'

'Is if you value your skin,' Renna said. Arlen squinted at her, but she met his eyes and after a moment he shrugged.

'Don't lose all my strength in the day,' he said. 'Even under the noon sun I reckon I could pick up a milk cow and throw it farther than you can skip a brook stone.'

'What makes you so special?' Renna asked.

Arlen gave her that look again, and she scowled, shaking a fist at him only half mockingly.

Arlen laughed. 'Tell you all once we get to my safehold. Honest word.'

Renna smirked. 'Kiss on it, and it's a deal.'

While she waited, Renna took out the warding kit Arlen had given her, placing a clean cloth on the ground and laying the tools out in a neat row. She took out her brook stone necklace and her knife, and slowly, carefully, lovingly, began to clean them.

The necklace was a promise gift from Cobie Fisher, a stout cord strung through dozens of smooth, polished stones. It was so long Renna needed to loop it twice, and it still fell below her breasts.

The knife had belonged to her father, Harl Tanner. He'd always kept it at his belt, sharp as a razor. He'd used it to murder Cobie when she ran away to be with him, and she in turn had used it to kill him.

If that hadn't happened, Renna and Cobie would have been man and wife when Arlen came back to Tibbet's Brook. The necklace was a symbol of her failure to be true to Arlen, a promise gift from another man. The knife was a reminder of a man who had kept her in a private Core her entire life.

But Renna could bring herself to part with neither. For better or worse, they were the only things in the world that were truly hers, the only parts of her day life that had come into the night. She had warded them both, the necklace with defensive wards, and the knife with offensive. The necklace could serve as a ward circle in need, but proved an even more effective garrotte. And the knife . . .

The knife had punched through the chest of a coreling prince.

Even now, its magic shone brightly to her warded eyes. Not just the wards – the entire blade had a dull glow to it. It drew blood on her finger at the barest touch.

She knew the power would burn away with the sun, but at the moment, the weapon seemed invincible. Even in the day, it would be stronger. Magic always left things better than it found them. Likewise, the barest brush of the polishing cloth brought the necklace back to a shine, the cord even tougher than when it was made.

Renna stood guard over Twilight Dancer until dawn. The morning sun struck the scattered bodies of the corelings, setting them ablaze. It was a sight she never tired of, though it came at a heavy price. Even as the demons burned, the blackstem wards on her skin began to tingle as their magic faded. The knife grew hot in its sheath, burning her leg. She had to lean against a tree for support, feeling like a Jongleur's puppet with the strings cut, weak and half blind.

The disorientation passed quickly, and Renna took a deep breath. With a few hours' rest, she would feel fitter than the best day of her life, but even that was but a pale shadow of how she felt in the night.

How did Arlen retain his power in the sunlight? Was it that his wards were permanent tattoos rather than blackstem stains? If so, she would take a needle and ink to her skin that very day.

The demon corpses burned hot and fast, in seconds leaving only scorched ground and ash. Renna stamped out the last few scrub fires before they had a chance to grow, and then finally gave in to her exhaustion, curling next to Twilight Dancer and falling asleep.

Renna was still next to Twilight Dancer when she awoke, but rather than the moss bed she had gone to sleep on, she was now lying on a rough blanket in the back of a trundling cart. She popped her head up and saw Arlen out front wearing the yoke. He pulled them along at an impressive pace.

The sight washed the last vestige of sleep from her, and Renna vaulted easily into the driver's seat, grabbing the reins and giving them a loud crack. Arlen jumped straight up in surprise, and Renna laughed. 'Giddyap!'

Arlen gave her a sour look, and Renna laughed again. She leapt down from the cart and kept pace with him. The road was poorly kept and overgrown in places, but not so much as to hinder them.

'Sweetwell's just up ahead,' Arlen said.

'Sweetwell?' Renna asked.

'S'what they named the town,' Arlen said. 'On account of how good the well water tasted.'

'Thought we were avoiding towns,' Renna said.

'None but ghosts in this one,' Arlen said, and Renna could hear the pain in the words. 'Sweetwell was taken by the night a couple years ago.'

'You knew the place before it was taken?' she asked.

Arlen nodded. 'Used to come here sometimes, back when I was a Messenger. Town had ten families. "Sixty-seven hard-workin' folk", they loved to say. They had some queer ways about them, but they were always glad to see the Messenger, and they made the harshest poteen you ever drank.'

'You ent had my da's,' Renna grunted. 'Worked same as drink or lamp oil.'

'Sweetwell's was so strong, the Duke of Angiers had it outlawed,' Arlen said. 'Struck the town from the maps and ordered the Messengers' Guild not to visit there any more.'

'But you still did,' Renna said.

'Corespawned right we did,' Arlen said. 'Who's he think he is, cutting a town off like that? Besides, a Messenger could make six months' pay with one poteen run to Sweetwell. And I liked the Wellers. They had their whole town warded, the place abustle day and night. You could hear them singing a mile away.'

'What happened?' Renna asked.

Arlen shrugged. 'Started working farther south, and stopped visiting for a few years. Wasn't until after I started warding my flesh that I came back this way. I'd spent months in the wild at that point. Got so lonely I used to talk out loud to Dancer, carrying the conversation for the both of us. I was cracking, and I knew it.'

Renna thought of all the times she'd talked to the animals on her father's farm the same way. How many heartfelt talks had she had with Mrs Scratch, or Hoofy? Even with Harl around, she knew lonely.

'Realized I was near Sweetwell one day,' Arlen said, 'and decided to wrap my hands and face in cloth and tell 'em some tampweed tale about how I was burned by firespit. Anything to talk to a person and have them talk back. But when I got to the town, it was quiet for the first time.'

They passed a stand of trees, and the village came into view, ten sturdy thatch-roofed houses and a Holy House in a neat circle around a central boardwalk with a great well at its eye. There were wardposts along the outer perimeter, and each house had two storeys, the top for living and the bottom a work space/shopfront. There was a smithy, a tavern, a stable, a baker, a weaver, and others less easily identified.

Renna felt unnerved as they crossed the boardwalk to the stable. Everything was so well preserved. There was no sign that demons had come, and it seemed that at any moment, people would come pouring out of the buildings. She could see their ghosts in her mind's eye as they went about their lives.

'Boardwalk was full of bones and blood and demonshit when I got in close,' Arlen said. 'Still stank, as if it had only been a few days. Days! If only I'd come sooner, I could have . . .'

Renna touched his arm, saying nothing.

'One of the wardposts looked like it cracked and blew over

in the wind,' Arlen went on. 'Wood demons must've found the gap and fell on the folk at evening supper. A few fled into the night, but I tracked them and found only remains.'

Renna could picture it vividly, the Wellers all gathered around the wooden tables on the boardwalk, sharing a communal meal, completely unprepared when the corelings struck. She could hear the screams and see the dying. Dizzied by it all, she dropped to her knees as her stomach churned.

Arlen put his hand on her shoulder a moment later, and Renna realized she'd been weeping. She looked up at him guiltily.

'Ent nothin' to be ashamed of,' he said. 'Took it a fair bit worse myself.'

'What did you do?' Renna asked.

Arlen blew out a breath. 'Blacked out a few weeks. Spent the days burying bones, drunk on poteen, and the nights killing every corespawn that came within ten miles of Sweetwell.'

'Saw fresh tracks on the way in,' Renna noted.

Arlen grunted. 'They'll be bonfires come tomorrow morning.'

Renna put her hand on the hilt of her knife, spitting on the boardwalk. 'Honest word.'

They moved on to the stable, and Arlen eased Twilight Dancer down to the floor. He grunted with the exertion, but managed the task easily enough. Renna shook her head, doubting she could have done the same even when charged with magic in the night.

'We'll need some water,' Arlen said.

'I'll fetch it,' Renna said, turning towards the central well. 'Want to taste water so sweet they named a town after it.'

Arlen grabbed her arm. 'Water ent too sweet any more. Found Kennit Sweetwell, the town elder, floating in the well. Rotted for more'n a week before I could climb down and haul what was left of him up. Well's poison now. Pump behind the tavern still runs clean, but it ent anything to name a town over.'

Renna spat again, fetching a bucket and heading to the

tavern. Again, her hand drifted to her knife, caressing the bone handle. Night couldn't come soon enough.

When Dancer was seen to, they took time to wash and ate a cold meal in the empty tavern. 'There's a rent room upstairs,' Arlen said. 'We can get a few hours' sleep before night falls.'

'Rent room?' Renna asked. 'When there are whole houses for the taking?'

Arlen shook his head. 'Dun't feel right to take someone else's bed after they been cored. That room was where I slept when I was a Messenger, and it's good enough.'

Love you, Arlen Bales, she thought, but there was no need to repeat what had already been said. She nodded and followed him up the stairs.

Even the rent room was bigger than any Renna had ever slept in before, with a large feather bed. Renna sat on it, amazed at its softness. She had never slept on anything softer than a straw mattress. She lay back. This was softer than a cloud.

Her eyes wandered the room as she sank further into the feathery embrace. Arlen had clearly spent some time here. There was his signature clutter on every surface – pots of paint, brushes, etching tools, and books. A small writing desk had been made into a workbench, and there were wood shavings and sawdust all over the floor.

Arlen crossed the room, folding a rug out of the way and finding a loose floorboard beneath. He pulled and an entire section of the floor came up with it, cleverly disguised with sawdust to hide the cracks. Renna sat up, and her eyes widened as she looked within. It was full of weapons – oiled, sharp, and heavily warded. She slid off the bed, moving to him and crouching for a better look, her eyes dancing along Arlen's warding.

Arlen selected a small goldwood bow and a quiver of arrows, handing it to her. 'Time you learned to shoot.'

Renna's lip curled in distaste. He was trying to protect her again. Keep her from fighting in close. Keep her safe. 'Don't want it. Don't want no spears, neither.'

'Why not?' Arlen asked.

Renna held up her brook stone necklace in one hand, and drew her knife with the other. 'Don't wanna kill corelings from some hiding spot. I kill a demon, I want it to die knowin' who did it.'

She waited for him to argue, but he only nodded.

'Know exactly how you feel.' Arlen continued to hold the weapon out to her. 'But sometimes you're outnumbered, or need to kill a demon quick before it cores somebody.' He smiled. 'And got to say, it ent a bad feeling, to just point at a coreling and kill it from afar.'

Renna took a deep breath. He was right of course. Yes, he was protecting her, but it was in the way he always had.

By teaching her to protect herself.

Love you, Arlen Bales.

She took the bow, marvelling at its lightness. Arlen handed her a small quiver of warded arrows, then began hauling out the rest of the weapons and rolling them in oilcloth.

'What do you need all them for?' she asked.

'Gonna need these and a lot more,' Arlen said. 'Doin' what I shoulda done a long time ago. Gonna give warded arms to every man, woman, and child strong enough to hold one. Been making these stores all over Thesa, but I kept them all to myself. No more. I don't need weapons to kill demons. I'm past that, now.'

'How's that?' Renna asked. She waited for his eyes to flick to the side as he decided how to evade the question. Love him or no, she would smack the top of his bald head if they did.

But Arlen looked right at her, his eyes dancing. 'Gonna show you tonight.' He reached out, caressing the wards of vision stained in circles around her eyes. 'Gonna need your night eyes to understand.'

Renna took his hands and rose to her feet. She backed away, pulling him along until her legs struck the bed. They sank into the feathered mattress, and kisses quickly turned to caresses.

Blood pounded in her ears, a thrumming that made her feel as alive as she did in the night.

The sun was setting as they came back to the taproom for supper. After they had eaten, Arlen rose and rummaged behind the bar. He reappeared a moment later with a heavy clay jug. 'Demons like to rise in the fields out back. What say we have a drink while we wait for 'em?'

They walked together in the gloaming, watching the lavender sky darken. The Wellers' fields were south of the town proper and ran for acres, mostly potato, barley, and sugarcane. The fields hadn't been tended in years, but a wild patchwork crop still clung tenaciously to the land. There were wardposts at regular intervals throughout the fields. Most were in poor repair – worthless, but here and there she saw fresh ones, their painted wards still crisp and clear. Her eyes ran over the posts, finding the pattern.

'You made this place a maze,' she said. 'Like the one in the desert you told me about.'

Arlen nodded, finding a clear spot and sitting. 'Good for cutting demons off from the horde, and a moment's succour is never more than a step away.' He took the heavy jug and filled two tiny clay cups with clear liquid.

'They have a spirit in Krasia that the *Sharum* sometimes drink before going into battle. Call it couzi. Say it gives a warrior courage.' He held a cup to her. 'I've found poteen to have a similar effect.'

'Thought you said the *Sharum* embrace their fear,' Renna said, sitting down next to him with the jug in between.

'Most do, and there ent no better way,' Arlen said. 'But embracing leaves a body cold. Don't want to be cold when I'm in a place like Sweetwell. Want to be mad as the Core itself.'

Renna nodded. That was something she could understand.

She ignored the tiny cups, sticking her finger through the jug handle. She braced the container on her arm and brought it to her lips with practised smoothness, taking a long pull.

The poteen was as strong as Arlen warned, and she coughed a bit, but it was sweeter than her father's brew, and the ball of fire that struck her belly soon calmed and spread warmth throughout her limbs.

Arlen dropped the cups, taking the jug and pulling as she had. They passed it back and forth until the light failed completely and the telltale mists began to rise, heralding the corelings. The mists began to coalesce into field demons, sleek and low to the ground, prowling on all fours like lions, faster than anything alive. A few wood demons appeared as well, the larger demons taking longer to form.

Renna got to her feet, swaying unsteadily for a moment before she regained her equilibrium. She moved towards a coalescing wood demon, carrying the much-lightened jug loosely with one finger.

She glared at the demon as she waited for it to materialize, thinking of the night she had spent locked in her farm's outhouse, screaming as demons rattled at the door. She thought of the empty buildings, and the poisoned well behind her.

She took one last pull of poteen and stoppered the jug. With her free hand, she reached into the pouch at her waist.

At last the demon solidified, opening its mouth to roar at her. The orifice was great enough to swallow her entire head, with row upon row of pointed teeth.

Before it could let out a sound, Renna flicked her hand at it, tossing an acorn into the gaping maw. The heat ward she had painted on the acorn activated when it made contact with the demon's tongue, exploding the nut with a flash and bang.

At that very moment, Renna spat poteen into the demon's face.

She stepped out of the way as its head exploded in flames. The demon fell to the ground, thrashing as its barklike armour burned.

There was a laugh, and Renna turned to see Arlen clapping his hands at her. 'Nice work, but I'll do you one better.'

Renna smirked, and crossed her arms, stepping over to the safety of a wardpost. 'Like to see you try, Arlen Bales.'

Arlen bowed. A field demon turned solid a few feet away from him, bigger than a nightwolf. It growled and tamped down, ready to pounce.

Arlen crossed his arms the same as Renna, standing his ground. His hood was down – he almost never put it up any more – but he still wore the rest of his day robes, covering the powerful wards tattooed all over his body. Field demons were fast as the wind, and without the protection of his wards, it seemed the demon would knock him down and savage him. Renna's hand dropped to her knife, and she gripped it tightly.

But the field demon passed through Arlen as if he had been made of smoke. His body swirled where the creature passed through it, returning after a moment to sharp clarity.

Arlen took a brief bow as the demon recovered. 'Nothing can touch me in the night now, Ren. Not if I see it coming.'

The field demon hit the ground and turned instantly, leaping back at him. Renna expected it to pass through him again, but this time Arlen flowed around the attack faster than her eye could see, wrapping an arm around the coreling's neck and sharply arresting its momentum. He quickstepped around the demon's back to avoid the flailing claws, maintaining the headlock with one arm. He reached his free hand around to draw a heat ward on the demon's chest with his bare finger.

The line he traced came alive with fire as he completed the symbol, and he let go his hold and backed away as the demon was consumed in flames.

Renna gaped, but Arlen wasn't finished with the lesson. He strode towards another field demon, provoking an attack. The demon obliged, roaring and coming at him with claws leading.

'Of course, if I don't see it coming in time to stop it . . .' Arlen was knocked back several steps and grunted as the demon's claws struck home, tearing into his abdomen.

Renna gasped as blood arced through the air. She pulled her knife and darted forward to interpose herself between Arlen and the demon.

But Arlen straightened and stopped her up short with a raised hand. The demon pounced again, but once more Arlen blew apart like smoke.

When he re-formed, there was no sign of his injury. Even his robe was mended. '. . . given a moment to catch my wits, I can heal just about anything that doesn't kill me.'

The demon came at him a third time, but this time Arlen drew a quick warding in the air, and the demon was thrown back as if kicked by a mule before it ever got close to him. His new power seemed limitless.

But as the demon struck the ground several yards away, Arlen staggered in his bow. To Renna's warded eyes, he had been bright with magic a moment before. Now the glow of his wards was noticeably dimmer.

Arlen caught the look she gave him, and nodded. 'I draw wards on a demon, the coreling powers them itself. I draw them in the air, they draw their magic from me, instead.'

The demon came back at him a fourth time, but this time Arlen seized it by the throat and pinned it to the ground in a *sharusahk* hold. As he held it down, Renna could see the wards on his hands throbbing with power, and his glow began to return even as the coreling's dimmed. The demon shrieked and thrashed, but Arlen held it as easily as a man might hold down a small child. The power in his hands built in intensity until the demon's throat collapsed. With a flex of his muscles, Arlen tore its head clean off.

Renna caught sight of a field demon stalking her and shifted position to look dim and helpless. It wasn't difficult. All she needed to do was recall the useless cow she had been all her life. The victim.

But that part of her had died with Harl. When the coreling pounced, it struck the forbidding like an invisible wall, and Renna pivoted in an instant, thrusting her knife into its chest. The wards along the blade flared, cutting through the demon's armour and sending a jolt of magic into her that warmed her limbs even more than the poteen. She bulled forward, stabbing again and again, each blow sending a thrill of power through her.

When the demon hit the ground, dead, she crouched and reached out her hand, tracing a heat ward on the demon's rough armour.

Nothing happened.

'How come you can do it and I can't?' Renna called as she scanned the field for more demons. There were some still circling, but they were wary of the two humans now, and kept their distance.

'Didn't know myself for a long time,' Arlen said. 'Didn't understand any of my powers. But when I fought that demon along the path to the Core, our minds touched, and a lot came clear. I really have become part demon.'

'Demonshit,' Renna said. 'You ent evil like them.'

Arlen shrugged. 'Most demons ent evil, either. Ent smart enough to be evil – or good, for that matter. Might as well call a wasp evil for stinging. The mind demons, though . . .'

'Them bastards are more evil'n Harl,' Renna said.

Arlen nodded. 'By a month's ride.'

Renna furrowed her brow. 'So you're saying . . . what? Corelings are just animals? I ent sold. Wasps don't burst into flame when the sun comes up. Even if demons ent evil, they ent natural, either.'

'That's day folk talking,' Arlen said. 'Folk who haven't warded their eyes. Look around you. Is magic unnatural?'

Renna considered. She looked at the way the power vented

up from the Core, drifting across the surface like a glowing fog swirling at their feet. She saw it at the heart of plants and trees, even animals and people. Would life even exist without it?

'Maybe not,' she allowed, 'but that don't explain why you think you're part demon, or why you still have powers in daylight when the sun burns magic away.'

Arlen hesitated, and his eyes flicked away, considering. Renna's eyes narrowed, and Arlen caught the look. 'Ent gonna lie to you, Ren, or hold back. It's just something I ent proud of, and I don't want you . . . thinking less of me.'

Renna moved in close, putting a hand on his cheek. His skin tingled with magic. 'Love you, Arlen Bales. Ent nothin' in the world ever gonna change that.'

Arlen nodded sadly, not meeting her eyes. 'It's the meat that gave me the power.'

'Meat?'

'Demon meat,' Arlen clarified. 'Ate it for months when I was living in the desert. Seemed only fair, the way they're always eatin' on us.'

Renna gasped and took a step back. Arlen met her eyes then, and she knew from his expression that the look on her face was horrified.

'You . . . *ate* them? Demons?'

Arlen nodded, and Renna felt sick to her stomach. 'Didn't have much choice in the matter. Left in the desert to die, no food, no hope. I was wretched as a man could be.'

'Think I would have let myself die.' Renna immediately regretted the words as a look of anguish crossed Arlen's face.

'Yeah, well,' he said. 'Guess I ent as strong as you, Ren.'

Renna rushed to him, taking his hands and pressing their foreheads together. 'You're stronger than I ever was, Arlen Bales,' she said, feeling tears well in her eyes. 'You hadn't slapped the fool out of me, I'd have let myself die to just keep the Tanner shame a secret. Ent no strength there.'

Arlen shook his head, and a tear of his own struck her lip, cold and sweet. 'Needed the fool slapped out of me more than once over the years.'

Renna kissed him. 'You sure it's the demon meat gave you these powers?'

Arlen nodded. 'Coline Trigg used to say that what you eat becomes a part of you, and I reckon that's so. I've absorbed the corelings' ability to store magic in their cells, but my skin has retained its proof against the sun. I've become like a battery.'

'Cells? Battery?' Renna asked.

'Science of the old world. It doesn't matter.' Arlen waved the questions away in that annoying way he had, keeping the knowledge from her simply because he thought it too tedious to explain. As if she wouldn't listen to him speak all night. As if there were a better sound in all the world. 'Think of it as a drain barrel after a night's rain. Full of water even after the sky clears and the ground dries up. Can't tap the magic in sunlight, but I feel it inside of me, healing my wounds, making me tireless and strong. At night I can let it out like opening a bung, and I'm only just scratching the surface of what can be done.'

Renna paused, considering. Whatever Arlen might say, it was nearly impossible to see corelings as anything but evil abominations of nature, an offence to the Creator. Despite the fact she was often covered in the foul ichor they called blood, the thought of putting it in her mouth was abhorrent.

But the power . . .

'Know what you're thinkin', Ren,' Arlen said, snapping her out of her reverie. 'Don't go tryin' this one.'

'Why?' Renna asked. 'Din't seem to hurt you none.'

'You don't know what it was like, Ren. I was crazed. Suicidal. Lived like an animal.'

Renna shook her head. 'Alone in the middle of nowhere, no one to talk to but Dancer and the corelings. Know what that's like. Apt to make anyone have a night wish, demon meat or no.'

Arlen looked at her, and nodded. 'Honest word. But eating demon ent like painting blackstem on your skin. Won't fade away after a few weeks, and you ent ready for it.'

'Who're you to say what I'm ready for?' Renna demanded.

'Ent giving you orders, Ren, I'm begging you.' Arlen knelt in front of her. 'Don't eat it, and if anyone asks, you tell 'em it's poison.'

Renna stared at him a long while, unsure if she should hold him or slap the fool out of him. At last she sighed, letting her swirling emotions drift away. 'Think on it. And won't tell anyone else. Honest word.'

Arlen nodded, getting to his feet. 'Then let's hunt. Need to be holding as much magic as possible when I heal Dancer.'

Twilight Dancer was lowing in pain when they returned to the stable, tongue hanging from his mouth. His feed was untouched, and the only water he had drunk was what they had poured down his throat. He laboured for breath.

With a single blow, the mimic demon had broken the great stallion's ribs, puncturing Creator only knew what inside, and launching him through the air. Dancer had struck a tree, breaking his back, and the fall had shattered his legs. Arlen had saved Dancer's life with his magic, but without further help he would never walk again, much less run.

But Arlen had suffused himself with so much magic his wards glowed of their own accord, lighting the stable bright as day. He seemed like the Creator Himself as he reached for one of Dancer's legs, pulling the broken bones into proper position and tracing wards on the skin around the fractures.

Dancer whinnied in pain as the bones and sinews knitted back together, a terrible sound Renna could hardly bear. Arlen's glow lessened a bit with each healing, and there were many. Soon his wards dimmed, and then winked out entirely. Still he worked, his sensitive fingers running over the horse's body, probing for places to focus his power. Dancer's chest inflated as the ribs healed, and he began to breathe normally. Renna sighed with relief until Arlen gave a slight groan and collapsed.

He was shivering when she carried him up to bed, his breath coming in short gasps. She could barely hear his heartbeat, and the glow of his magic had faded so much she thought it might wink out at any moment. She stripped and slipped into bed next to him, clutching him tight and willing some of the magic she had absorbed into him, but it seemed to make no difference.

'Don't you die on me, Arlen Bales,' she said. 'Not after all we been through.'

Arlen did not respond, and Renna stood, brushing back tears as she paced the room, her mind racing.

Needs magic, she thought. *Go and get him some.*

She had her knife in hand in an instant, grabbing her cloak and running out the door without bothering to pull her clothes back on. With the Cloak of Unsight around her, she was invisible to the corelings, and quickly found a field demon prowling not far from the wards.

She cast the cloak aside, and before it knew she was there, she had leapt on the demon's back, pulling its chin up with one hand while she cut its throat. She took a bucket from the stables, draining the creature's foul black ichor, rich with glowing magic.

Her naked skin was soon covered in the stuff, and she could feel her blackstem wards pulling at the power. She felt strong beyond belief, moving like wind back to Arlen's side. She laid him on the floor and dumped the reeking bucket over him, watching the wards on his skin brighten and absorb the magic, then dim as his internal aura brightened. He began to breathe easier, and Renna fell to her knees.

'Thank the Creator,' she whispered, drawing a ward in the air. The gesture was an instinctive one, but so similar to the way

Arlen healed Dancer. If only she had been able to do the same for him.

She looked to the bucket, a slimy piece of demon gut clinging to its lip. She scooped the black thing up in her hand, poking at it like jelly. It stank, and her stomach heaved. She had to breathe deeply to keep her supper down.

He'll pull away, I let him, she thought. *Strong as he is, he can't do this alone. Got to keep the pace, or I'll be left behind again next time he's pulled into the Core.*

'Done thinkin',' she muttered.

She held her breath, and put the meat in her mouth.

2

Promise

Renna woke not long after dawn. Arlen slept peacefully now, and she moved carefully so as not to wake him as she washed the dried gore from her skin.

With the curtains drawn tight, Renna still felt charged with power, but as soon as she went out into the sunlight, that strength burned away. She stretched experimentally, seeking some evidence that her disgusting meal had had an effect on her. If there was a change, she couldn't sense it. Arlen had eaten demon meat exclusively for months to achieve his level of power. Renna's stomach churned at the thought of even another nibble.

She moved to the stable, brushing down Twilight Dancer and giving him his morning feed. The stallion looked hale, showing no sign that just two nights ago he had been moments from death. Even his scars were faded things, barely visible.

When she was done, she went out into the field, harvesting potatoes and vegetables from the wild crop, enough to make a proper breakfast for once. She had it ready when Arlen stumbled into the kitchen looking haggard, as if he hadn't slept at all.

'Smells like Heaven in here,' he said.

'Ent got eggs or proper bread, but I caught a rabbit in the fields, so there's meat,' Renna said, spooning the stew into a pair of wooden bowls they took out into the taproom.

When they sat, Arlen looked at his bowl for a moment, then put his head in his hands. 'Might've overdone it last night.'

Renna snorted. 'That's undersaid.'

Arlen puffed his cheeks and blew out a slow breath. 'Regrettin' all that poteen now.'

'Eat,' Renna ordered. 'Your stomach will calm with something in it. And best drink all the water you can stand, sweet or not.' Arlen nodded and soon was eating voraciously, his bowl quickly emptied.

'There any more?' he asked, and Renna started. She'd been so busy watching him eat, she hadn't touched her own food.

'Take mine.' She slid the bowl to him and took his empty one. 'I'll get another.' She was pleased to see his second helping emptied by the time she sat back down.

'Feeling better?' she asked.

'Feel human,' Arlen said, a small smile tugging the corner of his mouth. 'Been a while.'

'Can rest up another day,' Renna said. 'Charge you up again tonight.'

Arlen shook his head. 'Miles to go today, Ren. Got one stop this afternoon and then it's straight on to the Hollow fast as we can manage.'

'What stop?' Renna asked.

Arlen smiled again, this time wider, with a glitter to his eyes. 'Need to pick you a proper promise gift.'

Arlen set a strong pace as they headed down the Messenger road. Renna could see it took a toll on him after a few hours, but he steadfastly refused to ride.

'Dancer needs the rest more'n me,' he said.

The sun was well past its high point when they came to a fork in the road and Arlen turned onto the less travelled way, little more than a bridle path heading into the wild hilly plain.

'What's off this way?' she asked.

'Rancher I know,' Arlen said. 'Owes me a favour.' Renna waited for more, but nothing was forthcoming.

It was an hour's walk before the ranch came in sight. There were three barns, each with its own wards in addition to the posts set around the exercise pen and yard. Wide grazing areas had been warded as well.

A boy appeared on the roof of the closest barn, holding a short bow with an arrow nocked and pointed at them.

'Whozzat?' he called.

Renna crouched at the sight, ready to dodge left or right if the boy should shoot. She gripped the familiar bone handle of her father's knife, though it would do her no good here. She'd hated Harl Tanner, but always felt safe when touching the knife she'd used to kill him.

Arlen seemed unconcerned as he shouted back to the boy, 'Someone who's going to regret not letting you get et by that wood demon, Nik Stallion, you don't put down that bow and fetch your da.'

'Messenger!' Nik shouted, lowering the bow and waving. 'Ma! Pa! Messenger's come, and he's brought Dancer!'

The boy slid down the roof to the porch awning, swinging easily to the ground from its lip. He ran to the garden and pulled up a couple of carrots before hurrying over to them, staring at Twilight Dancer in wonder. 'He's grown big as a barn!'

He eased carefully up to the great stallion, holding out the carrots. 'Easy, boy, it's me, Nik. You remember, don't you?' Twilight Dancer nickered, taking the carrots, but the boy stayed tense, ready to run.

Renna couldn't understand his tension. If the boy knew Dancer, he should know the horse was gentle as the dawn. 'He ent gonna kick or bite you, boy.'

Nik turned and seemed about to say something, but he paused mid-breath, noticing Renna for the first time. His eyes roamed her body, and she wasn't sure if he was looking at her blackstem wards or the flesh they were painted on. She didn't much care what he saw, but it was rude, and she put her hands on her hips and gave him a glare to remind him of his manners. The boy jumped and looked away so quickly Renna had to stifle a laugh.

Nik turned to Arlen, blushing fiercely. 'You *tamed* him?'

Arlen laughed. 'Hardly. Dancer's still the meanest horse alive, but he only bites and kicks corelings now.'

A low whistle came from behind them, and Renna whirled. Without thinking, her hand found the knife handle again. She took it away quickly, hoping no one had noticed.

And I meant to teach young Nik his manners.

The man who approached showed no sign that he had seen. Like the boy, he only had eyes for the horse at first. He approached calmly, giving Dancer time to get used to his presence. The stallion snorted and stamped a bit, but accepted his touch.

'He *has* grown,' the man said, running his hands over Dancer's heavy flanks. He was tall and lean, with a thick but close-cropped beard. His brown hair was long and braided in back. 'Must be two hands taller than his sire, and old Rockslide's bigger'n any horse I ever saw.' He picked up one of the stallion's feet. 'Could do with a shoeing, though.'

The man looked up at them at last, and like the boy he let his eyes range over Renna, examining her as if she were a horse. A low growl formed at the back of her throat, and the man gave a start when his eyes finally met hers and saw her glare.

Arlen stepped between them. 'Just a look, Ren,' he murmured. 'These're good folk.'

Renna gritted her teeth. Much as she hated to admit it, he was right about what the magic did to a person, even in the day. Passion came quick to her now. She took a deep breath and let her anger fall away.

Arlen nodded and turned to the rancher. 'Renna Tanner, this here's Jon Stallion and his boy Nik. Jon breaks and breeds wild Angierian mustang.'

'*Catches* and breeds, anyway,' Jon said, his eyes offering an apology as he put out his hand. 'Ent easy to tame something that can trample a field demon to death and outrun anything else in the naked night.' Renna took his hand, but let go quick when he winced at her grip.

'Know how they feel, sometimes,' she muttered.

Jon nodded back at Dancer. 'Take that'un. Caught him as a colt not six months old. Thought for sure I could break the wild out of one that young, but he wouldn't take so much as a halter, and kicked his way out of the barn more'n once.'

'The naked night ent forgiving,' Arlen said. 'Six months is a lifetime out with the demons.'

Jon nodded. 'Didn't think even *you* could tame him.'

'Didn't,' Arlen said. 'Just brought him back where he belonged.'

'Got him taking a saddle and reins, though,' Jon noted, 'but I guess I shouldn't be surprised. Back then, you were just the crazy tattooed Messenger who saved my boy. Now I hear tell you're the ripping Deliverer!'

'Ent,' Arlen said. 'I'm Arlen Bales out of Tibbet's Brook, and I just got more sack than sense, sometimes.'

'So you have a name, after all,' a woman said, coming out from the ranch house. She was plain, but had the vigorous look of one used to hard work. She wore men's clothes – high leather boots, breeches, and vest with a simple white blouse beneath. Her hair was brown and braided back much like Jon's.

'Don't mind the boys,' she told Renna. 'Ent gonna talk about much else when there's horseflesh about. I'm Glyn.'

'Renna.' Renna shook her hand, then clenched her fist as

the woman embraced Arlen. Was it the magic that made her resent another woman touching him?

'Good to see you again, Messenger. Can you stay for supper?'

Arlen nodded, showing the first warm smile Renna had ever seen him give another person. 'I'd like that.'

'What brings you out this way?' Jon asked. 'Ent just for the shoeing, I'd guess.'

Arlen nodded. 'I need another horse. A filly I can breed with Dancer.'

He looked at Renna and gave her a half smile. 'Startin' a family.'

Mack Pasture, who lived up the road from Renna's father's farm, had been a horse breeder. Renna visited his ranch often when her mother was alive. It was a good deal smaller than Jon Stallion's, but it worked much the same. After Dancer was brought to the farrier, Jon led the way towards a great fenced field where dozens of horses grazed under the watchful eyes of mounted ranch hands and barking dogs. On the way, they passed thick, heavy corrals, too high for even Twilight Dancer to jump in daylight, used for training and quarantine.

In one of these, Renna saw a giant black stallion cantering by itself, watched by two nervous ranch hands with ready whips. She stopped short.

'Ay, that's old Rockslide,' Jon said. 'Dancer's sire. Caught him on the plain with half a dozen mares and young Dancer. Call him Rockslide 'cause that's what it felt we'd been through when we finally herded him into a corral.

'Big bastard won't do a lick of work, but he'll kick holes in the barn all night long, you let him. Mean as a demon, and too smart by half. City breeders'll tell you wild horses ent smart because they won't follow commands, but don't you believe 'em. Mustang got their own smarts. Enough to survive the naked night, which is more than most folk can say. Rockslide liked to throw anyone that tried to mount, then trample them into the yard. Retired him to the breeding pen when we got tired of bone setting.'

Renna looked at the magnificent animal, and felt a profound sorrow. *You were a king out on the plains, and here they have you running circles in a pen and mounting mares all day.* She had to suppress an urge to walk right up to the gate and set him free.

'Good foaling this summer,' Jon said as they made their way out onto the field. 'Lots of fillies to choose from.'

'Your choice, Ren,' Arlen said. 'Any one you want.'

Renna looked out over the herd. At first glance, Jon's horses looked little different from Mack's, but as she drew closer and took in their scale, her eyes widened. The foals looked juvenile next to the mares, but even they were bigger than some of the stallions Mack kept. Jon had yearlings big enough for a grown man to ride, and there were no poor specimens. Demons had culled all but the strongest strains, and the remainder were giants, sleek and dark-coated.

There were a number of strong-looking fillies, but Renna found her eyes drawn instead to a grown mare who stood apart from the herd. The mare had a blotchy coat of brown and black, and stood a hand taller than the others. She had a surly look about her, and even the other horses gave her a wide berth.

'What about that one?' Renna asked, pointing.

Jon grunted. 'You got a good eye, girl. Most folk can't see past that ugly coat. That's Twister. Caught her last summer, right before the worst windstorm I ever seen. Stronger'n most stallions and barely five years old, she's tried to get away more times'n I can count. Go near her with a halter – night, go near her at all – and she gets all kinds of mean. Even bit old Rockslide when I put her in his pen to see if they'd get on.'

'Ent gonna need a halter,' Renna said, vaulting the fence and heading across the field.

'Telling you, that horse is dangerous,' Jon called after her. 'Sure you know what you're doin'?' Renna waved a hand dismissively, not even bothering to look at him.

Twister didn't back away as Renna approached. That was good. The mare seemed to be ignoring her, but the way her ears were pointed, Renna was sure she had the horse's full attention.

She held up her empty hands. 'Ent got a halter. Don't reckon I'd care to wear one, so I ent gonna ask you to, either.'

Twister let her get in close, but when Renna reached out to stroke the horse's neck, she moved fast, powerful jaws snapping. Renna barely snatched her hand away before it was bitten off.

'Weren't no call for that!' she snapped, slapping the mare hard on the nose. Twister went wild at the blow, rearing up and kicking her feet, but Renna was ready. Months of hunting demons and absorbing their magic had left her stronger and faster than she had ever dreamed, and now that her blood was up she could feel a new tingle in her limbs, a taste of night's power, even here under the sun.

Renna weaved like a barley stalk in the wind, feeling the whoosh of air as the kicking hooves missed her by scant inches. Again and again the frenzied mare tried to crush her. Powerful blows. And fast. Kicks that could break a field demon's back.

But Renna's moves were smooth and fluid like a dance, and she remained untouched. It went on for some time, and she began to wonder which of them would give in first. The new power in her limbs was only a fraction of what she felt in the night. The horse seemed tireless.

But at last, Twister's kicks began to slow, and she bunched her muscles, ready to flee. Renna rushed in before the mare could gallop off, gripping a handful of mane in her fist and vaulting onto the horse's bare back.

If Twister had been crazed before, her rage was tripled now.

She fought true to her name, leaping and writhing in mid-air, bucking and galloping in circles, trying to throw Renna.

But Renna had her seat, and wasn't giving it up. She threw her arms around the horse's throat, so thick she was barely able to clasp her wrists. Once she had the hold, that powerful neck became her entire world, her only adversary. Nothing else mattered.

She called upon every bit of power she could muster, and began to squeeze.

It seemed to go on forever, but finally Twister began to calm. She stopped bucking and galloped around the pen, setting the dogs into a frenzy as the other horses leapt from her path.

Renna continued to squeeze, slow and sure, and soon even that gallop slowed to a wilful canter. Renna smiled. Wilful was good.

She eased her grip from Twister's neck, taking two fists of mane and pulling hard to the left. She laughed aloud when Twister obediently turned. Gripping the horse's flanks with her knees and the mane in her fist, Renna drew her knife and slapped the horse's rump with the wide flat of the blade. 'Hyah!'

Twister leapt ahead, breaking back into a gallop. Renna sheathed her knife and took the mane in both hands. A tug here or there would turn the horse, but Renna let her have her head, exhilarated as the wind whipped her long braid about, and she was jarred again and again by the horse's powerful strides.

Renna leaned in, putting her mouth to Twister's ear. 'You belong in the night, girl. Ent gonna let you end up like Rockslide. Promise.'

Renna ran them back to the edge of the fence where Arlen and the others waited, pulling up short.

'Made your choice, then?' Arlen asked. 'Twister?'

Renna nodded. 'But Twister ent a good name. Gonna call her Promise.'

Dinner on the Stallion ranch was a family affair, and that family extended down to the last ranch hand and laundry girl, over thirty people in all. Even some of the dogs lay on blankets along the walls of the great hall, ready to leap for scraps. Renna and Arlen sat by Jon, Glyn, and Nik at the head of a long trestle table heavily laden with food and pitchers of water and ale.

Jon led them in a prayer to the Creator, and Renna saw some of the hands staring at Arlen's warded face. Even over Jon's intonation, her sharp ears caught the word 'Deliverer' whispered about the table. Unbidden, her fingers stroked the smooth bone handle of her knife.

Jon finished his prayer and straightened. 'Dunno about you lot, but I'm starved! Set to passin'.' At that, the still table came alive with motion as thirty diners began passing trays of meat, bowls of vegetables, crusts of bread, and boats of gravy around the table with practised efficiency.

Everyone filled their plate, laughing and talking as they ate and drank while the sun set outside. People continued to glance Arlen's way, but he pretended not to notice, filling his plate three times. But no sooner had the plates been cleared and the pipes lit than he was on his feet.

'Dinner was delicious as always, Glyn, but it's time we were on our way.'

'Nonsense,' Glyn said. 'It's full dark out there. We've plenty of room for you to spend the night.'

''Preciate the hospitality,' Arlen said, 'but Ren and I got miles to go tonight.'

Glyn frowned, but she nodded all the same. 'I'll have the girls pack you something for the ride. Creator only knows what you've got to eat in your saddlebags.' She rose and headed for the kitchen.

Arlen reached into his robes, handing Jon a pouch of coins. 'For Promise.'

Jon shook his head. 'Your coin's no good here, Messenger. Not after what you did for me and mine. Even beyond my boy,

66

those warded arrows you gave us have gone a long way toward everyone sleeping easy in the night.'

But Arlen shook his head. 'Hard times a-comin', Jon. Refugees from Rizon are pouring north in a flood, and don't think the war won't get here eventually. Krasians have their sights set on Miln and beyond, and now that folk are fighting back, don't expect the corelings to take it well. They'll be out in force at night, especially when the moon is dark.'

He pressed the bag into Jon's hands. 'Got plenty of gold. No reason I can't pay fair for what I take. Leaving you a couple warded spears, too. You're smart, you'll get your forge hands and Warders to copy them and make enough to go around.'

Renna put a hand on his arm, and when Arlen looked at her, she met his eyes with a pleading look. 'Take Rockslide, too. Ent right, him locked up like that. Meant to be out in the night.'

'Can't argue that,' Arlen said, 'but we got a long way to go in a hurry, and ent got time to drag another wild mustang all the way back to the Hollow.' He looked to Jon, counting out more coins. 'Can you send him on after us?'

'Owe you that much and more,' Jon said, 'but I can't risk my hands on a trip like that. Rocky will pull his stake and likely kick out the warding circles the first time they camp.'

Arlen nodded. 'I'll send Cutters to fetch him once I get to the Hollow. If anyone can handle a giant horse like that, it's them.'

They flew down the road now. Twilight Dancer had to slow his full stride to match Promise, but Renna knew that it was only a matter of time.

'I'm done wardin' you up,' she whispered in the mare's ear, '*he'll* be the one tryin' to keep pace with *you*.'

Already, Promise wore shoes Arlen had warded himself, same as Dancer. A wood demon stepped onto the road in their path, and Renna rode it down in a thunderclap of magic. She pulled up, trampling the hapless demon and laughing as Promise crushed the life from it and got her first taste of demon magic. She leapt on down the road after Dancer, closing the gap between them with new vigour.

They made camp not long before dawn. 'Stay with the horses,' Arlen said. 'Need to get a bit of my strength back.' He disappeared into the gloom.

Renna gave him a few breaths to draw away, then moved off after prey of her own. She caught sight of a field demon stalking not far from camp, and fell into the lack-witted stumble of the old Renna, heaving her chest and whimpering in fear.

The demon gave a growl and pounced, but Renna was ready and caught it in a *sharusahk* throw, bearing it down. Her fists were painted with powerful wards, and she beat it about the head until it lay still.

She drew her knife, and this time didn't even bother to cook the demon's flesh before she ate it, sucking down the ichor like Glyn's gravy. The taste was even fouler, but the remembrance of her power under the sun that day kept Renna's stomach strong.

She was cleaned up and back in camp, chewing a sourleaf and carving wards into Promise's hooves, when she heard Arlen returning.

'He ent gonna know what I done,' she told Promise. 'Ent no way he could. And so what if he does? Arlen Bales don't tell me what to do, promise or no.'

It was true enough, but it felt like a lie all the same.

She lifted her chin as Arlen appeared. He was glowing so brightly with magic that she had to squint her warded eyes to look at him. She understood why others thought him the Deliverer. There were times when the Creator Himself didn't shine like Arlen Bales.

3

The Oatingers

333 AR Summer
27 Dawns Before New Moon

*T*hey said little the next day as they raced down an ill-used Messenger road. Arlen's hood was drawn against the sun, but Renna knew the look of frustration it hid.

What business does Arlen have in Deliverer's Hollow that's so all-fired important?

It had to do with a girl, she knew. Leesha Paper. The name itched at her like a chigger. Arlen was evasive the first time Renna tried to ask who Leesha was to him, but they hadn't been promised then, and she'd no right to insist.

Reckon it's time to ask again, she thought.

'Look out!' Arlen cried as they turned a tight bend. Right in front of them, a cart was turned across the road, thick bushes to either side making it impossible to ride around. Renna dug her knees into Promise and pulled hard on her mane. The giant horse reared, whinnying and kicking wildly, and it was all Renna could do to keep her seat. Arlen watched, amused, from atop Twilight Dancer, who had already pulled up short and composed himself.

'Promised you no halter,' Renna said to the mare when she finally calmed. 'Din't say nothin' about no saddle. You think on that.' Promise snorted.

'Ay, Tender! We could use a hand!' a grey-bearded man called, waving at them with a worn and beaten hat. He and another man stood behind the cart, pushing as the skinny nag in front pulled.

'Let me handle this, Ren,' Arlen murmured, edging Twilight Dancer ahead of Promise. 'What happened?' he called.

The man came over to them, taking off his hat again to wipe the sweat from his brow with the back of his dirty hand. His hair and beard were mostly grey, the deep lines of his face streaked with dirt. 'Stuck in the rottin' mud. Think you might lend us one o' them big horses long enough to break free?'

'Sorry, can't help,' Arlen said, his eyes scanning the area.

The man's eyes gogged at him. 'Whaddaya mean, you can't help? What kind of Tender are you?'

Renna looked at Arlen, surprised he would be so rude to a greybeard in need. 'Dancer could pull them free in no time.'

Arlen shook his head. 'Cart ent stuck, Ren. This is the oldest trick in the bandit handbook.' He snorted. 'Didn't think folk still did this one.'

'Bandits? Honest word?' Renna looked around again, this time with her night eyes. She and Arlen were cut off in the middle of nowhere, in daylight when they were weakest. The mud wasn't even up to the ankles of the men, and the bushes on either side of the road could easily conceal more men. Her fingers drifted towards her knife, but Arlen whisked a hand at her and she left it in its sheath.

'Bad enough we got demons at night,' Arlen said. 'Now folk turn on each other in the day.'

'That's ridiculous!' the greybeard cried, but he was stepping back, and Renna could see the lie in his eyes now, so clear that she wondered why she hadn't seen it before. That day folk, even elders, could be just as bad as demons was no new lesson to her. Harl had been grey, and Raddock Lawry.

The man standing behind the cart ducked out of sight a moment, and then reappeared holding a crank bow. Two men came from the bushes, aiming drawn hunting bows at them. From around the bend behind them came three more men with spears, blocking their retreat. All were gaunt, with dark circles under their eyes and ragged, patched clothing.

Only the greybeard was unarmed. 'Ent looking to hurt anyone, Tender,' he said, putting his hat back on, 'but these are desperate times, and you're carrying an awful heavy load for a Tender and his . . .' He squinted at Renna. She was dappled in shadows, obscuring the wards on her skin, but there was no missing the scandalous cut of her clothes. The man with the crank bow let out a low whistle, moving forward for a closer look.

'Don't go gettin' any ideas, Donn,' the greybeard warned, and the crank bowman checked himself.

The greybeard flicked his eyes back to Arlen. 'In any event, we'll be taking any food, blankets, or medicine you got, not to mention those big horses.'

Renna gripped her knife, but Arlen only chuckled. 'Trust me, you wouldn't want the horses.'

'You don't get to tell me what I want, Tender,' the greybeard snapped. 'Creator abandoned us a long time ago. Now you two get down off those horses or my men will fill you full of holes.'

Arlen was off Twilight Dancer in an instant. Renna barely saw him move as he closed the distance to the greybeard, catching him in a *sharusahk* choke hold and twisting the old man between him and the bowmen.

'Like you said,' Arlen said, 'ent looking to hurt anyone. Just looking to be on my way. So why don't you tell your men to . . .'

He was cut off as one of the bowmen let fly. Renna gasped, but Arlen snatched the arrow out of the air the way a quick man might snatch a horsefly.

'This was apt to hit you more than me,' Arlen noted, holding up the arrow in front of the greybeard. He tossed it aside.

'Corespawn it, Brice!' the greybeard shouted. 'You trying to kill me?!'

'Sorry!' Brice cried. 'Slipped!'

'Slipped, he says,' the greybeard muttered. 'Creator help us.'

While all the attention was on the bowman, one of the spearmen took the opportunity to quietly move up behind Arlen. He was sneaky enough by day folk standards, but Renna didn't cry an alarm. She could tell just from Arlen's stance that he knew the man was coming. Was baiting it, even.

Just as the spearman lunged, Arlen shoved the greybeard away. The man put his spear horizontally over Arlen's head, meaning to come up under his chin in a choke. Arlen grabbed the shaft, bending forward with a twist that turned all the man's momentum against him, flipping him over to land heavily on his back. Arlen, now holding the spear in one hand, put his foot on the man's chest and looked at the others.

In the struggle, his hood had come down, and the men gaped at the sight. 'The Painted Man,' Brice said, and all the bandits began to mutter among themselves.

After a moment, the greybeard remembered himself. 'So you're the one everyone says is the Deliverer.' He squinted. 'You don't look like the Deliverer to me.'

'Never said I was,' Arlen said. 'I'm Arlen Bales out of Tibbet's Brook, and I ent gonna deliver anything but a whipping to anyone doesn't start acting neighbourly right quick.'

The greybeard looked at him, and then around at his men. He waved a hand and they put their weapons up, all staring at Arlen, who glared back at them like Renna's mam when she'd caught the girls at mischief and was readying a scolding.

Even the greybeard couldn't weather that stare for long. He wiped the sweat from his weathered brow again, wringing his hat in his hands. 'Ent gonna apologize,' he said. 'I got mouths to feed, and folk in need of proper succour. Done some things I'm not proud of to get by, but it ent from greed or malice. A man tends to forget himself when he's been on the road a long time with nowhere to go.'

Arlen nodded. 'Know what that's like. What's your name?'

'Varley Oat,' the greybeard said.

Arlen nodded at the surname. 'You're out of Oating, then? Three days' north of Fort Rizon, past the Yellow Orchards?'

Varley's eyes widened, but he nodded. 'You come a long way from Oating, Varley,' Arlen said. 'How long you been on the road?'

'Nigh three seasons. Since the Krasians took Fort Rizon,' Varley said. 'Knew the desert rats would come for us next, so I told folk to pack up everything they owned and set off right away.'

'You Town Speaker?' Arlen asked.

Varley laughed. 'I was the Tender.' He shrugged. 'Guess I still am, after a fashion, though I been doubting there's anyone watching from above.'

'Know that feeling, too,' Arlen said.

'Whole village of Oating left together,' Varley went on. 'Six hundred of us. We had Herb Gatherers, Warders, even a retired Messenger to guide us. Plenty of supplies. Honest word, we started with more than we could carry. But that changed quick.'

'Always does,' Arlen said.

'Desert rats came quickly,' Varley said, 'and their scouts were everywhere. Lost a lot of folk to the running, and a lot more to the winter. Krasians stopped chasing us eventually, but no one felt safe until we got to Lakton.'

'But Lakton wouldn't have you,' Arlen guessed.

Varley shook his head. 'We were looking a bit shabby by then. Folk would look the other way for a bit if we camped for a week in a fallow field or fished a bit in their pond, but no one was looking to take five hundred new folk into their town. Someone would accuse us of stealing something, and before you know it, whole town comes out with rakes and hoes to run us out.

'Went on from there to the Hollow, where they're taking in

Rizonans by the thousand, but folk there were chewing bark and digging bugs just to fill their bellies, and the Cutters roam the refugee camps, looking for recruits to get themselves killed in the naked night. Some of us lost everything to the Krasians, and they want us to start fightin' demons? Won't be no one left.'

'So you set off north,' Arlen said.

Varley shrugged. 'Seemed like the wisest course. I still had nigh three hundred folk to look after. Hollowers gave us a couple of warded spears and what help they could. Farmer's Stump wasn't half so kind, and the bastards in Fort Angiers turned us away at spearpoint. Heard there might be work up Riverbridge way, but that place was no better. Packed full. So now we're here, and got nowhere else.'

'Show me your camp,' Arlen said. The bandit looked at him for a moment, then nodded and turned to his men. The cart was out of the mud in an instant, and they were soon travelling off road through a narrow pass in the trees. Arlen dismounted, leading Twilight Dancer by the reins. Renna did the same, laying a hand on Promise's strong neck to guide her. The mare stomped and snorted when any of the men drew near, but she was growing used to Renna's touch.

It was over an hour before the Oatingers' camp came in sight, hidden well away from the road. Renna's eyes widened at the ragtag collection of crudely patched tents and covered wagons, thick with the stench of sweat and human waste. Perhaps two hundred souls were gathered there. Varley's men, ragged themselves, were the pick of the lot.

Women, children, and elderly stumbled about the camp, exhausted, filthy, and half starved. Many wore bandages, and most feet were wrapped in rags. Everyone was working – repairing and warding tattered and meagre shelters, tending gruel pots, airing laundry and scraping dishes, gathering fire-wood, preparing wardposts, tending scrawny livestock. The only idle were the sick and the wounded, housed under a poorly constructed rain shelter. Their moans of pain could be heard clear across the camp.

Arlen led Twilight Dancer through the camp, his back stiff as he looked in the lost and tired eyes of the people. They started when they caught sight of his warded face, and began to whisper among themselves, but none had the courage to approach him as he passed.

They came to the shelter for the sick, and Renna choked on the sight like it was demon meat. Almost two dozen folk spread out on narrow cots, covered in bloody bandages, filthy and reeking. Two of the patients had soiled themselves, and another was covered in her own sick. None of them looked apt to recover.

One frazzled woman attempted vainly to tend them all. Her grey hair was pulled in a tight bun, and her narrow face pinched. She wore no pocketed apron on her worn dress.

'Creator, they don't even have a proper Gatherer,' Arlen whispered.

'My wife, Evey,' Varley grunted. 'She ent an Herb Gatherer, but serves as one, for those in need.' Evey looked up, and her eyes widened in shock as she took in Arlen's and Renna's warded skin.

Arlen went to his saddlebag and fetched his herb pouch. 'I've some Gatherer's art, particularly when it comes to coreling wounds. Like to help if I might.'

Evey fell to her knees. 'Oh, please, Deliverer! We'll do anything!'

Arlen's brows knit in sudden anger. 'You can start by not acting the fool!' he snapped. 'I ent no Deliverer. I'm Arlen Bales out of Tibbet's Brook, and I'm just looking to help as I can.'

Evey looked as if he had slapped her. Her pale cheeks grew a bright red, and she got quickly to her feet. 'I'm sorry . . . I don't know what came over me . . .'

Arlen reached out, squeezing her shoulder. 'You don't have to explain. Know the ale stories the Jongleurs spin about me.

But I'm here to tell you I'm a man like any other. Just learned some old world tricks folk these days have forgotten.'

Evey nodded, finally looking him in the eye and relaxing.

''Bout sixty miles north of here is the village of Deadwell,' Arlen told Varley. 'I can draw you a good map, with places you can camp along the way marked off.'

'Why should they want us at Deadwell more'n anywhere else?' Varley asked.

''Cause there ent no one in Deadwell any more,' Arlen said. 'Corelings got in and killed every man, woman, and child there. But we just been there, and swept the place good. Might be cramped at first, but it's got everything you need to start a new life. Just make sure you brick up the well, and dig a fresh one.'

Varley gaped at him. 'You're just . . . giving us a village?'

Arlen nodded. 'Used to go there a lot. Place was special to me. I'd like it to be a home to good folk again.' He gave Varley a pointed look. 'Folk that take a dim view of banditry.'

Varley seemed unconvinced. 'Canon says, *Trust not the man who offers all you desire just when you need it most.*'

Arlen smiled. 'Creator abandoned you, but Tender Varley can't stop quoting Canon?'

Varley chuckled. 'World's full of contradictions.'

'Deadwell ent gonna do you any worse than you already are,' Arlen said. 'Your wards are weak. Could see that just passing through.'

Varley nodded and spat. 'Ent got so much as a Hedge Warder outside a hospit cot. Folk are just warding their carts and tents as best they can.'

Arlen nodded to Renna. 'This here's Renna Tanner, my intended. She's a fair hand at warding. I'd like you and your men to take her around the camp. Help her see if she can't grant you more succour.'

Evey bowed to Renna. 'It's a real blessing, you doing this for us.'

Renna smiled and grabbed Arlen's arm. 'Excuse us a minute.' She turned and dragged Arlen back between the horses.

'What are you playing at, Arlen Bales?' she demanded. 'Had to fight tooth and nail for you to let me ward my own backside, and now you trust me to ward this whole camp?'

Arlen looked at her. 'Saying you ent up to it? I shouldn't trust you?'

Renna put her hands on her hips. 'Din't say any such thing.'

'Then why we talkin' about this?' Arlen asked. 'Light's wastin', and you need to shore up them wards any way you can. Bully folk and slap the fool out of them if you have to, but get it done. Take a few spears and some warded arrows, to give to those as can use them.'

Renna blinked. No one had ever trusted her to ward more than the barn before. Or given her any responsibility, really, beyond milking the cow and making supper. Now, without a wave, Arlen was trusting her to be Selia Barren to these people.

Love you, Arlen Bales.

Renna quickly saw the wards were even worse than they feared. There was no proper circle around the camp at all. The Oatingers had spread haphazardly through the clearing, each of their carts, wagons, and tents individually warded, with varying levels of skill. The best of them were barely adequate.

'How many folk you losing every night?' she asked.

Varley spat. 'Too many. And more each night.'

'Only gets worse every night you stay in one place,' Renna said. 'Big camp like this, smell of fear and blood in the air, will draw corelings like ants to an apple core.'

Varley swallowed. 'Don't like the sound of that.'

'Shouldn't,' Renna said. 'You get these people on the road to Deadwell tomorrow, whatever it takes.' She stopped in front of one cart, surrounded by wardposts staked into the ground.

'Been seein' a lot of these posts,' Renna said.

Varley nodded. 'Our Warder made them before he was cored.

Used to be enough to surround the camp, but we've lost a few and ent been able to replace 'em.'

Renna nodded. 'Pull them all, if you please, and bring them over to the edge of the clearing.' She pointed. 'We'll circle the biggest wagons and put the posts in the gaps in between. Whole camp needs to squeeze in tight to fit inside.'

'Folk ent gonna take kindly to us pulling up their wards,' Varley said.

Renna gave him a hard look. 'Don't care what they like, greybeard, or you. 'Less you want to lose more folk tonight, you best mind me 'tween now and sunset.'

Varley's bushy eyebrows widened, and he took his hat off again, twisting it in his hands. 'Ay, all right.'

'I'll need paint,' Renna said. 'Any stain will do, darker the better, and a lot of it. And posts this high.' She held up a hand parallel to the ground. 'Many as you can put together. Take axes to live trees if you got to. They only need to last till you make Deadwell.'

'Donn,' Varley said. 'Collect posts. Anyone argues, you send 'em to me.' Donn nodded, picked a few men, and left. 'Brice,' Varley said. 'Paint. Now.' The man ran off, and Varley turned to the rest of his men. 'Fresh posts. Rip apart anything you need to.' He looked back at Renna expectantly.

'Wagons need to be in place before I start planting posts,' Renna said, 'and that means right now.'

Varley nodded, moving off to speak to the owner of one of the carts, pointing.

'That will practically put us in the midden!' she complained.

'You want the midden, or a coreling's belly?' Varley replied.

It was almost dark when Renna returned to Arlen. Some of the patients in the makeshift hospit seemed to be resting more comfortably, but many still suffered horribly. Arlen knelt by a cot, holding a young girl's hand. Her other arm ended before the elbow in a bandage soaked through with brownish yellow pus. Half her face was scabbed and oozing from firespit burns, still angry and red. Her skin had a grey pallor, and her breathing was shallow. Her eyes were closed.

'Demon fever,' Arlen said without looking up at her approach. 'Flame demon bit her arm off and left an awful infection. Gave her what cures I know, but the sickness is far enough along I doubt it'll even slow.'

The pain in his voice cut at her, but she embraced the feeling and let it pass. There was work to be done still.

Arlen looked out at the others in the sick tent. 'Might be I saved a couple, but I'm out of herbs and most are beyond my skill in any event.' He sighed. 'In the sunlight, at least.'

'Your rooster strutting this afternoon was bad enough,' Renna said. 'You start healing folk in the night and there'll be no end to this Deliverer business.'

Arlen looked at her, and she saw his face was streaked with tears. 'What would you have me do? Leave these folk to die?'

Renna looked at him, and her resolve weakened. 'Course not. Just sayin' there's a price.'

'Always a price, Ren,' Arlen said. 'This is all my fault.' He swept his hand out over the Oatingers' camp. 'Made this happen.'

Renna raised an eyebrow. 'How's that? You drove these people from their homes?'

Arlen shook his head. 'Woke the demon that did. Never should have brought the spear to Krasia. Never should have trusted Jardir.'

'What spear? Who's Jardir?' Renna asked.

'Mind demon was willing to kill to answer those questions,' Arlen said. 'Sure you want to know?'

'Killin' is all demons ever do,' Renna said, and pointed to the mind demon ward painted in blackstem on her forehead. 'And those bigheaded bastards ent ever gettin' inside my skull again.'

Arlen nodded. 'Jardir is the leader of the Krasian people. Met him a long time ago, and we became friends. Night, *friends* don't even cover it. Taught me half what I know, and saved my life more'n once. Couldn't have loved him more he was my own brother.' Arlen clenched a fist. 'And all along, he had a ripping knife to my back.'

'What happened?' Renna asked.

'Bought a black market map to a lost city in the desert, said to be the home of Kaji,' Arlen said.

'What's *black market*?' Renna asked. 'They only open at night?'

Arlen smiled, but there was little humour in it. 'Guess you could say that. *Black market* means the people I bought it from stole it.'

Renna frowned. 'That don't sound like the Arlen Bales I know.'

'Ent proud of it,' Arlen said, 'but had dealings with a lot of shady folk since I left Tibbet's Brook. Folk to make what Varley's doin' seem honest. When you're out beyond the wards, sometimes shady folk are all there are.'

Renna grunted. 'So you got a map to this Kaji place. Then what?'

'Kaji ent a place,' Arlen said. 'He was a man. The last general from the demon wars. The Deliverer, if you believe such things.'

Renna laughed. 'You, Arlen Bales, went huntin' the Deliverer? Now I know you're spinning an ale story.'

'Wasn't hunting the *Deliverer*,' Arlen snapped. 'Was hunting his *wards*. And I found 'em, Ren. Deliverer or no, I found Kaji's tomb and rescued his spear. The ancient battle wards, means to fight the corelings, brought back to the world! Took it to Jardir, and he had the nerve to say I *stole* it. That it belonged to *him*. Offered to make him a copy, down to the last ward, but that wasn't good enough.'

Arlen inhaled deeply, breathing in rhythm for a few moments as he centred himself. It was ironic that a Krasian meditation technique gave solace here, but Renna was glad for it nevertheless.

'What'd he do?' she asked after a moment.

'Took the spear in the night,' Arlen said. 'Laid a trap and smiled as his men threw me in a demon pit to be cored. Now he's come north, meaning to enslave us all for a new demon war.'

'So kill him and have done,' Renna said. 'World's better off without some folk.'

Arlen sighed. 'Sometimes I think that I'm the one the world would be better off without.'

'Say again?' Renna asked. 'You can't seriously be comparing yourself to that . . .'

'Ent excusing Jardir,' Arlen said. 'But try as I might, can't help but think none of this would have happened, not to you, the Rizonans, or anyone, if I'd just kept our promise and stayed on the farm. Everyone's looking to me to put things right, but how can I, when I'm the one made it all wrong?'

Renna gritted her teeth and slapped him in the face. Arlen recoiled, looking at her in shock. Evey and some of the patients looked up at the sound, but Renna ignored them.

'Don't you go looking surprised, Arlen Bales,' she said. 'You're the one told me to slap the fool out of any not helping shore the wards, and it's almost dark. You ent done nothing but true by anyone I seen, and we don't got time for another lick of this nonsense.'

Arlen shook his head as if to clear it, and then suddenly he was smiling at her. 'Love you, Renna Tanner.'

Renna felt a thrill rush through her, but embraced the feeling and let it pass. There was business to attend to. 'Scrounged and made enough posts to go three-quarters of the way around the camp. Had to draw wards in the dirt to close the circuit.'

'Never trust dirt wards,' Arlen said.

'Ent a fool,' Renna said. 'Posted guards with warded

spears, but half Varley's men are dozing like they're playing possum on the road, and the other half are ready to piss themselves.'

Arlen nodded, and that hint of smile was back in the corner of his mouth. 'Don't worry. I'm getting good at this next part.'

Renna led the way to where the guards stood, and just as she'd said, there were half a dozen who gripped their new warded spears with shaking hands, and then another group, Varley's bandits led by Donn and Brice, lounging on the ground playing Succour. Their warded weapons lay nearby, half forgotten. The wagons and warded tents were all shut, but there were plenty without such shelter that watched in fear as the sun set. Varley stood nearby, but still he held no weapon. He wrung his hat in his hands.

Everyone looked at Arlen as he passed. There were whispers from every part of the camp, and Renna even saw some of the wagon shutters and tent flaps peek open.

Arlen walked right over to Varley's men, kicking a shaking cup of dice right from Donn's hand.

'Ay, what's that about?' the man cried.

'The sun is setting and you're playing at dice is what it's about,' Arlen snapped.

'You crazy, Donn, talkin' back to the Deliverer?' Brice asked.

'He ent the Deliverer,' Donn said. 'Said so himself.' He turned to Arlen. 'Sun ent gonna set for ten minutes, and there's wards right there in the dirt for all to see.'

'Can't trust wards in the dirt,' Arlen said.

Donn looked up. 'Don't look like rain to me.'

'Ent just rain you got to worry about,' Arlen said, going to inspect the wards. 'Anything can scuff out a dirt ward.' With that, he reached out with his sandalled foot and rubbed out a yard of Renna's carefully drawn wards. She gasped, but Arlen laughed as the men scrambled to their feet, grabbing their weapons.

'Ten minutes doesn't feel like such a long time any more, does it?' he called loudly, for the whole camp to hear.

'Creator, are you cracked?' Varley cried, but Arlen ignored him, striding back over to the dicers.

He nodded to Donn, now gripping his new warded spear tightly. The others, too, had quickly grabbed their warded weapons. 'Now, you show respect for the coming night.'

Donn glared at him. 'You'd best be the Deliverer now, 'cause if you ent, you are made of crazy.'

Arlen smiled and moved to face the other men, who now seemed doubly terrified – and with good reason. Already it was dark enough that Renna's warded sight was coming to life. Luminescent wisps of magic, invisible to the others, were beginning to seep from the ground, pooling in the shadows and strengthening against the light. Soon the paths to the Core would open fully and the demons would rise.

Jered, who was barely sixteen, clutched his spear so tightly his knuckles showed white. 'Why'd you go and do that? Don't wanna die.'

'Everyone dies,' Arlen said. 'It's *how* we die that matters. Do you want to die because you were too piss-scared to defend yourself? You want your family to die because your knees buckled when you were supposed to protect them? Or do you want to take a coreling with you? Maybe more'n one?'

'You need to let demons into our camp to make your point, boy?' Varley demanded. He pointed as he did at the shapes of demons beginning to form just outside the clearing as full dark fell upon them.

'Ent no demon getting in this camp,' Arlen said, and he drew a deep breath. Renna watched as the soft glowing mist at Arlen's feet suddenly rushed towards him like smoke sucked into a bellows. The air around him grew dark as Arlen absorbed the magic, then brightened again as the wards on his skin flared to life. Even the unwarded eyes of the Oatingers could see it, and they gasped as one.

A field demon solidified and ran towards the gap in the wards. Somewhere in the camp a woman screamed. Arlen swept a hand through the air, drawing a large ward. It flared to life as the demon struck the spot, its leap checked in mid-air with a crunch. The magic rebounded, throwing the demon back away from the camp.

'Creator,' Varley whispered.

'Mind if I borrow your spear?' Arlen asked Jered, snatching the weapon from the boy's nerveless fingers.

Arlen stepped out beyond the ward, pointing to the recovering demon with the spear. 'See how the field demon had to thrash to get to its feet,' he called loudly for all to hear. 'There ent nothing faster on four legs, and their sharp scales can blunt the attack of even a warded spear . . .' The demon leapt at him, but Arlen stepped nimbly to the side, striking the demon with the butt of the spear. Impact wards flared, flipping the demon onto its back. '. . . but put it off its feet, and you expose its belly, which ent armoured for spit.' He struck hard, putting the spear directly into the demon's chest.

As he spoke, Renna moved to confront the next demon taking form. She inhaled as Arlen had, willing the ambient magic into herself. The air about her did not darken, but Renna could swear she felt something. The day's weariness was gone. She felt strong.

The field demon swiped at her, its arm like a whip, but Renna saw the move coming and was well ahead of the flashing talons. She darted in before it could recover, whipping her beaded necklace around its throat. The wards painted on the brook stones flared to life, crushing inward. The demon tried to scream, but it came out a hoarse gasp. Renna locked her legs around it, carefully tucked in behind the claws as it rolled and thrashed about. Another moment, then a flash of magic as the beads came free with a jerk and the demon's head fell free. She drew Harl's knife and watched the other demons that stalked the area as Arlen continued his lesson.

It was nearly morning when Arlen approached the healing tent. All the Oatingers were asleep except for the guards patrolling the wards. Renna had finished the remaining wardposts, and Arlen had given Varley a map to Deadwell. He drew a little skull over the town well.

'Sure you gotta do this?' Renna asked.

Arlen nodded. 'Can't turn a blind eye, Ren.'

'Don't suppose you can,' Renna said. 'So do it quick, while no one's looking.'

Arlen knelt by the young girl, armless and dying of demon fever, and drew wards in the air. The girl breathed in sharply as the magic swept through her, then relaxed again. The redness and blisters faded from her face, and a healthy pallor began to return to her skin.

'Where'd you learn healin' wards, anyhow?' Renna asked. 'You pull that from the demon's mind?'

'Sort of,' Arlen said. 'Ent exactly healing wards. Body wants to make itself well and knows what to do. The wards just give it power to do it fast.'

Arlen moved from one patient to the next, working quickly. He had charged himself with as much energy as he could hold, but it faded quickly with the healing. Soon he was swaying. Finally, his eyes half closed and he stumbled.

Renna was there in an instant to catch him. 'That's enough,' she whispered. 'Done what you could. Will you kill yourself to heal the rest?'

'Sneaks up,' Arlen said. 'Feel invincible one second, and like I'm drowning the next. Need to learn my limits.' He drew a deep breath, and again all the magic pooling across the ground like fog was drawn to him. The glow of his wards brightened, but it was nothing compared with the power he had radiated just a few minutes before. He looked haggard, and there were dark circles beneath his eyes.

'Time to go,' Renna said.

They galloped for several miles before Renna pulled up. Arlen wheeled Twilight Dancer around when he noticed her fall behind.

'Go,' Renna said.

'Eh?' Arlen asked.

'Hunt something,' Renna said. 'Ent light yet, and you need more than just the magic in the air to get back up to speed. This ent the time to be getting sloppy.'

Arlen tilted his head, considering her, and that hint of smile crept back onto his face.

Renna was cold to it. She pointed off the Messenger road to the plains. 'Go.'

He nodded and was off, leaping Twilight Dancer off the road and onto the grasses. Renna waited until he was out of sight, then turned Promise and galloped back the way they had come.

She didn't have a lot of time, but Renna didn't need a lot. The wood demon she had glimpsed a few minutes before was still lurking by the thick tree that had hidden it from Arlen's warded eyes.

She ran Promise right up to the tree and set her kicking, warded hooves exploding into the demon like thunderbolts, hurling it twisted and broken to the ground.

Renna leapt lightly from the horse, drawing Harl's knife. *Arlen's pushing himself hard.*

The demon thrashed as she came for it. Already, its magic was healing its wounds. In moments it would be ready to attack her again, but the demon did not have moments. Wood demon armour was a thick tough skin, gnarled and knobbed, with heavy bone plates jutting from beneath. The ridges between the plates were where they were most vulnerable. Renna struck hard, prising the demon's breast plates apart and cutting its heart out before it stopped writhing.

He'd have kept on healing folk until it killed him. Always trying to give his life for someone, Arlen Bales. That ent changed in all these years.

It almost seemed to frustrate Arlen that he could find no demon great enough to destroy him, no burden too great to bear. He would keep seeking until he found one. Always trying to die a Krasian death.

Renna bit into the demon's heart. It was foul and bitter, slick with black ichor, slimy and tough. There was a burst as her teeth met, sending some even fouler liquid spraying in her mouth. She thought there could be no viler taste until she retched, bile flooding around the half-chewn demon heart and up into her nostrils. She longed to spit the horrid mixture on the ground and give heave to her stomach, but she ground her teeth instead.

Arlen can't find his death here, he's gonna look for it in the Core, and I ent letting him go alone. Promised to stay with him, and never slow him down.

Renna swallowed, letting the tears stream down her face. She embraced the nausea, riding it like she had ridden Promise that first time, forgetting all else and holding on until her stomach finally calmed. Then she took another bite.

She had collected herself when Arlen returned, his glow restored. The dark circles were gone from his eyes, his movements sharp and agile once more. And his blood was up. She could hear it in his breathing and see the magic crackling around him, bringing with it primal urges not easily suppressed.

She felt much the same. Only the utmost concentration let her keep focus on the wards she was painting onto Promise's blotched coat. The mare swatted Renna with her tail, but didn't nip or pull away.

'Feeling stronger?' she asked.

Arlen nodded. 'Still feel off, though. Charged and exhausted at the same time. But it'll do. We got a long way to ride, and I don't mean to stop till we reach the Hollow.'

He pointed. 'Path up ahead will take us east to the Old Hill Road. Fell out of use 'round ninety years ago when the corelings destroyed Fort Hill. Should give us a straight, clear run to the Hollow. We ride on through tomorrow night and we'll be there noon the next day.'

Renna nodded. 'Who's Leesha Paper to you?'

Arlen breathed three times in rhythm, the surest tell he was embracing some feeling or memory, but there was no way to know what that might be. 'Leesha Paper is Herb Gatherer of Deliverer's Hollow, but she's more like Selia Barren from back in the Brook. People hop when she claps. Innkeep in Riverbridge said Jardir snatched her from the Hollow and forced her to his bed. Need to see if that's so. Pick up the trail, if I can. Find out Jardir laid a finger on her, gonna kill him.'

Renna smiled. 'Wouldn't be the man I love if you didn't. What he did to you, I'm part fixin' to kill him myself.'

'Don't you go tryin' that, Ren,' Arlen said. 'You ent a match for him, no matter what you think you've learned. Jardir's been fighting demons since before either of us was born.'

Renna shrugged. 'Still haven't answered my question. Din't ask "Who's Leesha Paper?" Asked "Who's Leesha Paper, to *you*?" Hear tell the Krasians been forcing a lot of women to their beds. Why's this the one that makes you come running?'

'She's my friend,' Arlen said.

'You don't talk about her like a friend,' Renna said. 'You go all stiff. Cold. Can't read you. Makes me think you're hidin' somethin'.'

Arlen looked at her and sighed. 'What do you want me to say, Ren? You've got your Cobie Fishers, and I've got mine.'

'Cobie Fisher is *one*,' Renna said, feeling her blood pounding in her veins. 'Da drove off any other boy who came to court more'n once. How many you got?'

Arlen shrugged. 'Two or three.'

'Well ent you popular.' Renna spat. She could feel the monster raging within her, the demon essence, shrieking for violence. She gritted her teeth. It was too big to embrace. It was overwhelming. She tensed, fighting back the urge to leap at him. To kill him, even.

'What?' Arlen snapped, seeing the fierce look in her eyes and returning it tenfold. 'Was I supposed to hold true because our das bartered us like cattle? I left Tibbet's Brook and never meant to come back, Ren.'

Renna recoiled. Arlen Bales, just the idea of him and the memory of that kiss in the hayloft and her words of promise, had been Renna Tanner's whole world when she was young. Dreams of Arlen had kept her going through hard times that would have broken other folk. That *did* break other folk. The thought that she had meant nothing to him back then, that she didn't even enter into his thoughts, was too harsh to bear.

Arlen rushed at her, and instinctively she drew her knife. He was quicker, grabbing her wrists and holding them down with the strength of a rock demon. She strained against him uselessly.

'Din't know the girl you were then,' Arlen said. 'Or the woman you'd be. I had, I would have turned right around to take you away with me.'

Renna stopped struggling and looked at him. 'You mean that?'

'Honest word,' Arlen said. 'You askin' if I got some past with women? Ay, I do. But past, as in done.' He reached out, cupping her face and lifting it so their eyes met. 'My future is Renna Tanner.'

Renna let her knife drop to the ground, but when he let her go, she still leapt on him.

4

Second Coming

333 AR Summer
26 Dawns Before New Moon

They galloped until dawn, then eased the horses into a walk as the sun burned their night strength away. Arlen took them off road, leading Twilight Dancer with confidence down a Messenger way so overgrown and twisted it was almost invisible. The path beneath Renna's feet never vanished, but it opened up suddenly before her and closed off quickly behind, like she was wandering through a thick fog.

Around midday, the path merged into a wide Messenger road, and they were able to mount again after a break for lunch and necessaries. Like the roads in Riverbridge, the Old Hill Road was made of stone, but most of it was now cracked and eroded into enormous potholes, filled with dirt and thick with stunted patches of scrub and weed. In more than one place, a full tree had broken through, leaving great blocks of broken stone, moss-covered and filthy. In other places, the road ran for long stretches as if untouched by time, miles of grey stone, flat and uniform with nary a crack or seam.

'How'd they haul stones that big?' Renna asked in wonder.

'Din't,' Arlen said. 'They made a muddy porridge called crete, which hardens into solid rock. All roads used to be like this, wide and stone, sometimes hundreds of miles long.'

'What happened to them?' Renna asked.

Arlen spat. 'World got too small for big roads. Now Old Hill Road's one of the last of her kind. Nature doesn't take them back quickly, but eventually she does take 'em back.'

'We'll make good time here,' Renna said.

'Ay, but night will be a race,' Arlen warned. 'Field demons are drawn here like pigs to the trough. Come up through the potholes.'

Renna smirked. 'Who am I to worry? Got the Deliverer with me.' Arlen scowled, and she laughed.

Renna wasn't laughing any more. Promise had relented to take a few strips of braided leather as a girth, but it was still all Renna could do to hang on as the giant Angierian mustang galloped flat-out over the ancient highway, leaping obstacles and barely keeping ahead of the reap of field demons at her heels.

Twilight Dancer fared no better, with as many of the corelings on his tail as Promise's. The demons seemed bred for the road, their long tireless strides eating up the pavement.

Above, the raptor cries of wind demons filled the night sky. Renna glanced up and saw the demons clearly by the glow of their magic, massive wingspans blotting out the stars. Even wind demons weren't quick enough to dive and take a galloping horse, but if they slowed . . .

'Do we fight?' Renna shouted to Arlen. Both their senses were far more acute in the night, but it was still hard to tell if he heard her over the thunder of hooves and the shriek of demons sensing a kill.

'Too many!' Arlen shouted back. 'We stop to fight, more will catch up! Keep on!'

His face was clear as day to her night eyes, lined with worry. He was in no danger, of course. Nothing could harm Arlen in the night. But Renna had no such security. Her warded cloak would not shield her at a gallop, and while she had painted much of Promise's splotchy coat, those wards wouldn't last long in a pitched battle against an ever-increasing number of demons. Even Twilight Dancer's warded barding had gaps necessary for mobility.

Renna's hand itched to go to her knife, but she kept her arms tight around Promise's powerful neck. A coreling nipped at the mare's heels, and caught a hoof in the face for its efforts. The wards Renna had carved into it flared, and the coreling's long, razor-sharp teeth shattered as the demon was thrown back.

Renna's satisfaction at the blow was short-lived. Promise stumbled, momentarily losing her stride, and the other corelings gained quickly, almost upon her. Back down the road, the demon she had kicked rolled to a stop and wobbled to its feet. Already its magic was repairing the damage. It would be back in the chase before long.

Arlen let go of Twilight Dancer's reins and turned, drawing a ward in the air. Renna felt a rush of air, and the corelings at her heels were thrown back like leaves in the wind.

Renna smiled and looked back at Arlen, but the curve fell from her lips as she saw how his glow had dimmed. He couldn't keep using that trick, and the field demons at his own back were barely a stride behind. She cursed her own stubborn refusal to practise with the bow he had given her.

A field demon leapt, its long hooked talons digging deep grooves into Twilight Dancer's hindquarters just beneath the barding as it tried to pull the massive stallion down.

Dancer broke stride to kick back, his warded hooves crushing the demon's skull, but the pause gave another of the demons time to climb atop an ancient pile of crete and hurl itself at Arlen.

Arlen twisted, catching a swiping paw in one hand and punching the demon hard in the head with the other. 'Don't slow!' he called as Promise ran past.

Magic flared from the wards on his fist as he struck again and again, leaving the demon's face a ruined mass. He hurled the demon back into the reap, knocking others to the ground in a jumble, then kicked Dancer back into a gallop.

They soon caught up, but Dancer's flanks were wet with running blood, and his speed began to lessen as the demons renewed their chase.

'Night!' Renna looked up the road, seeing another reap of demons charging at them from the opposite direction, spread as wide as the road. To either side the ground fell away in a thicketed ditch. There was no escape there.

Part of Renna longed to fight. The demon in her blood shrieked for the carnage, but the sense left to her knew it was a hopeless battle. If they couldn't break the ring and outrun the pack, it was likely only Arlen would survive to see the dawn.

The thought gave her some comfort as she leaned in to the charge.

'Stomp right through,' she whispered in Promise's ear.

'Follow my lead,' Arlen called. He had leached some power from the demon he'd killed, though it was still less than he'd started with. He drew a quick ward in the air, and the demons directly in front of the horses were knocked aside. He laid about with a long spear, jabbing at any demon that drew too close, but one was not fast enough and was trampled under Twilight Dancer's hooves, magic flashing in the night. Renna followed right behind, trampling the hapless demon further, leaving it crushed and broken.

Left to itself, the demon might have recovered from even these grievous injuries, but its reapmates sensed its weakness and temporarily gave up the chase, falling upon it viciously, rending its armour with their long talons and tearing away large chunks of flesh in their teeth.

Renna bared her teeth, and for a second, imagined herself joining them, feasting on demon meat and revelling in the power it brought.

'Eyes in front!' Arlen snapped, breaking her from the trance. Renna shook her head and turned away from the grisly scene, putting her mind back to the business at hand.

It looked like they might clear the trap, but the clash had slowed them enough for a wind demon to chance a dive at Renna, talons leading to snatch her right from horseback and carry her off.

The blackstem wards on Renna's arms and shoulders flared, forming a barrier that gave the demon's talons no purchase, but the force of the rebound threw Renna from Promise's back. She hit the ground hard, smashing her right shoulder with a pop and tasting dirt and blood in her mouth. The wind demon crashed shrieking down beside her, and she rolled, just barely avoiding the razor-sharp talon at the end of its massive wing.

Her shoulder screamed at her as she shoved herself to her feet, but Renna embraced the pain as wood embraces fire, awkwardly pulling her knife in her left hand. To lie still was to die.

Not that her chances of living were very good. Nearby, Promise reared and bucked, kicking at the field demons snapping and clawing at her from all sides. In a moment they would be upon Renna as well.

'Renna!' Arlen wheeled Twilight Dancer about, but even he couldn't be quick enough.

The wind demon struggled awkwardly to its feet. Wind demons were clumsy on land, and Renna used that to her advantage, kicking a leg out from under it and driving her warded knife deep into its throat as it fell. There was a hot splash of ichor on her hand, and she felt a wave of magic pump into her. Already, her injured shoulder felt stronger.

A field demon leapt upon Promise's back, and Renna reached into her pouch for a handful of chestnuts. The heat wards she had painted activated when they struck the coreling, and the nuts exploded with a series of bangs and flashes, scorching its coarse armour. The demon wasn't badly injured, but it was startled and stung, enabling Promise to buck it from its tenuous perch.

Renna didn't have time to see what happened next, as the corelings took note of her and several raced her way. Renna sidestepped the first and kicked it in the belly, the blackstem impact wards on her shin and instep flashing with power. The demon was launched away like a child's ball. Another hit her from behind, clawing through her tight-laced vest and scoring deep lines in her back. She fell to her knees as another came at her from the front, biting hard at her shoulder.

This time, her wards were not enough to turn the demon. Blood and filth had weakened them, and Renna screamed as the demon locked down, its four sets of talons raking at her. Some of her wards remained in effect, but others did not. The demon's claws skittered along the flash of magic until they found openings and dug in hard.

But the pain and the magic both were a drug to Renna. In that moment, she didn't care if she lived or died, she only knew that she would not die first. Again and again her arm pumped, stabbing her father's knife into the coreling, bathing in its ichor. Her power intensified even as its weakened. Slowly, she began to force it back, feeling its talons slide back out of her flesh inch by agonizing inch.

It was dead when Twilight Dancer scattered its reapmates to stand over her and Arlen leapt down, his robe cast aside. His wards flared bright as he prised open the snout of the demon and pulled it off her, hurling it into several others, all of them going down in a heap. Another came at him, but he took it down in a *sharusahk* pivot and stabbed a finger that sizzled like a hot poker through the coreling's eye.

Renna growled, raising her knife. Her body screamed at her, but the magic that gripped her was stronger. The night was a dizzy haze of blurred figures, but she could make out Promise's huge form, and the demons surrounding her. One swung wildly from her neck, grasping for purchase. If it found its grip,

Promise would be pulled down. Renna gave a mad howl and ran her way.

'Renna, corespawn it!' Arlen shouted, but Renna ignored him and waded into the demons' midst, kicking and shoving corelings aside and laying about with her knife as she struggled to Promise's side. Every blow sent a shock of magic thrilling through her, making her stronger, faster – invincible. She leapt up and caught one of the scrabbling hind limbs of the demon on Promise's back, pulling it into position as she stabbed it in the heart.

Arlen ran after her, collapsing into smoke as demons struck at him, only to turn deadly solid a split second later, striking hard with warded fists and feet, knees and elbows, even the top of his shaved head. He was beside her in an instant and gave a shrill whistle, calling Dancer to them.

The great stallion scattered another group of demons on the way, giving Arlen time to draw large field demon wards in the air around them. With her warded eyes, Renna could see the thin trail of magic he left to hold each symbol together. A field demon leapt at them, and two of the wards flared, throwing it back. The wards would only grow stronger the more they were struck. Arlen moved in a steady line, forming a circle around them, but ahead of him, several demons barred his path, continuing to snap and claw at Promise's flank. She moved for them, knife leading.

Arlen grabbed her arm, yanking her back. 'You stay put.'

'I can fight,' Renna growled. She tried to pull her arm free, but even with her night strength, he held her in place easily. He turned and drew a series of impact wards in the air, knocking the demons away from Promise one by one.

As he did, his grip weakened, and Renna used the opportunity to pull away from him with a snarl. 'You don't get to tell me what to do, Arlen Bales!'

'Don't make me slap the fool out of you, Ren!' Arlen snapped. 'Look at yourself!'

Renna looked down, gasping at the deep wounds gaping in her skin. Blood ran freely in a dozen places, and her back and shoulder were on fire. The mad night strength left her, and her knife dropped, too heavy to lift. Her legs gave way.

Arlen was there in an instant, easing her to the ground, and then moved off to complete the wardnet around and above them. More and more field demons came racing down the road, surrounding them like an endless field of grass, but even that great host could not pierce Arlen's wards, nor the flight of wind demons circling in the sky.

He was back at her side as soon as the net was complete, cleaning the dirt and blood from her wounds. There was a fallen demon inside the forbidding, and he dipped a finger in its ichor like a quill in an inkwell, writing wards on her skin. She could feel her flesh tightening, pulling as it knit back together. It was incredibly painful, but Renna accepted it as the cost of life and breathed deep, embracing it.

'Put your cloak on while I tend the horses,' Arlen said when he had done all he could. Renna nodded, pulling her warded cloak from the pouch at her waist. Lighter and finer than any cloth Renna had ever felt, it was covered in intricate embroidered wards of unsight. When drawn about her, it rendered Renna invisible to corespawn. She had never cared for the cloak, preferring to let the demons see her coming, but she couldn't deny its usefulness.

Lacking the warded barding of Twilight Dancer, Promise was easily the more wounded of the two horses, but she stamped and snorted at Arlen's approach, teeth bared and snapping. Arlen ignored the posturing, moving almost too fast to see as he swept in and took a great handful of Promise's mane. The mare tried to pull away, but Arlen handled her like a mother changing a struggling baby's nappy. Eventually, Promise relented and let him tend her, perhaps realizing at last that he was trying to help her.

The casual display of power might have surprised her a few

days ago, but Renna was used to surprises from Arlen now, and it barely registered. Again and again, she saw her gaping wounds in her mind's eye, terrified to think she'd been ignoring them as her life's blood drained away.

'That what happens to you?' Renna asked when he returned. 'Feel so alive you don't even realize it's killing you?'

Arlen nodded. 'Forget to breathe sometimes. Get so drunk on the power it feels like I shouldn't need to do something so . . . mundane. Then I suddenly break out gasping for air. Almost got me cored more'n once.'

He looked up, meeting her eyes. 'The magic will trick you into thinking you're immortal, Ren, but you ent. No one is, not even the corelings.' He pointed at the field demon carcass beside her. 'And the struggle never goes away. It's a new fight, every time you taste the power.'

Renna shuddered, thinking of the irresistible pull of the magic. 'How do you keep from losing yourself?'

Arlen chuckled. 'Started keeping Renna Tanner around to remind me I'm just a dumb Bales from Tibbet's Brook, and ent too good to breathe.'

Renna smiled. 'Then you got nothing to fear, Arlen Bales. You're stuck with me.'

Renna and the horses were well recovered by morning, but Arlen eased the pace, never taking Twilight Dancer above a trot, and stopping to rest twice before midday.

'Thought we were in a rush,' Renna said when they dismounted the second time.

'Day or two don't matter at this point,' Arlen said.

'That's not how you felt yesterday,' Renna said.

Arlen looked away, and his shoulders sagged. 'Had my priorities wrong, Ren. Sorry for that. Ent right to push you and the horses past your limits.'

Renna took a deep breath. She hated the way he turned from her when saying things he didn't think she'd like. Men were always doing that, thinking it spared feelings.

And maybe it does, Renna thought. *But only their own.*

'Don't mean you got to baby us, either,' she said.

'You came an inch from dying last night, Ren,' Arlen said. 'Promise and Dancer, too. Ent no harm in stopping now and again to stretch our legs and have our necessaries.'

He was right, but Renna didn't feel like she'd been close to death. In truth, she felt stronger and more alive than ever in her life. There was new pink flesh where her wounds had been, lighter than her natural tan and needing fresh blackstem, but smooth without even hint of scar. Her body thrummed with power.

Her eyes flicked to Promise, already knowing it was not the same. Arlen had used the same healing wards on the mare's flank as he had on Renna, drawn in demon ichor thick with magic. Nothing remained of Promise's wounds but a few strips of hairless flesh on her blotchy coat, but there was still a tenderness to the horse's movements, and she showed little sign of her usual wilfulness.

Renna looked up at the morning sun, and smiled. *Power's inside me now. And gettin' stronger, more I eat. Ent gonna slow you down, Arlen Bales. Soon, you'll need help to keep up with me.*

'Tell me about the Hollow, then,' she said. 'Everyone there think you're the Deliverer, too?'

Arlen sighed. 'There most of all. Two years ago, Cutter's Hollow was a town not even as big as Southwatch. But a flux hit last year, laying half of them low. Someone dropped a lamp in the inn, and fire spread quick, with no one to fight it. Wasn't long before the wards failed.'

Renna saw the disaster in her mind's eye and ground her teeth. She found herself clutching at the bone handle of her knife, and it took the full force of her will to let go. 'Trouble makes for trouble, my mam said.'

'Honest word,' Arlen said. 'Came on them the next day, and found more'n a hundred dead, and half the rest on their backs. With night coming, I warded their axes and taught those that could to fight. Put the rest in the Holy House and made our stand out front. Lot of folk died that night, but they gave better than they got, and more than not were on their feet come dawn. Built the town back from scratch, putting the roads and houses in the shape of a forbidding. Ent no demon setting foot in the Hollow now, not even the princes.'

Renna grunted. 'Sounds like you made quite the Jongleur's show of it. Figure you must *want* them thinkin' you're the Deliverer, at least a little.'

Arlen's face darkened. 'Last thing I want anyone thinking. Waitin' for the Deliverer's kept us hiding behind wards for three hundred years.'

'Ay, but the wait's over, ent it?' Renna said. 'Painted Man's come to save us all.'

Arlen scowled, but Renna dismissed it with a wave. 'Oh, you slap the fool out of any that bow to you and call you Deliverer, but you're just as quick to temper when folk don't take one look at you and start hopping to your words.'

Arlen pulled back, stung, but Renna matched his stare and didn't back down. Finally he gave a helpless chuckle and shrugged. 'Can't deny it helps get things done, Ren. And there's a lot to do. Folk ent got any idea of what's coming with the next new moon, and I ent got time to baby 'em.'

Renna smiled. 'Ent arguin', just keepin' you honest.' Quick as a rabbit, she darted in and kissed his warded cheek.

They rode for some time before splitting off from the Old Hill Road down a thickly overgrown Messenger way. Late in the day they met up with a new road of hard-packed dirt. There was a large warded campsite at the intersection.

'Huh.' Arlen hopped down from Twilight Dancer, moving to inspect the wards. 'Little clumsy, but thick and strong. Darsy Cutter painted these.' He grunted. 'Hollow must be growing like wildfire, they're this far north already.'

'Sun's setting.' Renna said loosening her knife in its sheath as magic began to seep into the lengthening shadows, opening the paths from the Core. 'We should get moving.'

Arlen shook his head, again not meeting her eyes. 'We're stopping here.'

'Ent going to hide behind the wards every night over one close shave,' Renna growled.

'Ent asking you to,' Arlen said.

'Then we're going,' Renna said.

'Going where?' Arlen asked. 'Right where we need to be.' He went to the camp's wood stores, then began laying kindling in the firepit. He did not meet her eyes, but there was a smugness about him, like this was a game.

Anger flared in her, hot and fast, and out of the corner of her eye Renna saw the magic drifting in gentle whorls and eddies at her ankles suddenly flow into her like smoke from a pipe. As soon as she noticed it, the flow stopped and nothing she could do could will it back.

She looked at Arlen, still laying a fire, proud as a cat with a mouse in its teeth, and grew angrier still. Magic came to him easy as breathing, but not to her? Why?

Ent eaten enough. Still got a way to go.

'Gonna hunt, then,' she said.

Arlen shrugged. 'Won't kill you to have some supper first.'

Renna wanted to slap the back of his shaved head. Her fists clenched, nails digging into her skin, drawing blood. She wanted to rend . . .

She caught herself. Magic pulsed through her, primal and powerful, awakening base desires and turning them into raging storms.

Maybe I've eaten too much already.

Renna breathed deeply, again and again in rhythm, the Krasian technique Arlen had taught during her *sharusahk* lessons. Slowly her fists began to unclench, and her heart stopped pounding in her chest, or at least slowed to a steady throb. She forced herself to dismount, brushing down Promise and letting her graze on the thick grass at the side of the road.

They had almost finished eating when Arlen craned his head as if listening to something far away. He smiled. 'There it is.'

'What?' Renna asked, but he stood quickly, scraping the remains from his bowl and stowing it with his cookpot. He drew a ward in the air, and the fire winked out.

'Come on.' Arlen leapt into the saddle and kicked Twilight Dancer into a gallop, tearing down the road.

'Son of the Core,' Renna muttered, dumping her own bowl and hurrying after. Promise had limbered as the day went on, but it was still several minutes until she caught up to Arlen as he pulled to a stop. Up ahead was a hazy glow and the sounds of battle, but he seemed unconcerned.

'Seems the Hollow's expanding again. Reckon the Cutters got it in hand.' Arlen dismounted and nodded into the woods. 'Put your cloak on and let's see if we can get a peek.'

He led them quickly through the trees. A wood demon stepped into their path, ready to strike, but Arlen hissed at it and the wood wards on his body flared, driving the coreling back. They soon came to a thin spot in the trees just outside a huge clearing, still full of stumps and the smell of fresh lumber. Here Arlen stopped, watching from the darkness.

In the centre of the clearing, bonfires burned in a large warded circle, full of tents and tools and draught animals. The fires gave light to the men and women moving about the clearing, fighting a great copse of wood demons and a ten-foot rock demon.

Every instinct in Renna's body told her to leap into the battle – her blood was on fire with the need to kill demons. She smelled ichor and felt her mouth water, ready to aid in choking down their foul meat.

But Arlen stood calmly, clearly having no intention to interfere. She forced herself to relax, taking her hand off the handle of her knife and letting her warded cloak envelop her fully, hiding her from demon eyes.

The cloak had changed since she began eating coreling flesh. She could feel the wards drawing off her own personal magic, but rather than flare brighter, they, and the cloak itself, seemed to dim and blur. Staring at it too long made her dizzy. She wondered how much demon meat she would need to eat before it faded from sight entirely. More than Arlen, it seemed, for he could still see the cloak, though she noted he never looked her way long when she wore it.

'What are they doing?' Renna asked, when silence and inaction began to weigh on her.

'Clearing a greatward,' Arlen said. 'They start by chopping trees to form a centre for the town, then they branch out, clearing land in the shape of a ward of forbidding miles wide. At night, they kill the demons that rise in the area, so they're culled and not just pushed to the edge of the forbidding when the ward activates.'

'Why doesn't everyone do that?' Renna asked. A ward that big would draw so much magic that no corespawn could penetrate it, and it would be almost impossible to mar.

'Reckon they used to, back in the demon wars,' Arlen said. 'But people forgot, and since the Return, folk have been too busy hiding to use their heads.'

Renna grunted and watched the battle more closely, recognizing the Cutters immediately. Cutter was a common name in the hamlets, the surname of most anyone who felled trees or sold wood. Even in Tibbet's Brook, hundreds of miles away, there were close to a hundred Cutters, living in a cluster by the goldwood trees. It was shocking how alike they were to the Hollowers.

The men were big and burly, dressed in sleeveless vests of thick leather, with banded bracers and biceps that seemed bigger than Renna's head. She could almost squint and see Brine Cutter, who had defended Renna in council, those months ago. She hadn't had the will to move that night, even to speak in her own defence, but she remembered every word as the elders of Tibbet's Brook condemned her to death. The Cutters had stood by her.

There were women as well, all armed with crank bows or heavy warded blades. At first Renna thought they wore heavy skirts, but when they moved she could see the skirts were divided, giving freedom of moment without sacrificing modesty.

Renna snorted. That was exactly the sort of ridiculous thing the goodwives in Tibbet's Brook would do, which was likely why they had never taken well to Renna and her sisters. The Tanner girls seldom hid much skin from the sun. Renna herself bared as much as possible, so the blackstem wards on her flesh could embrace the magic-charged night air.

Surrounding the women were a group of men that stood in stark contrast to the Cutters. Clad in thick wooden armour, lacquered with wards and fired hard, they wore heavy helms and carried matching spear and shield. At the centre of the warding circle on their shields was a painted toy soldier.

'Who're they?' Renna asked, pointing.

'The Wooden Soldiers,' Arlen said. 'Royal guard of Angiers. Duke Rhinebeck said he would send 'em here to train with the Cutters.'

'Looks like they haven't been at it long,' Renna noted. Despite their splendid armour, the men stood stiffly, clutching their weapons tight and casting nervous glances at the demons.

'City guards,' Arlen said. 'Used to bullying folk and maybe handing down a beating or two, but I doubt any of them ever so much as thrust a spear outside the practice yard before coming to the Hollow.' He pointed. 'And Prince Thamos looks to be the worst of the lot.'

Indeed, the man Arlen pointed to was clad as she imagined a prince might be, his steel armour gilded with golden wards and polished bright. He was tall and lean, powerfully built with a trim black beard lining a strong jaw.

But the prince shifted his feet, stretching his arms and rolling his head, trying vainly to limber muscles gone tense. Renna could smell his fear from across the clearing, and she knew the demons could scent it, too.

It was clear the Cutters had relegated the Wooden Soldiers to the back of the fray, given the specious duty of guarding the women, who seemed neither to want nor to need such protection.

Years ago, Renna's father had asked Brine Broadshoulders and some of the other Cutters in Tibbet's Brook to help clear some land for planting. Renna and Beni had watched the men work for hours, systematically felling trees, hauling off the wood, and tearing free the roots. Every movement smooth and practised, letting the weight of the tools power their swings, wasting no energy.

It was much like that to see the Hollow Cutters fight. They still carried the tools of their trade, now warded, and put them to work with brutal efficiency.

Two men wielding great long axes took turns hacking at the legs of a wood demon. It was tall and thin, with tremendous reach, but whenever it went after one man, the other came at it from the opposite side. When the demon's strikes came in too close, the men would catch them on their warded bracers, deflecting the blows with flares of magic. Finally, one of the axes took the demon in the back of the knee, and the limb buckled.

'Samm!' one of the axe-wielders called, and a third Cutter came up behind the demon, putting a giant boot into its back and knocking it facedown, his full weight holding it prone. The man carried a great, two-handed saw, and he bent to the task, sawing through the thick barklike armour of its neck in a shower of magical sparks and spraying ichor. In seconds the head fell free.

'Night,' Renna whispered.

Arlen smiled and nodded. 'That's Samm Cutter, but everyone calls him Samm Saw. Used to cut the limbs from trees the Cutters felled so they could be hauled off. Hundreds a day. Now he cuts off demon limbs just as quick.'

Another call came, and Samm turned to a Cutter who swung a heavy axe mattock, chopping at a wood demon. Each warded blow knocked the demon back a step, unable to recover its balance, but the demon showed no sign of real damage, healing as fast as the blows could come. Samm came in behind the demon, sawing through one of its trunklike legs while the demon still stood. It collapsed with a shriek, and the Cutter shouted thanks as he raised his mattock to finish it off.

Across the clearing, a dozen Cutters hauled on ropes looped around the rock demon's arms and shoulders, thrown this way and that as the coreling thrashed. Two women with crank bows fired repeatedly, the heavy bolts sticking from the obsidian carapace like porcupine quills, but they seemed to do little beyond provoke the rock demon's rage.

Three men and a boy stood by the scene, two younger men with small but heavy mallets, and the third, older, with a heavy sledge. The boy held a thick metal wedge.

'Tomm Wedge and his sons,' Arlen pointed. 'Watch.'

The rock demon set its feet to pull on the ropes, and the younger men darted in, jamming warded spikes into the gap in the armour plates at the demon's knees. Almost simultaneously, they struck with their mallets, once, twice, sending showers of magical sparks as they drove the spikes in.

The demon shrieked and staggered, teetering as the Cutters threw their full weight onto the ropes to bring it down. Its thrashing tail caught one cluster of men, knocking three of them to the ground, their rope flying free. The sudden release sent the demon staggering in the other direction, and it soon lost balance and fell.

Quick as a rabbit the boy was up on the rock demon's back, planting the warded metal wedge into a gap where the plates met on the demon's armoured back. Tomm Wedge went into action, swinging his hammer in a smooth arc to come down on the wedge with a thunderclap of magic. The flare was so bright Renna blinked, and when she opened her eyes the demon collapsed from the blow's rebound and lay still.

Practised. Efficient. No wasted energy.

'It's eerie,' Renna said. 'They might as well be felling trees.'

Arlen nodded. 'Wasn't time to make weapons or train folk to fight that first night. Had to ward whatever was at hand, and the Cutters gave me the most precious things they owned – their tools. More and more folk join the fight every day now and are handed mass-produced spears, but the best of them can't keep up with the Cutters. Using their old tools marks them. Sets them apart. Folk step lightly when they're about, and spin ale stories about them when they're not.'

'All because they were fortunate enough to meet Arlen Bales on a bad day,' Renna said. 'Like me.' Arlen looked at her, but she held up a hand to check him. 'Don't think you're the Deliverer any more'n you do, but you can't deny you've a knack for showing folk their spines,' she touched her knife hilt again, 'and teeth.'

Arlen grunted. 'Everyone's got a knack for something, I guess.'

'Doesn't hurt that the Hollowers are so big you'd have to jump to kiss them, as my sister used to say,' Renna noted.

'Didn't all start that way,' Arlen said. 'Magic's played its part. Sun may burn it off come morning, but not before it affects whatever it touches. Warded weapons don't tend to break or dull, and the Cutters have been soaking magic up nightly for nigh a year. Old ones get younger, and young ones grow into their full before their time.'

He pointed. 'See that one with the salt-and-pepper hair?'

Renna looked where he was pointing and saw a man with arms and legs bunched with thick-veined muscle, standing toe-to-toe with a seven-foot wood demon. She nodded.

'Name's Yon Gray,' Arlen said, 'and he's the oldest man in the Hollow. Hair was stark white a year ago. Needed a stick to even walk crooked, and his hands shook.'

'Honest word?' Renna asked.

Arlen nodded, pointing again, this time to a huge man in the prime of his life, charging in behind the demon while Yon kept its attention. 'Linder Cutter. Ent no more'n fifteen years old.'

One of the wood demons struck one of the huge men a backhand blow that lifted him from the ground and threw him back several feet. He landed with a heavy thump, his axe mattock flying from his grasp. Renna saw no blood, but the prone man had no time to rise as the demon charged.

Her knife was in her hand in an instant, but Arlen took hold of her shoulder as she started to move. She snapped a glare at him, but he only inclined his head back at the scene. Renna looked and saw an enormous wolfhound leap on the demon's back, bearing it down as the dog's huge jaws tore loose a chunk of the demon's rough, knobbed armour, sinking into the soft flesh beneath.

The man had recovered by then, and buried his mattock in the coreling's skull with a wet thwack. The dog looked up at him with its muzzle wet with black demon ichor, glowing bright with magic to Renna's warded eyes. It was the biggest dog Renna had ever seen, five hundred pounds at least, with gnarled charcoal fur and claws so great they couldn't fully retract. It growled at the Cutter, but he only laughed and gave it a scratch behind the ears. He whistled as he ran back into battle, and the dog licked the ichor from its teeth and followed.

'Creator,' Renna said. 'It's as big as a nightwolf.'

'Didn't used to be,' Arlen said, 'but it's been eating demon. Corespawned dog's bigger every time I see it.'

'That how nightwolves grew so big in the first place?' Renna asked.

'Reckon,' Arlen said.

An eight-foot-tall wood demon got past the Cutters in the heat of battle and came at the Wooden Soldiers. The men shrieked, forgetting their spears entirely to lock their warded shields together. They were pushed back by the rebound as the wards flared, stumbling into the women they were supposed to be guarding. One soldier lost his feet completely, taking down two women with loaded crank bows in the tumble. Another soldier screamed as one of the bows went off and the bolt took him in the back of the thigh, punching right through his lacquered armour.

The wood demon had barely lost balance when the attack was deflected, and moved for the gap with frightening speed.

Prince Thamos gave a shout, throwing off his fear as he leapt to interpose himself. With one swipe of his arm, he caught the demon's claws with his shield, sending them skittering off trailing sparks of magic as he followed through with a thrust of his short, stabbing spear into the demon's belly. Renna could see the magic that pumped up the weapon into the prince's arm, filling him with power.

It was a masterfully executed attack, but Thamos' blow had struck no vital area, and after a shocked instant the demon recovered and swung its branchlike arms at him again. Thamos ducked the first blow and caught the next on his shield, never letting go of his spear as he tried vainly to pull it free of the demon's thick, barklike armour. The piercing wards on the speartip had broken through easily enough, but there was nothing to aid him pulling it back out.

'Bad warding for such a nice spear,' Arlen noted. 'He's smart, he'll let go and let the women handle it.' Indeed, several women held crank bows at the ready, and would have fired had the prince not been in their way.

But Thamos surprised them. He gave a roar and, still holding

109

on to the shaft of the spear, raised his armoured boot and kicked repeatedly at the coreling's midsection. Impact wards flared on his boot heel, and the demon was bashed and battered as the prince hammered it off his spear and knocked it onto its back. He was on it in an instant, stabbing his newly freed spear right into the coreling's heart.

The prince put a foot on the demon's chest for leverage as he tore the weapon free in a spray of ichor, turning with a shout to assist a pair of Cutters in their own battle. He growled as he put his spear into the back of the demon they faced, pressing in so close the wards on his armour flared.

The frightened man Renna had seen was gone, the prince screaming like a madman as he ran about the clearing, fighting with abandon and little regard for his own safety.

There was a shriek, and Renna turned to see a wood demon bury its talons into a Cutter's chest. The man knocked the demon back a step with a weak blow from his axe, but the weapon fell from his fingers as he collapsed to the ground.

Renna tensed, but Arlen was already off and running. She followed on swift feet, but neither of them would be there in time as the demon moved in for the kill.

She saw a sudden blur and felt a familiar dizziness as a slender girl appeared, throwing back the folds of a warded cloak much like the one Renna wore. The girl was clad in bright motley – loose pantaloons and blouse, with a tight fitted vest. She was half the size of the Cutter who had fallen, and when she stepped in front of the great wood demon, it was like a house cat hissing at a nightwolf. Still, she stood boldly, meeting the demon's gaze, and when it reached its claws for her, she raised a fiddle and put bow to string, sending out a series of discordant sounds.

The demon shrieked and swiped at her, but the girl leapt away, tumbling across the ground and coming back to her feet, never ceasing her playing. The demon put its clawed hands to its ears and shrieked again, stumbling back.

Another dizzying blur, and a large woman appeared behind the demon, unnoticed until she swung a heavy warded blade, severing one of its thin arms. The wound, coupled with the grating sounds of the fiddle, proved too much for the demon and it fled the scene, coming right at Arlen and Renna. Arlen barely paused, catching the coreling by one of its horns and pulling it close as he drew a heat ward on its chest. He spun the demon aside, and it blazed into a ball of bright shrieking flames as he rushed to the wounded Cutter.

Both women's eyes flared at the sight of Arlen running their way, recognition mixed with shock and more than a little fear. The one who had severed the demon's arm shook her surprise away first.

"Bout time you got back,' she said, kneeling at the injured man's side and pulling implements from a heavy pocketed apron to treat his wounds. The young girl continued to stare open-mouthed at Arlen.

Arlen's mouth twisted. 'Good to see you again too, Darsy.' He looked to the girl. 'Mind on your music, Kendall.' He pointed his chin at her fiddle before kneeling beside the Herb Gatherer. Kendall straightened, bringing up her fiddle and scanning the area for other threats.

The Cutter gave a racking cough, blood splattering Arlen's face, and fell still. Arlen paid it no mind, holding the man steady as Darsy examined his wounds.

'Night,' she whispered. Three deep gashes ran from his breast to hip, and there was blood everywhere. 'Ent nothing we can do.'

'Demonshit,' Arlen said, grabbing the first gash and pinching it closed with one hand as he drew a series of wards in the air with the other. A soft glow surrounded them as he worked, Darsy and girl staring dumbfounded as the fatal wounds knitted closed.

The man suddenly pulled in a deep gasp of air, followed by a round of coughing as he attempted to rise. Arlen put a hand on his chest and held him back down. He opened his eyes, looking up at Arlen. 'You come back,' he croaked.

Arlen smiled. 'Course I came back, Jow Cutter.'

'They said you abandoned us,' Jow whispered, 'but I never lost faith.'

Arlen's mouth tightened, but he bent and lifted the man like a child, carrying him to the safety of the warded circle. There was a Tender there, an older man with a beard the grey of a rain cloud. Over his plain brown robes he wore a thick surplice emblazoned with wards of protection surrounding the crooked staff symbol of his order. The man caught sight of Arlen and his eyes widened, but he came in quickly with an acolyte by his side, taking Jow and bringing him to a warded tent, its flaps bearing the Tenders' staff. His eyes never left Arlen as they went, and he reappeared from the tent moments later carrying a staff of polished goldwood carved with wards, watching from the safety of the circle.

The battle was dying down now, and the prince, who had leapt from fray to fray, suddenly found himself without an opponent. He looked around frantically, panting, but when there was no threat to be found he gave a great shudder, suddenly leaning heavily on his spear. His men were by his side in an instant, crowding around him and blocking him from sight. Renna could make out the sound of his retching from within the ring of armoured backs.

'Always like this,' Darsy said. 'There's no one fiercer than the count when his blood is up, but it's slow to rise, and drops like a falling tree.'

'Ent nothin' to be ashamed of,' Arlen said. 'Felt that way myself plenty of times. Fact he's out in the night at all says a lot . . .' He paused. 'Count?'

Darsy nodded. 'Came with a fancy royal decree naming him "Lord of Cutter's Hollow and All of Its Environs", along with a train of carts a mile long. Soldiers, too. More than a thousand, with bowmen aplenty, to fortify against the Krasians. They already started building him a fort. Folk were so thankful for the food and blankets they didn't argue, especially with you and Leesha gone off to Creator knows where.'

'So you just handed him the Hollow?' Arlen asked.

'Din't have a lot of choice,' Darsy said. 'But it ent been so bad. Thamos mostly lets folk who know their business go to, and none can deny the aid he's brought, or the hope he's given to folk who ent got naught else.'

The fighting was over, but Renna could still see Arlen's training as the Cutters went through the clearing methodically, confirming their kills. Demons healed magically fast, and even against warded weapons they could recover in minutes from anything short of death or dismemberment. More than one seeming-dead demon lying in the field shrieked when the Cutters approached, slashing at them or trying to escape. These were quickly pinned, thrashing wildly as the Cutters began cutting at the thick armoured ridges around their necks. Taking the head of even a small wood demon took a few strokes of the axe, and even Samm Saw had to put his back into the task.

Renna came to stand by Arlen and the women, eyeing their dizzying warded cloaks.

'You warded their cloaks, too?' she asked Arlen, dreading his answer.

Darsy turned suddenly, noticing Renna for the first time, particularly the state of her dress, or lack thereof. She glanced at Renna's shoulders, and her nostrils flared. She grabbed the edge of Renna's cloak and held it up so she could see it better in the light, then turned to Arlen with a look of indignation and put a meaty finger in his face.

'You gave your Cloak of Unsight away?! Do you know how Mistress Leesha *slaved* over it? More than her own! You didn't even thank her, and ent worn it once! Now you just piss it away—'

'Ay, you stupid cow!' Renna shouted, snatching the edge of

her cloak back and moving to interpose herself between the two of them. 'Don't you talk to him like that!'

'Or what?' Darsy demanded, looming over Renna and bending so their noses practically touched. 'This doesn't concern you, girl, so shut your mouth or you'll go over my knee.'

Darsy might have been a Herb Gatherer, but Renna knew a fighter when she saw one. She was more than a head taller than Renna and had a heavy frame, packed muscle and not fat. She wore the same floppy pantaloons as the other fighting women, and her heavy warded knife curved inward like a scythe. It would serve equally in hewing thick herb stalks or the limbs of a demon. Its handle was well worn.

But none of that seemed to matter as Renna grabbed her by the throat and began to squeeze. Darsy struggled, her mannishly thick hands pulling at Renna's arm, but she might as well have been pulling at a bar of steel. She swung a heavy fist, but Renna diverted the blow easily, locking on to Darsy's wrist and yanking her arm straight, using the limb to increase her leverage. Darsy went red in the face, the veins in her neck distending.

'That's enough, Ren!' Arlen snapped, grabbing her arms. He squeezed hard, and both her grips lost strength. He pulled her aside as easily as a cat that had jumped on the counter to sniff the butchering block.

'She started the fire,' Renna growled, struggling against his iron grip much as Darsy had against hers. 'You saw.'

'Ay,' Arlen agreed quietly. 'She did. But that ent call to kill someone. Or were they right to try and stake you back in the Brook?'

Like he'd dumped a cold bucket on her head, Renna stopped struggling immediately. He was right, of course. Few would deny that Harl Tanner got what was coming to him when Renna stabbed him with his own knife, but this Darsy Cutter was no Harl.

Still, a part of her screamed for the woman's blood. Renna

breathed deeply, embracing the feeling and letting it pass. Arlen felt her relax and let her go immediately.

'You all right?' he asked Darsy, who was gasping and rubbing her throat.

'Fine,' Darsy croaked.

Arlen nodded, a sharp gesture. 'Then keep to mind that what I do with my own property ent any of your corespawned business. Don't think Leesha would care to hear you gossipmongering over her relations, either.'

'Ay,' Darsy coughed. 'Think maybe you're right at that.' She turned to Renna. 'My mum tried to beat some manners into me, but she never managed the task.'

Renna grunted. 'Guess I wasn't quite neighbourly, myself.'

The girl cleared her throat, and all eyes turned to her. She was perhaps seventeen summers and pretty, but up close Renna saw thick scars coming up over the neckline of her blouse. She had been near death once. Very near. And she could charm corelings with her music. Renna might have doubted Arlen's stories about the red-haired Jongleur, but this she had seen with her own eyes.

Arlen smiled and bowed to the girl. 'Your fiddling's gotten better, Kendall. Looks like Rojer's been working you and the other apprentices hard.'

Kendall looked at the ground, and there was a sadness in her eyes.

'Rojer's been gone for months,' Darsy said, her voice still hoarse, but getting stronger. 'Went to Rizon with Mistress Leesha. And the rest of his apprentices are more interested in playing reels than fighting demons.' She gave Kendall a gentle punch on the shoulder. 'But not our little fiddle witch. Worth a dozen men with spears, she is.' Kendall kept her eyes down, but Renna could see her pale skin flush, and a thin smile crept onto her lips.

'How long's Leesha been gone?' Arlen asked.

'Left with the Krasians going on two months ago,' Darsy said.

Arlen grunted. 'It true, then? Jardir came to the Hollow and stole her away?'

'After a fashion,' Darsy said.

Arlen's brow drew tight. 'What's that supposed to mean?'

Darsy took a deep breath and looked at him. 'He's asked her to marry him.'

Arlen's eyes bulged, and his jaw dropped. It was only a split second before the look dropped from his face, but it had been there, clear as day. Even the aura of magic surrounding him changed noticeably, its surface crackling and popping like green wood in a fire.

Renna had never seen anything take Arlen by surprise, and wasn't sure how to read it. Past Leesha Paper might be, but she still had power over him.

Arlen leaned forward, his face utterly serene, but his eyes intense. 'You telling me Leesha's gone to marry Ahmann Jardir? That lyin', rapin', murderin' son of the Core? That what you're fixing to tell me, Darsy Cutter?' His low voice grew louder as he spoke. Not loud, but louder. Again, Renna saw the ambient magic in the area rush to him, his wards beginning to glow. Darsy drew back from him as one might from a hissing rattlesnake.

'She ent said yes!' Darsy practically shouted. 'And she ent playing the fool. Said it was an excuse to see what he's done to the south. To count his troops and learn his ways. Didn't go alone, either. Took Rojer, Gared, Wonda, and her parents to watch over her.'

'Don't matter,' Arlen said. 'The fact she went at all, and took her da, tells the Krasians Erny's put her to market and is just waiting for the right price.'

Darsy scowled. 'How dare you! Mistress Leesha ent some cow to buy and sell!'

'To *them* she is!' Arlen snapped. 'Krasians don't treat women as free folk. Don't matter if they're a duchess or a milkmaid, women are just property to those people, bought and sold. And no one outbids Ahmann Corespawned Jardir when he sets his mind on a prize, Darsy Cutter. No. One.'

Darsy deflated, the fight gone out of her, and she nodded. 'Told her it was stupid to go, but she wouldn't listen. Stubborn as a coreling.' A pained look crossed her face, as if admitting fault in her precious mistress hurt her. Renna spat on the ground. Darsy flinched, but made no comment.

'Don't think she's in danger just yet, anyway,' she said. 'I've gotten regular letters from her, and the codes all say she and the others are well. Say one thing for the Krasians, they make excellent Messengers.'

'Codes?' Arlen asked.

'Said she wasn't playing the fool,' Darsy said, daring to meet his eyes at last. 'Mistress Leesha figured the Krasians would read her letters, but she gave me phrases and words to memorize so she could let me know how things stood even if they were forcing her hand. So far, Jardir seems to be keeping his word, but she says his army is spread out over all Rizon, and their numbers are impossible to count. She specifically asked that we not mention you, but she left a code to signal your return.'

'Tell her,' Arlen said, 'and tell her that she needs to get back to the Hollow right quick. Got news that can't wait and you ent got codes for it.'

'You'll get no argument from me,' Darsy said. 'Creator never meant me to be town Gatherer.'

'It's hard times, Darsy Cutter, and you got to shoulder what burdens come to you,' Arlen said. 'Something bad's coming with the new moon. Something to make Jardir look like a horsefly buzzing in our ear.'

Darsy's face grew pale. 'What is it?'

Arlen ignored the question. 'Who's been speaking for the Cutters with Gared gone?'

'Who else?' Darsy asked. 'The Butchers. Even the new count knew better than to mess with those wards. Gave them royal commissions, but he's yet to ask them to do anything they weren't already meaning to do themselves.'

There was a great bark, and a heavy shape bright with magic charged at Arlen. Renna drew her knife, but Arlen simply knelt and opened his arms as the massive wolfhound bowled him over. His laughter was infectious as the beast began to lick his face.

'Still ent taught this mongrel to heel, Evin Cutter?' Arlen asked its master as he approached.

'Shadow heels when he wants to, and no time other,' Evin replied. 'Good to have you back, sir.'

'How're Brianne and the boys?' Arlen asked, prising the giant dog back.

'Boys're shootin' up like weeds,' Evin said. 'Callen will be a Cutter himself soon, and Brianne's got another one growin' in her belly. Been prayin' on a girl this time around.' He looked at Arlen expectantly.

Arlen sighed. 'Babe is what it is, Evin. Ent convinced there's a Creator at all, much less one that takes my messages. Just hope if it's a girl she gets her looks from her mam.'

Everyone looked at him in shock, as if unable to believe Arlen had made a joke, but then Evin barked a laugh, and the others joined in, the tension broken.

Darsy cleared her throat, catching Arlen's eye and nodding to the killing field where Renna saw the count heading their way. He was wiping at his mouth with a silk kerchief, but his stride was determined. At his back were two fighters, a man and a woman.

'Dug and Merrem Butcher,' Arlen murmured to Renna. 'Used to be real butchers, till the Battle of Cutter's Hollow.'

The Butchers were both heavyset, with thick arms criss-crossed with scars and burns on their faces. Dug was bald and sweaty, wearing a thick leather butcher's apron reinforced with underplating and spattered with demon ichor. Like Darsy, Merrem wore loose pantaloons that gave the appearance of skirts. Her leather corset was armoured like Dug's apron and equally ichor-splattered. Either one of them looked strong enough to toss a cow. The heavy cleavers on their belts were little different from the one Harl used when he slaughtered a hog, but these were heavily warded, and Renna doubted they'd been used for butchering in some time.

They walked proudly, like Speakers on the way to town council. The rest of the Cutters drifted in their wake, covered in blood, sweat, and demon ichor, glowing fiercely with magic. All of them towered over Renna, giving her the feeling they were standing in a ring of trees. They whispered excitedly among themselves, pointing at Arlen and drawing wards in the air. By way of contrast, the Wooden Soldiers quickly fell into neat lines at the count's back, backs straight and spears in hand, ready to kill for their prince at a moment's notice.

Count Thamos was not as tall as the Hollowers, but he more than made up for it in his bright armour, polished and glowing powerfully with magic.

'No one in the Hollow has forgotten what you've done,' Darsy said quickly, before the count was in earshot. 'The Cutters will go where the Painted Man tells them and nowhere else.'

Arlen nodded. 'This "Painted Man" business is the first thing I mean to clear up.'

Thamos stopped a respectful distance from Arlen and stood haughtily while a smaller man Renna had not noticed appeared before him. The man wore armour and kept a short spear strapped to his back, but he did not have the look of a fighter. Both weapon and armour looked more ornamental than functional. His hands were smooth, likely more used to a quill than a spear. His tabard was embroidered with two emblems, a throne overgrown with ivy and a wooden soldier. He bowed.

'May I present His Highness Count Thamos of Cutter's Hollow, Marshal of the Wooden Soldiers, brother to Duke Rhinebeck of Angiers, and Lord of all the lands and peoples between the River Angiers and the southern border.'

Thamos looked at Arlen, giving him an almost imperceptible nod. Renna knew nothing of courtly manners, but she knew a rub when she saw one. She smiled, eager to watch Arlen break the man.

But to her surprise, Arlen bowed deeply. 'Count Thamos,' he said loudly, so all could hear. 'Thank you for bringing aid and succour to the refugees suffering on your lands. You honour the Hollow by standing with the Cutters in the night.'

Thamos' eyes narrowed, as if waiting for the hook, but Arlen only bowed again. 'We were never properly introduced,' he said, looking up to take in Darsy, the Butchers, and all the crowd. 'Ent been introduced to any of you, really. I'm Arlen Bales, out of Tibbet's Brook.'

Utter silence fell over the crowd at the words. Renna looked around and saw everyone holding their breath, waiting on his next words.

The silence only lasted a few seconds, though it seemed far longer. Then everyone began talking at once, a cacophony too great to make out the words of any one person. Even the Wooden Soldiers began to chatter in the ranks.

Thamos glanced to Dug Butcher, who turned back to look at the crowd. 'Shut it!' he barked, cutting through the din. 'This ent some Jongleur's show!' Immediately, the noise died down to a few mutterings, but Renna could see folk biting their tongues. It wouldn't last long.

Thamos pursed his lips, digesting Arlen's words. 'Tibbet's Brook,' he grunted. 'So you're Milnese, after all. Beholden to Euchor.' He spat the name as if it were poison.

Arlen shrugged. 'Lines on a map may say so, but truer is Euchor never gave a rip about Tibbet's Brook, and the folk there returned the favour. I grew up in the Brook, ay, but I'm my own man.' He met the count's eyes. 'Euchor no more tells me what to do than you.'

Thamos squinted and they locked stares. The count had killed several demons in the battle, and he and his armour glowed fiercely with Core magic. Renna could see the halo around him pulse with his breath, and knew the count would be inhumanly fast. Incredibly strong. And that the magic was screaming at him to attack.

She might have been concerned, but for all his power, the count was facing Arlen Bales. The tattoos on his skin were glowing fiercely now. Renna did not know if it was intentional, but the effect it had on the crowd was clear. Many of the Cutters began murmuring and drawing wards in the air.

The count and Arlen postured like two dogs presenting over a bitch, but Arlen had bigger teeth, and the loyalty of the pack. All around them, Cutters adjusted their grips on their tools, and the Wooden Soldiers shifted nervously.

Arlen ignored the tension, breaking the stare with a disarming smile. He turned to Renna, bowing and sweeping a hand at her in a smooth, practised gesture. He might not wait on proper manners most of the time, but it was clear he knew them.

'My apologies for not introducing my companion,' he said. 'This is Renna Tanner, also from Tibbet's Brook.' He stood, looking up over Thamos' head to the Cutters clustered around them. 'And my promised.'

Again Renna saw the collective jaw of the crowd drop, but this time she felt her own fall with them. His saying it aloud, in front of these people, made it seem far more real than it had just a moment before. She was promised to Arlen Bales. Again.

This time, Thamos was quicker to recover, moving to Renna and bowing, taking her hand and kissing it smoothly. 'An honour to meet you, Miss Tanner. Let me be first to offer my congratulations.'

Renna knew from Jongleur's pantomime that gentlemen kissed ladies' hands in the Free Cities, but she'd never so much as seen it done. She stiffened, not having the slightest idea how to respond. She felt her face colour, and was thankful for the cover afforded by the night.

'Th-Thank you,' she managed at last.

Thamos rose and turned back to Arlen. 'Now,' he said in a low voice, 'if you're quite finished making the bumpkins gasp, might we have a word or two in private?'

Arlen nodded, and the count's manservant escorted the leaders to a large pavilion of heavy canvas at the centre of the warded section of clearing. Inside, the tent was richly appointed with warm fur carpets, a four-poster bed, and a great table surrounded by a dozen chairs. At its head was what Renna could only describe as a throne, a heavy thing of polished wood with a high back and great ivy-carved armrests. It was the biggest chair she'd ever seen, and dwarfed every other seat in the room. Haloed in magic and wearing his bright armour, Thamos looked like nothing more than the Creator himself as he took the seat, sitting in judgement over the proceedings.

A moment later, Arther, Thamos' manservant, cleared his throat and held the canvas open for the Tender Renna had seen looking after Jow Cutter and the other wounded. He carried his warded staff, but though his beard was grey, he was still straight-backed and seemed to have no physical need for the support.

'Tender Hayes, High Inquisitor under Shepherd Pether of Angiers,' Arther announced. Arlen's brow furrowed, and Renna could sense his immediate mistrust of the man.

'Sent to replace Tender Jona, I recall,' Arlen said, looking to Thamos as if the count had been the one to make the announcement. 'Has Jona gone to your inquisition already?'

'That is the concern of the Tenders of the Creator, and none of yours,' Tender Hayes cut in acidly.

Arlen snorted, glancing to Darsy.

'They took him weeks ago,' Darsy said. 'Vika is beside herself with worry, but they wouldn't let her accompany him, and she has had no word since, despite all her pleas.' She nodded slightly Thamos' way.

Arlen looked to the count, but Thamos spread his hands

helplessly. 'As Tender Hayes says, this is a matter for the Council of Tenders. It is out of my hands.'

Arlen shook his head. 'Not good enough. A wife deserves word from her husband and proof that he is well . . . as he had best be.'

'How dare you!' Tender Hayes demanded. 'You may wear a Tender's robe, but you are not of our order, and it remains to be seen if you—'

'If I what?' Arlen challenged.

'Enough!' Count Thamos said. 'A Messenger will take a letter from Mistress Vika tomorrow, and return with one from her husband in one week. If she wishes to visit her husband, an escort will be arranged.'

Tender Hayes fixed the count with a stern glare. 'Your Highness—'

'I'm not your student any more, Tender,' Thamos cut him off. 'Spare me the lecture. If the council has a problem with my ruling, they can take it up with my brother and see who truly has his ear.'

They exchanged a look, and Hayes nodded, bowing. 'As Your Highness commands.'

Thamos grunted. 'Good.' He looked to Arlen. 'May we consider the matter closed, or do you have more veiled threats for me? We have taller trees to fell than some hamlet Tender preaching off Canon.'

Arlen nodded. 'Taller by far, Highness. The corelings have tired of our resistance. They mean to push back, and push hard.'

'Let them,' Merrem snarled. 'Every demon in the Core ent got half a wit between them. We'll make a bonfire so big the Creator will see it.'

Dug grunted in agreement, but Thamos said nothing, staring hard at Arlen over steepled fingers.

'We haven't seen a fraction of what the Core has to throw at us, Merrem,' Arlen said. 'Less than a week ago, me and Renna met a demon a good sight smarter than either of us. A mind demon. It had a bodyguard, a coreling that could change into anything it wished, and when the mind was around, the demons started behaving different.'

'Different, how?' Dug asked.

'Like soldiers with good generals,' Arlen said. 'It sent a copse of wood demons after me that attacked with clubs when their talons failed to pierce my wards.'

'Night,' Merrem shuddered, and Dug spat on the carpet. Renna looked to Thamos, but the count seemed not to have noticed. He had gone deathly pale, and she could smell his fear. She wondered what had happened to the powerful leader and savage fighter he had been just a moment earlier.

'My mother must hear of this,' Thamos mumbled after a moment.

Everyone looked at him curiously. Tender Hayes scowled. 'Mother, Your Highness?' he murmured. It was too quiet for the others to hear, but Renna heard the words as clear as day. Her senses were stretching farther every day.

Thamos gave a start, sitting up straight as some of the colour returned to his face. 'Brother,' he corrected. 'My brother, Duke Rhinebeck, must hear of this immediately. Arther, ready a Messenger!'

Arther moved to comply, but Arlen raised a hand to forestall him. 'I regret to inform Your Highness that there is worse news. Mind demons can reach right into your thoughts and eat them, knowing everything you do. They can even take over and work your body like a puppet.'

'Creator!' Merrem exclaimed. 'How are we supposed to fight against that?' The count's face looked so green Renna thought he might slosh up at any moment.

'The greatwards are proof against them,' Arlen said. 'And for the rest, there are mind demon wards.' He produced a sheaf of parchment and a warding brush from somewhere in his robes. The brush seemed an extension of his arm as he quickly drew a large mind ward, turning it to face the others at the table.

'This symbol can block their intrusion.' He pointed to the same symbol tattooed on his forehead, and the one in blackstem that now adorned Renna's. 'Mind demons are even more sensitive to light than regular corelings. Even moonlight stings them. They only come to the surface at the cycling of the new moon. Those three nights, anyone outside an active greatward needs to be wearing this ward on their head.'

Darsy traced a finger along the curves of the symbol. 'It's simple enough. We can make stamps and put them all over town.'

Arlen nodded. 'Do it.' He looked to the Butchers. 'And you're going to need to step up recruiting and get the Cutters ready for corelings that know how to fight smart.'

'Got recruits aplenty,' Dug said, 'but that just means there's a lot of raw wood running around with warded spears and not a clue how to use them.'

'They've got three weeks to learn,' Arlen said. 'I'll help as I can, but this is on you, Dug Butcher. You and Merrem,' he looked at Thamos, 'and your count.'

'Can't believe you just gave up an army of demon hunters,' Renna said as they went back to the horses.

'Never wanted to lead an army, Ren,' Arlen said. 'These days, any army I lead is apt to have more red on their spears than black. Folk need to stand together, day and night. I'd only get in the way of that. Let Thamos have his throne.'

He looked at her and smiled. 'I can always kick him back off it, if need be.'

Renna laughed, and a nearby wood demon glanced about excitedly at the sound, trying to find its source. She was only a dozen feet away, but in her warded cloak she could have walked right up to it unnoticed.

The cloak Leesha had so lovingly made for Arlen.

'Knew there was a reason I never quite liked this thing,' Renna said. She reached up, undoing the clasp and letting the cloak fall to the ground. The demon gave a shriek as it caught sight of her, coming in fast.

Renna let it come, standing her ground until the last moment before sliding aside, stabbing her knife into a fold in the demon's armour as it stumbled past.

The demon clutched the wound, but it was not fatal, and already its magic would be healing the damage. It turned back to her and shrieked again. Renna met its eyes and spread her arms, waiting.

The demon was more cautious when it came back at her, keeping its distance and using the reach of its branchlike arms to full advantage. Renna bided her time, giving ground freely as she wove around its attacks. Occasionally she hacked at a passing limb with her knife, but those shallow cuts did little more than sting the demon.

Still she waited, until the coreling set its feet a certain way. She dodged its next attack and came in hard before the demon could recover, stabbing into the gap between its third and fourth ribs on the right side, as Arlen had taught her. She felt the beating as her knife pierced the demon's heart, pumping raw magic into her as the light left its eyes.

Flailing, the wood demon clawed at her, but magic sparked along the blackstem wards on her skin, keeping it at bay. Finally, it collapsed.

She looked at Arlen. '*That* demon knows who killed it.'

Arlen looked down his nose at her. 'It's dead, Ren. It doesn't know anything.'

He bent, picking up the cloak and shaking the dirt and leaves from it before folding it carefully. 'Honest word, I never liked wearing it, myself. Don't like hiding any more'n you do. Less, I reckon.'

He grunted. 'Ever get a gift from someone and know they

put a lot of thought into it, but you open it and your first thought is *"This person don't know me at all"*?'

Renna nodded. 'Like when Da would buy a keg of Boggin's Ale to celebrate my born day, then drink it all himself.' She shrugged. 'Tanners ent ever been much for gift giving. Leastways not since Mam died.'

'How'd she go?' Arlen asked softly. 'Heard it was demons, but they never told the tale in town.'

'Couldn't say,' Renna admitted. 'She was cored sure enough, but there wern't a breach in the wards – she was out in the yard. Remember she and Da were fightin' something fierce that night. Didn't give it a lot of thought when I was little, but now I figure she ran out to get away from him. Night, thought about doing it myself a few times.'

'Glad you didn't,' Arlen said. 'One thing to run when you got something to run to, but if you gotta go out, better to go fightin' than runnin'.'

'Honest word,' Renna said.

'Cloak's got its uses, though,' Arlen said. 'We might've both been cored without it.'

'Guess I ought to thank Leesha Paper for savin' us, then.' Renna spat on the ground.

'*You* saved us, Ren,' Arlen said. 'Wern't the cloak or your da's knife that walked up to that corespawn and put him down. Mind demon came closer to ending me than any, and I've had some close calls at night.'

He held the bundle out to her, and Renna nodded, accepting it. She smiled. 'Can't say I won't enjoy when your Leesha sees me in it. Tells folk you put me first.'

Arlen smirked. 'Some folk. The rest will see it and think you're one of Leesha's apprentices.' Renna scowled, and he laughed.

5

Tender Hayes

333 AR Summer
25 Dawns Before New Moon

'Corespawn it,' Arlen growled.

'What?' Renna asked. They had dismounted after a hard ride, leading the horses through a thick stand of trees that had just opened into a small clearing with a jutting rock face.

'Someone's found my hideout.' He pointed.

Renna followed his finger to the rock face, but shook her head. 'Don't see anything.'

'It's there,' Arlen said. 'You'd have to walk right up to it before you saw the door. Got a metal gate covered in corkweed at the entrance, and the rest covered in moss and grass.'

Renna squinted. 'How do you know someone's found it?'

Arlen pointed at a thin trail of smoke drifting out the top of a dead tree that stood solemnly atop the small rocky knoll. 'That's my chimney. Didn't leave the hearth fire burning for three months.'

'Leave anything important there?' Renna asked.

Arlen shrugged. 'Some half-finished warding. Folk joining the Cutters were gobbling up weapons faster'n I could ward them, so I never really built up a cache. Just a place to lay my head.'

There was a squawk, and Arlen sighed. 'Made my nice stable into a corespawned chicken coop.'

'So now what?' Renna asked.

'Reckon we rent a room in town,' Arlen said, sounding tired. 'Starting tomorrow. Day or night, expect folk are going to swarm once we show our faces. Need a few hours' sleep before it starts.'

'Why can't we just camp like we been doing?' Renna said.

'Ent animals, Ren,' he said. 'Nothing wrong with sleeping in a bed, and we ent too good to get to know folk.'

Renna grimaced. She hadn't had a chance to hunt tonight, and expected that once they were in town, her opportunities to feed on coreflesh without Arlen's knowledge would be fewer still. The part of her disgusted by the act was fading quickly as her power grew. She was hungry, and mere food could no longer satisfy.

But the tired look on Arlen's face checked her. He was carrying the world on his shoulders, and she needed to support him in the coming days, no matter what.

'Fine. Tomorrow.' She went to him, taking his hands in hers and kissing him. 'Put down a circle, and I'll put you down proper.' She smiled. 'You'll sleep like the dead.'

The tired look left Arlen's face as she began to caress him. He was never so tired she couldn't rouse him by dropping her clothes to the ground.

It was hours later when Renna, lying awake as she listened to Arlen's breathing deepen into a snore, slipped from his embrace. She paused, watching him there in the circle. He looked so small, so vulnerable. For all his power, he wasn't too good to breathe, or to sleep. He needed someone at his back. Someone he could trust.

Someone strong.

She drew her knife and ran off into the night.

Renna woke with her face in the dirt. She must have rolled off the blanket at some point in the night. She spat and brushed absently at her face as she stretched out the morning kinks. It wasn't quite dawn yet, but the sky was light enough that she could use her normal vision while still watching the drift of magic as it weakened and fled for the shadows.

Arlen was already up and about, wearing only his bido as he dug in Twilight Dancer's saddlebags, grumbling to himself. 'Know I left 'em here somewhere . . .'

Renna smiled as she watched him. She'd gladly wake up with a mouthful of dirt every morning, if the first thing she could see was Arlen Bales. 'What's that?'

Arlen looked up at her as he continued to rummage, and the smile that lit his face was a reflection of hers. 'My clothes. Aha!'

He produced a crumpled bundle of cloth, shaking out a pair of faded denim trousers and a once white shirt. He pulled them on, and Renna laughed at how baggy they were. 'Still don't fit in your da's clothes?'

Arlen gave her a wry look as he tightened his belt and rolled up his shirtsleeves. 'Folk said I was lean back in my Messenger days, but I ate well enough. Think I lost twenty pounds since,' he swept a hand over his tattooed face, 'all this.' He cuffed the loose ends of his trouser legs.

His sandals sat atop his neatly folded robes, all of which he placed in a saddlebag. He pulled out an old pair of leather boots but, after a moment's consideration, grunted and tucked them back away, remaining barefoot.

It was strange to see Arlen in normal clothes. She squinted, trying to imagine the man he might have been if he had never left Tibbet's Brook, but it was impossible. The tattoos covering his forearms and calves – not to mention his neck and face – were all the more jarring coming from out the plain shirt and trousers. 'What's all this?' Renna asked.

'Started wearing robes because the hood let me hide my face in the day, and people were less apt to hassle travelling Tenders,' Arlen said. 'Plus they were easy to fling off at sunset.'

He shook his head. 'But I ent hiding any more, and the robes are giving folk the wrong idea. I'm no Holy Man. And if I need to show my wards in a hurry . . .' He snapped his fingers, momentarily turning to mist, and his clothes fell away. He solidified again in an instant, clad only in his bido, his wards revealed.

'That trick looks handy for more than just fighting demons,' Renna said, grinning.

Arlen smiled. 'Some things're worth doing the old-fashioned way.'

'So we're walking into town just as we are?' Renna asked. 'You're not going to ask me to cover up like you did after Riverbridge?'

Arlen shook his head. 'Sorry about that, Ren. I was just full of steam. Din't have no right—'

'You did,' Renna cut in. 'I gave you reason to boil. Ent holding it over you. Needed the fool slapped out of me.'

In an instant, Arlen was across the clearing, holding her in his arms. 'You done as much for me. More'n once.' He kissed her as the sun finally rose, touching them with gentle beams.

'No more skulking, Ren,' Arlen said. 'We are who we are, and folk can take or leave us.'

'Honest word,' Renna said, putting her hands on the smooth skin of his shaved head to pull his lips back to hers.

Soon after, Arlen took them to Deliverer's Hollow, walking on bare feet and leading Twilight Dancer by the bridle.

'The roads aren't warded,' Renna noted.

'The roads *are* the ward,' Arlen said. 'Or part of one, anyway. After the corelings razed most of the town, we rebuilt even bigger on a plan for a series of interconnected greatwards, like the one the Cutters were clearing up north. Each ring will take longer than the last, but a decade from now no corespawn will be able to set talon anywhere within a hundred miles of the Hollow.'

'That's . . . incredible,' Renna said.

'It will be,' Arlen agreed. 'If it can be done while the Core spews forth an army to knock us back into the Age of Ignorance.'

Even this early, the roads and paths were well travelled with regular folk going about their business. Arlen nodded to some as they passed, but said nothing and never stopped. All of them stared wide-eyed, some even bowing or drawing wards in the air. Almost all dropped whatever they were doing and followed. They kept a respectful pace, but the din grew as numbers increased, and more than once Renna caught the word 'Deliverer'.

Arlen seemed to pay it no mind, his face serene as he guided them towards the centre of town.

There were dozens of homesteads and cottages, all freshly built, and hundreds more under construction. The twists of the greatward left huge swathes of unmolested forest throughout, letting the Hollow retain a simple village feel quite unlike the crete streets, stone walls, and huge buildings of Riverbridge.

'Place almost feels like home,' Renna said. 'Like we could turn this corner and see Town Square and Hog's General Store.'

Arlen nodded. 'Here they call it the Corelings' Graveyard, and it's Smitt instead of Hog, but you squint a bit, it's hard to tell the difference. Think maybe it's why I settled in the Hollow awhile. Wasn't ready to go home, and this was the next best thing.'

They turned a corner, and the graveyard came into view. The cobbled central area was much like that of Town Square. At one end stood a stone Holy House that could as easily have been Tender Harral's on Boggin's Hill, but it was dwarfed by the foundation being laid around it, hundreds of men digging trenches and hauling stones.

Arlen stopped short, and for a moment, the serenity left his face. 'That Angierian Tender din't waste any time. Looks like he's building a cathedral to swallow Jona's Holy House like a frog does a fly.'

'You talk like that's a bad thing,' Renna said. 'Town's

growin' as much as you say, ent they going to need the extra pews?'

'Reckon,' Arlen said, but he sounded unconvinced.

There was a great platform at the far end of the cobbled square with a large stage and a shell to amplify sound. Renna was drawn to the chatter of a huge crowd, but one voice rose above the din. She saw Jow Cutter standing onstage, showing no sign that he had been injured near to death just a few hours before. Renna caught sight of a now familiar set of robes, and saw Tender Hayes standing at the edge of the crowd with one of his acolytes, leaning on his crooked staff and watching with cold eyes.

'Saw Him with my own eyes!' Jow cried. 'Woodie laid me clean open, an' I heard Darsy Gatherer say there wan't nothing she could do! But then the Painted Man came and waved His hands, and now I barely got a mark on me!'

'Get off that stage, Jow Cutter!' someone shouted. 'You may be a fool, but you're no Jongleur! Spin your tampweed tales somewhere else!'

'Swear by the sun!' Jow cried, and he held up his torn and bloody jerkin, showing the faded scars where the wood demon had mauled him. When the crowd still looked sceptical, he pointed at a man in the crowd. 'Evin Cutter, you seen it, too!'

All eyes turned to Evin, but his great wolfhound bristled, keeping them back.

'Din't see no magic healing,' he said after a moment. 'Leastways not with my two eyes. But ay. The Deliverer's returned.'

Arlen groaned, putting his face in his hand as the crowd turned back to Jow with renewed interest.

'Ay!' Jow cried. 'The *real* Deliverer's come back to bring Mistress Leesha home and put that desert rat down!' The crowd roared in approval.

'Dumb as a pile of rocks, but he ent all wrong,' Arlen muttered.

Just then Jow looked up, seeing Arlen and Renna at the edge of the crowd. 'There He is!' he cried, pointing. 'The Deliverer!'

Arlen put his hands on his hips as the entire crowd turned to him at once, looking at Jow like a dog that had shit inside the house.

And then suddenly the crowd closed in, everyone reaching, grabbing. Hundreds of people crushing inward, all shouting at once.

'Deliverer!'

'Bless you!'

'Bless me!'

'I need—!'

'You must—!'

Renna struggled in the press, even her new strength overwhelmed by the swarm of people. 'Get back!' she screamed, but they seemed not to hear, and Renna felt her blood come to a boil, her vision going red as she reached for her knife.

In that instant, Renna saw a bottle flying through the air at Arlen's head, but she was in no position to stop it.

She needn't have worried. Arlen's hand moved faster than her eyes could see, snatching the bottle out of the air. Everyone gasped, and a path opened up in the crowd along its trajectory, all those innocent of the deed stepping quickly away to reveal a group of three men glaring at Arlen. Their clothes were patched and threadbare, and there was a hollow look about them that bespoke hard times. They had thrown their bottle, but Renna knew drinkers when she saw them, and knew it could spur all sorts of mean. Again, her hand fell to the handle of Harl's knife.

'Deliverer!' one of the men spat on the ground. 'If you're the ripping Deliverer, where were you when the Krasians took my daughter?!'

'And my son!' another shouted.

'And my farm!' the third added.

'Show some ripping respect,' Linder Cutter growled, punching the lead man in the face. He went down heavily, and in response the other two tackled the giant Cutter. They struggled back and forth, the men's legs swinging freely off the ground as they tried to pull Linder down. The man he had punched was shaking his head and struggling to get back to his feet with murder in his eyes.

'Ay, he asked a fair question!' someone else in the crowd cried, and there were grumblings of assent and argument. Half a dozen Cutters were racing to the scene.

Arlen was there in an instant, crossing the distance inhumanly fast. 'Enough!' He picked the men off Linder by their shirt collars, holding them like insolent children. Linder looked smug until Arlen glared at him as well.

'Next time you punch someone in my name, Linder, I'll crack your skull.' Linder suddenly looked his age, the overgrown boy's face reddening.

Arlen tossed the other two men aside gently enough for them to land on their feet and reached out to the man on the ground, helping him up. When he spoke, his voice was gentle, but it carried as easily as Jow's in the sound shell so all could hear.

'Know you're hurtin', friend, and I'm sorry for your daughter, but throwing bottles and acting the fool ent helping her, and I'm not the one you ought to be mad at. Never claimed to be the Deliverer. I may be painted up, but I'm just folk like you.'

'But you Delivered the Hollow,' the man said, almost pleading.

Arlen shook his head, scanning the crowd as he did. Everyone was quiet, hanging on his words. 'Didn't deliver the Hollow. Hollowers did that themselves, bleeding right here on the cobbles under our feet. I threw in when they had a bad patch, ay, but so did Leesha Paper and Rojer Inn. So did Linder and Evin Cutter, and a hundred other folk. Even Jow, though it seems he's got it in his head to act the fool as well.' He glanced at Jow, who looked sheepish as he leapt down from the stage.

Arlen put his hand on the man's shoulder. 'Know what it's like to lose people. Apt to make you crazy and mad as the Core. But there's more storms comin'. I'm here to help, but what I do won't mean spit if I'm doing it alone. It's your choice if you want to throw in or drink and point fingers, but I don't owe you any explanations.'

He turned, taking in the crowd as his voice rose to a boom. 'Got more useful things to do than rabble-rousing in the Corelings' Graveyard! Wager that goes for the rest of you, too!'

Suddenly everyone was studying their feet and muttering about unfinished business. They left in a steady flow.

Jow Cutter came rushing up to them as Arlen turned to go. 'I'm sorry. Din't mean—'

Arlen cut him off. 'Ent mad at you, Jow. Had it comin' for being so mysterious last time and keepin' to myself.'

Jow seemed relieved until Arlen raised a finger. 'But that sound shell is for Tenders and Jongleurs and fiddle wizards, not any fool wants to shout. Don't want to see you up there again, 'less you're doing a song and dance. You ent got wood to chop, go ask the Butchers for something to do.'

Jow nodded eagerly and ran off.

Renna looked back to where the Inquisitor had stood, but he, too, was gone.

'Place is more like the Brook than I care for,' Renna said. 'They gonna stake us, we don't save them?'

'Everyone needs the fool slapped out of 'em now and again, Ren,' Arlen said as they led their horses into the stable behind the newly built inn. 'Times ent been easy, and we can forgive if folk're a bit excitable. Don't need to reach for your knife every time.'

Renna stiffened at that. 'Din't know I was that obvious.'

Arlen shrugged. 'It's a big knife.'

A young man, thin but well muscled, came to take their horses. He took one glance at Twilight Dancer and his gaze snapped to Arlen.

136

'Ay, Keet, it's me,' Arlen said. 'Know space is tight, but my promised Renna and I need a room for a few weeks.'

Keet nodded. He quickly stabled the horses and led them through a small side entrance to a mudroom. 'Wait here while I fetch my da.'

'His da, Smitt, is the innkeeper and Town Speaker,' Arlen said when he was gone. 'Good man, you don't cross him. More honest than Hog, but tough enough, time comes to haggle. His wife, Stefny, ent a bad sort in small doses, but she's always got a look like she ent been to the outhouse in a week and wants to take it out on any who come too close. Quick to get preachy, too, tellin' you this and that about how the Creator wants you to live, like someone out of Southwatch.'

Renna bristled. The Watches had been quick to condemn her to death and call it Creator's will.

Moments later a big man, thickly bearded and strong at around sixty summers, came into the mudroom followed by a small, thin woman with grey hair pulled back in a tight bun. Arlen was right about her face. She looked like she'd just eaten a bitter and was ready to spit it out.

'Thank the Creator you're back,' Smitt said, after the introductions were made.

'Creator ent got anything to do with it,' Arlen said. 'Got business in the Hollow.'

'Creator's hand is in everything, great and small,' Stefny said. The edge of a demon scar peeked from the high neck of her dress, and there was a hardness about her that recalled Selia Barren, Speaker of Tibbet's Brook, who had defended Renna when no one else would. Renna had never met a woman stronger than Selia.

Without thinking about it, Renna reached out to her, brushing the scar lightly. 'You fought, didn't you?' she asked. 'When the wards failed last year.'

The woman's eyes widened, but she nodded. 'Couldn't just stand by.'

'Course not,' Renna said, squeezing her shoulder. 'Can't ask any to do what you ent willing to do yourself.'

The pinched look left the woman's face and she smiled. It was an awkward gesture, twisting against the set lines of her face. 'Come. The inn's busy, but we keep a couple rooms open for Messengers. Let's get you settled and put some food in your bellies.' She turned and led the way up a back stairwell as Arlen and Smitt gaped.

They had barely settled in their room and finished the breakfast Stefny sent up when there was a knock at the door. Arlen opened it to find one of Tender Hayes' acolytes – the one who was always at his side.

He wore only plain sandals and tan robes, his warded surplice reserved for night. His trim brown beard was flecked with grey.

'I am Child Franq, aide to Tender Hayes, High Inquisitor and spiritual advisor to His Highness, Count Thamos of Cutter's Hollow,' he said with a minimal bow. 'Apologies for the interruption, Mr Bales,' he nodded to Renna, 'Miss Tanner, but His Holiness was most impressed by your words this morning, and requests the honour of your presence at dinner at six o'clock this evening in the dining hall of the Holy House. Formal dress.'

He turned to go, but Arlen's reply checked him before he could leave. 'You'll have to extend our regrets.'

Franq froze for a moment, and when he turned back, he still had a touch of surprise on his face. He gave another shallow bow. 'You mean to say you have . . . ah, more *important* plans on your calendar than seeing His Holiness?'

Arlen shrugged helplessly. 'Afraid my calendar is quite full. Perhaps after the new moon.'

This time, Franq could not hide his incredulity. 'That . . . that is your reply to His Holiness?'

'Shall I put it in writing?' Arlen asked. When Franq did not reply, he strode to the door, taking hold of it pointedly. Franq shuffled out, his face a mix of outrage and shock.

'Ent he a bit old to be a Child?' Renna asked when she heard his footsteps recede down the hall.

Arlen nodded. 'Looked close to forty summers. Tenders usually take orders by thirty even if the council ent found them a flock.'

'So what, he failed the test?'

Arlen shook his head. 'Means Hayes is powerful, as Tenders go. So powerful that being a Child and his aide is loftier than tending your own flock. Politics.' He spat the word.

'Then what's all this calendar business?' Renna asked. 'Din't seem neighbourly. We just walked into town an hour ago. Ent planned so much as our next privy visit.'

'Don't care.' Arlen waved irritably at the door. 'Corespawned if I'm going to be bullied into a ripping formal dinner just so some Tender can look important. Got no patience for posturing.'

He dropped his voice to Franq's low tenor. '". . . mean to say you have . . . ah, more important plans than seeing His Holiness?" Bah!'

'*Do* we have more important plans?' Renna asked.

'Thought we might spend a few hours knocking our heads against a wall,' Arlen said. 'That's about the same as talkin' to a Tender. They've all got that book memorized, but each one reads it different.'

'Tender Harral from back in the Brook was a good man,' Renna said. 'Stood by me when the town was out for my blood.'

'But not in front of you, Ren,' Arlen said. 'Best remember that. And Jeorje Watch, who was full of righteous fire at your staking, was a Tender, too.'

'You don't talk bad about the old Hollow Tender,' Renna said.

Arlen shrugged. 'Jona's as fool as the rest of them. Maybe

more, in some ways. But he always done right by folk. Earned his respect. Hayes ent earned anything.'

'Ent given him much chance,' Renna noted.

Arlen was silent a few moments, but at last he grunted. 'Fine, I'll send Keet to let him know we found space in our "calendar". But ent no way we're goin' in formal dress.'

There wasn't precisely a crowd outside the inn when Arlen and Renna emerged late in the afternoon to head to the Holy House for dinner with Tender Hayes, but there were hundreds of folk milling about the shops and street corners, attempting to look as if they had reason to be there. A frantic buzz began as they caught sight of the pair.

Renna sighed. It seemed nothing Arlen could say would change the minds of some folk, even those who hung on his every word like it was Canon.

There had been a steady stream of knocks at their door through the day. Smitt and Stefny did their best to keep the petitioners from swarming, but they did not deny access to any they deemed important, and there were many of those. The Butchers came with heavy ledgers and rolled maps they spread on the floor, showing their progress in recruiting and clearing land. Dozens of southern hamlets had fled the Krasians as they spread out to overtake Rizon, many of them resettling entirely on their own greatwards in Hollow County. There were six greatwards surrounding the Hollow proper now, though only two, New Rizon and Journey's End, were fully active. More were still in the early stages.

A glassblower named Benn brought beautiful warded items for Arlen to inspect, and Kendall had snuck in to talk about Angierian Jongleurs that had arrived with Count Thamos' caravan.

'Five masters from the Jongleurs' Guild,' Kendall said, 'and a dozen apprentices. Claim they're here to help Rojer get us better at controlling demons, but they seem more interested in gathering stories about *you*.'

And so it went. Warders, Messengers, Herb Gatherers, Speakers from refugee towns; one by one and in pairs, they came and went until Renna thought she might scream.

Arlen took it better, greeting many as friends and offering suggestions most folk seemed to take as commands. Still, it was a relief to be out of the room, even though it meant weathering the stares of countless eyes as they passed down the street.

Tender Hayes and Child Franq were waiting for them when they reached the Holy House. Hayes was clad in brown robes, but these were of a finer material than Renna had ever seen apart from her warded cloak. Over this the Tender wore a white chasuble, trimmed with green ivy needlework with a crooked staff stitched in glittering gold in the centre, surrounded by a circle of wards, many of which Renna did not recognize. His stole and skullcap were forest green, embroidered with wards in shining gold thread. His hands glittered with gold rings, one of which held a green stone the size of a cow's eye.

Franq, too, was formally outfitted with a green warded skullcap and a white surplice over his tan ·robe, stitched in green-and-gold thread with the same ivy-and-staff design as Hayes. A gold necklace set with a large red stone hung at his throat.

They stood in stark contrast with Arlen, barefoot in his faded denim trousers and shirt, and Renna, who was clad scandalously by anyone's standards, wearing only a high, leather vest and a calf-length skirt slit to the waist on either side. But if their plain clothes – or lack thereof in Renna's case – gave offence, the men showed no sign.

'Welcome to the House of the Creator, Mr Bales, Miss Tanner!' Hayes said loudly, his voice carrying far. 'We're honoured you could join us on such short notice.'

Renna listened for a hint of sarcasm in the old man's tone,

but he seemed sincere. 'Kind of you to have us.' She drew a holy ward in the air. Arlen simply grunted and gave a nod.

Hayes' smile shrank slightly. 'I must congratulate you on your promising. As you can imagine, it has caused quite a stir among the townsfolk. I would be honoured to perform the ceremony, if you wish.'

'That's awful kind,' Arlen said before Renna could respond, his voice carrying as easily as the Tender's, 'but I mean Tender Jona to do it on his return.'

There was another buzz that passed through the bystanders, now a crowd without doubt. Hayes pursed his lips, his mouth becoming a thin line that vanished in his thick beard and moustaches. 'Close to him, were you?'

Arlen shrugged. 'Din't always agree with him, but Tender Jona done right by the Hollow when the need was great. It's my hope he'll return soon.'

The smile left Hayes' eyes, and Franq cleared his throat. 'Perhaps we should adjourn inside, Holiness. The others are already here. They await you in the dining hall.'

'Very well, lead the way,' Hayes said. Franq bowed and led them inside, closing the great doors firmly behind them and leaving the prying eyes and ears behind.

From the small narthex beneath the choir loft, Renna could see a nave meant to hold perhaps three hundred souls. The floors were plain stone, worn smooth by the passage of countless feet over the years. The pews were similarly worn, fine wood with concave depressions where the lacquer had been rubbed away by generations of posteriors. The support beams were carved with wards, as were the stained windows, but they were otherwise unadorned. The main altar was similarly plain, though fresh cloth had been thrown over the table and podium, emblazoned with the ivy and crooked staff of the Angierian Tenders. Thick carpeting had been put down beneath.

'You'll have to excuse the meanness of the accommodations,' Franq said. 'Once the expansion is complete, we'll have a worthy

House of the Creator, with proper appointments more fitting for His Holiness to receive in.'

Renna's sharp ears picked up the sound of Arlen's teeth grinding, but he said nothing as Franq led them to a door to the side of the altar that opened to a narrow hall they followed to a small windowless dining chamber. The dining room was much more richly appointed than the rest of the building. The cold stone walls had been covered in heavy woven tapestries, and a heavy table of polished goldwood ran the length of the room, covered in velvet cloth. The table was laid with delicate porcelain plates, silver utensils, and a golden candelabra. A warm fire blazed in the hearth, and more candles burned overhead on a simple wooden chandelier.

Three men had been sitting at the table, but they rose quickly when the Tender entered.

'You recall Lord Arther, the count's aide,' Hayes said, indicating the man. 'Next to him is Squire Gamon, captain of the count's guard.'

Arther was clad in fine leggings and polished boots, wearing a white shirt cuffed with lace and a tabard bearing the count's insignia, the wooden soldier. Over the back of his chair was slung a harness containing a short polished spear. The weapon was warded, with an elaborate crossguard encrusted with precious stones. It was beautiful and well maintained, but Arther did not have the look of a fighting man to Renna, and she wondered if it had ever tasted coreling ichor.

Her mouth watered at the thought, and she had to suppress a wave of revulsion. What was she becoming, that such things should stir her appetite?

Gamon was clad in similarly fine clothes, though his cuffs lacked the lace, and he had the hardness of a warrior about him, with a close-cropped beard that did not grow over the puckered lines of a demon scar. His eyes were fixed on Arlen, sizing him up as if before a brawl, and his spear had a worn look about it. It rested against the wall in easy reach.

'Honoured,' Arther said as he and the captain bowed. 'The count sends his regrets, but he was delayed overseeing the construction of his keep.'

'Din't want to be seen dining with us, he means,' Arlen murmured.

'And this is the duke's Herald, Lord Jasin Goldentone, nephew to Lord Janson, first minister of Angiers,' Hayes said, indicating the third man. 'Jasin will be heading back to Angiers on the morrow, but we were fortunate that your arrival allowed him to meet you before heading on his way.'

'He'd have waited as long as it took to see us,' Arlen said, again too low for any but Renna to hear.

The herald wore a fine fitted jacket and loose silken trousers of emerald green, tucked into high brown boots of kid leather. His half cape was brown, emblazoned with the ivy throne of Angiers. He swept it out with a flourish as he bowed to Renna, and the inside flashed with the bright motley colour she expected from a Jongleur.

'I have never been so far as Tibbet's Brook,' he said, kissing her hand, 'but perhaps I should rectify that, if the women there are as beautiful as you.'

Renna felt her face colour. 'That's enough of that,' Arlen snapped.

'Indeed,' Hayes agreed, looking reproachfully at Jasin. 'Please, be seated.' He indicated settings for Arlen and Renna. Arther swept smoothly behind her and for a moment she nearly struck him until she realized he was simply pulling out the chair to slide it under her as she sat. The chair was padded with velvet. She had never sat on something so soft.

Franq clapped his hands, and acolytes appeared with wine bottles. The men – Arlen included – took their napkins off the table with a snap, placing them in their laps. Renna awkwardly did the same.

'We have a wonderful menu tonight,' Franq said. 'Roast pheasant stuffed with apricot grain in a wine sauce and suckling pig slow-roasted over applewood with plum jelly.' He turned to Renna. 'Do you prefer red or white?'

'Say again?' Renna said.

Franq smiled. 'Wine, child. What kind would you like?'

'There's more than one kind?' Renna asked, and she felt her face colour as Jasin, Arther, and Franq laughed. 'What'd I say?' she murmured to Arlen under her breath.

Arlen looked ready to spit fire. 'Nothing,' he said, making no effort to keep his voice low. 'They're being rude, looking down over their fancy food and drink while folk a mile from here are eating weeds and thanking the Creator they have that much.'

Franq paled, glancing at the Tender before looking back at Arlen. 'I meant no offence—'

Arlen ignored him, looking at Tender Hayes. 'That what you teach your Children, Holiness? That it's fair to mock regular folk? 'Cause where we come from, Tenders wear plain robes for a reason.'

Hayes' jaw tightened. 'It most certainly is not.'

'Not how I see it,' Arlen said. He looked back at Franq. 'What was it you said about this Holy House? That it was mean? That it was not worthy?'

Franq had the look of a cornered deer. 'I only meant that something more grand—'

'You don't know the meaning of the word,' Arlen cut him off. 'This Holy House is a symbol of the Hollowers' strength. When all else was lost, this building stood strong. We put the wounded here, some in this very room, while their kith and kin stood outside and faced the night to protect them. Ent nothing *mean* about this place.' He looked to Hayes. 'But you'd tear it down and build something bigger, so people forget who they were before you came along, and forget the Tender whose House it was.'

Hayes' face hardened at that. 'Again with Jona! You've taken off your brown robe but still speak as a Holy Shepherd, telling us how our order is to be run. The count already promised that Jona's wife would be allowed to see him, yet still you cause a scene outside in full view of the crowd, and again at my table.'

'It was your scene outside,' Arlen noted. He glanced at the others at the table. 'Know you think us fools because we come from the hamlets, but I worked long years as a Messenger, and know politics when I see 'em. Stood in the graveyard and told all that I was neither Holy Man nor Heaven-sent, but that wasn't enough for you. Had to push and make a show so folk think I'm in your flock,' he glanced at Arther, Gamon, and Jasin, 'while the Royals send their footmen through the back door to listen in and report back. Leave me out of your games. I hold to no Canon and swore no oath to the ivy throne.'

Renna leaned back in her seat, watching in amusement. No one paid her the slightest mind. The other men looked outraged, but Hayes held up a hand to calm them.

'Nevertheless,' Hayes said, 'the ivy throne is sovereign in Angiers, and all within its borders are subject to its laws. Duke Rhinebeck and Shepherd Pether have decreed that Cutter's Hollow is a Canonic holding, Mr Bales. If you reside here, you are subject to both the count's jurisdiction and my own.'

'Evejan law,' Arlen said.

'Eh?' the Tender asked.

'Religion and law are one in Krasia, as well,' Arlen said. 'Their holy book, the Evejah, is the basis for their entire culture, and as the Krasians conquer the southland, they press Evejan law on its people, forcing them to cover up and pray to Everam whether they like it or not. They rape the women and enslave the men, taking away their children to be indoctrinated fully. Even if they cease their advance now, in a generation everyone in their territory will be Evejan, quadrupling their numbers.'

'Then you see why we must resist them utterly,' Hayes said, 'and reject this false god with a renewal of faith in the true Creator.'

'In resisting them, you are becoming them,' Arlen said. 'And I won't stand for it here in the Hollow. Spout all you like from the pulpit. If you can sway folk, that's their choice. But you try some archaic nonsense like staking a fornicator out for the demons, I'll break the stake over my knee and shove half through your door and the other half through the count's.'

'You wouldn't!' Franq growled.

'You see if he don't,' Renna said.

'How *dare* you!' Arther shouted. Captain Gamon leapt to his feet, grabbing his spear. 'By the authority of Count Thamos, I place you under arrest for treason . . .'

Arlen snorted, not even bothering to rise. He casually drew a ward in the air, and the blade of Gamon's spear turned the grey-blue of a hazy sky. The air about the weapon began to shimmer, and both blade and shaft fogged and turned white as rime frost covered its length.

There was a creaking sound, and Gamon cried out and dropped the weapon, clutching his hand as if burned. Jasin leapt out of his chair as the spear struck the stone floor between them, shattering into a thousand pieces.

'Aaah, Creator, my hand!' Gamon shrieked.

'Quit acting the fool and sit back down,' Arlen said. He looked to one of the serving boys, staring wide-eyed and slack-jawed. 'Bring the squire a bowl of cool water to soak his hand in.' The boy ran off without so much as a glance to Hayes or Franq.

Hayes steepled his fingers. 'So you think yourself above the law of both man and Creator? Is this your way of informing me that your speech this morning was a lie? That you really do believe you are the Deliverer?'

Arlen shook his head. 'My way of informing you that I'm not some bumpkin you can push around. Came back to the Hollow because I've got work to do, not to pick a fight with you or the count. So long as you're doing right by folk – and it seems for the most part you are – want us to be friends. But

147

you been taking liberties, and need to know where the wards end. Got no interest in being a pawn in your politicking, and I'll have satisfaction the next time one of you is fool enough to mock my promised.'

Hayes nodded. 'I apologize for any insult to you and Miss Tanner. It was unintentional, and I assure you,' he glanced at Franq, 'my aide will be properly reprimanded.'

The Tender spread his hands. 'I want us to be friends, as well. Neither the count nor I wish to make an enemy of you, Mr Bales. Thamos' brother the duke commanded he come south, secure the border, and protect its people. My own mandate from Shepherd Pether is much the same. I am to minister to these people as your own Jona would have in his absence – a matter I have little sway over.'

'Is that your entire mandate?' Arlen asked.

Hayes shook his head. 'There is one more matter. You.'

'Me,' Arlen said.

'You are not the first would-be Deliverer in Angiers,' Hayes said. 'Tales of His return crop up every few years, especially in the hamlets. The Tenders of the Creator investigate every one for validity. I myself have investigated a dozen in my tenure – every one a fraud.'

Arlen smiled. 'Add one more to the list, because I ent Him.'

Hayes leaned forward. 'Perhaps, but neither are you a simple Messenger from the hamlets, no matter what you claim. You're quick to say what you're *not*, but you have yet to say what you *are*. You use demon magic; who is to say you are not corespawn yourself?'

Silence fell on the room, and Renna bristled. The other men leaned in to hear every nuance of Arlen's reply even as Hayes sat back. Jasin produced a small notebook and a tiny pencil. Tales were money to Jongleurs, and heralds most of all, though they had an audience of one.

'Saw me stand in the sun just this morning,' Arlen said. 'Can corespawn do that?'

148

Hayes shrugged. 'There's a first time for everything.'

'And the thousands of demons I've killed, including what you witnessed last night?' Arlen asked. 'Those just a ruse to gain men's trust?'

'You tell me,' Hayes said.

'Doesn't need to tell you anything,' Renna snapped. All eyes turned suddenly to her.

'Excuse me, young lady,' Hayes said, his tone reproachful, 'but—'

'Arlen din't want to come tonight,' Renna cut him off. 'Said this would happen. Said you'd try to use him, or accuse him. Said we'd be better off talking to a wall. I was the one told him to be neighbourly.' She stood. 'Regrettin' that decision now, and don't see any reason we need to stay for this kind of talk. Enjoy your pheasant.'

She strode for the door, and Arlen shrugged apologetically at the Tender, a grin on his face as he moved to follow.

The sun was setting outside, the streets of the Hollow bustling with activity. Squads of Cutters were forming in the Corelings' Graveyard, preparing for their nightly patrols, and vendors continued their brisk business, selling food, drink, and other items with no apparent plans to pack up for the day. Even the workers digging the foundation to the new Holy House continued to work. Renna knew the greatward kept them all safe through the night, but it hadn't truly dawned on her just what that meant. Freedom, night and day. In Hollow County, humans were not forced to live on the demons' schedule.

'Won't it be too dark to keep working soon?' Renna asked.

Arlen shook his head. 'Magic's about to rise. There'll be light enough for all before long.'

Renna wondered at that, watching for the telltale signs of

the rise, wisps of smoky light drifting up from the ground, visible only to her and Arlen's warded eyes.

But there was no sign of magic's fog on the greatward. Instead, the entire street grew warm underfoot, and began to glow. She thought she was imagining it at first, but it soon grew too bright to ignore. So bright that it was apparent everyone could see the light, warded eyes or no. The casual air of the people on the streets towards the growing dark now made sense. It was not as clear as day, but more than bright enough to see and work by.

'It's beautiful,' Renna said. She could see the edge of the greatward not far off. The magic there rose normally, but flowed towards the greatward in the same way it flowed towards Arlen when he called it. She could feel the ward tugging at her own personal magic, as well. That growing core of power that had been born when she first tasted demon meat was drawn like a lodestone towards an iron pot. Her footsteps felt heavy, and she felt weaker and slightly dizzy.

'Used to feel . . . off on the greatward,' Arlen said, as if reading her mind. 'Like I was walking through water, or had been out in the sun too long.'

'Used to?' Renna asked.

'Everything's different now,' Arlen said. 'Greatward draws so much power, and tapping into it's as easy as breathing.' He drew a deep breath, and his wards flared to life, brighter than she had ever seen them. He blew it back out, and they died away again. 'I can even let the excess back into the ward if I don't need it, strengthening the forbidding.' He looked at Renna. 'Powerful here, Ren. More'n I ever dreamed. Don't even need to kill for it. Can't say it'll be enough, but come new moon, whatever the Core sees fit to spew at us will be in for the fight of its life.'

He turned to another great building, this one situated on the other side of the cobbles. It was the only warded structure Renna had seen in the Hollow, its symbols large and strong, etched deep into the wood.

'Hospit,' Arlen said. 'Need to see Mistress Vika before she goes off to Angiers, and perhaps I can ease her burden before she goes. Time I'm done in there, she won't have so much as a kid with a sniffle.'

'Sure that's a good idea?' Renna asked. 'Liable to start this Deliverer business right back up.'

'That's happening like or not,' Arlen said. 'I ent the Deliverer, but I'm done hiding what I can do. We stirred up a hornets' nest, killing that mind demon, and unless I miss my guess, the stinging starts on new moon. Need everyone on their feet.'

Renna scowled.

'What?' Arlen caught the look. Renna crossed her arms, turning away.

A moment later she felt Arlen's arms around her, squeezing gently. 'Something's botherin' you, Ren, just say it. I learned a lot from that demon, but reading minds ent a trick I'm ready to try.'

Renna sighed. 'Don't like you healing.'

Arlen stiffened. 'What? Why? I should leave folk laid up? Crippled? Dying?'

Renna wanted nothing more than to stay in his arms, but she shook them off, rounding to face him. 'Ent that. Just think it ent safe. You call me reckless, but you near kill yourself every time you heal. Too stubborn to know when to stop. So ay. I'd rather some nit broke his leg heal the old-fashioned way than have you pass out tryin' to fix it.'

She expected him to shout at her, but Arlen only nodded. 'Still getting the hang of it. But I got the greatward to draw on, and I'll be careful, Ren. I promise.'

6

The Earring

333 AR Summer
29 Dawns Before Waning

'Ah! Aaaaah!'

Inevera fell into her breath as the cries of the Northern whore emanated from her earring.

The ring seemed a simple silver bauble, but it was etched with tiny wards and powered by a half pebble of demon bone at its centre. The other half of that pebble rode in the ring's mate, which she had given to Jardir on their wedding day, its true nature unknown even to him.

As you love me, you will never remove it, she told him that day.

The wards were normally out of alignment, but with a twist Inevera could activate them, and the bit of *hora* would resonate with its twin, sound carrying through to her like a child's toy of cups and string.

Including the sound of Leesha Paper moaning pleasure into her husband's ear.

I am the palm, Inevera told herself, *and this is only wind. I will bend, but I will not break.*

Her eyes flicked to Melan and Asavi, her closest advisors. They could not hear the ring – its magic tuned to the wearer alone – but it made little difference. Ahmann and Leesha played their lovegames openly now, at least inside the palace. Inevera was forced to smile and act unbothered, even as it eroded her power among the *dama'ting* and the men in Jardir's court.

She clenched her fist. There was little she could do to oppose them. Ahmann was Shar'Dama Ka, and by any accepted interpretation of the Evejah, it was his right to have any woman he desired. Inevera had worked for years to ensure his needs were met by her personally, or women she had carefully selected – ones that brought him power and children, but whom she could easily dominate or eliminate.

Leesha Paper was neither. She could indeed bring Ahmann power, but she was cagey with it, and haughty as an Andrah's First Wife. She would not be dominated, and Inevera had failed to eliminate her twice. The first time Inevera had commanded her eldest daughter Amanvah, betrothed to the red-haired Northerner Rojer, to poison Leesha. The girl was loyal but inexperienced, and bungled the job badly.

Leesha could have gone to Jardir then, making their fight public and ugly. Jardir would have been furious. Perhaps uncontrollably so.

But Leesha had said nothing, and even allowed Amanvah to remain in her presence. Inevera had been forced to concede her a measure of respect for that, and when she had her eunuch Watchers break into Leesha's bedchamber soon after, she had foolishly tried to bully the woman off rather than simply killing her. That same night she had been forced to save Leesha's life, that they might face the mind demon attempting to kill Jardir together.

Of course, if she hadn't, the demon might well have taken Jardir's life, and hers as well. Much as Inevera hated to admit it, the Northern hedge witch was formidable, and her power had only increased that night. Inevera had been unable to stop her from taking powerful *alagai hora* from the mind demon – much as Inevera herself had. She had sent eunuchs to retrieve the bones, but they returned beaten and empty-handed. Leesha would not be taken off guard again.

So Inevera listened. Listened and tried not to feel replaced. Supplanted. Humiliated.

She breathed, restoring her calm. The woman would be returning to her barbarian village soon enough, and good riddance. Inevera would reclaim her rightful place in Jardir's bed, and all would be as it was.

Perhaps.

The moans and cries of passion faded, replaced by gentle murmuring. Inevera strained her ears, trying to make out the muffled words. This was worse than the cries of passion and the slapping of flesh. Inevera had watched her husband with other women many times, and knew well the sounds he made, and those he drew from women. Confident in her pillow dancing, Inevera had no fear of anything Leesha could do in love. It was the quiet moments, when he and Leesha lay intertwined, that Inevera loathed.

'Marry me,' Jardir said.

'How many times must I refuse you, before you stop asking?' Leesha replied, feigning ignorance of the incredible honour she was being paid.

'If you refuse me ten thousand times,' Jardir said, 'I will ask ten thousand more. Come, there is still time. I am Shar'Dama Ka, and can marry us with a wave of my hand. Wed me now, in secret. Your mother and Abban can bear witness and sign the contracts. No one else need know until we deem otherwise, but *we* would know.'

Abban. Inevera's lip curled. He was wrapped up in this, making his own plays for power and Jardir's ear. He would need to be dealt with, as well.

'Ask me ten thousand times, or twenty thousand,' Leesha said, 'the answer is still no. You have enough wives.'

'I will deny them all my bed,' Jardir said, and Inevera bristled. 'All save Inevera,' he amended, and she found her breath again, still stunned at his foolishness. It was said *Sharum* could not haggle, and Jardir was *Sharum* to his bones.

'So I would only have to share you with one other woman instead of fourteen?' Leesha asked.

'You share me now,' Jardir growled, and Inevera bit her lip at the sound of their renewed kissing.

'We are alone, Ahmann,' Leesha said, and Jardir gasped in pleasure. 'For the next few hours, I am not sharing you with anyone.'

'Damajah!' Melan cried. 'Your hands!'

Inevera looked down and saw blood running from her clenched fists. Her long painted nails were sharp, and had cut hard into the heels of her hands. Numb, she hadn't even realized it. Even now, they seemed someone else's hands as Melan and Asavi took them, carefully cleaning and bandaging the wounds.

How had it come to this? How had she failed Ahmann, that he shamed her so? She had seen him trained and educated before the *Sharum* could beat the potential from him or see him killed in waste. She had handed him a unified Krasia, and given him the tools to drive the *alagai* all the way back to Nie's abyss. She had given him four sons and three daughters, and selected *Jiwah Sen* to keep his bed warm and provide him with yet more children.

'Perhaps I should have selected Northern whores for him to slake his lust for white skin upon,' she muttered.

'Men are predictable creatures,' Melan said.

'The first thing they do when they overpower something is hump it like a dog,' Asavi agreed. 'Many of the *Sharum* are developing a taste for pale skin.'

Still lovers after all these years, Melan and Asavi shared quarters and were always at each other's side. They had no personal interest in men beyond their seed, and had long since used the dice to choose a father for their daughter heirs, both doing the deed in one night and never seeing him again.

But for all their bias, the words rang true enough, and Inevera should have anticipated it. Now, because she hadn't, her husband was bewitched by an infidel whore in the perfumed chamber where they had lain so many times.

Already Leesha's whispered advice had begun to change Ahmann, making him rethink centuries of culture and tradition. Some of his resulting decrees were innocuous enough, but others were dangerous, alienating his own people for the sake of Northern sensibilities, forgetting they were meant to be his subjects, not allies.

They did not have years to treat with the *chin*. Sharak Ka was coming. In some ways, it had already begun.

7

Training
300 AR

Inevera always hated when her father brought *Sharum* to their home. She and her mother did all the cooking and serving while her father shouted and swatted at them, making a great show before his friends as they grew increasingly drunk and rowdy, playing Sharak with clay dice. Even before he took the black, Kasaad had forbidden Soli to do work of any kind. 'You're a warrior, my son, not some *khaffit* or woman!'

When she was younger, the men had ignored Inevera and leered at Manvah, but as she approached womanhood some of those leers had turned Inevera's way. One *Sharum*, a disgusting man named Cemal, had even tried to paw at her.

But though he could not cook or carry, Soli was always there to protect. Cemal's hand had barely begun to squeeze before her brother put a hard knee between the man's legs and broke his nose.

Kasaad had laughed, mocking Cemal and congratulating his son, but he hadn't so much as glanced at Inevera to see if she was all right. Worse, he had continued to invite Cemal into their home, and did nothing to stop the leering. Inevera knew the *Sharum* were only waiting for Soli's attention to lapse.

Serving her father and half a dozen drunken *Sharum* terrified

Inevera, but not half so much as serving Waxing Tea to the *dama'ting*.

A semicircle of velvet pillows was spread on the thick carpet of the dining chamber. Kenevah sat first at the centre, and was immediately served a steaming cup of tea by Melan. The girl was like a wisp of smoke, appearing to fill the cup and then vanishing again.

'Qeva, sit at my right,' Kenevah bade, gesturing at the pillow there. 'Favah, my left.'

Qeva sat as she was bade, as did Favah, a venerable Bride who looked older even than Kenevah. Asavi and another *nie'dama'ting* stepped forward to serve them.

Kenevah lifted her cup, and the three women drank. Then Kenevah invited two more Brides to sit, one on each side. They were served hot tea, and all five drank.

The tea for the next pair of women, served from the same pots, was barely hot. For the next pair, it was merely warm. By the time the last Bride sat and all of them drank, it was cold.

Food was served in the same order, with Kenevah's most favoured getting the choicest cuts of meat, though all dined on food finer than Inevera knew existed. The smell of it made her dizzy with hunger.

After these rituals, the *dama'ting* relaxed, talking quite amiably among themselves. Their handsome eunuchs did the cooking and most of the carrying, but it was up to the Betrothed to attend the Brides directly.

The *dama'ting* before Inevera finished her tea and set the empty cup before her. When Inevera did not immediately move to refill it, she glanced back with a raised eyebrow. Inevera hurried forward with the pot, spilling a single drop on the table. The *dama'ting* to her other side glanced at it, sniffing disdainfully.

When she returned to the service, Melan pinched her and it was all Inevera could do not to cry out. 'Idiot,' the girl whispered.

'We'll all pay for that. Spill again and next time you bathe we'll hold you under until you meet Everam.'

Even in such exclusive company, the *dama'ting* kept their veils in place, leaning over their bowls and using a pair of smooth sticks to quickly bring morsels to their mouths. Occasionally Inevera caught a glimpse of a mouth or nose, and immediately averted her eyes. The sight felt more obscene than watching Kasaad bend Manvah over a pile of baskets.

When the *dama'ting* had finished their supper, the Betrothed served themselves from the remains in the kitchen. Melan and the other girls shoved Inevera to the back of the line, and there was little food remaining when they were through. She managed to scrape a bowl's worth from what clung to the sides of the cookpots, but even then the other girls sat in tight circles, deliberately shutting her out. She ate alone, and followed numbly as Qeva ushered them back to the Vault at sunset.

The *nie'dama'ting* slept in a communal chamber, lit by a ceiling that glowed with clear wardlight. Inevera's eyes drifted up and stared at the magical symbols with unbridled wonder.

'You'll learn your warding soon enough,' Qeva said, noting her stare. 'Melan, where is your cot?'

There were several neat rows of cots at the centre of the room. Melan pointed to a corner spot, well away from the door.

Qeva nodded. 'Who sleeps there?' She gestured to the cot next to Melan's.

'Asavi,' Melan said, and the girl stepped quickly forward.

Qeva grunted. 'Your pillow sister will have to find a new place. Inevera will sleep next to you for the next twelve Wanings, that you may better instruct her.'

Melan gave an almost imperceptible hiss as Asavi moved to collect her possessions – books and writing implements, mostly. She glared at Inevera as she passed, and the look might as well have been knives.

'You have your liberty until the wardlight fades,' Qeva said, and left the room.

Inevera held her breath, waiting for the girls to come at her, but again they ignored her, breaking into small, tight circles, locking her out. Inevera went to her cot, took out the Evejah'ting, and began to read.

It was hours before the wardlight faded, but she had barely made a dent in the thick book. She set the ribbon on her page and passed into a fitful sleep.

Inevera woke to find someone hovering over her in the darkness. Her eyes were adjusted to the darkness, but it was still little more than a silhouette, moving cautiously to keep quiet. She caught her breath a moment, then remembered herself and began an even breathing to feign sleep. She let herself snore softly, as her mother often did.

Inevera had no possessions save for her Evejah'ting and *hora* pouch, nothing to use as a weapon, if such would even do her good against a room full of girls who despised her. Could they kill her here, in the dark, and get away with it? She tensed to run, though there was nowhere she could run to. Even if she could find the door in the blackness, it was barred from the outside.

But the silhouette moved past, shuffling to Melan's bed. There was a rustle as the blanket was thrown back.

'I think she might have heard me,' Asavi whispered.

There was a pause. 'She's asleep. I can hear her snoring,' Melan said. 'And who cares what the bad throw thinks?'

Inevera lay in her cot, trying to keep the rhythm of her snoring steady as she listened to the sounds of kissing and whispers of love from Melan's cot. She had never kissed another girl, never even considered it, but she did envy them. Inevera had never felt so alone.

Inevera woke again, this time to a stabbing pain in her side. She cried out, half sitting, and saw Melan drawing back her foot for another kick. 'Up with you, bad throw.'

The wardlights were active again, and most of the other girls had already woven their bidos. Aching to make water, Inevera moved quickly for the privy curtain, but Melan caught her arm. 'You should have woken sooner if you wanted time for that. The *dama'ting* will come at any moment, and if your bido isn't fully woven when she arrives, a full bladder will be the least of your worries.'

Inevera's face went cold, and in an instant she was leaping for a fresh silk, her discomfort forgotten. The other girls watched her with scowls on their faces as she quickly wove her bido.

Asavi spat at Inevera's feet. 'So she's a weaver's daughter. It proves nothing.'

Barely a moment after Inevera finished tying, the heavy doors to the sleeping chamber opened and Qeva stood waiting. The girls lined up in only their bidos, and Inevera followed them out of the Vault and into another great chamber of the underpalace.

'We begin each day with *sharusahk*,' Melan advised. 'You will not speak. Do exactly as the *dama'ting* does.'

Inevera nodded as the girls lined up in neat rows, each standing two paces apart. Qeva strode to a small dais at the front of the room, reaching to unfasten her robe. The silk fell away in a whisper, and she stood nude before the assembled girls, save for her veil and headscarf.

Slowly, she began doing a series of stretches. The other girls copied her, and Inevera struggled to do the same. Qeva's flesh was smooth and muscled, soon coated in a sheen of sweat and scented oil. Inevera wondered how such slow movement could make the woman sweat as if she had run in the hot sun for an hour.

The movements were gentle and precise – nothing like the broad, brutal motions Soli had practised. But though gentle in appearance, the poses proved far more complex than Soli's. Inevera was forced to attain positions she hadn't known possible and hold them for extended periods of time. Never-before-used muscles screamed at the strain, and she broke into a heavy sweat, heart thumping as she struggled for air. It seemed no amount of gasping could pull in a full breath, and she feared that at any moment she would lose control of her water.

Qeva leaned forward on her left leg until her body was perpendicular to the floor, arms out before her as if to embrace. Her right foot raised high into the air and curled back over, toes nearly touching her tailbone.

Inevera attempted the pose, but lost her balance, pitching forward onto her hands.

'Hold pose,' Qeva said, and the other girls were left balanced in that precarious position as she stepped down from the dais.

'Stand up straight,' the *dama'ting* commanded. Inevera got quickly to her feet, and Qeva put one hand on her bare chest and the other in the hollow where her shoulders met. 'Breathe in through your nostrils. Deeply.' She squeezed, and Inevera had to overcome the resistance to inflate her chest.

The *dama'ting* grunted. 'Out. Slow.' She continued to squeeze as Inevera slowly let the air out at an even pace.

'Again,' Qeva said. 'Breath is life. If you have breath, you have your centre. If you have your centre, nothing can truly touch you. You will not feel hunger or pain. Not love nor hate. No fear. No anxiety. Only the breath.'

Already, Inevera felt herself calming. The insistent cries of her full bladder and empty stomach faded as she followed the path of her breath from her nose to her belly and out again. Around her, the girls began to wobble, strain telling on their faces as they held the difficult pose.

'With me,' Qeva said. Still squeezing, she began to breathe in a slow rhythm, and Inevera paced her own breaths to match. 'As the breathing cleanses your mind, these will hone your body, until the two act as one.' When they were in sync, the *dama'ting* took her hands away and grabbed Inevera's arms, spreading them wide above her.

'Cobra's hood,' Qeva said, and glanced at the other girls. 'Resume.'

There were sighs of relief throughout the room as the girls all stood straight, reaching for the ceiling with arms spread.

'These are the *sharukin*,' Qeva said as she guided Inevera through the next several movements, gently correcting her posture. 'Vulture's beak. Jackal's spring.'

She leaned Inevera forward into the position she had stumbled in. 'Scorpion's tail.' The *dama'ting* stepped her left foot on Inevera's, holding her in place as she hooked her right foot around Inevera's right ankle and lifted her leg until she could catch it, pulling it higher and higher, then bending it over until Inevera felt her tendons straining to the limit. She gasped and wobbled.

'Breathe,' Qeva said. 'You are the palm, and breath is the wind. Use its power to lead you back to balance and guide you from one form to the next.'

Inevera returned to the rhythm, and found the steady breathing did indeed aid her. Qeva noted her renewed balance and nodded, returning to the dais.

The lesson went on for some time. Inevera still wobbled and felt awkward, her joints stretched into fire, but she kept her breath steady, and was relieved when Qeva finally relaxed, reaching into a box beside the dais. There was a clatter of metal and she came away with four tiny cymbals, one strapped to each thumb and forefinger.

At a nod, Melan went and took up the box, taking her own cymbals and passing it along. All the other girls did the same, and soon they were back in place, waiting for Qeva to begin this next part of the lesson.

Qeva turned to stand in profile, her hands held high, cymbals poised. One leg was stretched out before her, the other kept close.

The other girls assumed the same pose, and Inevera did her best to imitate it.

'Knees bent,' Qeva said. 'Weight on the balls of your feet.'

When Inevera corrected herself and found her centre, the *dama'ting* clapped her cymbals four times, each time snapping her round hips so they cracked like a whip.

'All,' she said, and repeated the move. The other girls copied her with practised precision, but Inevera found the move trickier than it looked.

'Again,' Qeva said. 'Watch closer.'

Again she rang the cymbals and snapped her hips, and again the move eluded Inevera. At first she could not figure out how to move her hips, and then her cymbals were out of sync with the others. Doing both at once seemed impossible.

Over and over Qeva took her through the move. Inevera could sense the irritation of the other girls as she struggled, but there was nothing she could do save try and try again.

Finally, Qeva seemed satisfied. She grunted and began to ring the cymbals in a continuous pattern, snapping her hips to match. Inevera fell into the rhythm, and soon it was second nature. She found herself smiling.

But then the *dama'ting* began to move, stepping around her dais with lithe grace, never ceasing the rhythm of the cymbals or her hips. It was beautiful. Mesmerizing. And when Inevera tried to imitate her, she walked right into Melan, bringing them both down in a heap.

'Idiot!' Melan snapped.

Qeva leapt from the dais, slapping Melan hard on the face, her cymbals rang with the impact. 'The fault is yours, Melan! The *Damaji'ting* assigned *you* to teach her the ways of the *nie'dama'ting*! What have you taught her? She did not know so much as cobra's hood or the first turn of the hips.'

She lifted a finger and put it in Melan's face. 'You must learn to take your responsibility seriously. Until Inevera can keep pace with the class, you are denied the Chamber of Shadows.'

All the other girls gasped, and Melan's eyes bulged.

'Point those wilful eyes at me a moment longer,' Qeva said, 'and you will find yourself living in the great harem, a plaything of the *Sharum*.'

Melan dropped her eyes, bowing deeply. 'Yes, Dama'ting.'

After *sharusahk*, the girls lined up by the kitchens where a pair of aging eunuchs gave each a ladle of thin porridge. Inevera could see in the eyes of Melan and the other girls that they meant to shove her to the back of the line, so she gave way freely. There was nothing to be gained in pointless confrontation. It was best to appear meek as she learned the ways of the *nie'dama'ting*.

Inevera's bowl was less than half full, the final watery remains of the porridge pot. Even so, she barely had time to gulp it down before Melan came for her.

'It is nearly dawn,' Melan said. 'The *dama'ting* leave for the pavilion shortly, and Nie take us if we are late.'

'The pavilion?' Inevera asked.

Melan looked at her as if she were an idiot. 'The *Sharum* will be returning from the Maze at dawn, and the injured are taken to the pavilion. We assist the *dama'ting* in the healing.'

Inevera remembered the screams of injured *Sharum* filtering through the canvas walls the day before, and imagined men all around her, covered in blood, howling as she helped the *dama'ting* cut and stitch their flesh.

She felt suddenly dizzy, and her face flushed hot. The thin porridge rose back up her throat.

Melan slapped her hard in the face. Porridge and bile flew in a spray, spattering the stone floor as the crack echoed off the chamber walls. Every girl in the room looked up at that, their gazes cold. There were no *dama'ting* present, and the eunuchs were mute as ever.

'Everam's balls, find your centre!' Melan snapped. 'The *dama'ting* take nothing so seriously as the healing. Already the Chamber of Shadows is denied me. If so much as a drop of *Sharum* blood falls because of your weakness, the *dama'ting* will have it from my hide a hundredfold.' She moved in closer, her voice dropping to a whisper. 'And if that happens, I will cut off your nipples and make you eat them.'

Inevera stared at her as the words sank in. Melan gave her no time to respond, grabbing her arm and pulling her back towards the Vault. The girls quickly washed their hands and faces, donning their white robes and lining up once again. Melan led the way back to the Vault doors, where they met the *dama'ting* who guided them out of the palace and through the Undercity to the catacombs beneath the Kaji *dama'ting* pavilion, where they waited for the *dama* to sing the dawn from the minarets of Sharik Hora.

Assisting the *dama'ting* in their healing was every bit as bloody and horrid as Inevera had feared. Her ears rang with the shouts and screams, half from *Sharum* too lost in agony to embrace their pain, and half from Melan and the *dama'ting*, cursing her slowness.

Once, while carrying a jug of instruments soaking in a harsh fluid that made couzi smell mild, she tripped and spilled a few drops. Melan punched her full in the face for that, with Qeva and another *dama'ting* looking on. Neither woman said a word, more interested in the instruments Inevera carried than her swelling cheek.

On the table before them, a warrior thrashed and flailed as they tried to cut the black robes away from a deep gash in his abdomen. The Brides tossed shattered bits of ceramic armour plates into a palm basket where they clattered, wet with blood.

Qeva threw a pair of silk cords to Melan. 'Pin him.'

Melan took one of the cords, handing the other to Inevera. 'Be swift, and do exactly as I do.' She wound the cord around her fists with perhaps a forearm's length between.

Inevera had no time to ponder those instructions before Melan moved in, impossibly fast and graceful as she wrapped the cord around the warrior's wrist, twisting back and using leverage to hold his arm out straight. He tried to resist, but Melan knew the angles where his arm was weakest and kept control.

'Now!' she shouted, as the man grabbed at her awkwardly with his other hand. Inevera rushed in, attempting to do as Melan had. She caught the *Sharum*'s wrist in a twist of silk, but she did not know precisely where to step or how to shift her weight as Melan had. The warrior caught her with a backhand blow that made Melan's punch feel like a kiss.

Inevera hit the floor hard and Qeva hissed, stabbing two stiffened fingers into the man's shoulder joint. His arm spasmed and lost its strength long enough for Inevera to recover her cord and pin him once more. Qeva glared at Melan in irritation, and Melan in turn glared at Inevera silently as they held the warrior prone. The *dama'ting* forced a sleeping draught down his throat, and he soon went limp. The Brides began to cut, oblivious to the blood and other, fouler fluids that stained their pristine white robes.

'This will not do,' Qeva said after a time.

'He needs *hora* magic, if he is to survive,' the other Bride agreed. She looked at Melan. 'Take him to the catacombs.'

Melan nodded, and she and Inevera heaved at the poles of the stretcher that hung limp at the sides of the operating table. The warrior easily outweighed the two girls combined, but Inevera was no stranger to hard work, and her steps did not falter. Asavi scurried ahead to open the trapdoor, and the *dama'ting* led them down into the darkness.

Asavi waited until Inevera and Melan had descended the steps, then pulled the door shut behind them, leaving them in perfect pitch until Qeva produced her glowing bit of demon bone, lighting the way to a stone chamber with another operating table. There was a steel door cut into the rock wall, and Qeva took a key from around her neck and opened it, revealing what looked like an assortment of coal lumps and blackened bones. *Alagai hora.* She selected a modestly sized lump and closed the door with a click as the locking mechanism re-engaged.

'Suction,' Qeva said, and Melan fetched a device of tubes and bellows, operated by a foot pedal. Inevera pumped the pedal evenly as Melan inserted one of the tubes into the warrior's open wound, siphoning the blood into a glass chamber.

The *dama'ting* cleaned the edges of the wound, first clearing the blood and then shaving the surrounding area. As they worked, Asavi prepared brushes and a bowl of ink.

'Inevera, step close,' Qeva said. Asavi took her place at the pedal, and Inevera approached the Brides, taking care to stay out of their way.

Qeva did not look at her as she spoke. 'First, the siphon ward, drawn at the north edge of the wound.' She dipped a brush in the ink and drew a strange symbol. Inevera watched intently, expecting the ink to glow, but there was no effect. 'Next, the wards for strength, endurance, and blood.' She drew quickly, moving her brush clockwise along the *Sharum*'s flesh, putting wards at each compass point around the wound.

'Now they must be connected,' Qeva said, drawing the same ward four times in the gaps between the others, forming an octagon.

When she was done, she gestured to the other *dama'ting*, who held forth the lump of demon bone from the cabinet. As soon as the bone was brought close to the wound, the wards Qeva had drawn did indeed glow, flaring fiercely to life.

'The wards are not magic,' Qeva said, 'but they leach magic from the demon bone and turn the *alagai*'s power to Everam's purpose.'

As Inevera looked on open-mouthed, the *Sharum*'s flesh began to knit back together, the wound closing like two cupped hands of water brought together as one. In moments the wound was gone without so much as a scar. The new flesh looked paler, untouched by the sun or ever-blowing sands, healthier even than the skin around it.

'Praise be to Everam,' Inevera whispered, awestruck. 'With such magic, no *Sharum* need ever die again.'

Qeva shook her head sadly. 'If only it were so. Even *hora* magic cannot cure the most serious wounds, and such power is not without its price.' She gestured to the lump of demon bone, which was crumbling away in the other *dama'ting*'s hand. 'Healing is the most taxing of magic, and not used lightly. The *alagai* may be an endless scourge, but harvesting their bones is costlier in lives than the bones can save. We must use the power sparingly.'

'And secretly,' the other Bride added sternly. 'The *Sharum* are already too reckless with their lives. Everam only knows what heights of idiocy they might reach if they knew we possessed such power. Better to let as many as possible heal naturally.'

Qeva nodded. 'We will keep this one from his brothers for some time, drugged senseless as he "heals".'

'But is he not needed to defend us from the *alagai*?' Inevera asked.

Melan laughed, and Qeva glanced her way. 'Thank you for volunteering to carry this warrior back up to the pavilion and wash bido silks for the rest of the day, daughter.'

Melan stiffened, but she bowed. 'I apologize for my disrespect, Mother.'

Qeva whisked a hand, dismissing her. 'Accepted. Take Asavi with you.'

Unsure of what to do, Inevera stood frozen as the two girls heaved the healed *Sharum* back up on the stretcher and carried him from the chamber. The other *dama'ting* led their way with a glowing demon bone.

When all were gone, Qeva turned back to her. 'Despite her lack of respect, Melan is not incorrect. It is the wardwalls, not warriors, that protect the Desert Spear. Until the Deliverer comes again, *alagai'sharak* is only the pride of men, throwing lives away for victories not worth their price.'

Inevera's eyes widened at the blasphemy. Soli and Kasaad risked themselves in the Maze every night. Her grandfathers, uncles, and male ancestors going back three hundred years had died in the Maze, as she had always thought her own sons would. It could not simply be the pride of men. 'Does not the Evejah tell us that killing *alagai* is worth any price?'

'The Evejah tells us that obeying the Shar'Dama Ka is worth any price,' Qeva said. 'And the Shar'Dama Ka commanded we kill *alagai*.'

Inevera opened her mouth, but Qeva raised a finger and cut her off. 'But the Shar'Dama Ka has been dead for three *thousand* years, and took the fighting wards to his grave. Each night, more men die in the Maze than are born each day. There were millions of us before the Return. Now, less than a hundred thousand, all because of men and their ridiculous game.'

'Game?' Inevera asked. 'How is defending the city's walls from demons in sacred *alagai'sharak* a game?'

'Because the walls need no defence,' Qeva said. 'Kaji built the Desert Spear with two wardwalls – one outer, at the city's ancient perimeter, and one inner, to protect the oasis and its surrounding palaces and tribes. Between them lies the Maze, built on the ruins of the outer city.' She paused, making sure to meet Inevera's eyes. 'Neither wall has *ever* been breached.'

Inevera looked at her curiously. 'Then how do demons get into the Maze each night?'

'We let them in,' Qeva growled. 'The Sharum Ka opens the gates wide till the Maze is well seeded, then closes them again, trapping the demons in the Maze for his men to hunt.'

Inevera felt much as she had earlier in the day, when Melan

slapped her. She felt dizzy, and put a hand to the wall to steady herself.

'Breathe,' Qeva said. 'Find your centre.'

Inevera did as she bade, drawing deep, rhythmic breaths and using them to steady both her limbs and her pounding heart.

The technique helped, but not enough to step away from all the anger she felt. Part of her wanted to slap every man in the city across the face. She had thought Soli and her father brave; their sacrifice great as they stepped into the Maze each night. But if the solution was to simply leave the gates closed . . .

'Those . . . idiots,' Inevera said at last.

Qeva nodded. 'But idiots or no, it is not the place of *nie'dama'ting* to make light of their sacrifice.'

Inevera remembered Qeva's punishment of Melan, and her face flushed. She bowed. 'I understand, Mother.'

Qeva's eyebrow arched. 'Mother?'

Inevera bit her lip. 'Is "Mother" not the proper form of address from a Betrothed to a Bride?'

Qeva's eyes crinkled in what Inevera took as a smile. 'No. Melan addresses me so because she is my daughter.'

The knowledge did nothing to quell Inevera's sudden tension. 'She called Kenevah Grandmother . . .'

Qeva nodded. 'And so she is. I am the *Damaji'ting*'s heir.'

Inevera felt her heart clench. Qeva had always seemed stern, but fair. Not a friend, perhaps, but neither an enemy. But now . . .

'Breathe,' Qeva said again, holding up a hand and waiting as Inevera found her centre. 'I am not your enemy. I've grown used to my place of power as second among the *dama'ting*, but I learned long ago to accept that I would not succeed my mother in leading the women of Kaji. Melan has yet to embrace this truth and bend before its wind, but I pray to Everam that she will in time.'

Qeva's placating hand changed into a pointing finger. 'But do not mistake my meaning. I am not your enemy, but neither am I your friend. It takes a special woman to lead the Kaji *dama'ting* with strength, competence, and humility before Everam as my mother does. If you prove not humble, competent, or strong enough to survive and advance to the white,' she shrugged, 'then that is *inevera*.'

Inevera's face went cold, but she focused on her breath and kept her centre. 'Yes, Dama'ting.'

'Good,' Qeva said. 'Come with me.' She strode from the chamber, and Inevera followed her through the hidden passages of the Undercity leading back to the Dama'ting Palace. Most of these tunnels were lit by glowing wards running in continuous lines along the top and bottom of the tunnel walls.

When they arrived at the *dama'ting*'s quarters, the eunuch Qeva had spoken to the day before admitted them, naked save for his golden shackles. Stoneless he might be, but his manhood hung heavy before her, and Inevera could not help but gaze at it.

'Impressive, is he not?' Qeva asked. 'Khavel is a favourite of mine, a skilled lover and a loyal servant. But you must tear your gaze from him now, I'm afraid. You will see his prowess first-hand during your pillow dancing lessons.'

Pillow dancing lessons? Inevera felt a wave of anxiety at the sound of that, though there was at least a little curiosity bound up in it.

Qeva gave her no time to ponder. She produced a square box of fine white sand and a slender stick. There was a track along the top and bottom that allowed her to slide a pane from one side to the other, smoothing the sand into an unblemished flat. She handed the stick to Inevera. 'You watched me paint five wards this morning. Draw them for me now.'

Inevera pursed her lips, but she took the stick, closing her eyes to visualize each ward before carefully drawing. As Qeva had, she drew an octagon, a ward at each of the points. Four were unique, and the fifth was repeated four times to connect them. She held the stick close to its end like a pen, forming the curved symbols with precise turns of her supple wrist. When she was finished, she looked up proudly.

Qeva studied her work for long minutes before grunting. 'You were better at *sharusahk*. Only two of these hold any power at all, and little enough at that.'

Inevera's face fell as the Bride slid the pane to clear her work and took the stick. 'Let us begin with the siphon ward. These are the demon's fangs,' Qeva said, drawing two curved marks in the sand as Inevera leaned in, studying the markings closely. 'They float next to or hide within every ward, drawing magic into the symbol. The shape of the ward is what guides that power into its final form.' She continued to draw, holding the stick at its far end. 'See how my wrist remains straight. I move the brush with my arm, not my hand. Wards are strongest when drawn in a single continuous line, and you cannot do that with your wrist alone.'

Quickly, Qeva drew the siphon, and Inevera saw just how poor her memory had been. Her cheeks coloured in shame, but Qeva seemed not to notice, clearing the sand and handing the stick back to her.

'Again.'

Inevera complied, but holding the stick as Qeva had shown was awkward, and if anything, her warding was worse the second time.

Qeva's eyes were expressionless as she cleared the sand again.

When Inevera at last returned to the Vault, her arm ached from holding the stick almost as much as her bladder, which was ready to burst. Her robes were still spattered with *Sharum* blood.

But these seemed distant things, physical discomforts easily ignored. With Melan and Asavi occupied, she was finally able to empty her water and use the baths.

There were scented oils and cakes of soap, tools for paring nails, and rough stones for smoothing skin. The other girls pointedly ignored her as she took a razor and finished the job they had begun the night before, shaving away the last ragged bits of hair from her head until it was completely smooth to the touch. It felt alien, like someone else's skin.

But while her body relaxed, Inevera's mind was in free fall. Everything she had ever known, ever believed, had been stripped from her or revealed as a lie. Nothing made sense any more. Nothing seemed to matter.

Inevera felt as if she had stepped outside herself at dinner. She was dimly aware of her body as she served the *dama'ting*, hopping at their need and vanishing just as quickly. Ironically, this seemed to be just what the women wanted, and she served better when giving the task no conscious thought. Not that she had thought to spare, still struggling to find a constant or truth to cling to. Even the Evejah she had been raised to, once believed to be the ultimate truth, was proving subjective now, the great deeds of Kaji and the laws the *dama* drew from them unravelling before her eyes. The Evejah'ting included the Damajah's perspective on those world-shaping events, and it was often very different from the male account.

Which was true? Kaji's account, or the first Inevera's? Or were both full of lies and half-truths? Did the events of thirty-three hundred years ago even matter?

She ached for her mother's arms, for the safety she felt when Soli roughed her thick black hair. But that hair was gone now, and Soli with it. Perhaps she would see him again, but more likely he would be killed in the Maze before she became *dama'ting*, if she ever did. She even felt a pang of regret for Kasaad and his drunken *Sharum* friends. Could she truly judge the actions of men forced into the Maze to needlessly face hordes of demons each night?

But for all her pain and turmoil, Inevera realized that even if she could wave a hand and take back the last two days, she wouldn't. She had spent nine years in darkness, and now for the first time there was a flickering light.

Magic. They were teaching her *hora* magic.

Inevera thought back to her revulsion at the sight of the tiny demon bone Qeva had used to light the way to her foretelling. Could it only be a day ago? It seemed a lifetime. Now she wanted nothing more than to clutch a demon bone in her hand and cure men's wounds with a wave.

She felt her heart thudding, and forced herself back into the rhythmic breathing of her centre. Soon she felt her body relaxing and was able to step outside it once more. The problems and questions continued to swirl around her, but they were more like blowing sand now, a nuisance that could be ignored.

She shuffled wordlessly along at the back of the *nie'dama'ting* food line, and managed to scrape a full bowl's worth from the eunuchs this time. She ate in silence and was escorted back to the Vault with the other girls.

Find your centre! Melan had snapped at breakfast, just before the slap. Inevera almost wished she would do it again, just so she could remember what it was like to feel.

Was this what finding one's centre meant? What it meant to be *dama'ting*? Did these women truly feel nothing as they looked into the future and made decisions that meant life or death for men and women alike – all the while living like *Damaji* in their great palaces, their every desire catered to?

When they were back in the Vault, the *dama'ting* left them to their nightly liberty until the wardlight faded. There was a heavy clicking of locks as she pulled the doors shut behind her. Inevera moved directly for her cot and the Evejah'ting that lay upon it.

She was barely aware that Melan was approaching her until she found herself flying through the air. She struck the ground hard, and a flash of pain brought her back to herself.

She looked up as she put her hands under her to rise. As in the baths, the other girls had formed a ring around her and Melan as the older girl approached.

She sighed. *Not this, again.*

'I am to teach you *sharusahk*,' Melan said. 'I am denied the Chamber of Shadows until you learn!'

Inevera slowly gave ground as Melan advanced until her back came to the ring of girls, and one of them shoved her forward.

'Scorpion!' Melan cried, bending smoothly at the waist and wrapping her arms around Inevera's hips as her foot came up behind her, kicking Inevera square in the face.

Inevera fell back, stunned, and took several moments to recover herself before she got back to her feet. Melan continued to hold the pose.

'Scorpion,' the girls around them chanted, each falling into the pose themselves. 'Scorpion. Scorpion . . .'

Inevera kept her breathing steady, and was surprised to find she was not afraid. Melan obviously meant to give her a beating, but it seemed pointless to resist. She doubted the girl would do her any lasting harm, and there was little she could do to stop it in any event. Best to submit for now, and learn what she could.

Her centre was strong as she assumed the scorpion pose, steady despite her rapidly swelling face.

Melan seemed more angry than ever at this response, as if expecting Inevera to cry and beg. Inevera pitied her in that moment. Melan's own mother, Kenevah's heir, had cast the bones that called her. What was all this anger and jealousy supposed to prove?

'Wilting flower!' Melan cried, moving in fast and low, thrusting the stiffened fingers of her right hand into Inevera's abdomen.

There was a blunt pain, and Inevera lost all feeling in her legs, collapsing to the floor.

'It is not just knowing how to strike,' Melan said. 'One must also know where.' Before Inevera could find the control of her limbs to rise, Melan pinned her on her back, knees pressed into her upper arms, keeping them helpless and without leverage.

Melan reached out, pressing the knuckles of her index fingers hard into Inevera's temples.

The pain was intense, like lightning arcing through her brain. She saw flashes of light and struggled helplessly, her breathing forgotten.

It seemed an eternity before Melan eased back, getting to her feet. Inevera lay there, breathing slowly until she could find her centre again.

'Wilting flower,' the other girls began to chant, each flowing into the gesture as they did. 'Wilting flower. Wilting flower . . .'

Inevera rose shakily to her feet and copied the move.

'This is a tunnel asp,' Qeva said to the girls, presenting a glass box for the *nie'dama'ting* to observe. Inside was a hollow bit of stone sitting on a sand floor, and within that hollow, a small coiled snake with dull grey scales. 'There is no deadlier creature under the sun.'

Inevera and the other Betrothed leaned in for a better look. Months had passed, and the days had fallen into a rhythm of sorts, beginning as always with *sharusahk* and treating injured *Sharum*, followed by lessons, some shared with other girls her age, and others with Qeva alone.

'It's so tiny,' she whispered.

'Do not be fooled by its size,' Qeva said. 'Tunnel asp venom makes scorpion stings feel like sweet kisses. A single bite can kill a *Sharum* in minutes. The tunnel asp strikes quickly, then retreats to wait for its prey to die. It can afford to wait. Other animals will not feed on those it poisons, lest the venom kill them in turn.' As she spoke, she took the lid off the box, rolling one of her silk sleeves up to the elbow. In one hand she held a small sand mouse by the tail. It squeaked and squirmed desperately, sensing the danger. She dropped it into the asp's box, just in front of the hollow stone.

Instantly, the snake uncoiled, snapping at the mouse, but fast as it was, Qeva was faster. Her hand was a blur as she caught the snake behind its head and lifted it from the case. It thrashed at first, but Qeva's grip was firm, and she cooed at it, stroking its head until it calmed.

'We can force the asp to reveal its fangs by applying pressure to the base of its skull.' She pressed with her thumb, and two curved fangs, previously flat against the roof of its mouth, extended. There was a tiny glass bottle on the table, its mouth covered with a thin membrane. Qeva pressed the fangs through this.

'The poison sacs are on either side of its head, here and here.' She pointed. 'Squeezing will empty them into our vial.' She did so, and a few drops fell into the glass. Qeva then dropped the snake back into the glass box, where it immediately coiled and stared at the mouse, head bobbing slowly from side to side. The mouse stared back, frozen in place save for its nose, which followed the dance of the snake's head precisely. At last, the snake struck, biting but once before retreating into its stone hollow, leaving the mouse to thrash in the sand. In moments it stiffened and lay still.

'Even milked of its poison, the bare residue on its fangs was more than enough to kill,' Qeva said as the snake slithered from the hollow to claim its prize, its jaw unhitching to swallow the mouse whole. 'The asp will feed, and sleep, and by this time tomorrow, its poison sacs will be full again.' She held up the tiny bottle, which held perhaps three teardrops' worth of venom. 'This is enough to kill everyone in this room. Who can tell me how the antidote is prepared?'

Several girls raised their hands, but none faster than Inevera.

Inevera and the other girls knelt in a ring around the pile of pillows, their backs straight and their eyes attentive. In addition to the *nie'dama'ting*, there were several *dal'ting* girls in black headwraps, sent to study in the *dama'ting* palace before going to the great harem.

Qeva stripped off her white robe, even her hood and veil. Beneath, she wore diaphanous leggings that flowed like lavender smoke about her calves and thighs, ending in anklets tinkling with golden bells above her bare feet, the toenails painted to match the lavender cloth. Her top, too, was transparent, loose around her firm breasts, leaving her smooth midriff bare save for a golden chain that secured her black velvet *hora* pouch and a small vial. Dozens of golden bracelets jingled at her wrists. Her sex was uncovered, shaved smooth like the rest of her save for her eyebrows and thick black hair, which fell in lustrous ringlets, bound in gold. Only her face remained covered, her silk veil an opaque purple that accented the diaphanous lavender. Her body shone from scented oil.

In the back of the room, a trio of aging eunuchs began to play a steady rhythm on zurna, tombak, and kanun. Qeva beckoned, and Khavel approached. The muscular eunuch was clad, as usual, in nothing save his golden shackles and a silken loincloth that hung like a flag from his great, stiffened member. Like many of the girls, Inevera felt her eyes drawn to it like metal to a lodestone. She shifted uncomfortably.

The *dama'ting* laughed. 'As you can see, already Khavel is prepared for his duty. But a man should always be tantalized to the point of madness before being allowed to sheathe his spear.' She took Khavel's arm and pivoted, using the eunuch's own weight to throw him onto the pillows.

Then she began to dance. Her hips swayed in time to the music, even as she beat a complementary rhythm on the tiny brass cymbals attached to her thumbs and forefingers. The golden bells on her ankles and the bracelets on her wrists added to the spell as she gyrated around the bed of pillows, her feet as quick and sure as they were at *sharusahk*. Indeed, many of the movements she made were the same as those practised each morning in the hours before sunrise.

Khavel stared at her, mesmerized like the mouse before the tunnel asp. His loincloth was taut, seemingly about to tear, and his great muscles were no different, tense and defined, veins pulsing with the pounding of his blood.

It went on until Inevera began to feel dizzy. The room was hot, filled with sweet incense smoke, and she began to sway to the music and the *dama'ting*'s endless rhythm. The other girls were no less affected, all watching intently as the Bride stalked her hapless prey.

Finally, Qeva struck, moving to the pillows and tugging Khavel's loincloth away to reveal his proud spear. She ran a finger along its length, and the tongueless eunuch moaned. Taking the vial from her waist chain, she dribbled oil into her palm and rubbed her hands together until both had a coating of the slick substance.

'There are seven strokes laid down by the Damajah, as she told of the nights she lay with Kaji,' the *dama'ting* said, reaching for Khavel's member. 'Watch closely as I demonstrate each one.'

Khavel soon threw his head back, moaning again, but the Bride squeezed tightly at the base of his mushroom-like tip, cooing softly as she waited for him to calm again. 'Though Khavel is stoneless – the men you will lie with will not be. In their loins lie the future generations of Krasia, and the Evejah'ting commands that none of their seed be spilled or swallowed.'

Several more times, the *dama'ting*'s ministrations brought poor Khavel to the brink, but each time, she applied pressure and patience until he regained control.

'Seven strokes,' the *dama'ting* said, as she moved to mount the eunuch, 'but there are seventy and seven ways to lie with a man. This is the first, *Jiwah Superior*. It is not enough to simply move up and down his spear. You must . . . twist.' She demonstrated, using many of the same gyrations of her dance, now practically applied.

'When you control a man's loins in the pillows, you control *him*,' the *dama'ting* said, 'and you can ensure your own pleasure besides. Most men barely know where to put it, and will simply hump like a dog if given their liberty.'

As she stretched for morning *sharusahk*, Inevera's muscles ached from countless hours spent practising the pillow dance. There were tiny calluses on her fingertips where the brass cymbals were held, and her feet were red with blisters. She would smooth them with pumice in the bath later.

But though she was stiff and sore, Inevera felt strong. Stronger than she had ever felt, even when hauling great stacks of baskets through the bazaar. She was ready to assume the *sharukin*, but Qeva did not remove her robe. Instead she beckoned the girls to form a ring around her, and summoned a muscular eunuch. It was not Khavel this time, but one named Enkido.

Like the other eunuchs, Enkido spoke with his hands in an intricate language of gestures that Inevera and the other *nie'dama'ting* learned as part of their studies. The *dama'ting* could give their servants complex commands with quick gestures, and receive equally detailed answers on the rare occasions when one was required.

But the similarity ended there. Unlike the other eunuchs, Enkido was always clad in black robes, though he still wore the gold shackles of servitude. His veil was red, meaning he had been a *Sharum* drillmaster before coming to the Dama'ting Palace, an expert in *sharusahk* and a master of the Maze. It was said that he had killed many *alagai*, fathered many sons, and taught many warriors before falling under a *dama'ting*'s spell and willingly allowing his stones and tongue to be cut from him.

Inevera heard he continued to wear the black to hide the terrible scars he incurred as a *Sharum*, but when the *dama'ting* clapped her hands, he pulled off the robe and she gasped aloud, as did several of the younger girls.

He did have scars, but they were long healed – more badges of honour than unsightly blemishes. It was not that which made the girls gasp, but the tattoos on his shaved, muscular skin. All over his body, there were lines and small circles, the black markings running up his limbs and all over his torso, onto his neck and shaved head.

Qeva dropped her robe as well and they stood nude, facing each other, though as always she kept her veil in place. She motioned, and Enkido attacked, moving with sudden, frightening speed. He outweighed the woman twice over, but it did not seem to slow him as they grappled and he put her quickly into a submission hold, lifting her feet from the ground so she could find no leverage.

But the *dama'ting* seemed unconcerned. She shifted slightly, then drove two stiffened fingers into one of the tattooed points on his chest. Immediately one of his arms slackened, and she pulled it away like the arm of a toddler, twisting from his grasp and flipping him onto his back.

'All of Everam's creatures are guided by lines of power and points of convergence, where their muscles, tendons, bones, and energy meet,' the *dama'ting* said. 'These are places of great strength, but also vulnerability. Touch the right place, and even the most powerful will lose their strength.'

She beckoned and again the warrior attacked, this time refusing to grapple, striking with lightning-fast kicks and quick, snapping punches like the strikes of a tunnel asp.

But the *dama'ting* bent like a palm in a windstorm, flowing this way and that, his blows never striking home. Finally, she reached out almost gently while he was mid-kick, pressing one of the points marked on his supporting leg. It collapsed under him, and while Enkido managed to control his fall and quickly come upright, his leg was now slack and would not support him. He stood balanced on the other, hands up protectively as he waited on the *dama'ting*'s command.

Instead, she turned back to the girls. 'Trained in Sharik Hora, Enkido was the greatest *sharusahk* master the Kaji *Sharum* had known in a hundred years. No man of any tribe could stand against him, and *alagai* quailed at the sight of him. More than one *dama'ting* sought his seed to bless their daughters, and through them he learned of our art. But though he begged time and again, he was forbidden to learn it. The Damajah teaches that no man can be trusted with the secrets of flesh. At last, the *Damaji'ting* took pity on him, and told him that only by yielding his tongue and his freedom would he be allowed to glimpse our secrets. He broke his spear over his knee right there, using the point to cut out his tongue and sever his own manhood, root and stones. Bleeding to death, he laid them at the *Damaji'ting*'s feet. No longer a man, he was healed and blessed with the right to aid in your training. You will accord him every honour.'

As one, Inevera and the other girls bowed to Enkido. Though he was only a eunuch, he looked at them all with the stern eye of a drillmaster assessing his *nie'Sharum*, and when he spoke with his hands, the girls quickly obeyed.

Inevera kept her hand on the Evejah'ting but did not open it, eyes closed as she recited the holy verse:

> 'And from the sacred metal did the Damajah forge
>   the three holy treasures of Kaji.
>
> First, the cloak,
> Sacred metal hammered into supple thread,
> Sewn into the finest white silk with wards of unsight.
> Months she laboured,

At Everam's will,
Until the eyes of the alagai slid from Kaji in his raiment,
As easily as her fingers coated in kanis oil,
Slid along his skin.

Second, the spear,
Sacred metal pounded thin as vellum,
Etched with wards,
Rolled seventy-seven times about a shaft of hora.
The blade she made of the same sheet,
Folded and fused with hora dust
Seven times seventy times
In the fires of Nie's abyss.
A year she laboured,
At Everam's will,
Until the edge she ground with diamond dust,
Could cut the skin of Nie Herself.

Last, the crown,
Sacred metal warded on both sides,
Masking the many powers she blessed upon it.
Fused to a circlet cut from the skull of a demon prince.
The nine points princeling horns,
Each set with a gem to focus its unique power.
Ten years she laboured,
At Everam's will,
Until the demon lord himself could not touch the
    thoughts of Kaji,
Nor approach if the Shar'Dama Ka did not will it.

With these treasures, Kaji became the most feared
    of all warriors,
And the cowardly princes of Nie
Fled the field whenever he drew the folds of his cloak.'

Qeva nodded as Inevera finished, gesturing to the workbench the *nie'dama'ting* had gathered around, where bowls of metal filings were arranged, ready to be melted down. 'Precious metals conduct magic better than base ones. Silver is better than copper, gold better than silver. But the transfer is never perfect. There is always loss.'

She looked at Inevera. 'What is more precious than gold?'

Inevera hesitated, though she knew better than to look to the other girls around the workbench for aid. At last she shook her head. 'Apologies, Dama'ting. I do not know.'

Qeva chuckled. 'You might truly be your namesake reborn if you did. The Damajah, blessings be upon her, gave us many secrets in her holy verses. But in her wisdom, she kept others still in her mind lest they be stolen by her rivals. Now many are lost to the millennia. The wards of unsight, the powers of the spear and crown, and the sacred metal.'

She took up a bowl. 'And so we begin our lessons with copper . . .'

Weeks passed, and Inevera found herself standing before a silvered glass, drawing wards around her eyes in soft pencil. She had practised the sigils a thousand times, as they were in the Evejah'ting, and inverted, as she must draw them in the mirror for full potency.

Some of the older girls, Melan and Asavi among them, had progressed beyond pencil, wearing delicate circlets of warded coins across their brows, but Inevera's first circlet was still a clinking collection of unfinished coins and gold wire in a pouch at her waist.

Qeva inspected her closely when she was finished drawing, holding her chin in a firm grasp and roughly turning her head this way and that. She said nothing, giving only a slight huff of satisfaction, but that breath meant more to Inevera than the most glowing compliment. If there had been the slightest flaw, the *dama'ting* would have announced it derisively to all and made her wash her face and draw anew.

Inevera felt a chill as the *dama'ting* touched a finger to a small bowl of black liquid. It looked like ink, but she would have known from the stench alone that it was the rendered ichor of demons.

It was warm when Qeva touched the barest smudge to her forehead, but it did not burn as Inevera feared. The spot tingled like static, and she could feel the magic crawling across her skin, drawn to the pencilled wards, dancing along their delicate lines.

And then her eyes came alive, and Inevera gasped for the wonder of it, her centre lost. The dim wardlight of the room was washed out by light from every corner, drifting across the floor and seeped in the walls, shining in the spirits of Qeva and the other girls. It was Everam's light, the line of energy they reached for and drew upon each morning in *sharusahk*, the fire in their centre that gave life and power to all living things. It was the immortal soul.

And she could *see* it, as clearly as the sun.

'Praise be to Everam in all his glory.' Inevera fell to her knees, shaking as she wept for the joy and beauty of it.

'Place your hands on the floor,' Qeva said. 'Let the tears fall free, lest they run through the pencil and rob you of the sight.'

Inevera immediately fell forward, terrified of losing this precious gift. Her tears spattered the stone floor, sending tiny whorls through the magic drifting up through the *ala*. She expected derision from Melan and the other girls, but there was only silence. Doubtless they had all been as overwhelmed as she when they first saw Everam's light.

When her convulsions eased, Qeva dropped a silk kerchief to the floor and Inevera carefully dabbed her eyes. The other girls stared silently at her as she rose.

Qeva pointed to a stone pedestal, its smooth surface carved with dozens of wards, some covered in smooth stones. Inevera had seen the *dama'ting* use the pedestal to control light and temperature in the chamber, but the pattern was far too complex for her to comprehend.

But now, her eyes awash in Everam's light, she could see the power as it moved through the net. The pattern that had been a mystery a moment before was clear now, a child's puzzle easily solved.

'Dim the lights,' Qeva commanded. 'We will not need them for this lesson.'

Inevera immediately complied, shifting the polished stones to other positions, and removing others entirely, setting them in a small basin.

Immediately the wardlight dimmed, but Inevera's vision only sharpened, an unneeded glare removed, allowing her to see even more clearly in Everam's light.

'The wardsight will be invaluable to you as you learn our craft,' Qeva said. 'It is forbidden only in the deep cells of the Chamber of Shadows where you carve your dice.'

Months passed, and Inevera's studies consumed her. She woke to *sharusahk*, assisted *dama'ting* in the healing, and attended regular classes in history, warding, potions, jewellery making, singing, dance, and seduction. The other girls continued to shun her, especially once they saw her carving wooden dice years ahead of many who had been born to the white.

And every night, Melan beat her, calling it *sharusahk* practice. Even after half a year, Qeva was not sufficiently pleased with Inevera's *sharusahk*, and Melan was still denied the Chamber of Shadows.

Each night Inevera slept alone with nothing save her Evejah'ting clutched to her breast as the other girls whispered to one another in the darkness, or shared beds and caresses. Even her dreams were haunted by the shapes of the seven dice that had ruled her life since the day of *Hannu Pash*. She would have wept, but for fear that Melan and Asavi, always together in the bed next to her, would take pleasure in the sound of her sobbing.

Inevera stood proudly as Kenevah inspected the large bowls. There in the sand Inevera had drawn the most complex circles she had ever attempted. Each was made of forty-nine wards, all linked to work in unison. Between the bowls lay her practice box, a single ward drawn at its centre.

The wards were crisp and clear in the fine yellow sand, but Inevera's warding had never truly been tested, and she had no way of knowing if they would hold power.

Qeva stood beside her mother, regarding the wards but saying nothing. She didn't have to. That she had thought Inevera worthy to test for *hora* after less than two years spoke volumes. Next to Qeva stood Melan, her face serene as her eyes cut at Inevera.

At last Kenevah nodded. 'Draw the curtains.' Inevera did as she was bade, and the *Damaji'ting* drew a large demon bone from the thick velvet of her *hora* pouch. Inevera wondered how much *Sharum* blood had been spilled to collect that bone.

Inevera made a cradle of her hands, and Kenevah placed the priceless bit of *alagai hora* in them. It was the first time she had ever touched demon bone, and though the Evejah'ting had told her what to expect, it was still an alien feeling, tingling with power and pulling at her blood as a lodestone might pull iron.

Carefully, reverently, she laid the bone atop the ward centred between the two bowls, and the wards began to glow softly, brightening as they drew power from the bone. They flared with a golden light even as the sand darkened in colour.

The circles began to swirl. At first was a slow churn Inevera thought she was imagining, but it grew faster, like whirlpools in a cookpot after vigorous stirring, flowing into one another in a figure of eight.

The demon bone disappeared into the centre of that vortex, and there was a bright flash of light before the bowls went black. Colours danced before Inevera's eyes in the darkness, leaving her dizzy and disorientated.

'It is done,' Kenevah said. 'Open the curtains.'

Inevera stumbled through the darkened room more by memory than sight, finding the thick layers of curtain and drawing them back, flooding the room with light.

She returned to Kenevah and Qeva's side, gasping as she saw the bowls, each sitting in a bright beam of sunlight. The sand within was gone, as was any sign of the demon bone laid between them. The bowl to the left was filled with clear water. The one to the right was filled with couscous, steaming and ready to eat.

In preparation for this trial, Inevera had fasted for six days, taking only one couzi cup of water each morning and one at night. Her throat was parched, and her stomach ached, hollow and sullen. It growled unexpectedly at the smell of the couscous.

Kenevah raised an eyebrow at the sound. 'Your fast may soon be over.' She handed Inevera a pair of ivory eating sticks, the handles capped with gold and jewels. 'If you formed your wards precisely, a mere stickful of the food will fill your stomach . . .' She produced a golden chalice encrusted with jewels, dipping it into the water and filling it. '. . . and the water will be the purest, sweetest draught you have ever tasted, quenching your thirst with but a sip.'

She looked at Inevera grimly. 'If not . . . you will be dead within moments of either touching your tongue.'

Inevera felt a chill run down her spine. Her hand shook as she took the chalice. 'Must I?'

Kenevah shook her head. 'You can set them aside, but if you

do, it may be years before I waste another *hora* on you – if I ever do.'

Inevera found her centre, and her fingers stopped shaking enough to steady the sticks. She reached out, lifting couscous smoothly to her mouth.

She chewed, and her eyes widened. The consuming hunger that had her stumbling on her feet vanished. Already, new strength was flooding through her limbs as she lifted the goblet and drank deeply.

Kenevah smiled as Inevera finished the cup, her eyes aglow. Indeed, she had never tasted water so sweet and refreshing. It was like a sip from Everam's own river.

The *Damaji'ting* took the sticks and chalice from Inevera, passing them to Melan. The girl's nostrils flared, and Inevera allowed herself a slight smirk. Short of dying at the taste, there was nothing Melan could do now to prevent Inevera gaining access to the Chamber of Shadows.

'Please, sisters,' she spoke the ritual invitation, 'eat and drink of my bounty, for we are all the Damajah's children.'

Melan snatched some of the couscous from the bowl, and dipped the chalice, drinking it quickly to wash the food down. 'The Damajah's children.'

Qeva took the items next, handling them with more reverence and not a little pride. She lifted her veil just enough to bring the sticks and chalice to her lips. Inevera caught a touch of smile at the corner of her mouth as the silk slipped back into place. 'The Damajah's children.'

Qeva refilled the cup for Kenevah, but the aged *Damaji'ting* handled the sticks deftly, quickly taking a mouthful without dropping so much as a grain. She chewed slowly, thoughtfully, then sipped the water, swishing it gently in her mouth. At last she swallowed, drinking again to empty the chalice. 'The Damajah's children.'

The *Damaji'ting* set the items aside and turned to regard Inevera. 'What are the best conductors of magic?'

Inevera stood silent a moment, sensing a trap. The *Damaji'ting* might as well have asked her two plus two. It was an idiot's question.

'Gold, Damaji'ting,' she said, 'followed by silver, bronze, copper, tin, stone, and steel. Iron will not conduct. There are nine gemstones to focus power, beginning with the diamond, which . . .'

Kenevah waved her off. 'How many wards of prophecy are there?'

Another simple question. 'One, Damaji'ting,' Inevera said. 'For there is only one Creator.' The ward was placed at the centre of one face on each of the seven dice, guiding the throw.

'Draw it for me,' Kenevah bade, signalling to Melan, who produced a brush, ink, and vellum.

Inevera had spent the last few months drawing in sand and the brush felt awkward in her hand, but she made no comment, dipping it carefully and wiping off the excess ink on the bowl's edge before beginning to draw on the valuable vellum.

When she was done, Kenevah nodded. 'And how many symbols of foretelling?'

'Three hundred and thirty-seven, Damaji'ting,' Inevera said. The symbols of foretelling were not wards, but rather words that represented different twists of fate, one adorning the centre of each remaining face and along each side of the seven polyhedral dice the *dama'ting* used to read the future. Instinctively, Inevera clutched at her *hora* pouch and the clay dice it contained, their edges now worn from a year of careful study.

Each die had a different number of sides – four, six, eight, ten, twelve, sixteen, and twenty. Each symbol had multiple meanings, based on the pattern of the surrounding symbols and context. The Evejah'ting contained detailed explanations of those meanings, but reading the dice was less a science than an art, and one that was much disputed among the *dama'ting*. Inevera had witnessed them arguing frequently over the results of a throw. In the most extreme cases, Kenevah was called upon to make a ruling. No one ever dared argue once the *Damaji'ting* spoke, but they did not always appear convinced.

Kenevah signalled Melan, who laid a fresh sheet of vellum before her. Inevera dipped her brush again. She drew the symbols smaller this time, and though her hand moved with quick precision, it was some time before she was finished. The *Damaji'ting* had been watching over her shoulder the whole time, and nodded immediately when she was done.

'Have you dice of clay?' Kenevah asked formally.

Inevera nodded, reaching into her *hora* pouch for the clay dice the *Damaji'ting* had first given her. Kenevah took them and set them on the table next to a block of ivory. This she lifted, smashing it down on the dice until they were little more than shattered lacquer and dust.

'Have you dice of wood?' Kenevah asked. Inevera reached into her *hora* pouch a second time, producing the dice that she had painstakingly carved, sanded, and etched from a solid block of wood. Her hands were crisscrossed with tiny scars from the work.

When Qeva had given her the block, Inevera had thought warding the dice would be the most difficult part of the process, but she had no skill at woodwork, and coaxing even the simplest shapes from the wood almost proved her undoing. She cut herself numerous times, casting aside uneven chunks of wood again and again before setting the block aside and carving from soap until she mastered the tools.

The simple shapes, four, six, and eight, came quickly after that, but even with the geometric calculations laid out in the *Evejah'ting*, it took hours to carve the ten-sided die, and even then one side was slightly larger than the others, coming up more often than not when thrown. She had to discard it and begin again. For her to pass the test for *hora*, the dice she gave Kenevah had to be perfect in every way.

Kenevah examined the dice carefully, then set them in a brazier. Melan squirted the precious things, the product of untold hours, with oil and set them ablaze. Inevera had known to expect this, but was still unprepared for how the loss cut at her. Melan looked up at her with a smirk of her own.

Inevera breathed deeply, finding her centre as Kenevah looked at her again. 'Have you dice of ivory?'

Inevera reached for her pouch a third time, emptying into her hands the dice she had carved from camel teeth, these done blind, with strands of bido silk woven over her eyes. They had taken even longer than the dice of wood, months of work, and every time she needed to request a new tooth, she had spent a week washing bidos.

Kenevah rolled the ivory dice through her fingers, studying them intently. Then she grunted, hurling them against the stone wall of the chamber with surprising strength. The fragile dice shattered on impact. She reached out and took the empty *hora* pouch from Inevera's hands, throwing it onto the pyre of her wooden dice. The velvet caught flame, giving off a thick, black smoke.

'You may enter the Chamber of Shadows,' Kenevah said, handing Inevera a new *hora* pouch, this even finer than the first, black velvet tied with golden rope. 'Inside you will find eight *alagai hora*. You will carve your seven dice from them, preserving every shaving. If you make no mistakes, the last is yours to use as you see fit; if you need more, it will be a year's penance for every bone.'

The Chamber of Shadows. Other *nie'dama'ting* spoke of it only in hushed whispers. Deep in the bowels of the palace, untouched by sun or candle or chemical light, it was said the chamber was so dark its walls seemed miles away at times, and closing in on one the next. A darkness so complete it seemed like the abyss itself, and if one was quiet enough, one could hear Nie whispering in the black.

Melan's eyes were those of a tunnel asp as Inevera took the pouch.

No sooner had the Vault doors closed for the night than Melan shoved Inevera to the ground. She was fifteen, and Inevera not yet eleven. The difference was clear in their size, though not as great as it had been when Inevera first came to the palace.

'My dice were nearly done!' Melan shouted. 'Another year at most, and I would have been able to take the white veil. The youngest since the Return! But instead I waste two years trying to teach *sharusahk* to a clumsy pig-eater, only to see her enter the Chamber of Shadows before me!'

She shook her head. 'No. This will be your last lesson, bad throw. Tonight I kill you.'

Inevera felt her blood run cold. Melan looked angry enough to mean it, but what would the *dama'ting* do if she carried out her threat? She looked to the other girls around them.

'I see nothing.' Asavi, ever loyal to Melan, turned her back on the scene.

'I see nothing,' the girl next to her said, turning as well.

'I see nothing. I see nothing.' It was repeated like the names of the *sharukin* as each girl turned her back.

Melan had the other girls well trained. And why not? She was the *Damaji'ting*'s granddaughter, and undefeated among the Betrothed in *sharusahk*. The other girls looked to her as their leader, and she had indeed been expected to become the youngest *dama'ting* since the Return. Only her own mother's order prevented that.

Inevera had never understood why Melan's punishment was so severe, and had held on so long. Inevera had excelled at dancing and *sharusahk*. By her second month in the palace, her forms were as good as the other girls her age. Now, after two years, they were as good as any. Qeva should have lifted the ban long ago, but she had not. Why? It served nothing but to antagonize Melan. If the *dama'ting* thought she could teach her daughter humility this way, she was a fool.

And then, suddenly, it clicked, as Qeva's words from two years gone came back to her.

If you prove not humble, competent, or strong enough to survive and advance to the white, then that is inevera.

Carving and warding were not the only tests barring the Chamber of Shadows. Qeva wanted the strongest leader for the Kaji, and she had set her own daughter to bar Inevera's path, whether Melan knew it or not.

'Scorpion,' Melan hissed, coming forward hard.

But Inevera was through pretending to be weak. She had spent two years humble before Everam. Now it was time for strength.

Inevera had never fought back during these nightly beatings. There had been nothing to gain. But she had watched, and waited, and planned. She knew Melan's weaknesses now, and in her mind she had fought this battle a thousand times.

She dropped down on one hand and the balls of her feet, driving her stiffened fingers into the point of convergence on Melan's thigh. 'Wilting flower,' she said as Melan's supporting leg lost strength and she collapsed to the ground.

Melan rolled quickly to her feet, massaging strength back into her leg, and Inevera gave ground freely, offering no aggression of her own. More than one of the girls forming a ring around them peeked over her shoulder.

'You see nothing!' Melan shrieked, and they quickly turned away.

'We see nothing,' they all echoed.

'Lucky,' Melan snarled. Inevera only smiled in return as the girl came at her again, meeting Melan's cobra's hood with a deft strike to her throat before melting out of her path.

'Shattered wind,' she said as Melan stumbled past, overbalanced and gasping for air. Girls were looking again, but Melan paid them no mind, turning and launching herself at Inevera, her kicks and punches moving like tunnel asp strikes, followed close behind by targeted strikes at Inevera's own convergence points.

But Inevera bent and swayed like a palm in wind, seeing the

lines of energy clearly as Melan set her feet and eyed her targets. Again and again she broke those lines, sometimes simply taking away her breath and balance, other times adding a sharp stab of pain to accentuate the lesson. She was careful to cause no permanent harm, though. Inevera had never told the *dama'ting* of how Melan and the other girls abused her, but she held no such faith in them. Qeva would be looking for excuses to deny her passage into the chamber, and killing or maiming her daughter would surely qualify.

But she was through being abused. Melan came at her again, appearing to use camel's kick, but then flowing unexpectedly into ram's horn, trying to smash Inevera's nose with her forehead.

Inevera caught Melan's robe, swaying to the side with a leg left in Melan's path to trip her into a throw. She kept a hold on Melan's arm, and if the other girl resisted, her arm would pop from its socket. As expected, Melan added her own momentum to the throw to avoid that, practically leaping along to crash into Asavi's back. Both girls went down in a heap, and the others around them gasped and scattered.

Melan let out a low growl, twisting and scissoring her legs around Inevera's feet, tripping her as well and rolling atop her. They struggled for several minutes on the floor, and here the older girl's strength began to tell as she worked her way behind Inevera into a hold, bashing her forehead against the stone floor more than once. There was a flare of light behind her eyes after each one, leaving Inevera's ears ringing and her equilibrium shattered.

She managed to free one arm as Melan pulled the cords of Inevera's bido around her neck, sacrificing control for the hold. After all, what could Inevera do with one arm and Melan firmly planted on her back? She threw her head back to strike Melan's nose, but the girl was wise to the trick, pulling her face back and to the side.

As Inevera knew she would. Quick as a flame demon, she

stuck her index and middle fingers into Melan's nostrils. Her fingernails were sharp, and they cut into the tender cartilage as she pulled hard, threatening to tear Melan's nose clean off.

'Will Asavi still want to kiss you when your nose is a ruined hole?' she whispered.

Melan wasn't the prettiest of the *nie'dama'ting*, but she was easily the most vain. She shrieked, dropping her hold in order to preserve her beauty. Inevera struck several quick blows in the ensuing chaos, then rolled away and got to her feet. Melan followed wobbling unsteadily. There was nothing she could do as Inevera scorpion-kicked her in the face, feeling Melan's cheek and nose crumple under the blow. Melan hit the floor hard and struggled to rise again.

'When she sees your face tomorrow, I think Dama'ting Qeva will lift your banishment,' Inevera said, holding up her new *hora* pouch. 'We will enter the Chamber of Shadows together. And I will finish my dice before you.'

8

Sharum Do Not Bend

302–305 AR

Inevera waited nervously in the *dama'ting* pavilion, her breath fogging in the bitter cold. Qeva was there, as well as three other Brides, seven Betrothed, and four eunuchs, including the powerful Enkido. The eunuchs were dressed in full *Sharum* blacks, night-veiled with spear and shield. Under their robes was linked armour of *dama'ting* craft, enough to turn even a demon's bite.

But despite the powerful gathering in a familiar space, Inevera shifted her feet nervously. It was deep in the night, and they were on the surface. Evejan law forbade this, even for Brides of Everam, but Qeva and the others stood chatting among themselves as easily as if they stood in the Dama'ting Underpalace. Inevera knew logically the chances of *alagai* passing the *Sharum* in the Maze and breaching the great wall was minimal at best – and in truth closer to infinitesimal – but still her heart thudded in her chest.

Fear and pain are only wind, she reminded herself, picturing the palm and finding her centre.

Standing by the tent flap, mute Enkido raised a hand and made a quick series of gestures with his fingers.

'*Oot!*' Qeva said. 'They come.'

Everyone quieted, and the Brides moved to stand in front, Qeva at their lead. She nodded to Enkido as he opened the tent flap.

Half a dozen *Sharum* approached the pavilion, one of them leading a camel with feet wrapped in thick black cloth. There was black cloth over its body as well, and wrapped around the wheels of the large cart it pulled.

Their blacks were dusty from the Maze, with fresh dents in their armour and ichor splattering their heavy shields. One walked with a slight limp, and another had a blood-soaked cloth tied around one thick arm. The *Sharum* all had their night veils in place, but Inevera recognized them immediately by their sleeveless uniforms with breastplates of blackened steel emblazoned with the golden sunburst of Dama Baden. Even without his characteristic swagger and white *kai'Sharum* veil Inevera would have recognized Cashiv, and even more so the man beside him. His *ajin'pal*.

Soli.

She had not seen her brother in years, but she knew him instantly even behind his veil. His eyes had the twinkle of her brother's easy smile, and she knew his walk, his stance, and his muscular arms as well as she knew her own. She suppressed a gasp, but could not help staring.

Next to her, Melan snorted. 'You have as much chance there, bad throw, as you do in beating me to the veil. Those are *push'ting*. Man lovers. There are said to be none finer in battle than Dama Baden's *Sharum*, but they would sooner bed a goat than you.'

Asavi snickered. 'And be better for it.'

'Silence!' Qeva hissed.

Cashiv and the other *Sharum* came before the *dama'ting* and bowed deeply. As they did, Soli's eyes passed over Inevera, but though her face was bare, there was no recognition in the dim light.

'Rise, honoured *Sharum*,' Qeva said. 'The blessing of Everam be upon you.'

Cashiv and the others straightened. 'Everam is great. All honour and glory begins and ends with Him. Our lives belong to Him and his sacred Brides. It is the first night of Waning after winter solstice. We have come to deliver Dama Baden's tithe.'

Qeva nodded. 'Your sacrifice in blood does not go unnoticed by Everam, or his Brides. What gift have you brought?'

Cashiv bowed again. 'Twenty-nine *alagai*, Dama'ting.'

Qeva raised an eyebrow. 'Twenty-nine? This is not a holy number.'

Cashiv bowed again. 'Of course the *dama'ting* is correct. Twenty-eight is the traditional tithe; seven sand demons, seven clay, seven flame, and seven wind. One each of the common breeds for every pillar of Heaven.' He paused, his eyes sparkling with amusement. 'But Dama Baden is grateful for the blessings of the *dama'ting*, and commanded us to lay a special trap. To honour the one Creator, we have also brought a single water demon.'

Several of the *nie'dama'ting* gasped. The Brides showed no obvious sign, but Inevera could read the shift in their stances as easily as if they were shouting in elation. Water demons were beyond rare in Krasia, and there were spells that could only be made from their bones. The spell to create water alone could be accomplished with a fraction of the *hora*.

'Everam is pleased with your gift to honour Him,' Qeva said. 'How did you accomplish this?'

'Dama Baden had us wall off a section of the Maze, removing the wards and breaking the sandstone floor that prevents *alagai* rising. We dug a deep pool, which the *dama* filled with water from his own stores, and seeded with fish and other life. It took many months, but at last, the bait was taken and a water demon took residence there. It killed one of my men and injured two others as we hauled it out in the nets this night, surviving far longer than we expected in the night air. It eventually died of suffocation, and is otherwise intact.'

The *dama'ting* exchanged a glance. The cost of this endeavour was not lost to them. The water alone was a *Damaji*'s ransom – tainted now and useless. It spoke of Dama Baden's incredible wealth . . . and of a favour he sought.

Dama Baden did nothing for free.

'This gift pleases us greatly, Cashiv asu Avram am'Goshin am'Kaji. Your honour, and that of your men, is boundless. The pleasures of Heaven will be yours forever when you pass from this life. Bring forth your wounded.'

The two most heavily wounded men stepped forth, and there was no hesitation as the *dama'ting* warded the skin about their injuries and drew forth small bits of *hora* to effect magical healing. The other men had only superficial scrapes and burns the Brides treated with more conventional means.

When it was done, Qeva turned back to the *Sharum*. 'Bring the gifts into the Rendering Chamber.'

Moving with the assuredness of men who had been this way many times, Cashiv and the others began unloading *alagai* corpses from the cart and carrying them down through a trap-door Inevera had never seen before, right in the entrance hall. Large punctures in the chests of the sand and wind demons told of death by stingers – arrows the size of spears, launched from wooden scorpions atop the walls. The armour of the clay demons was crushed by heavy stones dropped into demon pits. The smell of rank ichor was nauseating.

The flame demons – drowned in shallow pools – were unmarked, as was the water demon, a slimy mass of horned tentacles and sharp scales. Its mouth was enormous for its body, with row upon row of wicked teeth.

When it was done, Qeva gestured and Cashiv came to kneel before her. 'Four questions,' Qeva said, 'and a boon.'

Cashiv nodded. 'Thank you, Dama'ting. I humbly accept this gift, though we are yours to command, and act only to bring glory to Everam, not from thought of reward.' His words had the ring of practice, more a chant than speech. Inevera understood that this meeting likely played out every year, a business transaction that had become ritual. The way everyone smoothly gathered into a ring around the scene spoke of it as well.

Qeva knelt across from Cashiv as she reached into her *hora* pouch. 'Have you the *dama*'s blood?' Cashiv drew forth a polished wooden box. Contained within was a delicate porcelain vial. He passed this to the *dama'ting*, who emptied its contents onto her dice.

'Lower your veil.' When Cashiv complied, she asked, 'Do you swear now that this is the true blood of Dama Baden, and that you speak with his voice – his words and not your own – with Everam as your witness?'

Cashiv put his hands on the canvas floor of the pavilion and pressed his forehead between them. 'I do, Dama'ting. I swear before Everam himself, in the name of Kaji and on my honour and hope of Heaven, that this is Dama Baden's blood and I have memorized his questions precisely.'

Qeva nodded, raising her hand and causing the dice to flare with a harmless glow. Cashiv flinched in spite of himself. 'Then ask, *Sharum*. The dice will know if you lie.'

Cashiv swallowed hard and drew deep breaths, finding his centre in much the same way as a *dama'ting*. Their *sharusahk* might be vastly different, but the philosophy at its core was not.

Cashiv met Qeva's eyes, his words slow and careful. 'What will be my greatest loss this year, and how can I profit from it?'

'Well said,' Qeva congratulated. 'That was two questions last year.' Without waiting for a response, she shook the dice in her hands, chanting as they began to glow. She threw, then studied the pattern carefully.

'A sickness will spread through the goat herds this winter,' she said. 'Only two in five will see the spring, and those too weak to have much value. Tell Dama Baden to sell his stock now and buy as many sheep as he can afford.'

Cashiv bowed and asked his second question. 'As my palanquin passed through the city a month ago, a *khaffit* spat upon me from the crowd. How may I find this one again, to visit justice upon him?'

Inevera knew full well what 'justice' the *dama* meant. One fool enough to spit on a *dama* no doubt deserved it, but it said much of Baden's pride that he would waste such a valuable question on revenge.

Qeva showed no emotion at all as she consulted the dice. 'You will find him in the bazaar. His stall three hundred twenty paces east of the statue of the Holy Mother near the Jaddah gate in the Khanjin district. A seller of . . .'

Inevera tilted her head, studying the pattern still glowing softly on the dice. *Honey melon*, she read.

'Honey cakes,' Qeva said after a moment. Inevera stiffened, looking at the dice again, positive of her reading. She glanced at Qeva, and did not know what filled her with more fear, that Dama Baden was going to torture and kill the wrong man, or that her great teacher had made an error.

She hesitated. Should she speak? She quickly dismissed the idea. If she pointed out the mistake in front of the *Sharum*, it would likely mean her life, as well as that of all the warriors present, Soli included. The *dama'ting* could not be seen as fallible.

She breathed, finding her centre, and did nothing.

Cashiv bowed again. 'Dama Lakash is attempting to end the exception that the personal *Sharum* of *dama* need fight in the Maze only on Waning. How can this be prevented?'

Qeva grunted and threw the dice a third time. 'Dama Lakash's son-in-law and heir Dama Kivan has spoken ill of you in council. Claim insult and kill him, taking his *Jiwah Ka*, Lakash's eldest daughter Gisa, as your *Jiwah Sen* in recompense. Marry her that night, and get a daughter on her the third afternoon after the ceremony.'

Cashiv's face wrinkled at the thought. 'This brings me to the *dama*'s final question, Dama'ting: "I remain vigorous with men, but have lost my ability to lie with and seed my wives. How can this be restored?"'

Qeva snorted and put her dice away. There was a tinkling clatter of small corked bottles as she rifled through the pouch at her waist, finally selecting one. 'Apply this personally to the *dama*'s spear before he does the deed, and tell him to be quick about it.' She tossed the bottle to Cashiv. 'If that doesn't work, stick a finger in his arse.'

Cashiv and the other *Sharum* laughed at that.

'And the boon?' Qeva asked.

'My master has lost nine poison tasters in the year,' Cashiv said. 'He suspects one or more of his many sons.'

'Yet he wastes a question on a spitting *khaffit*,' Qeva noted.

Cashiv bowed low. 'My master's sons add to his power, and he would not wish to kill one, nor does he think it would deter the others if he did. He asks instead for a chalice, ornate as befits his stature, magicked to turn poison to water.'

'A precious gift,' Qeva said. 'Difficult to make.'

Cashiv smiled. 'My master prays it will be less so, with the bones of a water demon.'

Qeva nodded, rising to her feet. 'You may go. Tell your master his chalice will be ready on the first Waning after spring equinox. We will teach him a precise way to hold it, so that only he may activate its power.'

'The Dama'ting is generous beyond measure.' Cashiv touched his forehead to the ground and got to his feet. As he and the others turned to go, Soli looked back. For an instant, he met Inevera's eyes.

And winked.

The days that followed were a horror, as Inevera and the other *nie'dama'ting* who had earned the Chamber of Shadows rendered the demon's flesh with acid and fire, leaving the *hora* untouched. The bones were then polished with sacred oils as the *nie'dama'ting* chanted endless prayers to Everam until they were black and hard as obsidian.

The putrid acid slurry was neutralized with a base, the resulting liquid poison to the touch, but thick with magic the *dama'ting* could tap. It was drained into large vats connected to pipes that sent the stuff through the palace walls like a circulatory system, powering the wardlights, climate control, and countless other spells warded throughout the palace.

The work left the other girls pale and retching, their hands burned and eyes watering, but Inevera barely noticed. Her mind was far away from such inconsequential wind. She breathed through her mouth as she chanted, letting her hands work the monotonous task on their own as her thoughts danced with the image of Soli. She had worried greatly about him over the years, her heart clenching every day *Sharum* wounded were brought to the pavilion. It would have been enough to see him and know he was alive, but the wink had changed everything. He knew her fate and loved her still. He would tell Manvah that she was well and calm their mother's heart.

The chamber rang with the sound of Inevera's cymbals as she gyrated and spun, the grip of her bare feet sure on the polished stone floor. She was thirteen, but already she had a woman's body, lithe yet well curved. She snapped her hips at Khavel and saw him rock back with every thrust.

The younger girls watched in fascination. Inevera taught the beginner classes in pillow dancing now, though the bido wrap she wore meant she herself had yet to experience the dance in full.

Sacred law held that Everam's Betrothed remain virgins until they took the veil, as signified by the bido. That first night, the

Damaji'ting would break her hymen to consummate the marriage to Everam, and Inevera would become a full Bride.

The second night, she would be free to love any man or object as she pleased, for what were they, compared with Everam's embrace? Playthings.

Inevera met the eunuch's gaze as she writhed before him. Firmly under her spell, his eyes were glazed, head swaying in time with her movements. He was hers.

Khavel was a perfect physical specimen – the *dama'ting* settled for nothing less in a pleasure eunuch – with a handsome face, proud jaw, and muscular body glistening with oil. Trained from an early age in massage and all the other ways a man might give a woman pleasure, he would without question be a skilled lover. It was whispered that almost every *dama'ting* made use of him, and that he was on a constant diet of virility drugs, with a strict ritual exercise and sleep regimen. Practically every new *dama'ting* in the last decade had summoned him to her chambers on her second night, with none regretting.

But while Inevera could see the eunuch's beauty, he stirred no desire in her, no more than a perfect statue of a man might. Other girls might be eager to practise the pillow dance fully, but Inevera didn't spend years honing her skills to waste them on half a man. She would sooner bed a *khaffit*.

When her demonstration ended, she lined up the younger girls, helping them place their feet and practise the twist and snap of the hips that was the core of the pillow dance.

After the lesson, Inevera went to the baths, breathing steam deeply as the hot water soaked into her muscles. Melan and Asavi were there, pointedly ignoring her, but in the many months since Inevera's defeat of the older girl, most of the other *nie'dama'ting* had changed their attitude towards her.

'Bathe you, sister?' Jasira asked, holding a soaked cloth lathered with scented soap. She was two years older than Inevera, and had just passed the test of admission to the Chamber of Shadows. Inevera waved her off. Such offers were becoming common, as her power grew and Melan's waned. As Kenevah predicted, the other girls feared her, whispering among themselves that she would one day be *Damaji'ting*. Inevera could make willing servants of most of the *nie'dama'ting*, even so far as taking them as pillow friends and having her pleasure of them. But Inevera had no interest in such things. The girls did not shun her as they once had, but neither were they her friends.

More than anything, Inevera wished she could speak to her mother. Or her brother. The only people she could ever really trust.

As they were dressing, Inevera looked to Melan. 'Going to the chamber, sister? We could walk together.' Melan glared at her, and Inevera allowed herself a slight smirk.

'Smile now, bad throw,' Melan whispered. 'Today I finish my dice, and tomorrow I will take the veil.' She gave a predatory smile, but Inevera only smiled pleasantly in return.

'I will still be *dama'ting* before you,' she promised.

The girls sat in a semicircle before Qeva in the entrance hall to the Chamber of Shadows – seven Betrothed aspiring to one day take the white veil.

There was always a lesson before carving began, the *dama'ting*'s robes blood red in the dim wardlight – the only light allowed in the chamber.

Throughout the lesson, Melan fidgeted, shifting her weight and pursing her lips, rolling the velvet bag with her dice with one hand, eager to get back to carving.

It was always thus. Inevera and Melan had entered the Chamber of Shadows together, but even though Melan had years of work on Inevera and sneered about it publicly, she seemed to take seriously Inevera's threat to finish her dice first. When Qeva ended the lesson each day, Melan practically ran to a carving chamber, always last to emerge when the *dama'ting* called an end to the day's work. Inevera imagined she could hear the frantic scraping of her tools even through the thick stone walls.

If Melan took the veil before Inevera, it could be dangerous . . . perhaps deadly. All the Betrothed had heard Inevera's vow to finish first, and any power she had gained among the other girls with her defeat of Melan would vanish if her threat proved hollow. More, Melan would gain the near-limitless privilege of *dama'ting*, and her opportunities to have Inevera killed would increase manifold. There were others among the Brides of Everam who would surely support her.

The girls were finally dismissed, and padded down the cold stone passage to the long tunnel filled with small carving chambers. There were no wardlights in the tunnel, but Melan and the other girls lifted their unfinished dice, casting a red glow to see by. Only wardlight was permitted in the carving chambers, but even that was not given freely. It had to be earned by the girls' own hands. Without light, they would not be able to see their tools, their hands, or even the dice themselves.

The circlets of wardsight they left behind, forbidden in the carving cells. Inevera had heard it whispered in the Vault that a girl once tried to sneak her circlet into the cells that she might carve in Everam's light. Her eyes had been cut out before she was cast from the Dama'ting Palace.

Inevera walked unhurriedly as the other girls slipped into carving chambers. Qeva shut the doors behind them, leaving only the faint glow of wardlight leaking from under the door frames. One by one, the lights winked out until it was only by this faint glow that Inevera came to her own chamber. Qeva shut the door behind her, and she slipped off her robe, using it to stuff the bottom of the door, leaving her in perfect darkness.

Inevera, too, could call light from her dice, but chose not to in the Chamber of Shadows. The Evejah'ting warned that even wardlight could weaken the dice, leaching their power unnecessarily. The Damajah had carved in utter darkness, and Inevera saw no reason to do differently. *Everam will guide your hands, if you are worthy*, the holy book said.

Kneeling in the darkness, she said a prayer to her namesake as she took out her dice and warding tools, laying them out in a neat, evenly spaced row. She had finished the four-sided die, and the six, now working on the eight. Her work was slow and meticulous – shaping, smoothing, etching, all in rhythm with her breath.

Time passed. She did not know how long. Her trance was broken by a ringing sound that echoed through the silence of the chamber.

Melan had completed her dice.

Inevera quickly gathered her *hora* back into their pouch and put away her tools. There would be no more work tonight. She drew deep breaths and emerged from her chamber.

The other girls had already gathered, Melan in their centre, her face elated in the wardlight. She held up her dice and basked in the sounds of adoration and envy. When she caught sight of Inevera, her smile was one of cold triumph.

Inevera smiled in return, bowing politely.

They gathered in the lesson room, Melan kneeling with the *nie'dama'ting* surrounding her in a semicircle. Before long, *dama'ting* began to file into the room as well, nearly every Bride in the tribe forming an outer ring. Kenevah was the last to arrive, moving to the centre and kneeling to face her grand-daughter. Her face was unreadable as she produced an ancient, faded deck of cards. The sound of her shuffling echoed in the silent chamber.

The *Damaji'ting* laid three cards facedown on the floor between them. She produced a knife and handed it to Melan, who cut her own hand and let the blood coat her dice. As she did, the wards began to softly glow.

Kenevah pointed to the first card. Melan shook the dice until they glowed fiercely, then threw them to the floor, scattering them in the precise method the girls had been taught.

Inevera strained to see the markings, but the angle was wrong for any but Melan and Kenevah to read the pattern.

'Seven of Spears,' Melan said after a moment.

Kenevah pointed to the next card, and again Melan threw. '*Damaji* of Skulls.'

Again. 'Three of Shields.'

Kenevah nodded, her face still unreadable. 'One of the Brides announced to me this day that she carries a daughter. Which?'

Melan threw again. This time she took longer, studying the dice carefully. She glanced at the assembled *dama'ting*, and sweat trickled from her brow.

'Dama'ting Elan,' she said at last, naming one of the younger Brides who had yet to produce an heir.

Kenevah said nothing, turning over the first card. The *nie'dama'ting* gasped as the Seven of Spears revealed itself. Inevera felt her heart clench.

The next card was turned. The *Damaji* of Skulls. Inevera's heart moved into her throat.

Kenevah turned the third card, and there was a gasp from all. It was the *Damaji'ting* of Water.

Suddenly Kenevah lashed out, smacking Melan hard on the face. 'No Bride is pregnant, you idiot girl!'

She snatched the dice from Melan's hand, holding them up and studying them in the wardlight. 'Sloppy! Wasteful! Good enough for light, but naught else. Your dice of wood, carved when you were barely in your bido, were better! Where is your eighth?'

Melan's face was a mask of shock and horror, her centre lost. Numbly, she reached into her *hora* pouch, producing her eighth bone and handing it to the *Damaji'ting*.

Even from her vantage, Inevera could see it was a twisted ruin.

Kenevah held the dice under Melan's nose. 'Each of these is a year of your life. They will be shown the sun, and you will return to ivory. When you have made three perfect sets, you may return to the Chamber of Shadows, and carve one *hora* each year until you have completed a new set. Each die will be examined before you are given another, and Everam help you if there should be the slightest flaw.'

Melan's eyes widened, and the shocked look left her face as her shame and fate dawned on her fully. Inevera breathed deeply, finding her centre and suppressing the smile that threatened to pull at her lips.

Kenevah thrust the dice back into Melan's hands and pointed to the exit. Melan was weeping openly now, but she rose and stumbled out. Asavi gave a wail and tried to go to her, but Qeva caught the girl's arm and threw her roughly back.

Outside the chamber, the younger *nie'dama'ting* were waiting. They gasped as one to see Melan weeping, and all fell in line as Kenevah and every other Bride and Betrothed followed the procession.

They walked to the highest tower in the Dama'ting Palace. When Melan failed to climb fast enough, Kenevah shoved her with surprising strength. More than once the girl stumbled, and Kenevah kicked her until she rose and continued on up the spiralling stairs, coming at last to a high balcony that gave a view of all the Desert Spear.

'Hold out your hand,' Kenevah ordered, and Melan did so as the others all crowded behind her, some on the balcony and others in the topmost chamber of the tower. The girl's fingers were clenched tightly around her precious dice, the result of half a lifetime's work.

'Open your hand,' Kenevah said. It was late in the day, the sun low in the sky, but still it flooded the balcony with Everam's bright light. Weeping, Melan did as she was bade, uncurling her fingers and letting the sunlight strike the dice.

The result was immediate. The bones sparked and caught fire, burning with white-hot intensity. Melan screamed.

In an instant, it was over, Melan's hand smoking, the flesh blackened where it wasn't melted away. Her three largest fingers were fused together, and Inevera could see bits of scorched bone amid the ruin.

Kenevah turned to Qeva. 'Treat and bind her hand, but use no magic. She must always bear the mark of her failure, as a reminder to herself . . .' She turned, and her gaze took in the other Betrothed. '. . . and to others.' All the *nie'dama'ting* save Inevera gasped and stepped back at the words.

With Melan broken, Inevera put the politics of the *nie'dama'ting* from her mind, finding her centre and focusing on her studies. She continued to thrive in her training, mastering herbs and *hora* magic, teaching classes in *sharusahk* and pillow dancing, as well as indoctrinating the younger girls, whose training normally began at five.

On the following solstice, she glimpsed Soli again, and threw him a return wink that crinkled his eyes in pleasure. She floated for six months on the memory.

After a year, Melan completed her three sets of ivory and returned to the Chamber of Shadows. Qeva's ministrations had been skilled, but her daughter's hand was still a twisted ruin with little of its former dexterity. She grew her nails long and sharp on that hand, giving it the look of an *alagai*'s clawed appendage. The sight struck terror in the other *nie'dama'ting* – both of Melan and of the risk taken by all who aspired to the white veil.

But while the other girls were intimidated by Melan and her claw, she was nothing to Inevera – a pile of camel dung she had already stepped around. Blocking out all distraction, she continued her slow, methodical work on her dice. The fact that she worked in utter darkness was now common knowledge, whispered at mealtimes and in hallways as she passed. Rumour was that none of the *dama'ting*, not even Kenevah, had done the same. Many seemed to think this was a sign that

Inevera was indeed the chosen of Everam, meant to take the place of the aging *Damaji'ting*.

But the talk was just wind, and Inevera ignored it, keeping her centre. Working in the dark meant nothing if she grew overconfident as Melan had.

'I have ruined him for his wives,' Dama'ting Elan told Inevera one evening while Inevera served her tea. Just that morning, Elan had whisked away a handsome *kai'Sharum* to bless her with a daughter.

Each *dama'ting* was expected to produce at least one daughter to succeed her. The fathers were selected carefully, chosen for their intelligence and power, the choices and timing sanctified by the dice. When a *dama'ting* selected a man, a palanquin was sent for him, taking him to a private pleasure house the Brides kept outside the sacred palace – where no man could set foot with his stones intact.

No man was fool enough to refuse a summons from the *dama'ting*, and with their skills at herbs and pillow dancing, compliance with their wishes was assured, even if the man were *push'ting*. The men stumbled away drained and dazed, having no idea they had just fathered a daughter they would never meet.

Few of the Brides were above gloating about it. 'His *jiwah* will never satisfy him again,' Elan sneered. 'He will dream of me for the rest of his days, praying to Everam that I will dance for him once more.'

She winked. 'And I may. His spear was hard and true.'

Many of the *dama'ting* had warmed to Inevera in this way, taking the girl into their confidences and making efforts to befriend her. Since Melan's failure, it was widely accepted by the Brides that Inevera was to be Kenevah's heir. Some, like Elan, tried to impress her. Others tried to dominate, or offer gifts with strings attached.

Inevera kept her eyes down, her ears open, and her words noncommittal. While she had put the politics of the Betrothed behind her, the politics of the Brides were a weave she was still learning – one that made tying the bido seem like braiding one's hair.

'Even among the *dama'ting*,' she told Elan, 'your pillow dancing is regarded.'

Regarded poorly, she added silently, but she had her centre, and the *dama'ting* saw no sign of her true feeling.

'He will never again see the like,' Elan agreed.

Inevera turned away, only to see Asavi coldly glaring at her from across the room. Older than Melan by two years, Asavi had recently taken the veil, and Inevera stepped lightly when she was about, giving her no excuse to take offence. With the Vault doors between them, Asavi and Melan could no longer hold each other in the night, but Melan was summoned frequently to Asavi's new quarters during the daylight hours, and Inevera did not doubt their pillow friendship continued.

One dawn in her fifth year as Betrothed, Inevera was in the *dama'ting* pavilion when a familiar shout heralded a group of *Sharum* rushing in their wounded. It was the morning after Waning, and casualties had increased in recent years.

'Let me through, *push'ting* scum! That's my son!'

Inevera felt her blood run cold. Even after half a decade, she knew her father's voice.

Lifting her robes, she ran without a shred of *dama'ting* composure to the surgery, where a familiar crowd of sleeveless *Sharum* stood in their black steel breastplates. Cashiv's face was wet with tears as he faced Kasaad, each of them with warriors at his back. Kasaad's eyes were bloodshot, and he stood unsteadily, likely still feeling the effects of the couzi he drank for courage in the Maze.

Several warriors were being treated, but Inevera only had eyes for one, running to Soli's side with a shout. Her brother's handsome face was covered in sweat and dust, his eyes glazed, and his skin pale. His good right arm was slashed at the bicep by *alagai* talon, nearly severed. A tourniquet had been tied just below his shoulder, and though the sheet below him was soaked with blood, Inevera imagined much more lay on the Maze floor, and the path from there to the pavilion.

She was Betrothed to Everam now, with neither family nor name, but Inevera didn't care, taking her brother's head in her hands and gently turning him to meet her eyes.

'Soli,' she whispered, brushing the sweat-soaked hair from his face. 'I'm here. I will care for you and make you well. I swear it.'

A dim recognition came to his eyes. Soli tried to laugh, but it came out as a cough that flecked his lips with blood. His voice was a wet wheeze. 'It is my duty to care for you, little sister, not the other way 'round.'

'No more, brother,' Inevera whispered, feeling tears begin to well.

'We will not be able to save the arm,' Qeva said at her back. 'Not with herb or *hora*. It will have to be amputated.' If she was bothered by Inevera's lack of composure, she gave no sign.

'No!' shouted Kasaad. 'Bad enough Everam has cursed me with a *push'ting* for a son, but I will not have him a cripple as well! Send him down the lonely path now, and pray Everam forgives him for wasting his seed!'

Cashiv gave a shout of anguish, leaping on Kasaad and easily wrestling him to the floor, pressing his head down savagely. Kasaad's friends moved to intercede, but Cashiv's warriors blocked their path. 'Soli never meant anything to you!' Cashiv cried. 'He is everything to me!'

'You have twisted him with your *push'ting* ways!' Kasaad growled. 'A true *Sharum* would not suffer life as a cripple!'

Qeva tsked and shook her head. 'As if their opinions matter

a whit.' She clapped her hands, a loud crack that sounded like thunder. 'Enough! Out, all of you! Any unwounded *Sharum* still in this pavilion by the count of ten will be *khaffit* before the sun sets!'

That got everyone's attention. The excess warriors scrambled outside, and Cashiv released Kasaad immediately, getting to his feet and bowing deeply. 'I apologize for bringing violence to this place of healing, Dama'ting.' He cast a pained look at Soli and fell to his knees, pressing his forehead to the floor. 'I beg you, honoured Bride, please do not hold my actions against Soli. Even one-armed, he is worth a hundred other men.'

'We will save him,' Inevera said, though it was not her place. 'I will not let my brother die.'

'Broth . . .' Kasaad looked up. 'Everam's beard, Inevera?!'

Recognition lit his face, and he moved with surprising speed, grabbing his spear off the floor and kicking his daughter aside. Caught off guard, Inevera hit the floor hard, looking up just in time to see Kasaad bury the point in Soli's chest. 'Better dead than a *push'ting* cripple spared by his sister's soft heart!'

Cashiv had him in an instant, standing behind Kasaad with one iron arm around his throat and a long curved knife at his belly. Inevera rushed to Soli, but her father's thrust had been true, and her brother was dead.

'You do not deserve to die by *alagai* talon or spear,' Cashiv growled in Kasaad's ear. 'I will gut you like a *khaffit* guts a pig, and watch as the life bleeds out of you. You deserve a thousand deaths, and in Nie's abyss you will have them.'

Kasaad laughed. 'I have done Everam's will, and will drink from his rivers of wine in Heaven. The Evejah tells us, *Suffer not the* push'ting *nor the cripple!*'

Qeva approached. 'It also says, *Drink not of fermented grain . . .* and *It is death to strike one of Everam's Betrothed.*'

It was true. The punishment for striking a *nie'dama'ting* was the same as for a *dama'ting* – the striker was made *khaffit*, then executed. Only the offended woman could spare him.

Qeva took her own curved knife and began cutting the blacks from Kasaad. He screamed and thrashed, but she struck swift, precise blows to shatter his lines of power, and his limbs fell weak.

'You are *khaffit* now, Kasaad of no name worth mentioning. You will forever sit outside Heaven's gates, and should Everam in His wisdom one day take pity on your soul and send it back to Ala, pray you are less stupid in the next life.' She turned to Inevera, handing her the knife. Cashiv pulled hard, arching Kasaad's back and presenting her an easy target.

Kasaad wailed and begged, but there was no sympathy in the eyes around him. Finally he calmed and looked at Inevera. 'If you will waste a true warrior for the sake of a one-armed *push'ting*, then so be it. Make it quick, daughter.'

Inevera met his eyes, rage boiling in her veins. The silver knife handle was hard and warm in her hand, moist with her sweat.

'No, I will not kill my own father,' she said at last. 'And you do not deserve for it to be quick.'

She looked at Qeva. 'The Evejah says I may spare him, if I wish.'

'No!' Cashiv shouted. 'Nie take you, girl, you will give your brother justice! If your flesh is too pure to sully, only say the word and I will be your striking hand.'

'You understand what sparing him means?' Qeva asked Inevera, ignoring Cashiv completely. 'Everam must be paid in blood for the offence given him.'

'He will be paid,' Inevera said.

Qeva nodded and took a tourniquet, wrapping it firmly around the leg Kasaad had kicked Inevera with. She looked to Cashiv. 'Hold him tightly.' The warrior nodded, tightening his iron grip.

Inevera didn't hesitate, taking the sharp knife to her father's knee like a butcher working a joint. Hot blood poured over her as his lower leg was severed with a pop right where the bones met. Kasaad's screams carried all through the pavilion, but it was a place used to such sounds, and it seemed not amiss.

Inevera grabbed her father by the beard, cutting off his screams as she yanked his agonized face to look at her. 'You will go to Manvah and serve her. Serve her like she is the *Damaji'ting*. Do this for the remainder of your days, and I *may* take pity and let you die in black.

'But if you ever strike my mother again, or fail to obey her slightest whim, I will hear of it and take the other leg, and your arms as well. You will live a long life with no limbs to get you into trouble, and when you die as *khaffit*, you will be left for dogs to gnaw upon and shit onto the streets.'

Cashiv dropped Kasaad to the floor, bringing a fresh scream of anguish. He pointed a finger in Inevera's face. 'A limb? The limb of a worthless, drunken fool? That is how you value Soli?'

Inevera moved quickly, grabbing his finger and breaking it as easily as she broke the line of energy in his leg with a single raised knuckle. The limb collapsed and she caught him in a throw that put him heavily on his back. 'You presume to judge my love of my brother? You think my ties of blood weaker than yours of semen?'

Cashiv looked at her, his eyes cold. 'My soul is ready for the lonely path, Inevera vah Kasaad. I have killed many *alagai*, fathered a son, and I have not struck you. It is your right to kill me if you wish it, but you cannot deny me Heaven as you did your father. I will sit in Everam's great hall by Soli's side, and comfort him under the camel's piss his sister pours on his memory with every breath that pig-eater takes.'

He sneered. 'Strike. Do it!' A madness came into his eyes, and Inevera realized he wanted her to. He was begging for it.

Inevera shook her head. 'Begone from here. I will not kill you for loving my brother, even if it has made you a fool.'

After she returned to the palace, Inevera went quickly to the Vault. Few girls were there at that hour, and those hurrying to get ready for classes. Inevera was due to teach one herself before entering the Chamber of Shadows later that afternoon.

She saw *nie'dama'ting* Shaselle weaving her bido after a bath and snapped her fingers, getting the girl's attention. Though older, Shaselle jumped at the sound. 'I have matters to attend,' Inevera said. 'Take over teaching basic herbs to the second-years.'

'Of course, nie'Damaji'ting.' Shaselle bowed and scurried away to attend the matter.

Nie'Damaji'ting. Kenevah's heir apparent. It was no formal title – likely any girl caught using it would be punished severely.

Inevera had never ordered another girl to teach for her, nor did she have any right to, but at the moment she didn't care. All that mattered was she was alone at last. She threw herself onto her tiny cot and cried. She sought to capture the water in tear bottles she might offer to Everam with prayers for her brother's soul, but her hands shook with her sobs, and the task was impossible. She buried her face in her pillow, letting the rough cloth soak up the tears.

Soli was gone. She would never again see his easy smile or handsome face, never again be comforted by his words, or feel the safety of his presence. In an instant, all those futures had vanished. She wondered if the *dama'ting* had seen it in the dice at the end of his *Hannu Pash*.

And Kasaad? Had she done the world any favours by sparing him, or would he be an even greater drain to the Desert Spear? Was Cashiv right? Had she failed to avenge her brother as he deserved?

Time passed, and the afternoon bell was rung. The Chamber of Shadows beckoned, but still Inevera did not rise. Since her admission, she had never missed a session, but there was no law forcing her attendance. If she wished to take a lifetime to carve her dice, it was within her rights.

At last, the Vault door opened and Qeva entered, standing by the door. 'Enough, girl, you've had your tears. There isn't water enough to spare in the Desert Spear for you to gush all day. Find your centre. Kenevah has summoned you.'

Inevera drew a deep breath, then another, subtly wiping her eyes on the cuff of her sleeve. When she rose, she had regained her composure, though her insides still felt torn to shreds.

Kenevah was waiting in her office when Inevera arrived. The teakettle was steaming, and at a signal Inevera poured for them both and took a seat across from the *Damaji'ting*.

'You never told me your brother was one of Baden's men,' the old woman noted.

Inevera nodded numbly. 'I feared you would keep me from him each year if you knew.' The confession was tantamount to admitting lying to the *Damaji'ting*, but Inevera found she lacked the strength to care.

Kenevah grunted. 'Likely I would have. And perhaps he would be alive today if you had.' Inevera looked up at her, and she shrugged. 'Or perhaps not. The dice can let us glean much of the future, but on the past they are silent.'

'*The past is gone,*' Inevera said, quoting the Damajah, '*it is pointless to chase it.*'

'Then why have you spent the day weeping?' Kenevah asked.

'My pain is a mighty wind, *Damaji'ting*,' Inevera said. 'Even the palm must bow before the wind, straightening only when it passes.'

Kenevah lifted her veil just enough to blow steam from the surface of her tea. '*Sharum* do not bend.'

Inevera looked up at that. 'Eh?'

'They do not bend, they do not weep,' Kenevah said. 'These are luxuries *Sharum* cannot afford in the Maze, when life and death are a hair's breadth apart. Where we bend before the wind, *Sharum* embrace their pain and ignore it. To the untrained, the effect seems much the same, but it is not. And as a great wind can break even the most supple tree, there are pains too great for *Sharum* to hold. When this happens, they hurl themselves into its cause in hopes they might die an honourable death with no submission on their lips.'

'Cashiv wanted such a death,' Inevera said. 'He and my brother were lovers.'

Kenevah sipped her tea. 'Other *Sharum* lock their loved ones away in the Undercity at night when they go into the Maze. *Push'ting* stand side by side with them. They fight more wisely because of this, but also feel the loss more keenly when one of them is taken.' She looked at Inevera. 'But you denied him this death. And your father, too, though the Evejah demanded it.'

'The Evejah gave me a choice,' Inevera said, 'and why should Cashiv be given a release from suffering over Soli's death when I am not?'

Kenevah nodded. 'We have become too free with death in Krasia. A frequent but unwelcome visitor has become like an old friend, greeted with open arms. Three centuries ago there were millions of us, filling this great city and all the lands beyond. We fought among ourselves even then, but a few lives lost over stolen wells was nothing when we were as numerous as grains of sand in the desert. Now we are scarce as raindrops, and every life matters.'

'The *alagai*—' Inevera began.

Kenevah whisked a hand dismissively. 'The *alagai* may be taking most of the lives, but it is our own foolishness that keeps feeding them.'

'*Alagai'sharak*,' Inevera said.

'Millennia of tribal feuding are not forgotten at sunset, no matter what the Andrah and Sharum Ka say,' Kenevah said. 'They are corrupt, putting the Kaji first in all things and doing what they can to cull their rivals. The Sharum Ka is old and remains in his palace at night, leaving no true leadership in the Maze, but still we funnel our strongest men into that meat grinder night after night, losing warriors faster than they are born. The *dama'ting* do all we can to keep every fertile womb in Krasia full with child, but there are simply not enough wombs to keep pace with men determined to rush to extinction.'

'But what can be done?' Inevera asked.

Kenevah sighed. 'I do not know if there is anything to be done. Our power has its limits. It may be that you will one day inherit my veil, only to preside over the end of our people.'

Inevera shook her head. 'I do not accept that. Everam is testing us. He will not let our people fall.'

'He has been letting it happen for three centuries,' Kenevah said. 'Everam favours the strong, but also the cunning. Perhaps He has lost patience suffering fools.'

She continued to work with calm precision, but Inevera felt the tension grow as she drew closer and closer to finishing her dice. Another week, two at the most, and she would test for the veil. At fourteen. The youngest in centuries.

Unbidden, her mind flashed to Melan as her dice burned in the sunlight. The sound of her screams. The smell of burning flesh and the putrid smoke that stung her eyes. Even now, after many cuttings and more than one suspected *hora* healing by Asavi, Melan's hand was like a sand demon's paw, misshapen and scarred.

Would that be her fate? Inevera's instincts told her no, but there were no absolutes, even in Kenevah's foretellings.

She woke from a nightmare, her heart pounding. It was still dark in the Vault, but Inevera guessed morning was not far off, and knew there would be no further sleep for her. She slipped quietly from her cot and padded to make her ablutions and take fresh bido silk from the pile, wrapping it as quickly as a man might don his robes. She was ready when the wardlights activated, and quickly had the younger girls dressed and ready for *sharusahk*.

Casualties were low in the pavilion that day, and she was about to head back to the palace when a pair of boys still in their bidos arrived. One was surprisingly fat – she knew the drillmasters all but starved the *nie'Sharum* – and supported another boy, shorter and skinnier by far, little more than stringy muscle and bone. He could not have been more than ten years old, his arm broken so badly the bone jutted white from his torn flesh and blood streamed down the limp appendage. His face was pale and sweaty, but he did not cry, and walked on his own feet to the table where Qeva was to set the arm. As soon as Qeva nodded, the fat one bowed and vanished.

Inevera had helped treat broken bones many times, and knew the herbs and implements to bring the *dama'ting*. For the boy she brought a stick wrapped in a thick layer of cloth for him to bite upon. He looked at her with eyes glazed from pain, and her heart went out to him.

She set the stick in his mouth. '*Dal'Sharum* embrace their pain.'

The boy nodded, though the confusion was clear upon his face. He bit hard as Qeva set the arm, but then, after a moment, his body went limp and his jaw slackened, the stick falling away. Inevera thought he must have passed out – perfectly understandable – but his eyes were open, calmly watching as the *dama'ting* fitted his broken bones together and treated the wound. It was impressive. Inevera had seen full *Sharum* turn away from the stitching of their flesh. When she was done, Qeva gave him a potion to dull him to sleep and keep him from moving while Inevera prepared the plaster.

'Drillmasters.' Qeva spat the word. 'That boy is the last of the Jardir line, his father killed senselessly in a Majah well raid. Bad enough our men are slaughtered in the night, but I tire of patching up boys in *sharaj*. Many never even reach the Maze, crippled or killed just in the training. It must stop.'

'It will stop,' Inevera said. 'I will find a way.'

'You?' Qeva scoffed. 'Do you think yourself the Damajah, then?'

Inevera shrugged. 'Is it better to wait idly by waiting for her to appear?'

Qeva's eyes narrowed. ''Ware your words, girl. They ring close to blasphemy.'

Inevera bowed. 'None was meant, Dama'ting.'

Inevera watched the boy as he slept, long after she might have gone back to the palace. He was good looking, perhaps enough to catch a *dama'ting*'s eye, but she did not imagine this one would give up his stones for life as a eunuch. There was power in him. She could sense it. Perhaps that was why she felt the need to speak to him again.

He stirred, opening his brown eyes, and she smiled. 'The young warrior awakens.'

'You speak,' the boy croaked.

'Am I a beast, that I should not?' Inevera asked, though she knew full well what he meant. *Dama'ting* did not deign to speak to *nie'Sharum* in the pavilion. They left that duty to the girls.

'To me, I mean,' the boy said. 'I am only *nie'Sharum*.'

Inevera nodded. 'And I am *nie'dama'ting*. I will earn my veil soon, but I do not wear it yet, and thus may speak to whomever I wish.'

She lifted a bowl of porridge to his lips. 'I expect they are starving you in the Kaji'sharaj. Eat. It will help the *dama'ting*'s spells to heal you.'

The boy nodded, sipping hungrily, and soon emptied the bowl. He looked up at her. 'What is your name?'

Inevera smiled again as she wiped a bit of porridge from his mouth. 'Bold, for a boy barely old enough for his bido.'

'I'm sorry,' the boy said.

Inevera laughed. 'Boldness is no cause for sorrow. Everam has no love for the timid. My name is Inevera.'

'As Everam wills,' the boy translated, and nodded his head, as if pointing to his chest with his chin. 'Ahmann, son of Hoshkamin.'

Inevera bit back a laugh. Did he mean to court her, this boy? She nodded politely, wondering what it was that drew her to him. She wondered if this bold, strong boy would be one of those killed in training, his life wasted before it truly began, or if he would be sacrificed to the Maze and the will of fools, like Soli.

Inevera returned to the palace, going directly to the Chamber of Shadows. There was no more time to delay. She had questions only the dice could answer. She went right to a chamber and laid out her tools, running sensitive fingers over the bones as she took them from her *hora* pouch. Smoothed by ten thousand handlings and polished with holy oils, their surface was like glass, broken only by the grooves of the symbols.

A ward of prophecy for each, and then one symbol of foretelling for each side and the centre of the remaining faces. The four-sided die alone had sixteen symbols. The six had thirty. The eight, thirty-two. And so on. One by one, Inevera traced the symbols in the darkness, testing their perfection as she had countless times before. They grew smaller as the sides increased, but she knew them all as if etched into her soul.

Finally, she lifted the twenty-sided die. The last of the set. Still in her *hora* pouch lay the eighth bone, untouched since Kenevah had first given it to her. Most girls made mistakes along the way and needed the spare. There was no shame in using it, but to 'make it in seven' was a special honour, and it was only with great reluctance that a bone was discarded. That eighth was hers to use if it was kept pure. Magic of her discretion.

The twenty was almost complete, with but three more symbols to carve. In the past, she had done it slowly, running her etching tool gently over the precise spot, barely scratching the surface as she drew a symbol so shallow it could be polished away in moments. Then, after running her fingers over it, she would trace it again, this time slightly deeper. And again. And again. A hundred times if necessary, until the lines were deep and unmistakable.

But not this day. This day she felt Everam's power in her fingers, and she dug deep with her tool, etching the first symbol in a single smooth motion. It was reckless – foolish – but she could not help herself, turning the die and going right into the next tiny symbol, and after that the third, accomplishing in seconds what had taken weeks with the other sides. Her hands shook as she took her polishing cloth and buffed away the shavings, afraid to run her fingers over the symbols. Had she made a mistake? Had she ruined the die? It would be a year's work if she did, and no third chance. Not without a burning.

At last she found her centre and dared touch the surface, marvelling at its perfection. Without a moment's hesitation, she took her sharpest carving tool and sliced the web of flesh between her thumb and forefinger, letting her blood mingle with the dice, settling into the ward grooves. As she did, she prayed.

'Everam, Creator of Heaven and Ala, Giver of Light and Life, your children are dying. We fight among ourselves when we should band together, throw away lives when we should succour them. How can we return to your favour and be saved from passing from this world?'

As she whispered the words, she shook the dice gently in her cupped hands, feeling them warm to her touch as the magic activated. Light peeked through her fingers, making her hands glow red and sending thin beams to dance along the walls of the chamber.

It was forbidden to test the dice alone. The law was clear that she ring the chime for a testing before trusting in her dice, but Inevera did not care. She felt the power building in her hands, and could wait no longer.

She threw.

The dice scattered on the floor, flaring with magic. Inevera watched as they turned unnaturally, the pattern dictated by the wards rather than laws of physics and geometry. Then they lay still, some symbols throbbing dully, others glowing brightly, and still more dark. Reading them was an art as much as a science, but to Inevera, their meaning was as clear as words on parchment.

– A boy will weep in the Maze on the 1,077th dawn. Make him a man to start the path to Shar'Dama Ka.—

Inevera felt her face flush, and breathed deeply to find her centre. She was to find the Shar'Dama Ka reborn? Did this mean she truly was the Damajah, as Qeva had scoffed? She would never know, for the dice could read the fortunes of others, but never the thrower.

'Make him a man,' she whispered. The symbols here were vague. Did they represent the traditional veiling ceremony all *Sharum* went through? Sexual deflowering? Education and training? Marriage? The dice did not say.

She shook again. 'Everam, Creator of Heaven and Ala, Giver of Light and Life, what must I do to make this boy a man?'

Again the symbols spoke to her, though their answer was no clearer, and only filled her with new dread.

– Sharak Ka is near. The Deliverer must have every advantage.—

Sharak Ka. The First War. Without the Deliverer, the well of humanity would dry out for good, the last of Everam's light extinguished from the Ala.

The Deliverer must have every advantage.

Quickly she gathered the bones, holding them aloft. Using her fingers to manipulate the symbols, she cast bright light over a chamber she had spent countless hours in, yet never truly seen. The light reflected off a tiny nook cut into the rock wall where the silver chimes lay.

Gone were her days of living in darkness. From now on, the dice would light her way.

The test for the veil came and went in moments. Inevera had no doubts, and answered instantly, even though Kenevah asked far more questions of her than she had of Melan, or indeed any of the girls who had taken the veil since.

The *Damaji'ting* threaded her questions with tricks and half-truths, trying again and again to confound Inevera. Around the chamber Bride and Betrothed alike began to murmur at this, wondering if Inevera had made an error early on that Kenevah was testing against. The dice were subjective, and errors did occur. One might be permitted, but never two.

But though she sensed the speculation, to Inevera it was only wind. She felt Everam's wisdom flowing through the dice, and spoke with the assurance of His voice. There were no wrong answers, and both she and Kenevah knew it. At last the aged woman nodded. 'Welcome, sister.'

The true *dama'ting* held their composure, though their quiet chatter halted instantly. There was a cheer from some of the *nie'dama'ting*, but not all. Inevera's eyes passed over them, meeting Melan's, staring back hard.

The girl gave an almost imperceptible nod of respect, but her eyes were hard. It was difficult to tell if she was humbled or vengeful. Inevera supposed it did not matter.

Right there in the Chamber of Shadows, with all watching,

Inevera was stripped from her robes and bido wrap, making her oaths to Everam.

'I, Inevera vah Kasaad am'Damaj am'Kaji, Betrothed of Everam, take Him as my first husband, His wishes above all others, His love my greatest desire, His will my greatest command, for He is the Creator of all things great and true, and all other men are but pale shadows of His perfection. I do this for now and all eternity, for on my death I will join my sister-wives in the Celestial Harem, and there know His sacred touch.'

'I hear this oath, and hold you to it,' Kenevah said, lifting her dice in the air and causing them to flare with magic.

'I hear,' Qeva said, lifting her own brightly glowing dice.

'I hear,' the other *dama'ting* echoed one by one, each lifting her dice in turn.

'I hear. I hear.'

Inevera was led to a marble table and made to kneel, putting her hands down flat in front of her and pressing her forehead down. Worn depressions in the stone marked where countless knees, hands, and foreheads had been placed before her.

Kenevah produced a large piece of marble that looked as if it had once been shaped like a man's organ, but centuries of use had worn the bulbous head down to little different from the shaft.

Qeva took a chalice of blessed water, pouring it over the phallus, whispering prayers as she did. Then she produced a vial of sacred kanis oil, dribbling it over the marble and stroking it in a circular pumping motion as if pleasuring a man. All seven sacred strokes were used, spreading the oil evenly over every inch.

Kenevah took the shaft from her, moving behind Inevera, who clenched her thighs in spite of herself, knowing it was the worst thing she could do.

'Fear and pain . . .' Kenevah said.

'. . . are only wind,' Inevera finished. She followed her breath, finding her centre, and let her thighs relax, opening herself.

229

'With this, I consummate your union to Everam,' Kenevah said, and did not hesitate as she thrust the phallus into Inevera, making her gasp. Kenevah pumped repeatedly, twisting it as she did. Pain blew over Inevera, but she bent as the palm, revelling instead in the elation of her wedding to Everam. He was her true husband, and spoke to her through the *hora*. Finally, she understood what it meant to be one of Everam's Brides. She would never be alone again. Always, He would guide her.

At last Kenevah withdrew. 'It is over, Bride of Everam.'

Inevera nodded, getting slowly to her feet, cognizant of the pain and the blood running down her thighs. Her legs buckled as she stood, but she kept her feet as she turned to Kenevah, who produced a cloth of smooth white silk, tying it around Inevera's face.

She bowed. 'Thank you, Damaji'ting.' Kenevah bowed in return, and Inevera turned and strode, nude save for the *hora* pouch about her waist, past the other women and out of the chamber. Her back was straight. Her bearing proud.

She was given her own chambers in both the palace and the underpalace. They were huge, opulent things full of expensive carpets, silk bedclothes, and thick, velvet curtains; with services of silver, gold, and delicate porcelain. Lit by wardlights she could brighten or dim, there was a private marble bath, surrounded by heat wards that could warm or chill the water or her rooms as needed. A *Damaji*'s ransom in magic for her simple comfort, all controlled by one of the stone pedestals she had learned to manipulate while still in the bido.

As soon as she was alone, Inevera went to the closet where a dozen sets of pure white silk robes hung. She selected two. The first she laid out on the wide, four-poster bed. The second she took her knife to.

The eunuchs had already warmed the bath. She slipped into

the deliciously hot water and scrubbed herself carefully. She felt the barest stubble on her bald head and smiled. She would never need to shave it again, but continued her daily shaving of her legs and nethers.

Smooth, she took brush and ink, painting wards around her womanhood. The blood had ceased to flow, its crust washed away, but Inevera could still feel the ache of her consummation with Everam.

She shut the thick curtains, calling wardlight from the room's walls, and knelt on the floor, breathing to find her centre as she prayed. Then she reached into her *hora* pouch and drew forth her eighth bone. It was rough, like a chunk of obsidian hacked free of the *ala* with a pick.

It was a priceless gift – magic of her own discretion. The ichorous slurry that ran through the palace walls like blood was limited in its uses, but there were countless spells this bone could power. It would be a year before she could have another to use for anything outside the healing pavilion. No doubt there was already speculation about what Inevera would do with the bone, perhaps warding it as a weapon or defensive shield, as many *dama'ting* kept about their person.

But Inevera did not hesitate, touching it to the wards she had painted on her skin, feeling them warm and activate, flaring with power in the dim wardlight. She felt her thighs clench, and she shivered in something that was not quite pleasure, not quite pain.

Healing was the strongest of magics, the most draining. The eighth bone crumbled away to dust in her hand, and she reached between her legs, probing. It had done its work.

Her hymen was restored.

If there is even a chance I am to marry the Deliverer, I should come to him a proper bride, unknown to man.

She reached for the silk robe she had cut into one long, continuous strip, and fell into the familiar weave, retying her bido.

The familiar kiosk was gone, replaced with one much larger and finer.

'Baskets!' a call came, and Inevera's head snapped up in surprise, seeing her father, dressed in *khaffit* tan and leaning on a cane as he walked on a peg leg. 'The finest baskets in all of Krasia!'

Inevera waited until a customer entered the kiosk, drawing Kasaad's attention, then slipped around behind him, gliding behind the counter and through the curtain in back.

Her mother was there, unchanged by time as she held a hoop between her feet, weaving. She was surrounded by a dozen other weavers, some young with bare faces, and others of middle years or venerable. There was a hiss as Inevera passed through the curtain, and all of them looked up sharply. Only Manvah returned to her work.

'Leave us,' Inevera said quietly, and the weavers dropped their hoops and scrambled to their feet, hurrying past. Even veiled, Inevera thought she recognized a few of them.

'You've cost me an afternoon's work, at least,' Manvah said. 'Likely more, since those crows will caw about nothing else for days.'

Inevera loosened her veil, letting it fall from her face. 'Mother, it's me. Inevera.'

Manvah looked up, but there was no surprise or recognition in her eyes. 'I was given to understand *dama'ting* had no family.'

'They would not be pleased to know I'm here,' Inevera admitted. 'But I am still your daughter.'

Manvah snorted, going back to her work. 'My daughter would not stand around with so much weaving to be done.' She glanced up. 'Unless you've forgotten how?'

Inevera gave a snort so like her mother's, it gave her a moment's pause. Then she smiled, replacing her veil and slipping off her sandals. She sat on a clean blanket and took a half-finished hoop between her feet, tsking. 'You've prospered to have Krisha and her sisters weaving for you,' she removed several strands before reaching for the pile of fresh fronds, 'but their work is still sloppy.'

Manvah grunted. 'Much has changed since your father became *khaffit*, but not that much.'

'Do you know the truth of how it happened?' Inevera asked.

Manvah nodded. 'He confessed to all. At first I wanted to kill him myself, but Kasaad hasn't touched a couzi bottle or dicing cup since, and turned out to be a better haggler than a warrior. I've even managed to purchase sister-wives.' She sighed. 'Ironic we should all be more proud married to a *khaffit* than a *Sharum*, but your father chose well when he named you. Everam wills as Everam will.'

As they wove, Inevera related the events of her last few years. She held nothing back, up to and including her first throw of the dice, and what they said – something she had told no one else.

Manvah looked at her curiously. 'These demon dice you say speak for Everam. Did you consult them about coming here today?'

'Yes,' she said. 'But it was always my intent to see you again once I took the veil.'

'What if the dice had told you not to?' Manvah asked.

Inevera looked at her, and for a moment considered lying. 'Then I would not have come,' she said at last.

Manvah nodded. 'What did they tell you? About today?'

'That you will always speak true to me,' Inevera said, 'even when I do not wish to hear.'

The flesh around Manvah's eyes crinkled, and Inevera knew she was smiling. 'A mother's duty.'

'What should I do?' Inevera pressed. 'What did the dice mean?'

Manvah shrugged. 'That you should go to the Maze on the one thousand and seventy-seventh dawn.'

Inevera was astonished. 'That's it? That's your advice? I may meet the Deliverer in three years, and you want me to just . . . not think on it?'

'Fret over it if you prefer,' Manvah said. 'But the years will pass no faster.' She looked pointedly at Inevera. 'I'm certain you can find a way to be productive in the meantime. If not, I have plenty of weaving to be done.'

Inevera finished her basket. 'You're right, of course.' She stood to add it to the pile, noting as she did that even the cloth she sat upon had left dust on the posterior of her pristine robes. 'But I accept your invitation to come weave with you again,' she brushed at herself, sending dust flying, 'provided you can arrange a cleaner place to sit.'

'I'll purchase white silk for your precious *dama'ting* bottom,' Manvah said, 'but you'll weave till the cost is off the ledger.'

Inevera smiled. 'At three draki a basket, that could take years.'

Manvah's eyes crinkled. 'A lifetime, if I buy fresh silk each visit. A *dama'ting* should have no less.'

9

Ahmann
308–313 AR

Inevera strode through the darkened streets of the Desert Spear, feeling none of the apprehension she'd once experienced at being on the surface at night. Even if the dice had not already promised she would see the boy at dawn, three years had passed. Inevera's *hora* pouch now contained bones enough to defend her from almost any assailant, demonic or otherwise, and only Qeva was still considered Inevera's match at *sharusahk*.

It was peaceful, the ancient city at night. Beautiful. Inevera tried to peel back the years to a time when the paint and gilding had been fresh, the pillars and moulding unworn. To visualize what Krasia had been like before the Return, just three hundred years ago.

The image came readily, sweeping Inevera away in its wonder. The Desert Spear had been the seat of a vast empire at the height of its power, the city proper containing people in the millions. Aqueducts made the desert bloom, and there were great universities of medicine and science. Machines did the work of a hundred *dal'ting*. Sharik Hora was still Everam's greatest temple, but hundreds of others dotted the city and surrounding lands in praise of the Creator.

And there had been peace. The closest thing to war had been nomadic tribes outside the walls raiding one another for women or wells.

But then came the demons, and the fool Andrah who called for *alagai'sharak* even after it became clear the fighting wards were lost.

Inevera shivered and returned to herself. The empty city seemed no longer peaceful, no longer beautiful. It was a tomb, like the lost city of Anoch Sun, claimed by the sands thousands of years past. That would be the fate of all Krasia if the tide of attrition was not turned. Sharak Ka was coming, and if it came tomorrow, all humanity would lose.

'But that will not happen,' she promised the empty streets. 'I will not allow it.'

Inevera quickened her pace. Dawn was approaching, and she must perform her foretelling before the sun crested the horizon.

Drillmaster Qeran nodded as she approached, making no comment about her wandering unescorted in the dark. She had been expected, and *Sharum* did not question *dama'ting* in any event.

She had consulted the dice about this day many times over the years, but no matter how many ways she posed her questions, the *hora* were evasive, full of might-bes and unknown conditions. The future was a living thing, and could never be truly known. It rippled with change whenever someone used free will to make a choice.

But there had been pillars even among the ripples. Bits of truth she could glean. Numbers of steps and turns, given randomly, that enabled Inevera – after weeks spent poring over maps of the Maze – to calculate precisely where the boy would be found.

– *You will know him on sight* – the dice had told her, but that was no great revelation. How many boys could there be, alone and weeping in the Maze?

– *You will bear him many sons*—

This had given Inevera pause. *Dama'ting* could take a man

and bear his daughters in secret, but sons were forbidden outside marriage vows. The dice had told her she was fated to marry this boy. Perhaps he was not the Deliverer himself, but that one's father. Perhaps the Shar'Dama Ka was meant to come from her own womb.

It was a thought so full of honour and power that her mind could hardly grasp it, but there was disappointment as well. The mother of Kaji was blessed above all, but it was the Damajah who whispered wisdom in the Deliverer's ear and guided his way. It could be that another woman would share his bed and have his ear.

The thought grated on Inevera, and for a moment she lost her centre. Had she been insincere in her prayers? What was more important to her, saving her people, or taking the mantle of her namesake?

She inhaled slowly, feeling her breath, her life's force, and letting it lead her back to her centre. With no hubris, she knew of no woman more worthy than herself to guide the Deliverer. Should she find such a woman, she would step aside. If not, she would marry him no matter the cost, even if it meant divorcing her husband, or marrying her own son.

– *The Deliverer must have every advantage*—

She heard cries ahead, the sound of violence, and forced herself to slow. She would not be in time to make a difference. When the dice spoke clear, they marked a fixed point, like a large stone jutting from time's river. She was to find the boy alone and weeping. In effect, it had already happened, and it was pointless to resist such wind.

A *Sharum* appeared, laughing as he retied his pantaloons. His night veil hung loose about his neck, and there was blood on his lips. He stopped short, paling at the sight of her. Inevera said nothing, making note of his face as she raised an eyebrow and tilted her head back the way she had come. The warrior bowed and quickly shuffled past her, then turned and ran as fast as he could.

Inevera resumed her approach, hearing the boy's sobbing. She kept her breath a steady rhythm, walking at her normal, steady glide. Turning the last corner she saw the boy shuddering on the ground. His bido was around his knees, and his shoulder bled where the *Sharum* had obviously bitten him when his lust reached its climax. There were other bruises and abrasions, but if they came from this assault or *alagai'sharak*, she could not say.

He noticed her approach and looked up, tears glittering on his face in the starlight. And as foretold, she knew him.

The *nie'Sharum* she had met years ago, the night she finished her dice. Ahmann Jardir, who had embraced his pain and watched wordlessly as the *dama'ting* set his broken arm. Ahmann Jardir, who at twelve had somehow killed his first *alagai* and survived a night in the Maze. It seemed to be a glimpse of Everam's holy plan.

She wondered for a moment if he would recognize her as well, but she was veiled now, and he had been dull with pain when they last met. The boy remained frozen for a moment, then remembered himself, quickly pulling up his bido as if it could cover the shame written clearly on his face.

Her heart pounded once, a heavy throb going out to this brave boy who had suffered such humiliation when he should be triumphant. She wanted to go to him and fold him in her arms, but the dice had been clear.

– *Make him a man*—

She hardened herself and clicked her tongue like the crack of a whip.

'On your feet, boy!' she snapped. 'You stand your ground against *alagai*, but weep like a woman over this? Everam needs *dal'Sharum*, not *khaffit*!'

A look of anguish crossed the boy's face for an instant, but he embraced it, getting to his feet and palming away his tears.

'That's better,' Inevera said, 'if late. I would hate to have come all the way out here to foretell the life of a coward.'

The boy snarled, and Inevera smiled inwardly. There was steel in him, if unforged. 'How did you find me?'

Inevera psshed, dismissing the question with a wave. 'I knew to find you here years ago.'

He stared at her, unbelieving, but his belief meant nothing to her. 'Come here, boy, that I may have a better look at you.'

She grabbed his face, turning it this way and that to catch the moonlight. 'Young and strong. But so are all who get this far. You're younger than most, but that's seldom a good thing.'

'Are you here to foretell my death?' Ahmann asked.

'Bold, too,' she muttered, and again suppressed a smile. 'There may be hope for you yet. Kneel, boy.'

He did, and she spread a white prayer cloth in the dust of the Maze, kneeling with him.

'What do I care for your death?' she asked. 'I am here to foretell your life. Death is between you and Everam.'

She opened her *hora* pouch, emptying the precious dice into her hand, throbbing with power. Dawn was approaching quickly. If she were to read him, it must be now.

Ahmann's eyes widened at the sight, and she lifted the objects towards him. 'The *alagai hora*.'

He recoiled. Inevera could not blame him for it, remembering her own reaction the first time she had seen demon bone, but if there was weakness in him, it must be crushed.

'Back to cowardice?' she asked mildly. 'What is the purpose of wards, if not to turn *alagai* magic to our own ends?'

Ahmann swallowed and leaned back in.

He finds his centre quickly, she thought, and there was a strange pride in it. Had she not first taught him to embrace pain?

'Hold out your arm,' she commanded, drawing her curved knife, the jewelled hilt of silver with etched wards on the steel blade.

Ahmann's arm did not shake as she cut and squeezed the wound, smearing her hand with blood. She took up the *alagai hora* in both hands, shaking them.

'Everam, giver of light and life, I beseech you, give this lowly servant knowledge of what is to come. Tell me of Ahmann, son of Hoshkamin, last scion of the line of Jardir, the seventh son of Kaji.'

She could feel the dice flaring with power as she shook. 'Is he the Deliverer reborn?' she murmured, too low for the boy to hear.

And she threw.

Inevera lost all sense of centre as she leaned in, staring hungrily at the dice as they settled into a pattern in the dust of the Maze. The first symbols made her blood run cold.

– The Deliverer is not born. He is made.—

She hissed, crawling in the dust, mindless of how it clung to her pure white robes as she studied the rest of the pattern.

– This one may be, but if he takes the veil or knows a woman before his time, he will die and his path to Shar'Dama Ka will be lost.—

Made, not born? The boy before her *might* be the Deliverer? Impossible.

'These bones must have been exposed to light,' she muttered, gathering them up and cutting the boy again for a second throw, more vigorous than the first.

But despite the move, the dice fell in precisely the same pattern.

'This cannot be!' she cried, snatching up the dice and throwing a third time, putting a spin on the *hora* as she did.

But still, the pattern remained the same.

'What is it?' Ahmann dared to ask. 'What do you see?'

Inevera looked up at him, and her eyes narrowed. 'The future is not yours to know, boy.' He drew back at that, and she returned the bones to her pouch before rising and shaking the dust from her robes. All the while she breathed, reaching for her centre though her heart was pounding in her chest.

She looked at the boy. He was only twelve, uncomprehending of the enormity of the burden that hovered around him in the endless possibilities of the future.

'Return to the Kaji pavilion and spend the remainder of the night in prayer,' she ordered, and left without so much as a backward glance.

Inevera walked slowly back out of the Maze. Dama Khevat, Damaji Amadeveram's liaison to the Kaji *Sharum*, would be waiting for her. Likely the whole tribe was holding their breath, as they did whenever it was time to read a potential *Sharum* at the end of his *Hannu Pash*. But the tribe did not concern her. It was Khevat. The *dama* was shrewd and powerful, from a family with ties all the way back to the first Deliverer's advisors. He was in full favour of his *Damaji*, the Sharum Ka, and the Andrah himself. Even a *dama'ting* was wise to step carefully about one such as Dama Khevat.

But what could she tell him? Traditionally, there were but two answers to a reading: yes and no. Yes, this boy is worthy to take the black veil of warrior and be called a man. No, this boy is a coward or weakling who will break like brittle steel when struck. The *dama'ting* saw more in the foretellings, of course, glimpses and possibilities, but these things were not for men to know, not even the *dama*.

It was possible to give a bit of detail. The dice often showed untapped potential, giving glimpses of futures where they make names for themselves as Warders or marksmen or leading men. These last were watched closely by the *dama*, and after a year the best of them were sent to Sharik Hora for *kai'Sharum* training.

Sometimes the dice spoke of failings. Bloodlust. Stupidity. Pride. Every *Sharum* had his share, and the *dama'ting* rarely spoke them unless they were apt to bring down others around them with their folly.

But once Inevera gave Ahmann the black, these would be mere hints and suggestions the *dama* and the Sharum Ka could heed or ignore as they saw fit.

– *Make him a man* – the dice had said, and even at twelve, there was no doubt in Inevera's mind that Ahmann Jardir was worthy of the black. But potential Deliverer or no, he was vulnerable now, as proven by the state Inevera had found him in. It was impossible for someone to rise so fast without making enemies. If anyone understood this fact, it was Inevera. And the dice had said if he was given the veil before his time, he would die.

– *Deliverers are made, not born* – Was she expected to intercede? Was that why the dice had sent her to him, and now? Or were there a hundred other potential Deliverers out there among the tribes, waiting for a chance to be made?

Inevera shook her head. It was too great a risk to take. She had to protect the boy, her husband-to-be. Protect his honour, but, more importantly, his life.

There was only so much she could do, once he took the black. She could not deny him the Maze, or the *jiwah'Sharum* in the great harem. She could not protect him from every knife and spear aimed at his back.

– *Make him a man, but not before his time* – But how was she to know when that time came? Would the dice tell her? If she denied him the black, was there a way for him to regain it?

She turned a corner and, as expected, found Khevat waiting. The drillmaster must have fetched him. She found her centre and glided up to him, her eyes a mask of serenity.

'The blessings of Everam be upon you, holy *jiwah*.' Khevat bowed to her, and she acknowledged it with a nod.

'You have foretold the death of Ahmann Jardir?' he asked.

Inevera nodded silently, offering nothing more.

'And?' The barest hint of irritation entered Khevat's voice.

Inevera kept her own voice level. 'He is too young to take the black.'

'He is unworthy?' Khevat asked.

'He is too young,' Inevera said again.

Khevat frowned. 'The boy has enormous promise.'

Inevera met Khevat's gaze and shrugged. 'Then you should never have sent him into the Maze so young.'

The *dama*'s face darkened further. He was powerful, and had the ear of those even more so. Not a man used to being questioned – or dictated to – by anyone, much less a woman. The *dama'ting* stood below the *dama* in the city's hierarchy. 'The boy netted a demon. Everam's law is clear . . .'

'Nonsense!' Inevera snapped. 'There are exceptions to every law, and putting a boy still half a decade from his full growth into the Maze was madness.'

The *dama*'s voice hardened. 'That is not for you to decide, Dama'ting.'

Inevera drew in her brows and saw doubt cross the *dama*'s face. He might outrank her, but where they had sway, the *dama'ting*'s power was absolute.

'Perhaps not,' she agreed, 'but whether he takes the black is, and he will not, because of your decision.' She raised her *hora* pouch, and Khevat flinched. 'Shall we take the matter to court? Perhaps Damaji Amadeveram will have me read you as well to determine if you are still worthy to run his *sharaj* after needlessly costing the Kaji a warrior of great promise.'

Khevat's eyes widened, the muscles in his face trembling with barely contained fury. Inevera was pushing him to his limit. She wondered if he would lose control. It would be regrettable to have to kill him.

'If the boy returns to the Maze before he is grown, he will die, and I will not abide such waste,' she said. 'Send him back to me in five years and I will reconsider.'

'And what am I to do with him until then?' Khevat demanded. 'He cannot go back to *sharaj* after setting foot in the Maze, nor back to the Kaji pavilion without the black!'

Inevera shrugged as if the boy's fate meant nothing to her. 'That is not my concern, Dama. The dice have spoken. Everam has spoken. You created this problem, and you must find a solution. If the boy is as exceptional as you say, I'm sure you can find a place for him. If not, there is no doubt use for a strong back among the *khaffit*.'

With that, she turned and walked away, her steady glide belying the emotions roiling inside her like a sandstorm. She had purposely enraged the *dama* so that he would be determined to keep the boy's honour intact, if only to spite her. There was only one place Khevat could do that: Sharik Hora.

Ahmann was old to be called as *nie'dama*, and ill suited in any event, but perfect for *kai* training. So far as Inevera knew, no *nie'Sharum* had ever been called before taking the black, but the Evejah did not forbid it. In Sharik Hora, Ahmann would learn letters and mathematics, philosophy and strategy, warding, history, and higher forms of *sharusahk*.

Knowledge a Shar'Dama Ka would need.

I must seize for him every advantage, Inevera thought.

As Inevera had hoped, Ahmann was sent to Sharik Hora the very next day. Dama Khevat smirked the next time they met, believing he had outmanoeuvred her. Inevera allowed him the notion.

She watched Ahmann's progress often, lurking in the shadowed alcoves of the undertemple where the *nie'dama* trained. The boy was woefully behind in many regards, and took special resentment to his early lessons, believing he had already learned all there was to know in *sharaj*.

He was quickly disabused of this notion, and the resentment beaten out of him. Before long he applied himself fully to his studies, and progressed quickly from there on.

Almost seven years to the day after her burning, Melan rang the chimes once more. Inevera watched her testing calmly, though she knew there were many who would flock to Melan if she passed.

Kenevah's voice was sharp, her examination of the dice scrutinous, and her questions complex. Melan passed all without flaw, gathering the dice with her good hand and casting with the claw.

Later that day, Inevera was walking through the long hall of the underpalace to her personal chambers when she found Melan waiting by her door. She was newly robed and veiled, but even if the older woman's stance were not already familiar, the twisted hand, nails long and sharp like *alagai* talons, marked her.

Melan pointed one of those claws at Inevera, the rest curling back stiffly. 'You tricked me.'

There was no one else in the passageway, but Inevera did not back away. The dice had not warned her to expect an attack, but that did not mean one would not come. The *hora* revealed mysteries beyond what a woman could discern on her own. They might warn her of a hidden poison, but an attack that she saw coming was her own concern. Everam had no sympathy for the weak.

She shook her head. 'No, Melan, you tricked yourself. All I had to do was nudge, and you were off running. If you'd kept your centre, you'd have finished your dice a year before me. But you let your pride and your jealousy rule you, and were fool enough to treat carving the sacred dice like a camel race. You didn't deserve the veil.'

Melan's eyes darkened. 'And do I deserve it now?'

'It must have been crushing to fall as you did,' Inevera said. 'The pain, the humiliation, and the scars – a constant reminder. Most girls would have been broken by that and left the Dama'ting Palace. Even a failed *nie'dama'ting* is a sought-after bride. Wealthy *dama* would have happily overlooked the scarred hand for your training at pillow dancing alone, not to mention knowledge of healing and *sharusahk* and *hora* magic. You could have arranged a marriage and secured yourself a comfortable position as *Jiwah Ka* to a worthy husband.'

Melan breathed hard, causing her veil to suck in, then billow.

'But it didn't break you,' Inevera went on. 'It took incredible courage to ignore the stares and derision and return to the chamber day after day these long years, and indomitable will to keep centred enough to carve a perfect seven. You deserve the veil.'

Inevera flicked her eyes to Melan's clawed hand for an instant. Not in fear, just a reminder to Melan of her stance, attempting to menace Inevera like a bully in the bazaar.

Melan looked at her hand and shook her head, as if coming out of a reverie. She breathed again and took a half step back, dropping her arm.

Without giving any indication, Inevera readied herself. If an attack was to come, it would come now. 'We can end this right here, Melan. I bear you no ill will. Whatever our motives, I needed the lessons you gave me, as you, I think, needed mine. Now we are reborn as Brides of Everam, and should leave the feud between us in the Vault where it belongs.'

Inevera held out her arms. 'Welcome, sister-wife.'

Melan stood there, eyes wide, for a long moment. Stiffly, she moved into Inevera's arms, meaning a token embrace, but Inevera held her tightly, in part to cement the moment, and in part to keep a lock on that dangerous, clawed hand.

Slowly, and then more powerfully, as if a dam were cracking and then finally gave way, Melan began to cry.

On the day Jardir took the black – the first ever to do so with a white veil – Inevera strode through the halls of the Dama'ting Palace to the *Damaji'ting*'s wing.

She encountered a group of Brides, and they made a show of stepping from her path in a precise, orderly flow that reminded Inevera of a flock of birds. The first to clear her path were the youngest and least influential, the last the oldest and most powerful.

Tea politics. Kenevah served Waxing Tea each month without fail, controlling the seating precisely to show the women their place in her regard. The places closest to the *Damaji'ting* seldom shifted, but those farther out did often, and there was a constant struggle for a rise in status. The *dama'ting* wasted endless hours fretting over every opportunity to impress the *Damaji'ting* and her closest advisors.

Inevera suppressed her derision. Over the years, she had moved up the table to sit at Kenevah's left hand, second only to Qeva at her right. The concerns of the other Brides meant nothing to her. Sharak Ka was coming, and she had little patience for petty feuds over imagined slights, talk of who had which *dama* by the bido, whether he had the Andrah's ear, how much gold was in his purse or how many wives in his harem.

To some, her refusal to play at tea politics only made her seem more powerful. What secrets did she hide, that let her rise above the intrigues of the palace? Most gave her a wide berth, believing – rightfully – that she knew something they did not.

But others saw weakness in her lack of involvement in palace intrigues. Kenevah was an expert at playing the Brides against one another, and by keeping Inevera at her left, her veil still white rather than black, she signalled that Inevera had not been formally named her heir. This led some to speculate that Kenevah was not convinced Inevera was fit to lead the tribe and might have her killed and name Qeva *Damaji'ting* until the dice called another.

Already, there had been attempts on Inevera's life. Three times, her food and drink were poisoned. Once, there was a tunnel asp in her bed, and another time a passing eunuch whirled on her with a knife.

Each time, the dice had warned her. The viper she caught and boxed, and the poisons she pretended to ingest with no sign of ill effect. The eunuch she killed, offering no explanation save that he gave her insult. Nothing more was required of a sister.

Never once did Inevera retaliate, or seek the identity of her attackers. It was irrelevant whether the attempts came from the *Damaji'ting* herself or simply other sisters sensing weakness. She'd no time to waste preparing poisons or planting rumours in return. If the dice were giving warning, she was in Everam's favour, and there was nothing to fear. What was her sister-wives' regard in comparison with that?

Ahmann was her only concern. Making sure he was safe, and ready to grasp at power when it passed his way. Planting the seeds of that power. If he was allowed to come into his full, all the politics in Krasia would be obsolete. And if not, her people would destroy themselves in a generation.

But today, with his veiling, matters had changed. So long as he slept in Sharik Hora, Ahmann had been protected. Few had known he was even there, and there was no *alagai'sharak* beneath the temple of bones; no rival who would strike at him.

But now he was *kai'Sharum* and would lead men into nightly battle. She feared little for his safety against the *alagai*, but with his skill and prowess, he would quickly come to the notice of the other *kai'Sharum* and the Sharum Ka. The *dama* might not – yet – fear so promising a warrior, trained as one of their own, but the more powerful *Sharum* would see him as a threat to their status. *Sharum* did not do their business with poison and hidden knives, but at any sign of weakness they would challenge him like wolves.

She needed to be by his side, to cast for him daily and keep death at bay. Krasia needed him, and he needed her. The Deliverer could not go unbridled.

– *Make him a man—*

The words had echoed in her mind as she pressured him

into betrothal, and the thrill she felt upon his acceptance was not all in duty to Everam. Illiterate and barely more than a savage just a few short years ago, Jardir could now debate tactics, strategy, and philosophy with the wisest *dama*, and break any that faced him in *sharusahk*.

And he was handsome. All those hours spent watching him in his bido as he grew into manhood had put a longing in her. She ached to unwrap her bido weave for the last time on their wedding night and never tie the cursed thing again.

Inevera reached Kenevah's chamber and saw Enkido standing watch without. The *Sharum* eunuch had a touch of grey in his hair now, but he was still strong and dangerous, the only man in the world privy to the fighting secrets of the Kaji *dama'ting*. He allowed women to defeat him at practice to show how a move should be correctly applied, but Inevera had watched him closely, seeing how he was always in control. Any *dama'ting* who underestimated Enkido was a fool.

She signalled him in the secret hand code of eunuchs, her nimble fingers speaking quickly, her stance conveying respect but not deference.

He was still a eunuch, after all.

I must speak with the Damaji'ting, her hands said.

Enkido bowed. *I will inform her, mistress*, his hands replied. He knocked at the door, and entered upon a call from Kenevah. A moment later he re-emerged.

The Damaji'ting *bids you wait here in the vestibule.* He gestured towards a silken divan. *May I provide you some refreshment?*

Inevera shook her head, dismissing him with a whisk of her hand. The eunuch resumed his marble-like stance outside Kenevah's door. Inevera was left waiting – in comfort, but full view of any passerby – for almost an hour.

Inevera gritted her teeth. More useless tea politics. Kenevah was not in audience with anyone. She was simply making Inevera wait, publicly, to illustrate that she could.

At last there was a ringing of bells, and Enkido signalled her to enter. Inevera moved through the portal, and the eunuch closed it behind her. Inevera bowed deeply. The *Damaji'ting*'s office windows were covered in thick velvet curtains, allowing no natural light. Wardlight kept the room aglow.

'You do not often grace my doorway, little sister.' Kenevah regarded her with unreadable eyes.

'There have been pressing matters to attend, Damaji'ting,' Inevera said, 'and your time is too valuable to waste.'

'Pressing matters,' Kenevah grunted. 'May I ask what those are? Your skills are second to none, and yet you spend little time in the palace, or at court. Even in the healing pavilion, you give only the time required of you and not an instant more. My informants have spotted you all over the city, even in territory controlled by other tribes.'

I've been blooding boys, searching for more like Ahmann, Inevera thought.

– Deliverers are made, not born—

She shrugged. 'I would know the Desert Spear and its people, that I might better serve them.'

'It gives poor appearances,' Kenevah said, 'and it is dangerous to set foot in the territory of other *dama'ting*.'

'More dangerous than walking these very halls?' Inevera asked.

Kenevah pursed her lips. It was not a signal that she had ordered the attempts on Inevera's life, but it was a clear sign that she was aware of them. 'If my time is so precious, what brings you to me now?'

Inevera bowed. 'I have decided to marry.'

Kenevah raised an eyebrow at that. 'Have you, now? And who is this fortunate *dama*? Khevat, perhaps? Or will you marry Baden, since you seem to have no real interest in male company?'

Inevera's throat tightened. Kenevah did indeed have spies everywhere, but how much had she guessed? Her spell to restore her maidenhead was likely still a secret, but Inevera could not hide the fact that no eunuchs were allowed in her chamber save those too old to use their spears. *Nie'dama'ting* did most of her attendance. It had given her a reputation for liking young girls abed.

'It is not a cleric, Damaji'ting,' Inevera said. 'He is *Sharum*.'

'*Sharum?*' Kenevah asked in surprise. 'Curiouser still. The boy you had shuttled into Sharik Hora?'

For an instant Inevera's *dama'ting* calm slipped, and she feared her eyes had told Kenevah much when the old woman laughed. 'Do you think me a fool, girl? Even if you hadn't caused one holy stench in the Kaji palace after refusing the boy the black, your hours spent haunting the catacombs to observe his training were obvious to all.'

Kenevah held up her hand, holding an ancient set of dice. 'And I have bones of my own.'

Inevera's fingers itched to reach for her *hora* pouch. Her most powerful bones could send a blast of magic at the old woman, killing her instantly. Black veil or no, with no other called by the dice, Inevera could immediately lay claim to the *Damaji'ting*'s throne, though she would likely have to kill Qeva and a few others to hold it.

I have bones of my own, Kenevah said. It was a reminder of her ability to foretell, but a threat as well. Inevera had a handful of *hora* she had collected since taking the veil. Kenevah likely had hundreds. No doubt she was protected in ways Inevera could not see, and a failed assassination attempt could have only one result.

She relaxed, and Kenevah nodded, slipping her dice back into their pouch. 'You did not consult me on the match.'

'I consulted the dice,' Inevera replied.

A flash of anger crossed Kenevah's eyes, though it never touched her face. 'You did not consult *me*. What if you read the dice wrong? No *Damaji'ting* has married in a thousand years. Everam is our husband. Do you truly have no interest in my office?'

'There is nothing in the Evejah'ting that says I cannot take the black headscarf if I marry,' Inevera said. 'That it is rare is irrelevant. The dice have instructed me to bear him sons, and I shall, in accordance with Evejan law.'

'Why?' Kenevah demanded. 'What makes this man so special?'

Inevera shrugged and gave a slow smile. 'The Evejah'ting says that the right wife is what makes a man special.'

Kenevah's eyes darkened. 'Off with you then, if my counsel means so little. I'd thought to guide you in your role as heir, but I can see my time is better spent looking for poison in my tea . . . or preparing my own.'

Inevera felt stung, but there was nothing for it. That the *Damaji'ting* was aware of Ahmann at all was a danger. She could say nothing without risking further scrutiny of the man.

Ahmann gripped Inevera's hand tightly as he led the way to their wedding chamber. She went willingly, but it seemed he would drag her if she did not keep his frantic pace. He moved like a wolf that knew it was being stalked as it brought a kill back to the den.

The men saw this as eagerness, cheering him on as he drew his new bride to the bedchamber and shouting crude suggestions. Warriors loved to boast their sexual exploits, thinking themselves djinn simply for being able to make a woman grunt.

But countless pillow dancing classes had taught Inevera to see and exploit inexperience in a man. Ahmann was still a boy in that regard. He had never so much as seen a woman unclad, much less shared a kiss or caress. He was terrified.

It was adorable.

They were both virgins of a sort, but while Ahmann had no idea what to expect in the pillows, Inevera knew they were going to her place of power. She knew the seven strokes and the seventy and seven positions. She would dance and weave him into her spell, coaching him on to glory without ever letting on that he was not in control.

– *Make him a man*—

They reached the perfumed and pillowed chamber, carefully prepared by the Brides. Incense smoke scented and thickened the air, and candles cast a dim, flickering glow. There was a broad area of floor for her to dance in, surrounding a pile of pillows on all sides. She would toss him into those pillows, and he would be hers, caught like a fly in a spider's web.

Inevera smiled beneath her veil as she drew the heavy curtains behind them. 'You seem ill at ease.'

'Should I be another way?' Ahmann asked. 'You are my *Jiwah Ka*, and I do not even know your name.'

Inevera laughed. She did not mean it cruelly, but it was clear from the look on Ahmann's face that he took it as such, and she immediately regretted it.

'Do you not?' she asked, slipping off her veil and hood. Since becoming a *dama'ting* she had regrown her hair, which hung long and thick in ebony waves, banded with gold. Her bido wrap was now secured at her waist alone.

Ahmann's eyes widened. 'Inevera.'

She felt her heart skip at his recognition. He had seen her face but once, and been dulled by pain at the time, but even after all these years he remembered. The terror left his eyes, replaced by a smoulder that seemed to burn through her. Suddenly it became harder to draw a full breath in the perfumed air.

'The night we met,' Inevera said, 'I finished carving my first *alagai hora*. It was fate; Everam's will, like my name. I needed a question to ask. A test to see if the dice held the power of fate. But what question? Then I remembered the boy I had met that day, with the bold eyes and brash manner, and as I shook the demon dice, I asked, "Will I ever see Ahmann Jardir again?"'

'And from that night on, I knew I would find you in the Maze after your first *alagai'sharak*, and more, that I would marry you and bear you many children.'

Inevera had rehearsed the tale so many times that she spoke with utter conviction, despite the lies and half-truths. But in the end, her words did not matter. Their union had been destined by Everam. They were *meant* for each other. That was why he was looking at her that way, making her face heat and her *dama'ting* calm slip. She was caught in his wind.

She almost broke and told him everything. Looking into his honest eyes, she had little fear this one would grow into a monster. He was chosen by Everam. If any could shoulder the burden, it was he.

But how does one tell someone he might be the Deliverer? It was too much, and this night was too important. It must be perfect.

She shrugged her shoulders, and her white robes fell away with a sigh of silk. She was clad only in her bido now, finger cymbals tucked into its weave. She rubbed her thumbs over the smooth tips of her index fingers, limbering them. She would step into him, allowing him to caress her until his breathing laboured; then she would use *sharusahk* to break the line of power in his leg, a whisper touch that would send him stumbling back onto the pillows. Then she would slide her fingers into the cymbals and beat a rhythm to set his loins ablaze.

And then she would dance, slowly unweaving her bido for the last time. The dance, like the speech, had been rehearsed so carefully every move was a part of her.

When Ahmann was firmly under her control, she would fall into the pillows and ruin him so utterly that every woman to come after her would prove a disappointment.

But he was still staring at her, and the smoulder in his eyes was brightening into fire. She felt its heat, and flushed. The incense hung heavy in the air as she tried to breathe, making her dizzy, her centre elusive. She knew she should act, but the thought came as if from outside her body.

She watched helplessly as Ahmann stripped his outer robe and went to her bare-chested, crushing her to him and running his hands over her body. He inhaled the perfume at her throat and let out a growl that seemed to resonate between her legs. He held her close to him, kissing her and stealing her breath, her centre. She felt the stiffness in his pantaloons, and knew all her plans might be undone if she allowed him to take her like a common *jiwah*, but somehow he had broken the lines of power in her limbs, and she was helpless as he threw her down to the pillows.

He was on her in an instant, hands and mouth roaming her body, kissing here and biting there, squeezing so hard in places that she squirmed. His hands found their way between her legs, caressing the silk of her bido weave. Inevera groaned, grinding into him further.

I must take control, she thought desperately, *or he will ever have of me as he will.*

She twisted and rolled atop him, undoing the laces at his waist and untying his bido. There was oil in the chamber, and she wet her hands in it, taking him in the first of the seven strokes.

Ahmann grunted and fell back, caught in ecstasy, and Inevera began to breathe again.

I have him now.

But she didn't have him for long. The strokes were designed to take a man's arousal to a steady pace and hold him there, but Ahmann only became more incensed. She altered her strokes, but still they were not enough for him. He took her in his powerful arms and reached down, sticking fingers into her bido and attempting to yank it off.

But the *nie'dama'ting* bido wrap was made of stronger stuff, and thwarted him. He grunted and yanked harder. Inevera gasped.

Ahmann growled, fumbling at the weave for its ends and failing to find them. He locked his fingers into the weave and tried to snap the silk, but it resisted even when he ground his teeth in strain.

'You will not get through until I unweave it,' Inevera told him, pushing him back into the pillows. 'I will dance . . .'

'Later.' Ahmann grabbed her arm hard, pulling her back down with him. He reached into his pantaloons and pulled forth a knife.

'You cannot . . .' she gasped.

'I am your husband,' he said. 'I have been dreaming of you for years, and now you are in my arms. It is *inevera*, and I will not wait a moment longer.'

She could have stopped him. Could have numbed his knife arm, or twisted away, but she hesitated. In an instant the silk was cut and he was inside her.

None of Inevera's lessons had prepared her for the rush of pleasure as her husband took her. She might have been overwhelmed, but for the countless hours spent practising the pillow dance. Her hips moved of their own accord, twisting as her thighs gripped him, pulling him into her more forcefully at times, and holding him at bay at others.

But Ahmann was no meek eunuch, and she found the practised poses harder to hold when her own senses were aflame. Ahmann made up for his lack of experience in passion, and they wrestled in the pillows for control. Inevera felt her own climax building and against all wisdom let it take hold, racking her from skin to centre. She howled, and Ahmann began to thrust with abandon. She tightened, her nails digging into his hard buttocks until he roared and they both collapsed panting and spent.

They slept for a time, and then Inevera woke to Ahmann caressing her again. His breathing was deep and even.

Even in his sleep, my wolf paws me, she thought with pride, and wriggled her hips back into him, feeling his night stiffness.

But Ahmann was not quite as asleep as he seemed. He pushed her onto her stomach and mounted her like a dog mounts a bitch, grunting softly as he ground into her.

When you control a man's cock, you control him, Qeva had taught, but Inevera felt no control here. In some ways, she wanted none. How was this possible?

Because he's not just a man, a voice within her said. *He's the Deliverer.*

She groaned into the pillows.

You have the Deliverer's cock in you.

Her groans became a cry. She thrust back at him hard, and soon he was spent as well, and fell into a deep sleep.

But Inevera did not sleep again. She lay awake through the rest of the night.

The dice were tricky, giving only half-truths at times.

She had known she was to make him a man, but she hadn't expected him to make her a woman as well.

10

Kenevah's Concern

313–317 AR

'**M**y son promised me he would one day give me a palace,' Kajivah exulted as she danced through Ahmann's *kai'Sharum* quarters in the Kaji palace. It was not even truly Ahmann's, much less Kajivah's, but the woman did not seem to care – nor did Ahmann's three younger sisters, Imisandre, Hoshvah, and Hanya, who ran shrieking about the rooms.

'He promised me, and though Everam knows we'd never had much good fortune, I believed him. They said I was cursed for having three girls after him, but you know what I say?'

Inevera closed her eyes and took a breath. *It's only wind.* 'That Everam blessed you with a son so great, he needed no brothers?' There was no hint of sarcasm in her tone, though she had heard these words a thousand times since meeting Kajivah on her wedding day, barely a week past.

'Precisely!' Kajivah bleated. 'A mother knows these things. I always knew my son was destined for greatness.'

You have no idea, Inevera thought. Indeed, how could she? Kajivah and her daughters were illiterate and uneducated, with little to distinguish them. Dim-witted women who had loved the one male in their family too much and one another not enough. Until recently, they had subsisted on the unskilled work she and her daughters did cleaning the homes of affluent families and the charity of local *dama*.

Now, Kajivah would never work again, and live always in opulence. That fact alone was almost more than she could contemplate. True greatness was beyond her, like the sky was beyond the fish.

Kajivah continued to prattle on as she surveyed her new surroundings. She was harmless enough, and respectful of Inevera's white veil, but she was forever underfoot, and doted on her son overmuch when Inevera wanted him hard.

She wished she could marry the woman off. She'd had Ahmann betroth his insipid sisters to his lieutenants before they'd even said their vows. They were comely enough, and the marriages would cement the loyalty of his men. The girls had cried with joy when he informed them, not even asking which of them would be betrothed to whom.

But Kajivah was too old to bear new children, and none of the men Inevera had suggested was good enough for Ahmann to agree to give them his sacred mother. And so she was consigned to their household and Inevera's sufferance.

She'll be good enough at watching the children, Inevera supposed, *until they turn five and begin to outwit her.*

'Mother! Look at this!' Ahmann cried. Inevera turned to see her husband, reaching tentatively to touch the water tinkling from the fountain in their receiving room. Before his fingers touched the water, he snatched his hand back as if he had been about to profane something holy. Having spent the last ten years sleeping in a tiny stone cell, it must seem an impossible luxury.

Inevera remembered her first visit to the Dama'ting Palace, and smiled as Kajivah ran to her son and the two of them began to unknowingly use a porcelain chamber pot as a water pitcher, drinking right from its rim. The girls heard their laughter and came running with a great many shrieks and whoops, all of them tasting of the fountain.

259

Inevera shook her head, finding peace easily. Kajivah was harmless, and her care was a small price to bring such happiness to Ahmann.

Three years passed, and each summer, Inevera presented Ahmann with a child. Two sons, Jayan and Asome, to be his firstborn heirs, then a daughter, Amanvah, to be hers. She acquired two sister-wives, Everalia and Thalaja, after interviewing every unmarried *dal'ting* in the tribe and casting the bones over the best of the lot. They were essentially servants, but fit to breed Ahmann sons to increase his status and holdings. Soon both were with child.

Ahmann had proven an excellent *kai'Sharum*. Given a beginning command of fifteen men, the *dama* had scoffed when he chose many of his former classmates in *sharaj* over older, more seasoned veterans. But Ahmann's men knew him from when he had been *Nie Ka*, and were used to obedience. His unit had tighter discipline than any other among the Kaji, and they fought more fiercely, taking so many *alagai* that the other *kai'Sharum* had begun whipping their men to try to stir them to equal frenzy. Soon Ahmann was commanding fifty men, the largest unit in the tribe, and the least of his warriors held a kill count to impress any drillmaster.

Now the other *kai'Sharum* eyed Ahmann warily. 'Kai Haival dreams of skewering me like a lamb,' he told her one day as she bathed him. 'I can see it in his eyes, though he does not have the courage to challenge me.'

'I will need his blood,' Inevera said.

Ahmann looked at her. 'Why?'

He had always been bold, and that trait grew stronger as the years went by. He continued to obey, but as if Inevera were an advisor, like Shanjat, rather than the voice of Everam. He had begun to question.

'To read his fate,' she said. 'To ensure it does not include killing you.' *And to keep searching*, she added silently, *in case there are more like you.*

'I just told you he did not have the courage,' Ahmann said, turning away and leaning back against her. He closed his eyes, serene as she massaged his sore muscles in the steam. Stubborn.

'Cowards kill as often as heroes,' Inevera said. 'Only they do not strike from where they can be seen. A knife in the back; a lie in other men's ears; venom in your food.'

'Even then, he would have to get past my fifty, and then me.' Ahmann had no need to boast of his own unmatched vigilance and strength. It was true the chance of another man harming him was remote.

But where there was one man driven towards jealous fantasy, there would be others. If protecting the Deliverer meant casting for every man, woman, and child in the Desert Spear, she would do it.

'And if he lashes instead at your wives?' she asked. 'Or your children? The histories are full of such tales. Can you protect all of us, all the time? What harm is there in knowing how deep his hate?'

Ahmann sighed. 'He does not hate me now. He is simply jealous. But he will begin to hate when I must break his nose tomorrow, that I might bring you the bloody glove. You speak of unity, of our people coming together, but how will that ever be reality if your mistrust of even our own tribesmen is so strong?'

Inevera stiffened, but she bent in the wind and calmed before Ahmann could notice. 'Perhaps you are right, husband.' She dried him and led him from the bath. After a night's battle and a hot soak, even Ahmann's hard muscles were relaxed, and she danced for him before mounting him and putting him down.

Later, as he snored contentedly, Inevera slipped from his embrace and padded away to one of her personal chambers. Ahmann's words continued to haunt her. They were foolish. Naïve.

And yet they were the very sorts of wisdom Kaji gave in the Evejah. The Damajah had trusted no one, but the Shar'Dama Ka always reached for the best within people, inspiring them to acts of incredible loyalty.

Perhaps he really is the Deliverer.

She knelt on a velvet pillow, spreading a casting cloth on the floor before her and taking out her dice. She kept a vial of Ahmann's blood on her always, and sprinkled a few drops of the precious fluid on them as she shook.

'How can Ahmann unify our fractured people?' she whispered, and threw.

– The Deliverer must have brides to give him sons and daughters in every tribe.—

Inevera started. Often the dice were so cryptic their advice was meaningless, or gave only the barest shred of knowledge. Other times they were a slap in the face. Not only was marrying outside the tribe certain to get Ahmann – and her – ostracized, the symbol for 'bride' was the same as the one for '*dama'ting*'. Did Everam wish her to share her husband with other *dama'ting*? It was too much to countenance. Everalia and Thalaja might breed with Ahmann, but they had none of Inevera's wit or skills at pillow dancing, no beauty to match her, or skill with magic or healing. Another Kaji *dama'ting* would be challenge enough as *Jiwah Sen*, but one of another tribe? Eleven of them?

Inevera breathed to find her centre. She was Everam's servant, the instrument of His will. If the dice commanded this, so it would be.

She gathered the dice again, daring a second throw. 'How do I select Ahmann's brides?'

– They have already been selected.—

Inevera was kneeling in a small casting alcove in the Andrah's Palace when Belina arrived. There were many such chambers.

When council was in session, the Andrah and *Damaji* frequently demanded minor spells and foretellings that were beneath the *Damaji'ting* to cast personally. These were delegated during recess to an army of senior Brides from each tribe who attended their mistresses at court.

As Kenevah's third, Inevera was expected to attend, though sacred law did not require it. The older women had all been scandalized when she first skipped a session at the demands of her dice, collecting advantages for her husband. It happened many more times over the years, and the implied insult to Kenevah had not been without consequences.

The tribes might often be at odds, but all *dama'ting* took their wisdom from the Evejah'ting, and thus all called their new leaders from outside the palace. A few years after Inevera had begun coming to court, the first of these girls appeared – to a one younger than she.

Since then, all had taken a black veil. All save Inevera. Whenever she was at court, it was a constant reminder of her sacrifice for Ahmann. *Dama'ting* could speak volumes with their eyes, and to a one the new heirs sneered at Inevera, standing still as they moved forward.

She hated them. Belina of the Majah, most of all. The diminutive *dama'ting* had nothing but disdain in her eyes when she looked at Inevera.

And so it was all the more unexpected when a day earlier, Inevera had passed her a note in the hall, so swiftly that none but they two noticed the exchange.

Inevera's casting chamber was richly appointed, as befitted her place as third of the Kaji. It was secure from sunlight, lit in the soft glow of wardlight. A silver tea service rested next to Inevera, heat wards keeping it steaming.

She poured as Belina entered. It was a calculated gesture, though Inevera rankled at the submissive stance before one she must dominate. 'I thank you for coming, sister.'

Belina accepted the cup gracefully. She was a tiny thing, a

full inch shy of five feet. But her frame was sturdy, with a small waist, big, heavy breasts, and round hips. She looked fit to breed an army. She cast a suspicious eye upon Inevera. 'I am still not certain why I am here.'

Inevera kept her eyes down as she poured her own cup. 'Let us not play games, Belina. We both cast the bones before this meeting. Tell me what your dice told you, I will tell you what mine told me.'

Belina's teacup twitched – the only sign of her surprise, but for a *dama'ting* she might as well have dropped it to the floor. Casting was a private communion with Everam, and while Brides sometimes debated meanings with their closest and most trusted allies, it was the height of rudeness to ask outright what another had seen.

They watched each other silently a while, sipping their tea. Finally, Belina shrugged. 'They said you would give me a gift, and then offer me your husband.'

She looked at Inevera with hard eyes. 'But I have no interest in marrying some piddling *kai'Sharum*, especially one of another tribe. They say your own *Damaji'ting* denies you the black veil over it. No gift you can give will change this.'

Inevera let the insult pass. 'I will not ask you to agree to marry a *kai'Sharum*. It is the Sharum Ka you will marry, and the Sharum Ka has no tribe.'

This got the other woman's attention. Her eyes narrowed. 'Ahmann asu Hoshkamin am'Jardir am'Kaji will be the next Sharum Ka? You know this?'

Inevera nodded, suppressing a smile. Even now, her 'piddling' husband's name was known to the *dama'ting* of other tribes. 'It is *inevera*.' She made no mention of the price she must pay for it. That, too, was Everam's will, and not to be denied.

Belina sipped her tea. 'The Andrah himself has not had a *Damaji'ting* wife in five generations. Even the Sharum Ka would be beneath me . . .' She met Inevera's gaze with a hard one. '. . . and I would never accept being beneath you.'

Inevera nodded. 'And so the gift, at the command of my own dice. Blood to show you part of Everam's plan. Hold out your dice.'

Belina looked at her warily. Her hand went to her *hora* pouch, but whether it was to clutch it or draw forth protective magic, she seemed to have no intention of removing her dice. 'You offer me your husband's blood?' That would be an incredibly powerful gift – one that could give Belina great power over Ahmann. Like asking about another's casting, it simply wasn't done.

But Inevera shook her head. 'Not his.' She drew her knife and sliced the meat at the base of her fist. 'Mine.' Belina gasped as Inevera held out the fist, blood welling into the first drop. 'Hold out your dice.'

No one trained in *hora* magic would pass up such an offer. This time, Belina obeyed instantly.

It's a start, Inevera thought.

Command what only a fool would refuse enough times, the Evejah'ting taught, *and even the proudest* Jiwah Sen *will become accustomed to obedience.*

Inevera watched the Andrah begin to wheeze as she danced for him. He was grossly fat, and seemed to labour under the weight of simply inflating his enormous chest.

He will have trouble performing. She had already laced his food and drink with potions to keep him aroused, but there was only so much that could be done with such a man.

When she had his robe off, she had to search under the rolls of his belly to even find his member, and it took all seven strokes to stiffen it enough for her to mount him. Twice, he came close to Heaven in her hands, but she pinched him down, knowing that her husband's fate depended on their union. When it was in, she made it quick, howling for his benefit, false sounds that barely covered her disgust, but nevertheless drove him to frenzy. With a twist and a clench, she finished him and left him panting in the pillows.

'Fine,' he gasped at last, struggling to rise and pull on his robes. 'The son of Hoshkamin will be the next Sharum Ka.'

Inevera was the palm, bending in the wind as she left, but when the curtains fell around her palanquin, the tree snapped, and she wept. She had known for years that she and Ahmann were fated to marry, but she had not anticipated falling in love with him.

Mere hours after Ahmann took the white turban of Sharum Ka and petitioned the *Damaji* for a bride from each tribe, Kenevah summoned Inevera to her office. The lesser tribes had been thrilled, their *Damaji'ting* all but drooling at the prospect of placing agents in the Sharum Ka's pillow chamber – not yet knowing their own heirs would be chosen, and thus fall under Inevera's command.

But the Kaji had been first among the tribes for as long as any could remember, and Damaji Amadeveram had been enraged at the idea of mixing Kaji blood with that of a lesser tribe. Kenevah had given no sign in court, but her eyes were hard when Inevera entered.

'I had thought your husband clever when he made his mad request,' the old woman said. 'Imagine my surprise when my dice,' she rattled the bones in her hand, 'told me that you were behind the move.' She did not appear surprised.

Inevera said nothing, and this seemed to irritate the *Damaji'ting* even more.

'Are you mad?' the old woman snapped.

Inevera spread her hands, knowing the futility of the gesture, but required to attempt it all the same. 'Is this not what you wanted? What we spoke of, those many years ago? The Andrah and Sharum Ka are corrupt, you said, favouring the Kaji in ways that were dividing and killing our people. I swore to find a solution, and I have. Now there is a Sharum Ka who is brave and true of heart who will be bound to all the tribes.'

'And to you most of all,' Kenevah sneered. 'Do not think me such a fool as not to see it. And of the Andrah? Will you replace him, too? A few years' study in Sharik Hora doesn't make your upstart husband a *dama*.'

Inevera shrugged. 'Kaji was no *dama*. He rose out of the blood of *alagai'sharak* and united the world under his spear.'

Kenevah laughed. 'You think you're the first Inevera to try to fashion herself the next Damajah? The *Damaji'ting* histories are full of their bloody failures. Or are you fool enough to truly think your husband the Deliverer reborn?'

'I have seen futures where he is,' Inevera said. 'I will ensure they come to pass.'

'Will you?' Kenevah asked. 'How do you think he will react when he learns you had to sheathe the Andrah's own spear to win him the Spear Throne?'

Inevera felt her face grow cold. Kenevah knew? The gentle wind had become a sandstorm that could flay the bark from the supplest palm.

Again Kenevah laughed. 'You think you're special? That old pig has *dama'ting* offering to work his limp spear for favours every day. I bedded him myself, long before you were a cup of couzi in your father's pathetic hand. Brides of Everam have never been above whoring for a favour, though it seems you're better at it than most. Do you think Ahmann will strike you when he hears? It would be delicious irony to end your grab for power by putting your husband to death for hitting his *dama'ting* wife.'

Inevera felt a wave of fear pass over her. *No blood runs hotter than a cuckolded* Sharum, the Evejah'ting taught. It was possible Ahmann would fly into a rage and kill her or the Andrah or both. To take the Skull Throne he would need to kill the fat old man one day, but he would not be in a position to hold it until he had *nie'dama* sons in every tribe. A decade, at least.

'What do you want?' she asked.

'A vial of your husband's blood, to start,' Kenevah said. 'I will cast him myself—'

Inevera cut her off. 'Absolutely not.'

'You forget yourself, child,' Kenevah growled. 'I am still your mistress. You can refuse me nothing.'

Inevera whisked her hand dismissively. 'The dice have called no other girl. By law, I will be *Damaji'ting* on your death whether you support it or not.'

'If you live that long,' Kenevah said. 'I will have Ahmann Jardir's blood, even if I must drain yours first. If he is truly fated for greatness, perhaps he can still be of use as a eunuch after you are safely locked away.'

Inevera sighed. 'I had hoped to avoid this,' she said, pulling a flame demon skull from her *hora* pouch.

Kenevah threw back her head and cackled. 'A flame skull? You disappoint me, Inevera. I expected more of you.' No doubt there were anti-flame wards all around her desk. She spread her arms in the air, palms out to show they were empty. 'Strike. The dice will call another after I have killed you.' She shook her head and tsked. 'Such waste.'

'Indeed,' Inevera said, nodding. She turned and let loose a great blast of flame, but not at Kenevah. Instead she struck at the thick velvet curtains that covered the *Damaji'ting*'s great windows. They burst into a roaring flame so intense they came apart in seconds. Bright sunlight poured in, bouncing from the smoke to reach every nook and corner.

A circle of *hora* around where Inevera stood, obviously meant to trap her, exploded, leaving burning holes in the thick carpets. There were more bangs on Kenevah's desk, and the old woman shrieked, pelted with burning shrapnel.

Inevera had already hidden her flame skull back in its protective pouch. She stalked calmly around the desk to stand in front of the old woman. The smoke stung her eyes and burned her lungs, but it was bearable. 'No magic to aid you, old crone. We will settle this with *sharusahk*.'

To her credit, the old woman did not hesitate. A lifetime of *sharusahk* was not easily forgotten, even if she had not fought another woman in decades. Her attack, wind snaps palm, was perfectly executed.

But it was slow. Her form might be perfect, but Kenevah was fifty years Inevera's senior, and it told in speed. Swaying branch diverted wind snaps palm and she stepped past, delivering a kick to the back of the old woman's knee. Her leg collapsed, and Inevera took hold and bore her down.

Kenevah twisted and actually managed to reverse the hold as they struck the floor. *Sharusahk* taught to steal free energy whenever possible, and even an old woman could be formidable, given enough force to divert. They rolled about in the smoke and dwindling flames, grunting and growling. There was a pounding at the door, but Inevera had barred it securely.

Kenevah proved more formidable than expected, but the outcome was not in doubt as Inevera ceased giving the *Damaji'ting* energy to steal and instead pitted muscle against muscle in a slow push until she achieved the desired hold. Seconds later she popped one of Kenevah's hips from the socket. The *Damaji'ting*'s howl was cut short as Inevera worked her way around, wrapping her legs tightly about Kenevah's waist and reaching for the black veil that should have been hers long ago. She found it and pulled it tight around Kenevah's throat, holding the *Damaji'ting* prone as her face reddened and seemed to inflate. Soon the old woman's struggles ceased. Inevera held on a bit longer, then eased her grip and untied the silk.

She was holding the black hood and veil when the doors exploded in a blast of magic and Qeva and Enkido stepped in, followed by a dozen women, *dama'ting* and *nie* alike.

Qeva took in the destruction with horror in her eyes. Most of the flames had died out, but the room was filled with wreckage, charred and smoking. She took in the still form of her mother on the floor, stripped of her veil, and turned to Inevera with murder in her eyes.

'Kenevah was old and weak,' Inevera said loudly. 'It is time the black hood passed on.'

'How dare you?' Qeva demanded. Killing a *Damaji'ting* to open a succession was certainly not without precedent, but to do it so openly was unheard of. 'My mother and I taught you everything you know. For you to betray her after we took you in . . .'

Inevera laughed. 'Took me in? I was not some beggar on the street or *nie'ting*. Do not reweave history to make yourself my saviour. You dragged me from my mother's arms without a word and threw me in a pit where your own daughter tried to kill me.' Melan was in the crowd, her clawed hand unmistakable. Inevera met her eyes, daring her to contradict.

'And when I did not turn out as she wished,' Inevera went on, 'Kenevah tried to have me killed. Seven times, the dice tell me. I at least gave her the courtesy of doing it face-to-face.'

'You lie,' Qeva growled.

Inevera shook her head. 'Why would I lie when my words are irrelevant? I am the only one the dice have called to succeed Kenevah. While I live, the Kaji *dama'ting* are mine.'

'If you live,' Qeva corrected, moving forward into a *sharusahk* stance. As she came out of the shadowed alcove, sunlight struck the *hora* she had used to blast open the doors, and the bone exploded in her hand. Qeva shrieked, and her concentration was lost as the concussion knocked her from her feet.

Inevera moved swiftly to finish her while she was distracted. A quick kill, and then only Melan could make a claim against her.

But Enkido stepped between them, delivering a camel kick that sent Inevera sprawling across the room.

'Kill her!' Qeva commanded as Inevera struggled to her feet. 'You would have a eunuch settle who leads the women of our tribe?' Inevera asked loudly. As she'd hoped, all eyes snapped to Qeva for her response. In that moment she slipped her hand into her *hora* pouch, clutching a bit of warded bone tightly in her fist, careful that no light should strike it.

'You are not worthy to lead if you cannot defeat Enkido,' Qeva growled. 'My mother made him to be her spear beyond the grave.'

Inevera had no time for a retort as Enkido came in fast and hard, his *sharusahk* like nothing she had ever seen. The size and ferocity of a *Sharum*, the grace of a *dama*, and the precision of a *dama'ting*. She had never once sensed anger in the man, but it radiated from him now.

All Sharum *must avenge the death of their* dama *master, even if it mean their death*, the Evejah taught, and Kenevah had been no less his master for being a woman. She had mutilated him, crippled him, but Enkido loved *sharusahk* above all, and she had given him that to his heart's content. Enkido came at Inevera with everything he had, and – she had to admit – without the aid of magic he would have been the end of her.

But the warded bit of demon bone in her hand pumped raw magic up her arm, flooding her limbs with strength and speed beyond anything mere flesh and bone could duplicate. She could sense Enkido's confusion as his first strike missed and she jabbed stiffened fingers at his kidney.

It should have been a telling blow, but it was her turn to be surprised. Enkido was armoured. Her fingers struck one of the hard ceramic plates *Sharum* wore sewn into their robes in the Maze. She felt it shatter on impact, but the force of her blow went with it, leaving her fingers aching.

She managed to evade his return strike, barely, but he reversed again, catching her with a backhand blow to the face that cracked her head back like a whip. His following kick broke ribs and sent her crashing into Kenevah's burning desk, which collapsed under her weight. There was a collective gasp from the crowd gathering in the office, encircling them.

Inevera had to strain to keep her fist tight and not lose the *hora* stone as she absorbed the impact, tucking into a ball and using some of the energy to roll to her feet past the wreckage. Enkido came on, but she had firm footing, and did not underestimate him again.

Back and forth they paced, Enkido striking and missing, Inevera landing quick blows in return that were largely shrugged off or turned by his armour. Both were wary now, and gave no real openings, no free energy. Inevera glanced at Qeva, waiting patiently just inside the ring of women around their battle, fresh and ready to take up where Enkido left off, should he be defeated.

And she would have *hora* of her own.

Enkido came at her with wilting flower, and Inevera could have slipped away, but on impulse she let the blow strike home. Her leg collapsed and Enkido pounced to take advantage, but Inevera drew on the power of the demon bone, restoring strength to her wilted limb. She came up at him hard, jabbing fingers into a space between his armour plates and causing him to clench his abdomen reflexively. While he was bent she landed several precise strikes to the lines of power in his neck and shoulder, then broke his knee with a hard stomp.

The eunuch did not cry out as he fell to the ground, even as much as a tongueless man might. He struggled to rise again, but though the strain showed in his brow, his remaining limbs would not obey. He calmed then, breathing deeply and looking up at her with quiet dignity, unafraid as he waited for her to finish him.

But Inevera had no interest in killing the eunuch. 'You have honoured your mistress, Sharum, but Everam still has a plan for you.' She felt the *hora* in her hands crumble into dust, drained, and wondered if she would regret the mercy. She was already labouring for breath, coughing in the smoky air.

Qeva took a *sharusahk* stance, but Inevera did not respond in kind.

'Are we blind *dama*, following the most skilled fighter?' Inevera asked the assembled women. 'The Evejah'ting gave us the *alagai hora* that we might never descend into such savagery.'

She looked at Qeva. 'It was you who first cast the bones for me. You who pulled me in when you could easily have turned me away. Why? What did you see?'

'Your future was hidden,' Qeva said. 'It was that, my mother told me to seek.'

Inevera nodded. She had known as much. 'It is hidden no longer. Cast the bones again. Now, in the Chamber of Shadows for all to see.'

Qeva's eyes widened at that, then narrowed, sensing a trap. A frantic whispering broke out among the surrounding women, and it closed on her.

Command what only a fool would refuse.

The two contenders for the black hood led the way down into the underpalace, followed by every woman and girl in the palace. When they had barred themselves into the chamber, out of sight of men, Qeva produced her dice and moved up to Inevera, hatred in her eyes. 'Just a few drops of your blood now, but don't fear, I shall take the rest before the day is out.'

Inevera lifted her veil, spitting blood from her split lip onto Qeva's dice. She didn't think it was possible to double the woman's rage, but she could see in her eyes that she had managed it. *I am sorry, Qeva, but you must be broken like a* Jiwah Sen *for all to see.*

The assembly held their breath as Qeva shook the dice and chanted her prayers. The *hora* glowed fiercely, casting a sinister light over the crowd, but Inevera did not fear it, or them. She stood tall over Qeva as she knelt. A single well-placed kick could kill the woman while she was intent on the casting, but Inevera had no wish to kill Qeva, even less than she had Enkido.

Honour demanded Qeva kill her, but Inevera's dice had told her more of the woman's heart.

– You are more daughter to Qeva than her own get. She may kill you, but she will never betray you.—

Qeva threw, and as the dice settled, the other women lost composure, Bride and Betrothed alike moving forward in a rush to see the pattern.

Some, like Qeva and Melan, saw the heart of it immediately and gasped, much as Belina and the others had. Most stared at the dice for several moments before their meaning became clear.

Qeva looked up at her, and Inevera held out the black hood. It was a paltry thing, and she had no interest in it. In truth, she never had. It was a rung in a ladder she had only to grasp long enough to leave behind her.

'You will wear the black hood, sister Qeva,' she said, and turned to Melan. 'And you, sister Melan, the black veil. I have my husband to see to, and little interest in Kaji tea politics. I have my own palace, and higher goals.'

Qeva nodded, reaching for the hood. Inevera moved it slightly out of reach, and there was an intake of breath around the room.

'You will speak for the Kaji at court,' Inevera said, 'but though it be your voice, the words will be mine.'

Qeva bowed. 'Yes, Damajah.' She reached again, and this time Inevera allowed her to take the hood.

She held the black veil to Melan, who bowed even more deeply. 'Yes, Damajah.'

Inevera raised the veil, forcing Melan's eyes to rise to meet hers. 'You are not to speak that name aloud.' Her voice carried throughout the chamber, but she turned, meeting the eyes of each woman and girl in turn. 'None of you – not yet.'

Three more times over the next six months, Inevera needed decrees from the Andrah, and each time he took payment the same way. He pawed at her boldly now, like she was some pillow wife. When he dared to bite her breast, she nearly stabbed him.

Long enough, she thought. *Ahmann has made his name. The Andrah cannot take the white turban back, and no decree is worth this.*

That morning she called Qasha, her Sharach *Jiwah Sen* and Ahmann's favourite, to her.

'I will invite the Andrah again tonight,' she said. 'Let slip to Ahmann that he visits the Palace of the Sharum Ka while its master is away. I want Ahmann to find us together. It is time to teach the Andrah to fear, and time for Ahmann to learn more of his destiny. I will suffer the fat man's touches no longer.'

11

Last Meal

333 AR Summer
28 Dawns Before New Moon

'Stop pacing, Rojer,' Leesha said. 'You're making my head hurt.'
Indeed, the motion of the Jongleur's garish motley had set
off a throbbing behind her right eye. She worried her temple with
the heel of her hand.

Ahmann had invited them to breakfast at his table before
they joined the caravan back to Deliverer's Hollow. Leesha
assumed he meant at dawn, the traditional time for breakfast
before a long journey, but the Krasians seemed to be dragging
their feet. They had been left waiting in one of the receiving
rooms for hours.

After the first hour, Rojer produced his fiddle and began to
play, but as always his emotions came through in the music, a
piercing melody that reminded Leesha of nothing more than
fingernails on slate. She had asked him to stop, but it was too
late. She felt her sinuses constrict. No stranger to the feeling,
Leesha knew a headache cycle was beginning.

She had known headaches her whole life. Sometimes the pain
and nausea lasted an hour. Other times it would come and go
for a week or more, like rain in springtime. Most of the time
the aches simply made her irritable, and many were fended off
with easily mixed remedies and avoidance of triggers. Other

times, Leesha had a choice between blinding pain or such powerful medicine that she was delirious for hours. On the worst – and thankfully least frequent – occasions, there was nothing to do but find a private place and weep.

The cycles worsened as she grew older and took on more stress and responsibility, and were regular visitors by the time she became Herb Gatherer of Deliverer's Hollow. Now, in Everam's Bounty, surrounded by their enemies, it was a near-constant state, like a long winter with no sign of spring.

She wasn't alone in her discomfort. Tension was thick in the air as the delegation from Deliverer's Hollow waited on this last formality before they could begin the long trek home. Her father, Erny, had stood and strode urgently to the privy room seven times in the last hour, and he blushed furiously as her mother harangued him about it.

'It ent natural, Ernal, piddling in drips and drops. You should have Leesha examine you.' Elona was across the room, but Leesha's sense of smell would put a wolf to shame when a cycle was upon her. She caught the scent of her mother's perfume, and it nauseated her. The pressure in her skull increased.

Like everyone else, the Cutters pretended not to hear. Wonda, who fancied herself Leesha's bodyguard, sat hunched forward in a chair much too small for her massive frame. Her giant warded bow, unstrung, was slung with her quiver of arrows over the chair back, and a heavy knife hung at her belt.

Big enough to wrestle strong men to the ground, Wonda Cutter was just sixteen, and when she was nervous, as now, she rocked slowly back and forth, tracing the demon scars on her face with her fingers.

Gared Cutter, close to seven feet tall and thick with muscle, was the only one in the room built on Wonda's scale, though they were only distantly related. Bored and with nothing to kill, he was attempting to carve a wooden horse, but his massive hands – perfect for throttling a downed wind demon – were unsuited to the careful work. He put too much pressure on the knife, and for what felt like the hundredth time the blade skipped from the wood and nicked his hand.

'Corespawn it!' He stuck his bleeding thumb in his mouth and made as if to throw the bit of wood, but Leesha raised an eyebrow at him, and he restrained himself. She immediately regretted the gesture, minute though it was, as a stab of pain struck her eye.

Rojer rounded on her. 'Can't pace, can't fiddle. What *can* I do, Your Highness?' Everyone looked up at that. Leesha wasn't known for tolerating that tone even in her best moods.

But the last thing Leesha needed at the moment was an argument. There was still hope to blunt the attack, and every heated word would halve her chances. She took a dose of headache powder with a sip of water from her mixing flask. The liquid splashed in her empty stomach, making it roil with a mix of hunger and nausea. The last thing Leesha wanted was food, but if she didn't eat soon, it would be all the worse.

She cursed herself silently for passing on the tea and pastry Abban's wives had put out that morning in the Palace of Mirrors, but she had just cleaned her teeth, and wanted her breath fresh when she greeted Ahmann. His invitation was for breakfast, a last meal before their journey began, but the sun was already high in the sky.

Idiot girl, she heard Bruna say in her head, *chew a mint leaf next time*. Leesha knew her old mentor's spirit was right. She fumbled in the pockets of her apron for something to eat, but for all the thousand and one medicines she could brew from their contents, she did not have so much as a nut.

Rojer kept glaring at her, and she suppressed the desire to snap at him. 'I'm sorry, Rojer. I'm as frustrated as you. At this rate, it will be past noon before we're on our way.'

'If they let us go at all,' Rojer said. 'Every minute we're kept waiting makes me all the more sure I'm going to end up in a dungeon with my stones on a chopping block by sunset.'

Rojer had good reason to be afraid. Ahmann had sent his

eldest daughter Amanvah – a full *dama'ting* – and his niece
Sikvah to Rojer as potential brides some weeks past. The two,
selected by Inevera, had proven to be spies, pretending not to
speak Thesan when in fact they were fluent, and attempting to
poison Leesha when she threatened the status quo in Everam's
Bounty.

Nevertheless, and much to Leesha's annoyance, Rojer had
allowed himself to be seduced by them, bedding Sikvah while
Amanvah coaxed them on. Since that night he had been on
edge, wondering if at any minute the Spears of the Deliverer
would come and take him away for despoiling the girls without
first agreeing to marry them.

'Perhaps you should have shown some self-control,' she said.

'Like you should tell,' Rojer said.

'And what is that supposed to mean?' Leesha asked.

Rojer's face became one of such comic incredulity Leesha
almost laughed, but for the lash of words that followed. 'Do
you honestly think there isn't a person in this room, this palace
– this city, even – who doesn't know you've been sticking
Ahmann Jardir?'

Leesha closed her eyes and took a breath. 'I made a calculated
decision with Ahmann, pondering all the variables. Your
calculus was done solely with your cock.'

'Calculus?' Rojer laughed. 'I grew up in a brothel, Leesha, I
know all about that sort of maths.'

'That is enough, Rojer!' Leesha's temper flared, and a bright
ball of pain flared hot in her skull, giving her strength as she
surged to her feet.

But Rojer refused to back down. 'Or what? I'm getting tired
of your holier-than-thou attitude, Leesha. You're not the
Duchess Mum of Angiers. I don't have to do as you say, and
I won't have you acting better than me after whoring yourself
to the demon of the desert.'

Gared rose to his feet, pointing at Rojer with his carving
knife. 'Can't have you talking to Leesha like that, Rojer. Painted

Man said to keep you safe, but I'll scrub your mouth with soap, you say that again.'

A knife spun into Rojer's hand. 'Try it, you backwoods bumpkin, and you'll have a knife in your eye.'

Gared blanched, and then his face narrowed into the look of an angry predator. Wonda had her bow strung in an instant, arrow nocked and ready. 'You throw that knife, and I'll—'

'Stop it, all of you!' Leesha shouted. 'Wonda, put up your bow. Gared, sit back down.' She whirled on Rojer. 'And you, mind your ripping manners and remember that my "whoring" may be the only reason your stones remain attached!'

'Leesha Paper!' Erny barked, and all eyes turned. Erny was close to sixty, much older than his wife, but he looked older still. He was thin, with only a few wisps of grey hair atop his head. He wore wire-rimmed spectacles and his pale skin was almost translucent. A moment ago his head was down, looking ill as Elona harped at him, but now he met Leesha's gaze and his eyes were sharp. 'Is that how I raised you? You demand respect, and that's your due, but you give it in return and tell honest word.'

Leesha felt her face go cold, and for a moment her headache was forgotten. Her father didn't speak up often, and he took that tone even less, but when he did there was nothing for it but to obey, because he had the right of things.

'I'm sorry, Rojer,' she said. 'I have an empty stomach and a splitting headache and I was out of line. The whole reason they sent those girls to you in the first place was because they think you can pass on your talent for charming demons to your sons. Not much chance of that if they kill you, or take your stones. If you were some *khaffit* or *chin* off the street caught sleeping with the Deliverer's niece out of wedlock, you might have to worry. But after Inevera made such a show of Sikvah not being a virgin, I think it's safe to say this was planned from the start.'

Rojer cocked his head. 'What, like a trap?'

Leesha smiled wanly. 'One you fell right into. The question is, what will happen now that it's sprung?'

Elona snorted. 'May be they'll lock you in a harem for the rest of your life, breeding and training them an army of little fiddle wizards.'

Gared roared a laugh, slapping a gigantic paw on his knee. 'Beats cuttin' wood all day, ay?'

Rojer did not seem to share his enthusiasm, paling and beginning to pace again. He rubbed his chest, where his family medallion rested safely beneath his shirt.

'Why is everyone ignoring the obvious answer?' Elona said. 'Idiots, you and my daughter, both. Just marry them, you nit.'

'Even if I wanted to,' Rojer said, 'they'll expect a dower worthy of them. I have nothing to offer.'

'The only thing they want from you is your seedpods.' She grabbed a handful of material at the crotch of her seated dress and gave it a meaningful shake. 'You have a power no one has ever seen or heard of outside a Jak Scaletongue story, and they want to know if you can breed it. Jardir told you as much when he offered to find you brides in the first place. And who knows? Maybe he's right, and it's something in your blood that lets you charm demons. Can't hurt to check.'

'I couldn't . . .' Rojer said.

But Elona didn't relent, her voice a lash that made the pain in Leesha's head flare. 'Couldn't what? Accept the best marriage offer anyone's ever heard of? Jardir is rich and powerful beyond belief. Sit next to me and shut up for ten minutes alone with Inevera and the girls, and you can have it all. Lands. Titles. Peasants to tax and rule. More gold than a Milnese mine.'

'Stolen gold,' Leesha said. 'Stolen people. Stolen lands.'

Elona waved a dismissive hand. 'Everything's stolen in the end, land most of all. Those people it was taken from ent getting it back in any event, and Rojer'll be a better lord than some Krasian.'

She turned back to Rojer. 'And let us not forget daily bed

rights to two beautiful women. Creator! They'll even help you pick more! Do you think offers like that come every day? Believe me, boy,' her eyes flicked to Erny, just for an instant, 'they don't.'

'I—' Rojer began.

Elona cut him off with a cruel grin. 'Or do you prefer boys? Ay, maybe that's why you chase my unattainable daughter instead of more willing lasses. No shame if you want a man to bend you now and again, but you should still accept and put a pair of brats in those girls. Just close your eyes and picture Gared for the deed.'

'Ay, now!' Gared cried.

'I don't prefer boys!' Rojer snapped.

Leesha leaned forward, massaging her temples. 'If I don't eat soon, I may scream.'

'*Sharum* break their fast late,' a voice said, and Leesha turned to find Abban standing in the doorway. 'It comes from sleeping in after staying up all night killing demons. But fear not. I will escort you to the Deliverer shortly.'

Leesha wondered how much he had overheard as the fat *khaffit* hobbled over to her on his camel-headed crutch. Wonda tensed as he reached into his robes, but Abban bowed slightly to her, pulling his hand free to show he held only a ripe red apple. Leesha knew then he had heard everything. She wouldn't put it past Abban to have engineered the entire delay, just for the chance to listen in.

'Thank you.' Leesha took the apple and immediately bit into it, the first delicious wet crunch as welcome a medicine as any in her herb pouches. Like smell, her senses of taste and touch were heightened during an attack, and she closed her eyes to savour every chew.

'Remember, mistress,' Abban said in a low tone the others could not hear. '*You* may be a creature of calculation, but Ahmann is one of passion. His blood tells him right from wrong, and he reacts immediately and without remorse. It is a trait that serves him well as a warrior and leader of men, I imagine.'

'What of it?' Leesha asked.

'It means the Deliverer believes that one day, you are *fated* to marry him. That it is Everam's will. He may let you go now, but he will never stop pursuing you.

'As for you, Jongleur,' Abban continued, raising his voice and hobbling Rojer's way, 'I would worry less about the Deliverer and Damajah, and more about Hasik. If he learns you have lain with his daughter without marrying her honourably, he will consider it rape. The moment Ahmann turns his gaze elsewhere, he will return it tenfold on you, and your little knives might as well be silken kerchiefs, for all they will hinder him.'

Rojer's mouth fell open, and he clutched for his medallion again. 'Hasik is Sikvah's father?' They knew Jardir's brutal, hulking bodyguard well.

'That's if Hasik finds out, Rojer,' Leesha cut in, 'and he won't. Don't let Abban scare you.'

The *khaffit* shrugged helplessly. 'I speak only truth, mistress.' He bowed. 'Variables, for your calculus.'

'Give them all, then.' Leesha took another bite of her apple. She was close to the core now, nibbling it down to nothing but seed and stem. 'We both know it's not in Sikvah's or Inevera's interest to tell anyone. Evejan law forbids women to bear witness to rape. Ahmann would have to take Rojer's word over theirs, and even if he didn't, the admission would mean Sikvah's death as well.'

'Honest word?' Rojer asked.

'Disgusting, but true,' Leesha said.

'Evejan law can be flexible where the blood of the Deliverer is involved, mistress,' Abban said. 'Consider the insult of refusing the girls as unworthy.'

'Hasik is going to kill me if I don't accept,' Rojer said, as if testing the words.

'Rape and kill, yes,' Abban agreed.

'Rape and kill,' Rojer repeated numbly.

'Bah, he's no bigger'n Wonda,' Gared said, slapping one of his great paws on Rojer's shoulder. 'Don't you worry, I ent gonna let him hurt ya, even if yur acting the fool.'

Rojer was a foot and a half shorter than Gared, but still seemed to look down at him. 'Don't shine yourself, Gared. You're used to being the biggest kid at the swimming hole, but truer is Hasik would have you on the ground in seconds.'

'And bugger you in front of the other *Sharum* so all see your shame,' Abban agreed. 'He is known for that.'

'Why you fat little . . .' Gared lunged, reaching for the *khaffit*'s throat, but Abban stepped smoothly aside on his good leg, then delivered a sharp rap of his camel-headed crutch to the back of the giant Cutter's leg.

Gared roared in pain and fell to one knee. Stubborn, he turned to grab again, but froze when he found the crutch pointed right at his throat, a thin blade extended from its tip.

'Ah,' Abban said, lifting the blade into Gared's beard, making him gulp. 'I haven't been in *sharaj* since my stones dropped, but even I recall enough *sharusahk* to put down a brainless oaf, and I have my tricks to keep them down.'

He stepped back, and the blade disappeared into his crutch with a well-oiled click. 'So listen to me when I offer you wisdom. When Hasik comes to my house without Ahmann to hold his leash, I bow and stay out of his way, no matter what, or who, he does. That one is a killer of killers, and I have seen many. Heed Drillmaster Kaval and you may one day be his match, but it is not this day.'

He looked at Rojer. 'Learn from your Mistress Leesha. If you do not wish to accept the girls, delay.'

'How?' Rojer asked.

Abban shrugged. 'Say your custom is to be . . . promised, you say?'

'Promised,' Rojer agreed.

'Say your custom is that you be promised for a year, or that you must first compose some great work of music to bless the day. Say you will not marry until you learn the Krasian tongue, or until the first day of spring. It does not matter *what* you say, son of Jessum, only that you save face for my master and the girls and give yourself time to get far away from here.'

Rojer and the others followed Abban into Jardir's huge dining hall. Sunlight streamed in from high windows, filling the room with light. The main section of the marble hall was a collection of long, low tables, surrounded by pillows where hundreds of *Sharum*, the elite Spears of the Deliverer as well as the personal guards of the *Damaji*, sat cross-legged, spears and shields at hand as they gorged themselves on bread, couscous, and spits of roast meat, served in beautifully painted pottery by boys clad only in white bidos.

Rojer gave no outward sign, walking as casually as he would through a field of flowers, but he could feel his heart beating wildly as he passed the warriors. There would be no running from this room, no trick of smoke or fiddle that could spirit them past such a host. They would leave at Jardir's sufferance, or not at all.

Abban led them through the warriors to a stair to the dais where sat the *Damaji*, Jardir's sons and heirs, and various other ranking clerics. There was thick carpet on the floor and warm tapestries on the wall. They sat on silken pillows and ate delicately from rich food piled upon moulded silver wares served by women clad in black from head to toe.

The clerics watched with hate-filled eyes as the Hollowers passed and ascended above them to the next dais. There was no change in his casual stride, no hint of it on his face, but Rojer felt his chest constrict as if the air were being slowly squeezed from his lungs. He knew the skill with which the clerics fought, deadlier with open hands than a Cutter with an axe.

On the next and smallest dais, though still a huge space rich with thick carpet and gilded marble, sat Jardir's own table. The pillows were embroidered in gold, like the gem-studded bowls, pitchers, and plates, which were served by Jardir's own women, many of them black-veiled *dama'ting*. Rojer's stomach twisted at the thought of eating at a table where almost every server was skilled in poisoning. They were all covered from head to toe, but Rojer nonetheless caught sight of Amanvah and Sikvah among them, their shapes and the graceful way they moved etched forever into his mind.

Jardir sat at the head of the table with Inevera at his right, the Damajah clad as ever in diaphanous silk that drew the eye, yet promised a painful death to any man whose gaze lingered too long. At the foot of the table sat Damaji Ashan and Aleverak, their heirs Asukaji and Maji, Jardir's first- and secondborn sons, Jayan and Asome, *kai'Sharum* Shanjat, and, of course, Hasik.

Despite the obvious futility, Rojer felt a mad urge to run for his life. Subtly, he slid a finger between the buttons of his motley shirt to touch the cold metal of his medallion. As he did, he felt much of his tension ease.

The medallion was the highest award of bravery from the Duke of Angiers, given to Rojer's adoptive father Arrick Sweetsong as reward for throwing him and his mother to the corelings and then later lying about it. Even Arrick had been unable to stomach that, and when he gathered his things before being expelled from the duke's palace, he had left the medallion behind even as he took everything else of value he could get his hands on.

But where Arrick abandoned him, others stood fast that night. Geral the Messenger had thrown his mother a shield, and he and Rojer's father interposed themselves between mother and child and the demons that poured through the ruin of their front door. They had died, much as Arrick many years later, protecting Rojer.

Leesha had etched the names of all who had given their lives for Rojer into the medal of valour, and it had become his talisman. It was a comfort when fear threatened to overwhelm him, but also a reminder that his remaining days were bought with the lives of everyone who had ever cared for him. He wanted to believe it was because there was something special about him, something worth saving, but in truth he had never seen much evidence that was the case.

Leesha took the pillow to Jardir's left with Rojer after, followed by Elona, Erny, Gared, and Wonda. Abban took his customary place, kneeling a pace behind Jardir, almost invisible in the backdrop.

Sikvah immediately set a tiny cup of thick coffee in front of him, and as he caught her eye, she winked at him, her lashes thick and black. No one else caught the look, and it was a warm, artful gesture that sent a little thrill through Rojer. But he had practised such looks in front of a mirror enough times not to be taken in. Amanvah and Sikvah might be fond of him, and willing to be his brides, but they did not love him. Did not know him well enough for it to be true even if they believed it.

Neither did Rojer love them. They were brilliant, beautiful creatures, but beneath the surface they were still a mystery to him.

But there was something . . .

He thought back often on the night they seduced him, but it was not the lovemaking that he recalled. At least, not most often. It was the *Song of Waning* they had sung for him in duet. There was power in their voices. Power that Rojer, raised by arguably the greatest singer of his time, knew was rare and potent.

Inevera and Elona had done everything in their power to pressure Rojer into accepting the brides. Abban wanted him to dance around the promise. Leesha seemed to want him to turn them down on the spot, though she herself danced Abban's dance like she was in the centre of a reel.

No one seemed at all interested in what Rojer himself wanted.

The meal seemed to drag forever, with endless prayers and formal pleasantries, often delivered through thinly veiled expressions of mistrust. Ahmann kept most of his attention on Leesha, to the obvious annoyance of the Krasians at the table. They were arguing again over how many *Sharum* would act as escort for their journey back to the Hollow.

'We agreed to ten,' Leesha said, 'and not a one more. Gared tells me there are closer to thirty in the caravan.'

'We agreed to ten dedicated *dal'Sharum*,' Jardir agreed. 'But you need men to drive the wagons with my gifts to the Hollow tribe, to hunt your food, care for the animals, prepare your meals, and wash your clothes. Those will not lift their spears unless the need is dire.'

'Are those not jobs traditionally done by your women?' Leesha asked. 'Let your ten warriors bring their wives and children.' She didn't say *as hostages*, but Rojer heard it all the same.

'Even so,' Jardir said, 'ten is insufficient to ensure your safety. My scouts tell me the roads to the Hollow have grown dangerous with *chin* bandits.'

'Not *chin*,' Leesha said.

'Eh?' Jardir asked.

Careful, Rojer thought.

'You taught me that *chin* means "outsider",' Leesha said. 'These are people living in the land they were born to, or driven from it by your army. You are the *chin* here.'

There were angry murmurs from the Krasians at that. Here in Everam's Bounty, Jardir's power was absolute, his slightest whim no different than law. In truth, his decrees could, and often did, supersede laws that had stood for thousands of years. No one, especially not a woman – and an outlander at that – dared speak so boldly to him in open court.

Jardir lifted a finger, and they fell silent. 'A trick of words that changes nothing of the danger. Twenty warriors. Ten *kha'Sharum* and ten *dal*, including Drillmaster Kaval to continue the lessons to your own warriors, and my Watcher, Coliv. All will bring their first wives and one child of their blood.'

'Half of them girls,' Leesha said, 'and not a one old enough for *Hannu Pash*. I don't want twenty boys pulled from *sharaj* a day before they are to lose the bido.'

Jardir smiled and flicked a finger over his shoulder. 'Abban, see to it.'

Abban touched his forehead to the floor. 'Of course, Deliverer.'

'Twenty-one,' Inevera cut in. 'A holy number. Amanvah is *dama'ting* and must have a dedicated eunuch guardian. I will send Enkido with her.'

'Agreed,' Jardir said.

'It is not—' Leesha began, but Jardir cut her off.

'My daughter must be protected, Leesha Paper. I think your honoured father,' he gestured to Erny, 'can agree that this is not a negotiable point?'

Leesha glanced his way, but Erny gave her a stern look. 'He's right, Leesha, and you know it.'

'Perhaps,' Leesha said. '*If* she returns with us. There has been no agreement about that.'

Inevera smiled over the golden chalice she used to sip her water. 'Another thing, daughter of Erny, that is not yours to decide.'

All eyes turned to Rojer, and he felt his guts clench tight. He focused his thoughts on the medallion, heavy against his chest, and drew a deep breath. He reached into his multi-coloured bag of marvels, producing his fiddle case.

'Great Shar'Dama Ka,' he said, 'I have been practising a tune your daughter and her handmaiden taught me, the *Song of Waning*. You said music in praise to Everam was welcome in your court. May I play it for you?'

There were curious looks from around the table at the

evasion, but Jardir waved a hand and nodded. 'But of course, son of Jessum. We would be honoured.'

Rojer opened the case, removing the ancient fiddle the Painted Man had given him, a carefully preserved relic of the old world. The strings were new, but the lacquered wood was still strong, producing a rich resonance that surpassed any instrument Rojer had ever held. He paused carefully, then looked up as if a thought had just occurred to him. 'Would it be appropriate to ask Amanvah and Sikvah to add their voices to the song?'

'The *Song of Waning* is an honoured one,' Jardir said, and nodded to the young women. They moved silently over to him like birds to the falconer's wrist, coming to kneel on the pillows a step behind him.

As well I can't see them, Rojer thought. *Can't afford distraction. Not here. Not now.*

He took the fine horsehair bow in his crippled hand and closed his eyes, blocking out the taste of Krasian coffee from his mouth, the smell of food from his nostrils, the general din of the dining hall from his ears. He focused until there was nothing in the world but the feel of the instrument in his hands, and then he began to play.

He started slowly, a long improvisation around the opening notes of the tune. It was soft at first, but as he layered in more and more of the true melody, he let it grow louder until it filled Jardir's dais, spread out over the *Damaji*'s level, and finally echoed through the entire hall. Rojer was dimly aware of the silence that fell over the crowd, but it was meaningless to him. Only the music mattered.

When the melody was complete, Rojer let the fiddle grow quiet again, and began assembling the notes anew. He gave no other signal, no nod or stroke of his bow as he might to his apprentices, but nevertheless Amanvah and Sikvah joined him instantly on the repeat, softly singing wordless notes to complement Rojer's previous improvisation as he built the complexity and volume back to its former height and beyond.

Oh, the lungs, he thought, feeling the air thrumming with the strength of their voices. He felt a stiffening in his crotch, but ignored it like every other distraction. A good performance could have that effect. Fortunately, Jongleurs wore loose trousers.

This time when the melody was built again in full, the women began to sing. The words were still beyond Rojer's very limited understanding of Krasian, but they were beautiful nonetheless – mournful but with a tone of warning. Amanvah and Sikvah had explained their meaning, but the women's knowledge of Thesan, while fluent, was insufficient to translate the artistry and harmony that resonated between the music and the original Krasian lyrics.

It was a challenge Rojer was hungry for. There was power in the *Song of Waning*. Ancient power.

After each verse, there was a wordless chorus, a call to Heaven beseeching Everam for strength in the night. Amanvah's and Sikvah's voices blended into a union that made it nearly impossible to determine where one ended and the other began.

He played the first chorus exactly as the women had first shown him, but before the second verse ended, Rojer began to thread in a new variation, improvised around the original. It was a minor change, but a difficult one for a singer to follow. They did so effortlessly, changing their harmony to follow his playing. On the third chorus, he took them farther still, building the music into something that would stop a coreling in its tracks. Again they followed, as easily as if he led them down a garden path, arm in arm in arm.

The fourth verse spoke of Alagai Ka, the father of demons, who stalked the land when the moon was new. Rojer did not know if such a creature existed, but the demon prince that had tried to kill Leesha and Jardir on new moon a few nights past was terror enough. The music had a frightening tone, and when the next chorus was reached, Rojer turned the music into a piercing, discordant wail that would send even a rock demon fleeing beyond earshot.

And again, Amanvah and Sikvah, without practice, without prompting, followed.

Verse after verse, Rojer tested them, working his fiddle magic – if that was what this was – to its fullest, bathing the great dining hall in his power. They were with him every step of the way, even as he improvised a new closing to wend the music down into silence.

When the last resonance left the wood, Rojer lifted bow from string and opened his eyes. As if coming out of a deep slumber, reality was slow to focus. Everyone at the table, even Jardir and Inevera, sat in stunned silence, watching him. Rojer looked out farther, seeing the dozens of clerics at the table below similarly entranced, as well as the hundreds of *Sharum* on the floor proper.

Then, as if given a cue, the room burst into a roar of approval. The *Sharum* shouted and ululated, stomping their feet so hard the floor seemed to shake. The clerics were more controlled, but their applause was thunderous nonetheless. Gared slapped him on the back, nearly knocking the wind from him, and Leesha flashed him a smile that once would have stopped his heart in its tracks. Even Hasik clapped and stomped his feet, staring at his daughter with obvious pride.

Jardir and Inevera did not react, however, and soon all fell silent, eyes upon the Deliverer to see his response. The demon of the desert smiled slowly, and then, to the astonishment of all, bowed deeply to Rojer.

'Everam speaks to you, son of Jessum,' he said, and with that, the roars and clapping began anew.

Rojer bowed in return, as deep as the table before him would allow. 'I wish to marry your daughter and niece, Ahmann asu Hoshkamin am'Jardir am'Kaji.' Leesha let out a slight gasp, and Elona a satisfied huff.

Jardir nodded, gesturing with his right hand towards Inevera and his left towards Elona. 'Our women will arrange . . .'

But Rojer shook his head. 'I wish to marry them here. Now.

There is nothing for the women to negotiate. I have no need or want of groom gifts, nor have I money for dower.'

Jardir steepled his fingers as he regarded Rojer, his face an unreadable mask that would do a master Jongleur proud. He looked as apt to order Hasik to crush him like a bug as to accept the offer. Indeed, his bodyguard had dropped a hand to his spear.

But Rojer had his audience now, and there was no fear in him as he pressed on. 'But no gold or jewels could ever be worthy of Amanvah and Sikvah in any event. What are such things but baubles to Shar'Dama Ka? Instead, I will translate the *Song of Waning* into Thesan and play it for my people. If Sharak Ka is coming as you say, all should remember to fear the new moon.'

'You think I will sell you my daughter for a song?' Inevera said.

Rojer bowed her way. He knew he should fear her, but the rightness was on him, and he smiled instead. 'Apologies, Damajah, but that is not yours to decide.'

'Indeed,' Jardir said, before Inevera could retort. She gave no outward sign of agitation, but there was a cold calculation in her eyes that frightened more than an outburst.

Rojer turned back to him. 'You say Everam speaks to me. I cannot say if this is so or not, but if true, He is telling me there was real magic in your court just now. Magic older and deeper than warding. He is telling me that if I pursue that magic with your daughters, we may learn to kill *alagai* with song alone.'

'He tells me the same, son of Jessum,' Jardir said. 'I accept.'

Hasik gave a whoop of delight that would have sent a chill down Rojer's spine just a few minutes ago. There was more applause and stomping of feet from below, and congratulations from around the table.

'You sly son of the Core,' Gared said, grabbing Rojer's shoulder in a great paw and giving him a teeth-rattling shake. Even Inevera seemed pleased with the result, though Rojer knew his slight to her would not soon be forgotten. The only sour look was from Elona, no doubt mentally cataloguing all the wealth he had just turned his back on.

But Rojer had no love of wealth save as a means of survival, and he had gold enough for that already from the Painted Man. And even without, his fiddle had never failed in the past to bring him a full belly and a place to lie his head.

Jardir gestured to Amanvah, and she stepped forward, bowing. 'Rojer, son of Jessum, I offer you myself in marriage in accordance with the instructions of the Evejah, as set down by Kaji, Spear of Everam, who sits at the foot of Everam's table until he is reborn in the time of Sharak Ka. I pledge, with honesty and in sincerity, to be for you an obedient and faithful wife.'

Jardir turned to him. 'Repeat my words, son of Jessum: I, Rojer, son of Jessum, swear before Everam, Creator of all that is, and before the Shar'Dama Ka, to take you into my home, and to be a fair and tolerant husband.'

Rojer reached into his shirt, producing his medallion and clutching it in his fist. 'I, Rojer, son of Jessum, swear before the Creator of all that is, and before the spirits of my parents, to take you into my home, and to be a fair and tolerant husband.'

There were some murmurs of discontent at that. Rojer heard ancient Damaji Aleverak's voice among them, but Jardir gave no sign that he even noticed the shift, though Rojer was not fool enough to think that the case. 'Do you accept my daughter as your *Jiwah Ka*?'

'I do,' Rojer said.

The vows were repeated with Sikvah, and Amanvah reached for her, removing her black veil. 'Welcome, sister-wife, beloved *Jiwah Sen*,' she said, tying a veil of white silk in its place.

Hasik rose, spear and shield in hand. For a moment, Rojer was sure the giant *dal'Sharum* meant to kill him, but instead Hasik clattered his spear against his shield and gave out an ululating cry. Instantly, every warrior in attendance was doing the same, and the hall shook with their cacophony.

'You could have at least said something if that was your plan, Rojer,' Leesha said as Abban escorted them to the caravan.

'I hadn't decided anything until the song was done,' Rojer replied, 'but even if I had, what business is it of yours who I marry? Let us not pretend you would consult me if the positions were reversed.'

Leesha gripped her skirts tightly in her fists. 'Need I remind you that those young women tried to murder me?'

'Ay,' Rojer agreed. 'Yet you're the one that treated Amanvah when the antidote made her sick, and offered asylum to her and Sikvah both.'

'Don't fool yourself,' Leesha said. 'They're still Inevera's creatures.'

Rojer shrugged. 'Perhaps. For now.'

'You really think you can change them?' Leesha asked.

Rojer shrugged. 'Do you think you can change *him*?' They reached the caravan, and Rojer, who had been given an opulent carriage to ride in with his wives, quickly disappeared inside.

'Do not underestimate the son of Jessum,' Abban said to Leesha. 'He gained much power today.' He gestured to a woman who stood at the head of the caravan with a ledger. 'My First Wife, Shamavah. She will accompany you to the Hollow, and has personally chosen the *kha'Sharum* who will drive the carts with their wives and children. All of them, wives or husbands, are family, or work for me. They will give you no trouble.'

'It's not the *kha'Sharum* I'm worried over,' Leesha said.

Abban nodded. 'And you are wise in that. I have had no say over the *dal'Sharum*. They will report to Kaval, and though Ahmann has told the drillmaster that you are still his intended and to answer to you in all things, I expect it will be Amanvah they follow in practice.'

'Then we'd all best hope Rojer's confidence is justified,' Leesha said.

'I am saddened to see you leave, mistress,' Abban said. 'I will miss our conversations.'

Rojer fell into the wedding carriage with a contented sigh. It was of Rizonan make, fine wood and gilded paint with a metal suspension to take away the jolts and bumps of the road. A nobleman's carriage, and a rich one at that.

But the Krasians had made alterations, removing the seats and covering the floor with thick colourful carpets and embroidered silk pillows. The walls and ceiling were covered in dark velvet of red and purple, and scented herbs hung from the ceiling in bronze pots punched with holes. The windows were glass, but could be cracked to let in air, as they were now, but curtained in velvet for privacy. Bronze and glass oil lamps hung from the walls, lighting and extinguishing themselves with the twist of a key.

Rojer had been in brothels less suited to lovemaking.

They don't want me to waste any time, it seems. He couldn't deny that he was eager for it, as well. Sikvah had lain with him already, but refused to let him spend in her until they were wed, and Amanvah was still a virgin. He would have to be gentle with her.

He took a pencil and notebook from his bag of marvels, continuing his notes on the *Song of Waning*. He could read well enough, and write in a cramped hand, but neither letters nor the musical symbols Arrick taught him came as naturally as fiddling.

'Not everyone can hear a song once and play it forever,' Arrick scolded when he had complained of the lessons, punctuating the advice with a clout to the ear. 'You want to sell a song, you've got to be able to write it down.'

Rojer had hated his master in that moment, but now he was thankful for the lesson. He had already put down the tune and the meter of the lyrics. It would take time to translate the meaning fully, but they would be two weeks at best on the road to the Hollow, with nothing else to do.

Rojer smiled, stroking one of the silken pillows. *Well, almost nothing.*

He heard voices, and peeked through a crack in the curtains, seeing Amanvah and Sikvah approaching with a pair of white-clad *dama*, a strange-looking *Sharum*, and two other women.

Rojer immediately recognized Jardir's son Asome and his nephew Asukaji. The warrior must be Amanvah's bodyguard, Enkido. He wore the standard warrior blacks, but his wrists and ankles were bound in golden shackles that seemed permanently welded in place.

The women he did not recognize. Both wore black robes, but one had a veil of white like Sikvah's. The other's face was bare, indicating she was unmarried and unbetrothed.

Asome and Amanvah walked in front, arguing. They stopped in front of the carriage, whispering harsh words that Rojer could not understand. Asome grabbed Amanvah by the shoulders and shook her, his face a scowl. Her supposed bodyguard looked on but did nothing. It seemed doubtful any Krasian would dare strike the Deliverer's son, much less a lowly *Sharum*.

Rojer felt a chill of fear. He knew Asome could kill him. He had seen *dama* fight – the least of them could use his head as a tackleball. But he couldn't just watch. He ran through his mummer's repertoire, thinking of the most fearless person he knew and putting him on like a cloak.

He kicked open the door of the carriage, startling everyone.

'Get your hands off my wife!' Rojer said in the low growl of the Painted Man. He flicked his good hand, and a throwing knife appeared in it.

Asukaji hissed and looked ready to leap at him, but Asome let Amanvah go and used a hand to forestall him.

'Apologies, son of Jessum,' Asome said, though he did not bow. His Thesan was clear, but heavily accented like Amanvah's. 'A disagreement among siblings, only. I meant no disrespect on your wedding day.' The anger in his tone was barely contained. Had any man ever dared threaten him with a knife before?

'Got a funny way of showin' it,' Gared said, appearing off to one side of the carriage. His huge axe was held casually in one hand, his warded machete in easy reach. Out of the corner of his eye, Rojer saw Wonda quietly appear to the other side, bow in hand. Rojer knew she could nock and fire an arrow in the blink of an eye.

Asukaji moved to interpose himself between her and Asome. There was a cold calm about him, and Rojer wondered if even Wonda could fire before the *dama* reached her, and if she would hit anything if she did. All around, their *dal'Sharum* escort was watching.

Rojer gave a shallow bow, little more than a nod, tucking his knife away in a blink and showing his empty hand. 'You honour me, brother, by coming personally to bless our wedding day and present your sister and cousin to me.'

Amanvah gave him a warning look. Rojer knew he was walking a line taking such a familiar tone with men who would as soon kill as speak to him, but he had a handle on the scene now. The *dama* would not dare attack the Deliverer's new son-in-law in public as long as he kept his words polite.

'Indeed,' Asome agreed, though there was nothing of agreement in his tone. His return bow was the exact depth and duration as Rojer's. Asukaji did the same. 'Blessings upon this day . . . brother.'

Asome looked at Amanvah and said a few words in Krasian, then the two *dama* turned on their heels and strode off to the collective relief of all.

'What did he say?' Rojer asked.

Amanvah hesitated, until he turned and met her eyes. 'He said, "We will speak of this another time."'

Rojer nodded as if it were of no import. 'It would please me, wife, if you would introduce the rest of your escort.'

Amanvah bowed, gesturing for the other women to step forward. First was the woman with the white veil. Up close, Rojer could see she was young, perhaps no older than Sikvah.

'My sister-in-law and cousin Ashia,' Amanvah said, 'firstborn daughter of Damaji Ashan and the Deliverer's eldest sister, holy Imisandre, *Jiwah Ka* to my brother Asome.'

Rojer hid his surprise as the woman bowed. 'Blessings upon your wedding day, son of Jessum. My heart is filled with joy to see my blessed cousin wed to you.' Her tone held none of Asome's insincerity. Quite the contrary, she looked as if she might kiss him.

He turned to the other young woman, her uncovered face showing her to be of an age with the others.

'My cousin Shanvah,' Amanvah said. 'Firstborn daughter of kai'Sharum Shanjat, leader of the Spears of the Deliverer, and my father's middle sister, holy Hoshvah.'

'My blessings as well, son of Jessum.' Shanvah's smooth bow was so low her nose nearly touched the ground. Rojer knew trained dancers who would give anything for such strength and flexibility.

'The four of us have trained together under Enkido in the Dama'ting Palace since we were children,' Amanvah said, nodding to include Sikvah. 'They have come to hold their goodbyes until the last moment, as it may be some time before we are together again.'

Enkido bowed deeply to Rojer as Amanvah indicated him.

'Rojer asu Jessum am'Inn am'Bridge,' Rojer said, giving his name in the Krasian fashion as he stuck out his hand. The warrior looked at it curiously a moment, then reached out and clasped his wrist. His fingers were like bars of steel. He did not reply.

'Enkido is a eunuch, husband,' Amanvah said. 'He has no

spear, so he may be trusted to guard us in your absence, and no tongue to whisper our secrets.'

'You let them cut off your tree?!' Gared blurted in shock. All eyes turned to him, and he blushed. Enkido only looked at him mutely.

'Enkido does not speak your heathen tongue,' Amanvah said, 'so he is unaware of your rudeness.'

Gared flushed even more deeply at that, fumbling his axe back into the harness on his back and bowing as he backed away. 'Sorry 'bout that. I . . . ah . . .' He turned and moved quickly to tend his horse.

Rojer bowed again to draw attention back to himself. 'I am honoured to have so many of the Deliverer's blood come to see us off. Please, do not let me interfere with your goodbyes. Take as long as you need.'

He moved away as the women began their tearful embraces, nodding to the two Cutters. 'Thanks.'

'Just doin' our jobs,' Gared said. 'Painted Man said to keep you safe, and that's what we aim to do.'

'Glad we're leavin',' Wonda said. 'Sooner we're gone the better.'

'Honest word,' Rojer agreed.

'What was all that about?' Rojer demanded of Amanvah as soon as they were alone in the carriage.

'A matter between—' Amanvah began.

'Is this how we begin our marriage, my *Jiwah Ka*?' Rojer cut her off. 'With half-truths and evasions?'

Amanvah looked at him in surprise, but she quickly dropped her eyes. 'Of course you are right, husband.' She gave a slight shiver. 'You and your companions are not the only ones eager to leave Everam's Bounty.'

'Why was your brother so angry?' Rojer asked.

'Asome believes I should have refused my mother when she told me to wed you,' Amanvah said. 'He argued with her, and it . . . did not go well.'

'He doesn't want your house allying with a greenlander?' Rojer guessed.

Amanvah shook her head. 'Not at all. He sees the power you command and is not blind to its uses. But Father has many *dama'ting* daughters whom he feels would serve. He has ever meant me as a gift for Asukaji, though it is not a brother's right to give away his sister while their father lives.'

'Why you?' Rojer asked.

'Because nothing less than his eldest full-blooded sister would do for Asome's beloved Asukaji,' Amanvah spat. 'He cannot bear his lover's children himself, so he tries to use the closest thing, as Asukaji did when he convinced Uncle Ashan to offer Ashia to my brother. Only my white robes have protected me thus far.' She looked at him. 'My white robes, and you.'

Rojer felt nauseous. 'Where I come from, it's considered . . . improper to marry your first cousin, unless you're in some remote hamlet and haven't got a choice.'

Amanvah nodded. 'It is not favoured among my people either, but Asome is the son of the Shar'Dama Ka and Damajah. He does as he pleases. Already, Ashia has been forced to bear him a son that he and Asukaji treat as their own.'

Rojer shuddered, and breathed his relief as the carriage began to sway in its suspension, a sign they were finally moving.

'Think on it no more, husband,' Amanvah said, taking his right arm as Sikvah moved to his left. 'It is our wedding day.'

12

The Hundred

333 AR Summer
28 Dawns Before Waning

Abban gasped for breath, sweating onto the fine silk sheets of the master bed in the Palace of Mirrors. The very bed where Ahmann first took Mistress Leesha, a bed yanked out from under Damaji Ichach at Abban's suggestion. It pleased him to steal his own pleasure there, marking the silk while the leader of the Khanjin tribe laid his head in some lesser place.

Shamavah was already on her feet, pulling on her black robes. 'Up with you, fat one. You've had your draining, and time is short.'

'Water,' Abban groaned as he sat up. Shamavah went to the silver pitcher cooling on the table. Beads of water ran down the metal as she poured a cup, much as beads of sweat ran down his skin.

'One of these days your heart will give way, and control of your fortune pass to me,' she taunted, quenching her own thirst before refilling the cup and bringing it to him.

Had any of his other wives dishonoured him so, Abban would have taken the cane to her himself, but for Shamavah he only smiled. His *Jiwah Ka* had never been the most beautiful of his wives, and her fertile years had long since waned, but she was the only one he bedded for love.

'You already control my fortune,' Abban said, taking the cup and draining it as she began helping him into his clothes.

'Perhaps that is why you send me away,' Shamavah said.

Abban reached out, taking her face in his free hand. He knew she was only teasing, but still it was too much to bear. 'I will curse every minute we are apart.' He winked. 'And not just because I will need to work twice as hard without you.'

Shamavah kissed his hand. 'Thrice.'

Abban nodded. 'But it is for that very reason that I trust no one else to begin our dealings with the Hollow tribe. We must secure our operations and win the greenlanders over, even if it means red in the ledger at first.'

'Nie take me first,' Shamavah said. 'It did not take long to buy the Hollowers' trust, and they sold it cheaply. They do not have the stamina to hide their weakness for long.'

It was true enough. When they first set out from Deliverer's Hollow, the Northerners all quieted whenever Abban drew near, mistrustful of any with a dusky tone to their skin. But Abban always came bearing gifts. Nothing so bold as gold or jewels – that would offend these people. But a silk pillow casually offered to one rubbing a sore backside from long days on a cart bench? A flattering word when it was needed? Exotic spices to flavour their cookpot? A few bits of common knowledge about his people?

These things the Northerners accepted freely, congratulating themselves over learning to say 'please' and 'thank you' in his language as if it were some great deed.

And so they began talking to him, still guarded, but with increasing comfort, letting him lead a conversation about the weather into talk of harvest festivals and holidays, marriage customs and morality. The Northerners loved the sound of their own voices.

It wasn't the information Ahmann wanted, of course. The Deliverer wanted troop sizes and positions, points of military or symbolic significance, and maps. He wanted maps most of all. The Rizonan Messengers' Guild had burned theirs the day the

Krasians attacked, and the idiot *Sharum* had not bothered to stop them. The maps in Duke Edon's library were extensive for his own lands, but for those outside his borders they were a decade old. To the north, Deliverer's Hollow was growing exponentially. Small villages were swelling with refugees, and new settlements were forming, many far away from the Messenger roads Ahmann needed to move the full strength of his forces.

'The landscape is changing,' Ahmann had said. 'We cannot achieve victory without understanding that change.'

It was sound military thinking, but gullible though they were, the Hollowers were not such utter fools as to reveal such information. Yet while Ahmann might turn up his chin at gossip and bickering, Abban knew it for the power it was.

Great things can be found in small talk, his father Chabin used to say.

Shamavah had done much the same when the greenlanders came to the Palace of Mirrors. All Abban's wives and daughters spoke Thesan, but on her orders they had pretended only a handful of words, turning simple interactions into such complicated pantomime that the Hollowers had quickly stopped bothering to speak to them despite their near-constant presence. They silently brought food, cleared away refuse, changed linens, and carried water, all but invisible.

After weeks on end, the greenlanders no longer bothered to hide their petty squabbling. Even when they thought they were alone, more often than not they stood near one of the palace's many air vents, and Shamavah had women 'cleaning' the central shafts continually. Abban read their reports, detailing everything from privy habits to sexual encounters. Some he read with more pleasure than others.

Now the leanings of the Northerners' hearts were open scrolls. *Know a person's desires,* his father had told him, *and you can charge whatever you wish to fulfil them.*

Like the steps of a ladder, he had built their trust, keeping their secrets and offering sound advice. Occasionally he even seemed to suggest a course not to his master's advantage, a tactic any child in the bazaar knew to mistrust. But the trick always seemed to work on greenlanders, the best of whom were poor hagglers.

Most delicious was when he could offer up a secret about Inevera, buying their trust even as he helped thwart the manipulations of the Damajah.

She was beginning to suspect his hand now, but it mattered little. He had made his opening moves too subtly for her to oppose him openly, using unwitting agents – including Ahmann himself. The Shar'Dama Ka might publicly heap abuse on Abban, but he tolerated none of it from others, brutally putting down even his sons and closest advisors when they tried to bully the *khaffit*.

But it was not enough. Sooner or later, Inevera or one of the others would have him poisoned, or killed in his bed, unless he vastly increased his protections.

'I fear for you while I am gone,' Shamavah said, as if reading his thoughts. 'You and the rest of our family, now that we must leave the Palace of Mirrors.'

'Look to your own concerns in the coming months,' Abban said. 'I can see to my own protection, and that of our women, while you are gone.'

'And our sons?' Shamavah asked.

Abban let out a deep sigh as he straightened his turban in the mirror and reached for his camel crutch. 'That will be more difficult,' he admitted. 'But one problem at a time. For now, you have a caravan to catch.'

When he had seen his wife and the greenlanders off, Abban limped back to Ahmann's palace. Duke Edon's manse was the most impressive and defensible structure in Everam's Bounty, though it was dwarfed by the palaces of the Desert Spear.

Abban himself had larger holdings in Krasia, though his were disguised as crumbling warehouses in poor districts. It was unwise for a *khaffit* to advertise his wealth to the local *dama* and *Sharum*.

The *Damaji* and most powerful *dama* had claimed all the grandest structures in Everam's Bounty when the city was captured, and the *Sharum* had snatched up the best of what remained. Abban had been left with a humble abode in the poorest and most remote section of town, the building not even large enough to properly house all his wives, daughters, and servants. His pavilion in the new bazaar was grander.

In the short term, Abban had solved the problem by moving everyone into the Palace of Mirrors while he quietly bought all the land in his poor neighbourhood. Slaves worked day and night, secretly tunnelling the perimeter. He would fill the tunnels with poured stone to found his outer wall, the materials already stockpiled. By the time anyone knew what was happening, the wall would be up, and safe from prying eyes, though even those would see only a squat block of a building with nothing to note the splendour within.

But a wall was nothing without warriors to guard it. Abban was no warrior, but he knew their value. He had many muscular *chin* slaves, but they were no match for true *Sharum*. If he wasn't prepared, the *Damaji* would take his new palace from him the moment the final brick was laid.

The halls of the Shar'Dama Ka's palace were full of *dama* and *dama'ting*, with *Sharum* marching to and fro, guarding every archway and door. Black-clad *dal'ting* scurried about carrying trays and laundered linen. Abban kept his eyes down, exaggerating his limp as his crutch thumped a steady beat on the thick carpet.

Always appear weaker than you are, Chabin had taught, and Abban had taken the lessons well. Shattered decades ago, his leg pained him still, but not half so much as he let on, even to Ahmann. A simple cane would have sufficed, but the crutch made him seem that much more helpless. As intended, almost everyone avoided him with their eyes, that they not show their disgust.

Hasik stood outside the throne room, and glowered as Abban approached. Ahmann's entire inner circle despised the *khaffit*, but Hasik had a capacity for hatred and sadism that surpassed any man Abban had ever met. Tall and muscular enough to wrestle the Northern giants in Deliverer's Hollow, he had been given special training in *sharusahk* since becoming bodyguard to the Deliverer. Pain meant nothing to Hasik, and even *kai'Sharum* feared to face him. For Hasik did not simply defeat his enemies. He left them crippled and humiliated.

They knew each other from *sharaj*, when Abban and Ahmann had been friends, and Hasik Ahmann's greatest rival. Now Hasik served Ahmann fanatically, but his hatred of Abban had only grown, especially since Abban took every chance he could to flaunt the fact that Hasik was only a bodyguard, while he had the Deliverer's ear.

Unable to strike at Abban directly, Hasik vented his frustrations on Abban's women, coming often to his pavilion and home on some errand for the Deliverer, always making time to break some item of great value or rape whichever of Abban's wives or daughters was nearest to hand.

In the Palace of Mirrors, his women had been safe from Hasik, and denied this pleasure the brutal warrior's loathing had multiplied. His nostrils flared like a bull as the *khaffit* approached, and Abban wondered if he would be able to control himself.

'Don't just stand there, open the door,' Abban snapped. 'Or shall I tell the Deliverer you delayed my answering his summons?'

Hasik gaped and looked like he was going to choke on his own tongue. Abban watched in amusement as he sputtered, but he did at last open the portal.

Ahmann had made enough examples of those who would hinder Abban that even Hasik dare not do so. His eyes promised vengeance as Abban passed, but the *khaffit* only smiled in return.

There was a knot of *Damaji* and various hangers-on around Ahmann as Abban limped into the throne room, but Ahmann dismissed them with a wave. 'Leave us.'

The men all shot glares at Abban, but none dared disobey. Ahmann led the way into a smaller side chamber. There was a great oval table of dark polished wood surrounded by twenty chairs, a throne at its head. Behind the throne was a great map covering an entire wall, and the table was laden with fresh food and drink.

'She has left?' Ahmann asked when they were alone.

Abban nodded. 'Mistress Leesha has agreed to allow me to set up a trading post for the Hollow tribe. It will help facilitate their integration, and give us valuable contacts in the North.'

Ahmann nodded. 'Well done.'

'I will need men to guard the shipments, and the stores at the post,' Abban said. 'Before, I had servants for such heavy duty. *Khaffit*, perhaps, but fit men.'

'Such men are all *kha'Sharum* now,' Ahmann said.

Abban bowed. 'You see my difficulty. No *dal'Sharum* will take orders from *khaffit* in any event, but if you would allow me to select a few *kha'Sharum* to serve me in this regard, it would be most satisfactory.'

Ahmann's eyes narrowed. He was guileless, but no fool. 'How many?'

Abban shrugged. 'I could make do with a hundred. A pittance.'

'No warrior, even a *kha'Sharum*, is a pittance, Abban,' Ahmann said.

Abban bowed. 'I will pay their family stipends from my own coffers, of course.'

Ahmann considered a moment longer, then shrugged. 'Pick your hundred.'

Abban bowed as deeply as his crutch allowed. 'I will need a drillmaster to continue their training.'

Ahmann shook his head. 'That, my friend, I cannot spare.'

Abban smiled. 'I was thinking perhaps Master Qeran.' Qeran had been one of Abban and Ahmann's own drillmasters when they were in *sharaj*. He was harsh, bigoted, and hated *khaffit* with a passion. He had also had his leg bitten so badly by a field demon that the *dama'ting* had been forced to amputate it. The drillmaster had healed, but his pride had not.

Ahmann looked at him in surprise. 'Qeran? Who struck me for not dropping you to your death?'

Abban bowed. 'The same. If the Deliverer himself decided to spare me, and has come to see my uses, perhaps the drillmaster will, too. He has been having a difficult time of late it seems. He still teaches in *sharaj*, but the *nie'Sharum* do not respect him as they once did.'

Ahmann grunted. '*Nie'Sharum* are ever fools until blooded, but there will be blood for all soon enough. If you wish Qeran to work for you, you may ask him, but I will not command it.'

Abban bowed again. 'Will your promises to the mistress of the Hollow tribe alter your plans?'

Ahmann shook his head. 'My promises affect nothing. It is still my duty to unite the people of the Northland for Sharak Ka. We will march on Lakton in the spring.'

Abban pursed his lips at that, but nodded.

'You think it a mistake,' Ahmann said. 'You would have me wait.'

Abban bowed. 'Not at all. I am told you have already begun recalling your forces.'

Ahmann nodded. 'We have angered Alagai Ka by killing the demon princeling. The next Waning will bring the opening salvos of Sharak Ka. I can feel it in my heart. We must be ready.'

'Of course,' Abban agreed. 'The *chin* are pacified and will offer little resistance even as you remove most of your warriors from their lands. Their women properly scarved, their sons taken for *Hannu Pash,* and their men enslaved. It will be years, though, before the boys are old enough to test as *dal'Sharum,* and their fathers, the *chi'Sharum,* are not progressing well in their training, I hear.'

Ahmann raised a brow at him. 'You hear much from the *Sharum* pavilions, *khaffit.*'

Abban only smiled. 'My leg may be crippled, my friend, but my ears are sharp.'

'The boys taken for *Hannu Pash* have been separated from their families, and are young enough to forget the old ways,' Ahmann said. 'Many of them will be fine *dal'Sharum,* and a few of them valuable *dama* we can use to proselytize in the green lands. Their fathers, however, remember too much and learn too little. Most will never open their hearts to the honour we offer them by training them to fight in Sharak Ka.'

'First you ask them to fight Sharak Sun against their greenland brothers,' Abban noted. 'That is a difficult thing for any man.'

'The Daylight War has been foretold,' Ahmann said. 'It cannot be denied if we are to win against the *alagai* and rid the world of their taint forever.'

'Prophecies are vague things, Ahmann, oft misunderstood until it is too late. All the stories in the Evejah tell us so.' Abban held up his ledger, a heavy book with huge pages, all filled with neat, tiny lines of indecipherable code. 'Profit margins speak clearer truth.'

'So we will make of them a blunt instrument,' Ahmann said. 'Fodder for the slings and arrows of the enemy. They will be the shield of my army, even as the true *Sharum* are its spear.'

'Your spears will have fine mounts, at least,' Abban said. 'We pride ourselves on our breeding in Krasia, but the herds of wild horses roaming the grasslands of Everam's Bounty put them to shame. Mustang, the *chin* call them. Enormous, powerful beasts.'

Ahmann grunted. 'They would have to be, to survive the night.'

'The *dal'Sharum* have proven exceptional at hunting and breaking them,' Abban said. 'Your armies will be quick, and little will stand in the way of their charge.'

Ahmann nodded in satisfaction. 'Spring cannot come soon enough. Every day we wait, our enemies have time to gather their forces.'

'I agree,' Abban said. 'Which is why you should not wait. Attack Lakton on first snow.'

Ahmann looked at him in surprise, but Abban kept his face blank. It pleased him to so shock his friend.

'Since when does Abban the coward ever suggest attack?' Ahmann asked.

Abban held up his ledger. 'When it is profitable.'

Ahmann looked at him a long time, then went and poured himself a goblet of nectar, sitting on his throne. He gestured at Abban to sit. 'Very well. Tell me your prophecy of profit. How am I to know when the first snow will come? Are you now *dama'ting*, to see the future?'

Abban smiled and took a goblet of his own, sitting at the table and opening his ledger. 'First snow is not an event, but a specific date in the Thesan calendar. Thirty days after autumn equinox. In Lakton, it is significant because it is when the harvest tithe from the hamlets is due to the Laktonian duke.'

'And you want us to steal it,' Ahmann surmised.

'Spears are useless when carried by men with empty stomachs, Ahmann,' Abban said. 'Your army almost starved this past winter, especially after that fool *dama* set fire to the grain silos. We cannot afford another such blunder.'

'Agreed,' Ahmann said, 'but now we control the largest swathe of farmland in the North. What need have we for more?'

'We do,' Abban agreed, 'but so, too, has your army grown. There are now *chi'Sharum* in the thousands, and you have a growing nation to hold and feed. More than that, you must deprive Lakton of their winter stores. The city is built on a body of water so great, they say that from its centre one cannot see the shore in any direction.'

'It seems impossible,' Ahmann gestured to the great map on the wall, 'but the greenlanders would appear to agree.'

'No scorpion bolts or arrows will reach the city from the shore,' Abban said. 'If they can take their ships to the city full of provision, it may be a year or more before you can dislodge them.'

Ahmann steepled his fingers. 'What do you propose?'

Abban rose heavily, leaning on his camel crutch as he limped over to the great map on the wall. Ahmann turned to regard the *khaffit* with interest.

'Like Everam's Bounty, Lakton has an eponymous city proper.' He pointed with the tip of his crutch to the great lake and the city close to its western shore. 'And dozens of hamlets throughout the duchy.' He moved the head of his crutch in a circular motion around a much larger swathe of land. 'These hamlets have land as fertile as Everam's Bounty, with harvests nearly as prodigious, and they are all but unguarded.'

'Then why not simply annex the hamlets and have done?' Ahmann said.

Abban shook his head, waving his crutch over the area again. 'The land is too vast to simply take. You do not have enough men, and would then need to harvest them yourself, if the inhabitants did not burn the fields the moment they saw your army on the horizon. Many would slip through your fingers, reaching the city in time for the dockmasters to pull stores and weigh anchor, locking the city tight.

'Better to wait for first snow, and attack here.' He pointed to a large village on the lake's western shore. 'Docktown. It is here the *chin* will bring their tithe, to be tallied by the dockmasters, loaded onto ships, and sent to the city on the lake. The dockmasters' entire fleet will be docked or at anchor, waiting to fill their holds.

'Docktown is weakly fortified, and will not be expecting an attack without warning so late in the season. But your army will be quick atop their mustang. An elite group could capture the entire harvest, the majority of Lakton's docks, and half its fleet. Send your blunt instrument in behind to crush the hamlets once the surprise is done. Focus first on those along the lake-shore, denying safe harbour, and the Laktonians will be trapped on their island all winter without proper provision. Come spring, they may surrender without a fight, and if not, you will have ships of your own to fill with *Sharum* to take the city.'

Ahmann stared at the map a long time, frowning. 'I will think on this.'

You will consult Inevera's dice, you mean, Abban thought, but he was wise enough to keep silent about it. It would be well enough to consult the *hora* before such a risky undertaking.

With Ahmann's writ in hand, Abban limped into the training grounds, headed for the Kaji'sharaj.

He was spotted immediately by Jurim, who had trained with him when they were both boys. Jurim had laughed when Abban fell from the Maze wall – shattering his leg – and had himself been cast down by Drillmaster Qeran as punishment. But while Abban remained forever crippled, Jurim had recovered fully. And he had not forgotten.

The warrior was taking his ease with others by the Kaji pavilion, enjoying cups of couzi and playing Sharak. It was a game Abban had been surprised to learn the greenlanders played as well, though they called it Succour and had different rules. One *Sharum* clattered the dice in a cup and threw, roaring with victory to the scowls of the others.

'What are you doing here among men, *khaffit*?' Jurim cried. The other warriors looked up at that. Abban's heart sank at the sight of two of them, Fahki and Shusten.

His own sons.

Jurim rose to his feet, showing no sign that his back had been whipped raw barely a week past. He had always been a quick healer, even before he began absorbing demon magic at night.

The warrior approached, looming. Abban was by no means short, but Jurim was taller still and blade-thin, while fat Abban was stooped by weight and forced to lean on his crutch.

Jurim did not dare touch Abban – even with Ahmann nowhere in sight – but like Hasik, he missed no opportunity to hurt and humiliate his former classmate. While Hasik took his hatred out on Abban's women, Jurim and Shanjat cut as deeply through his sons. The older men were Spears of the Deliverer after all, the most famed – and deadly – of the Shar'Dama Ka's warriors, seasoned by battle and kept young and strong by the magic they absorbed on a nightly basis. Fahki and Shusten worshipped them.

The young men followed Jurim, but there was no greeting for Abban, not so much as the slightest acknowledgement in their eyes. Indeed, they looked at the ground, each other, off into the distance – anywhere save at their father. In a culture where the name of a man's father was more important than one's own, there could be no greater insult.

'Your sons have made fine warriors,' Jurim congratulated. 'They were soft at first – as expected for blood of *khaffit*,' Fahki spat in the dust at that, 'but I have taken them under my shield, and found the steel in them.' He smirked. 'They must get it from their mother.'

All three warriors laughed at that, and Abban gripped the ivory haft of his crutch so tightly his hand ached. Its hidden blade was poisoned, and he could put it into Jurim's foot before he ever saw the blow coming. But while it might earn him a moment's respect in the eyes of his sons, it would be short-lived. Poison was a coward's weapon after all, and it was death for a *khaffit* to strike a *Sharum* for any reason. Had he been anyone but the favourite advisor of the Deliverer, even speaking disrespectfully could earn him a spear in the chest.

Fahki and Shusten glared at him with barely hidden disgust. If he struck, they would turn him in to the nearest *dama* without hesitation, and his sentence would be carried out before Ahmann ever heard of it.

Abban kept his face blank and forced himself to bow, holding up the scroll with the Deliverer's seal. Jurim, like many warriors, could not read, but he knew the crown and spear well. 'I am here on the business of Shar'Dama Ka.'

Jurim scowled. 'And what business is so important that you must sully the ground of warriors?'

Abban straightened. 'That is not for you to know. Take me to Drillmaster Qeran, and be quick about it.'

Shusten snarled. 'Do not take that tone with your betters, *khaffit*!'

Abban snapped a cold glare at him. 'You may have inherited your mother's steel, boy, but obviously not her brains if you would hinder the will of Shar'Dama Ka. Go find something useful to do or the next time I speak with him, I will mention to the Deliverer how his *Sharum* waste their days playing Sharak and drinking couzi when they should be training.'

The boys blanched at that, glancing at each other before hurrying off. Abban felt a cold satisfaction, but it did nothing to stem the blood from the knife twisting in his heart. That other men sneered at him for his crippled leg and coward's heart, Abban had learned to live with. But a man that did not have the respect of his own sons was no man at all.

Soon, he promised himself. *Soon*.

Many of the *Sharum* flouted the restrictions of the Evejah, drinking couzi to give them courage in the night, and to forget the nights in the day. Few, though, were fool enough to get so drunk they could not stand at attention should a *dama* pass them by.

Qeran was that drunk and more. The drillmaster sat on a stained pillow with his back supported by the tent's central pole, his black robes wet and stinking of vomit. Next to him lay his fine warded spear, a special crossbar added to allow him to use the weapon as a crutch. His left leg ended just below the knee, the leg of his pantaloons pinned back. Strapped to the stump was a simple wooden peg.

He glared at Abban as the *khaffit* entered, small eyes hard with hatred. 'Come to gloat, *khaffit*? I'm nearly as useless as you now, but at least my place in Heaven is secure.'

Abban let the tent flap fall closed, leaving the two men alone. Then he spat at Qeran's feet.

'I am not useless, Drillmaster. I serve our master every day, and never once have I whined like a woman over my fate, much less drunk myself into a piss pool. Everam blessed you with a strong body, but I see without it, your heart is weak.'

Qeran's face twisted with rage and he grabbed for his spear, meaning to leap to his feet and thrust it through Abban's heart. But he was new to his wooden leg, and unsteady from the couzi. He stumbled, and it was all the time Abban needed to strike the peg hard with his crutch, knocking it clean off the drillmaster's leg. As Qeran fell, he struck again, knocking away the spear.

The drillmaster hit the ground hard, and there was a click as Abban's hidden blade snapped open, pointing right between his eyes.

'You have killed many demons in your day, Drillmaster,' Abban said, 'but will even your place in Heaven remain secure if you are killed in your own filth by the crippled *khaffit* you cast from *sharaj* in shame?'

Qeran remained still a long time, his hard eyes nearly crossed as they watched the blade hovering at the bridge of his nose. 'What do you want?' he said at last.

Abban smiled, stepping back and retracting his blade so he could lean on his crutch as he bowed. From within his brightly coloured vest he produced the scroll marked with the Deliverer's seal. 'Why, to make you great again.'

Abban and Qeran drew many stares as they limped through the training ground toward the Kaji *khaffit'sharaj*. The drillmaster had been stripped by one of the *jiwah'Sharum*, doused in clean water, and dressed in fresh blacks. Abban knew without doubt that his head was pounding from the couzi as he squinted in the bright light of day, but the drillmaster had recovered something of himself and showed nothing of his discomfort. His back was straight as he walked, head high. As was the custom, Abban walked a step behind him, though he could easily have outpaced the slow gait Qeran required to walk with dignity.

They came to a section of grounds where tan-robed *kha'Sharum* trained – thousands in the Kaji tribe alone. Most practised the simple spear and shield forms Abban remembered from what seemed a lifetime ago, turning in unison, shields overlapping as they thrust their spears as one. A smaller group practised more advanced techniques.

Qeran spat. 'Most of these men should still be in bidos, or better yet carrying water and polishing shields.'

A handful of young *Sharum* walked the ranks. They wore black, but the veils hanging loose around their necks were tan, marking them as *khaffit* drillmasters.

'Pups,' Qeran sneered, 'sharpening their teeth on *khaffit* in hope of earning the red.'

One of the young drillmasters caught sight of them and approached, eyeing them with wary disdain until his eyes lighted on Qeran's red veil. His eyes flicked up and lit with recognition as he met the drillmaster's face. Qeran had been among the Spears of the Deliverer, and his reputation was well known. He and Drillmaster Kaval had trained the Shar'Dama Ka himself.

The young drillmaster bowed, ignoring Abban completely. 'I am Hamash asu Gimas am'Tesan am'Kaji.'

Qeran returned his bow with a slight nod. 'I trained your father. Gimas was a fierce warrior. He died well in the Maze.'

Hamash bowed again, more deeply this time. 'What brings you to the *khaffit'sharaj*, honoured Drillmaster?'

Abban limped forward, holding out his writ. Drillmasters, like *kai'Sharum*, were given special training that included letters and warding, but from the way Hamash's brow furrowed as he stared at the writ, he had obviously fallen short in his lessons.

Abban let the failing pass. It was to his advantage. 'The Deliverer requires ten of your best *kha'Sharum*. I am to select them.'

'You, a *khaffit*, mean to select warriors?' Hamash said, eyes flicking to Qeran.

Abban smiled. 'Who better? They are *khaffit* warriors, after all.'

'Warriors, still,' the young drillmaster growled.

'Drillmaster Qeran will ensure they are fit to fight,' Abban said. 'I am to ensure they have brains in their heads.'

'Only ten?' Qeran asked quietly, too low for Hamash to hear. 'You told me the Shar'Dama Ka commanded a hundred.'

'The Deliverer has no tribe, Drillmaster,' Abban said. 'We will select ten from each.'

'That is more than a hundred,' Qeran said. There were twelve tribes of Krasia.

Smart for a Sharum, Abban mused. 'I remember your training methods well, Drillmaster. There will be those who will not survive its rigours, and others who will not be fit for battle when you are finished.' He tapped his own leg pointedly with his crutch. 'We will start with one hundred and twenty, that you may kill or cast out those who fail you.'

318

Qeran grunted, and Hamash, who had been watching the exchange, met his eyes. His lip curled slightly in disgust. 'Even a crippled drillmaster should not allow a *khaffit* to speak so boldly to him.'

Qeran's calm eyes revealed nothing of his intentions as his spear haft snapped upward, taking Hamash between the legs. The young drillmaster bent forward, and Qeran spun the weapon, cracking it hard against the side of his head, knocking him to the ground.

Hamash was quick to roll aside, but Qeran anticipated the move, slamming the metal butt of his spear down just as he rolled into the blow. Hamash's cheek tore open as several of his teeth shattered. He coughed blood and shards, trying vainly to regain his feet, but the beating did not stop there. Qeran had firm footing, and struck again and again. Most of the blows were painful but not meant for lasting damage, but when the young drillmaster continued to resist, there was a sharp crack as Qeran's spear butt broke his right arm at the elbow. He roared with pain.

'Embrace the pain and be silent, fool!' Qeran hissed. 'Your men are watching!' Indeed, drillmasters and *kha'Sharum* alike had stopped their training, watching with mouths hanging open.

Qeran turned to look at the other drillmasters. 'Strip the men to their bidos and form squads for inspection!' he roared, and they scrambled as if the command had come from the Deliverer himself. In moments their spears and shields were neatly stacked, robes folded, and the men stood at attention in nothing but their tan loincloths.

Qeran jabbed the butt of his spear into Hamash, still writhing on the ground. 'On your feet and heel me. I will already have your tan veil. Fall behind or disrespect me again and I'll have your blacks as well.'

Abban resisted the urge to smile as Hamash struggled to his feet, his face pale and bloody. He had chosen his drillmaster well.

Looking pale and dazed, blood running down his face, Hamash stumbled after as they limped over to the first squad. Another tan-veiled drillmaster stood at attention before them. His bow to Qeran was so low, his beard nearly touched the ground.

They walked the line, Qeran calling each man forth, treating them no differently than slaves on the auction block.

'Flabby,' Qeran noted of the first, pinching at his arm, 'but a few months of gruel and carrying stones as he runs around the city walls would cure him of that. Perform the first *sharukin*.' The man began to sweat, but he complied, moving slowly through the series of movements.

Qeran spat in the dust. 'Pathetic, even for a *khaffit*.'

'What was your profession before you answered the Deliverer's call to *sharak*?' Abban asked the man, taking out his ledger and pen.

'I was a lamp maker,' the man said.

Abban grunted. 'Were you master or apprentice?'

'Master,' the man said. 'My father owned our business, but left me to train my sons.'

'What difference does this make?' Qeran demanded, but Abban ignored him, asking several more questions before moving to the next in line. He was so thin his bones showed through his skin as he stood in his bido. His eyes squinted as they came to stand before him.

Abban held up three fingers. 'How many?'

The man squinted harder. 'Two.' There was doubt in his voice.

Abban took several steps back, and the squinting stopped. 'Three,' the man said more decisively.

Qeran gave the spindly man a shove and he fell onto his back in the dirt.

'On your feet, dog!' one of the tan-veiled drillmasters shouted, whacking at him with a spear butt, and the man quickly got back in line.

'This one does not even belong here, much less among the Deliverer's elite,' Qeran said.

Again Abban ignored him, still facing the man. 'Can you read? Do sums on a bead lattice?'

The man nodded. 'I can, when I have my lenses.'

They continued on thusly, Qeran pinching and prodding the men as Abban interrogated them. Some few were ordered to stand apart from the others, a group of potentials for Abban and Qeran to choose from.

They approached one who stood a head and more higher than all the others, his chest broad and his arms thick with muscle. Abban smiled.

'You will not want that one,' one of the drillmasters advised. 'He is strong as a herd of camels, but he cannot hear the signal horns – or anything else for that matter.'

'You were not asked,' Abban said. 'I remember this one. He was one of the first to answer the Deliverer's call. What is his name?'

The drillmaster shrugged. 'No one knows. We simply call him Earless.'

Abban made a few sharp gestures, and the giant left the line to stand with the other potentials.

There were over a thousand Kaji *kha'Sharum* in the capital. When the *dama* sang the curfew from the minarets, they had barely seen half of them. They culled from the potentials as they went, but still there were more than fifty men following them. Abban and Qeran took these into the pavilion, testing and interrogating them further until the group was narrowed to twenty, then ten, until at last they agreed upon four, including the deaf and mute giant.

Qeran argued against the giant. 'A warrior who cannot hear the horns is a liability.'

'In *alagai'sharak*, perhaps,' Abban agreed, 'but as the *dama'ting* have their tongueless eunuchs, I can make good use of a man who will never overhear anything he shouldn't.'

They returned the next day after court, spending every moment until sundown inspecting, testing, questioning, and arguing until satisfied. Six times, Qeran threatened to quit if Abban overruled him on a particular man.

'Go, then,' Abban said over the seventh, a pit dog from Sandstone. He was a powerful brute, but his eyes were glassy with stupidity, and he could barely count his fingers. 'I will not have idiot soldiers.' The brute glared at Abban, but Earless towered behind him, arms crossed, and he thought better of speaking.

Qeran glared at him, but Abban glared right back. At last, the drillmaster shrugged. 'Would that you had such steel when you were a boy, I could have made a man of you.'

Abban smiled and gave a slight bow. 'It was always there, Drillmaster. Just not for battle.'

'You have a good eye,' Qeran offered grudgingly in the end, as he looked over his ten new recruits. 'I can make warriors of these men.'

'Good,' Abban said. 'Tomorrow we will go to the Majah *khaffit'sharaj* and begin again.'

It was another day to vet the Majah, a third for the Mehnding. It went more quickly after that, the tribes shrinking in size as they went down the line of pavilions in the training ground. The smallest was the Sharach with only three dozen full *dal'Sharum* and barely a hundred *kha'Sharum*.

'We passed over hundreds of better men in the Kaji,' Qeran noted after they had selected the best the Sharach had to offer. Like many of the older warriors, trained before Ahmann united the tribes, Qeran was fiercely loyal to his own and would prefer the majority of his recruits share his blood.

Abban nodded. 'But the Sharach are masters of the *alagai*-catcher.' Indeed, they had watched the Sharach warriors drilling with the weapons, long hollow spears with a hoop of woven steel jutting from the butt end to loop around the neck of a demon or man. A lever near the crosspiece could quickly widen or constrict the hoop. There were *sharusahk* forms to leverage the weapon, keeping control of the victim.

'I can teach the weapon well enough,' Qeran said.

'Well enough is not good enough, Drillmaster,' Abban said.

The drillmaster showed his teeth. 'I taught the Deliverer himself to fight. That is not good enough?'

Abban was unimpressed. 'You taught him much, but the *dama* taught him more, and it was blending the two that gave him true mastery. Ahmann studies the *sharukin* of all tribes now, and you will, too. You will teach these men, but you will also learn all they know. The Nanji spear and chain. The Krevakh ladder techniques. Everything. And if you are not up to the task, I will find one who is.'

'I can learn the tricks of lesser tribes,' Qeran growled.

'Of course,' Abban agreed. 'And improve many of them, no doubt. I chose the greatest living drillmaster for a reason. You will make the least of these men more than a match for any *kai'Sharum*.'

Qeran seemed mollified by that. *Sharum* were such simple creatures. A bit of lash with a compliment at the end, and they were yours.

'I cannot teach them the secrets of the *dama* that *kai'Sharum* learn,' Qeran admitted.

Abban smiled. 'Let me worry about that, Drillmaster.'

A wooden palisade had gone up around Abban's compound by the time he and Qeran marched in the 120 *kha'Sharum*. The stakes were planted deeply and lashed tight to give no sign of what went on behind them, but they were carefully worn to look haphazard and weak. The wards along its length were strong, but painted with no artistry – nothing to draw attention to what might be going on behind.

It was, of course, an elaborate disguise. Once inside, Qeran gaped. Hundreds of *chin* slaves laboured to haul and mortar fine cut stone into the true wall – already waist-high – just inside the palisade. Others cleared rubble from the remains of the shoddy greenland homes that had previously populated the area. Great pavilions had been raised, some venting great plumes of smoke. The sounds of ringing metal, smashing stone, and shouting workers filled the compound.

'You're building a fortress,' Qeran said.

'A fortress from which we will arm and armour the forces of Sharak Ka,' Abban said. 'A fortress that must be protected, especially now, when it is weakest.'

For perhaps the first time since Abban had come upon him in a drunken stupor, Qeran smiled, his trained eyes dancing along the palisade and the foundation of the inner wall. 'Leave that to me. Your *kha'Sharum* will be patrolling in shifts by nightfall.'

'That will do for now, but it will not be enough,' Abban said. 'My agents have purchased many slaves from the auction block, and their labours have made them hard, but they are not warriors. You must train them as well.'

'I have never been comfortable with Shar'Dama Ka's decision to arm the *chin*,' Qeran said. 'The Evejah tells us to disarm our enemies, not train them.'

'Your comfort is irrelevant, Drillmaster,' Abban said. 'The Shar'Dama Ka has spoken. These are not enemies, they are slaves, and I do not mistreat them. They sleep in warmth with full bellies, many of them beside their own families, safe from predation.'

'You are a fool to trust them,' Qeran said.

Abban laughed in spite of himself, forced to stop walking and clutch his crutch for balance. He wiped a tear from his eye as he looked at Qeran, who scowled, unsure if he were the butt of the joke. 'Trust?' He chuckled again. 'Drillmaster, I do not trust anyone.'

Qeran grunted at that, and they continued their tour. Abban led him to the armourer's pavilion, where metal rang and the forges burned hot. Even with fanned vents along the walls, the air inside was stifling, thick with smoke, heat, and the steam of quenching troughs. Artisan stalls ran the length of the pavilion – forges of metal or glass, blacksmiths, grinders, woodworkers, fletchers, weavers, and warders.

Each stall was run by several women in the thick black robes of *dal'ting*, seemingly oblivious to the damp heat. Qeran, too, showed no sign of discomfort, though he had taken on the rhythmic breathing of a *Sharum* embracing pain.

Abban took a deep breath of the hot, foul air and let out a contented breath, as if tasting the finest tobacco from his hookah. It was the atmosphere of profit.

In the centre of the pavilion were neat, growing stacks of finished products: spears, shields, ladders, hooks and lines, *alagai*-catchers, as well as the smaller – though no less deadly – weapons Watchers concealed about their persons. Scorpion stingers by the gross, and the giant cart-driven bows to launch them.

The drillmaster selected a spear at random from a pile, setting his peg leg firmly and putting it through a series of spins and thrusts. 'It's so light.'

Abban nodded. 'The greenlanders have a tree called the goldwood, and true to its name, it is worth its weight in precious metal. Goldwood is lighter and stronger than the rattan used for *Sharum* spears in Krasia, and needs less lacquer to harden the wards carved along its length.'

Qeran tested the tip against the meat of his palm, smiling broadly as the point slid in easily with only the barest pressure. 'What metal is this, to hold such an edge?'

'No metal,' Abban said. 'Glass.'

'Glass?' Qeran asked. 'Impossible. It would shatter on the first blow.'

Abban pointed to a cold anvil in one of the forge stalls, and Qeran did not hesitate, limping over and bringing the spear down on it hard enough to break even a steel blade. But there was only a ringing in the air, and a notch in the anvil.

'A trick we learned from the Hollow tribe,' Abban said. 'Warded glass – lighter and stronger than steel, and hard enough to hold the sharpest edge. We silver the glass to obscure its nature.'

He took Qeran to another stall, handing him a ceramic plate. 'These plates are what *dal'Sharum* currently wear in the pockets of their robes.'

'I am familiar,' Qeran said drily.

'Then you know they break on impact, proof against one blow at most, and often making a powerful hit all the worse with shrapnel,' Abban said.

Qeran shrugged.

Abban gave him a second plate, this one of clear, warded glass that glittered in the light of the forge. 'Thinner, lighter, and strong enough to break a rock demon's claw.'

'The Deliverer's army will be unstoppable,' Qeran breathed.

Abban chuckled. 'No ordinary *dal'Sharum* could afford such armament, Drillmaster, but nothing is too good for the Spears of the Deliverer.' He winked. 'Or my Hundred. Your recruits will be better equipped than all but the Shar'Dama Ka's elite.'

Abban saw the glitter of greed that shone in the drillmaster's eyes at that, and smiled. *One more gift, and he will be mine.*

'Come,' he said. 'No drillmaster in my employ will hobble on a cheap peg.'

Abban watched in satisfaction as Qeran paced before the *khaffit* and *chin* he had selected for training. The drillmaster's peg had been thrown on the fire, replaced by a curved sheet of warded spring steel. It was simple, elegant, and gave him the potential to regain almost all the combat ability he had lost. He still used his spear for balance, but was becoming more sure-footed by the moment.

The men had been stripped down to bidos, their robes and other clothing burned. The *khaffit* wore tan, the *chin* a cloth the colour of green olives.

'I do not care what titles the paltry excuses for drillmasters in *sharaj* gave you,' Qeran shouted. 'You are all *nie'Sharum* to me, and will be until you have proven yourselves. If you do well, you will be rewarded. A warrior's robes and veil. Fine weapons and armour. Better food. Women. If you shame me,' he stopped, looking just over the heads of the crowd, seeming to stare in all their eyes at once, 'I will kill you.'

The men stood stock-still, backs arched and chests thrown forward, more than a few sweating and pale, even in the cool morning air. Qeran turned to Abban and nodded.

'Now,' Abban murmured to his nephew Jamere, but the young *dama* was already striding forward. He was tall but not thin, having never partaken in the dietary restrictions of the Evejah. Neither was he fat, moving with the fluid grace that marked Evejan clerics. Jamere had lived in Sharik Hora most of his life, and had copied or pilfered the secret *sharusahk* manuals of almost every tribe, mastering forbidden techniques. Skills he was all too happy to sell his uncle.

'Kneel before Dama Jamere!' Kaval barked, and the men fell immediately to their knees, none hesitating to put their palms in the dust.

Jamere held up his hands. In one, he held the writ Ahmann had signed, and in the other, the Evejah. 'Loyal *nie'Sharum*! Ahmann asu Hoshkamin am'Jardir am'Kaji, Shar'Dama Ka and Everam's voice on Ala, has given you to his servant Abban. It was Abban who brought the Deliverer's eyes to you, giving men cast from Everam's light a chance at redemption, a chance to prove your loyalty.'

He swept his gaze over the assembled men. 'Are you loyal?'

'Yes, Dama!' they shouted as one.

'Everam is watching!' Jamere cried, sweeping his hands up to the sun. 'Those who serve with loyalty and faith will see their rewards both on Ala and in Heaven. Those who break their oaths or fail in their duty will suffer greatly in their final hours before He casts their spirits down into Nie's abyss.'

Abban suppressed a snicker. The fanatical light in his nephew's eyes was nothing but a practised act, like that of a Northern Jongleur. The man was utterly faithless, and had been since before he was called by the clerics.

But the fear in the eyes of the men showed that his veil was perfect. Even Qeran seemed cowed as Jamere held out a copy of the Evejah.

'Your spear hand,' Jamere commanded, and the drillmaster laid his right hand on the worn leather.

'Do you swear to serve Abban asu Chabin am'Haman am'Kaji?' Jamere asked. 'To protect him and obey him and no other save the Deliverer himself, from now until your death?'

Qeran hesitated. His eyes flicked to Abban, his brows bunching together in outrage. When the three men had met earlier to rehearse the oath-taking, no one had mentioned the drillmaster would be included. It was one thing for Abban to demand oaths from *khaffit* and *chin*, but another to expect one from a *dal'Sharum* drillmaster of Qeran's stature.

Abban smiled in return. *Make your choice, Drillmaster*, he thought. *Everam is watching, and you cannot take it back. Serve me, or go back to walking on a cheap peg and sleeping in your own vomit.*

Qeran knew it, too. Abban had given him a path to glory, but glory had its price. The drillmaster looked to the waiting *nie'Sharum*, knowing that every second of hesitation would be a doubt he would have to beat from the men.

'I swear to serve Abban,' he growled at last, meeting Abban's eyes, 'until my death, or the Deliverer relieve me of the oath.'

Abban reached into his vest, producing a flask of couzi. He lifted it in salute to the warrior and drank.

13

Playing the Crowd

333 AR Summer
28 Dawns Before New Moon

Leesha looked at the darkening sky and had to press a palm to her eye socket, easing a throb of pain. With their late start from Ahmann's palace, the caravan to Deliverer's Hollow made little progress that first day – perhaps ten miles. A Messenger might make the trip from Fort Rizon to Deliverer's Hollow in under two weeks. The Spears of the Deliverer, fearing no demons and travelling at speed even at night, had done it in half that. Even the ride out had been swift as these things go, despite a slow cart to accommodate her parents, unaccustomed to the road.

Leesha's father had never been robust even when young, and he was far from young now. Erny had back spasms daily on the journey out, and she'd been forced to give him relaxants that made him sleep like the dead. They rode in a far more comfortable carriage for the return, but while he never complained, Leesha saw him rubbing his back when he thought no one was looking, and knew the journey would be hard on him.

'We should stop soon for the night,' she told Shamavah, who shared the carriage with Leesha and her parents – at least when she wasn't out shouting at the other women. Krasian women had their own pecking order, and it did not matter that Shamavah was the wife of a *khaffit*. All of the women – and the *kha'Sharum* as well – hopped at her commands, keeping the caravan in proper order.

Still, the heavily laden carts moved at a crawl that seemed to chafe at the jet-black chargers of the *dal'Sharum* and even the sturdy garrons Gared and Wonda rode. Leesha remembered Ahmann's warning of bandits and bit her lip. Even in Krasian lands, there were many who would wish her dead. Beyond, the cartloads of food and clothing in the caravan might make them too much to resist for those who had lost everything when the Krasians came and took their homes. The *Sharum* would deter smaller bands, but there were women and children to hostage, and Leesha knew well that bandits would exploit such weaknesses.

'Of course.' Shamavah's Thesan was almost as flawless as her husband's. 'There is a village, Kajiton, just over the next hill, and riders have already been sent to prepare a proper reception.'

Kajiton. The name of the Krasian Deliverer with a Thesan suffix. It said much about the state of Rizon . . . or Everam's Bounty, as she had best get used to calling it. Ahmann had given land to his tribes like a man slicing a birthday cake for his family, and while the hamlets had not been taken as brutally as Fort Rizon itself, it was clear from Leesha's carriage window that the tribes had dug in, and Evejan law taken a firm hold.

There was no sign of any men of fighting age, save for those weak or infirm, and the Thesan women toiling in the fields did so in dresses of dark, sombre colour that covered them from ankle to neck, hair wrapped carefully in scarves. When the *dama* sang the call to prayer, or even came in sight, they were quick to prostrate themselves. The smell of hot Krasian spices drifted on the air, and a pidgin, part Krasian and part Thesan mixed with hand signs and facial expressions, was emerging.

The duchy she had known was gone, and even if the Krasians were somehow driven off, it was doubtful it would ever return.

'Proper reception' turned out to be almost everyone in the village bowing and scraping as they rode past, and the town inn emptied save for the staff. While thousands of people had fled the Krasian advance, forming refugee groups that swelled every hamlet and city north and east of Everam's Bounty, it was clear that far more stayed behind, or were captured and herded back. There were hundreds of Thesans still in Kajiton alone. The land in Rizon was fertile, and the population was greater than all the other duchies combined.

As they rode into the town square, Leesha saw a large stake at its centre with a woman hanging limply from wrists chained high above her head. She was obviously dead, and the marks on her naked body, as well as the small stones that lay scattered about her, made clear the cause. A sign atop the stake had a single word in flowing Krasian script, but Leesha needed no translator, having seen it often enough in the Evejah.

Adulterer.

The pain in her head flared again, and she thought she might throw up in the carriage. She fumbled in the pockets of her apron, taking a root and a handful of leaves, popping them into her mouth without bothering to brew them into something palatable. They chewed into a bitter cure, but it settled her stomach. It would not do to show the Krasians her weakness.

They pulled up, and children scattered flower petals from the carriage doors to the steps of the inn, acting as if there were not a rotting corpse a few dozen feet away.

'Children can adapt to anything,' Bruna used to say, and it was true enough in Leesha's experience, but no child should have to adapt to this.

The local *dama* awaited them, looking like he was carved from solid oak. His beard was iron grey and his eyes the blue of slate. Kaval, leading the procession, reined and leapt from his horse with an agility that belied the grey streaks in his beard, bowing to the *dama* and exchanging a few words. The cleric gave a shallow bow as Leesha stepped down from her carriage.

'So this is the Northern witch who has beguiled Shar'Dama Ka,' he muttered to Kaval in Krasian.

The scent of the petals under her feet did not cover the smell of death, and pain and outrage made her feel murderous. Now he presumed to judge her as well? It was all Leesha could do not to pull the knife from her belt and bury it in his throat.

Instead she gave him the imperious stare she had learned from Inevera. 'The Northern witch understands you, Dama,' she said. 'What is your name, that I may tell Ahmann of your words of welcome?'

The cleric's eyes widened in shock. In Krasia, unmarried women spoke only when spoken to, and would not dare take such a tone with a *dama*, who could – and often would – kill them for such an affront.

But Leesha had spoken the words in Krasian, showing she knew their ways, and her use of the Deliverer's given name showed a familiarity that would make all but the most powerful *Damaji* wet their robes.

The *dama* hesitated, pride and the instinct for self-preservation at war on his face. In the end he bowed again, this time so deeply his long beard swept the dust. 'Dama Anju. Apologies, Holy Intended. I meant no disrespect.'

'In my land, those who mean no disrespect remember to speak respectfully,' Leesha said. She kept her words simple, her Krasian far from fluent. 'Now remove that woman's body and return it to her family to lay to rest according to their own custom. This is the wedding day of the Deliverer's eldest daughter to Rojer asu Jessum am'Inn am'Hollow, and its presence is an offence.'

She was not entirely within her rights to speak for Rojer, but by calling him 'am'Hollow' – rather than the proper 'am'Bridge' for his birth city of Riverbridge – she had named him as Hollow tribe, which made them family in the eyes of the Krasians.

Dama Anju's eyebrows began to twitch. Only *dama'ting*

332

dared take such a tone and order *dama* about, and then only because it was clearly stated in the Evejah that it was death and a denial of Heaven to harm or physically hinder one in any way. Leesha was no *dama'ting*, but her tone made it clear she believed her position as holy intended accorded her the same rights.

The *dama* stopped breathing, and Leesha knew she had pushed him too far. She watched his face redden as his anger built and reached into her apron for a pinch of Bruna's blinding powder. He would come at her in a moment, and she would put him down before everyone.

Anju began to move his feet.

'Do not,' Kaval warned, his voice a soft murmur.

The *dama* looked to the drillmaster and saw Kaval's hand was on his spear. There were other sounds, and Anju turned to see the *dal'Sharum* of Leesha's escort had done the same. Wonda had her bow trained on him, and Gared had his axe and machete in hand.

Anju eased into a more submissive posture, but his face was swollen and his breath quick and shallow. Leesha could not resist twisting the knife, meeting his eyes boldly. 'To honour this holy occasion, it would please the son of Jessum if you released seven *chin* slaves, one for each pillar of Heaven.'

The impotent rage she saw in the *dama*'s slate eyes was bittersweet. *The barest taste of what you deserve*, she thought.

Leesha swept away before Anju could respond further, heading for the inn. In her wake, she heard her orders being carried out, and kept her face serene, showing nothing of what she felt.

She was learning.

'Here we go again,' Leesha groaned as the singing stopped.

Rojer and his wives were a week married, but still the sounds from Rojer's carriage were a constant pendulum between the young women's singing and their wails of passion.

Sikvah began to cry out not long after, and Amanvah soon joined her. Leesha put her head in her hands, massaging her temples. The headache cycle had continued all week. The pain had receded, but there was tightness in the muscles around her left eye, a constant threat that it could return in force at any moment. 'Night, can't those tramps shut it for five minutes?'

'Not likely.' Elona sighed wistfully. 'Ent nothing like the dangle of an eighteen-year-old boy. They harden every time the wind blows, and get right back up ten minutes after you put them down.'

'Seems more like every three hours,' Leesha muttered.

Elona laughed. 'Still gets my respect, and I don't give it easy. That cock's got two young brides to please and from the sound of it, he lasts a lot longer than most boys his age . . . and some a good deal older.' Her eyes flicked to Erny, who looked like he wanted to crawl between the seat cushions. 'I take it back. You might have done well to keep that one for yourself.'

The cacophony increased, and Leesha shook her head. 'They're exaggerating. No one wails like that.'

'Well of course,' Elona said. 'Any new bride with half a mind knows to make her husband feel like king and explorer both, charting new territory to rule.' She looked at Leesha. 'Still, I think there's a bit of green in your eyes. Missing your Krasian lover?'

Leesha felt her face redden, and Erny looked at the door as if considering leaping from the moving carriage. 'It's not like that, Mother. I just don't trust them. They're spinning a spell around Rojer, but they're still loyal to Inevera. A fool could see it.'

'Clearly not,' Elona said, 'since the professional fool is missing it, though you're right enough. It's what I'd do. You, too. Did you leave the demon of the desert with a single seed in his pods before you left?'

Leesha sighed and put her head out the window, breathing

334

deeply of the fresh air as they trundled down the road. 'I'll just be glad when we're safe in the Hollow. We'll be leaving Everam's Bounty tomorrow.'

'Good riddance,' Elona said, spitting from her own window.

'Ay,' Leesha said, 'but the *Sharum* that keep us so safe here will attract attention we don't want outside the borders. Bandits and duke's men will be looking at our caravan hungrily, and Ahmann was right that twenty warriors might not be enough.'

'He offered more,' Elona noted.

Leesha nodded. 'But twenty warriors, however skilled, can only cause so much mischief in the Hollow. Any more begins to be a problem, and we have problems enough. Have you seen a single boy over the age of six since we left the city?'

Elona shook her head. 'They've all been taken for Hanna Pats, or whatever.'

'*Hannu Pash*,' Leesha said. 'Training and indoctrination. They'll speak Krasian like natives before long, and hold to the Evejan ways. In ten years, they will have an army that can crush the Free Cities like a child crushes an anthill.'

'Creator above,' Rojer gasped, gulping at the skin of cool water Sikvah brought to his lips. Amanvah stroked his sweat-matted hair, cooing softly as she nibbled his ear.

He had thought the Krasian women repressed, and perhaps they were in public, but alone with their husbands, it was a different tale. In the privacy of their carriage, Amanvah and Sikvah removed their plain robes, dressing in bright silks as garish as a Jongleur's motley. Half the cloth was so thin it was transparent, and the rest not much thicker, lined with thread-of-gold, lace, or embroidery. They still wore veils, but these were ornamental – colourful, diaphanous silk starting at the tip of their noses and ending just past their lips. Their hair was uncovered, oiled, and bound in gold.

'Our husband wields his spear better than a *Sharum*,' Amanvah said. Blood had marked her a virgin on their wedding day, but she was no less skilled at 'pillow dancing' than Sikvah.

'Jongleurs get a lot of practice,' Rojer said. 'Women used to throw themselves at my master, and I daresay I learned a trick or two, but – no offence – the two of you do things that would make the whores in Duke Rhinebeck's brothel blush.'

Sikvah laughed. 'The women of your Northern duke's harem were not trained in the Dama'ting Palace.'

Rojer shook his head. 'And I can't shake the feeling that you're still holding back.'

Amanvah kissed his ear so softly he shivered. 'There are seventy and seven ways to lie with a man,' she whispered, 'and we have years to share them all with you.'

Amanvah and Sikvah had proven to be nothing like he imagined. He thought them much alike at first, but the more he got to know them, the more he saw how unique they were. Amanvah was taller, with smaller breasts and long, lithe limbs. Sikvah was more rounded at the hips, with thicker arms and legs. Both women were incredibly muscular, definition showing in every move. It was the stretching they did every morning. They called it *sharusahk*, but it was nothing like the violent wrestling Rojer had seen the *Sharum* and the Painted Man teach.

Where Amanvah was unflappable, Sikvah was easily roused to emotion. He had expected Amanvah, in her white robes, to be the more conservative of the two, but Sikvah was always the first to gasp at indiscretion.

'Sleep now, husband,' Amanvah said. 'You must regain your vigour. Sikvah, the curtains.'

Immediately Sikvah moved to pull the heavy velvet curtains over the translucent ones covering the carriage windows. It seemed 'First Wife' was more than just a title. Amanvah took the lead in everything from conversation to seduction, ordering Sikvah around like a servant. Sikvah never resisted in the slightest, performing every task as if it had been her idea all along. She spoke little save when spoken to, unless Amanvah was out of the room, or her attention turned elsewhere. It was then Sikvah truly came to life.

He smiled, feeling himself drift off to sleep as his wives began a soft lullaby in Krasian. He was used to taking naps during the day, a common Jongleur trick allowing them to stay fresh and alert for nighttime performances. Most folk couldn't read worth spit, and there was little to do once the sun set and the supper plates were cleared.

'When others' work ends, ours begins,' Arrick used to say.

He woke with a jolt as the carriage came to a halt. He lifted one of the heavy curtains, and shut it quickly against the glare. It was late afternoon and they were outside a modest inn. Amanvah and Sikvah had pulled plain robes and veils over their colourful silks.

'Ent it a bit early to be stopping for the night?'

'This is the last village before we pass from Everam's Bounty, beloved,' Amanvah said. 'Shamavah thinks it best to rest and restock before moving on. If you wish to sleep further, please do so while the *khaffit* unload our things.'

That would give him a lot of time. His wives did not travel light. Rojer rubbed the sleep from his face. 'Ay, that's all right. My legs could use a stretch.' He moved to put his clothes on, and immediately both women began to assist.

He soon hopped from the cart and walked about a bit, beginning the ritual of stretches and tumbles he used to keep his skills sharp. The ritual was a show in itself, full of cartwheels and running flips, rolls and backbends.

As usual, the miniature performance began to draw attention. Passersby, Krasian and Thesan alike, stopped to watch, and when he began walking on his hands, a few children ran after him, cheering.

337

Instinctively, Rojer led them towards the centre of the cobbled square, circling to clear himself a wide space. The ring he created quickly filled with people – local villagers, and the *Sharum*, *khaffit*, and *dal'ting* of whatever tribe had claimed the place. A *dama* watched him coldly, but did not seem foolish enough to interfere with the Deliverer's son-in-law.

Amanvah and Sikvah were watching him, too. Sikvah laughed and clapped along with the rest of the crowd at his antics, perhaps the most enthusiastically of all. Amanvah was the exact opposite, her eyes cold as she watched him.

'Only thing worse than a woman who laughs at every pratfall,' he heard Arrick say, 'is one who doesn't think anything's funny.'

He moved over to them. 'Husband, what are you doing?' Amanvah asked.

'Playing the crowd,' Rojer said. 'Just watch. Sikvah, please fetch my bag of marvels.'

'Immediately, husband,' Sikvah said, bowing and vanishing into the crowd. Amanvah continued to stare at him, but Rojer winked at her and went back to warming the crowd. He kept it simple, not sure which of his bawdy jokes and songs might offend the Krasians. Music in Krasia was limited to the private bedroom or praise to Everam. His wives had taught him some of these, but the fanaticism of the lyrics made him uncomfortable. Until his translation of the *Song of Waning* was complete, Rojer kept things instrumental, soon getting even the Krasians to stomp and clap to a beat.

When it came time for magic, obedient Sikvah was the perfect assistant, obeying his every command without hesitation. If only she weren't clad in featureless black robes and veil. *Wear your pillow dancing silks, love, and we'd have the best act in Thesa.*

The crowd was his effortlessly. Even the *dama* laughed in spite of himself a few times. Only Amanvah was unmoved.

The sky was darkening when the performance ended. Rojer

was still rising from his final bow when his First Wife turned on her heel and strode into the inn. Sikvah came to him immediately.

'Your *Jiwah Ka* apologizes for not being here to greet you, but the holy daughter is moved to prayer over your fine performance,' she said, as if this were natural.

Hated it, she means, he thought. *I've stepped in something, and I don't even know what.*

'Gone off to her secret room?' Rojer asked. Sikvah nodded.

Rojer was used to having a single small room at an inn, but Amanvah always demanded a minimum of three – a common, one for Rojer, and a private one for her alone to retreat to whenever she wished. Amanvah accepted nothing less than the finest rooms, richly appointed with her own things. Each night the *khaffit* carried in heavy rugs, lamps and incense burners, silk sheets, and a collection of paints and powders that would make even a Jongleur's jaw drop. Here, the innkeeper and his family had been put out of their own rooms to accommodate the daughter of Ahmann Jardir.

As they retired, Rojer saw the door to Amanvah's room shut tight, with Enkido standing guard. Even if he knew what was bothering Amanvah, even if he knew what to say, there would be no getting past the giant eunuch to tell her.

Food was brought up by the innkeeper's daughter, a meaty woman in her late forties who kept her eyes down and hopped at their every word. With no men to see, Sikvah changed back into her bright embroidered silks, serving him attentively as he ate and only taking quick nibbles of her own food at his urging.

'Would you like your bath soon, husband?' she asked when he was finished eating. 'Your amazing performance must have tired you.'

It was like this every night. Amanvah would go quiet at some point, and then excuse herself and vanish into her secret room for hours. Sikvah would swoop in, attending his every need and burying him in flattery until she returned.

Normally Sikvah's attention was indeed an effective distraction, but Rojer had never seen Amanvah so disapproving. There was an argument brewing, and he wanted to get into it and have done.

'What in the Core is she doing in there?' he grumbled.

'Communing with Everam,' Sikvah said, beginning to clear the bowls.

'Dicing,' Rojer said.

Sikvah seemed offended at his tone. 'The *alagai hora* are no game, husband. Your *Jiwah Ka* consults the dice to help guide your path.'

Rojer tightened his lips, not entirely liking the sound of that, but he said nothing. He found himself craving a cup of wine badly, though he doubted there was any to be had. Alcohol was one of the first things the *dama* abolished in the hamlets. He imagined what his master Arrick's reaction would have been to that. He might have wept, or saved himself the trouble and tied his own noose.

Just then Amanvah's door opened. You could tell a lot from how a person opened a door – every Jongleur who ever worked a stage knew that. Amanvah did not open it in the tentative way of one chastened, nor the aggressive way of one in full fume. It was a calm, decisive action. She had her mask in place, and still wore her white robes.

Corespawn it, Rojer thought, putting his Jongleur's mask on as Amanvah came to sit across from him, her eyes calm but piercing. He shifted slightly to feel the weight of the medallion on his chest.

'This is what it means to be a Jongleur?' Amanvah asked. 'To dance on a ball and pretend to fall on your face to get peasant children to laugh?'

Rojer kept his face smooth, though the words made him want to bare his teeth. It was no more than he had heard from self-involved Royals in Angiers, looking down their noses at his kind even as they hired them for their balls and parties, but the words cut deeper coming from his own wife.

Night, what have I gotten myself into?

'You didn't seem to mind performing for the *Sharum* and *dama* in Everam's Bounty,' Rojer noted.

'That was in the Deliverer's court, praising Everam before honoured guests and loyal *Sharum*!' Amanvah hissed. Sikvah moved quickly away, busying herself around the room. 'Your honour was boundless that day, husband, but you cannot mean to compare it to debasing yourself playing the fool for *khaffit* and *chin*.'

'*Khaffit*,' Rojer said. '*Chin*. These words have no meaning to me. All I saw in that square were people, and each and every one of them deserves a little joy in their life.'

Amanvah's mask was a good one, but Rojer caught the pulse of a vein in her forehead and knew he had niggled her. *Point to me.*

Amanvah stood. 'I will be in my chamber. Sikvah, tend to Rojer's bath.'

Sikvah bowed. 'Yes, *Jiwah Ka*.' Amanvah swept out of the room.

'Shall I draw your bath, husband?' Sikvah asked.

Rojer looked at her, incredulous. 'Of course. And cut my stones off while you're at it.'

Sikvah froze, and Rojer immediately regretted it for the frightened look on her face. 'I . . . I do not . . .'

'Forget it,' Rojer cut in, getting to his feet and putting on his motley cloak. 'I'm going downstairs a bit.'

Sikvah looked at him in concern. 'Is there something you need? Food perhaps? Tea? I will fetch whatever you wish.'

Rojer shook his head. 'I just need a walk and a few moments alone with my thoughts.' He gestured towards the bedroom. 'Warm the bed for me.'

Sikvah did not seem pleased with the instructions, but Rojer's command was clear, and he had learned she would not refuse such a tone without good reason and a nod from Amanvah, of which she had neither. 'As you wish, husband.'

He left the room, finding Enkido and Gared just outside in the hall. The gold-shackled eunuch stood straight and stiff before Amanvah's door, giving no reaction as Rojer exited the room.

In contrast, Gared lounged on a chair tilted on its back legs, tossing cards at a hat a few feet away. His weapons rested against the wall in easy reach.

'Ay, Rojer. Figured you were off to bed by now.' He winked, and then laughed as if he had just made a clever joke.

'You don't have to stand watch all night, Gar,' Rojer said.

Gared shrugged. 'Don't, but I usually wait till you're off to bed before I sneak off to find my own.' He nodded at Enkido. 'Dunno how that one does it, standing like a tree all night. Don't think he sleeps.'

'Come downstairs with me,' Rojer said. 'I'm off to rummage under the bar and see if anything stronger than tea escaped the local *dama*'s glare.' Gared grunted and stood. Rojer collected the cards with practised speed, snapping and shuffling them as he headed down the stairs.

The taproom was empty save for the innkeep, Darel, who was sweeping the floor. As at all the inns they had visited on the Messenger road through Everam's Bounty, the other guests had been ejected for the night to accommodate Leesha's caravan. She and her family, Gared, Wonda, Rojer, and his wives were all given their own rooms, as were the full *dal'Sharum* and their wives. The women, children, and *kha'Sharum* slept in the carts circled outside.

Darel was a fit man, but well past fighting age, with more grey in his beard than his natural sand colour. 'Honoured masters.' He bowed. 'How may I serve you?'

'Cut that demonshit, for starters,' Rojer said. 'Just us *chin* here.'

The man relaxed visibly, heading behind the bar as Rojer and Gared took stools. 'Sorry. Never know who's watching, these days.'

'Honest word,' Gared said. 'Like worrying you got a ward wrong somewhere.'

'Got anything real to drink?' Rojer asked. 'I've a powerful thirst, and not for water. Been so long, a bottle of disinfectant will do.'

Darel hawked into a clay spittoon. '*Dama* smashed all my wine casks the day they came to town. Used the stronger stuff to make a pyre to burn everything "sinful" in town. Took my granddaughter's stuffed doll. Said its dress was indecent.' He spat again. 'Girl loved that doll. Lucky they din't take her, too, I guess.'

'It bad as all that?' Rojer asked.

The innkeeper shrugged. 'First week was rough. *Dama* came with a paper from the demon of the desert that said the town belonged to his tribe now. Some folk disagreed, and the *Sharum* put 'em down hard. Most fell in line after that.'

'So you just let 'em take over?' Gared growled.

'We ent fighters like you Hollow folk,' Darel said. 'I saw the biggest man in town have his arm broke like a twig by a *dama* half his size, just for refusing to bow. Needed to look after me and mine, and couldn't do that dead.'

'No one's blaming you,' Rojer said.

'S'not so bad once you learn the rules,' Darel said. 'Most of the Krasian holy book is the same as in the Canon, and like us, some of them are preachier than others,' he cracked a smile as his voice dropped to a whisper, 'and some are hypocrites.' With that, he produced a small clay flask and two tiny cups. 'You boys ever try couzi?'

'Huh-uh,' Gared grunted.

'Heard stories,' Rojer said.

Darel chuckled. 'For all their talk of the sin of spirits, them sand folk brew a drink that'll take the varnish off your porch.'

Rojer and Gared took the cups he offered, looking at them curiously. Even in his crippled hand, Rojer could hold his easily. The one Gared held looked like something a child might use to serve tea to a doll. 'It's barely a mouthful. Do you taste it or toss it?'

'Toss the first couple,' Darel advised. 'Gets easier after that.' They touched cups and threw them back, eyes widening. Rojer had been drinking since he was twelve and thought himself used to the worst burn alcohol could bring to bear, but this was like drinking fire. Gared started coughing.

Darel just smiled, filling their cups again. Once more they tossed them back, and this time, as he said, it was easier. Or maybe their tongues and throats were just numb.

Gared sipped the third cup thoughtfully. 'Tastes like . . .'

'. . . cinnamon,' Rojer finished, swishing the liquid in his mouth.

'The Krasians are like couzi,' Darel pulled at his whiskers, 'or this corespawned itchy beard they make all the men grow. Take some getting used to, but not so bad after a while. They let me keep my business so long as I pay my taxes and keep to the rules, and if I arrange a marriage for my granddaughter by the time she bleeds, I don't have to worry about the white witches arranging one for her.'

He paled suddenly, looking sharply at Rojer.

Rojer smiled and held up his scarred hand. 'Keep your pants dry. I may have married a *dama'ting*, but that doesn't mean they're any less scary to me. Might want to get out of the habit of calling them white witches, though. "An act practised in private will eventually be seen", as my master used to say.'

'Ay,' Darel agreed. 'Fair and true.'

'You were saying?' Rojer prompted. 'Krasians aren't so bad?'

'Find that hard to swallow,' Gared said. 'Like saying it's not so bad having a boot on your back.'

Darel poured himself a cup of couzi, tossing it back with a practised quickness. 'Ent saying I don't miss the old days, and plenty have it worse than me, but generally, you remember when to bow and keep your nose clean, the Krasians leave you be. You have a dispute with your neighbour, it still goes to the

Town Speaker first, and then he takes it to the *dama* if it ent something he can settle on the spot. The *dama* are generally fair, but they take all that ear-for-an-ear business in the Canon literally. Know a feller lost a hand for stealing a chicken, and another who raped a girl, and had to watch the same done to his sister.'

Gared balled a fist. 'And that ent so bad?'

Darel threw back another cup. 'It's bad, ay, but I don't steal chickens and rape girls. Reckon there'll be a lot less of that in the future, too. Evejan law is harsh, but can't deny it gets results.'

'And them taking all the boys?' Gared asked. 'I had a son, I wouldn't stand for that.'

Darel swished his third cupful in his mouth, swallowing thoughtfully. 'Got a grandson they took. Ent happy about it, but they let him come home every month on new moon. Waning, they call it. Boys're getting it rough, coming home with bruises and broken bones, but no worse'n the Krasian boys. They're picking up the language and rules quicker than the rest of us, and the *dama* says that the ones who earn the black will be full citizens, with all the rights of a *Sharum* lord. And the ones who don't are kicked out as *khaffit*.' He smiled, scratching his neck. 'Which ent too different from my lot, 'cept without the itchy beard.'

Rojer sipped his fourth – or was it his fifth? – cup of couzi. His head was beginning to spin. 'How many boys did they take from . . . where are we, anyway?'

'Used to be Appleton,' Darel said. 'Now it's some long bunch of sand words. We just call it Sharachville, 'coz that's our tribe now. There were thirty boys here the right age for *Hannu Pash* or whatever.'

Rojer had to steady himself on Gared as they climbed back up the steps. He had drunk a big mug of fresh water and chewed a sourleaf, but he doubted his wives would be fooled if he stumbled over his own feet on the way to bed. Fortunately,

Rojer was Arrick Sweetsong's apprentice and had a lot of practice pretending to be sober when he was anything but.

'They're building an army bigger than all the Free Cities combined,' he said quietly. 'Lakton doesn't have a chance.'

'Gotta do something,' Gared said. 'Find the Painted Man, fight, something. Can't just sit back and let 'em take everything south of the Hollow.'

'First thing is to warn folk in Lakton what's coming,' Rojer said. 'Got some ideas about that, but I need a night's sleep and maybe a pot to sick up in first.'

It took all his mummer's skills and acrobatics to keep steady as he walked by Enkido. If the giant eunuch took any notice of him, he did not show it. Inside, Amanvah was still in her private chamber, the evil glow of wardlight shining from under the door. He made his way into bed without a problem. Sikvah was waiting for him, but she said nothing as he collapsed face-first into the pillows. He felt tugging as she pulled off his boots and clothes, but while he did not resist, neither did he have strength to assist. She stroked his back gently, cooing as he fell fast asleep.

14

The *Song of Waning*

333 AR Summer
20 Dawns Before New Moon

Rojer's head was pounding when he was woken an hour before dawn. The novelty of Sikvah waiting on his every need – bathing him, picking his clothes, dressing him – had begun to wear thin, but he was thankful for it now. His head felt like it was kicked by a mule, and his mouth stuffed with cotton.

'Haven't gotten sauced like that since Angiers,' he muttered.

Sikvah looked up. 'Eh?'

He shook his head. 'Nothing. Going to need you to entertain Erny and Elona in the carriage this morning. Need to talk to Leesha.'

'That is not appropriate, husband,' Amanvah said, sweeping in from her personal chamber carrying a small wooden box, varnished black and polished to a shine. Had she been in there all night? Rojer had no recollection of her coming to bed, but he had been far gone. 'The daughter of Erny is unwed and my father's intended, and you are a married man. You cannot . . .'

Sikvah was buttoning his shirt cuff, but Rojer yanked his hand away so fast she gasped. 'Demonshit. I swore to be a good and loyal husband, and that was honest word, but that don't mean I gave up my right to talk to my friends in private. If you think it does, we've got a problem.'

Sikvah seemed scandalized, and Amanvah was silent a long moment, looking down at the box she held, tapping it against one hand. Rojer knew that was as irritated as he would likely ever see her, even if she were about to put her knife in his eye, or have Enkido break his fingers.

But at that moment, Rojer didn't care. 'Marriage is the death of freedom,' his master used to say. He shook his head, deliberately buttoning his own cuff. *Not for me. Corespawn me if it is.*

At last Amanvah looked up and met his eyes. 'As you wish, husband.'

Leesha was a little surprised when Rojer asked to ride with her that morning, but did not question it. She told herself she was still annoyed with his decision to marry, but truer was she missed him terribly. Rojer had been her best friend and closest confidant for over a year, and she felt an emptiness when he was not close by.

Amanvah and Sikvah had put up an impenetrable wall with more than their singing and wailing. When they stopped for the night, they guarded Rojer like lions around a kill. This was the first time Leesha had been alone with him since the trip started, and even now they were forced to leave the curtains of the carriage open as a nod to Krasian decency. *Sharum* rode by regularly, not even bothering to hide their spying as they checked to ensure that she and Rojer remained clothed and on opposite benches.

But they had privacy nonetheless. Gared and Wonda rode to either side to keep everyone out of earshot, and Leesha had selected a driver she was sure did not speak a word of Thesan. Most of the Krasians who knew more than *please* and *thank you* in Thesan tended to keep it secret as Amanvah and Sikvah once had, but the Hollowers were wise to the trick now, and had ferreted most of those out over the last week. Elona had proven particularly adept at the game, making outrageous statements and watching closely for tics and tells.

'I think my mother liked your carriage a little too much,' Leesha said. 'You may find her unwilling to trade back after we stop for lunch.'

'It's a bit cold at the moment,' Rojer said. 'Amanvah and Sikvah did not care for the idea of us being alone together.'

'Well they're just going to have to get over that.' Leesha nodded out the window to where Kaval was passing by on his horse. 'Ahmann as well. I didn't agree to cut every man out of my life when I slept with him, regardless of what his people think.'

'My point exactly,' Rojer agreed, 'but I think it will be an ongoing battle.'

Leesha smiled. 'That's marriage, as I understand it. Are you regretting the decision?'

Rojer shook his head. 'No one gets to dance for free. I'll put my coins in the hat, but corespawned if I'll be overcharged.'

Leesha nodded. 'So what was worth risking the wrath of your wives to discuss?'

'Your intended,' Rojer said.

'He's not—' Leesha began.

'You're throwing your weight around with the Krasians like he is,' Rojer cut in. 'So which is it?'

Leesha felt a twinge in her temple and pretended to brush back her hair so she could rub it. 'What business is it of yours? You didn't consult me on your betrothal.'

'My wives aren't kidnapping every able-bodied boy under fifteen,' Rojer said. 'If just half of them make it through *Hannu Pash* . . .'

'In a few years Ahmann will have an army of Thesan fanatics big enough to conquer everything from here to Fort Miln,' Leesha finished. 'I'm not blind, Rojer.'

'So what are we going to do?' Rojer asked.

'Build our own,' Leesha said. 'The Hollow must keep expanding, and training Cutters in battle. Ahmann has named us tribesmen, and will not attack us if we do not attack him first.'

'Do you really believe that?' Rojer asked. 'I'll admit he's not what I expected, but do you trust him?'

Leesha nodded. 'Ahmann is many things, but he is honest. He has made no secret of his plans to conquer everyone who does not willingly join him in Sharak Ka, but that does not necessarily mean all must bow to him in the day.'

'And if it does?' Rojer asked.

'Then perhaps he will take my hand as a symbolic conquest,' Leesha said. 'It's not my first choice, but better than open war pitting neighbour against neighbour.'

'That may save the Hollow,' Rojer said, 'but Lakton is still on the gibbet. The city might hold up better than Fort Rizon did, but the hamlets are indefensible. The Krasians will begin swallowing them soon.'

'Agreed,' Leesha said. 'But there's not a lot we can do about that.'

'We can warn them,' Rojer said. 'And have them pass it on. Offer sanctuary and training in the Hollow now, while the roads are still passable.'

'And how are we supposed to do that?' Leesha asked.

Rojer smiled. 'Play your princess act. Demand a roof over your head every night as we pass through Lakton, and no more kicking out everyone else at the inns. I am going to debut my new song, and need an audience.'

'I do not think this is a good idea, mistress,' Kaval said. He was the ranking *Sharum*, his red veil hanging loose about his throat in the midday sun. They had stopped briefly for lunch, and to allow folk to stretch their legs. The drillmaster's tone was polite, but there was frustration under its veneer. He was not accustomed to explaining himself to women.

'I do not care what you think, Sharum,' Leesha said. 'I will not sleep on the roadside with rocks for pillows when there are perfectly good inns until two days out from the Hollow.'

Kaval frowned. 'We are no longer in the lands of Shar'Dama Ka. It is safer—'

'To camp on the road where bandits can come on us at night?' Leesha cut him off.

Kaval spat in the dust. 'The *chin* cowards will not dare come at us on the road at night. The *alagai* would slaughter them.'

'Bandits or demons, I don't care to spend the night out with either,' Leesha snapped.

'Mistress has shown no fear of *alagai* before,' Kaval pointed out. 'I would worry more about hidden spears in some unknown *chin* village.'

'What is this?' Amanvah asked, coming over to them.

Kaval immediately went to one knee. 'The mistress wishes to sleep in a *chin* village tonight, Dama'ting. I have told her this is unwise . . .'

'She is correct, of course,' Amanvah said. 'I have no more desire to sleep in the naked night than she. If you're afraid of a few local *chin*,' she made a mockery of the word, 'then by all means, leave us at the inn and put a tent out in the woods to hide till dawn.'

Leesha bit back a smile as she watched Kaval bow deeper to hide the grinding of his teeth.

'We fear nothing, Dama'ting,' the drillmaster said. 'If this is your wish, we will commandeer—'

'You will do nothing of the sort,' Leesha interrupted. 'As you say, this is not the Deliverer's land. Our beds will be bought and paid for, not taken at spearpoint. We are not thieves.'

Leesha could swear she heard the grinding of teeth. Kaval's eyes flicked to Amanvah, waiting for her to countermand the order, but the girl was wisely silent. She had regained something of her former haughtiness, but they both remembered what happened the last time she crossed Leesha.

'Call the *Sharum*. All twenty-one, and have them sit there,' Leesha pointed to a small clearing. 'I will address them while they eat. I want no misconceptions about what is acceptable behaviour, both for the runners we send ahead and the bulk of the group when we reach town.'

She swept away, heading over to the cauldrons where the *dal'ting* prepared lunch for the caravan under Shamavah's watchful eye. Most would receive a heavy brown soup of beef stock and flour with potatoes and vegetables, along with a half loaf of bread. The *Sharum* ate better, with spits of lamb and couscous in addition to their soup, which had large chunks of meat. Leesha, her parents, Rojer, and his wives all ate better still, herb-encrusted roast pheasant and rack of lamb, their couscous spiced and thick with butter.

Leesha came over to Shamavah. 'I am addressing the *Sharum* over lunch. I will need you to translate for me.'

'Of course, mistress.' Shamavah bowed. 'It would be my great honour.'

Leesha pointed to the place where the warriors were already beginning to gather. 'See to it they are seated in a half-moon and given bowls.' Shamavah nodded and hurried off.

Leesha went to the woman preparing the *Sharum*'s soup, taking the ladle from her and tasting it. 'Needs more spice,' she said, taking a few handfuls from the bowls of spice the cooks had laid out and tossing them into the soup. Along with a few herbs from her own apron.

She pretended to taste it again. 'Perfect.'

Rojer held the last note of the *Song of Waning* for a long time, eyes closed, feeling the hum of the wood in his hands. He cut the note hard, and Amanvah and Sikvah followed him easily.

'The hush before the roar,' Arrick used to call it – that precious moment of silence between the last note of a brilliant performance and the applause of the crowd. With the heavy curtains pulled, even the myriad sounds of the caravan were muted.

Rojer felt his chest tighten, and suddenly realized he was holding his breath. There was no one to applaud, but he heard the sound anyway. He could say with no ego that as a trio, they exceeded anything he had ever done alone.

He let his breath out slowly, opening his eyes at the exact moment Amanvah and Sikvah opened theirs. Those beautiful eyes told him they, too, sensed the power of what they had wrought.

If you only knew, Rojer thought. *Soon, my loves. Soon I will show you.*

My loves. He had taken to calling them that, in his head if not aloud. He had meant it as a joke, calling women he barely knew 'love', but it had never been funny. There were times when it was passionate, and times, like last night and this morning, when it was bitter.

And there were times like right now, when the void left by the music's end filled with a love as true as he could ever imagine. He looked at his wives and what he felt at the sight of Leesha Paper paled in comparison.

'My master used to say there was no such thing as perfection in music,' Rojer said, 'but corespawn it if we aren't close.'

The original *Song of Waning* had seven verses, each with seven lines, each with seven syllables. Amanvah had said that this was because there were seven pillars of Heaven, seven lands on the Ala, and seven layers to Nie's abyss.

The translation made his previous crowning achievement, *The Battle of Cutter's Hollow*, seem a cheap ditty. The *Song of Waning* had power over human and coreling both, music that could take a demon through the full range of reaction and words that would tell the Laktonians all they needed to know.

The Painted Man had asked for more fiddle wizards like him, but Rojer had failed at that, even questioning whether the talent could be taught at all. He had begun to feel like he was standing still, peaked at eighteen winters. But now he had stumbled onto something new, and felt his power building once more. It was not what he or the Painted Man had been seeking. It was something stronger still.

Provided, of course, his wives would perform it with him, and the Krasians didn't realize what he was doing and have him killed.

Amanvah and Sikvah bowed. 'It is an honour to accompany you, husband,' Amanvah said. 'Everam speaks to you, as my father says.'

Everam. Rojer was getting sick of the name. There was no Creator, by that name or any other. 'Not much difference between Holy Men and Jongleurs, Rojer,' Arrick used to say in his cups. 'They spin the same old ale stories and tampweed tales over and over, bedazzling bumpkins and half-wits to help them forget the pain of life.'

Then he would laugh bitterly. 'Only they're better paid and respectable.'

An image flashed in Rojer's mind – the evil red glow coming out from under the door to Amanvah's private chamber each night. Had she spent the entire night there?

Your Jiwah Ka *consults the dice to help guide your path.*

Rojer didn't pretend to understand the bone magic of the *dama'ting*, but Leesha had explained enough of it for him to grasp that there wasn't anything divine about it. Hadn't the science of the old world harnessed 'the lightning in the sky and the wind and the rain'? He didn't know what the dice were telling her, but it wasn't the word of the Creator, and he didn't like the idea of dancing to their bidding.

'Do your dice agree?' he asked, keeping his tone carefully neutral. Sikvah inhaled sharply, but Amanvah had her mask in place, giving not a hint to her true feelings. The Jongleur in him railed against that. It was a common pastime in the guild hall to try to make other Jongleurs laugh or otherwise break character while practising their routines. Rojer considered himself a master at it.

He cocked his head at her. *Will I spend the rest of my life trying to trick a real reaction from you?*

'The *alagai hora* are never absolute, husband. They are a guide only.'

'And what do they tell you about me?' Rojer asked.

Sikvah hissed. 'It is forbidden to ask . . .!'

'The Core with that!' Rojer asked. 'I won't dance to an imaginary tune.'

Amanvah turned to reach into a large velvet bag, the kind *dama'ting* kept their demon bones in. With the heavy curtains drawn, there was no natural light in the carriage, perfect for *hora* magic. He froze, wishing he'd kept a knife strapped to his wrist.

But Amanvah simply removed a wrapped package and handed it to him with a bow. 'The dice tell much and little about you, husband. Your power is undeniable, but your life's path is scattered with divergences. There are futures where hordes of *alagai* dance to your tune, and others where your gift is squandered. Greatness and failure.'

Rojer untied the bright cloth wrapping, discovering the small wooden box she had held early that morning. 'But when I asked them if I should marry you, they told me yes, and when I asked what marriage gift could help you to greatness, they guided me to this.'

Suddenly Rojer felt boorish. She had been spending all that time alone making him a marriage present? Creator, was he expected to provide presents as well? No one had told him that. He made a mental note to ask Shamavah the custom when they stopped for the night, and get her advice on a gift, if need be.

Amanvah bowed as deeply as he had ever seen, her head

nearly touching the carpeted floor of the carriage. 'Please accept my apologies, for taking so long presenting it to you. I began the work two weeks ago, thinking I would have months to prepare. The dice did not predict that you would move to speaking our vows so quickly.'

Rojer ran the three fingertips of his right hand over the smooth surface of the box, feeling the wards that had been burned into the wood before it was lacquered. Some were wards of protection, but most he did not know. Rojer had never had any skill at warding.

What's inside? he wondered. What did the demon dice command her to make him? An image flashed in his mind of Enkido. *If it's a pair of golden shackles, I am grabbing my bag of marvels and going straight out the door, moving carriage or no.*

He opened the box and his eyes widened. Inside, on a bed of silk, was a fiddle's chinrest of polished rosewood with a moulded gold centre, affixed to a golden tail clamp. The piece was covered in wards, etched into the gold and cut sharply into the lacquer of the wood, filled with gold filigree. It was beautiful.

Like all modern instruments, Arrick and Jaycob's fiddles had chinrests, but the ancient instrument Rojer had taken from the Painted Man's treasure room did not, perhaps dating back to days before the innovation. A chinrest allowed the player to hold the fiddle in place with just his neck, freeing his hands for other things if necessary.

'The piece comes from Duke Edon's instrument maker, designed for the royal herald.' Rojer reached out reverently to touch the object as Amanvah spoke. 'It has taken me many nights to ward it and infuse it with *hora*.'

Rojer recoiled, snatching his hand back as if from a hot kettle. '*Hora?* There's a demon bone in that?'

Amanvah laughed, a musical sound he heard all too infrequently. *Is that real*, Rojer wondered, *or just part of the mask?*

'It cannot harm you, husband. The evil will of Nie dies with

356

the *alagai*, but their bones continue to carry the magic of Ala, made by Everam long before Nie created the abyss to pervert it.'

Rojer pursed his lips. 'Still . . .'

'The bone is little more than a thin slice,' Amanvah said. 'Bound in wards and solid gold.'

'What does it do?' Rojer asked.

Amanvah smiled so widely Rojer could see it through her translucent veil, and even to his practised eye, it seemed truly genuine and sent a thrill through him.

'Try it,' Amanvah whispered, lifting his fiddle and handing it to him.

Rojer hesitated a moment, then shrugged and took the instrument, affixing the clamp to the tail piece where the resonance would be greatest. He turned the threaded barrels carefully to tighten it without damaging the wood, then set it beneath his chin, holding the instrument without the use of his hands. There was a slight tingle where it touched his chin, like a limb gone to pins and needles.

Rojer waited a moment. 'What's supposed to happen?'

Amanvah laughed again. 'Play!'

Rojer took the bow in his crippled hand and the frets in the other, playing a quick tune. He was shocked at the resonance. The instrument had become twice as loud. 'That's amazing.'

'And that is with most of the wards covered by your chin,' Amanvah said. 'Lift away and the sound will only grow.'

Rojer cocked an eyebrow at her, then went back to playing. At first, he kept the wood covered, and the instrument seemed little louder than normal. Slowly, he lifted his chin, revealing some of the wards, and the volume began to increase. He lifted more, and the sound doubled, and doubled again, rattling his teeth even as his wives moved to cover their ears. Finally, he had to stop from sheer pain, with much of the rest still covered.

'This will drown out your beautiful voices,' Rojer said.

Amanvah shook her head, lifting her veil to show a golden choker with a warded ball at its centre, resting in the hollow of her throat. Sikvah revealed a similar bit of jewellery at her own neck. 'We will match you, husband.'

Rojer shook his head, stunned. *Perhaps bone magic and dice ent so bad after all.*

'I don't know what to say,' he managed at last. 'This is the most amazing gift anyone has ever given me, but I haven't anything to give in return.'

Amanvah and Sikvah laughed. 'Have you already forgotten the song we just sang?' Amanvah said. 'It was your marriage gift before our holy father.' She laid a hand on his arm. 'We will sing it with you tonight for the *chin.*'

Rojer nodded, suddenly racked with guilt. They had no idea what the song would say to the Laktonians.

The village of Greenmeadow appeared deserted when their caravan arrived, fields empty of humans and livestock. The few fleeting glimpses of movement vanished quickly over hills and into the woods. They left the caravan on the Messenger road while the carriages headed into the village proper. Even then they saw no one.

'I do not like this,' Kaval said. Coliv said something to him in Krasian, and he grunted.

'What's that?' Leesha asked.

'He says the *chin* make only slightly less noise than thunder. They are all around us, watching from every window and around every street corner. I will dispatch him to scout our path . . .'

'You won't,' Leesha said.

'He is a Krevakh Watcher,' Kaval said. 'I assure you, mistress, the greenlanders will never even know he is there.'

'I'm not worried about them,' Leesha said. 'I want him where I can see him. These people have reason for caution, but we aren't going to do anything to threaten them.'

A moment later the town square came into view, surrounded

by homes and shopfronts. There were five men waiting on the inn steps, two with nocked hunting bows, and two more with long pitchforks.

Leesha called a halt and stepped out of her carriage. Immediately she was joined by Rojer, Gared, Wonda, Amanvah, Enkido, Shamavah, and Kaval. 'Let me do the talking,' Leesha said as they approached the inn.

'They do not appear interested in talking, mistress,' Kaval said, nodding to both sides, where she saw bowmen at every window around the town square.

'They will not shoot unless we give them cause,' Leesha said, wishing she was as confident as her words. She spread her pocketed apron so that all could see she was a Herb Gatherer. Rojer's patchwork cloak announced him as a Jongleur – another point in their favour.

Rojer and Enkido placed themselves between the bows and Amanvah, with Gared in turn protecting Rojer. Leesha was similarly surrounded by Kaval and Wonda.

'Ay, the inn!' Rojer cried. 'We mean no harm, seeking only safe succour, for which we can pay. May we approach?'

'Leave your spears right there!' one of the men cried.

'I'll do no such—' Kaval began.

'Your spear or yourself, Drillmaster,' Leesha cut in. 'It's a fair request, and they could as easily drop you where you stand.' Kaval let out a low growl, but he bent and laid down his spear, as did Enkido.

'Who're you, then?' the lead man asked when they made it to the porch.

'Leesha Paper,' Leesha said.

The man blinked. 'Mistress of the Hollow?'

Leesha smiled. 'The same.'

The man's eyes narrowed. 'What are you doing so far south? And with the likes of them?' He nodded at the Krasians.

'We are returning from a meeting with the Krasian leader,' Leesha said, 'and wish to spend the night in Greenmeadow.'

'Since when do Herb Gatherers go on diplomacy missions?' the man asked. 'That's Messenger work.'

Rojer stepped forward, extending a hand with a sweep of his motley cloak. 'I am the herald of Deliverer's Hollow. Rojer Halfgrip, former apprentice to Arrick Sweetsong, one-time herald of Duke Rhinebeck of Angiers.'

'Halfgrip?' the man asked. 'The one they call the fiddle wizard?' Rojer smiled widely at that, nodding.

'You have our names, but have not given yours,' Leesha said. 'I'm guessing you are Havold, the Town Speaker?'

'Ay, how d'you know that?' the man demanded.

'Your Herb Gatherer, Mistress Ana, once wrote to me for advice on curing your daughter Thea of the gasping cough,' Leesha said. 'She is well, I take it?'

'That was ten years ago,' Havold said. 'She has children of her own now, and I don't care for the thought of them sleeping not half a mile from a bunch of murdering Krasians. We heard the stories from those that passed through last winter, running from them.' His bearded lip curled at Kaval and Enkido, showing the tip of one of his canines.

Leesha prayed the drillmaster would not rise to the bait, and breathed a sigh when he remained silent. 'I cannot speak for the people as a whole, but I can vouch for the men in my caravan. If left alone, they will keep to themselves and harm no one. Most will remain in their carts on the road, but my parents are elderly and I would dearly appreciate a few beds for the night. As my herald told you, we can pay, in both gold and entertainment.'

Havold's mouth was a hard line, but he nodded.

Leesha sat in the taproom with her parents, Gared, Wonda, Kaval, and Enkido as Rojer tuned his fiddle. He sat in a plain hard-back chair in a dimly lit corner, Amanvah and Sikvah kneeling on clean cloth to either side of him. Leesha could tell

the drillmaster and eunuch were uneasy with Amanvah and
Sikvah on the stage – such things were unheard of in Krasia
– but they kept their peace after a few harsh whispers from
the *dama'ting*. The other tables and bar stools were packed
with Meadowers, with more standing at the back. A Jongleur
would draw a crowd in any event, but Leesha could see as
many eyes on the Krasians at her table as on the stage, not all
of them friendly. The general din kept her from making out
details, but there was angry murmuring throughout the room.

At least until the music began.

Rojer had done nothing to warm the crowd as he had the
day before. No acrobatics or juggling, no magic tricks, jokes,
or stories. With his wives on stage, he played and nothing more.

As he had in Ahmann's dining hall, Rojer began with a slow,
quiet melody, building in complexity and volume until the sound
filled the room, wrapping everyone in its spell. The crowd fell
silent, eyes glazing. In her heart, Leesha knew his playing was
not truly magic, but the way human and demon both were
moved by it belied that fact. He had a gift none could deny.

When the music built to a crescendo, Amanvah and Sikvah
began to sing, wordlessly at first, but then in perfect Thesan:

> *Everam the Creator*
> *Saw the cold blackness of Nie*
> *And felt no satisfaction*
> *Creating Blessed Ala*
> *He sparked sun and moon for light*
> *And men in His own image*
> *Everam was satisfied*
>
> *Nie was vexed by Creation*
> *Marring Her perfect dark void*
> *She reached out to crush Ala*
> *When Everam stayed Her hand*
> *Nie spat blackness on His world*

The Mother of all demons
Alagai'ting Ka uncurled

Everam blew a great breath
Spinning all His Creation
The Demon Queen fled before
The holy sun and moonlight
Cursing Alagai'ting Ka
Slipped into the dark abyss
At the centre of Ala

But Ala turned and night fell
Heralding Nie's dark children
Get of Alagai'ting Ka
The destroyers, alagai
Everam against Nie's might
Bade man to defend himself
Steadfast in the cold moonlight

Moonlight is always Waning
Alagai power growing
And when the moonlight falls dark
Alagai Ka walks Ala
Ward your mind when Waning teems
Lest the father of demons
Devour your thoughts and dreams

Everam Great and Mighty
Sent His children one last gift
Gave us the Deliverer
Shar'Dama Ka leads the way
To glory and Heaven's light
Unite Everam's children
To purge the Demon Queen's blight

Shar'Dama Ka is Coming
To unite mankind as one
Kneel to him and Everam
Or be levied with the spear
To bathe in alagai gore
Joining glorious battle
Of Sharak Ka, the First War

Leesha felt an ache in her hand, and realized she had been clutching her teacup so hard her knuckles showed white. She forced herself to relax and glance around a room holding its collective breath. At the last verse she expected the Krasians to suddenly produce weapons – though those had all been left in their rooms – or the Meadowers to riot. Instead, all burst into a cacophony of sound. Kaval and Enkido roared and stomped their feet, sending bits of dust drifting down from the rafters. The clapping of the Thesans was like an entire box of festival crackers.

Not for the first time, she had underestimated Rojer. He seemed a boy, eighteen summers old, with only the barest whisper of hair on his face. Often his actions made him seem younger still – petulant, impetuous, and downright foolhardy. Leesha was forever fretting when he ignored her advice, sure she knew better than he, sure she could solve all his problems if he would only listen and do as he was told.

But Rojer had done more with a song than she could have ever imagined, telling the Meadowers everything they needed to know about the Krasians and their beliefs, warning them about the danger of the coming new moon, and telling them in no uncertain terms that Ahmann's army was coming their way.

Most of all, he had done it right under the Krasians' noses, revealing nothing their *dama* did not shout from their pedestals and minarets. He might as well have said the sky was blue. Amanvah and Sikvah thought they were singing their father's glory, when in fact they were telling folk to pack their things and run as fast and far as they could.

Leesha was accustomed to knowing best, but suddenly it was she who felt directionless, and Rojer the one who could see the net for its wards.

'That was beautiful, Rojer,' she said, rising as they took their bows and returned to the table. Kaval and Enkido were on their feet instantly, moving to surround the women protectively.

'Thank you,' Rojer said, 'but it was a group effort. I could never have done it without Amanvah and Sikvah.'

'My husband is too modest,' Amanvah said. 'We taught him a song everyone knows, and helped him understand the meaning of its words, but it was he who put it in your language, finding rhymes and words we could never have hoped to.'

Leesha smiled. 'I think you, too, are being modest, Amanvah.' She looked at Rojer. 'But it's true Rojer added . . . subtle touches that were nothing short of brilliant.'

Just for an instant, Rojer shot her a glare, too fast for the others to notice. Amanvah looked at her curiously, and Leesha realized Rojer wasn't the only one she was underestimating. The *dama'ting* might be young, but she was no fool.

Havold came over after the performance, and Leesha taught him the mind demon ward, and how to make headbands with it for use on new moon.

'You mean those things are real?' Havold gaped.

'Every threat in that song is real, Speaker,' Leesha said. 'Every one.'

Rojer woke the next morning at the gentle rebound of the feathered mattress as Amanvah and Sikvah slipped to the floor. They were making an effort not to wake him, but after many nights among the skilled pickpockets of the Jongleurs' Guild, he had learned to sleep lightly.

He kept his breathing even, pretending to shift in his sleep to give himself a better view as the women lit oil lamps and began their morning ritual. It was not yet dawn, and Rojer could likely sleep another hour before needing to rise and rejoin the caravan, but some things were preferable to sleep.

Watching his wives exercise was one of them.

Amanvah and Sikvah were clad only in loose diaphanous pants and tops, leaving little to the imagination as they moved through their *sharusahk* poses. Rojer felt himself stiffen and shifted under the blankets to put a bit of pressure on himself, swallowing a groan of pleasure as he mused about how lucky he was.

As always, the women seemed to have a sixth sense when it came to his arousal. They turned to regard him, and Rojer was not quick enough to close his eyes. Immediately, they ceased their exercise and moved towards him.

'No, please,' Rojer said. 'Don't let me interrupt. I enjoy watching.'

Sikvah looked to Amanvah, who shrugged, and the women resumed their posing.

'Your *sharusahk* is nothing like what Gared and Wonda are learning from Kaval,' Rojer noted.

Amanvah snorted. '*Sharum sharusahk* is like wolves howling at the moon. Even the *dama* are only a cricket's song. This,' she fell into a series of poses, 'is music.'

Rojer concentrated, thinking of Darsy Cutter, the homely Herb Gatherer of Deliverer's Hollow. He undressed the woman in his mind's eye until his arousal faded, then rose from the bed, moving over to face Amanvah, imitating her as she shifted from stance to stance.

It was surprisingly difficult, even for one trained to the stage. Rojer could walk on his hands, tumble, flip, and dance every dance from royal ballrooms to country reels, but the *sharukin* tested muscles he didn't even know he had, forcing him to hold more balance than it took to walk a ball while fiddling.

Sikvah laughed. 'That is quite good, husband.'

'Don't lie to me, *jiwah*,' Rojer said, smirking to let her know it was only teasing. 'I know it was awful.'

'Sikvah does not lie,' Amanvah said, moving to adjust his pose. 'Your form is good, it is only your centre that is off.'

'My centre?'

'Imagine yourself a palm tree, swaying in the wind,' Amanvah said. 'You bend, but do not break.'

'I would,' Rojer said, 'but I have never seen a palm tree. You might as well tell me to imagine myself a fairy pipkin.'

Amanvah did not frown, but neither did she offer him a smile. In her eyes, there was no humour in *sharusahk*. He swallowed his smirk and let her guide his stance.

'Your centre is the invisible line that connects you, the Ala, and Heaven,' Amanvah said. 'It is balance, but also so much more than that. It is the calm place of silence, the deep place you fall into when you embrace music, the soothing place where you ignore pain.' She grabbed his crotch. 'It is the hard place you use to seed your wives, and the safe place you use to sway with the wind.'

Rojer groaned at her touch, and this time, Amanvah did smile. She took a step back, signalling to Sikvah. Both women reached into pouches at their waists, slipping their fingers into the tiny cymbals used for the pillow dance.

For the next few days, the scene was repeated in one Laktonian village after another, talking the townsfolk down from their fear of the *Sharum*, and then performing for them. Rojer felt a bit of guilt for duping his wives about the message they were giving, but since they hadn't even bothered to tell him they spoke his language at first, he managed to keep the feeling at bay. It wasn't a betrayal. He was just spreading news they already thought common knowledge.

Each morning, Amanvah and Sikvah continued his *sharusahk* training while Enkido looked on the proceedings, his face carved from stone. It seemed more a lark than a concerted effort, but it was pleasurable enough. Leesha had told him of the deadly nerve strikes Inevera had attempted, and the ease with which the woman had wrestled her into a choke hold. There was none of that in his wives' lessons. He improved ·slightly, but not enough to even attempt some of the more difficult poses.

'You must walk before you dance,' Amanvah said.

They were moving at a faster pace now as they moved farther from the Krasians' control. Once, their caravan was attacked – a quick strike on horseback by a dozen bandits with throwing spears and short bows, meant to distract as another group raided one of the baggage carts. The *Sharum* were not fooled. They killed four of the bandits and injured several more before they broke and ran. The caravan was unmolested after that.

Less than a week out from Deliverer's Hollow, they were beginning to feel more comfortable, with Leesha's familiarity with the local Gatherers growing with proximity to home. Some were women she had corresponded with for years but never met. In the village of Northfork, there were actually tears and hugging, but all Rojer could feel was a growing tension. The folk here felt safer from the *Sharum*, and that made them bold.

That night in the taproom, after he finished the *Song of Waning*, there was polite applause, but then the barkeep called, 'Ay, play *The Battle of Cutter's Hollow*!' The request was followed by a chorus of ays, with much hooting and stomping of feet.

Rojer suppressed a furrow of his brow that threatened to mar his Jongleur's mask. Two months ago, he was touting that song from every rooftop, and had sold it dear to the Jongleurs' Guild.

He looked to Amanvah. 'Please play if that is your wish, husband. Sikvah and I will return to our table. We would be honoured to hear a song of our new tribe's heroism in the night.'

They smoothly rolled back onto their heels and stood. Rojer wanted to kiss them as they passed, but while they seemed to be growing more comfortable with Northern customs, that was too far for any Krasian woman short of the Damajah herself to be expected to go in public.

Our new tribe. Rojer gritted his teeth. Did they really know what they were asking for? He had not been fool enough to sing *The Battle of Cutter's Hollow* while in the confines of Everam's Bounty – it bordered on blasphemy.

But they weren't in Everam's Bounty. They were in Laktonian lands now, and surrounded by Thesans who deserved to know that their cousins in the North were growing in power, and had their own saviour to rally to. Rojer didn't really think Arlen Bales was the Deliverer any more than he did Ahmann Jardir, but if folk needed to look to one for strength in the night and a way forward, he would still take the Painted Man over the Shar'Dama Ka. He wasn't going to spend the rest of his life lying about it and hiding that fact from his wives.

Now was as good a time as any.

Slowly, he began to play. As he fell into the music, his fear and anxiety began to drift away like demon ashes in the morning breeze. He had been so proud of the song when he had written it, and as his fingers danced across the familiar notes, he found he still was. *The Battle of Cutter's Hollow* might not have the sheer power of the *Song of Waning*, but he could weave a shell of protection in the night with it, keeping corelings at bay, and it had power over the hearts of all good folk. It was already sung far and wide, and would likely outlive him, lasting into the ages like the ancient sagas.

He fell into the trance that playing always brought, blocking out his wives, the *Sharum*, Leesha, and the patrons. When he was ready, he began to sing.

He had kept the song simple, both so country folk could clap and sing along, but also for his own benefit. His voice was nothing compared with Amanvah's and Sikvah's, or with that of his famed master, Arrick Sweetsong. Even in his cups, when folk laughed and called him 'Soursong' and he could forget lyrics midsong, Arrick still had levels of vocal ability Rojer could never match.

But he had been trained by the best, and while he lacked the lungs and natural talent, Rojer could carry a tune well enough, his voice high and clear.

> *Cutter's Hollow lost its centre*
> *When the flux came to stay*
> *Killed great Herb Gatherer Bruna*
> *Her 'prentice far away*
> Not a one would run and hide,
> They all did stand and follow
> Killing demons in the night
> The Painted Man came to the Hollow
>
> *In Fort Angiers far to the north*
> *Leesha got ill tiding*
> *Her mentor dead, her father sick*
> *Hollow a week's riding*
> Not a one would run and hide,
> They all did stand and follow
> Killing demons in the night
> The Painted Man came to the Hollow
>
> *No guide she found through naked night*
> *Just Jongleur travel wards*
> *That could not hold the bandits back*
> *As it did coreling hordes*
> Not a one would run and hide,
> They all did stand and follow
> Killing demons in the night
> The Painted Man came to the Hollow
>
> *Left for dead no horse or succour*
> *Corelings roving in bands*

They met a man with tattooed flesh
Killed demons with bare hands
Not a one would run and hide,
They all did stand and follow
Killing demons in the night
The Painted Man came to the Hollow

The Hollow razed when they arrived
Not a ward left intact
And half the folk who called it home
Lay dead or on their backs
Not a one would run and hide,
They all did stand and follow
Killing demons in the night
The Painted Man came to the Hollow

Painted Man spat on despair
Said follow me and fight
We'll see the dawn if we all stand
Side by side in the night
Not a one would run and hide,
They all did stand and follow
Killing demons in the night
The Painted Man came to the Hollow

All night they fought with axe and spear
Butcher's knife and shield
While Leesha brought those too weak to
The Holy House to heal
Not a one would run and hide,
They all did stand and follow
Killing demons in the night
The Painted Man came to the Hollow

Hollowers kept their loved ones safe
Though night was long and hard
There's reason why the battlefield's
Called the Corelings' Graveyard
Not a one would run and hide,
They all did stand and follow
Killing demons in the night
The Painted Man came to the Hollow

If someone asks why at sunset
Demons all get shivers
Hollowers say with honest word
It's 'coz we're all Deliverers
Not a one would run and hide,
They all did stand and follow
Killing demons in the night
The Painted Man came to the Hollow

'The true Deliverer!' someone in the crowd shouted, and there was a cheer of agreement.

There was the sound of a chair hitting the floor, and Rojer opened his eyes to see Kaval moving his way, seething with anger. Gared leapt to his feet, putting himself between them. The giant Cutter was eight inches taller and a hundred pounds heavier. He grabbed Kaval and for a moment seemed to have control, but the drillmaster gave his great log of an arm a twist and Gared roared in pain just before he was thrown halfway across the room. Kaval gave him no further notice, picking up speed as he went after Rojer.

Wonda had instinctively reached for her bow, but when she realized it was in her room, she did not hesitate to attack the drillmaster unarmed. She kept to the balls of her feet, guard up as she threw quick, economical punches and kicks, wisely refusing to grapple. She lasted a few seconds longer than Gared, but then Kaval diverted one of her punches and chopped her in the throat with the edge of one hand. He grabbed her arm as she choked and twisted in close, sending her crashing onto the centre of a table, cracking it in half with the impact. Wonda hit the floor under a spray of splinters, ale, and shattered glass.

The barkeeper had produced a cudgel and people were shouting all over the room, but none of them was close enough to aid Rojer. He flicked his wrist to produce a throwing knife, but fumbled in his panic and dropped it as Kaval closed in.

Then Enkido was there, hooking Kaval's armpit and turning his momentum into a throw. The drillmaster was wise to the move, quickstepping around and managing to keep his feet. He shouted something in Krasian as he came back in with a kick, followed by a snapping punch. Neither blow landed, Enkido slipping the kick and catching Kaval's wrist to divert the punch. His free arm snapped out, punching the drillmaster hard in his shoulder joint. Enkido let the limb go and it fell limp. Kaval struck with his other fist, but it was like hitting at smoke. Enkido flowed out of its path and then struck Kaval's other shoulder, rolling smoothly around to kick at the back of Kaval's knee.

With frightening ease he got behind the drillmaster, locking his limp arms and forcing him down to the floor. Kaval's face was agonized as his tendons screamed, but he did not cry out. Enkido was silent as always, his face expressionless.

'Enough,' Amanvah said, and the eunuch immediately released the drillmaster and took a step back. Kaval turned to the *dama'ting*, speaking through his teeth in Krasian. Rojer could not understand what he was saying, but the meaning was clear in the fanatical look in his eyes.

Amanvah responded in Thesan, her voice cold. 'If you or any *Sharum* lays so much as a finger on my husband, Drillmaster, you will spend eternity sitting outside the gates of Heaven.' Kaval's eyes widened at that. He put his forehead on the floor, but there was still rage on his face.

Amanvah turned to Rojer. 'And you, husband, will not play that song ever again.'

Rojer did not need to touch his medallion for strength. The flare of anger was enough and more. No one was going to tell him what he could and couldn't play. 'The Core I won't. I'm no Holy Man. It's not for me to tell folk what to believe. All I do is tell stories, and both of these are true.'

The little vein on Amanvah's forehead throbbed, signalling anger that did not touch her eyes. She nodded.

'Then my father will hear of this. Kaval, select your strongest, fastest *dal'Sharum*. I shall write a letter he is to put in the hand of Shar'Dama Ka and no other. Tell him to take two horses, kill no *alagai* but those that would hinder him, and that Sharak Ka itself may depend upon his swiftness.'

Kaval nodded and rolled back onto his heels to rise and comply, but Leesha stood and moved in front of him, crossing her arms. 'He won't make it,' she warned.

'Eh?' Amanvah asked.

'I've poisoned your *Sharum*,' Leesha said, 'with something that far outlasts the weak antidote I've been putting in their soup. You are several days from the nearest ally, and without the antidote, your man won't last half that time.'

Amanvah stared at Leesha a long time, and Rojer wondered if it was honest word. Surely not. Leesha was capable of many things, but killing with poison? Impossible.

Amanvah's eyes narrowed. 'Kaval, do as I command.'

'I'm not bluffing,' Leesha warned.

'No,' Amanvah agreed, 'I do not believe you are.'

'But you will send a man to his death anyway?' Leesha asked.

'It is you who have served him death,' Amanvah said. 'I am doing what I must to protect his brothers in Everam's Bounty. I will throw the dice and prepare herbs for him to take, but if you have truly poisoned him and I do not guess the cure, he will go to glory as a martyr, and his soul will weigh against you when you are judged by the Creator at the end of the lonely road.'

'Neither of us will go to him clean after this,' Leesha said. 'You make no difference to these people by frightening them and confusing them with lies and half-truth. When my father chooses to take their lands, they will be taken. These people will be stronger for it, and have a chance at glory and Heaven.' Amanvah flicked a finger, and the drillmaster was off. A few of the men in the taproom looked like they might hinder him, but Kaval bared his teeth and they wisely stepped from his path.

With a final glare at Rojer, Amanvah and Sikvah stormed off, heading up to their rooms with Enkido in tow. Rojer watched them sadly as they ascended the steps and vanished from sight. It was true he would never stop playing *The Battle of Cutter's Hollow*, but he need not have sprung it on them onstage. He knew what it was like, to feel left out in the middle of an act.

When the shock wore off, Rojer realized he and the other Hollowers were completely alone for the first time since the journey began. Wonda and Gared seemed to have more injury to their pride than their bodies, and kept watch as the others spoke.

'Well that was terrifying,' Rojer said.

'You were lucky,' Leesha said. 'It's one thing to use the *Song of Waning* to tell the locals to get out of the Krasians' path without their realizing what you're doing, but quite another to sing of another Deliverer right under their noses. You may as well have spit on everything they believe in.'

'So we should pretend the Battle of Cutter's Hollow never happened?' Wonda demanded. 'That we fought for nothing? That my da just up and died, rather than went down taking a copse of woodies with him? That the Painted Man didn't do just what happened in the song?'

'Gettin' sick of pretending up is down and black is white,' Gared said.

'Of course not,' Leesha said. 'But we're vulnerable on the

road. We'll be back in the Hollow soon enough. Between now and then, I suggest we tread carefully.'

'Ay, everyone all right?' the innkeeper asked, bringing over a fresh tray of drinks. He was accompanied by Gery, the Speaker for Northfork, and Nicholl, the Herb Gatherer.

'Ent been better,' Rojer said, motioning for them to sit. 'Night's got no flavour if I don't almost get killed.'

Gery blinked, but he and Nicholl took the offered seats. 'Just what in the Core is going on? You said they were with you, but it looks to me like you're with them. They holding you prisoner?'

Rojer knew they were expecting him to reply, but he felt numb and cloudy and had no answers. Leesha shook her head, and he was happy to let her have the floor, at least until she spoke.

'It's more complicated than that, Speaker,' Leesha said, 'and not your concern. We'll be safe enough. The woman in white is the daughter of the Krasian leader . . .'

Rojer stiffened and leaned forward. *Be careful*, he thought.

'. . . and married to Rojer. After tonight, none of the warriors will dare harm us without word from the Shar'Dama Ka, and that won't come quickly. We'll be safe in the Hollow by then, and better prepared for what's coming than the people of Northfork.'

'What's that supposed to mean?' the Speaker demanded. 'You tell us one thing, sing another, and show us a third.'

'It means the Krasians are coming this way,' Leesha said. 'They may not be as brutal as they were with the Rizonans if you aren't stupid enough to fight, but the effect will be the same. Every boy taken to be trained in demon fighting, every man made a second-class citizen, every woman a third. Your village will be put under an overseer and you will all be subject to Evejan law.'

'You're telling us we shouldn't fight that?' Gery asked. 'We should just take it like a mare when they come to stick us?'

'She's telling you to run while you can,' Erny said. 'You're right on the road they will march their army through. You're smart, you'll harvest whatever's still growing, pack up everything you can, and get out of their path.'

'And go where?!' Gery demanded. 'My family's been in Northfork long as anyone can remember, and the same goes for most of the folk here. We should just abandon the place?'

'Yes, if you value your lives more than the land,' Leesha said. 'If you want to keep to your duke, head for Lakton proper, if they'll have you. I sent word of the threat to them months ago. The city on the lake should be safe, at least for a while.'

'Only seen the lake once, and it scared the piss out of me,' Gery said. 'Don't think any of us're suited to living on that much water.'

'Then come to the Hollow,' Leesha said. 'We're not yet able to extend this far, but our reach is growing. Any who come will not be turned away, and allowed to keep their community and leaders. Good land will be allotted you, safely warded, and we'll give you warded weapons and training to use them. It will soon be the safest place short of Duke Euchor's fortress in Miln.'

'And either way, every able-bodied man'll be drafted to fight that which ent meant to be fought.' Gery spat on the taproom floor.

'Ay!' the innkeeper shouted.

'Sorry, Sim,' Gery said. 'All due respect, Mistress Paper, but we're simple folk in Northfork, and not lookin' to be demon killers like you Hollowers.'

'Might be easier to just kidnap this Krasian princess,' Sim said. 'Ransom the town for her. Those black-robed bastards are tough, but we got 'em outnumbered.'

'You don't want to do that,' Rojer said.

'He's right,' Leesha said. 'You lay a hand on her, and the Krasians will kill every man, woman, and child in Northfork and burn it to the ground. It is death to lay hands on a *dama'ting*.'

'They gotta catch us first,' Sim said.

The knife was in Rojer's hand in a blink, and he had Sim by the collar, pinning him to the table, the blade drawing a thin line of blood on his throat.

'Rojer!' Leesha shouted, but he ignored her.

'Forget the Krasians,' Rojer growled. 'You don't want to do that because she's my ripping wife.'

Sim swallowed hard. 'Just ale talk, Master Halfgrip. Din't mean it for real.'

Rojer snarled, but he released the man, his knife vanishing.

Gery gave Sim a hand up. 'Go wipe the bar down and keep your fool mouth shut.' Sim nodded quickly and scurried off. Gery turned back to Rojer. 'Apologies for that, Master Halfgrip. Got a couple woodbrains in every village.'

'Ay.' Rojer was still caught in the rush of adrenaline, seething, but his Jongleur's mask was back in place, and he returned to his seat.

'No one's pushing you to go one place over another,' Leesha told the Speaker. 'But staying here puts you right in the path of a storm you're not prepared for. You saw what one angry *Sharum* was capable of. Imagine ten thousand of them bearing down on you, along with forty thousand Rizonan slaves.'

Gery paled, but he nodded. 'I'll think on it. Rest easy tonight. Ent no one going to be fool enough to cause trouble between now and you leaving for the morning.' With that, he pushed up from his seat and gave Nicholl a hand as they left the inn.

'That one's got nightmares waiting in his bed tonight,' Elona said.

'Why should he be different from the rest of us?' Leesha asked.

Just then a young *Sharum* in full armour entered the inn with Kaval, carrying spear and shield. The two men headed up to Amanvah's chambers. The young warrior came back down at a run a few minutes later, shooting out the door like an arrow.

'You didn't really poison the *Sharum*, did you?' Rojer asked.

Leesha looked at him a moment, then took a deep breath

and stood, heading down the hall beside the bar towards her room, Wonda at her heel.

Rojer sighed, taking the full mug of ale before him and throwing it back in three gulps, the cool liquid leaking from the corners of his mouth and down his chin. 'Best I go face the music.'

Erny looked over at him, using the reproachful look he sometimes used to check his daughter. 'You're a fine fiddler, Rojer, but you have a lot to learn about being a husband.'

Gared walked Rojer up to his room, expecting to see Enkido guarding the door, but the eunuch was not in sight, which meant he was inside. Not comforting.

'Want I should go in with ya?' Gared asked.

Rojer shook his head. 'No, that's all right. You just stand by in case some other fool takes Sim's suggestion and tries to kidnap Amanvah. I have this.'

Gared nodded. 'I'll be out here in the hall. But I hear a commotion, I'll be through that door in a second.'

An image flashed in Rojer's mind, the splintering of wood as the rock demon had smashed through the door of his father's inn, fifteen years past. Rojer had no doubt Gared could break through the heavy wood with similar ease.

He left unvoiced what they both knew. Kaval had taken Gared down like he was a child, and Enkido had done the same to Kaval. Infuriating as the burly Cutter was at times, Rojer had no desire to see him killed in a fight he had no hope of winning. If he couldn't get out of this without fighting, he wasn't getting out.

Rojer pretended to adjust his tunic, needing to touch his medallion. Immediately he felt calmer. 'We all need something for the pains of life,' Arrick said when Rojer asked why he drank so much wine, 'and I'm too old for Jongleur's tales.' He reached for the door handle.

Inside, Rojer immediately noticed Enkido standing off to one side of the door, arms crossed. As always, the eunuch seemed to take no notice of Rojer.

Amanvah and Sikvah had changed into their coloured silks, which Rojer took as a good sign, but they glowered at him as he entered.

'You and Leesha are working against us,' Amanvah said.

'How?' Rojer asked. 'Your father knows we do not bow to him. He offered us a pact, and we are considering it. I made no oath to serve his every interest.'

'There is a difference between not supporting his interests and opposing them, husband,' Amanvah said. 'My father does not know you are telling tales of false Deliverers, or that Mistress Leesha has poisoned his warriors.'

'Your father knows all about the Painted Man and his connection to the Hollow. We told him as much when he first visited.' Rojer lowered his eyebrows. 'And you're in no position to lecture anyone about poison.'

Amanvah did not let her mask slip, but the pause before her retort was enough to let him know he had struck a nerve.

'But you tell your people to flee us,' Amanvah said, 'though we have no plans to march. You tell them to pack and go to the great oasis city, or come to your Hollow to strengthen your own tribe to stand against us.'

Rojer felt his temper flare again. 'And how do you know that? Are you spying on me?'

'The *alagai hora* tell me much, son of Jessum,' Amanvah said.

'Creator, I am so sick of your cryptic answers and your ripping dice!' Rojer snapped. 'You put more stock in the bones of demons than you do in people's lives.'

Amanvah paused again, holding her calm. 'Perhaps we can't stop your blasphemy when you return to the Hollow, husband, but there will be no more village stops on the road. And even when we reach the Hollow, Sikvah and I will never sing your infidel song, or suffer it in our presence.'

Rojer shrugged. 'Never asked you to. But I was in the Battle of Cutter's Hollow, wife. I lived it and know it for true. I'm not going to pretend those things never happened just because it hurts your father's case. If he's really the Deliverer, it doesn't matter. And if he's not . . .'

'He is,' Amanvah hissed.

Rojer shrugged and smiled. 'Then you've got nothing to fret over, do you?'

'My father is the chosen of Everam,' Amanvah said, 'but Nie is strong. He can still fail, if his people are not true.'

Again Rojer shrugged. 'These are not his people, at least not yet. If he wishes them to be, he must earn it. I will fight against the demons when Sharak Ka comes. Who I fight for is yet to be determined.'

Amanvah snorted. 'You are many things, son of Jessum, but a fighter is not one of them.'

It was an unexpected slap in the face, and Rojer felt his Jongleur's mask slip. His face showed his true anger as he got to his feet, such that even Amanvah flinched.

'As your husband, I order you to come with me,' he said, taking his bow and fiddle and turning to leave the room.

Enkido stepped smoothly to block his way.

Rojer walked right up to him, tilting his head back to look into the eunuch's dead eyes. 'Wife, remove your gelding from my path.'

Rojer caught the flash of understanding, though it was gone in an instant. 'Don't speak our tongue, my red shorthairs. You big ball-less bastard. You're getting every word. So either kill me or move aside.'

For the first time, the eunuch began to show emotion – a simmering anger that rivalled the look Kaval had shown when he came for Rojer. But Rojer was past caring, matching the stare with one of his own.

'Enkido, step aside,' Amanvah said. The eunuch looked surprised, but he did as commanded immediately. Rojer opened the door and stormed into the hall, making Gared jump.

Amanvah and Sikvah followed after as he strode towards the steps. 'Just where do you think you are going?' Amanvah demanded, but he did not bother to reply.

The taproom was mostly empty as they descended the steps, just a small cluster of townies left at the bar. They looked at Rojer in surprise, their eyes widening as they saw the Krasian women in their coloured silks.

'Husband!' Sikvah cried. 'We are not dressed!'

Rojer ignored her, crossing the room and unbarring the front door.

'Ay, what in the Core are you doing?' Sim cried, but Rojer ignored him as well, stepping outside.

As in most Thesan towns, the inn was right at the edge of the cobbled town square. There were interconnected warded porchways between many of the buildings on the perimeter to allow folk to gather at the inn after dark, but the main square was too large to ward effectively. The cobbles prevented demons from rising there, but wind demons knew to watch the spot, and would swoop on anything they saw moving. Other demons would occasionally wander into the area from the road.

Outside on the inn porch stood Kaval and two other *Sharum*, all fully armed and armoured.

'Out of my way.' Rojer pushed past them as if their obedience was expected and his due, and the *Sharum* backed away as he stepped out into the square. Rojer spotted two small wood demons prowling the far end, testing the wards of the buildings, searching for an opening. They froze in place at the commotion, looking like nothing more than a pair of twisted trees.

Rojer heard the warriors gasp as his wives followed him onto the porch, and smiled as they all turned to avert their eyes. His wives were blood of the Deliverer and married. Looking lustfully upon them was asking to have one's eyes put out.

Without his warded cloak, the woodies caught sight of him as he moved beyond the protection of the wards and began to stalk slowly his way. Rojer ignored them, not even bothering to raise his fiddle. Above, a wind demon's cry split the night.

Amanvah and Sikvah stopped at the porch rail. 'Enough of this foolishness!' Amanvah snapped. 'Come back inside!'

Rojer shook his head. 'You don't give me orders, *jiwah*. Come to me.'

'The Evejah forbids women to enter the naked night,' Amanvah said.

'And to let other men see us unveiled and in colour! The Damajah has women stoned for this,' Sikvah cried. He glanced back and saw her hunched over, trying to cover herself.

The demons were closer now, tamping their legs, muscles bunched as they prepared to spring. Unafraid, Rojer finally turned to them and lifted the bow in his crippled hand.

Demons were creatures of primal emotion. Manipulating those emotions was the key to controlling them. Right now, their entire attention was fixed on him. Rojer took hold of that feeling and enhanced it, projecting concentration in his music.

Here I am! he told them. *Focus on this spot!*

Then he stopped playing and took two quick steps to the side. The demons shook their heads, confused at the way he had vanished, and Rojer began to play once more, enhancing that feeling as well.

Where did he go? I don't see him anywhere! he told the demons. They began to frantically scan the area, but even as their gaze swept over him, their frustration at being unable to find him remained. Rojer stepped carefully around them, keeping a casual air to his Jongleur's mask.

'I could say the Evejah also commands you to obey your husband,' he told his wives, 'but the Evejah hasn't been where we're going. Female Jongleurs wear bright colours, and you are in the green lands now. Inevera would have to stone every woman outside Everam's Bounty.'

A crowd was forming at the porch rail. Gared was there, weapons in hand, as was Leesha and Wonda with her warded bow, a cluster of townies, and the three *Sharum*. The women hesitated, but then Amanvah huffed, drawing herself to her full height, and strode out to join him, Sikvah at her heels.

'Dama'ting, no!' Kaval cried.

'Silence!' Amanvah snapped. 'It is your rash action that has brought us to this point!'

Gared and the warriors moved to follow them onto the square, including Enkido, who now held a spear and shield.

'Stay behind the rails, Gar,' Rojer called. 'That goes for the rest of you, as well. We need no spears tonight.' The *Sharum* ignored him until Amanvah whisked a hand at them. They retreated, but looked ready to ignore her command and leap into the night if the demons got too close.

The woodies did fix on the women, but they had tested the wards around the square and knew they were out of reach. Rojer took that feeling, and held it. He tilted his head, taking his chin off the wards in the demons' direction to aim the music their way.

They are warded, he told the demons, even as his wives crossed into the open, unprotected area. *You cannot touch them. There will be light and pain if you try. Seek other prey.*

The demons did as instructed, and as Amanvah and Sikvah came to him, Rojer led his melody into the opening notes of the *Song of Waning*. Immediately they began to sing, accompanying Rojer's lead in harmony, an echo and a highlight that increased the effect of his playing manifold. With that power, he wove a spell of music around the three of them that made them invisible to the corelings. The demons could smell them in the air, hear them, even catch fleeting glimpses, but the source of their senses was gone, their eyes slipping away from them again and again.

Safe from assault, Rojer added another layer to the tune, and Amanvah and Sikvah picked it up immediately, sending a call out into the night. Slowly, Rojer lifted his chin, revealing more of Amanvah's wards. His wives put hands to their throats, manipulating their chokers in some way, and matched him as his volume increased.

The sound carried far, drawing first the locals around the square to their windows and porches. Lanterns appeared, shedding dim light over the cobbles. The folk looked on in stunned silence as the song did its work, drawing every demon in the area.

They came slowly at first, but soon there were more than a dozen corelings in the square. Five wood demons stalked, snuffling the air, seeking victims that could not be found. Two flame demons shrieked and cavorted, trailing orange fire as they raced from one end of the square to the other, unable to pinpoint the source of the music, but unable to resist its call. Above, three wind demons circled in the sky, their raptor calls echoing in the night. Two field demons prowled low to the ground, bellies scraping the cobbles as they tried to stay invisible for the hunt. There was even a stone demon – a smaller cousin of the rock, but still bigger than Gared, who was near to seven feet. It stood as still as its name, but Rojer knew it was extending every sense to seek them, and that it would explode into motion if he were to allow them to be seen.

Leesha had described the power of the mind demons, the vibrations in her mind forcing her to act at their bidding. Perhaps music had a similar effect, Rojer mused. Perhaps an attempt to mimic that power was why music was first created, why some melodies brought forth the same emotions in any who heard them.

Such was the power of the *Song of Waning*. Rojer had sensed it the first time his wives had sung it for him, a power akin to his, but . . . faded. Lost in the thousands of years since it was last needed.

But now Rojer brought that power back to life. Under his direction, the song's insistent call kept the demons' attention on something they could never find, to the ignorance of all else. If they had wanted, Gared or the *Sharum* could have walked right up and struck at them. A blow would break the spell and give the demons an immediate threat to respond to, but from a *Sharum* spear or Gared's axe, a single blow could easily cripple or kill.

But Rojer had spoken true when he told them weapons were not needed this night.

He began the first verse of the song, Amanvah and Sikvah singing of the glory of Everam, and threaded in his first spell, one he and his wives had practised many times in their carriage. By the time the refrain came, the women wordlessly calling to the Creator, the demons had forgotten their hunt, dancing to his tune like villagers spinning a reel at solstice.

They carried that on into the next verse, when Rojer changed his tune to another practised melody. He began to stroll casually about the square, his wives following him. The demons trailed them like ducklings following their mother to water.

He let this go on through the refrain and the verse that followed, but added a note to signal his wives to the abrupt change about to come. As the verse ended, the demons were in the position he wished, and the three of them spun, hitting the demons with a series of piercing shrieks that had them howling and running from the square like whipped dogs.

They were almost out of range when he began the next verse. The corelings stopped short and froze in place like hunters trying not to be seen, lest they frighten off their prey. With contemptuous ease, he raised their tension until they could not bear it any longer, running about the square slashing and snarling, desperate to find the source of the music and put an end to it.

Rojer continued to lead them, offering false hints of where their quarry lay. There was an old hitching post outside the wardnet. He draped music over it.

There I am! Attack now!

Immediately, the demons shrieked and charged. The field demons leapt first, claws digging great furrows in the wood. A wind demon swooped out of the sky to strike the post, knocking one of the field demons free. The two corelings hit the cobbles in a tumble, biting and clawing. Black ichor splattered the square, and the wind demon barely escaped alive, taking to the air again with multiple tears in its leathern wings. The flame demons spat fire on the hitching post, and in moments it was ablaze.

Next Rojer laid the music over the stone demon. The field demons leapt at it as well, but the stone demon caught one by the head in its talons and crushed its skull against the cobbles. It took the other by the tail, swinging it like a man might swing a cat. Another wind demon swooped in, but veered off as the stone swung the field demon at it, then threw the field demon so hard it smashed against one of the porch wardnets in a lightning flare and fell to the ground, smoking and still. A flamer spat on the stone demon's feet, setting them ablaze, but that did not save it from being kicked clear across the square to strike the wardnet with a flash of magic. When the flame died, the stone demon's feet were unharmed.

Rojer allowed himself a smile. It was all teachable. All these refrains, these 'spells' he had cast on the demons, were melodies they had practised and written down. Other players might not be able to bring the power and harmony of their trio to bear, but they could learn by rote how to call demons or repel them, how to hide from them or send them into a frenzy.

But that was only the barest surface of the power Rojer felt with the women at his side. The truly subtle work he could never hope to write down. It had to be lived and felt in the moment, dependent not only on the demon breeds, but local variables as well, building on the very atmosphere.

This was what he had never been able to teach. He looked back at his *jiwah*, seeing awe in their wide eyes, and a little fear. Even Amanvah had lost her mask, her *dama'ting* serenity overwhelmed. They could imitate him, but not innovate.

There's more, my loves, Rojer thought, turning back to regard the demons again. He took on a predatory demeanour, stalking the corelings as he and his wives herded them, separating them by breed. The song was done now, but Rojer kept on playing, building the final refrain louder and stronger, adding shifts and changes as quickly as Amanvah and Sikvah could pick them up. The demons backed into tight knots, hissing and clawing at the air, terrified of the power that was building but afraid to run lest they turn their backs on whatever hunted them.

And then Rojer began to hurt them, driving the music into them in jarring, discordant waves that seemed to strike the creatures like physical blows. They screamed, some falling to the cobbles, clawing at their own heads as if they could tear the sound out and be free of it. Even the wind demons above shrieked in agony, but the music held them fast, and they could not flee, circling endlessly.

Rojer looked up and changed his tune again, calling the wind demons down from the night sky. *The source of your pain is here! Strike now and silence it!*

The windies dived with terrifying speed, but Rojer and his wives were not where the music led – off to the side, and several feet low. The wind demons struck the cobbles with incredible force, their hollow bones crunching and splintering on impact. In seconds, the square was littered with their corpses.

He turned to the wood demons next, howling like trees bent near to breaking in a gale. Rojer thought of the fire-eaters, Jongleurs in Angiers who pretended to swallow fire, then spat it back out again with a spark and a mouthful of alcohol. It was generally thought a 'low' act – dangerous flash used to hide a lack of talent. Jongleurs who did it often got hurt, and in the forest fortress, spitting fire was against the law save in very specific circumstances. It was usually an opening act for a Jongleur of more renown.

I have flame demons to open my act now, Rojer thought as he made the flamers spit fire on the wood demons, aiming them as easily as Wonda might her bow.

The wood demons caught fire immediately, and unlike the stone they were not immune to its effects. They shrieked and flailed, snatching up the flame demons and crushing the life from them, but it was too late. Black smoke billowed into a thick stinking cloud as they collapsed to the ground, immolated.

Only the stone demon remained, close to eight feet of muscle and sinew, covered in indestructible knobs like river stones. It stood silent as a statue, but Rojer knew it was desperately seeking them, a killing rage barely contained. He smiled.

The trio began to circle, intensifying the refrain, notes going ever higher even as they revealed more and more of the wards of amplification. The demon began to shriek, covering its head in its talons and looking frantically about for an escape, but they tightened their circle, and it seemed the pain came from all sides. The demon wobbled, then dropped to one knee, letting out a roar of agony as sweet as any music.

Even the folk around the square were covering their ears now. Rojer's own head was ringing, ears aching, but he ignored the pain, taking his chin from the fiddle entirely.

The stone demon gave a final twist, and there was a *crack!* like an old oak snapping in a windstorm. Fissures spiderwebbed through the demon's armour, and it fell to the ground, dead.

Rojer stopped playing instantly, and his wives followed. The square fell silent, and Rojer inhaled the hush before the roar.

15

The Paper Women

333 AR Summer
16 Dawns Before New Moon

'Close your mouth, dear,' Elona told Leesha. 'You look like a woodbrained bumpkin.'

Leesha turned to retort, but realized she was indeed standing with her mouth open. Her teeth clicked as she snapped it shut, just as everyone around the Northfork town square burst into a roar, hooting and clapping and stomping their feet. One of the *Sharum* let out an ululating cry of delight, and even Kaval looked as if he had forgotten his rage.

It was understandable. The *Sharum* respected nothing more than a man's ability to kill demons, and Rojer had just displayed incredible power, killing corelings without even touching them. Even the Shar'Dama Ka could not do that. They looked at him awestruck, but no less so than the local villagers. Even Gared had that fanatical gleam in his eye, the one she thought reserved for Arlen alone.

But the power was not all Rojer's. She had heard him charm demons with his fiddle many times, but never so loudly her ears rang and the floorboards rattled. There was *hora* magic at work, she would bet her bottom.

At barely seventeen, it was easy to think Amanvah just a girl – one Leesha had dominated before. But she wore the white of *dama'ting*, and that meant she was schooled in the secrets of demon bone magic. Magic Leesha had seen Inevera display to powerful effect. She had done something to Rojer's fiddle, as well as the golden chokers she and Sikvah wore, using the magic to amplify their music.

Leesha understood the principles now – using bones to power wardings even when there were no demons about. Already she had begun to experiment, but the Krasian holy women had centuries of experience to draw on, while she was only just now feeling her way.

The crowd was still cheering when she left the porch, going out to the trio. Rojer was bowing like a master showman, gesturing for his wives to do the same. Sikvah did, bowing lower than her husband, as was the custom, though in her bed silks the move was downright scandalous. Amanvah looked decidedly uncomfortable at the idea of bowing to her lessers, and settled for nodding to the crowd like the Duchess Mum acknowledging a curtsy.

Rojer beamed at Leesha as she approached, and she embraced him, ignoring Amanvah's hiss. 'Rojer, that was incredible. Amazing.'

Rojer's boyish smile threatened to take in his ears. 'I couldn't have done it without Amanvah and Sikvah.'

'Indeed.' Leesha nodded to the women. 'You sounded like the Creator's own seraphs.' Both women's eyes widened at the compliment, and Leesha turned her attention back to Rojer before they could recover.

'Did Amanvah ward your fiddle?'

Rojer nodded. 'Just the chinrest. The wards let me play loud enough to break the barn. And using it makes me feel . . .'

'Energized?' Leesha asked. 'You should be half deaf after that.'

Rojer started, wiggling a finger in his ear. 'Huh. Not even a ring.'

'May I see?' Leesha asked, her tone casual. Rojer unclipped

the piece and handed it to her without a thought. Amanvah moved to stop him – too late. Leesha snatched it and took a quick step back. She unbuttoned a special pocket on her apron, slipping out the pair of gold-rimmed spectacles Arlen had made for her.

The lenses were not corrective, but wards in the frame and glass granted her the same wardsight Arlen used, letting her see the flow of magic. The chinrest was bright with power, its wards shining as if carved from lightning. She recognized almost all of them, wards of siphoning and linking, along with projection and . . . resonance.

'There's more here than just amplification, Rojer,' she said. 'There are resonance wards.'

Rojer looked at her blankly. 'What does that mean?'

'It means anything said near this fiddle will resonate somewhere else.' Leesha turned to Amanvah. Several of the many piercings in her ear glowed bright with magic. 'With an earring, perhaps?'

Amanvah kept her expression calm, but her hesitation betrayed her nevertheless. Rojer looked at his wife and his joyous expression fell into a stung look. 'Is that how you knew what we said in the taproom?'

'You were conspiring—' Amanvah began.

'Don't hand me that demonshit!' Rojer snapped. 'You spent weeks making that chinrest. This wasn't a reaction to anything I did on the road, it was your plan all along to spy on me.'

'You are my husband,' Amanvah said. 'It is my duty to support you and keep you from trouble, sending aid when you are in need.'

'Always lies with you!' Rojer shouted. The *Sharum* stiffened at that – shouting at a *dama'ting* was an unthinkable crime, but they did not move to intercept as they might have before, still awestruck at Rojer's power. Even Enkido hung back, waiting for a signal from his mistress.

'You are so fast to quote the Evejah when it suits you,' Rojer went on, 'but does it not command truthfulness?'

'Actually,' Leesha cut in, 'the book expressly states that oaths and promises to *chin* are meaningless if they in any way hinder service to Everam.' Amanvah glared at her, but Leesha only smiled, daring her to contradict.

'The Core with this,' Rojer said, snatching the chinrest back from Leesha and lifting it high to hurl it down at the cobbles.

'No!' Amanvah and Leesha shouted at once, both reaching to grab his arm and forestall him. Amanvah looked at her curiously.

'You saw the power it gave you,' Leesha said. 'Don't throw that away in your anger.'

'The mistress speaks truth, husband,' Amanvah said. 'It would be a month and more to make a new one, if we could even find a piece so fine to work with.'

Rojer looked at her coldly. 'When you first gave me the box, I wondered if it might be a pair of golden shackles. Seems I wasn't far off. I won't be your slave, Amanvah.'

'Are we slaves to fire because it can burn us?' Leesha asked. 'You are wise to its power now, Rojer. I can paint wards of silence on a box for it. Put it away when you want your privacy, but don't destroy it.'

'Throwing it to the stones would do little in any event,' Amanvah added. 'The magic strengthens the metal and wood. You will find it hard to destroy, and there is none other worthy of its power.'

Rojer seemed to deflate. He looked at the object sadly, then shoved it into a pocket and turned back to the inn. 'I'm going to bed.' He headed off without waiting to see if anyone followed. Amanvah and Sikvah heeled him like dogs, Enkido with them.

A few villagers had wandered out into the square to look in fascinated horror at the demon corpses, but a wind demon cry cut the night and sent them scurrying back inside. Leesha moved to do the same, though the wards on her shawl were enough to turn any coreling attention from her.

Before she went inside, she took one last look down the way to the Messenger road, where even now one of the *Sharum* raced back towards Everam's Bounty.

Alone in her room, Leesha wept.

She did not fully understand the demon dice, their secrets of foretelling closely guarded by the *dama'ting*. The Evejah spoke of a ward of prophecy, but it was not shown, and Leesha did not think she would ever persuade a Bride of Everam to willingly let her examine a set.

But from what she gathered, the dice did not provide specific predictions, only facts that hinted at what the future might hold. Odds were Amanvah had not guessed the poison Leesha had given the *Sharum*, and its cure was tricky and time-consuming to prepare. Given the speed with which the warrior left, Leesha doubted she had done anything to aid him. In a day, he would weaken. In two, he would be dead.

There had been no choice. She didn't know how Ahmann would take the news she meant to militarize the Hollow as a bulwark against him. She couldn't keep it from him forever, but she needed time. Time to warn the Laktonians and Duchess Araine. Time to fill the Hollow and prepare, both for the coming Waning and for Sharak Sun. But that made her feel no less wretched as she crawled into bed, throwing the coverlet over her head.

For the first time, Leesha wished she'd never gone to Everam's Bounty. Night, she wished she had never left Cutter's Hollow, never gone to Hag Bruna's hut and learned Herb Gathering. She'd have been a wonderful papermaker, and it would have made her father so happy.

But much as she would have liked to shift the blame, Leesha knew that was too easy, and a lie.

'Why must I learn poison?' she had asked, all those years ago.

'So you can cure it, girl,' Bruna told her. 'Learning the mixtures and signs won't turn you into some stinkhearted Weed Gatherer.'

'Weed Gatherer?' Leesha asked.

Bruna spat. 'Failed Herb Gatherers. They sell weak cures and poison the enemies of nobles for coin.'

Leesha was aghast. 'Women actually do that?'

Bruna grunted. 'Not everyone is as sweet and moral as you, dearie. I had one of my own apprentices turn that way. Corespawn me if I let it happen again, but you need to know what you're up against.'

I'm up against myself, Leesha thought. *Killing men for my convenience. Am I any better than a Weed Gatherer?*

She sobbed again, her body racked until exhaustion took her and she passed into slumber. Even there she found no peace, her dreams haunted with violence. Inevera, turning purple under her choking hands. Ahmann, standing by as his warriors killed Rizonan men and raped the women. Gared, his throat slashed by the blade of Abban's crutch. Rojer, strangled in his bed by his own wives. Kaval, beating Wonda to death and calling it 'training'. The Cutters and *Sharum* locked in a bloody storm of spear and axe as Arlen and Ahmann pointed them at each other.

A lone *Sharum*, dead on the road.

She woke with a start, her stomach roiling, and practically fell from bed in her desperation to get the chamber pot. It sloshed as she dragged it from under the bed, but she was not fast enough even so, and vomit mixed with last night's urine on the floorboards. She knelt there, shuddering and retching, tears streaming down her face. Her eye socket ached, and she knew another cluster of headaches was on its way.

Oh, Bruna, what have I become?

There was a knock at the door, and Leesha froze. Dawn was

only a purple hint outside the window. Too early to leave for the caravan.

Again the knock. 'Go away!'

'You open this door, Leesha Paper, or I'll have Gared break it down,' her mother said. 'You just see if I don't.'

Leesha stood slowly, her legs watery and her stomach still roiling. She found a clean cloth and wiped her face, then pulled a robe over her stained nightdress, cinching it tight.

She went to the door and lifted the bar, opening it a crack. Elona's face, looking like she'd just swallowed a lemon, was never the first thing she wanted to see in the morning.

'Now isn't a good time . . .' Leesha began, but Elona ignored her, pushing into the room. Leesha sighed and shut the door behind her, dropping the bar back in place. 'What do you want, Mother?'

'Thought you'd grown out of waking me and your father with your blubbering,' Elona said. 'Feeling bad about what you did, killing that boy?'

Leesha blinked. No matter how many times her mother read her mind and cut to the quick, it never ceased to shock her.

'Well don't,' Elona snapped. 'You did what you had to, and that boy knew what he was getting into when he picked up his first spear.'

'It's not that simple—' Leesha began.

'Pfagh!' Elona waved a hand dismissively. 'How many Rizonans you think he killed when they took the city? How many lives are you saving by keeping him from telling tales?'

Leesha felt her legs giving way, and fell to a seat on the bed, trying hard to make it seem as if she had meant to sit all along. Her stomach felt like a boiling pot, stirred too quickly and threatening to foam over the rim. 'I wouldn't have done it otherwise, but that doesn't mean I should be proud of it.'

Elona grunted. 'Maybe not, but for what it's worth, *I'm* proud of you, girl. Know I don't say it as much as you deserve, but there it is. Didn't think you had it in you to stand up like that. Glad to see something of me in there, after all.'

Leesha frowned. 'Sometimes I think there's too much of you in me already, Mother.'

Elona snorted. 'You should be so lucky.'

'Why the change of heart?' Leesha asked. 'You were the one pushing me to marry Ahmann and let him make me a queen.'

'Had a better look at his rule since then,' Elona said. 'Ent no way I'm spending the rest of my wrinkle-free days with everything except my eyes wrapped under seven layers of cloth.' She hefted her breasts, barely contained in a dress with a swooping neckline. 'What's the point of having paps like these if you can't put 'em on display and laugh as men drool and women simmer?'

Leesha raised an eyebrow. 'Wrinkle-free?'

Elona glared, daring her to say more. 'Letting that warrior go would have jeopardized everything you've worked for. You might have laid the drama on a bit thick, but there's no denying this trip was good for the Hollow. You bought a conditional peace, scouted the enemy camp, whispered wisdom and doubt into the ear of its leader, learned of those mind demons and bone magic. All that, and you got your toes curled in the process. Hag Bruna was still around, she'd be prouder than Jan Cutter showing off his prize bull.'

Leesha smiled wanly. 'I hope so. I was just thinking I'd disappointed her.'

Elona turned to the window, looking over her reflection with a critical eye. Though there were no men to see, she reflexively straightened her hair and smoothed the bosom of her dress. 'A bit, perhaps. Any apprentice of Bruna – night, any daughter of mine – should have been able to enjoy a few rolls in the feathers without making a child.'

Leesha felt her face flush red. 'What?'

Elona pointed to the disgusting mixture on the floor, making no effort to help clean it. 'Seen you throw your hysterics a lot of times, girl, but ent never seen it sick you up. Night, I can't recall you sloshing up ever. You got more than Mum's paps

396

and posterior. You got my iron belly.' She smiled, patting her stomach. 'But I was sick as a cat the whole time I was carrying you.'

Leesha felt her boiling stomach freeze over. She tried to swallow as she ticked off the days since her last flow, but the lump in her throat prevented it.

Could it be true?

With more desperation than she had reached for the chamber pot, Leesha went for her pocketed apron. Like a Jongleur's coloured balls, she juggled herbs and instruments, grinding and mixing until she had a tiny vial of milky fluid. She swabbed at herself and put it in the vial, holding her breath.

Her lungs gave way well before the time the chemics took to react. She turned pointedly and began to count by thousands to mark the minutes until she could turn back and see if the chemics had gone from milk white to pink.

One thousand. Two thousand. Three thousand . . .

'You already know what it's going to say,' Elona said. 'Quit biting at your fingers and figure out what you're going to do about it.'

Leesha raised an eyebrow. 'Do?'

'Don't play dim with me, child,' Elona snapped. 'I was apprenticed to Bruna as well. You could flush the problem right out if you wanted.'

'Really, Mum?' Leesha asked bitterly. 'You, who've pushed me to have children my whole life, would tell me to kill the child?'

'Ent a child, it's a notion,' Elona said. 'And a bad one, at that. Doesn't take a genius to see that babe would be a gap in our wards big enough for the mother of all demons to ride through.'

One hundred thousand. One hundred and one thousand. One hundred and two thousand . . .

Leesha shook her head so hard she felt it rattle. 'No. If it's far enough along for me to be sick, it's a life, not a notion. You complained I missed my most fertile years, Mum, and you weren't wrong. If this is how the Creator wants to give me a child, then I'm going to take it.'

Elona rolled her eyes. 'You picked a bad time to go all Canon, girl.' She shrugged. 'But if you're not going to flush it, you'd best seduce someone else, quick and public, to buy yourself time.'

Leesha felt her mouth fall open. 'I swear, Mum, if you so much as say Gared's name . . .'

But Elona surprised her with another disgusted wave of her hand. 'Pfagh! You can do better than Gared Cutter! Have another go at the other Deliverer, now that you have the knack. It's clear as day he's pent and needs a draining. Do him as good as you did the demon of the desert, and you can have the both of them eating out of your hand and brought to heel by winter.'

'Or brought to blows, all our respective men behind them,' Leesha said.

'That's gonna happen no matter what, and you know it,' Elona said. 'Best you can do is guide the where and how.'

Leesha grimaced. 'There is nothing in this world I hate more than when your words make sense, Mother.'

Elona cackled.

'Making the Painted Man think it's his might not be possible,' Leesha said. 'He won't touch me any more. He's terrified of making a child tainted by his demon magic.'

Elona shrugged. 'So tell him you're taking pomm tea. Leach some leaves and leave them out where he can see. Tell him it's just a release.'

Three hundred fifty thousand. Three hundred and fifty-one thousand. Three hundred and fifty-two thousand . . .

Leesha shook her head. 'He's not that gullible, Mother.'

'Demonshit,' Elona said. 'He's a *man*, Leesha. Every single one of them needs his pecker put down now and again. Lure him back by using your mouth on him once or twice. Make him feel safe, then get him drunk and pounce. It'll be over before he knows what hit him.' She smirked. 'Do a good enough job, and he'll even be back for more.'

Leesha felt her stomach roil again. Was she really considering this? 'And in less than a year, when he sees the child has an olive tint to its skin and an upward twist to its eyes?'

Elona shrugged. 'Never know. Babe might take after you. There's nothing of Erny in you that the eye can tell, and that's for the best.'

'Better I got his heart,' Leesha agreed. 'And what's between his ears.'

'Ay, but you got my stones,' Elona said, 'and you can thank the Creator for that. The day the Krasians come to the Hollow, the only thing Ernal Paper is going to do is piss himself. You ent helpless, but when the time comes, you're going to want a strong man at your side.'

Leesha wanted to shout at her, but could not find the energy. Her mother had been making more and more sense of late. Was she changing, or was Leesha?

Seven hundred thousand. Seven hundred and one thousand. Seven hundred and two thousand . . .

'I don't trust the Painted Man any more than the demon of the desert,' Leesha said.

Elona shrugged again. 'Then find another. I was wrong about the fiddle-boy. He's got power and would stand by you even if the babe came out with Jardir's forked beard, but you've missed your chance there – unless you want to play a dirtier game.'

'Rojer's marriage is in enough trouble without my help,' Leesha said.

Elona nodded. 'There's really only one other choice, then.'

Leesha looked at her mother, and saw a triumphant smile on her face. 'Mother . . .'

Elona held up her hands. 'You told me not to say his name and I won't, but you think on it. He's strong as an ox and braver than any other man in the Hollow. The Cutters all look to him when the Painted Man ent about. And he loves you. Always has, in his own brutish way. All that, with a pea-sized brain. You could rule the Hollow through a man like that.'

One million, Leesha thought, turning to look at the vial. Her heart fell.

A handful of herbs leached in boiling water calmed Leesha's stomach, but nothing she dared take had the slightest effect on the throbbing pain in her head. When she and Elona finally emerged from her room, they found Gared, Wonda, and Erny in the taproom already, waiting by empty bowls of porridge.

Shamavah was haggling with the innkeeper. As usual, she found fault with everything, and based on Sim's posture, he looked inclined to let her name her price, if she would only go.

Without shifting her attention, Shamavah pointed a finger and one of the black-clad *dal'ting* women moved to take Leesha's bag. Normally she would have protested, but Leesha was exhausted, head hurting and knees weak. A bowl had been set out for her, but she ignored it, waiting impatiently. All she wanted was to climb into her cart and be left alone.

In truth, no one seemed much inclined towards talking, looking around uncomfortably as Shamavah berated Sim over things that had been totally acceptable. It went on and on until Leesha wanted to scream.

'Night, just ripping pay him, already!' she snapped at last. 'The rooms were fine!' Everyone jumped at the sound.

Shamavah bowed. 'As the intended wishes.' The words were tight. She quickly counted out the coins, and they were on their way. Enkido, standing atop the steps, knocked on a door then, and Amanvah, Sikvah, and Rojer emerged.

Rojer's wives surrounded him like bodyguards as they went

down the steps and out the door, glaring as if daring Leesha to approach.

Not that Leesha had the slightest desire to do so. The pendulum had swung back and forth so many times last night that she could barely remember who was mad at who for what. She could not get to her carriage fast enough.

Light pained her when the headaches were this bad. Just the few feet from the porch awning to the carriage steps felt like Ahmann's description of the beating sun on the cracked flats of the Krasian desert. Inside, she pulled the curtains close.

Erny took the far corner, closing his curtains without being asked, though he left himself a sliver of sunlight to illuminate the book on his lap. Elona sat across from her but was blissfully silent, staring at nothing, her thoughts far away.

She was still beautiful, Leesha had to admit. So much so that one who did not know her might take that stare for the blank one of a pretty, dim-witted thing. Like her every other pose, Elona had cultivated that look. She was anything but dim-witted, as many learned to their regret. Everyone always said Leesha got her brains from her father, but she wasn't so sure. Elona Paper was many things, but she was no fool.

There was no music from Rojer's carriage as the morning wore on, nor cries of pleasure. But there was shouting. Plenty of that. And worse, long painful silences.

When they stopped for lunch, Leesha stepped out long enough to make water and have a bowl brought to her carriage. She caught a glimpse of Rojer stretching his legs, but kept her distance so as not to provoke Sikvah, who stood close by.

Krasians of all castes grew silent as Rojer drew near, pointing and whispering as he passed. Word of his exploits had obviously spread.

Leesha felt much better by evening. Without asking, the Krasians had bypassed the next hamlet and circled the carts some miles down the road. Leesha moved about the camp, inspecting the wards, but the Krasian circles were strong.

Sharum patrolled the perimeter, killing any demons that drew near with neat spear thrusts from behind the safety of the wards. Wonda did the same, picking off corelings with her bow to clear the area. Gared moved in each time, finishing them quickly with chops of his warded axe and machete.

Leesha looked at him, thinking of what her mother had said. Indeed, Gared was handsome, and Leesha had loved him once, before he proved selfish and possessive to a degree she could not abide.

But did that make him so different from the other men she'd known? None of them had ever truly met her needs. Was Gared any worse than Rojer, Marick, or Arlen, or even Ahmann?

She was given her own tent, its carpeted floor warm and the cluster of pillows that served as the bed inviting. Wonda stood watch outside the flap, her bow ready.

At her request, the girl had provided Leesha with a small bowl of demon ichor from one of her kills, glowing brightly in wardsight. Leesha took a horsehair brush and her plainest shawl, painting wards of misdirection and confusion, adding wards gleaned the night Inevera had used magic to trap Leesha in her pillow chamber. Wards that would direct the power towards humans as well as demons.

The wards glowed dimly as she threw the shawl over her shoulders and lifted the tent flap. Wonda stiffened, looking around and listening carefully, but her eyes slipped away from Leesha as easily as Rojer had done to the corelings. She moved to inspect the flap, peeking inside to see the blankets and pillows Leesha had arranged to appear as her sleeping body. She grunted and replaced the flap, resuming her station outside the tent.

Hidden in plain sight, Leesha passed through the camp towards Gared's tent, ignored by the *Sharum* sentries. She still wasn't entirely sure what she meant to do. Even if she went through with it and lay with him, she did not think she would have the nerve to let herself be caught at it as her mother instructed. And if not, what was the point?

She drew a deep breath, decided, and reached for the tent flap. A deep voice from within checked her.

'Ma'am, we can't keep doin' this. It ent right.'

'You didn't mind me teaching you what goes where with your da asleep ten feet away,' Elona said, 'but now it's so wrong?'

There was a shuffling sound, and Gared groaned.

'One last time,' Elona said. 'Just so you don't forget me.'

'We'll get caught,' Gared said, but there was more shuffling, and this time Elona groaned.

'We ent been caught at it yet,' she gasped. A rhythmic slapping of flesh followed, and Leesha felt ill. She threw open the tent flap and strode inside, tossing back her shawl. Elona's arms were around Gared's neck, and he held her suspended in mid-air, skirts around her waist and his breeches around his ankles.

'You have now,' Leesha said.

'Night!' Gared shouted, dropping Elona, who gave a yelp as her bare bottom hit the hard canvas floor of the tent.

Leesha put her hands on her hips. 'Every time I think I've seen the lowest you can sink, Mother, you find a deeper place.'

'Oh, if that ent the night calling it black,' Elona muttered, getting to her feet and smoothing her skirts. Gared had yanked up his breeches and was attempting to force his still-stiffened member back inside. It was a futile task.

'When I tell Da . . .' Leesha began.

'You won't,' Elona said, 'if not out of respect for what it would do to your poor father, then on your Gatherer's oath.'

'This isn't Gatherer's business,' Leesha said.

'Everything is Gatherer's business when you wear the apron!' Elona shot back. 'Did Bruna ever belie the affairs of the town? I promise you, she knew every one.'

She looked down her nose. 'And besides, I'm not the only one with a secret. What are you doing here in the middle of the night, Leesha?'

Leesha glanced at Gared, but he had turned his back on them, still fumbling. Her mother had her checked, and she knew it.

'Come along,' she said, lifting one side of her shawl to wrap it around Elona's shoulders. It would protect them both as they went back to the tents where they belonged.

Gared finally managed to lace his trousers back up and turned back to them, a guilty look on his face.

'You've disappointed me again, Gared Cutter,' Leesha said. 'And just when I was beginning to think you a changed man.'

Gared looked stricken. 'It ent my fault!'

'Course not,' Elona snapped as she stepped into Leesha's shawl and they turned to go. 'Mrs Paper had her way with you and you were helpless as a Rizonan girl when the *Sharum* came.'

Leesha was prepared for the morning sickness this time, and managed to deal with it without alerting anyone that anything was amiss. By lunchtime, she was feeling normal.

Gared came to her as she stretched her legs. 'All right if we talk a bit?'

Leesha sighed. 'I don't think there's much you can say, Gar.'

Gared nodded. 'Guess I deserve that.'

'You guess?' Leesha asked. 'Gared, you had sex with my mother!'

'What's it to you?' Gared demanded. 'You declared our promise broken a long time ago, and I ent bothered you since. I don't owe you anything.'

'What about my father, who took you in when your home was destroyed?' Leesha demanded. 'Did you owe him anything? Or your own da?'

Gared spread his hands. 'You don't know what it was like, Leesh. After Bruna made me tell the town I'd lied about you, no girl would let herself be caught alone with me for a second. Even after you left town for Angiers, I was as popular as itchweed.'

'I don't blame them,' Leesha said.

Gared swallowed a scowl, keeping his patience. 'Ay, maybe so. But it was lonely, too. Yur mum was the only woman in the whole town paid any attention to me. Only one who acted like I was worth more'n spit.'

He sighed. 'And in the right light, she looked just like you. I could close my eyes and pretend . . .'

'Ugh!' Leesha cried. 'I do *not* need to hear that you thought of me while you . . .' She felt her nausea returning, tasting bile in her mouth.

'Sorry,' Gared said. 'Just tryin' to give honest word. Never stopped wanting you.'

Leesha spat the sour taste from her mouth at his feet. 'Could have had the real me fifteen years ago, you'd kept your mouth shut.'

'Know that,' Gared said. 'Curse myself for it every night. It's why I was always so angry. But I wonder, maybe it was the Creator's Plan?'

'Eh?' Leesha asked.

'Whole world would be different, we'd kept our promise,' Gared said. 'You might never have trained with Bruna, or gone away to study in the Free Cities. Might not have brought the Deliverer back with you.'

'The Painted Man is not the Deliverer, Gared,' Leesha said.

'How do you know?' Gared asked. 'What makes you so sure you got it all figured out? Maybe the Creator din't make him perfect for a reason. Maybe he's testing the rest of us, too. Maybe the Deliverer's just supposed to show the path, and we're the ones to walk it.'

Leesha looked at him curiously. 'Why, Gared Cutter, when did such deep thoughts climb into that thick head?'

Gared scowled. 'Just an idiot to you, ent I? Not worth the attention of that big brain of yurs?'

'Gared, I didn't mean—'

'Course you did,' Gared cut her off. 'Yur always so humble,

but it's all an act as you talk to the simpletons.' He turned to leave.

Leesha reached out, taking his arm. 'Don't go.'

But Gared yanked his arm away, refusing to even look at her. 'No, I get it. I'm just a strong axe and a hard cock to the Paper women.'

He stormed off, leaving Leesha feeling lonelier and more confused than ever.

16

Where *Khaffit* Cannot Follow

333 AR Summer
28 Dawns Before Waning

Inevera tugged at the thick cloth, stifling in the humid greenland summer. Every breath into the veil seemed to add a blast of steam into the hood. It clung to her hair, matting it with sweat. It had been years since she had been forced to wear even the robes and veil of *dama'ting*, so white the brightest sun slid off them and so fine her skin could breathe as if bare. Save for these few excursions, she had never been forced to wear the blacks of *dal'ting*, and wondered how women could bear them.

She took a breath. *It is only wind. There is nothing other women can bear that you cannot.*

The disguise was necessary, and worth any discomfort, for it allowed her to escape the palace and move through the New Bazaar unmolested. She did not fear for herself – few would dare attack her, and more would leap to her defence if any was needed – but the Damajah could not travel without an entourage, and would draw a gawking crowd like scattered crumbs did birds, risking her most precious secret.

Without her dice, she needed her mother's counsel more than ever, a respite from the wind threatening to snap even the most supple palm.

The New Bazaar of Everam's Bounty wasn't yet as big as the Great Bazaar in Krasia, but it grew daily, and would soon rival even that monument of commerce. Abban had put up the first pavilion in the *chin* village just outside the city proper when Everam's Bounty first fell to the Deliverer's forces. Six months later, the New Bazaar had swallowed the village and spilled out into the lands beyond, a focal point for merchants, traders, and farmers throughout the land.

The merchants and their *dama* masters had spared no expense protecting their wares, laying out the streets in the shape of a greatward, much like the Hollow tribe to the north, with low walls to add strength to the warding, and guards to patrol and keep the streets clear when night fell. In the day, however, goods filled every inch of free space, with *dal'ting*, *khaffit*, and *chin* loudly hawking their wares.

Inevera made her way along the wending streets, occasionally stopping in this stall or that kiosk to add to her basket, looking like nothing more than a simple *Jiwah Sen* shopping for her family's evening meal. She fell into the role, haggling over bits of produce and a small block of salt as if she, like most women, had to make every draki stretch. She remembered what it had been like for Manvah, trying to feed four on barely enough money for three. It was strangely relaxing – Inevera knew every woman in the Bounty envied the Damajah, but some days she longed to have her greatest worry be convincing merchants to sell items below market value.

She was almost to her destination when a *Sharum* guardsman pawed at her behind. It took every bit of her self-control not to break his arm, and several steadying breaths as he and his fellow warriors strode off laughing to keep from killing the lot of them with her bare hands. If she had been in white, she would not have hesitated, and would have been well within her rights. In black, well, who would take the word of a *dal'ting* over a *Sharum*?

I should come to the bazaar more often, she thought. *I have lost touch with the common people.*

Her father stood at the entrance to her mother's pavilion, calling to prospective buyers in a loud voice. Though there was grey at his temples, the years had been kind to Kasaad. His peg leg was gone, replaced with a fine limb of polished wood, jointed and sprung. He still carried a cane, but used it more to wave at onlookers and gesture to his wares than for support.

Still sober, she marvelled, and when he laughed, a rich booming sound that carried far, it warmed her heart. This was not the jackal laugh he used to share with the other *Sharum* when they were deep into the couzi. This was the laugh of a man happy and at peace.

So different was he to the man she knew, it seemed impossible this could be her father – the man who had murdered Soli.

Inevera could have breathed away the tears in her eyes, but she let them fall, hidden by the sweat on her face and the thick black *dal'ting* veil. Why should she hold back tears for her brother, or her father? It seemed both men had died that night, and Manvah had gained a new husband, one more worthy of her, if without a *Sharum*'s honour.

Her mother's pavilion had continued to grow over the years, booming into a diversified business that went far beyond simple basket weaving. This was well, as the palm trees that had given her material were now hundreds of miles to the south. There were carpets and tapestries instead, and weavings of greenland material, wicker and corn husk. There was pottery, bolts of cloth, incense burners, and a hundred other things.

Inevera had offered the dice to Manvah more than once, to use as Dama Baden did to keep ahead of his rivals, but her mother always refused. 'It would be a sin against Everam to use *dama'ting* magic to fill my purse,' she had said, adding with a wink, 'and it would take away all the fun.'

'Blessings of Everam upon you, honoured mother,' a boy said as she entered the pavilion. 'May I assist you in finding anything?'

Inevera looked at him, and her heart clenched. He still wore the tan of a boy not yet called to *Hannu Pash*, but it seemed she was looking at Soli, or the boy he had once been. Instinctively, she reached out, tousling his hair the way her brother used to do to her. It was an overly familiar gesture, and the boy seemed taken aback by it.

'Forgive me,' she said. 'You remind me of my brother, taken by the night long ago.' When the boy looked at her blankly, she rubbed his hair again. 'I will look first, but I will call you when I am ready to buy.' The boy nodded, all too happy to run off.

'All Kasaad's sons have that look, no matter the wife,' a voice said, and Inevera turned to see her mother standing before her. Black robes or no, the two of them could never fail to recognize each other. 'It makes me wonder if Everam in His wisdom has sent back the soul of my firstborn, taken from me too early.'

Inevera nodded. 'Your family is blessed with many fine children.'

'You are the clay seller?' Manvah asked. When Inevera nodded, she went on. 'As I told your messenger, your price is too high.'

Inevera bowed. 'Perhaps we can discuss the matter privately?'

Manvah nodded, then led her through the pavilion to a stone door. A large building backed the pavilion; there the family lived and the most valuable goods were stored. Manvah led the way to a private office with a desk piled with ledgers and writing implements, two greenland chairs, and a small private space for weaving.

Manvah turned, holding out her arms, and Inevera fell into them gladly, sharing a crushing embrace.

'It's been years since you visited,' Manvah said. 'I was beginning to think the Damajah had forgotten her mother.'

'Never that,' Inevera said. 'If you but say the word . . .'

Manvah held up a hand to forestall her. 'The Deliverer's court does not need to know the Damajah's father is *khaffit*, and I have no interest in tea politics and poison tasters. My sister-wives have given me children and grandchildren, and I see my daughter and her sons often enough, even if I must watch from the crowd.'

Manvah clapped her hands outside the flap, and soon a young girl brought in a fine silver tea service, the pot steaming. They ignored the chairs, moving to the pillows in the weaving area and setting the tea tray on the floor. Manvah poured, and the two of them, alone in the office, removed their veils and hoods that they might look upon each other. Manvah's face was more lined than it had been, and there were streaks of grey in her long hair, bound in gold. She was still beautiful, and radiated strength. Inevera felt something in her relax. Here was the one place in the world she could truly be herself.

Manvah gestured with the spout of the teapot at a pile of pliable wicker strips. 'It's not quite the same as weaving palm, but we must all adapt to the new path the Deliverer has taken us on.'

Inevera nodded, watching for a moment as Manvah took strips and began to work a weave. After a moment, she reached into the pile and began her own basket, her strong fingers growing in confidence as she felt the peace of weaving flow over her once more. 'Some adaptations are harder than others.'

Manvah chuckled. 'And how is dear Kajivah?'

Inevera hissed as a splinter lodged into her finger. 'My honoured mother-in-law is well. Still dim as a guttering candle, and still wasting everyone's time with her inane prattle.'

'Still no luck finding her a husband?' Manvah asked.

Inevera shook her head. 'She wants no man to come between her and her son, and Ahmann thinks no one worthy of her in any event.'

'And your dice have no answers?' Manvah asked.

I have no dice, Inevera thought, and needed to breathe and calm herself. 'I consulted the dice once. They told me Ahmann would accept Dama Khevat as his father-in-law, and that

Kajivah could not refuse if he were to ask Ahmann for her hand. Unfortunately, Khevat's response to the suggestion was that he would rather marry a donkey.'

Manvah cackled, and Inevera laughed with her. It felt good to laugh. She could not remember the last time she had done it.

'If you cannot find her a husband, assign her a task, like any *Jiwah Sen*,' Manvah said.

'This is the mother of the Deliverer,' Inevera said. 'I can hardly set her to carrying jugs of water, and any real task would be beyond her.'

'Then give her a false one,' Manvah said. Her fingers continued to work, but her lips pursed as she stared off at the wall for a moment. 'Ask her if she will plan the Shar'Dama Ka's monthly Waxing Party.'

'There is no—' Inevera began.

'Invent one,' Manvah cut her off. 'Convince Kajivah it is a great honour, and will please her son and keep him in Everam's favour. Assign her a dozen assistants to help her plan food, decorations, music, ceremonies, and guest lists. You'll hardly ever see her again.'

Inevera smiled. 'This is why I come to you, Mother.'

Manvah finished the base of her basket, and began creating the frame for its walls. 'Everyone in the city knows the deeds of my grandsons, but there has been no word of my grand-daughters. Are they well? Progressing in their studies?'

Inevera nodded. 'Your granddaughters are all well, and will soon be *dama'ting*. Amanvah has already taken the veil and married.'

'And who is the lucky suitor?' Manvah asked.

'A *chin* from the Hollow tribe,' Inevera said. 'He is nothing to look at – small, weak, and dressed in more colours than a colour-blind *khaffit* – but Everam speaks to him.'

'The boy who charms *alagai* with his music?' Manvah asked. Inevera raised an eyebrow, but Manvah dismissed her with a wave. 'Everyone in the city speaks of the *chin* in the Deliverer's court.

The boy, the giant, the woman warrior,' she looked pointedly at Inevera, 'and the greenland princess.'

Inevera turned and spat on the floor.

Manvah tsked. 'That bad?'

'I forbade him to marry her,' Inevera said, not bothering for once to mask the venom in her voice.

'There was your first mistake,' Manvah said. 'Never forbid a man anything. Even Kasaad, meek as he is since you stripped him of his blacks, can be stubborn as a mule when forbidden, and your husband is Shar'Dama Ka.'

Inevera nodded. 'It is written in the Evejah'ting: *Forbid a man something, and he shall desire it tenfold.* But my heart spoke before my mind.'

'And how did the Deliverer react?' Manvah asked.

Inevera felt her spittle gather again, but swallowed it, breathing deeply. 'He told me I did not have the right. He said he would make her his greenland *Jiwah Ka*, with dominion over his Northern wives.'

Manvah paused her weave, looking up to meet Inevera's eyes. 'Did you expect that he would keep his wedding vows when you have not?'

The words stung, and part of Inevera regretted telling her mother of her infidelity with the Andrah, but she breathed deeply and let the feeling blow by.

– She will tell you truths you do not wish to hear—

'I at least had the decency to do it in private.' Inevera bit the words off. 'He flaunts her, taking her in my own pillow chamber and shaming me before the entire court.'

'I didn't think I had raised a fool,' Manvah said, breaking off a long end of wicker with a snap, 'but it must be so, if you think the distinction matters a whit to a cuckold. You hurt him, and he is returning it on you threefold. This was a bill you should long have expected to come due. But in truth, what difference does it make if he bent some Northern whore? Great men are expected to conquer women, and you remain *Jiwah Ka*.'

'In title, but no longer in truth,' Inevera said. 'I have not taken his seed in almost two Waxings.'

Manvah snorted. 'If that is what defines a *Jiwah Ka*, I stopped being Kasaad's decades ago. I have not had him since Soli.'

'Kasaad is not the Deliverer,' Inevera said.

'Then stop your posturing and go to his bed,' Manvah said. 'Show him you remember he is Shar'Dama Ka,' her eyes flicked to meet Inevera's, 'and remind him you are his Damajah. The woman is gone, I hear, and without accepting his proposal. Make him forget her.'

Inevera sighed. 'It is not so simple. The Northern witch brought more than just her gates of Heaven to Ahmann. She has whispered poison in his ear.'

'Poison?' Manvah asked.

'It was bad enough she and her harlot mother walked the palace unveiled,' Inevera said, 'but now they have brought the notion that our women should fight *alagai'sharak* like the Northern savages. To please her, Ahmann has decreed that any woman to take an *alagai* in battle will be *Sharum'ting*, and accorded all a warrior's rights.'

Manvah shrugged. 'What of it?'

Inevera gaped. 'You cannot possibly approve.'

'Why not?' Manvah asked. She picked at her blacks. 'You think I like having to wear these? I look at the Northern women and dream of being so free. Of owning my own pavilion, instead of running Kasaad's. And why should I not? Because Kaji's clerics saw women as cattle, and worked oppression into the holy verses? It is easy for you to cast a dim eye. You get to strut about the palace in the nude.'

'I am hardly nude, Mother,' Inevera said. Manvah looked at her, and she cast her eyes down, knowing dissembling did not work with her mother. Inevera dressed as she did to tweak the noses of the *Damaji* and remind them of her power, but there was no point denying that she gloried in it, as well.

'You never approved of *alagai'sharak* when it was Soli at

risk,' Inevera said. 'Should we add our daughters to the fight as well as our sons?'

'I hated *alagai'sharak* when it was a meaningless sacrifice of our men to the Andrah's pride,' Manvah said. 'But have not your precious dice told you Ahmann is the Deliverer, sent by Everam to lead us through Sharak Ka?'

'They said he *might* be,' Inevera reminded her.

Manvah levelled a look at her. 'You'd best pray he is, or you have wasted the last quarter century of your life. And did they not say Sharak Ka was coming in any event? *Alagai* kill women as well as men, daughter. Do not let the fact that allowing us to defend ourselves is a Northern notion blind you to its power. You remember Krisha and her ugly sister-wives beating your father. There are women built to fight. Let them. Nie, *encourage* them. Make the Northern custom your own and you will steal the fruit from this mistress of the Hollow's tree.'

'There will be uproar,' Inevera said.

Manvah nodded. 'There will be shouting in public, and cold anger in private. A handful of idiots with flaccid cocks will pick a few women at random to vent their rage upon. But none will dare oppose the Shar'Dama Ka publicly, and soon enough it will become accepted.' She smirked. 'As when you began baring your sex in public.'

Inevera feigned a shocked look, and Manvah winked at her. 'But the women of Krasia worship you for it, even if they dare not admit it aloud. Give them this, and you will own their hearts forever.'

Inevera moved quickly through the bazaar after her meeting with her mother. She hated leaving Manvah. Each time it hurt anew, knowing it might be months before she could visit again. But she had been gone too long already, and did not wish to raise suspicion that might lead back here. Manvah and Kasaad were secrets even Ahmann was not privy to. Qeva might remember, but the dice had said the Kaji *Damaji'ting* would never betray her.

But then, in a coincidence so great it was hard to believe it occurred without the aid of her dice, she saw him, strutting her way through the bazaar in his familiar sleeveless robe and black steel breastplate with its sunburst of hammered gold.

Cashiv.

He looked no different than he had all those years ago, which said much for his prowess in battle. His face had the immortal look of the Spears of the Deliverer, so charged with magic each night that they moved a few hours back towards their prime, though their eyes and expressions remained those of older men. In the older warriors like Kaval it took longer for the signs to tell, but the younger ones moved quickly and stayed there. Cashiv was close to fifty, but he had the look of a man in his thirties, still strong and full of fight.

A step behind, he was flanked by two other *Sharum*, both young and beautiful of body and old of eye. Inevera recognized them both, and for a moment almost expected to see Soli among them.

It had been years since she had thought of the warrior. Dama Baden was a strong voice in the Deliverer's court, but Inevera had not seen his favourite *kai'Sharum* since he had cursed her for sparing Kasaad's life. Had he ever forgiven her?

She froze. *Inevera* was a common name, and she did not know if Cashiv even knew his dead lover's sister was now the Damajah. But if he were to see her here . . .

Dama Baden was not a man she wanted to know where the Deliverer's mother-in-law was hidden. He might not be foolish enough to threaten her openly, but it was a weakness Inevera could not afford.

I will have to kill him, she realized. *Quickly, before he can tell the others . . .*

She readied herself, only to have Cashiv and the others pass by without taking the slightest notice of her. One of the warriors said something, and Cashiv brayed a laugh as they turned a corner.

Inevera blew out a breath. They had not seen her.

Of course not, idiot, she realized. *You're all in black.*

Inevera waited in Ahmann's bedchamber for his return. She wore her pillow dancing silks and jewellery, including a new circlet of white-gold coins, adding wards copied from Ahmann's crown to protect her from a mind demon's intrusion to those that gave her wardsight and enhanced senses. She could see the glow of magic as it drifted in whorls across the floor like sand devils, drawn by the many wardings around the room.

She had her own chambers, of course. Finest among all Ahmann's wives, though each had her own private receiving rooms and a richly appointed pillow chamber for sleeping and entertaining the Deliverer, should whim take him to her door. All were freshly shaved and oiled at all times, ready in an instant for his pleasure.

The magic men absorbed during *alagai'sharak* – leached as they thrust their warded spears into demon flesh – did more than keep them young, more than give them night strength and heal their wounds. It awakened animal passion – to hunt, to kill, to breed. Even before he had tasted the magic, Ahmann had been a man of great lust. Now his desires were endless, and left many of his wives easing soreness in the bath under the massaging touch of the eunuchs.

But while each wife had fine rooms, none could match Ahmann's own, and it was there he most often took his ease. His *Jiwah Sen* took it in turns to await him there with bath and refreshment, clad in bright, diaphanous silk.

The schedule was managed by Inevera herself, one of her many duties as *Jiwah Ka*. Occasionally she used the dice to adjust the schedule to ensure women were kept with child, but even that was at her discretion. Much like Kenevah's Waxing Tea, Inevera used the schedule to show favour to those who most pleased her, and disfavour to those who did not.

Those selected would wait upon her as well, and have the Shar'Dama Ka's touch only when she allowed it, which was seldom. Inevera suffered other women to touch Ahmann for the good of her people – that his ties to each tribe remain strong, and his lust be sated when there were other matters for her to attend – but she took him to the pillows personally more than all his other wives combined. Her near-constant use of *hora* magic had kept her body young and strong, and her own passions were formidable. Ahmann could seldom relax without a woman to put him down, and she, too, felt her patience thinning when it had been too long since she had taken her pleasure. The other women had her leavings, and thanked Everam for them.

But none of his wives had serviced the Shar'Dama Ka since he took Leesha Paper to bed. Inevera had refused to see him in her ire, and his other wives had been turned away as a man with a new stallion will turn down a ride on camelback.

Despite her mother's words, Inevera still had to fight to hold her centre at the thought of the Northern whore. When she threw the dice for Ahmann's first trip to Deliverer's Hollow and the bones told her he would fall in love with a *chin* woman and get a child on her, she had scarcely believed them. It was the first time in years she had doubted a throw. Not since the coming of the Par'chin.

Inevera prayed nightly while he was gone that her husband's heart would hold true, for the dice told only what might be, and not necessarily what would.

But her mother spoke true. Ahmann had not forgotten the Andrah. Killing the man had brought him little peace. She hadn't touched another since, not even her *Jiwah Sen*, but it did not matter. She could sense the distrust in her husband like a gap in her wards.

Bedding Leesha Paper and shaming his *Jiwah Ka* would prove no better balm, but that was something Ahmann would have to learn for himself. Surely the man who allowed Hasik to live – to wed his sister, even – could learn to forgive his First Wife.

Everything has its price, the Evejah'ting taught. Ahmann needed her to win Sharak Ka, and she needed him to give her the powers to do it. As Damajah, she could seize advantages for him that would otherwise be beyond her reach. They must reconcile, and quickly, before the schism became insurmountable.

It was because of that she waited for him this night.

That, and not the ache in her heart.

There was a soft vibration in one of her many rings, and she knew the outer doors to her husband's chambers had opened. She'd left orders not to be disturbed, so it could be none other than Ahmann himself who approached.

Inevera felt the wind of fear. Would he turn her away as he had the others? Even Qasha and Belina, his previous favourite *Jiwah Sen* in the pillows, had been cast aside in favour of the greenland woman. Was he bewitched by white flesh as Melan and Asavi had warned? What would become of their people's unity if it were so? The *Damaji* and *Damaji'ting* might suffer his taking a *chin* woman as a well prize and pillow wife, but to put her on his dais would enrage them beyond reason. Her *Jiwah Sen* would look to her for a solution, and if Inevera had none, their respect and her power would dissolve like smoke.

But fear had no place in the decisions of an ordered mind. She bent and let it pass over her, falling into her breath and finding her centre. She would confront the problem and repair the damage now, before it was too late.

The doors opened, and Ahmann entered. His breathing was even, but there was the scent of sweat and blood on him, as well as the stink of demon ichor. It was the scent of a man returning from *alagai'sharak*, and she knew her husband had been at the front of the line, leading men where other leaders commanded from safely behind.

The smell intoxicated her. Countless times he had taken her like that, his lust roaring with the magic that flowed in his veins. She would dance for him, and he would forget bath or sweat room until he had bent her over the nearest bit of furniture and had his way. The memory sent a shiver through her.

All about the room items of *hora* magic glowed dimly, their power contained by the metal shells that protected their demon bone cores from light. There were wards as well, glowing to heat the water in the bath, to cool the summer air, and to protect the chamber from intrusion and spying.

None of it glowed as brightly as Ahmann himself. The ward scars she had cut into his skin shone with the power he had absorbed in the night's battle, his crown flared even brighter, and the Spear of Kaji shone like the sun itself.

But for all that he was brimming with power, Ahmann's shoulders slumped as if weary of a burden.

Inevera waved her hand, activating a ruby ring on her littlest finger that contained a tiny bit of flame demon bone. Candles flared to life around the room, and his favourite incense began to burn.

It was then Ahmann noticed her. He sighed, setting his shoulders and straightening his back, eyeing her warily. 'I did not expect to see you tonight, wife.'

'I am your *Jiwah Ka*, Ahmann,' Inevera said. 'This is my place.'

Ahmann nodded, not relaxing at all. 'It is also your place to facilitate my acquisition of new brides. Yet you made no effort to come to a term with Leesha Paper, despite her obvious value.'

'I serve Everam and Sharak Ka before you, husband,' Inevera replied. 'As should you before me. Whether you choose to see it or not, half your *Damaji* would have been enraged had you named Leesha Paper your *Jiwah Ka* of the North.'

'Let them rage,' Ahmann said. 'I am Shar'Dama Ka. I do not need their love, only their loyalty.'

'You *might* be Shar'Dama Ka.' Inevera made the word a lash. 'Or you might be only what I have made of you. And yet you would halve my power as casually as you tear a loaf of bread, all for a woman you know nothing of. The dice told me to seize you every advantage, but I cannot do that for a fool who pisses on those who would die for him and showers his enemies with gold.'

'It would never have come to that, had you not refused to take her as *Jiwah Sen*,' Ahmann said. 'Where was the wisdom in that? I came home with a woman to honourably marry, one who could bring thousands of warriors to Sharak Ka and wards spells even you cannot. Abban had already negotiated the dower with her mother, and it was a pittance. Some lands, some gold, a meaningless Northern title, and recognition of her tribe. Yet you dismissed it out of hand. Why? Do you fear her?'

'I fear what the witch has done to your mind,' Inevera said. 'You value her far beyond her worth. She should have been carried off like a well prize, arriving slung over your saddle, not brought to court and given a palace.'

'The Damajah of old feared no woman,' Ahmann said. 'The true Damajah would have dominated her. So tell me, did the dice tell you that you *were* the Damajah, or that you *might* be?'

Inevera felt as if he had slapped her. She breathed to remain calm.

'You did not see her people, or spend weeks with her on the road,' Ahmann said. 'The Northerners are strong, Inevera. If the cost of securing their alliance is that there be a single woman in all the world who need not bow to you, is that too high a price?'

'Is it for you?' Inevera asked. 'The Painted Man, the one the Northerners call Deliverer, is the key to Sharak Sun, Ahmann. Even a blind fool can see it! And your precious Leesha Paper is protecting him, keeping him safe to put a spear in your back.'

Ahmann's face darkened and Inevera feared she had pushed him too far, but he did not lash at her. 'I am not such a fool.

We have agents in the Hollow now. If this Painted Man appears I will hear of it, and kill him if he does not bow to me.'

'And I will bring you the daughter of Erny, or proof of her disloyalty to Everam,' Inevera promised. She rose from the pillows, rolling her hips and turning so the candles behind her made the vaporous silks she wore seem to disappear, revealing her every curve. The incense was heavy in the air as she came to him, and Ahmann held his breath as she wrapped her arms around his neck.

'I believe that you are the Deliverer, beloved,' she said. 'I believe with all my heart that Ahmann Jardir is the man to lead our people to victory in Sharak Ka.' She lifted her veil boldly and kissed him. 'But you must have every advantage if you are to defeat Nie on Ala. We must stay unified.'

'*Unity is worth any price in blood,*' Ahmann said, a quote from the Evejah. He kissed her in return, thrusting his tongue into her mouth. She felt his tension, and knew where it was building. In an instant she had him out of his robes, leading him to the bath. As he stepped down to soak in the hot water, Inevera slipped her fingers into the cymbals hanging from her belt and began to dance in the smoke and candlelight, twirling in her diaphanous silk.

'I mean to attack Lakton in less than three months,' Ahmann said quietly, as they lay together. He held her close, his muscular body nude save for his crown, which he seldom removed now, and never at night. Inevera wore only her jewellery. 'Thirty days after equinox, the day the greenlanders call first snow.'

'Why that date?' she asked. 'Have the *Damaji* ascribed some significance to it in their star charts?' She did little to hide the derision in her tone. The *dama*'s art of reading omens in the Heavens was primitive nonsense compared with the *alagai hora*.

Ahmann shook his head. 'Abban's spies report that is the day the greenlanders bring their harvest tithe to the capital. A precise strike will leave them unsupplied through the winter while we wait out the snows in plenty.'

'You take your military advice from a *khaffit* now?' Inevera asked.

'You know Abban's value as well as I,' Ahmann said. 'His prophecies of profit are nearly as accurate as your *hora*.'

'Perhaps,' Inevera said, 'but I would not gamble the fate of all men on them.'

Ahmann nodded. 'And so I come to you, to confirm his information. Cast the bones.'

Inevera felt her jaw tighten. Ahmann had been fighting the demon prince's bodyguard, and had not seen the mind demon drain the magic from her bones, collapsing them into dust. Thus far, she had kept the loss a secret to all, even him.

'The *alagai hora* tell what they will, beloved,' she said. 'I cannot simply demand they verify information.'

Ahmann looked at her. 'I've seen you do it a thousand times.'

'The conditions are not—' Inevera began, but a flare of magic from one of the gems on Ahmann's crown cut her off.

'You're lying,' Ahmann said, his voice hard and sure. 'You're hiding something from me. What is it?' The crown continued to brighten as his eyes bored into her, and Inevera felt powerless before them.

'The demon prince destroyed my dice,' she blurted, hating the admission, but afraid to dissemble further until she understood what was happening. He was using one of the hidden powers of the crown.

According to the Evejah'ting, the sacred metal was etched with wards on both sides around the demon bone core. Inevera hungered for the secrets of those wards, but she could not unravel them without taking the precious artefact apart, and even she would not dare such sacrilege.

Ahmann's look was sour. 'You could have simply told me.'

Inevera ignored the comment. 'I have begun carving a new set. I will be able to cast the bones again soon.'

'Perhaps one of your *Jiwah Sen* should cast in the meantime,' Ahmann said. 'This cannot wait.'

'It can,' Inevera said. 'First snow is three months away, and you have more immediate concerns.'

Ahmann nodded. 'Waning.'

Inevera woke with Ahmann's arms clutching at her possessively, even as he slept.

Careful not to wake him, she put her thumb into a pressure point on Ahmann's arm, numbing it long enough for her to slip free of the bed. Her bare feet sank into the rich carpet, and she padded so softly across the floor that the belled anklets she still wore did not make a sound.

Ahmann grew more powerful every day, sleeping less and less, but even the Deliverer needed to close his eyes for an hour or three, and she had seen to it that he was relaxed. His seed ran slowly down her leg as she strode to the terrace. She wondered if a child would come of their union. Without the dice she could not know for sure, but their loving had been powerful, and it was too long since she had borne him a son.

Eunuch guards opened the great glass doors. Inevera paid them no mind as she strode past, relishing the warm breeze and the feel of sunlight on her skin. The guards who shadowed Ahmann's wives had neither stones nor spears, and would not dare so much as glance at her bottom.

Inevera leaned on the marble railing looking out over Everam's Bounty, the green land once known as Rizon. There was a rush of power as she surveyed the land, tingling like the sun on her skin and the seed on her thigh.

Ahmann's greenland palace was a paltry thing. Its previous owner, Duke Edon of Fort Rizon, had been a weak ruler, coming from a long line of such. Surrounded by vast riches, they had been unable to squeeze forth more than a trickle of gold from their subjects. With such abundance, Edon could have had a palace to make an Andrah sigh with envy. Instead his seat stood a mere four storeys and had but two wings, its walls thin and low. Inevera knew a dozen *dama* who held better back in Krasia. It was hardly fit for Shar'Dama Ka, though still preferable to the pavilions they had used on their journey through the desert.

Already her finest artisans were drawing plans to tear this 'manse' down and build in its place a palace so grand its spires would touch the bottom of Heaven itself, and an underpalace reaching so deep into the Ala that the mother of demons would tremble in the abyss.

But while the line of Edon was weak, they had not been utter fools. The hill they had chosen for their seat had an incomparable view. Everam's Bounty spread out before her, blooming as far as the eye could see, full of rich soil and an abundance of rivers and streams. Neat rows of crops and trees, cut into straight edges by wide dirt roads, fanned out from the inner city like the spokes in a wheel, here a cornfield, there an orchard. A hundred tributary villages, easily divided among the tribes to sate their lust for plunder after the difficult passage through the desert and hard winter's march.

The greenlanders outnumbered her people greatly, but they were not warriors. Between Inevera's foretellings and Ahmann's *Sharum*, they had taken the duchy as easily as a cat takes a mouse. Their wealth had made the *chin* soft.

It was fitting that Ahmann build a seat of power here, but it would not do for their people to grow too comfortable in this land of plenty. She had cast the dice while red blood was still wet on the warriors' spears, and seen the same fate awaiting her own people if they did not press on to further conquest in the green lands. The desert had made them hard, and that hardness was sorely needed in the war to come.

Much as she hated to admit it, there was merit in the *khaf-fit*'s plan to strike Lakton before winter.

Inevera went back inside, signalling her servants for hot water and scented oil. They clad her in translucent red silk. Another woman might have felt vulnerable leaving her pillow chamber in so little, but Inevera was the Damajah, and none would dare molest her.

Silently, she descended the stair her slaves had cut deep into the rock of the hill, leading down into a great natural cavern. Eunuch guards drifted in her van and wake, though Inevera felt no threat as she approached her place of power. She was blind without her dice, unable to foretell danger, but even if a mad assailant or rogue *alagai* got past her guards, she was not without defences of her own.

At last she reached a great stone door, and the guards took places to the sides as she produced the only key from a pouch at her waist. The key itself was a fake, turning with a meaning-less click, but as her hand drew near the locks, the gold-plated *hora* on her bracelet warmed, specially warded to matching bones within the locks, sliding the heavy bolts free. Even if a thief skilled at warding guessed the trick, the bracelet would be impossible to duplicate, and Inevera kept it on her person at all times. Though it weighed tons, the door swung inward silently at a touch, and closed just as smoothly behind her.

Within, she drifted through passages never touched by Everam's light. She carried no lamp in the blackness, but the chain of thin warded gold coins around her head warmed slightly, opening her senses to the magic all around her. The power of the abyss hummed in the walls and drifted in the air like smoke, lighting her way as if she strode in clear day.

Inevera did not fear the power around her. Rather, she gloried in it. Everam had created the Ala, and the power at its centre was His as well. The servants of Nie might exploit the magic at its source, but it was not theirs. Warding was the art of stealing that power back and turning it to Everam's purposes.

She glided along until she reached a special spot in the rock wall, then knelt, shifting a stone aside to reveal her warding tools, *hora* pouch, and the rendered bones of the demon prince Ahmann had killed, glowing more fiercely with magic than any *hora* she had ever known.

Ahmann did not believe it to be Alagai Ka, father of demons, but no doubt the creature was his get, powerful in ways even Inevera did not fully understand. It had taken her *hora* pouch and absorbed its magic effortlessly, leaving her nothing but ashes in place of her connection to Everam.

But while Inevera was blind, she did not waste time on tears, carving boldly into the demon's bones. Her skill had increased tenfold since her years as Betrothed, and now she could see her work clearly in the wardlight. Already three of the seven dice were restored to her, more powerful by far than those lost. Would that they could give her even partial seeing, like a man with one eye, but the seven worked in harmony, the parts useless without their full sum.

The sun was nearing its apex when she emerged from the Chamber of Shadows and returned to the palace proper. Melan and Asavi were waiting for her as she approached the throne room, falling in behind her as the *Sharum* guards bowed and opened the doors to admit her.

'What word?' Inevera murmured.

'The Deliverer is just beginning court, Damajah,' Asavi said. 'You have missed only ceremony.'

Inevera nodded. It was a calculated move, excusing herself from the formalities of court, filled with long lists of deeds and tedious prayers. The Damajah was above such things, her time better spent in the Chamber of Shadows until her full power was restored. Prayer was pointless to one used to speaking to Everam directly.

Her eyes flicked to the *hora* pouches of her companions. Had their own dice informed them their Damajah was blind? Melan and Asavi had served her loyally for many years, but they were still Krasian. If they sensed weakness, they would exploit it, as she would in their place. For a moment Inevera considering confiscating their dice or those of a lesser Bride to regain her sight until she had completed her new set.

She shook her head. It was within her power, but the insult would be too great. She might as soon demand they cut off a hand and give it to her. She must trust that Everam would not inform them of her weakness unless she had lost His favour, and now that she and Ahmann had reconciled, there was no reason to think she had.

With a breath to return to centre, she strode through the doors.

As ever, the throne room was crowded. The twelve *Damaji* stood council to the Deliverer, clustered to the right of the dais. They were led by the heads of the two strongest tribes, Ahmann's brother-in-law Ashan of the Kaji and ancient, one-armed Aleverak of the Majah. Each of the *Damaji* was attended in turn by the second sons of Ahmann's *dama'ting* brides – save for Ashan, who was shadowed by both Inevera's son Asome and her nephew Asukaji.

Ahmann had promised leadership of the Kaji to Ashan's son, though that left Asome, the second eldest of Ahmann's seventy-three children, heir to nothing.

But there was no animosity between the cousins. Quite the contrary, they were of an age, and had been pillow friends since they were boys in Sharik Hora.

Inevera didn't care that they were lovers – but she had been furious when Asome arranged to marry his cousin Ashia, that she might bear him the son her brother could not. It had pained Inevera to give Amanvah away to a greenlander, but better that than risk Ahmann giving her to Asukaji in further incest simply to strengthen his already unbreakable ties to Ashan.

To the left of the dais were the twelve *Damaji'ting*, led by Qeva. Like the *Damaji*, these women were followed by their successors – Melan for the Kaji and Ahmann's *dama'ting* wives from the other tribes. Both groups of women were extensions of Inevera's will. While the *Damaji* argued loudly with one another in open court, the *Damaji'ting* stood silent.

Hasik was standing inside the doors, and he snapped his feet together at the sight of her, thumping the metal butt of his warded spear loudly on the marble floor. 'The Damajah!'

Inevera did not spare a glance for her husband's bodyguard. Hundreds of *alagai* had fallen to his spear, and he was her brother by marriage, married to Ahmann's worthless sister Hanya. But Hasik was the one who had attacked and bitten her love that fateful night in the Maze. Ahmann had broken him to heel, but he was still little more than an animal. He knew better than to touch the Deliverer's youngest sister with anything but the gentlest hand, but he had not grown out of taking pleasure in inflicting pain on others. Hasik had his uses, but he was not worthy of her gaze save when she wished to set him to a task.

Everyone looked up at the announcement, turning like a flock of birds to bow as she approached. The *Damaji* watched her like raptors, but she ignored them, meeting Ahmann's eyes and never breaking the gaze as she crossed the room. She set her hips to swaying as if in the pillow dance, and in her vaporous robes it seemed as if she were caressing the entire room on her way to her husband.

She could feel the mix of desire and hatred radiating from the *Damaji* as she passed them on the way to the dais, and suppressed a smile. It was humiliating enough that a woman sat above them, but the lust she aroused was worse still. She knew that many of the *Damaji* had pillow wives chosen specifically because they looked like her, and took vigorous delight in dominating them. Inevera secretly encouraged the practice, knowing it only put them further under her spell.

'Mother.' Jayan bowed respectfully. Her firstborn waited at the base of the dais, clad in his warrior blacks and the white turban of Sharum Ka.

'My son.' Inevera smiled with her nod, wondering at his presence. Jayan had little patience for clerics and politics. He'd claimed one of the greenland manses as his palace and built a new Spear Throne, spending his days holding court with the *Sharum*. Whatever else she might say about him, Jayan had made a fine First Warrior.

Two steps down the dais to Ahmann's left knelt the fat *khaffit*, Abban, dressed in fine colourful silk and ready as ever to whisper in her husband's ear. His presence offended many, though after a few abject lessons, none dared protest it to the Deliverer's face.

For her part, Inevera found Abban's advice to have more sense than that of any other man in the room, but this only made her more cautious of him. Ahmann despised Abban at times, but he trusted him as well. Should it suit the crippled *khaffit*'s purpose, it would be simple for him to whisper poison instead of wise counsel. The dice had never been clear as to his motives, and she had reason to doubt him.

Inevera let the thought blow over her, bowing before its wind. She would deal with the *khaffit* in his time. She raised her eyes once more to Ahmann.

He had brought the Skull Throne with him from Krasia, and sat atop it on a seven-step dais, looking every bit the Shar'Dama Ka. He wore the Crown of Kaji as comfortably as another man might wear a worn and faded turban. He used the invincible Spear of Kaji like part of his arm, making even casual gestures with it, his every word a blessing and command.

But there was a new element now, the silken warded cloak given him by the greenland whore on their first meeting. Inevera felt her nostrils flare and breathed, becoming the palm.

The cloak was beautiful, Inevera could not deny. It was pure white, embroidered in silver thread with hundreds of wards that came to life in the night, causing *alagai* eyes to slide off the wearer like water on oiled cloth. The fabled Cloak of Kaji, sewn by the Damajah herself, had similar powers, but it had been lost to the ravages of time, found in tatters in the sarcophagus where they had found the Deliverer's spear.

Ahmann caressed the silk with his free hand like a lover, and its place about his shoulders said much to the assembled men and women. By wearing Leesha's cloak openly, Ahmann was saying that not only was she his intended, but she had a connection to the divine.

As I once did, Inevera thought bitterly. She might have been clad only in vaporous silk, but it was her missing dice that truly left her feeling naked.

Still, she smiled brightly as she presented herself before her husband, slipping into his lap brazenly and lifting her veil to kiss him as she squirmed for all to see. Ahmann was used to this display, but he had never been comfortable with it. She quickly slithered off him and over to the bed of pillows to the right of the throne. As she did, she caught sight of Abban's stare. There was no lust in it, but there was respect.

Remember that, khaffit, she thought. *You tried to follow me into Ahmann's bed with your Northern whore, but she is gone.* She arranged her hair, subtly turning the bottom of her earring to listen to the words Abban whispered to her husband.

'How have you fared in mustering our forces, my son?' Ahmann asked.

'Well,' Jayan said. 'We have increased the garrisons in the inner and outer city, and begun organizing patrols.'

'Excellent,' Ahmann said.

'But there has been cost,' Jayan said, 'in recalling and conscripting warriors from the *chin* villages and equipping them in time for the coming Waning.'

'In decorating his palace, he means,' Abban said softly. 'The Sharum Ka's war tax coffers should have been more than sufficient.'

'How much?' Ahmann asked his son.

'Twenty million draki,' Jayan said. He paused. 'Thirty would be better.'

'Everam's beard,' Abban muttered, rubbing his temple as the *Damaji* began to buzz in agitation. Inevera could not blame them. It was an obscene amount.

'Do I even have that much to spare?' Ahmann asked quietly.

'We could increase the rate we melt and recast the greenlanders' treasury, and the production yield of your gold mines,' Abban said, 'but I think you would be a fool to give the boy a single slip of copper without a full accounting of where the war tax has gone and how the new funds will be spent.'

'I cannot cost my son such face,' Ahmann said.

'The *khaffit* is correct, beloved,' Inevera said. 'Jayan has no concept of the value of money. If you give this to him, he will be back for more in a fortnight.'

Ahmann sighed. He himself had never been particularly good with money, but at least he trusted his advisors. 'Very well,' he said to Jayan. 'As soon as you have your *khaffit* deliver a full accounting of how you have spent the war tax to Abban, along with your projections for the additional funds.'

Jayan stood frozen, his mouth moving but no sound coming out.

'Perhaps I can assist, brother,' Asome said. 'You have ever been more adept with the spear than the pen.'

'I need the help of *push'ting* no more than I do *khaffit*,' Jayan growled.

Asome did not rise to the bait, bowing with a smug grin. 'As you wish.' He may have been heir to nothing, but it was no secret that both Ahmann's eldest sons aspired to succeed him, and they were quick to cut at each other's favour in their father's eyes.

In the meantime, Asome had asked more than once for his father to reinstate the position of Andrah with him on the throne. Thus far, Ahmann had denied him that honour. Asome was younger than any Andrah in history by a quarter century, and the appointment would put him above his older brother.

Jayan was impulsive where Asome was cautious, quick to anger where Asome was calm and soft-voiced, brutal where Asome was subtle. If Asome were placed above him, there would be blood, and many of the *Damaji* would support Jayan. The Sharum Ka served the council of *Damaji*. The Andrah commanded them. It was one thing to take orders from Ahmann, and another entirely to take them from a *dama* barely a year out of his bido.

'I will have the ledgers brought to you, Father,' Jayan said, glaring at his younger brother.

His *zahven*.

17

Zahven

326–329 AR

— *He will hear a voice from his past, and first meet his* zahven—

Inevera pondered the throw for a long time. Some of the symbols of foretelling were direct and easy to understand, regardless of context. Most were not. Inevera was more skilled at deciphering them than any woman alive, but even she found more confusion than truth in the *alagai hora*.

Zahven was an ancient symbol that had taken many meanings over the years, and none could be taken lightly. It could mean 'brother' or just as easily 'rival', 'counterpart', or 'nemesis'. Men referred to those of other tribes with equal standing in the social hierarchy as their *zahven*, but Everam was also considered *zahven* to Nie.

But who could be *zahven* to Ahmann? He had no brothers or even cousins of blood, and his *ajin'pal* was Hasik, someone Ahmann had already met. Was there another Deliverer in the making? A challenger? Or was he to meet Nie's representative on Ala? It was Waning, when the *alagai* were strongest, and Alagai Ka was said to rise from the seventh layer of the abyss. Was the prince of demons to come to the Maze this night?

Inevera breathed deeply, letting the fear and anxiety blow over her like wind, maintaining serenity.

But even safe within her breath, another part of the foretelling continued to niggle her. What voice from Ahmann's past, and why did she not know of it?

The past calls when its debts are due, the Evejah'ting taught. Inevera remembered the night Soli and Kasaad had entered the *dama'ting* pavilion, and could not disagree.

It was just before dawn on the first day of Waning, when debts were paid and oaths fulfilled. *Sharum* would be sent home with their wages, and sons released from *sharaj* to see their families.

Inevera put the dice away, breathing until she had her centre, then stood smoothly and went to the pillow chamber where Ahmann slept. Most nights he returned to the palace once the Maze was free of *alagai* – usually still hours before dawn. He would sleep until the sun was high, rising at noon to begin his day.

But on Wanings, he rose at dawn, that he might have as much time as possible with his sons.

She slipped from her robes and crawled into the pillows to wake him.

Inevera leaned against a marble pillar, watching Ahmann with Jayan and Asome. The elder boys were closest to their father, and he stood with them in the centre of the room before a practice dummy hanging suspended in the air, giving them lessons in spearwork and *sharusahk*.

Her sister-wives were in attendance of course, along with their sons, who knelt in a ring around the room, a small army in and of themselves. Inevera had taken to calling the *Jiwah Sen* her 'little sisters', much as Kenevah had with her. The diminutive did not please them – women in line to hold sway over their respective tribes – but none dared protest its use. It was Waning, and Ahmann would give each of his wives and sons his attention in turn before the great meal.

'One day, *I* will be Sharum Ka!' Jayan shouted, thrusting his spear at the practice dummy.

Inevera looked sadly at her firstborn, now twelve. He had been bright, once. Not clever like his brother Asome, but inquisitive enough. Three years in *sharaj* had burned the brightness from his eyes, leaving him with the dead look of all *Sharum* – that of a brutal, unthinking animal. One that looked upon life and death and saw more value in the latter. Jayan was first in his class at fighting, but struggled with simple sums and texts that Asome, a year his junior, had advanced beyond years since. He was more apt to wipe himself with paper than read the words upon it.

She sighed. If only Ahmann had let her put him among the *dama*, but no, he wanted *Sharum* sons. Only second sons were allowed to take the white. The rest were sent to *sharaj*.

But as she watched Ahmann with the boys and saw the love in his eyes, she could not fault him.

As if reading her mind, Ahmann turned and met her gaze. 'It would please me if my daughters could return home for Waning each month, as well.'

You would spend them like spare coin on men not worthy of them, Inevera thought, but gave only a slight shake of her head. 'Their training must not be disturbed, husband. The *Hannu Pash* of the *nie'dama'ting* is . . . rigorous.' Indeed, she had been training them since birth.

'Surely they cannot all become *dama'ting*,' Ahmann said. 'I must have daughters to marry to my loyal men.'

'And so you shall,' Inevera replied. 'Daughters no man dare harm, who are loyal to you over even their husbands.'

'And to Everam, over even their father,' Ahmann muttered.

And to you, most of all, she heard Kenevah say. 'Of course.'

There was a stirring of the guard, and Ashan came into

the room. As personal *dama* to the Sharum Ka, he was seldom seen on Wanings, off giving services and blessings. Asukaji entered with him, and the boy immediately went to stand beside Asome. They looked more like brothers than cousins, far more similar than Asome and Jayan.

Ashan bowed. 'Sharum Ka, there is a matter the *kai'Sharum* wish you to settle.'

Inevera felt every muscle in her body clench. *This is it.*

Ahmann raised an eyebrow as she rose to accompany him, but he made no move to stop her – not that he could have. They left the palace and descended the great stone stairs to the courtyard, which faced the *Sharum* training grounds. At the far end was Sharik Hora, and on the long sides between were the pavilions of the tribes.

Near the base of his steps, well inside the palace walls, a group of *Sharum* and *dama* surrounded two men. One was *khaffit*, grossly fat and dressed in brighter silks than a pillow wife. He wore the tan vest and cap of *khaffit*, but his shirt and pantaloons were of bright multicoloured silk, and the cap was wrapped in a turban of red silk with a gem set at the centre. His belt and slippers were of snakeskin. He leaned on an ivory crutch, carved in the likeness of a camel, with his armpit resting between its humps.

The other was a Northern *chin*, dressed in worn clothes faded and dusty enough to be taken for a *khaffit*'s tan, but he carried a spear, something *khaffit* were forbidden to touch, and had nothing of the deference any sane *khaffit* would have when surrounded by so many warriors. A Messenger from the green lands. Inevera had seen them in the bazaar, but never spoken to one.

Inevera watched Ahmann, seeing recognition in his eyes as they took in the *khaffit*.

The voice from his past.

Inevera looked closer, studying the man's face. She had to look past the thick jowls and cast back years, but at last recalled the boy who had carried Ahmann to the *dama'ting* pavilion all those years ago. A boy who had visited the pavilion himself years later, and left with a limp the *dama'ting* were not sure would ever heal. Abban, son of Chabin, the merchant who used to sell couzi to her father. That was reason enough to dislike him.

'What makes you think you are worthy to stand here among men?' Ahmann demanded. The anger in his tone surprised her. Perhaps the debt of his past was to be collected, rather than paid. Why else would a *khaffit* come to the First Warrior's palace and risk his wrath?

'Apologies, great one.' Abban dropped to his knees and pressed his forehead into the dirt.

'Look at you,' Ahmann snarled. 'You dress like a woman and flaunt your tainted wealth as if it is not an insult to everything we believe. I should have let you fall.'

Fall? Inevera wondered.

'Please, great master,' Abban said. 'I mean no insult. I am only here to translate.'

'Translate?' Ahmann glanced up and noticed the Northerner for the first time. 'A *chin*?' Ahmann turned to Ashan. 'You called me here to speak to a *chin*?'

'Listen to his words,' Ashan urged. 'You will see.'

Ahmann studied the greenlander a long time, then shrugged. 'Speak, and be quick about it,' he told Abban. 'Your presence offends me.'

'This is Arlen asu Jeph am'Bales am'Brook,' Abban said, gesturing to the Messenger. 'Late out of Fort Rizon to the north, he brings you greetings, and begs to fight alongside the men of Krasia tonight in *alagai'sharak*.'

Ahmann gasped, and Inevera, too, felt a wave of shock. A Northerner who wished to fight was like a fish asking to swim in hot sand.

The men began to argue over whether the man's wish should be granted, but Inevera ignored them. 'Husband,' she said quietly, touching Ahmann's arm. 'If the *chin* wishes to stand in the Maze like a *Sharum*, then he must have a foretelling.'

Inevera led the greenlander to a casting chamber. Ahmann insisted on accompanying her, and she could think of no easy way to deny him. He was naïve at times, but her husband was no fool. He sensed her interest in the man, and if the Northerner were indeed his *zahven*, he could likely sense that, too.

'Hold out your arm, Arlen, son of Jeph,' he told the Northerner when she drew her knife. The *chin* frowned but didn't hesitate to roll up his sleeve and hold out his arm.

Brave, Inevera thought as she made the cut. The dice seemed to hum in her hands as she shook and threw.

A chill ran down her spine as she read the result.

No . . .

She pressed her thumb into the *chin*'s wound. He grunted but did not resist. Inevera wet the dice afresh and threw them again.

And a third time.

The fate of Arlen asu Jeph am'Bales am'Brook spread out before her, the same on the third throw as it had on the first. Inevera had cast the bones for countless warriors, but never since Ahmann had she seen the like.

Could he be the Deliverer? She glanced at the greenlander. He was not much to look at, neither short nor tall, his hair the colour of sand and his face bare like a *khaffit*. He wasn't uncomely, but neither was he as handsome as Ahmann.

But his eyes were hard like her husband's, and the same potentials buzzed around him like insects drawn to a lamp – futures where men called him Deliverer, where he was martyred, or died alone, or failed, driving humanity into extinction.

If only I could take husbands like Ahmann takes wives. Her mind ran through the possibilities, but in the end it was impossible. Her powers were not infinite, and even a *dama'ting* could not take two mortal husbands. Just one pushed the boundaries. This greenlander, for all his potential, could not be the leader her people followed, and there could not be two such men, north and south. The land was not big enough for both. They would tear it asunder, losing Sharak Ka in the process.

And so it must be Ahmann.

'He can fight.' She put away her dice and daubed the cut, soaking up the welling blood. She administered a salve and bound the *chin*'s wound with fresh cloth, pocketing the bloody one.

Ahmann and the *chin* left the chamber immediately, and she could hear her husband shouting orders in the hall. She knelt and drew her dice once more, squeezing the bloody cloth over them.

'How can Ahmann take the son of Jeph's power for his own?' she asked as she threw.

– When the *zahven* finds power, he will share the secret with his true friends, but die before giving it up.—

Inevera quickly scooped the dice back into the pouch, getting to her feet and exiting the casting chamber. Ahmann was down the hall, about to leave for the training grounds. She caught his arm.

'The *chin* will be instrumental in your rise to Shar'Dama Ka,' she whispered. 'Embrace him as a brother, but keep him within reach of your spear. One day you must kill him, if you are to be hailed as Deliverer.'

Alarms burned in the city that night, echoed by bells and the screams of women throughout the Undercity. The first wall had been breached.

It was unthinkable. Unheard of.

And yet it was Waning, and the dice had said Ahmann was

to meet his *zahven*. Had the greenlander killed him? What if they had not been speaking of the greenlander? What if Alagai Ka had indeed risen this night and Ahmann was facing him this very moment? Was he ready if Sharak Ka began tonight?

It seemed the next morning that it had, and he was. A rock demon had smashed open the great gate, slaughtering warriors by the score and clearing the way for hundreds of other *alagai*. Such a thing had not occurred in the history of the Desert Spear, a calamity great enough to chill the blood of the bravest man.

But Ahmann had beaten them back, resealing the gates and rescuing countless warriors. He and the greenlander had faced the rock demon together on the Maze floor and trapped it for the sun. It was only by sheer luck it had escaped.

But the price had been high. Over a third of Krasia's warriors dead in one night, and the demon, it happened, was a personal foe of the greenlander. The Andrah had wanted him dead, and Ahmann had put his reputation on the line to save the man in open defiance of his leader, calling him Par'chin, the brave outsider. It was only the broad support of the *Sharum* and key *dama* that had saved the Northerner and kept Ahmann's head on his shoulders.

'I will need more of the Par'chin's blood,' Inevera said.

Ahmann laughed. 'Easily done. The Par'chin bleeds often in the Maze, but always at great cost to the *alagai*.' The next time he brought her a rag so soaked in the greenlander's blood that it filled an entire vial when squeezed. Inevera had attached a piece of *hora* to the glass under layers of opaque glaze and warded it for cold to preserve its essence.

Inevera herself served the Par'chin tea the night he brought the spear. Ahmann looked at her incredulously, but she wanted to get as close to the item as possible. The greenlander said nothing of its origins as the other *Sharum* gazed at the spear in wonder, but he had privately admitted to Ahmann that he had taken it from the ruins of the holy city of Anoch Sun.

The heavy curtains of the dining chamber were pulled tight, and she wore her warded circlet. It was years since she last served tea, but the precise movements of the ritual had been ingrained in her as *nie'dama'ting*, letting her focus on the spear. It glowed like the sun itself in Everam's light – power that could only come from a demon bone core. The hundreds of interconnected wards were beauty beyond belief, and the metal was something she had never seen before.

'You honour me, Dama'ting,' the Par'chin said when she bent to fill his cup. His Krasian was flawless, his manners impeccable. His smile was without guile. Either he was a master thief, every expression sheer artistry, or he did not realize what her people did to grave robbers.

'The honour is ours, Par'chin,' she said. 'You are the only Northerner ever to add your spear to ours.' *And to dare look us in the eye as you attempt to steal from us*, she added silently.

She looked back to the spear. She longed to examine it properly, but *dama'ting* were expressly forbidden to touch weapons. A great irony, as this spear had unquestionably been made by one.

That it was a genuine Sunian artefact with a demon bone core was already beyond doubt. Regardless of its origin, the spear would bite the *alagai* like no weapon in millennia. But in the time of the Shar'Dama Ka there had been many such weapons, carried by the sons and lieutenants of Kaji. Was this one of those, or was it truly the Spear of Kaji, made from the sacred metal by the Damajah herself? There was one way to be sure.

It took only the slightest flick of her arm to hook the flowing white silk of her sleeve on the point of the spear. It came up with her as she straightened, then tore the cloth.

Inevera gasped and pretended to stumble, spilling the tea.

Around the low table, kneeling *Sharum* averted their gazes that they not witness her embarrassment, but the Par'chin was quick, catching the teapot with one hand and steadying her with the other.

'Thank you, Par'chin.' Inevera looked to where the spear had rolled on the floor, seeing what she had hoped. Along its length was a thin, almost imperceptible seam. Without her wardsight, it might have been invisible.

The seam where the Damajah had rolled the thin sheet of sacred metal about the core.

The Par'chin had brought back the Spear of Kaji.

'Tonight is the night,' Inevera said, pacing in excitement. She had known the Par'chin would find power, but this was beyond her wildest dreams. 'Long have I foreseen this. Kill him and take the spear. At dawn, you will declare yourself Shar'Dama Ka, and a month from now you will rule all Krasia.'

She was already plotting his ascent. The Andrah would move to have him stopped or killed, but the *Sharum* were already more loyal to Jardir. If the warriors witnessed Ahmann killing *alagai* on the Maze floor, they would flock to him in droves, starting with those most beholden to him.

'No,' Ahmann said.

It took a moment for the word to register. 'The Krevakh and the Sharach will declare for you immediately, but the Kaji and Majah will take a hard line against . . . Eh?' She turned back to face him. 'The prophecy . . .'

'The prophecy be damned,' Ahmann said. 'I will not murder my friend, no matter what the demon bones tell you. I will not rob him. I am the Sharum Ka, not a thief in the night.'

Inevera's flash of anger was more than even she could bend against. She slapped him, the retort echoing off the stone walls. 'A fool is what you are! Now is the moment of divergence,

443

when what *might* be becomes what *will*. By dawn, one of you will be declared Deliverer. It is up to you to decide if it will be the Sharum Ka of the Desert Spear, or a grave-robbing *chin* from the North.'

'I tire of your prophecies and divergences,' Ahmann said, 'you and all the *dama'ting*! All just guesses meant to manipulate men to your will. But I will not betray my friend for you, no matter what you pretend to see in those warded lumps of *alagai* shit!'

Inevera felt as if everything she had built for over twenty years was crashing down around her. Had she come so far only to fail because her fool husband had not the spine to kill a man who had defiled the grave of Kaji? She shrieked and raised her hand to strike him again, but Ahmann caught her wrist and lifted it high. She struggled for a moment, but he was stronger than her by far.

'Do not force me to hurt you,' he warned.

Now he dared threaten her? The words brought Inevera back to herself. A lifetime of training with Enkido had taught her strength could be taken with a touch. She twisted, driving stiffened fingers to break the line of energy in his shoulder. The arm holding her went limp and she twisted out of his grasp, slipping back a step to straighten her robes as she breathed back to centre.

'You keep thinking the *dama'ting* defenceless, my husband, though you of all people should know better.' She took his numb hand in hers, twisting the arm out straight as she pressed her other thumb into the pressure point in his shoulder, restoring the line of energy.

'You are no thief if you are only reclaiming what is already yours by right.'

'Mine?' Ahmann asked.

'Who is the thief?' Inevera asked. 'The *chin* who robs the grave of Kaji, or you, his blood kin, who takes back what was stolen?'

'We do not know it is the Spear of Kaji he holds,' Ahmann said.

Inevera crossed her arms. 'You know. You knew the moment you laid eyes on it, just as you've known all along that this day would come. I never hid this fate from you.'

Ahmann said nothing, and Inevera knew she was reaching him. She touched his arm. 'If you prefer, I can put a potion in his tea. His passing will be quick.'

'No!' Ahmann shouted, pulling away. 'Always the path of least honour with you! The Par'chin is no *khaffit*, to be put down like a dog! He deserves a warrior's death.'

I have him, Inevera thought. 'Then give him one. Now, before *alagai'sharak* begins and the power of the spear is known.'

But Ahmann shook his head, and she knew he would not be swayed. 'If it is to be done, I will do it in the Maze.'

The next morning, Ahmann returned to the Palace of the Sharum Ka triumphant, the Spear of Kaji held high for all to see. *Sharum* cheered and *dama* looked on – some in religious fervour, others in terror. Their world was about to change forever, and any with half a mind knew it.

But though he looked every inch the proud, fearless leader, his eyes were haunted. He was surrounded by a crowd of lieutenants and sycophants, but Inevera knew it was imperative she speak to him alone immediately. She gestured, sending her little sisters. No man would impede a *dama'ting*, and the eleven *Jiwah Sen* quickly formed an impenetrable ring around Ahmann, cutting him off from the others and guiding him to a private chamber where they might speak freely.

'What happened?' she demanded. 'Is the Par'chin—'

'Gone,' Ahmann cut her off. 'I put the spear between his eyes and left his body out on the dunes, far from the city walls.'

'Thank Everam,' Inevera exhaled, unclenching muscles she

hadn't even realized were held tight. Even the dice had not been able to say with certainty that he would murder his friend.

And it was murder, despite the honeyed words she'd used to make bitter betrayal easier to swallow. The greenlander was a godless grave robber, but he had not been raised to Everam's truths, and she would have robbed the grave of Kaji herself had she known where it lay and what it contained. Already she counselled Ahmann to return there as soon as possible.

She reached out, putting a hand on his shoulder. 'I am sorry for your loss, husband. He was an honourable man.'

Ahmann pulled his shoulder roughly from her grasp. 'What would you know of honour?'

He stormed away from her, going into the small shrine to Everam where he said his private prayers. Inevera did not attempt to follow, but she turned her earring, breathing deeply as she listened to her husband weep.

Was Ahmann the Deliverer? If such a man was made and not born, would she ever know for sure if she had succeeded, short of him killing Alagai'ting Ka, the Mother of All Demons?

Surely Inevera had seized advantages for him, but if it was anyone, it had to be him. He had excelled at every test in his life, and even if he took it by force, the spear *had* come to him as if by fate. Any other man would have stabbed the greenlander without a second thought, but for all his power and station, Ahmann still wept over the betrayal.

Would he have seized the moment, if she had not commanded it? Even if she had never met him? If he was the strong but illiterate and racist animal that the Kaji'sharaj usually produced, would he have befriended the Par'chin all the same, and killed him when it was time? Was there something divine in Ahmann that would have clawed its way to power no matter how low his station?

She did not know.

'Today,' Ahmann said as Inevera helped him into his armoured robes.

It was almost half a year since he took the spear, the last press for the Palace of the Andrah. He could have taken the city sooner if he had wished for vast bloodshed, but Ahmann was content to wait and let men come to him, as more did each day.

'We have more men inside the palace than he does now,' Ahmann said. 'They will open the gates at dawn, killing the last remaining *Sharum* who hold to the old ways. By noon I will sit the Skull Throne. I will send a runner when it is safe for you and your *Jiwah Sen* to enter.'

Inevera nodded as if this were great news, though she had listened in on his secret meetings with his generals and confirmed his conclusions with the dice. She had needed to say or do little once the spear was in Ahmann's hands. She had groomed him to conquer and lead, and he took to those things like a bird to the sky.

Ahmann left to meet his men, and Inevera called her little sisters. They stripped her of her white silken robes, and she stepped into the steaming bath where Everalia and Thalaja waited to scrub her skin and massage her with scented oil.

'Bring me my red pillow dancing silks,' she told Qasha, who hurried to comply.

'Clever,' Belina said, smiling. 'You will wear them under your whites, the quicker to help our husband celebrate his rise.'

Inevera threw back her head and laughed. 'Oh, little sister. I am never wearing my whites again.'

Inevera lay on the pillows beside the Skull Throne of Sharik Hora. The temple of heroes' bones itself was their palace now, and there was old magic here. Not as flashy as that given by demon bones, but no less potent. Millions of men had died proudly to decorate this place, their spirits bound to the stone.

Knowing their ancestors were watching made her feel all the more wanton, lying on a bed of silk pillows clad only in transparent silk. The pants were slit up each leg, gathered with gold at the cuffs, and would flash long strips of bare leg as she moved. The top was a long strip of silk that barely covered her breasts, and did nothing to hide them. It was tied in a simple knot beneath her shoulder blades, the long ends streaming loose along her arms and fastened to golden bracelets. Her hair was oiled and bound in gold.

But there was power in that, too. Ahmann hated seeing his wife displayed so, but it was good to remind him publicly that even as Shar'Dama Ka, his power was not infinite. Thus, he was forced to pretend it was his choice.

It was an important lesson, and unless she missed her guess, she was about to teach it again. Before them stood Kajivah, Ashan, Imisandre, Hoshvah, and Hanya, along with Ahmann's nieces Ashia, Shanvah, and Sikvah.

'*Hannu Pash* has called my son Asukaji to take the white, Holy Deliverer,' Ashan was saying, 'but my daughter Ashia, blood of your blood, has been given blacks by the *dama'ting*. It is an insult.'

'You should cherish your daughters, Ashan,' Ahmann said. 'If they enter the Dama'ting Palace, you may never see them again. There is no dishonour in being *dal'ting*.' He gestured to Kajivah.

Ashan bowed deeply to the woman. 'I mean no disrespect, Holy Mother.'

Kajivah bowed in return. 'There is none taken, Damaji.' She turned to her son, and even though he sat seven steps above her, it seemed she was looking down at him.

'There is no dishonour in *dal'ting*, my son, but there is burden. Burden your sisters and I carried for many years. Would you have the law defend a husband who strikes a child of your blood?'

Ahmann turned to Inevera, but she cut him off before he could speak. 'The dice did not call them.' The words were quiet, for him alone, a benefit from sitting on high with him. 'Would you take a cripple as *Sharum*?'

Ahmann scowled, but kept his voice equally low. 'Are you saying my nieces are no better than cripples?'

Inevera shook her head. 'I am saying they were meant for other things. One need not take orders to be great, beloved. Witness yourself. If you wish, I will take the girls into the Dama'ting Palace and train them, as you were trained in Sharik Hora.'

Ahmann looked at her a moment, then nodded, turning back to the others. 'The girls shall be taken into the Dama'ting Palace as *dal'ting*, and trained. They shall emerge as *kai'ting*, and once married wear a white veil with their black headscarves and robes, as shall my mother and sisters from this day forth. As with the *dama'ting*, any man caught striking a *kai'ting* will lose either the offending limb or his life.'

'Deliverer—' Ashan began.

Ahmann cut him off with a subtle wave of his spear. 'I have spoken, Ashan.'

Inevera rose as the *Damaji* fell back, humbled. She clapped once, rubbing her hands together as she took in the three girls, still so young and pliable. In truth, she had no idea what she would do with them, but that was sometimes the way.

Plant the seeds you have, the Evejah'ting said. *For they may bear unexpected fruit.*

Inevera escorted the girls out of the great chamber through her own personal entrance. There, just inside the door, stood Qeva and Enkido, who would have heard, by way of precise acoustics, every word in the main chamber.

'The girls will be taught letters, singing, and pillow dancing for four hours each day,' Inevera told Qeva. 'The other twenty, they belong to Enkido.'

Ashia gasped at that, and Shanvah clutched at her. Sikvah began to cry.

Inevera ignored them, turning to the eunuch. 'Make something worthy out of them.'

18

Strained Meeting

333 AR Summer
11 Dawns Before New Moon

Leesha felt the roiling in her stomach calm as the familiar outskirts of the Hollow came into sight. It was good to be home. The refugee villages, each on its own greatward, were coming together with incredible speed.

But then a shout, and the caravan came to an abrupt halt. Leesha stuck her head out the window and saw a company of Wooden Soldiers at the border of the central greatward. Fifty of them stood blocking the road on heavy destriers, their lacquered wooden armour polished and shining in the sun. A rustling in the scrub to the side of the road heralded archers, lightly armoured in leather, each with a drawn bow and two more arrows in hand.

Behind them were hundreds of Cutters, some with spears, but others with the original implements of their craft. Some were faces she knew. Most were not.

'What is the meaning of this?' Kaval shouted, and Leesha knew the idiot was reaching for his spear. She wrenched the door to her carriage open, tripping in her haste and ending up sprawled on the ground. She momentarily clutched her stomach in fear, but gritted her teeth and pushed herself up.

'Mistress Leesha!' Wonda cried, vaulting down from her

horse. Leesha made her feet before the girl reached her and waved her off. As she expected, the Krasian men all had spears in hand, and the bowmen looked ready to cut them down and ask questions later.

'Put up your weapons!' she shouted. Her voice did not have *hora* magic to augment it, but the ability to boom was another thing Leesha had got from her mother. All eyes turned her way. No one made a move to disarm.

'Who are you, to order the soldiers of Count Thamos?' one of the mounted soldiers asked. He rode a fine destrier rather than one of the sleek Angierian coursers that carried the other Wooden Soldiers, and his cloak was held in place with gold chain. There was a captain's tuft on his helm.

'I am Mistress Leesha Paper, Herb Gatherer of Deliverer's Hollow,' Leesha said, 'and I'd appreciate being spared the trouble of sewing up wounds from overeager men with itchy bow fingers.'

'*Cutter's* Hollow,' the captain corrected. 'And you're late. Your sand Messenger arrived over a week ago, and said nothing about you bringing half the Krasian army with you.'

Kaval chuckled at that. 'If one hundredth of the Deliverer's army was on the road, the thunder of our footsteps alone would knock you off your horse, boy.'

The captain bared his teeth, and Leesha stormed into the road to stand between them. 'Keep your tongue still, Drillmaster, I won't have you shame my homecoming.'

Gared and Wonda moved to flank her, Wonda on foot, and Gared towering above the biggest mounted soldiers atop his heavy garron. The Wooden Soldiers began to whisper among themselves at the sight of him. Gared's reputation preceded him. Another thing her mother had been right about. She wished she could get the sight of them stuck together like dogs out of her head.

'Who in the Core are you?' Gared demanded of the captain. The big man's anger was palpable. 'Don't care to have spears pointed at me and mine on ground we bled for. You'd best lower them before they get shoved up your arse.'

451

The captain smiled. 'You're in no position to make threats, Mr Cutter. You don't command here any more.'

'Ay?' Gared put his fingers to his lips and gave a shrill whistle. The Cutters standing behind the Wooden Soldiers broke ranks at the sound, flowing to either side around the count's men. They were led by Dug and Merrem Butcher, and Leesha saw others she knew in the van. Yon Gray and his son and grandsons, all looking of an age with one another. Samm Saw, Ande Cutter, Tomm Wedge and his sons. Evin Cutter and his gigantic wolfhound.

The Cutters didn't threaten, but they didn't need to. The shortest of them was a head taller than any of the count's footmen. Even the mounted men in armour looked cowed. Shadow was almost of a size with the horses, and they whinnied and pranced in fear as he passed. If the beast got any bigger, Evin would soon be riding it instead of his garron.

The Wooden Soldiers hesitated, glancing at their captain for instructions. By then it was too late and they were encircled, cutting the captain off from his men.

More Cutters appeared in the trees, and bowstrings were eased back under their glare. Dug and Merrem saluted as they came to stand next to Gared.

'You were sayin'?' Gared asked smugly.

The captain's face had gone slack, but he shook his head, regaining his composure. He raised a hand and gave his men a complex series of gestures. They lowered their spears, seeming relieved, but looked ready to raise them again in an instant.

The soldier dismounted, removing his helmet and giving a curt bow to Leesha. 'My name is Squire Gamon, captain of the count's guard. We are here to escort you to His Highness.'

'And you need seventy men to do that, Captain Gamon?' Leesha asked. 'Is the very heart of the Hollow so dangerous now?'

'You have nothing to fear here, mistress,' Gamon said, 'but by order of Count Thamos, no Krasian is to enter the city bearing arms.'

'Nie take me first,' Kaval growled in Krasian. Leesha turned to him, raising an eyebrow.

'Forgive me, mistress,' the drillmaster said, 'but my spear was a gift from the Deliverer himself, and I will not surrender it to some soft greenland *chi'Sharum*.'

'You will,' Gamon told him, 'or we have orders to take them, no matter who stands in our way.' He looked to Gared and Leesha. 'You may have us outnumbered here, but the count commands a thousand Wooden Soldiers. Do you wish to spill blood over His Highness's efforts to keep his people safe from known invaders?'

Leesha rubbed her temple. 'If that was his goal, he has a funny way of showing it.' She shook her head. 'But no, we're not.' She turned to Kaval. 'You will not surrender your weapons to him, Drillmaster, you will surrender them to me.'

'I'm afraid that will not be good enough, mistress,' Gamon said.

Leesha looked down her nose at him. 'They're disarmed, Captain. Don't insist on taking the coreling by the horns.'

Gamon's mouth opened, but no sound emerged. It was answer enough. She turned back to Kaval. 'Collect the spears from your men, *dal* and *kha'Sharum* both, and stow them underneath my carriage. You have my word they will be returned to you when you leave the Hollow.'

Kaval hesitated, glancing over his shoulder. Leesha hissed at him. 'Don't look for the *dama'ting*,' she said in Krasian. 'Ahmann gave your command to me, not her. Do as you're told. Now.'

The drillmaster curled his lip, but he bowed and complied, taking the weapons from his men and stowing them safely out of reach. Doubtless they still had knives, and Coliv a host of other hidden weapons, but there was a limit to Krasian honour. If she or Captain Gamon tried to search them, there would be blood.

Darsy appeared out of the crowd to stand at her side. She didn't curtsy, but gave Leesha a hug that blew the wind from her. 'No idea how glad I am you're back.' Leesha returned the embrace, remembering how greatly Darsy had once resented her. The shift was not new, but it continued to surprise her.

'Now, Captain,' she said, 'if you'd care to escort us to His Highness, I would very much like to speak with him.'

The soldier nodded, replacing his helm and climbing back atop his horse. The Cutters opened their ring, allowing him to rejoin his men, but kept close, giving Leesha a sense of safety and protection she had not felt in months. It was good to be home.

Darsy moved to take the reins from the Krasian driving Leesha's carriage, and the man hopped down as she and Leesha took the bench so they could speak privately as the caravan began to move once more. Wonda kept close on her horse, while Gared led his garron so he could consult with the Cutters.

'You get my last message?' Darsy asked. 'Never got a reply.'

Leesha shook her head. 'We've been on the road for weeks. Must have missed the Messenger. What's been happening? I knew Thamos would be looking to flex his muscles when we returned, but I didn't expect an armed welcome. Have things soured?'

Darsy shook her head. 'Truer is the count's been good to the Hollow. Been fair to the people, and brought a steady stream of supplies from the North. His engineers have done a lot to speed along the new greatwards and put roofs over people's heads. New Tender's much the same. Bit stricter than Jona, but folk like him well enough. Things keep on as they've been, and we'll be bigger than Angiers in a year.'

'It's not surprising,' Leesha said. 'It was bold of the duke to give him the Hollow outright, and even if he does have a thousand men, he's still outnumbered. Best not to give us any reason to oppose him till his power's secure. He's going to need all the goodwill he can get when the Painted Man returns.'

Darsy cleared her throat. 'That's what my message was about. He's been back for two weeks. But he's . . . different.'

Leesha looked at her sharply. 'Different how?'

'Calls himself Arlen Bales now,' Darsy said, 'and changed his

Tender's robes for clothes like regular folk. Says he's from a place called Tibbet's Brook, a town on the arse end of nowhere in Miln.'

'Honest word?' Leesha felt a wide smile break out on her face. Had Arlen finally faced his demons and found himself again? She thought of their last awkward parting, how much she had wanted him to go, but how safe she had felt in that final embrace.

'Ay, seen it myself,' Darsy said. 'But there's more. He has . . . powers now.'

Leesha looked at her. 'He's always had powers, Darsy. The wards—'

'More'n that,' Darsy cut in. 'First night he came back, Ande Cutter was laid open like a butchered pig during a demon purge. I was there, and ready to let him go to the Creator. Wern't nothing I could've done. You neither. But Painted Man just waved a hand, and the wounds closed up right before my eyes. Ande was up and about like nothing happened the next day.'

'He just waved his hands?' Leesha asked. 'He didn't draw wards on Ande's flesh in demon ichor?'

'Course not!' Darsy was aghast. 'What kind of sick soul would put demon ichor near a wound?'

'Never mind that,' Leesha said. 'Was he just gesturing, or was he drawing wards in the air?'

Darsy thought a moment. 'Might've been drawing wards, I guess. But not ones I know.'

Leesha nodded. 'I'd like to speak to Ande later.'

'Speak to half the town,' Darsy said. 'Next night he went to the hospit, and cleared it out. Not so much as a hangnail left to treat.'

'Creator,' Leesha said. She had learned some secrets of healing with *hora* magic while in Everam's Bounty, but nothing on such a scale. The mind demon she and Inevera faced had cast spells by drawing wards in the air, but it hadn't worked for her, even when she did it with the demon's own horn in hand. Where was Arlen getting the power? The amount of magic he must have expended was staggering.

'Ay,' Darsy agreed, 'and he's been out to the refugee towns each night since, doing the same. All over there are tales of those at death's door back on their feet. Still claims he ent the Deliverer, but less and less folk believe him. Night, startin' to believe it myself.'

Leesha frowned. 'How is the count handling it?'

'Same as with Gared just now,' Darsy said. 'Tried to throw his weight around a bit, and got put in his place. Painted Man ent opposing Thamos openly, but any fool can see he's got the count and new Tender cowed behind closed doors and pickin' their words careful where others can hear.'

Leesha rubbed the ache in her temple, wishing Arlen were there to cure her headache the way he had every other ill in the Hollow. 'Anything else I need to know?'

'He fought some kind of smart demon last new moon,' Darsy said. 'Gets inside your head, and makes other corespawn fight like they got a good general. He's got everyone making warded headbands before the moon goes dark again.' She held out a strip of cloth, and Leesha took it, examining the mind ward there, same as the one she had been passing around the hamlets on her way home.

She nodded. 'That all?'

Darsy shook her head, lowering her voice. 'He ent alone.'

The ache became a stabbing pain. Darsy hadn't given detail, but it was there in her tone. 'Oh?'

'Got a girl with him,' Darsy confirmed. 'Renna Tanner. Says she's from back home in the Brook.' Darsy paused, fixing her gaze on some far-off point. Her voice went flat. 'Says they're promised.'

Darsy kept her eyes staring off into nothing, waiting for Leesha to react. Almost everyone in the Hollow whispered about how Arlen had charged into the Holy House during the Battle of

Cutter's Hollow bellowing her name when he thought she was in danger. They whispered of how he had first appeared at her side and how he was seen coming and going from her cottage at all hours. They whispered, and speculated. It was no secret the whole town was praying they would just get on with it and wondering what was taking so long. Leesha had often wondered herself.

Leesha realized she was holding her breath, and forced herself to blow it out. It was ridiculous for her to be upset. She had long since tired of waiting for Arlen and begun looking for other prospects. Night, the sickness that came on her each morning confirmed how she had moved on. Yet she'd wanted him. If he'd wanted her in return, she would have given herself to him without reservation.

But he hadn't wanted her. He claimed it was his curse. That he could not create a family with his blood tainted by demon magic. Somehow, that only made her love him more, his sacrifice so noble, so proud. She felt weak for having sought the arms of others in the light of it.

But had it been honest word? Now, a scant few months later, he had gone from swearing off love to promising himself to another. Had all his claims just been an act? The thought filled her with anger. How dare he? Did he think her so weak, so desperate for his love, that she couldn't handle the truth? That she required a lie to sugar the medicine as he rebuffed her? Coward.

All this went through her head, but she had learned her lessons from the *dama'ting*, and her face showed none of it. 'That's well,' she managed at last. 'He deserves to be happy, and a good woman will help keep his feet on the ground.'

'Not this one,' Darsy muttered. Leesha looked at her curiously, but the big woman rubbed at her throat and did not elaborate further.

To Leesha's surprise, they did not head for the Corelings' Graveyard, turning instead to another area of the greatward. She was wondering at the destination when Thamos' keep came into view.

The fort was still under construction, but already a huge palisade wall had been erected, tarred logs lashed tightly together, thick and high enough for soldiers to patrol the ramparts with crank bows, and crenellated to give them cover while firing.

The palisade gate swung open, showing a courtyard more than large enough to accommodate their entire caravan. As the soldiers waved for them to enter, it became clear Thamos intended just that, taking everyone inside the walls and shutting the gates behind them. Leesha worried that once inside, the Krasians might never emerge. She had always known they were hostages and spies both, freely given by Ahmann as a show of good faith, but her intent had been to treat them as any other folk, letting them see the goodness of her people up close.

She doubted Count Thamos would do the same. He had made a show of benevolence thus far, but his mission had always been clear: get control of the Hollow, learn the secrets of demon killing, and draw Angiers' line in the sand against the Krasians. The attitude at court had been one of loathing for the desert people. It was not undeserved after their attack on Rizon, but escalation was the last thing they needed right now. Ahmann could crush the Hollow – and likely Angiers itself – if given cause.

'Stop the carriage,' she told Darsy, and the woman complied immediately. The rest of the caravan stopped with them, and Leesha got down and opened the door to the carriage.

Elona looked out, taking in the count's keep. She let out a low whistle. 'Prince has been busy these last months. Is he married?'

Leesha sighed. Even now, she could not bear to look at her mother. 'I hope not. Court gossip has him bedding every young thing bats a lash at him.'

'Just needs the right one to spin his head a bit,' Elona said.

'I said *young*, Mother,' Leesha said. 'I don't think you're his type.'

'Ay, don't talk to your mother that way!' Erny said. Leesha

looked at him and wanted to scream. Even now, he defended her. It would likely be the same even if he knew about Gared. Night, he probably did. Erny wasn't half the fool people thought he was when it came to his wife, but Elona had been right about his courage.

Leesha pretended her father had not spoken. 'I am going in for an audience with His Highness now. I'll have some of the Cutters escort you back home. When you're there and no one is looking, take the Krasian spears and hide them in the paper shop. Somewhere no one will find them.'

Erny seemed nonplussed at both Leesha's and Elona's lack of response, and nodded after a moment. 'Ay, I know just the place. I've a slurry vat with a false bottom.'

'Oh, *really?*' Leesha asked. 'And what, might I ask, did you need that for?'

Erny smiled. 'To keep inquisitive young girls poking around my papermaking chemicals from getting themselves hurt.'

'I've been mixing worse for fifteen years,' Leesha said.

'Ay,' Erny agreed. 'But I haven't had reason to bring up since.' He raised a finger. 'And you'll know my secrets when I decide it, young lady, and not before. You mind your tone if you ever want to know where the gold's hid.'

'He ent bluffing,' Elona muttered. 'Been with him near thirty years, and still ent got a clue.'

Captain Gamon rode back to where they stood. 'The count is waiting,' he said impatiently. 'What is the delay?' With the count's seat of power – and crank bowmen – at his back, he seemed to regain something of the haughtiness he had first shown on the road.

'I am sending my parents home while I meet with His Highness,' Leesha said. 'And the rest of the caravan could use a bit of ease.'

'They can have that inside the count's keep,' Gamon said. 'Accommodations have been made. They will be safer inside.'

'Safer from whom?' Leesha asked.

'Many of His Highness's new subjects come from the south, and remember what these people did to their homes,' Gamon reminded her.

'I am aware of that,' Leesha said, 'but these are guests and not prisoners.'

She turned to Gared and the Cutters, who had come to stand beside her. 'I think the Cutters can keep peace with a group of unarmed Krasians, don't you?'

'Don't you worry none, girlie,' Yon Gray said, slapping his axe handle against his palm. 'Anyone woodbrained enough to start trouble'll soon regret it.' It was eerie, hearing the old man's voice come from a man now in his prime. She had been documenting Yon's slow shedding of years for some time, but the sudden change after months apart was still a little jarring. Most of the grey had fled his hair, and he looked a man of forty rather than one in his seventies.

'Ay,' Dug said. 'We'll see to it.'

Gamon shook his head. 'The royal summons mentions you and your wife by name, Mr Butcher, along with Captain Cutter, Master Inn, and Miss Cutter.' He indicated Wonda.

'Me?' Wonda asked. 'What's the count want to see me for?'

'I'm sure I don't know.' Gamon's tone was derisive. Angierians gave their women more rights than Krasians, but not by much. They didn't approve of women involving themselves in politics or military matters. Leesha opened her mouth to fire off an acid response, but Gared beat her to it.

'Mind yur manners,' Gared growled. 'She's got more coreling corpses to her name than yur whole runty company combined.'

Gamon's eyebrow became a hard V. Here beside the keep the Wooden Soldiers were more numerous, but more and more Cutters arrived by the moment. He pursed his lips, saying nothing.

Gared grunted and turned to Yon. 'Keep watch on the caravan while we're inside. No one bothers 'em, but no one leaves, either. Extra eyes on the ones in black.'

Yon nodded. 'Ay, boy. Don't fret on it.'

Rojer appeared a moment later. In the Krasian fashion, Amanvah followed a step behind him; Kaval, Coliv, and Enkido a step behind her; Shamavah a step behind them.

'Where is Sikvah?' Leesha asked. 'Is she well?'

Amanvah shook her head with a tsk. 'You play at understanding our ways, Mistress Paper, but your knowledge is obviously lacking if you think a man should bring his *Jiwah Sen* to court.'

Amanvah's tone was haughty as ever, but Leesha could sense the anger beneath. She bowed. 'I meant no insult.' Amanvah did not reply.

'His Highness has not summoned you,' Captain Gamon told her. 'You and your savages can wait in the courtyard.'

Amanvah's gaze snapped to him, her *dama'ting* serenity broken at the rudeness. Kaval and Enkido tensed, but she flicked a hand to calm them. 'My father is Ahmann asu Hoshkamin am'Jardir am'Kaji. Shar'Dama Ka and Deliverer, who will unite mankind. He will take it a grave insult if I am left rotting on the pillows by some minor princeling.'

'I don't care if your father is the Creator Himself,' Gamon snapped. 'You'll wait until you're called for.'

Amanvah's delicate eyebrows seemed to thread together, but she did not argue further.

Leesha felt the situation deteriorating and turned to Evin, absently stroking the back of his wolfhound, its massive shoulders almost as high as his. She had disliked Evin when they were young – he had been cruel and selfish and never one to be counted – but like so many folk, the coming of the Painted Man had changed him. 'Evin, will you see my parents home, please?'

Evin nodded, springing into the driver's seat of their carriage himself. Shadow followed alongside the carriage, and the horses stamped and pulled at their harnesses, whinnying in fear.

Evin gave a shrill whistle. 'Ay, Shadow! Go and find Callen!'

461

The wolfhound gave a bark that sounded like a thunderclap and ran off. Evin pulled hard at the reins, getting the horses under control, then gave them a crack and the carriage rode off. The rest of the caravan was left at loose ends under the watchful eyes of the Cutters and Wooden Soldiers as she and the others passed through the gates.

The count's keep was still under construction, but the foundations were laid and portions of his manse were already raised and functional. A group of Wooden Soldiers gathered at the main entrance, spears and shields at the ready.

Leesha moved over to Gared, dropping her voice. 'Gared, if the count tries to give you a title and a uniform, don't accept right away.'

'Why not?' Gared said, not bothering to keep her hushed tones.

'Because you'd be giving away our army, you idiot,' Rojer said, coming up on his other side. His voice, too, was too low for the others to hear.

Gared turned an angry glare the Jongleur's way. 'Just a big joke to you, too, ent I? Painted Man told me to keep you safe while he was gone, Rojer. I swore by the sun and promised I would. Stood in the way of charging demons and Krasians and Creator knows what else to keep it.'

He loomed forward suddenly, and the smaller man, his bearing so proud a moment before, shrank back from the sheer menace of his presence. 'But he never told me I had to eat yur shit, and you been takin' a lot of liberty. Way I see it, him back in town means my promise is kept and done. Watch yur own back from now on, you crippled little runt. And next time you call me idiot? Gonna put your teeth out.' He licked two fingers and held them up high enough to catch the sun topping the count's walls. 'Swear by the sun.'

'Gared,' Leesha said carefully, as Rojer stood shocked. 'You have every right to be angry about how we've taken you for granted, and for my part, I'm sorry. I blame you for everything wrong in my life sometimes, but truer is, you didn't do anything a million other boys haven't done. I forgive you. You've made up for it many times over.'

Gared grunted. 'Corespawned right.'

'But Rojer has the right of it,' Leesha said. 'If you let the count give you a title, it's the same as saying the Cutters are part of the Angierian army.'

Gared shrugged. 'Ent we? You two act like I'm the dim one, but it seems to me like you've forgotten whose side we're on, carrying on in the sheets with Krasians and forgetting who was there for us when we needed them.'

'It sure as the Core wasn't Duke Rhinebeck,' Rojer said.

Gared nodded. 'Know that. Was the Deliverer done it. Painted Man's letting the count lead the Hollow for now, that's good enough for me. Tomorrow he says chop the count's head off, I'll do that, too.'

'And all the Cutters with you,' Leesha said in disgust.

'Ay, that's right. They follow *me*. Not you, Leesh.' He nodded to Rojer. 'And not fiddle-boy here, either. You two can go back to pickin' herbs and spinning reels. The men got this.'

'Creator help us,' Leesha muttered as he turned his back and strode ahead.

'The Hollow has changed since you were last here, mistress.'

Thamos sat on a heavy throne atop a raised dais at the head of his receiving hall. Still under construction, the walls and high ceiling were partly bare wood and partly beams covered in heavy tarp. The air was thick with dust and the smell of mixing crete, amplified by her headache. Freshly swept sawdust crunched beneath her shoes. Still the room was daunting in its sheer size, and would likely be breathtaking when fully appointed.

Adding to the trappings of power, the count was dressed in

full armour, his spear close to hand. His beard was impeccably groomed to accentuate a sharp, handsome jaw, his waistline trim, and his shoulders broad. He looked every inch a noble soldier. A servant stood behind him, holding the count's helm and shield as if he might be called to battle at any moment.

At Thamos' right hand was Tender Hayes, the man Araine had promised in their meeting those months ago. Honest in his faith and fair, she said, but Angierian in his heart.

The Duchess Mum was behind everything the Angierians did, whether they knew it or not. Leesha had witnessed the woman's power first-hand on her last visit to court. The duke and elder princes were kept in line by her first minister, Janson, but Leesha had long suspected that the youngest reported directly to her.

In that meeting, Araine had promised to send Thamos and his soldiers as well, but left out the part about making him count. *I should have seen this coming*, Leesha thought. *The woman's played me for a fool again, even after scolding me to keep up with the dance.*

In front of the throne, Lord Arther stood at a small writing podium, pen in hand with an open ledger and a fresh pot of ink. Captain Gamon stood to the left, straight-backed with his spear planted firmly on the floor. Behind him, a footman held his helm and shield.

'Changed quite a bit it seems, Your Highness,' Leesha said with a curtsy. 'We don't normally surround our citizens with drawn bows on their return from a journey.'

'Our citizens did not used to go off into our enemies' midst without permission from the crown,' Thamos said.

'Perhaps that's because we never had enemies before,' Leesha said. 'I had fifty Krasian warriors in my town with an army at their backs, and did the best I could to keep my people safe. We didn't have a week and more to wait on a response from the crown, and there's nothing in the town charter that says I can't come and go as I please in any event.'

Thamos sighed. 'You've gotten used to having your own way

in Cutter's Hollow, mistress. Well enough when all you were good for was a few caravans of wood each year, but all that has changed. I am lord of the Hollow and its environs now. Your town council answers to me, and not the other way around. I can wipe my arse with your charter.'

Leesha smiled. 'Do as you please, Highness, but do not be surprised to find the Hollowers don't take it kindly if you do.'

'Threats, mistress?' Thamos asked. 'After the ivy throne has answered your plea for aid, sending food, supplies, engineers, Warders, and soldiers to succour the refugees and fortify against the Krasians?'

'No threat,' Leesha said. 'We are thankful for your aid and grateful to His Grace for the consideration he has given. I am simply offering a piece of advice.'

'And what "advice" do you have regarding the company of enemy soldiers you brought with you?' Thamos asked. 'Can you give me a reason not to arrest and execute the lot of them?'

'I have seen the Krasian army,' Leesha told him. 'Harming my escort, sent in good faith to keep us safe on the road and open relations between our peoples, would be tantamount to starting a war we cannot hope to win.'

'You're a fool if you think we will surrender an inch of ground to them,' Thamos growled.

Leesha nodded. 'Which is why you should smile and bide your time while the Hollow gets its feet under it. Treat our guests with courtesy. Show them our way of life is a good one, and that we, too, are strong.'

Thamos shook his head. 'I will not have Krasian spies living and moving freely about the greatwards of the Hollow.'

Leesha shrugged. 'Then you shall not. I will let them stay on my land.'

'*Your* land?' Thamos asked.

'Bruna was given a thousand acres of hereditary land by your father, Duke Rhinebeck the Second.' She smiled. 'A gift for midwifing Your Highness, I believe.'

Thamos' face reddened, and Leesha let the grin slip from her face. 'When Bruna died, she left me the land in her will. I have deliberately kept every acre off the greatwards.'

'The land around the cottage Darsy keeps?' Thamos asked. 'You doubt my sincerity in offering my walls to these people, and then suggest instead they live on unwarded land?'

'My lands are safer than you might expect, Highness,' Leesha said. 'Without their spears, there aren't enough of them to cause a real problem, especially with their wives and children in tow. The Krasians bring gifts and goods to trade, with the promise of more. Let them do business, and send merchant spies of your own in return. If we cannot avert war, it is in our best interest to delay it while we build our forces and learn our enemies' ways.'

Thamos wiped the frustration from his face, losing most of the tension in his shoulders. 'Mother said you'd be like this.'

Leesha smiled. 'The Duchess Mum knows me well. She is in good health, I presume?'

Thamos seemed to brighten a bit at the mention of his mother. 'Not as vital as she once was, but I think in the end she will outlive us all.'

Leesha nodded. 'Some women have too much will to die before their work is done.'

'Mother sends her regards,' Thamos went on. 'And gifts.'

'Gifts?' Leesha asked.

'First things first,' Thamos said, turning his gaze on Gared. 'Gared Cutter?'

Gared stepped forth. 'Ay, Yur Highness?'

Arther took a small scroll from his podium and broke the seal, unrolling it to read: '"Gared Cutter, son of Steave of the village of Cutter's Hollow, in the name of His Grace, Duke Rhinebeck the Third, Wearer of the Ivy Crown, Protector of the Forest Fortress and Duke of Angiers, you are hereby requested and required, in the year three hundred and thirty-three after the Return, to assume the rank of captain of the

466

Cutters in service to His Grace, and the title of Squire at court. You will be given a district of the Hollow to oversee and tax for the upkeep of your household, and report only to His Highness Lord Thamos, Marshal of the Wooden Soldiers." Do you accept this honour, and this duty?'

A wide grin split Gared's face. 'Captain, eh? Squire?'

'Do. Not. Accept,' Leesha said through gritted teeth. It was a meaningless title. Gared was already the leader of the Cutters. This was all just a ploy to get him to swear fealty to the crown, and admit that the Cutters were part of Rhinebeck's army and not a private force.

Gared chuckled. 'Don't worry. Not gonna.'

He looked up at the count. 'Thanks all the same, Yur Highness, but there's a lot more Cutters in the Hollow than Wooden Soldiers.'

Everyone in the room tensed. Thamos' hand found the haft of his spear. 'And just what are you saying, Mr Cutter?'

Gared thrust his chin at Gamon. 'Corespawned if I'll be the same rank as that pissant. Wanna be general. And . . . ay, like a baron or something.'

Gamon scowled, but Thamos nodded. 'Done.' Leesha put her face in her hand, feeling her temple throb again.

'Idiot,' Rojer whispered for her ears only.

Thamos rose and pointed his spear at Gared. 'Kneel.'

Gared gave Leesha a triumphant grin and stepped forward, falling to one knee. Thamos laid his speartip on the Cutter's burly shoulder. Tender Hayes came forward as well, holding out a worn but beautiful leather-bound book, its cover illuminated in gold leaf. 'Place your right hand on the Canon, my son.'

Gared did, his eyes closed.

'Do you swear fealty to His Highness, Count Thamos of Hollow County, answering to him and no other, from now until your death?'

'Ay,' Gared said.

'Do you swear to uphold his law,' Hayes went on, 'to administer fair justice to your subjects, the people of Cutter's Hollow, and to smite its enemies?'

'Ay,' Gared said. 'And twice for the last.'

Thamos gave a grim smile. 'By the power given me by my brother, Duke Rhinebeck, Wearer of the Ivy Crown, Protector of the Forest Fortress and Lord of All Angiers, I name you General Gared of the Cutters, Baron of Cutter's Hollow. You may rise.'

Gared got to his feet, taller than the count even with Thamos standing on his dais. The count gestured to the Butchers. 'A uniform and armour will be provided for you. Please confer with your lieutenants after the audience and prepare your troops for muster and inspection. The Butchers have handled elevating most of the petty officers, but you of course can change their decisions if you feel it necessary.' His tone made that sound like a terrible idea.

'Ay,' Gared nodded, sticking his hand out. 'Thanks.'

Thamos looked at the hand as if Gared had just wiped himself with it, but he shrugged and shook it all the same. 'I know you will do great honour to the ivy throne, General Cutter.'

Gared smiled a wide grin. 'General Cutter. Like the sound of that.'

Thamos grunted. 'And so, General, what is your assessment of the Krasian army?'

'Big, like Leesha says,' Gared said, 'but scattered. They'll get here eventually, but it'll be a while. Got time to get ready for 'em.'

'So you agree with Mistress Leesha that they should have free run of the Hollow?'

Gared shook his head. 'I'd keep an eye on 'em, sure. But I seen 'em fight, corelings and men, and there's no denyin' they got a lot more practice at it than us. They sent men to teach us tricks to killin' demons. Think we'd be fools not to let 'em.'

'Very well,' Thamos said. 'Have your men escort the caravan

468

to Mistress Paper's land. Keep men posted on the border. Train with the *Sharum*, but they are to be under watch at all times, two to one.'

'Three to one, we're smart,' Gared said.

Thamos nodded. 'Do as you think best, General.'

How do I keep getting myself into messes like this? Rojer thought.

But he had no choice but to speak. He'd be corespawned if he was going to start camping in Leesha's backyard when there was a fine room waiting for him at Smitt's.

Rojer cleared his throat loudly, and all eyes turned to him. 'What about my wives? Can they at least stay in town?'

'Your heathen marriage means nothing here,' Tender Hayes cut in. 'Taking more than one wife is an abomination. The Creator will not recognize it.'

Rojer shrugged. 'It may mean nothing to you, Tender, but that doesn't mean a corespawned thing to me. I said my vows.'

'And failing to recognize the union would insult the Krasians beyond measure,' Leesha added.

Hayes looked ready to retort, but Thamos silenced him with a wave. 'You get one wife in Angiers, Mr Inn. Pick one. If you want the other to live in your chambers and warm your bed, the servants won't ask any questions.'

'Chambers?' Rojer asked. 'Servants?'

Thamos nodded. 'I ask that you serve me as your master did my brother, as royal herald of the Hollow.'

Rojer kept his Jongleur's mask in place, though his shock could not have been more complete if Thamos had turned a somersault and broken into song. He remembered what it was like, back when Arrick had been royal herald of Duke Rhinebeck. Gold and wine flowed in equal measure, and he and Rojer wore the finest silks and suede. Lords and ladies alike had bowed to Arrick as an equal, and his voice carried the power of the throne behind it as he ranged far and wide. They had rich apartments in the duke's own manse, and access to his exclusive brothel. Arrick had spent almost every night there, and left young Rojer in the ladies' care when he was away, or drunk, or with a woman.

In other words, almost every night.

But all of that had ended in an instant, when Rhinebeck had stumbled drunk into the bed of his favourite whore, where Rojer was fast asleep. In his inebriated state, the man hadn't known the difference, yanking down Rojer's bedclothes and casually overpowering his struggles.

'Like to play the unwilling, eh, lass?' the duke had slurred, his breath reeking of alcohol. He chuckled. 'It will do you no good. Best bend and take it. Be over quick.'

It was only when Rojer cried out and elbowed him in his fat stomach, leaping from the bed, that the duke had roused and lit the lamp. He found Rojer quivering across the room, holding a small knife as he yanked his bedclothes back up.

The duke had roared, and Arrick had returned from the hamlets to find his royal commission torn to shreds. He was given barely an hour to remove his possessions and himself from the duke's manse. The duke had never spoken publicly of the reasons for his expulsion, and there had been a few patrons to take him in at first, but Arrick began drinking more and more, alienating one after another until he and Rojer seldom knew during the day where they would stay that night. They owed money to every bartender and innkeep in the city.

Rojer relived all that in an instant, and looked at Thamos, wondering if he was as fickle as his brother. Not that it mattered. Arrick, for his part, had been the duke's man, happy to tell people of new taxes or privations, secure in his own position. Rojer had no such desire to speak for Thamos, a man he knew only for his reputation as a short-tempered womanizer.

He made his best leg, his face calm. 'You honour me, Highness, but I fear I must refuse.'

Arther and Gamon both tensed, but kept silent. Tender Hayes shook his head as if Rojer were a fool.

'Think carefully about this, Mr Inn,' Thamos said. 'With your heathen bride, you would be an ideal ambassador to the court of the desert demon, and your own mistress advises that we need just that. The throne would be most generous. You could even take lands and a title, as General Gared has.'

Rojer shrugged. 'Leesha Paper isn't my mistress, and I want none of what Gared has. I want only to train my apprentices and the Jongleurs who came to the Hollow with you to charm corelings.'

Thamos' eyes became hard. 'I see no reason to allow my Jongleurs to train with someone who will not swear fealty to me.'

Rojer bowed. 'With all due respect, Highness, they're not your Jongleurs. They are mine, bought and paid for legally from Guildmaster Cholls. I have the writs. If you deny me those men, not only will you be wasting power to save lives, but every performer in Angiers will soon be singing that Count Thamos of the Hollow does not honour other men's debts.'

For the first time, Thamos looked truly angry, but Tender Hayes laid a gentle hand on his arm, calming him.

'Very well,' he said. 'Your little entourage can stay at the inn if Speaker Smitt will still have you. But I will not forget this.'

Rojer made another leg. 'Thank you, Your Highness.'

Thamos took a calming breath. 'Now, as for the gifts from my mother . . .'

Thamos gestured to Arther, who produced a small scroll bound in green ribbon, handing it to Leesha. 'Her Grace still controls the affairs of women in Angiers, and has appointed you Royal Gatherer of Hollow County.'

Leesha fought to keep her face calm. The Duchess Mum had her in check and she knew it, for she could not sidestep as Rojer had. Legally, a Royal Gatherer outranked all others. Leesha couldn't refuse without having someone else take the spot and begin to leach away at her own power in the Hollow, but accepting it was little different than Gared accepting a title. She would be legitimizing Thamos' rule and accepting his dominance. Also, her position would effectively make her his personal Gatherer. The idea of having to see the count unclothed sickened her, though that was becoming her natural state these days. She stroked her bodice, imagining the life taking root beneath.

The room was deathly quiet, waiting for her response. Thamos looked as if he expected her to refuse as Rojer had. She wasn't sure if that would please him or not.

'Maybe you'll get a uniform to go with that fancy title,' Gared said smugly, and she wanted to throw a dash of pepper in his face.

At last she curtsied, a slight tug at her skirts and a shallow dip. 'I'm honoured to consider the offer, Highness. You'll have my answer within the week.'

Thamos pursed his lips, then shrugged. 'We look forward to your response. Please have it by Seventhday, in case I need to send to Angiers for another to take the position instead.'

Leesha nodded her assent, and Thamos turned to Wonda. 'As for you, Miss Cutter, I have no lands or titles to offer you, no rank or station, but my mother has taken an especial liking to you, and has sent you a gift.' A servant wheeled in a clothing rack holding dozens of doublets, each emblazoned with Duchess Araine's seal, a wooden crown set over an embroidery hoop.

'Women cannot hold rank in the military, but the bow-women of the Hollow are legendary, and Mother wishes to be your patroness.'

The servant selected one of the doublets and approached Wonda. 'May I?'

Wonda nodded numbly. The man removed her warded cloak, and she bent as he lifted the thick doublet over her head. Wonda stroked it in wonder. She bowed. 'Ent ever had clothes so fine. Please thank Her Grace.'

Thamos smiled. 'The doublets are a trifle. You may give them to other women you deem worthy, but Mother was adamant that the first go to you. The crown will also give purse for a team of bowyers, fletchers, and their materials.' He gestured again, and the guards opened a wall flap, allowing in a middle-aged man, thin, with wiry muscles and a doublet emblazoned with the hammer and chisel of the Artisans' Guild. He was followed by three young men who carried bundles of oiled cloth they carefully laid on the floor. They unrolled them to reveal fine wooden armour, beautifully warded and shining with enamel just like that worn by the Wooden Soldiers. Wonda gasped.

'A proper fitting can be arranged later, but indulge us and try the breastplate, at least,' Thamos said.

Wonda nodded, and the artisan took the piece and began strapping it on. Leesha had half expected it to give her a woman's shape, implying breasts where there were none to speak of, but the duchess was cannier than that, and the breastplate fit perfectly. She looked magnificent.

'It's so light,' Wonda marvelled.

The artisan nodded, smiling. 'We had first thought to make you a proper metal mesh, but archers must be quick and agile. Wooden armour will protect you as well as the finest Milnese steel at a fraction the weight.'

Leesha sighed. It was another ploy by the Duchess Mum to leach at her power. Wonda had made her loyalties clear at their tea, and Araine had not been pleased by it. Leesha wanted to tell Wonda to send the armour back with her regrets. The girl would do it in an instant if Leesha told her to, but looking at her face, beaming with happiness as it so seldom did since the demons took her father and left her scarred, Leesha did not have the heart.

Rojer had begun to relax while everyone cooed over Wonda's new breastplate, but Thamos met his eyes again and he felt his muscles clench right back up.

'Now,' Thamos said, rubbing his hands together. 'I suppose we should see to our guests.' Arther signalled the door guards, who admitted Amanvah, Enkido, Kaval, and Coliv.

'Princess Amanvah of Krasia,' Arther called loudly, his voice easily filling the great hall, 'His Royal Highness Count Thamos, Prince of Angiers, Marshal of the Wooden Soldiers, and Lord of Hollow County, bids you and your counsellors welcome to his court.'

'There had best be a good reason why I have been kept waiting,' Amanvah said, 'and for the rudeness of your *chi'Sharum* when we came to your court in peace and goodwill.' She flicked a derisive finger at Captain Gamon. 'In Krasia, we have men whipped for showing such poor manners to their betters.'

Rojer sighed. This was not going to go well.

Thamos seemed caught off guard by her aggressive posture. 'Apologies, Princess, if you were treated rudely upon your arrival.' He glanced at Gamon. 'I assure you I will school my man in proper etiquette in the future. As to the delay, surely you cannot begrudge me a brief audience alone with my subjects before receiving you.'

'Made Gared a general,' Rojer said, 'and offered me a commission as his royal herald.'

Amanvah glanced at Rojer and laughed, a sharp bark that echoed in the chamber.

'This amuses you?' Thamos asked. His voice was hardening as his patience grew thin.

Amanvah looked back at the count, her eyes narrowing. 'As if my husband would refuse the patronage of the ruler of all that is and give himself instead to a minor princeling. The very notion is ridiculous.'

'Minor princeling?' Thamos asked, his voice a razor.

Amanvah turned to Rojer. 'Count. This is beneath a duke in your culture?'

'His Highness is third in line to the ivy throne,' Rojer supplied.

Amanvah nodded and turned back to Thamos. 'My father met one of your Northland dukes – Edon the Fourth, of Rizon. When Duke Edon knelt with his head pressed to the floor and tearfully begged for his life, he was made to swear utter fealty to Shar'Dama Ka, and lick the dirt from the sandals of all twelve *Damaji*. He would have sucked their cocks, if my father had even hinted that it would have pleased him.'

Thamos' look of impatience turned to one of rage. His face reddened, and Rojer could almost hear the sound of his teeth grinding. His hand gripped his spear so tightly it looked like the shaft would break in half.

'It doesn't matter!' Rojer snapped. 'I have no patron, and want none! I will write what I want to write and sing what I want to sing, and to the Core with anyone who says otherwise!'

Amanvah nodded. 'As it should be.'

Rojer looked curiously at the comment, but shrugged it off. 'And you, wife, will keep a civil tongue behind your veil.'

'Your husband speaks wisdom,' Thamos said. 'Your father will not find Angiers as weak as Rizon. We are ready for him.'

'The Rizonans were weak once,' Amanvah said. 'My father is making them strong. He sees the Hollow is already strong, and offers to make you an independent tribe, autonomous and with your own leaders. In return, he asks only two things.'

'And what are those?' Thamos demanded. 'What is a fair price to buy back what we already have?'

'First,' Amanvah said, 'that you accept that he is Shar'Dama Ka, and follow him when the First War begins.'

'First War?' Thamos asked.

Tender Hayes leaned in to him. 'The Final Battle, Your Highness. When the Deliverer unites mankind and leads us to drive the demons back to the Core.'

Amanvah nodded. 'It is foretold in your Canon much as in the Evejah, is it not, Tender?'

Tender Hayes nodded. 'Indeed. But we have seen nothing to hint that your father is the one foretold. The Deliverer may already be among us, or come tomorrow, or a thousand years from now. Nothing in the Canon tells us that he will bring rape, murder, and heathen religion with him.'

'All wars bring bloodshed and loss,' Amanvah said. 'It is the price of unity, and a fair one. But my father is offering you peace, and you would be wise to take it.'

Thamos scowled. 'And what is the second price of this generous peace?'

Amanvah smiled. 'That Mistress Paper agree to be his bride, of course.'

There was a rustling from off to the side, and the Painted Man stepped out from behind the heavy tarp that served as a wall. 'That ent gonna happen.'

Everyone stood shocked. It had only been a few months since Leesha had seen him last, but as Darsy said, Arlen had changed greatly in that time. Gone were his Tender's robes – he was clad now in simple dungarees and a faded white shirt, unlaced at the front to show part of the great ward tattooed there. His warded feet were bare as he padded on the cold floor.

But rather than humanizing him as she might have expected, the change only made Arlen stand out more, the hundreds of intricate wards on his neck and shaved head marking him in ways the Tender's robes and hood had kept hidden.

A step behind him stood the one Darsy had spoken of. Renna Tanner. His promised. Leesha scanned her critically, but the young woman's looks were so outlandish she was nearly impossible to judge. She was perhaps in her early twenties, her hair roughly hewn on top with a long, thick braid hanging down her back. She was barely clad, wearing only a tight vest and a rough homespun skirt slit almost to the waist on either side. At her belt was a heavy knife, a leather pouch, and a long beaded necklace. Like Arlen, she was covered from head to toe in wards, though they had the faded look of blackstem about them rather than true tattoos.

Corespawn him, Leesha thought. *This after making me swear an oath not to do the same.*

'What makes you think you have a right to tell me who I will or will not marry?' she demanded as Arlen approached her.

'Know your prospective bridegroom a lot better than you,' Arlen said. 'You were gone much longer, I was coming to save you.'

Leesha felt another flare of anger and didn't bother to hide it. 'I didn't need saving.'

'This time,' Arlen said. 'Don't be fooled by the silk pillows and fancy manners. Krasians come to you with smiles, but there are fangs beneath. Ahmann Jardir most of all.'

'Who are you, to speak so familiarly of my holy father?' Amanvah demanded.

Arlen turned to the *dama'ting*, dipping a shallow bow and switching smoothly to Krasian so flawless he sounded like a native. 'He is my *ajin'pal*. I am Arlen asu Jeph am'Bales am'Brook, known to your people as . . .'

'Par'chin!' Kaval growled. He turned to Coliv and made a quick gesture across his throat.

The Watcher reacted instantly, reaching into his black robes and flinging out an arm, sending a spray of sharpened metal triangles flying at Arlen. Leesha feared he would be killed, but Arlen didn't even flinch or step aside. His arm was a blur as he batted the spinning blades away as easily as leaves borne on a gentle breeze. They clattered to the ground harmlessly, but the drillmaster and Watcher were already moving to attack him from opposite flanks. Both had produced hidden weapons – Coliv a sickle with a long, weighted chain attached, and Kaval two short staves.

'I taught you to fight, Par'chin,' Kaval said. 'Do you honestly think yourself the match of true *Sharum*?'

Arlen smiled as he set his feet in a fighting stance. 'I've come a long way since the last time you and Coliv tried to murder me, Drillmaster. And you had more men then.'

Murder? Leesha thought, but before the full weight of it sank in, Coliv hurled the weighted end of his chain at Arlen from behind. It wrapped around one of Arlen's wrists, but Arlen grabbed it and yanked hard, pulling Coliv off balance. Kaval attempted to use the distraction to launch his own attack, spinning the staves in a blur of motion, but Arlen had grabbed a length of chain in his free hand, pulling it taut to block the first two blows. The third he caught fast in a twist of chain and heel-kicked the drillmaster onto his back.

Leesha heard ribs crack with the blow, but the drillmaster rolled to his feet instantly, tossing the remaining staff to his left hand as he pulled a knife with his right.

'Stop this madness!' Leesha shouted, but no one was listening. Thamos' guards looked ready to intervene, but the count gave no command, watching the battle with great interest. Gared and Wonda, too, looked on in dumbfounded amazement.

Coliv had managed to keep his feet, detaching the sickle from its chain and using a short punch-dagger in his free hand. His attacks were quick and precise, full of feints and reversals, but Arlen blocked them casually, toying with him as Kaval moved back into the fight, knife leading for Arlen's back.

Renna rushed to stop him, but she passed too close to

Amanvah, and Enkido moved to intercept her. He grabbed at her but she was too quick, slipping out of reach then coming back in fast with a roundhouse kick that connected solidly with his solar plexus.

The eunuch made no sound and never lost control, rolling with the blow and spinning to place himself back-to-back with her. He caught her trailing braid and pulled it hard over his shoulder.

Leesha thought the fight would end there, but the young woman surprised her, springing with the pull to somersault right over the eunuch, placing them face-to-face again as she punched him in the gut.

This time Enkido gave a slight grunt, but he did not release his grip on her braid, yanking her head into his fist, sending a spray of blood from her mouth. Before she could recover, he stabbed stiffened fingers into a nerve cluster that collapsed her leg. He caught her wrists and twisted hard, forcing her down to one knee.

Both Leesha and Enkido thought it done, but Renna Tanner was full of surprises. She let out a feral growl, arresting her downward momentum. Leesha would have sworn she would not be able to use her leg again for several minutes and Enkido outweighed her more than twice over, but, gritting her teeth, Renna slowly forced herself to her feet against his straining muscles. The eunuch's cold eyes widened in disbelief as their positions reversed and he was the one forced back, his spine bending like a bow and his legs quivering with strain.

She has powers in daylight, Leesha realized. *Like Arlen*.

Suddenly Renna twisted her arms, easily breaking Enkido's grip on her wrists. She caught one of his, so thick her hand could not close even halfway, and yanked the man towards her, grabbing his belt. The eunuch landed a few more flailing blows as she lifted him clear over her head, but the girl ignored them, hurling him across the room to smash through one of the wood-panelled walls. Dazed, he struggled to rise from the wreckage.

The battle between Arlen and the *Sharum* continued to rage. Kaval and Coliv attacked as fiercely as Leesha had ever seen, but Arlen dodged and blocked easily, his expression one of calm focus. Occasionally, he returned a blow, simply to show he could do so with impunity. He took the knife from Kaval, slapping the drillmaster on the side of his head with the flat of the blade, knocking him into Coliv. When the Watcher next came at him, there was a brief tussle that ended with Coliv's own punch-dagger stuck in his buttock as Arlen danced out of reach.

Leesha didn't pretend to understand how warriors thought, but she knew enough of Krasian culture to understand that Arlen was intentionally humiliating the men. To charge into battle against a more powerful foe and be killed with honour was the dream of every warrior. But to be defeated and survive was the stuff of nightmares. She could feel the shame and helpless rage radiating off them, and felt almost pity.

Almost.

But they had tried to murder Arlen. She had it from his lips now, and despite her other doubts, this she knew to be true.

The Painted Man was born on the Krasian desert, four years ago, Arlen had told her, when she asked his age on the road last year.

And the man beneath the wards? Leesha had asked. *How old was he when he died?*

He was killed, Arlen said, though he had never said by whom.

Leesha watched as Arlen fought the two *Sharum,* and knew she was looking at two of the killers. Two of the men who had kicked him onto the path that led to the madness of warding his own flesh. Had Ahmann been one as well? Probably, if Abban's warning had been true.

If you know the son of Jeph, if you can get word to him, tell him to run to the end of the world and beyond, because that is how far Jardir will go to kill him. There can only be one Deliverer.

Whatever he had done to her, Arlen was a good man. A good

man these men had tried to murder, and very nearly succeeded. A shameful part of her wanted to see them hurt, and to spare the anaesthetic when she splinted their broken bones.

The two *Sharum* were positioning for another pass when a piercing ululation filled the air. They froze as Amanvah shouted, 'Stop this at once!' in Krasian.

Kaval and Coliv stayed their next attacks, but they did not stand down. The drillmaster spared a glance to the *dama'ting*, keeping one eye on Arlen. 'Holy Daughter, there is much about this one you do not know. He is a blood traitor, laying false claim to the title of Shar'Dama Ka. Honour demands his death.'

Coliv nodded. 'The drillmaster speaks true, Holy Daughter.'

Arlen smiled. 'Tell me, *Sharum*, if Everam exists, how will He punish your lies?'

Amanvah turned to regard him. 'So you do not claim to be the Deliverer?'

'The Deliverer is all of us,' Arlen said. 'Everyone who stands tall in the night instead of hiding behind their wards . . . or underground.' He looked at her pointedly.

'My people no longer do that, Par'chin,' Amanvah said.

'Nor do mine,' Arlen said. 'All of us work to deliver humanity from the *alagai*.'

'Holy Daughter, do not listen to this lying *chin*,' Kaval said. 'Justice and your father's safety demand that we kill him now.'

'As if you could,' Arlen growled. 'We have a blood debt, true, but it is you who owe. I could have collected today, but I kill only *alagai*.'

'Why is this man such a threat?' Amanvah asked Kaval. 'From his own lips, he makes no claim on my father's title.'

'He diminishes it with his words,' Kaval said. 'Leaching your father's honour with his heathen talk while he bides his cowardly time, waiting for the moment to strike.'

Amanvah's face was unreadable. 'It is you who attacked first, Drillmaster. My father used to speak often of the Par'chin, and never as anything except a man of honour.'

'His honour was lost when he betrayed your father in the Maze,' Kaval said.

Arlen stepped forward, his eyes seething. 'Shall we speak of the Maze, Kaval? Shall I tell all gathered what happened that night, and let *them* judge who lost their honour?'

The drillmaster did not answer, exchanging a look with Coliv. Amanvah stared at him. 'Well, Drillmaster? What have you to say?'

Kaval cleared his throat. 'It is not a matter we may speak of. We have sworn an oath of silence to the Shar'Dama Ka. You must trust my judgement in this.'

'*Must?*' Amanvah asked, her voice a quiet lash. '*Dal'Sharum*, do you presume to tell a Bride of Everam what she must or must not do?' The men stiffened, but still they held their aggressive posture, ready to spring at a moment's notice.

'Please, Par'chin,' Amanvah said. 'Enlighten us about the night of which you speak.'

Arlen shook his head. 'You want to know? Ask the Spears of the Deliverer. Ask your father. And if they won't tell you, perhaps you ought to wonder why.'

Amanvah squinted at him, then turned to Kaval. 'Stand down and heel me. You will pursue this matter no further without my blessing, and I do not give it now.' When the men still hesitated, she added, 'I will not ask again.'

There was a finality in her tone that shook even the warriors, and they complied at last, weapons disappearing as they glided to stand at the young *dama'ting*'s back.

'It appears your new neighbours will keep you entertained, Miss Paper,' Thamos said, and Leesha couldn't help but feel that perhaps his smug tone was justified.

Arlen came over to stand next to Leesha, his voice dropping to a murmur. 'Glad to see you back safe.'

'And you,' Leesha said.

'Ought to talk,' Arlen said. 'Tonight after dusk. Just the four of us at your cottage.'

'Four?' Leesha asked before she could stop herself. Clandestine meetings with Arlen were nothing new, but it had always been three. Herself, Arlen, and Rojer.

It was a pointless question, only confirming what she already knew. 'Renna and I are promised. Where I go, she goes.'

She was surprised to find the words, though expected, still cut at her. 'Rojer and Amanvah are married,' Leesha noted. 'Yet you would deny his bride the same right?'

Arlen shrugged. 'It's your house, Leesha. You keep whatever company you like, but you want the whole story, it's just us four.'

Leesha gestured at Renna with her chin. The young woman caught the look, her eyes fierce. 'Didn't you beg me not to paint blackstem wards on anyone?'

Arlen sighed. 'Ent the first time I been wrong about somethin', Leesha Paper. Don't reckon it's the last, either.'

'How far to your palace?' Amanvah asked, as their carriage trundled along the road into Deliverer's Hollow.

'Palace?' Rojer asked.

Amanvah bowed. 'Forgive me, husband, I forget you have no palaces in the North. Your . . . manse?'

'Ah . . .' Rojer said. 'I don't exactly have one of those, either. I live at Smitt's.'

'I do not know this word,' Amanvah said. 'What is *smitz*?'

'Smitt,' Rojer said. 'Is a person. He owns the inn.'

'And you live at this . . . *roadhouse* Waxing and Wane?' Amanvah was incredulous.

'What?' Rojer asked. 'They change the sheets for me once a week and I never have to cook a meal.'

'Unacceptable,' Amanvah said.

'Well it's going to have to be,' Rojer snapped, 'because it's all I've got! I told your father I had no money, and I meant it.

Bad enough you picked a fight with the count, but now you need to piss on how I live?'

Amanvah bowed. 'Apologies, husband. It was not my intent to offend. I meant only that one so touched by Everam should live in a home worthy of his greatness.'

Rojer smiled. It was hard to argue with that.

Much of the town had gathered by the time they reached the inn, but Rojer paid them little mind. He wanted his wives settled as soon as possible so he could meet the Painted Man after dusk and find out just what in the Core was going on.

'Going to need a few extra rooms,' he told Smitt.

Sikvah took his hand, gently pulling him back. 'Please, husband. Such transactions are beneath you. If you will allow me . . .' She stepped ahead of him, beginning to negotiate in much the same manner Shamavah had on the road. Smitt looked shocked at first, then exasperated, then conciliatory. In the end, Sikvah counted out a number of gold coins into his hand, and Smitt turned, calling to one of his sons. Haggling seemed to be something Krasians had in their blood.

'The merchant must eject some of his residents and prepare our rooms,' Sikvah said on her return. 'We are invited to wait here or in our husband's old room.'

'Old?' Rojer asked. 'I loved that room. Best acoustics in the whole ripping inn.'

'It was not fitting, husband,' Sikvah said, and Rojer sighed. This was not an argument he could hope to win.

The front door opened, and a group of Jongleurs entered, easily visible by their instrument cases and bright motley. A young woman was with them, and the sight of her filled him with a horrible guilt. Kendall, his apprentice who had nearly lost her life to his stupidity.

A memory flashed in his mind, Gared carrying Kendall, cut and bloody, from the battlefield. He shook his head to clear it.

'Rojer!' Kendall cried, rushing over to him and wrapping him in a hug. 'They said you were back! We were so worrieAUGH!'

She was pulled away from him, and Rojer saw Sikvah twisting the young woman's wrist with two fingers, immobilizing her as easily as she might an impudent toddler. 'Who are you, to lay hands on my husband?'

Kendall looked at her, and even through her grimace of pain, a look of surprise took her. 'Husband?'

'Sikvah!' Rojer snapped. 'Release her! This is Kendall, one of my apprentices.'

Sikvah let go of Kendall's wrist immediately and the young woman snatched it back, rubbing. Sikvah and Amanvah began circling her like wolves, appraising her from every angle.

'You greenlanders allow your slaves great liberty,' Amanvah noted, 'but she seems fit enough. How many others do you own?'

'Ent his slave,' Kendall snapped. 'Nobody owns me.'

'She's right,' Rojer said. 'She and the other apprentices are all free folk, and Kendall is the most talented of the lot.'

His wives continued to circle the girl as the other Jongleurs came over. Rojer knew them all by reputation if not personally. Their leader was Hary Roller. Once, early in his career, Hary had played while standing upon a great ball. He hadn't done the trick since, but the name *Roller* had forever stuck.

Hary was old now, retired from performance and teaching, but he was respected both as a composer and a cellist. Guildmaster Cholls had promised masters, but it seemed the established ones had little interest in risking themselves in the Hollow. Sly Sixstring was even older, the guitar over his shoulder worn and weathered. Rojer had seen him perform once and was stunned at the nimbleness of Sly's wrinkled fingers, but that was a decade ago at least.

The others were younger, performers Rojer had been competing with for street corners little more than a year ago. Wil Piper had still been an apprentice then. Rojer wondered if he'd been elevated just for agreeing to this assignment.

Hary shook Rojer's hand. 'We're happy to see you returned,

Master Halfgrip. In your absence, I have been following your agreement with the guildmaster and teaching sound signs to your apprentices. They were . . . undisciplined, but I have made some progress . . .'

Undisciplined. Rojer snorted. That was one way to put it. They were a bunch of bumpkins he had sat in a circle and taught to play by ear. There had been none of the formal training of the guild, something Roller was known to be a stickler for.

But those days were coming to a close.

'Forget all that,' Rojer said, reaching into his satchel for the pages of music he had prepared, outlining the *Song of Waning.* He slapped them against the man's chest, and Roller reflexively took them. 'New song I need everyone to learn. Ask your apprentices to make lots of copies.'

Roller looked at the pages, startled. 'A theory . . .?'

'Tested,' Rojer said. 'Worked for my trio. Let's see if it works for others.'

Rojer's room was just as he'd left it, but after so much time in the Palace of Mirrors and the best rooms of every inn from here to the Bounty, he saw it in a new light. It was small and cramped, just a bed to flop on and a sundry trunk.

Always keep your bags packed, Arrick used to say.

Rojer went to the trunk and began rummaging in it, but Sikvah put a hand on his arm. 'Please, husband. Let the servants handle that. Your labour shames us.'

'Don't have servants,' Rojer said.

'Then I will have Smitt's people move your things when the new rooms are prepared.' Sikvah pulled at him until he relented and went to sit on the bed.

He looked at Amanvah. 'What did you mean, "As it should be"?'

486

'Eh?' she asked.

'Back in the count's hall,' Rojer said. 'When I said I had no patron, and needed none.'

Amanvah bowed. 'I have cast the bones since our . . . disagreement, husband. They tell me you must be free of fealty if your power is to remain pure. I apologize for doubting you. Sikvah and I are yours now. Whatever path you take in your battle with the *alagai*, we will follow. This is why my father wed us to you, and we will no longer forsake you. If you command we strip to our coloured silk and sing in the night, we will do this.'

'And if I command you sing *The Battle of Cutter's Hollow?*' Rojer asked.

'We will do as you command, and find ways to make you regret it.' Amanvah winked. 'We are your wives, not slaves.'

Rojer was stunned a moment, then laughed out loud.

'Do you trust this Painted Man?' Amanvah said. 'Do you know what happened between him and my father?'

'Yes, I trust him, but no,' Rojer shook his head, 'I don't know what happened. I will speak with him tonight. Maybe I'll learn something.'

'Will you share what he tells you with us?' Amanvah asked.

Rojer looked at her a long time. 'If he asks me to keep his counsel private, I will.' He frowned, then shrugged. 'Unless I decide I shouldn't.' He smiled at her. 'Gotta be free, don't I?'

19

Spit and Wind

333 AR Summer
11 Dawns Before New Moon

Leesha sat in Bruna's favourite rocker, wrapped in the old woman's shawl as she worked her needlepoint, trying to ignore the blinding pain behind her eye. Darsy had taken care of the cottage in her absence, but the garden showed the woman still had a brown thumb, and she was hopeless at keeping things in their proper place. It would be days before the place was restored to Leesha's satisfaction, everything just so.

Even so, simply being back in her mentor's chair and shawl was an enormous comfort. Many times in recent weeks she had doubted she might ever see home again. Even now, it seemed almost surreal.

But why shouldn't it? She was home, but in countless ways things would never be the same. There was a Royal in the Hollow now, determined to throw out their old ways, and much of Leesha's power in the process. Could Leesha stop him? Should she?

There were Krasians building a tent city in her backyard, on land Bruna had entrusted to her. Would they help bring about the peace Leesha dreamed of, or be a cancer in the centre of the Hollow, as she saw in her nightmares?

Arlen, whom she had thought would always keep the Hollow

safe, had left them to fend for themselves, and come back a changed man. It remained to be seen if this was for better or worse.

And there's a baby in my belly.

Even if the chemics hadn't confirmed it, every day made her more and more certain of the life growing within her. Ahmann Jardir's child. It had to be, for she had lain with no other – but that, too, seemed surreal. Arlen had feared putting a demon child in her, and she told him she did not care. Now the demon of the desert had planted a child in her, and she told herself the same, but was it true? The child, she would love and cherish, but how many lives would be lost when Ahmann came forward to claim it? She could not hide her state forever. Night, the *dama'ting* might already have seen it in their foretellings.

She stroked her belly, feeling a tear begin a slow drift down her nose. *Please be a girl.*

The thought filled her with shame. Would she love a boy any less? Of course not. But Ahmann would not likely bring an army north for a daughter.

Again, she thought of her mother's words. *Find a man and bed him quick.* Elona certainly knew how to do that.

But while her mother was vile, she was often right. Elona saw the world through the lens of her own desires, and understood the desires of others in a way logical Leesha never could. Was what Leesha had planned to do with Gared – bedding him and convincing all that her child was his – any less vile than Elona having her way with the son of her old lover behind her husband's back?

Night, Leesha thought. *I think my plan was worse.*

The worst of it was, she was still considering it. Not with Gared, of course, but surely there were other candidates – no shortage of brave, strong men in the Hollow. Even Yon Gray was increasingly young and handsome, and fifteen years a widower. He had pinched her bottom enough times to let her know he was interested, but it had been harmless at the time – the hopeless fancies of a dirty old man. Now . . .

She shuddered at the thought, remembering his toothless grin. *No, not Yon.* But there were others. How many lives could be saved if her child's heritage was kept secret?

Of course, Ahmann might as soon march north to kill the man who had laid hands on his intended. Night, Kaval would likely do it for him. It was a terrifying thought, but not easily dismissed. Ahmann might truly believe he was doing what was needed to save the world, but he was ruthless in pursuit of that goal, and he had decided Leesha – or at least, what was between her legs – was his gateway to the North. He would murder anyone who tried to touch her.

Just like he tried to murder Arlen. She didn't want to believe it, wanted to heap it with Arlen's dissembling about why he did not want her, but both would-be Deliverers were honest to a fault. If he said it, she believed him. But as with Ahmann's dancing around the subject of the Par'chin, so, too, were Arlen's comments cryptic. It was time to make him come clean.

Night, what will he think when he sees my belly swell?

In the distance she heard music, heralding Rojer's approach. They had agreed to speak privately before Arlen arrived, but Leesha hadn't realized it was so late. She looked to the window and saw it was near twilight, her needlepoint lying forgotten on her lap. The sky was darkening earlier and earlier each day. Solstice was well past, and the light grew shorter as darkness drew strength. She shuddered at the thought.

But as the music drew nearer, it drove away Leesha's fears and worries the same way it did demons. She put a kettle on the fire and left the door open for him, knowing Wonda was patrolling the yard, keeping other visitors safely at bay.

Rojer entered soon after, holding his fiddle and bow in one hand. Leesha's eyes flicked to the base, but the warded chinrest was absent.

'Left it back at the inn,' Rojer said. He pointed with his bow at Bruna's ancient shawl about Leesha's shoulders. 'Couldn't wait to wrap that old rag around you, could you?'

Leesha fingered the old knitted yarn, mended countless times over the years by the woman's skilled fingers. There were greybeards in the Hollow who said she had worn it when they were lads, half a century and more ago. Leesha never washed it, and it still smelled of Bruna, taking her back to a time when this cottage was the safest place in the world. 'You have your talismans, Rojer, and I have mine.'

Rojer threw his motley Cloak of Unsight, warded by Leesha herself, over a chair back, completely disregarding the cloak hooks by the door. He slung his bag of marvels atop it and plopped into the chair, putting his feet on the table, fiddle tucked under his chin. 'Fair and true.'

Leesha gave his chair a kick as she went to fetch the teacups and biscuits, knocking his feet down. 'What did you have to tell your wives to let you come unescorted?'

'Easier than you'd think,' Rojer said. 'Got a pat on the head and some nonsense about dice, then she sent me on my way.'

'Nothing about those dice is easy,' Leesha said, bringing the tea.

'Honest word,' Rojer nodded. 'But their power seems real enough.'

Leesha fought the urge to spit. 'A crutch to educate their guesses a bit, but if they were as powerful as the *dama'ting* would have us think, the Krasians would already have every woman in the North in a veil and every man in a spearwall.'

'Good crutch,' Rojer said, taking a sip of tea. His face screwed up. 'You always skimp on the sugar.' He took a flask out of his pocket and poured a bit of caramel-coloured liquid into the cup. Leesha frowned, but he simply smiled, raising the cup to her before taking a sip. 'Fixed. But we can talk bitter tea and demon dice later. Time is short to discuss the crazy girl.'

Leesha didn't have to ask whom he meant. An image of

Renna Tanner flashed in her mind, the young woman lifting Enkido over her head. Leesha had got a good look at her then. Under all the blackstem wards and snarls was a pretty round face, and a body that put even Leesha's to shame – rippling with muscle while lacking nothing of a woman's curve.

Is that what he wanted? she wondered. *A woman who can strangle a demon with her bare hands?*

If so, it wasn't Renna's fault. It wasn't fair to blame her. 'We don't know that she's any more crazy than he is, Rojer.'

Rojer laughed. 'Hate to be the Messenger, Leesha, but Arlen is crazy as demonshit. I owe him my life and I won't forget that, but the man is always turning left when sane folk go right.'

'That's why he's powerful,' Leesha said. 'And the same could be said for you.'

Rojer shrugged. 'Never met a sane Jongleur, either.' He drank again. 'They say he's promised her. Think he means it?'

'That isn't any of our business, Rojer,' Leesha said.

'Demonshit,' Rojer said. 'It's the whole corespawned world's business – yours most of all.'

'How is that?' Leesha demanded. 'We were stuck together for all of five minutes, a year ago, and haven't spoken of it since.'

'Quick shooter, eh?' Rojer asked. 'You never hear that in the sagas.'

'We were . . . interrupted,' Leesha said, remembering the wood demon that had pulled them from their embrace. She had never hated a coreling as much as she had in that moment. 'It still doesn't make where he's put it since any of my business.'

'Did you know they're staying at Smitt's?' Rojer asked. 'Right down the corespawned hall. I'll have to hear it every night. Smitt's daughter Melly says they make the walls shake after they've been out hunting demons.'

Leesha's teacup began to shake, she gripped it so hard. Rojer pointed to it with the bow of his fiddle. 'That right there? That's why it's your business.'

'Not far now,' Arlen said. They had gone perhaps a mile from the edge of the greatward of Cutter's Hollow to reach the Herb Gatherer's cottage. There was a warded road, but Arlen led them on a more direct path through the trees. At one point, Renna noticed a familiar spot.

'Awfully close to that old hideout of yours.'

'Leesha needed mindin',' Arlen said. 'Smart girl, but it gets her in trouble sometimes.'

The memory of Leesha Paper in the count's throne room flashed into Renna's mind as it had been doing for hours. The woman had been bad enough imagined – brave and smart and rich, practically worshipped by the Hollowers – but of course Arlen had never mentioned she was also pretty as a sunrise, with that soft, helpless look men loved. 'You stayed close so the Painted Man could swoop in and save her like the hero in an ale story?'

Arlen stopped walking and sighed. Then he turned and met her eyes. 'Make you a deal, Ren. You tell me every last detail of how you shined on Cobie Fisher, and I'll tell you every bit of how I shined on Leesha Paper.'

Renna felt her anger rise, and saw the ambient magic rush to her, feeding on the emotion and amplifying it. Strong emotions were visible in the aura of magic that surrounded people at night. Her rage was a crackling glow that must have been unmistakable to Arlen, but he only looked at her calmly. He didn't back down, but neither did he offer further offence, forcing her to simmer.

He was right. She had done things – felt things – with Cobie Fisher that had nothing to do with Arlen, and he didn't need to know. Wasn't his business.

But how then could she not grant him the same? He'd left

Leesha behind in the Hollow for months to be with Renna, and given her his word in promise. What did it matter what he had felt, or what they'd done?

But it did. 'Cobie Fisher's dead,' she said. 'Leesha Paper's inviting us to tea.'

Arlen sighed. 'What do you want me to do about that, Ren?'

She breathed deeply, in the rhythm Arlen had taught her, embracing the anger as she did pain. Awash in the feeling, she stepped back suddenly and let it go. Her magic cooled.

'Wern't fair of me,' she said at last. 'This ent easy.'

Arlen laughed. 'Honest word. Ent no treat for me, either, Ren. Just . . . don't hit anybody doesn't hit you first, all right?'

Renna chuckled. 'Ay, I can give you that. No promises about anything else.'

'Good enough,' Arlen said as they joined another road, this one made up of large squares of fresh-poured crete. Powerful wards had been inscribed in the stone, forbidding access to any corespawn. They glowed softly, drawing the ambient magic venting from the Core.

The wards became more intricate as they drew closer to their destination. The road ended at the entrance to a massive garden, larger than Harl's entire field, but it wasn't made up of any edible crops Renna knew. Weeds and herbs only. A Gatherer's garden.

A dirt path led through the garden, with plants growing in patches throughout the area as it curved this way and that. Painted wardstones circled each patch, warming some plants and cooling others, drawing moisture from the air to nourish roots.

'Fancy,' Renna grunted, knowing it was far more than that. There were wardnets too complex for her to understand. Even as she watched the magic ebb and flow, she could only guess at their effects. She hadn't even been formally introduced to Leesha Paper, yet already Renna didn't like her. She was like a sorceress from a Jongleur's tale.

They came out of the garden into a wide yard with a small cottage at its centre. A plain and unassuming place amid all the splendour and beauty. For some reason, this made Renna dislike Leesha Paper all the more.

She shivered though the night was warm, drawing her cloak closer, hating that it had been a gift from *her*.

There was a dizzying blur as a woman stepped out of the shadows, drawing back her own Cloak of Unsight. She held a nocked bow pointed down, and looked different in wardsight, awash with glowing magic, but Renna recognized her. Wonda Cutter, another of Arlen's apprentices, looking impressive in her new wooden armour.

The young woman loomed over them, taller than any woman had a right to be and twice as wide. She smiled, and the magic around her turned warm and inviting as she bowed deeply. 'Deliverer.'

'Told you more'n once I ent the Deliverer, Wonda,' Arlen said, but the scorn that usually came to his tone at the subject was absent. He liked this young woman. 'Call me Arlen.'

Wonda shook her head, eyes down. 'Don't think I can do that, sir.'

'Mr Bales?' Arlen suggested.

Wonda brightened. 'Ay, reckon that would be all right.' She turned to Renna, bowing again. 'Welcome to the cottage, Miss Tanner. Honoured to meet you. Saw what you did to Enkido in the throne room, and I seen him fight before. Hope to be half as good as you one day.'

There's a price, Renna thought, but she nodded, looking to Arlen. 'Had a good teacher.'

Wonda smiled, looking at Arlen with near worship in her eyes. 'Ay.' She glanced back at the cottage. 'Mistress Leesha's in there with Rojer. You don't mind waitin' a moment, I'll announce you.'

'Like her,' Renna said as the young woman moved off.

Arlen nodded. 'I had a hundred Wonda Cutters at my back, I'd storm the Core itself.'

Wonda appeared at the door an hour after dark. 'They're here, Mistress Leesha.'

'Thank you, Wonda,' Leesha said. 'Be a dear and send them in, then walk the yard and make sure we're left be.'

Wonda nodded. 'Ay, mistress.' A moment later Arlen appeared, looking more relaxed than she had ever seen him. Renna Tanner came next, her eyes roaming with predatory suspicion. She caught Leesha's eyes, and Leesha realized she was staring impolitely.

Elona's voice rang in her head. *Say something, idiot girl.*

Leesha shook herself and went over to her. 'Welcome to my cottage. Renna, I believe?' Her eyes flicked to Arlen. 'We were never formally introduced. I'm Leesha Paper.' She reached to take the young woman's cloak, only to gasp at the sight. It was the Cloak of Unsight she had made for Arlen.

He gave it to her? There was a flare of anger as she remembered how hard she had worked on that cloak, putting in more effort than on her own and Rojer's combined. She had wanted so badly to impress him, to show the power of her warding, but Arlen had barely glanced at it as she put it on his shoulders, and hadn't worn it since.

Was that your promise gift? she wondered bitterly. Suddenly their relationship seemed like it very much *was* her business.

'Know who you are,' Renna said.

Something about the look she gave made Leesha want to grab Bruna's stick and thump her, but she kept her smile pleasant. 'Tea?'

'Please,' Arlen said, putting an arm around Renna and steering the women apart.

Rojer rolled from his chair into a handspring, somersaulting into a low leg. 'Rojer Halfgrip, at your service.'

Renna laughed and clapped her hands, suddenly looking like an innocent girl. 'Renna Tanner,' she said as he kissed her hand. 'Arlen told me all about you.'

'Don't believe a word of it,' Rojer advised with a wink.

Renna smiled at him, and Leesha wanted to scream, but she kept a sunny smile on her face.

'Come help with the tea, Rojer,' she said. He complied, and as they stood at the counter amid a clatter of cups and saucers, she whispered, 'Night, whose side are you on?'

'Oh, there are sides now?' Rojer asked sweetly. 'I thought it was none of our business.' Leesha kicked at him, but he danced away, not spilling a drop of the tea he carried to Renna and Arlen in the sitting room. Leesha brought their cups from the kitchen table and saw Arlen and Renna together on her couch and Rojer on the closest seat. She wondered if the men were purposely trying to keep her and Renna as far as possible from each other.

'Soooo,' Rojer said with an exaggerated stretch. 'Ah. How have you been?'

'Busy,' Arlen said. 'Hollow's expanding faster every day, swallowing hamlets whole even as folk flock here from all the Free Cities. Work's started on the pattern of greatwards we plotted over the winter, and already some of them are activating.'

Arlen's eyes twinkled at her. 'It's working, Leesha. Greatwards keep growing, some day fighting demons will be irrelevant. Nothing to fight, they're all trapped in the Core. This rate, "Count" Thamos will be calling himself duke before long, and Rhinebeck won't be able to say much about it.'

'But you will,' Rojer said.

'Ent my business,' Arlen said. 'Don't care who sits what throne, so long as the greatwards are built and folk prepared for what's comin'.'

'And what is that?' Leesha asked.

'War,' Arlen said. 'The demons will move to stop us, now, before the greatward system can reach critical mass.'

'Demonshit.' Rojer glanced to Leesha, then back to Arlen. 'Sick of hearing you two say things ent your business even when you're standing right in the thick of them. Those people are flocking here from the Free Cities, building greatwards and arming themselves, because of you, Arlen Bales, the ripping Painted Man, not Count Thamos.'

Arlen shrugged. 'Maybe. Or maybe they're just tired of hiding and want to fight for the chance to be free. I'm a banner to flock to, ay, but that don't give me a claim to the throne even if I wanted it – and I don't. Why should I oppose Thamos? Bit taken with himself, but he's doing what a good Royal should do – building roads and towns, helping folk ward their homes and plant crops, appointing magistrates and ministers to keep peace, collect trash, lend money, and keep everyone fed and working to common good. His taxes are steep but fair, he's open to new citizens so long as they swear to Angiers, and he doesn't have enough men to really bully anyone.'

'I heard he had a thousand Wooden Soldiers,' Rojer said.

Arlen shook his head. 'A thousand who can put on a wooden helm and march holding a spear, ay, but he's got barely two hundred Wooden Soldiers. The rest can put an arrow near a target more oft than not, but they're mostly Warders, engineers, and construction crew.'

'And now Gared and the Cutters, thanks to you,' Leesha said.

Again Arlen shrugged. 'The count can make better use of them in the day. In return, I get them at night, along with the Wooden Soldiers. Thamos himself even comes out at night, and puts his spear where I tell him.'

'For now,' Leesha said.

'Thamos knows I can kick his keep gate down any time I like,' Arlen said. 'So long as I'm around, he'll keep in line.'

'And when you're not around?' Leesha asked.

Arlen smiled. 'You'll have to keep him in line yourself, and not pull a vanishing act like you did at court.'

Leesha fumed silently at his smirk. Her 'disappearing act' had been a pretence to meet with Duchess Araine, who was the real power in Angiers – her sons little more than puppets. Arlen's own meeting with the duke and his brothers had been a sham. But of course, she could say nothing of the sort without breaking Araine's trust.

I have to let him think me a fool instead. The thought angered her. 'What word from Duke Euchor?' she asked to change the subject.

'Rhinebeck will never pay the price Euchor demands for aid,' Arlen said. 'Not unless the Krasians are massed right outside his walls, and maybe not even then. There will be no alliance.'

The finality of the statement fell on the room like a weight. It meant Angiers would have to face Ahmann alone, which meant in turn that there would be no aid to Lakton before the Krasians turned their eye that way. How long did the Laktonians have now? A year? Three at the most?

'What did he want?' Rojer asked.

'Rhinebeck still has no son,' Arlen said. 'Euchor wants him to divorce Duchess Melny and marry one of his own daughters, all of whom have borne sons of their own.'

'Hypatia, Aelia, and Lorain,' Rojer said. 'Famous throughout the Free Cities for being indistinguishable from stone demons. He might as well have asked Rhinebeck to drop his pants and lie over the barrel.'

Arlen nodded. 'If the Krasians take Angiers, the metal throne will block their path at Riverbridge.'

'Euchor is a fool,' Leesha said.

'More than you know,' Arlen said. 'Euchor has the secrets of fire, Leesha, and schematics to turn them into horror like you never dreamed.' He produced an ancient, leather-bound book and tossed it to her. The cover read: *Weapones of the Olde Wyrld.*

'Rest up before you read it,' Arlen advised. 'Be a week before you can sleep again.'

Leesha took the book, looking into Arlen's eyes as she did. They seemed so calm, so at peace. The look of a man who had stopped worrying over tomorrow to focus fully on today.

'You've changed so much. The plain clothes, going back to your proper name . . .' *Your eyes*, she wanted to say, but wisely held her tongue.

'Got back to my roots,' Arlen said, nodding towards Renna. 'Ent gonna forget them again.'

'Get another kicking, you do,' Renna said, laying a hand on his leg.

Arlen put his hand atop hers, squeezing gently. Such a tiny gesture, but it spoke volumes. Leesha suppressed a shiver as Arlen looked back at her. 'Know what I am now, Leesh. *Who* I am. No more doubts and worries.'

'How?' Leesha asked.

Arlen's tone grew serious. 'Last new moon, a demon tried to kill me.'

Rojer chuckled. 'How's that different from any other night?'

'This wasn't just some worker drone, Rojer,' Arlen said, his voice taking on a hint of the Painted Man's rasp. The smile fled Rojer's face.

'A smart demon,' Leesha said. 'Darsy told me. Gets in your head.'

Arlen tapped his temple. 'And I got in its. Not for long, but enough to know what we're up against, and to see magic the way they do. And now that I seen, I can't unsee.'

He lifted his hand, drawing tiny wards in the air. One by one, the lamps in the room winked out. Leesha reached into her apron for her warded spectacles, but before she could put them on, he traced a light ward in the air above them and it flared, filling the room with more light than when the morning sun struck the windows full-on.

'Creator,' Rojer whispered.

'That's just the tip.' Arlen got to his feet, drawing a knife from his belt. 'Almost impossible to hurt me now, and if something does . . .' He slashed at his hand, drawing a bright line of blood.

'Arlen!' Leesha cried, rushing to her feet to inspect the cut.

It was down to the bone – she caught a flash of white before blood welled, gushing to the floor. Even with stitching, it might never heal the same. She glanced at Renna, but the girl seemed unconcerned.

'. . . I can heal it in an instant,' Arlen finished. His hand collapsed into smoke, falling through Leesha's fingers, and then re-formed, perfectly whole and unblemished save for the intricate pattern of tattoos that danced along its surface. Even the blood on the floor was gone.

Leesha put her warded spectacles on to examine more closely. In wardsight, Arlen glowed brighter than she had ever seen, and – she noted with little surprise – Renna, too, shone with power.

'I can heal others as well,' Arlen said, 'and kill demons without touching them. Every day I discover new powers. The potential is limitless.'

'Darsy told me about you emptying the hospit,' Leesha said, 'but bright as you are, you're still not carrying enough for that kind of magic. Where did you get the power? *Hora*? Ichor?'

Arlen shook his head. 'Crutches. You were right about why the greatwards make me weak, Leesha. They pull at my magic, sucking it out to strengthen their field.' He smiled. 'But now I can reverse the pull.'

He took a deep breath, and Leesha gasped as the ambient magic drifting along the floor rushed to him. The wards painted and carved all around the cottage, previously glowing with power, dimmed as Arlen grew so bright it became difficult to look at him.

'You learned all this from the mind demon?' Leesha asked.

Arlen nodded. 'But don't underestimate them just because I got lucky and killed one. I'm just scratching the surface of powers that are as natural to them as breathing. There'll be more of them, and they won't underestimate me again.'

'It was manlike, but shorter?' Leesha asked. 'With a bulbous head and vestigial horns?'

Arlen's eyes narrowed. 'Never told anyone that.' He glanced to Renna.

'Don't you look at me like that, Arlen Bales,' she said. 'Ent breathed a word 'bout what happened.'

'One of them attacked us in Everam's Bounty,' Leesha said.

Arlen glanced at Rojer. 'Not *that* us,' the Jongleur said. 'I was in the bath. Missed the whole thing.'

Arlen seemed taken aback. 'What happened?'

Leesha bit back a wave of revulsion at the memory. 'It came at Waning, same as yours. It . . . took control of me.'

Renna looked at her, empathy in her eyes for the first time. 'Forced you to do things?'

Leesha nodded. 'It was there to kill Ahmann or, better, to discredit him. Used me and his wife Inevera against him like puppets.'

'How'd you break the spell?' Arlen asked.

'Ahmann touched us, and the wards on his crown flared,' Leesha said. 'The demon's control was broken instantly. Ahmann killed it, though it might have had him if we hadn't distracted it first.'

Arlen nodded, glancing to Renna. 'Man ent nothin' without a good woman beside him.' Renna smiled at him, and Leesha had to swallow the bile that threatened to rise in her throat.

'Was it alone?' Renna asked.

Leesha shook her head, and saw in the woman's eyes that she already knew what was coming next. 'It had a . . . bodyguard. A shape changer.'

'Mimic demon,' Arlen said. 'They can turn into anything they can see or imagine. Under normal circumstances, they can't imagine much, but with a mind demon controlling them . . .'

'Ahmann said it was one of Alagai Ka's princelings,' Leesha said. 'And that there would be more come the next Waning.'

Arlen nodded. 'That bastard might be a coreson in need of putting down, but he ent wrong. New moon's a week and a half away. Done my best to ready the Hollow, but things are going to get ugly enough to make the Battle of Cutter's Hollow look like a game of Tackleball.'

Leesha nodded. 'Here and in the Bounty as well. The mind demons are afraid of Ahmann, just like they are of you. You'd be giving them a real *gift* by killing him.' The words were meant to sting, to remind him of his oath to oppose the corelings in all things, as they once had in a cave they had taken shelter in on the road from Angiers.

She expected him to be shocked, or angry or sad, but Arlen only looked at her patiently. 'Can't manipulate me just because I told you a promise I made as a boy, Leesha. Made a lot of promises in my life, and I'll be my own judge of when and how they're kept.'

'What promise?' Renna asked.

'Talk about it later,' Arlen said, and there was a hint of tightness in his voice. Renna didn't look pleased, but neither did she press the issue.

'Abban and Ahmann both spoke of the Par'chin as a friend,' Leesha said.

Arlen laughed, and if he was surprised she had heard his Krasian name before, he did not show it. 'Abban has no friends, Leesha! Only profitable acquaintances, of which I most certainly was one. And Ahmann Jardir has two faces, one kind and just, and another – the real one – he shows more seldom. The one that will do anything for power.'

'What happened in the Maze?' Leesha asked bluntly. 'What did he do to you? Enough riddles! If you want us to mistrust this man, then tell us why!'

For the first time, the calm left Arlen's eyes. Rojer held out his flask, and Arlen traced a casual ward in the air, sending it flying into his hand like iron filings to a lodestone. He unscrewed the top and took a long pull, sitting hunched with his arms on his thighs, eyes down.

'Ahmann Jardir was my *ajin'pal*,' he began. 'No doubt you've heard the word, but I don't think anyone can understand what it means. He took me into my first true battle with the demons, stood at my side, shed blood with me . . .'

'Like you did for the Hollowers,' Rojer said.

'And for me,' Renna said.

Arlen nodded. 'Ay, but it was different. The Krasians didn't want me fighting. Didn't think me worthy. Jardir stood for me when they would have strung me up. Welcomed me into his palace, learned my language. He was a brother to me, taught me things about the world and myself it would've taken a lifetime to learn on my own.'

'So you were truly friends,' Leesha said, though the words did not dispel the mounting dread she felt at Arlen's tone.

'For my part,' Arlen agreed. 'But looking back I think maybe he was always ready to plant a spear in my back when I ceased to be of use to him, always planning to come north, and pulling his plans from my head.'

He blew out a breath. 'But maybe not. Maybe it was what came next.'

The room was silent, everyone leaning in to hear Arlen's words, even Renna.

Guess he doesn't tell her everything, after all, Leesha thought.

'Wasn't just fighting alongside the Krasians in those days,' Arlen said. 'Kept regular work as a Messenger, and spent years ruin hunting. Blew through more gold than most folk ever see buying up old maps that usually led nowhere, and almost got myself killed more times'n I can count. But then, a few years ago, Abban promised me a map to Anoch Sun.'

'The final resting place of Kaji,' Leesha said.

Arlen nodded. 'Nearly died getting my hands on the map, copied right from under the *dama*'s noses. Spent weeks wandering the desert looking for the place. The Krasians said it was lost to the sands, but I got a stubborn streak.'

'Honest word,' Leesha agreed.

Arlen's eyes glittered. 'But I found it, Leesha! Anoch Sun, the ripping lost city of Kaji, and I found it! It was half buried, but even so, more beautiful than any place you ever saw. Its palaces dwarfed anything the dukes reside in, perfectly preserved beneath the sand. In the greatest of these, I found a stair into the catacombs, and searched.'

Rojer was leaning forward eagerly now. 'What did you find?'

'Kaji,' Arlen said. 'Or one of his descendants. He was embalmed and wrapped in cloth, arms still gripping his spear.'

'The Spear of Kaji,' Leesha said, a cold feeling growing in her gut. *Ahmann's spear.*

Arlen nodded. 'I brought it to Krasia to share its secrets. They all thought me a liar until it first flared to life, killing a demon in the Maze. An hour later, I was leading the charge, all the *Sharum* chanting my name. Two hours after that, Jardir and his men laid a trap to steal it from me, Kaval and Coliv among them. They beat me and took the spear, throwing me into a pit with a live sand demon.'

'Creator,' Renna said, her eyes wide. Her lip curled into a snarl, and she gripped the bone handle of the huge knife sheathed at her waist.

'How did you escape?' Rojer asked.

'Killed the demon and climbed out of the pit,' Arlen said. 'So Jardir cracked me on the head and they dumped me out on the dunes to die.'

Renna growled. 'I'll gut those sons of the . . .'

Arlen laid a hand over hers, and she calmed. 'Kaval and Coliv were just following orders. Ent their fault. They're just drones. Jardir's the mind.'

'He must have seen your looting the sacred city and the tomb of Kaji as a terrible violation,' Leesha said.

Arlen shrugged. 'Should I have left the lost magics to sleep under the sand?'

'Of course not, but you must understand their perspective,' Leesha said.

Arlen looked at her, incredulous. 'What I understand is that Jardir stole the greatest weapon in the world from me, and instead of sharing its secrets, he is using it to murder and enslave his way across Thesa. What I cannot understand is why you continue to defend that son of a camel's piss . . .'

His eyes widened. 'You stuck him.'

'That is *none* of your business!' Leesha had not meant to shout, but anger had been building in her all night, along with a constant brewing nausea and a searing in her head that could brand a cow. She knew the outburst confirmed his words, but that only made her angrier. 'And you should talk!' She whisked a hand at Renna.

Renna said nothing, but she rose from her seat, striding around the tea table to advance on Leesha. Their eyes met, and Leesha knew how Rojer must have felt when Kaval came at him. She fumbled at her apron for something to defend herself with, but Renna caught her wrist and snatched it away.

'Got something you want to say to me, I'm right here,' she growled.

'Ahhh!' Leesha gasped as the young woman twisted.

Arlen was there in an instant, grabbing Renna's own wrist. 'That's enough, Ren!' He pulled at her, but for a moment, she resisted him. Arlen, who was strong as a rock demon, and she resisted him. He looked as surprised as Leesha, and for a moment she wondered if Renna might kill her. The wild young woman leaned in, their noses nearly touching, and Leesha shrank back, worried she might wet herself and lose what little dignity remained to her.

But Renna just spoke, her words low and even. 'He said the words of promise to me, Leesha Paper. Did he say them to you?'

Leesha gaped. The words were almost identical to those Gared Cutter had said to Messenger Marick, right before they came to blows over Leesha. 'N-no,' she stuttered at last.

'Then you mind your own business about us.' Renna let go of Leesha's wrist and stepped back. Arlen let go of her arm, and she turned on her heel, storming out of the cottage.

Leesha rubbed her sore wrist and cast Arlen a withering glance. 'Lovely woman you've found.'

Arlen glared at her, and immediately she regretted the words. She reached out to him, but her hand passed right through as he dissipated into smoke and vanished.

For a moment, she and Rojer just stared at the spot where he'd been. Finally, Rojer shook his head and turned to Leesha with a grin. 'Could've been worse.'

Leesha glared at him. 'Shouldn't you be getting back to your wives?'

Rojer shook his head, coming over and putting his arms around her. 'They can wait a bit.'

Leesha tried to pull away, but he held her tight, and after a moment, she stopped resisting. Still he held her, and she slowly raised her arms to return the embrace.

And then she wept.

Renna strode past the Cutter girl with nary a glance, picking up speed as she entered the garden maze. Wanting to put as much distance as possible between her and that witch's cottage, she broke into a trot, and then a full run. But no matter how fast she went, the pain and anger followed her, and she found them impossible to embrace.

She pulled free her knife. She would hunt, killing a coreling and feasting on its magic-infused flesh. The power would ease her pain – lost in the rush, she would feel nothing but ecstasy.

She remembered the feeling of Arlen grabbing her wrist. He had pulled hard, and she had resisted him. He could still have forced her arm away if he had mustered his full strength, but even that was coming closer to her grasp. Soon, she would be as strong as he was.

A mist rose on the path in front of her. For a moment Renna tensed, thinking it was a coreling to kill. But the sun had long since set, and she had never seen a demon rise at any other time. It was Arlen.

One of his new tricks. He had not lied when he said there were more each day, and his comfort in using them, at least in front of Renna, was growing. He called this one 'skating' – slipping just beneath the surface and riding currents of magic, travelling from one place to another in an instant.

Renna had attempted it, but thus far dematerializing was beyond her. Whether she had not eaten enough coreflesh, or if it had not yet had enough time to change her was unclear. It might be months. Or years.

But I'll get there, she promised herself. *Sure as the sun rises.*

Arlen solidified, catching Renna as she ran into him. 'What in the Core was all that about? Promised to hold your temper.'

Renna shook her head. 'Promised not to hit anyone. Din't.'

Arlen sighed. 'Fair and true if you're playing to the letter, but you're a grown woman, Ren. Can't just bully everyone.'

'Witch needed a bit of bullying, and a reminder that you ent hers,' she glared at Arlen, 'and she ent yours, even if you two used to slap stomachs and never saw fit to mention.'

She began moving again, picking a direction at random and striding so Arlen had to hurry to keep pace. 'Never asked who you've had in the hayloft, Ren. We agreed past was past.'

Renna waved a hand at him. 'Can't blame you. Know I come with my trials, and Miss Prissy Perfect's got everything a man could want. Money, magic, and loved by all. And oh, look at that! She helped kill a mind demon, too! I was you, I'd set me aside, too.'

Arlen grabbed her, turning her roughly to face him. 'Ent setting you aside, Ren. Not now, not ever. Ay, Leesha's got her sunny bits, but she's got her own mess of crazy, too, and whatever she might have done, you stared her down cold.' He laughed. 'Never seen her intimidated like that. Thought she was going to wet herself.'

Renna smirked. 'Was hoping she would.'

'Heard it from her own lips,' Arlen said. 'Ent promised to her, Renna Tanner. Promised to you.'

Renna looked at him, wanting to believe the words, but it all seemed like demonshit. They'd danced this dance before. Arlen would talk up a storm, telling her she was the centre of his world and how he could never want another. He'd go on about how she was his sunrise and sunset.

She knew if she listened long enough, she'd be convinced by his arguments – or get so sick of hearing them she'd agree just to end the barrage.

But in the end, it was all just words.

'Renna Bales,' she said.

'What?' Arlen asked.

'Not Tanner,' Renna said. 'If you're speakin' honest word, you'll get a Tender and keep your promise. Tonight. Elsewise it's just spit and wind.'

20

A Single Witness

333 AR Summer
11 Dawns Before New Moon

Arlen looked at Renna a long time. She felt as naked under that gaze as she had when the coreling prince slipped into her mind. She wondered – not for the first time – if Arlen had learned that trick as well. There was judgement in his eyes.

'Think you're ready for that, Ren?' he asked quietly.

Renna straightened, steeling herself and staring right back at him. 'Ay. Been ready a long sight.'

'Man and wife oughtn't have secrets,' Arlen said.

'Know that,' Renna said.

Arlen put a hand to his face, rubbing his temples with thumb and forefinger. 'Think I'm stupid, Ren? Think I can't see you been eating demon meat? I can smell it on your breath, see it in your blood, taste it in your magic. Very night I begged you not to, you done it. And every chance you got since.'

Renna gritted her teeth, trying to quell a flare of anger and failing. He was judging her? After she had done it to save his life? Magic rushed into her, filling her with strength and multi-plying the rage tenfold. It was all she could do to keep it contained. 'Told you before, Arlen Bales, you don't get to tell me what to do.'

No doubt Arlen saw her magic rising, saw the growing anger

on her face, but he seemed unconcerned. He nodded. 'You did. And I haven't. Said my piece on it. You want to ignore me, that's your business. Ent even that you kept it from me. I can't stand in the sun and say I never kept things. People got a right to their privacy.'

'Then what's the problem?' Renna demanded.

Arlen sighed. 'Said it already. How can I marry someone thinks I'm a fool?'

With those words, the anger fled as quickly as it came, replaced with a guilt so strong Renna didn't think she could bear it. Arlen blurred as tears filled her eyes. Her legs felt weak, and she fell to her knees.

Arlen was there in an instant, supporting her, and she leaned into him, soaking his white shirt with her tears. He held her tightly, stroking fingers through the spiky remnants of her hair. 'There, Ren. Ent as bad as all that.' He put a hand on her cheek, tilting her head up to meet his gaze. 'Creator knows I ent perfect.'

'Only wanted to keep up,' Renna said. 'Know you got a hard road ahead, and I promised to walk it with you. Can't do that if you slip into the Core and I'm left up here, calling.'

Arlen pulled back enough to smile at her. 'Your calling saved me from being sucked down there forever, Ren. Don't haggle down your worth.'

'Ent enough,' Renna said. 'You're going there, sooner or late. Seen it in the sad look you get sometimes, staring off at a path to the Core. Ent telling you not to, but ent letting you go alone, either.'

Arlen stared at her, his expression blank, but a tear welled in his eye. 'You'd do that for me, Ren? Go down to the Core itself?'

Renna nodded. 'Go anywhere, Arlen Bales, long as it's with you.'

He sobbed, and suddenly it was her holding him, and not the other way around. 'Can't ask you to do that, Ren. Can't ask that of anyone. Don't think there's any coming back from that place.'

She took his face in her hands, making him look at her. 'You din't ask. But you don't get to tell me what to do.'

She kissed him then, and for a moment, he froze. It seemed he would pull away, but then he leaned in and returned the kiss, his arms crushing her to him.

'Love you, Arlen Bales,' she said.

'Love you, Renna Bales,' he said.

The Corelings' Graveyard was full of activity when they returned to town. More than a dozen Jongleurs milled around the sound shell tuning instruments, and the Krasian drillmaster was instructing a group of new recruits – raw wood, as the Cutters called them. General Gared, easily the biggest man Renna had ever seen, strode across the square with the Butchers at his back, shouting orders. A Cutter patrol assembled, waiting for blessing from Tender Hayes before heading out into the night.

Arlen moved towards them, and the Holy Man caught sight of them, stumbling over his prayer. He quickly regained composure and continued, but not before heads began to turn their way. Buzzing whispers picked up as they always did when Arlen was about.

Gared moved to approach, but Arlen stayed him with a hand, waiting quietly as the prayer was completed and the Tender drew wards in the air over the warriors. Under normal circumstances, the Cutters would have left immediately, but they stood rooted in place as Hayes turned to face Arlen.

'Mr Bales, Miss Tanner,' the Inquisitor said with a bow. His voice was tight – they had not spoken directly since she and Arlen had left his dinner, giving each other a wide berth. 'What can I do for you?'

'Sorry to bother you, Tender,' Arlen said. 'I . . . need a favour.'

The Inquisitor lifted an eyebrow at the request, glancing at the crowd as those nearest passed the words on. The whole yard began chattering.

For a moment, the Inquisitor did not respond, and Renna worried that they had offended him too greatly. But at last he nodded. 'Of course. Let us retire to my chambers in the Holy House . . .'

Arlen shook his head. 'The altar.' Renna took his hand at that, and Hayes did not miss the gesture. 'Said you'd marry us. Want you to do it. Tonight. Now.' The buzz of the crowd became a cacophony, excited whispers turning to shouts and whoops. Others hissed for quiet, hanging on every word.

'Are you certain?' the Inquisitor asked. 'Marriage is something done under the sun, not rushed into in the middle of the night.'

Arlen nodded. 'Been promised fifteen years, Tender. Time it was kept.'

'And to spare,' Renna said.

Hayes turned to Franq. 'Ready the altar.' He glanced at the growing crowd. 'We don't have enough space in the pews . . .'

'Just us for this, Tender,' Arlen said. 'Don't need a fancy ceremony. Ent some Jongleur's show.'

There were cries of disappointment that filtered through the crowd, growing into a roar of disapproval. Gared pulled his axe and blade, banging them together with a resounding ring. 'Shut it! Man saved this town, and he wants privacy, he's gonna get it!' He turned to the Cutters. 'You heard the man! Clear the way! No one gets near the Holy House!'

Immediately the Cutters formed up, encircling them and opening a path through the crowd.

'You'll need a witness, at least,' Hayes said.

Arlen turned, looking at Gared. 'Will you stand with me, Gar?'

'Me?' Gared squeaked, suddenly sounding more like a pubescent boy than the giant general of the Cutters.

'Stood by my side 'gainst a horde of demons,' Arlen said. 'Think you can handle this.'

'Ay,' Gared said. 'Be honoured.'

'The baron will do,' Hayes said, nodding to Franq. 'Have everyone else wait outside.' The Child nodded and moved quickly to the Holy House. A stream of people left as the Inquisitor and his guests approached. They pressed close, following along as they went, but the Cutters kept them back.

'Have you the rings?' Tender Hayes asked Arlen.

'Don't need any . . .' Renna began, but the words died in her throat as Arlen reached into his pocket, producing two rings – woven gold and silver, covered in tiny wards. Even at a glance, she recognized his delicate script. The rings drew on his magic, shining brightly with power.

She looked at him, and Arlen grinned like a cat. 'Think I ent been planning this, Ren? Meant it for after new moon, we were still alive, but I finished these days ago.'

Renna felt tears welling in her eyes, and made no effort to stop them falling as Arlen slipped the smaller of the rings on her finger. Her hands shook as she took the larger one and slid it onto his. 'You are going to get *such* a wedding night,' she whispered.

The Tender coughed. 'In the name of the Creator, here in His house, I pronounce you man and wife. Go forth and multiply in His name. You may kiss . . .'

Renna threw herself into Arlen's arms, pressing her mouth against his, and if the Tender finished the sentence, it was lost in the thrumming of blood in her ears.

'Owe you a favour,' Arlen told the Tender when they finally broke. 'Won't forget.'

Hayes smiled. 'Nor will I.'

'Congratulations,' Gared said, slapping Arlen on the

back when he turned the baron's way. The slap would have knocked most men across the room, but Arlen stood his ground. 'Honoured to be yur witness. Don't deserve it.'

'Honour's ours, Gared Cutter,' Arlen said. 'Hollow's got good men looking after it now.'

Gared looked suddenly sad. 'Ent been as good as I should. Even after you come to the Hollow. Made . . . mistakes.'

Arlen smiled, reaching a hand high to put it on the giant Cutter's shoulder. 'We all make mistakes, Gared. But those that can see 'em are halfway to being better men. Whatever you done, I forgive you.'

The light that came over Gared's face was unmistakable. He straightened to his full height, towering over even the Inquisitor – a step higher on the altar – then bowed low. 'Gonna make the other half of that trip, startin' now.' He glanced at Hayes. 'Creator as my witness.'

'Love you, Arlen Bales,' Renna whispered. Arlen took her hand and led her back down the aisle.

Gared rushed ahead of them, pushing the great doors as if they were weightless. They slammed open with a boom, revealing hundreds of people swarming about the Holy House with a steady stream coming from every street, filling the Corelings' Graveyard. Folk stood on balconies around the square for a better view, and children sat atop their parents' shoulders.

Renna froze. The only time she had seen such a crowd was the night the whole of Tibbet's Brook had gathered in Town Square to see her staked out for the demons. A thousand souls, come to watch and not lift a finger while the corelings tore her apart.

She felt her heart stop, and before she knew it she was reaching for her knife.

'Man and wife!' Gared roared, and the cheer that arose from the crowd was deafening, shocking Renna back to her senses. She stood stunned as hastily picked flowers began to rain on them and the Jongleurs in the sound shell struck up a reel.

Arlen bowed, offering her his arm, his voice too low for any without their enhanced hearing to catch. 'They ent here to hurt you, Ren. Just wanna give their regards and dance.'

Renna took his arm as he led her out into the crowd. An older woman appeared, a nervous smile on her face as she curtsied. 'Meg Cutter,' she said. 'My family was proud to stand with your husband at the Battle of Cutter's Hollow. None of us would be here, not for him.'

She pressed a beautifully painted pot into Renna's hands, adorned with a few half-wilted flowers. 'Pot's been in my family a hundred years. Don't know if it's true, but my grandda said he bought it from a Messenger said it come from before the Return. Know it ent much, but I'd love for you to have it, to bless your wedding.'

Renna froze, not knowing what to say. The woman was acting as if the gift was nothing, but it was clear in her eyes she treasured it. Such a thing was not given lightly.

'I . . . Thank . . .' she began at last, but the woman was swept away by the crowd as another took her place. Renna knew the woman's face but not her name. She loved the rosebush in the woman's yard and had once told her so in passing.

'Sandy Tailor.' The woman curtsied awkwardly, thrown off balance by the huge bundle of roses she held in her arms, tied together with red silk. Renna could see the cuts and scrapes where she had torn her sleeves and flesh hurriedly pulling them. She must have denuded her entire bush to make the bundle. 'Know you like roses, and a bride should have a bouquet.' Her face flushed redder than the flowers, and she turned to go, then looked back, pointing at the bow. 'That's real Krasian silk,' she noted before vanishing into the crowd. Renna tried to add them to the pot, but they would not fit and was left holding both awkwardly.

She felt drunk as people came on. Her night senses, instincts that kept her alive when she was out among the corelings, screamed at her, expecting them to rush forward – grabbing, clawing. But folk kept bowing and offering hastily chosen gifts. The Hollowers did not have money, but again and again they came forward with things Renna knew were more precious by far.

'Stood with your husband . . .'

'. . . please accept . . .'

'. . . Mairy Blower . . .'

'. . . please accept . . .'

'. . . husband saved my life . . .'

'. . . my son's life . . .'

'. . . every last one of us . . .'

'. . . please accept . . .'

'. . . please accept . . .'

'. . . please accept . . .'

Even with her night strength, it became hard to hold all the baskets and bundles. Before long she felt like a Messenger's pack mule, and still the well-wishers came on, hundreds in the line. Thousands.

Amazingly, it was a Krasian woman who saved her.

She appeared from the crowd, covered from head to toe in black cloth in the southern fashion, but her eyes were kind. 'What is this?' she said loudly. 'A bride should not carry her own gifts on her wedding night!' Around her, everyone froze, and the woman, her tone one of comfortable command, pointed to a few of the women who had already given her gifts. 'Find tables to lay them on, that such precious things not touch this ground, hallowed by the blood of your people in *alagai'sharak*.'

The women nodded eagerly, drafting still others, and the gifts were pulled back from Renna's hands. The Krasian woman looked at her, and from the crinkling around her eyes, Renna knew she was smiling. 'Please allow me to introduce myself. I am Shamavah, First Wife of Abban, son of Chabin, of the line of Haman of Kaji.' Arlen looked up sharply at that, and she met his eyes. 'My husband was always a true friend to the Par'chin.'

Arlen looked at her a moment, then smiled and nodded. 'It

is good to see you again, First Wife of Abban. I hope your sister-wives and daughters are well.'

Shamavah bowed. 'And to you, son of Jeph. It is my fondest wish that you and your honoured family have prospered in these years.' She turned back to Renna. 'If you will allow me to facilitate, it would be my great honour to assist the *Jiwah Ka* of the Par'chin on this sacred night.'

Renna blinked, then nodded, stuttering, 'A-ay.'

Shamavah bowed again, producing a small writing board, paper, and a pen. When the next woman presented her gift to Renna, Shamavah recorded her name and the gift, then instructed her to lay it on the tables that the folk were putting together and covering in white cloth.

'I can set guards on the tables if you wish,' Shamavah said when she caught Renna looking.

'No need,' Arlen said. 'Ent no one gonna steal anything here.'

Shamavah nodded. 'As you wish.'

It went on for some time, and Renna felt herself slowly unclenching as the Krasian woman handled everything with smooth efficiency. Whoever this Shamavah wife of whatever was, she was a lifesaver.

There was a shout, and a group of Wooden Soldiers broke through the crowd, their lacquered armour and polished shields shining as they pushed the revellers back. Renna felt Arlen tense a moment, and even Shamavah stiffened. But then the soldiers split, opening a path for Count Thamos, looking as dashing in silk and velvet as he did in his armour. His heavy medallion of office hung at his chest, and he wore a golden circlet of ivy in his hair, a mind ward moulded at its centre.

The count walked right up to Renna, dropping smoothly into a court bow that had one knee hovering barely an inch off the cobbles.

'Congratulations to you on your wedding night.' He kissed her hand. 'Please accept this small token from the people of Hollow County.' He waved behind him, and Arther ran forward, looking a bit breathless. He, too, wore finery, but it seemed more hastily thrown on. He held out a box of black velvet that the count took, opening it as he turned, still bowing, to present it to Renna.

There, on a bed of silk, was a necklace of delicate gold, at its centre a cluster of gemstones surrounding an emerald the size of a dog's eye. Renna was still getting used to the idea of money – something they had little use for in Tibbet's Brook – but she knew a fortune when she saw it.

She reached out, brushing the sharply cut stones with her fingertips. 'It's beautiful.'

Arther came smoothly forward once more, taking the box as Thamos lifted the necklace high for all to see. 'It will look more beautiful still about your throat,' he said loudly.

It was an incredible gift, worth more by far than all the others, but something about it rang false. The Hollowers were giving the most personal things they had. Thamos, his fingers bedecked with gem-studded rings, was just giving her money. Did he really care she was married, or was this just politics?

With the pad of her thumb, Renna rubbed at the woven band about her finger. The necklace was indeed beautiful, but she had all the jewellery she would ever need.

She smiled, raising her voice to match the count's. 'Thank you, Your Highness. I would be honoured to wear it tonight, but I cannot accept such a gift while folk still go hungry in Hollow County.'

Shamavah hissed, and there was a slight twitch at the corners of Thamos' smile, but he recovered smoothly, bowing again as he fastened it about her throat. 'It is yours to do with as you please, Mrs Bales. Sell it on the morrow, and you will fill many an empty belly.'

Renna smiled and nodded, and the crowd cheered again. Arlen took her hand, squeezing. She could feel his love in that simple gesture.

Leesha looked up as Wonda came to the door, knocking at the same time she opened it as was her habit. She and Rojer were back at the table, having spent the better part of an hour staring at their cups, lost in thought.

'Sorry to disturb, Mistress Leesha,' Wonda said, 'but there's a commotion down in town. Dunno what's goin' on, but you can hear it all the way out here, so I doubt it's good.'

Leesha set down her cup and reached for the half-warded cloak she had been making to replace the one she had given Ahmann. The ever-present headache, faded for a moment, flared back to life. 'Creator, is a quiet night too much to ask?'

Rojer was out of his chair in an instant, grabbing his cloak and fiddle case. 'Amanvah and Sikvah are down there' was all he said, going for the door.

'Rojer, wait!' Leesha cried, but he was already gone, running like all the Core was at his heels.

Wonda watched him go and sighed. 'Hope those Krasian girls know what they've got. Give anything for a man to feel like that about me.'

Leesha put a hand on her shoulder. 'Magic's put you in body of a woman, Wonda, and I know you've been with boys in the . . . heat that follows a demon hunt, but you're only sixteen. There's time still to figure out men and try a few on for size. And you don't need a man to run and save you like most girls.'

Wonda nodded. 'Ay, think that's the problem.' She waved a hand over her scarred face. 'That and this. I'm good for a sticking, ay, but no one's looking to bring me to the solstice dance.'

'If any man looks at you and only sees the scars, he doesn't deserve you,' Leesha said.

'Might be better off stuffing a sock in my trousers and chasing girls than waiting for one who does,' Wonda said as they started out along the path to town.

'Nonsense,' Leesha said. 'You keep your head held high, and

they'll be fighting over you before long, Wonda Cutter. You mark me.'

They set a strong pace, but Leesha resisted the urge to break into a run. Years of keeping pace with Bruna's slow shuffle had taught her patience. 'If folk can't live long enough for me to get to 'em, there isn't much I could do anyway,' her teacher used to say. 'No good to anyone if I fall and break my hip.'

There was a large rock beside the path about halfway to town, and a silhouette stood atop it, barely visible in the wardlight. Wonda trained her bow on it as they approached, but as they drew nearer they saw it was only Rojer, listening intently.

'Whatever it is, it ent trouble,' Rojer said, hopping down beside them. 'Sounds like a party.' His relief was visible, but – never one to miss a party – he pressed for them to quicken the pace even more.

The music and cheers and laughter grew louder as they approached the Corelings' Graveyard, creating an ever-present din. Leesha could see poles waving in the air as men hurriedly put up festival pavilions, and there were Jongleurs in the sound shell with women dancing on the stage.

'What in the Core . . .?' Rojer wondered.

Smitt's young granddaughter Stela ran by, carrying a basket of freshly cut flowers. 'Ay, Stela!' Wonda called. 'What's goin' on?'

Stela slowed and turned to look at them, but did not stop. 'Ent you heard? Deliverer just got married!' She turned back and took off, vanishing into the throng ahead.

Rojer and Wonda's eyes snapped to Leesha. She could see them holding their breath, waiting to see her reaction.

'Wonda,' she said, 'be a dear and run back to the cottage and fetch the festival flamework. Careful with it on your way back.'

Wonda looked at her a minute, then unstrung her bow, tucking it over her shoulder before setting off at a run.

'You all right?' Rojer asked.

Leesha shrugged. 'He's made his choice, Rojer. How I feel about it doesn't really matter. Arlen Bales saved us, and this town, and if this is what he wants, what gives him peace . . .'

Rojer looked at her. 'Then we shut up and dance.'

Leesha smiled. 'Ay.'

Stela rushed by them again, and returned a few moments later with more flowers. This time Leesha stopped her, pressing a coin into her hand and taking a handful.

'This way,' Rojer said, moving towards a collection of Krasians, standing apart from the rest of the throng. At their forefront were Amanvah and Sikvah, a knot of *dal'Sharum* around them. Rojer quickened his pace, and Leesha had to lift her skirts to keep up.

Amanvah saw their approach and immediately went over to him, Sikvah a step behind. 'Greetings, husband. It appears we have returned on an auspicious day for the Hollow tribe. It is said the Par'chin and his new *Jiwah Ka* gave no warning. Your tribesmen were not prepared, and were . . . chaotic in their joy. I sent Shamavah to facilitate for the bride before she was overwhelmed.'

'That was very kind of you,' Leesha said.

Amanvah bowed, but she did not take her eyes off Rojer. 'It is an honour to observe your Northern wedding customs.'

Rojer shook his head. 'Wedding celebrations aren't meant to be observed, Amanvah. They're meant to be enjoyed.'

Amanvah shook her head, and even Sikvah looked taken aback. 'This is not our tribe . . .'

'The Core it isn't,' Rojer said. 'Are you my wives or not?'

Amanvah blinked. 'Of course we are . . .'

'Then . . .' Rojer took her arms and drew in close to her, smiling as their noses touched through the thin white silk of her veil. '. . . please honour me by shutting up and dancing.'

With that, he took them both out into the wide space cleared in the Corelings' Graveyard. People were reeling, spinning wildly into one another's arms with practised efficiency. Amanvah and Sikvah watched the dance warily. No doubt there was nothing like it in Krasia. Any unmarried men and women so casually touching one another was against Evejan law, and no doubt touching a *dama'ting* who was not your wife would get a man's hand cut off. Out of the corner of his eye, Rojer could see Enkido lurking nearby.

'Look at me,' Rojer commanded, and the women both turned to him. 'I know this dance looks daunting, but it's really quite simple. Watch my feet.' He traced a quick series of steps, moving in a figure of eight. 'You try,' he said, continuing to move in the repeating pattern.

'Good!' Rojer cried as they did. 'Now clap your hands and stomp your feet to the beat of the music.' He began to clap as his feet beat a steady pattern on the cobblestones.

'Ay, now you're getting it,' Rojer said and moved his pattern to intersect Amanvah. 'When we swing close, lock my arm, and I'll use your momentum to spin you about and back into place. Then you just keep on.'

'Like in *sharusahk*.' Amanvah nodded. She caught his arm smoothly, leaping slightly to assist as he spun her. She kept the beat easily, and a laugh escaped her as she touched down and kept on.

'Now Sikvah!' Rojer said, turning to his other wife and bowing as he danced her way. Sikvah squealed with delight as he lifted her.

And so it went, as they fell into a pattern with him alternating between them. Both women were laughing openly now, and Rojer felt his heart swell.

'This way!' Rojer shouted, and caught both their arms, dancing them into the crowd. The women both shrieked as other men came at them, but then a thick-armed Cutter swept Amanvah off, setting her back just in time for Rojer to catch her arm next.

'Everam's beard,' Amanvah gasped, breathless, but there was joy in her voice.

'You honour us by sharing in our traditions,' Rojer said before she was swept off by the next man in line. He turned just in time to catch Sikvah from one of Benn Blower's apprentices.

'I can't believe I just did that!' Sikvah shrieked with glee.

It went on for some time. The sight of a *dama'ting* dancing drew other Krasian men and women into the crowd, clapping and stomping. They kept to families, but began to imitate the dance, laughing as they spun one another about.

One of the Jongleurs on the stage spotted Rojer and pointed with the bow of his fiddle, shouting, 'Halfgrip!'

It went through the crowd with a roar. 'Halfgrip! Halfgrip! Get up on stage!' The dancing stopped cold, and all eyes turned to him. Rojer bowed to his wives, pausing to whisper briefly in Amanvah's ear, then pulled out his fiddle case and leapt up the steps into the sound shell as the women moved away. The Hollowers cheered as one as he walked centre stage.

From the new vantage, Rojer could see the happy couple, Arlen and Renna, surrounded by a throng of people, waving and shaking hands. Shamavah stood on Renna's free side, Gared at Arlen's, keeping everyone respectful and tending their needs.

'It's an honour to be here on such a special night,' Rojer said loudly. He didn't have his magic chinrest to amplify the sound, but the shell was almost as good, and Rojer knew how to project in any event. The crowd quieted, and he saw Arlen and Renna look up at him. He waved broadly in return. 'I wouldn't be here tonight, ay, none of us might, if not for that man, there.' He pointed. 'Arlen Bales. He's saved my life more times than I can count, once in this very place.'

From all over the square, there were cries of agreement. Rojer let them go a moment, heightening the sense, then patted the air till they died out. He cast about the crowd, and, seeing a man with a foaming mug of ale, gestured, taking the cup and raising it high. 'And now, our friend has chosen a beautiful bride.' He swept another hand. 'I give you Renna Bales!'

There was a roar, and hundreds of Cutters drank as one as Rojer quaffed the entire mug, tossing it back to the man, who held it up like a trophy.

'I see a lot of new faces on this stage,' Rojer said, turning to the masters of the Jongleurs' Guild and their skilled apprentices, 'but I'm going to play a song I wrote, and I hope they can follow along.' He smiled to the crowd. 'Maybe you can help them with the words.'

With that, he took his fiddle and began the opening notes to *The Battle of Cutter's Hollow*. Folk recognized them and began to cheer anew, stomping their feet so hard Rojer could feel the sturdy stage rattling. He saw Kendall lingering stage right and beckoned her, twirling his bow until she began to play as well.

Together they began the melody, a song they had played together a thousand times. The other Jongleurs had obviously learned the song, because they joined the pair smoothly, accompanying their lead as Rojer began to sing. He kept the tempo slow, letting each verse be its own little world as he took the Hollowers through all the trials and triumph of that night.

There was a solo in the piece, but Kendall kept playing even as the other players fell silent. Her fiddling had improved greatly since he'd seen her last, and she smirked at him.

Never one to back down from a musical challenge, the solo became a battle, as each of them played increasingly complex tunes, Kendall keeping pace to the point where Rojer laughed aloud and let her have the final round before he went into the next verse of the song. People threw up their hands and cheered when the last note fell and the players went silent. Throughout the audience, folk were wiping at tears.

He caught a flash of colour out of the corner of his eye, and turned back to see Amanvah and Sikvah approaching, his *Jiwah Ka* in bright red and orange silks, his *Jiwah Sen* in blue and green.

The cloth was opaque, but as thin and flowing as one would expect of Krasian silk. They were bedecked in warded jewellery, and wore their warded chokers.

They ascended the stage as the Hollowers stared and gasped. The cut was more modest than they wore in the bedchamber, but still showed far more skin than any Krasian woman, even a *dama'ting*, would dare in public. Even by Northern standards, the attire was scandalous.

Amanvah bowed, presenting Rojer with his chinrest. 'Thank you, my *Jiwah Ka*,' he said, taking the rest and attaching it to the base of his fiddle.

He turned back to the crowd. 'I've learned a new song while I was away. I had to translate it into Thesan and make a few changes, but it's about something important to us all, and I think the warded couple would like to hear it.' He nodded to Arlen. 'I hope you enjoy it.'

And with that, he began the *Song of Waning*. There was no hesitation now, and Amanvah and Sikvah joined him smoothly. With the wards amplifying them and the sound shell directing the sound, the song shook the crowd with its power.

The other players stayed silent, afraid to join in as they listened intently. The Hollowers did the same, their eyes wide.

When it was over, there was utter silence. Rojer looked up at Arlen and raised an eyebrow. The man was more than a hundred yards away, but Rojer did not doubt he caught the gesture. He nodded, and began clapping loudly. Soon the entire throng was clapping along, hooting and stomping their feet.

'Now,' Rojer called with a smile, 'let's shut up and dance!' He kicked back into another reel, and the other players fell over themselves to ready their instruments and join in.

Leesha could have cut the line. She was Mistress of the Hollow, and these were still her children. If she had walked right up to the couple, none would have barred her way. Indeed, they would bow from her path as soon as they saw her face.

But Leesha was in no hurry, content with time to sort through her thoughts. Her fingers worked nervously at the flowers as she watched Arlen and Renna. The young woman was smiling broadly, the thanks on her lips and in her eyes sincere as the Hollowers came to pay their respects.

You don't know a corespawned thing about her, Leesha told herself, but even as she did, she knew it for a lie. She did know one thing. Arlen loved her. If she truly cared for him, that should be enough.

Still, even with Rojer's playing, the line moved alarmingly fast, and before long it was her turn and she stepped up before them.

Everyone froze for a moment, even Gared. Only Shamavah was unfazed. 'Mistress Leesha Paper, daughter of Erny,' she advised Renna as she wrote the name on her list.

Leesha smiled and gave a curtsy. 'A bride should have a proper wreath for her hair,' she said, holding up the circlet she'd woven from the flowers in Stela's basket.

Renna looked at her, and her eyes said so much more than any words could. They shimmered, wet with tears. 'It's beautiful, thank you.' She bowed as Leesha reached up to place it atop her head.

'Blessings upon your marriage,' Leesha said, turning to Arlen. He opened his arms, and she fell into them, squeezing him tightly once and then quickly letting go.

She hoped he didn't notice the tears on his shirt. Wonda appeared, holding the reins of a heavily laden mule, and Leesha excused herself to hurry over to the girl.

'Got all the good ones,' Wonda said.

'Thank you,' Leesha said, handing a passing boy a twist of festival crackers and a match. His smile took in his ears and he gave a delighted shout, running off with his prize. 'Do you think you could see about getting me a drink?'

'O' course,' Wonda said. 'Tea? Water?'

Leesha shook her head. 'Something that could take the varnish off my porch.'

Rojer laughed as his wives swung the reel together onstage, their bright silks billowing to the gasps and cheers of the crowd. With a dozen Jongleurs playing, they pulled Rojer into the dance, and Kendall as well, all of them clapping and laughing. Flamework began going off in the crowd, toss bangs, festival crackers, flamewhistles, and firewheels. A space opened up in the centre of the graveyard where Leesha stood, setting off rockets and shooting stars that lit the night sky.

The dancing died down as people stood in awe. Amanvah and Sikvah watched wide-eyed as Leesha put a rocket into the air, and clapped in amazement when it exploded into bright showers of colour.

'Good time to pay our respects,' Rojer said, leading them to the stairs stage left, closest to where Arlen and Renna stood. His wives dragged Kendall with them.

'Tell us more of your Northland wedding customs,' Amanvah said to the girl.

'We usually give gifts when we pay respects,' Kendall said. 'But after that song . . . think any gift would pale.'

'We must give something if that is tradition,' Sikvah said.

Amanvah nodded. 'We shall, in the manner we have been shown.' Rojer didn't know what to make of that, but he had little time, as the crowd parted to make way for them.

Arlen reached out, pulling Rojer into an unexpected hug. It was shocking. Since when did the Painted Man hug?

'That was beautiful, Rojer. Heard the *Song of Waning* before, but never like that. It had . . .'

'Power,' Rojer said. 'Power to kill a rock demon where it stands.

You'll have your fiddle wizards, as I promised.' He turned and made leg to Renna, smiling. 'A gift for your special day.'

Renna blushed as Amanvah went to her. 'I am Amanvah, First Wife of Rojer, son of Jessum of the Inns of Hollow tribe.' She turned to her companions. 'This is my sister-wife, Sikvah, and my husband's apprentice Kendall.' The women bowed in turn, and Amanvah reached into her pouch, producing a piece of pure white silk.

'Kendall tells me wedding gifts are traditional among your people. This is so among my people as well.' She held up the cloth. 'You are the Par'chin's *Jiwah Ka,* and should have a bridal veil. This is my own veil, woven of purest silk and blessed in the Dama'ting Palace.'

Renna was silent as Amanvah tied the silk around her face, hiding her ward-stained face from nose to chin. 'How long I have to wear it?'

Sikvah laughed. 'Until the Par'chin removes it to kiss you.'

Renna snorted. 'Core with that.' She turned to Arlen, lifting the veil herself and kissing him deeply. Amanvah, Sikvah, and Kendall all laughed and clapped, and more folk cheered.

'How was that?' Renna asked, turning back. The veil fell back into place, and she made no effort to remove it.

Amanvah smiled. 'Wedding traditions are not so different among my people.' She looked to Rojer. 'Sometimes I lament I will never have such a celebration.'

Rojer looked at her, seeing sadness in his wife's eyes. Every Northern girl dreamed of her wedding day, and he realized the Krasians were the same way. He had shoved all tradition aside by marrying them on the spot, and, he suddenly realized, trodden their dreams at the same time. He would have to make it up to them.

'You din't?' Renna asked. 'Then share mine and come dance with me.' She took Amanvah's hand and reached out to Sikvah and Kendall, dragging them all into the dancing area. There was a great cheer, and the Jongleurs struck up another song.

'You got two minutes, Arlen Bales,' Renna cried, 'then I better see you out here!'

'Ah, marriage,' Rojer said, and Arlen laughed.

'Every time it gets tough, I'll remember you got two,' Arlen said, watching the four women dance. 'You know what you're doing? Marrying any *dama'ting*'s no light thing, and Jardir's own blood . . .'

Rojer shrugged. 'Could ask the same of you. Sometimes I think I know what I'm doing, and sometimes . . .'

'. . . you're just swept along with the current,' Arlen finished.

Rojer nodded. 'Ay. But you heard the power of the *Song of Waning*. And I'm finding myself happy, more oft than not.'

'Know what you mean,' Arlen said. 'We might all die come new moon, but right now I ent ever felt so peaceful.'

'That's a gloomy thought for your wedding night,' Rojer said. 'All the more reason we have a dance.'

'Ay,' Arlen said, and they moved out onto the cobbles. He surprised Rojer with his skill in the dance, laughing as he swung Renna from one arm and Kendall from another. The Hollowers all moved in, taking turns linking with bride and groom, ecstatic looks on their faces.

'What dances do you do at weddings in Krasia?' Renna asked Amanvah when the players gave the Hollowers a moment to catch their breath.

'We do not dance in public,' Amanvah said, 'but there is a dance we do for our husbands when we retire to the bridal chamber.'

'Oh, you must show me!' Renna cried. Amanvah and Sikvah looked at each other, then at Rojer.

'Dancing is no sin here.' Rojer smiled. 'Just leave your clothes on.'

Amanvah shook her head. 'There are some things no man but a husband should see.'

'Ay, this we gotta see,' Brianne Cutter said. 'Ladies, form a circle! Krasian girls are going to show us their dance!' In moments, the tall women of the Hollow surrounded Renna and Rojer's women. Rojer was allowed to stay, but even Arlen was expelled, moving off to greet more well-wishers.

'I have not given you a bride-gift,' Sikvah said to Renna, taking the finger cymbals from her belt pouch. 'Please accept these, to aid your dancing.'

She helped Renna put the cymbals on as Amanvah slipped her own onto her fingers. In moments she was beating out a rhythm and the Hollow women were clapping along. Rojer picked up the tune on his fiddle, using the warded chinrest to amplify the sound, and soon the Jongleurs began to play along, though they could not see into the tight circle of women.

Safe from the eyes of other men, Amanvah began by teaching Renna the twisting snap of the hips that she could use with such hypnotizing power. The young woman was quick to pick up the move, and many of the Hollow women, including Kendall and Brianne, followed along. Sikvah moved among the women, helping correct their steps and the swing of their hips.

Rojer felt a familiar twitching in his groin, and blushed, flicking his cloak to add some cover to his loose motley trousers. He had only seen his wives dance so before lovemaking, and it seemed they had trained him well. Renna and Kendall both took to the dance as if born to it, and Rojer felt himself blushing further, even as the Hollow women squealed with glee at the racy moves. Other Krasian women joined them, helping demonstrate the moves at their *dama'ting*'s example. At last Rojer excused himself, feeling as if he were peeping into bedrooms where he did not belong.

Some time later the circle broke, Krasian and Hollower alike flushed and laughing. The Cutters brought out the wedding poles then, and ushered the couple back together. A wedding pavilion had been raised at the far edge of the graveyard.

'What is this?' Amanvah asked.

'The bride and groom will sit on those chairs,' Rojer said, pointing, 'which the Hollowers will raise up on poles and carry them around the square for all to see. Normally the procession goes to the couple's new home, but when they don't have one, they use the wedding pavilion. The Par'chin will carry his bride over the threshold, and the whole town will cause a ruckus while they . . . Ah . . .'

'Stick each other,' Kendall supplied.

'Consummate,' Rojer said. He glanced to see if his wives would be offended, but Amanvah and Sikvah seemed delighted at the prospect. They followed along eagerly as the procession circled the Corelings' Graveyard three times, then arrived at the pavilion. Arlen leapt lightly down from the high perch, catching Renna as she fell into his arms. He kissed her as they entered the pavilion and closed the flap behind them.

Immediately Amanvah gave an ululating cry, amplified tenfold by her warded choker. Sikvah and the other Krasian women followed suit as the rest of the Hollowers began to cheer and clap and stomp their feet, banging pots, pans, and ale barrels, clashing mugs, and doing whatever else they could to form a cacophony. Leesha set off more flamework.

Only the *Sharum* did not participate. Kaval glowered at the tent, and Rojer feared he would try to torch it.

Amanvah caught his stare. 'If you cannot be polite, Drillmaster, then make yourself useful. Take your men and kill seven *alagai* in honour of the union, one for every pillar of Heaven.'

Kaval looked frustrated as he bowed. 'We do not have our spears, *dama'ting*.'

Amanvah's eyebrows formed a tight V, and both Rojer and Kaval knew she was losing patience. 'For more than three hundred years, *Sharum* killed *alagai* without warded spears, Drillmaster. Have the battle wards made you weak? Have you forgotten your skills?'

Kaval knelt and pressed his forehead to the cobbles. 'Forgive me, *dama'ting*. It will be done.' He seemed almost relieved as he signalled the other men and they left the Corelings' Graveyard.

Any excuse to kill demons, Rojer thought.

'If they're killin' seven, then we're killin' seventy,' Gared said to Wonda. 'Cutters! Get your axes! We're going to give the Deliverer a wedding present: a demon pyre so big the Creator will see it from Heaven!'

Amanvah watched the Cutters muster and head off into the night, and she sighed, taking Rojer's arm.

'Father is right,' she said. 'Your people are not so different from ours.'

Wonda had done as Leesha asked, bringing her a small bottle of amber liquid. Leesha was not used to strong drink and had no idea what it was, but it burned her throat and warmed her limbs like the couzi Abban had given her, and soon she was in a comfortable fog, taking joy in the excited faces of children and adults alike in her displays of flamework.

But when they paraded Arlen and his new bride around the whole ripping graveyard three times before taking them to the wedding pavilion, it almost seemed like her children were mocking her. They all knew she shined on Arlen Bales. It had been the talk of the town.

Just like it had been with Marick. And Gared. It seemed no matter what she did, her love life was always the subject of whispers at her back.

The Hollowers' raucous laughter cut at her. Did they delight in humiliating her so? Had she truly become her mother?

Again she saw Elona with Gared in her mind's eye. But then Gared vanished and it was Arlen, whose bare warded flesh she had spent so many hours studying, holding her mother aloft with little more than his cock. Elona looked at Leesha and laughed, continuing to grind her hips and bounce atop him. Then her mother was replaced with Renna Tanner, shrieking with delight as Arlen thrust into her.

She could swear she heard the sound of them coupling in

the wedding pavilion, even over the roar of the crowd. She set off festival crackers, but it did no good. She pulled a large rocket from her dwindling supply of flamework and set its stick base between a pair of loose cobbles, hoping the boom would put a ringing in her ears for the next few hours.

But she had trouble getting the rocket to stand straight, and when she struck the match, she burned her fingers and dropped it with a yelp, sucking them as tears ran down her face.

'Night, look at you, you're piss drunk,' a voice said, and Leesha turned to see Darsy looming over her.

'Give me those,' Darsy said, snatching the matches from Leesha's hand. 'They call me woodbrained, but even I know drink and flamework don't mix. Are you trying to lose a few fingers? Set a house on fire? Kill someone?'

'Don't you lecture me, Darsy Cutter,' Leesha snapped. 'I am Gatherer of the Hollow, not you.'

'Then act like it,' another voice said, and Leesha saw Elona come to stand beside Darsy. The last person in the world she wanted to see. 'What would Bruna say if she saw you like this?'

We guard the secrets of fire for a reason, Bruna said. *Men cannot be trusted to respect such power.*

Suddenly Leesha felt horribly ashamed. Bruna would have spat at her feet right now, or struck her with her stick for the first time.

And Leesha knew she deserved it. The idea of letting down her mentor so was too much, and she shook, beginning to weep.

Darsy caught her and held her close, hiding the moment of weakness from the crowd. 'S'all right, Leesha,' she whispered. 'We all have our moments. You go on with your mum. I'll handle the flamework.'

Leesha sniffed and nodded, wiping her eyes and standing up straight as they broke apart. She walked slowly over to her mother, trying hard not to stumble on the uneven cobbles.

When Elona offered her arm, Leesha took it with dignity. Only her mother knew how heavily she leaned on it.

'Just a bit farther and you can rest,' Elona said. They moved over to one of the many benches that surrounded the cobbles, and the goodwives there quickly rose, dipping quick curtsies as they yielded the seat.

'All right,' Elona said. 'How much have you had?'

Leesha shrugged. She fumbled in her apron, pulling out the bottle Wonda had given her and handing it to her mother. Elona held it to the light, then pulled the cork and sniffed at it. She snorted and took a pull. 'I'd be starting to feel a tingle myself if I drank that much, so I'd wager you must be ready to slosh up everything you've eaten since the morning purge.'

Leesha shook her head. 'Just need a minute to catch my breath.'

'Well you're not going to get it,' Elona said, straightening and giving the laces of her dress a subtle tug to lower her neckline the way she did any time a man entered the room. 'Eyes in front. Don't slosh.'

Leesha looked up, seeing Count Thamos approaching, looking splendid in his fine clothes and jewels. A few Wooden Soldiers shadowed his steps, but the count seemed not to notice them, his handsome smile relaxed and easy. He made a leg in that smug way Royals had, bowing when their station did not demand it.

'A pleasure to see you again, mistress,' he said, and turned to Elona. 'Surely I would have heard if you had a sister, so this beautiful woman must be your mother, infamous Mrs Paper.'

Leesha rolled her eyes. She had at least expected the prince to be more original. If she had a klat for every time a man used that line to ingratiate himself with Elona, she'd be richer than Duke Rhinebeck.

Elona's response was likewise identical each time, tittering like she had never heard such cleverness while looking down and blushing fetchingly. Leesha doubted anything could truly make Elona blush, but her mother could do it on command.

Elona offered her hand for the count to kiss. 'I'm afraid the stories are all true, Your Highness.'

That's honest word, Leesha thought, taking a deep breath to steady herself.

Thamos' smile was positively predatory, like the wolfish grin of Messenger Marick. Leesha could not stand the thought of Thamos looking at her mother like that. Not when she was right here. Not tonight. She put a smile on her face and gave her own dress laces a tug.

'Enjoying the festivities, Highness?' she asked, pulling his eyes back to her and holding his gaze as best she could. His eyes kept dipping lower and then flicking back, but like Elona, she pretended not to notice.

'I've never been to a wedding in the hamlets,' Thamos said, 'and I see now what a loss that is. This makes court balls seem dreary by comparison.'

'Oh, you flatter,' Leesha said. 'How can Hollow women in their homespun dresses compare to painted courtesans in silk and gold?'

Thamos' eyes flicked downward again, and Leesha felt her smile widen. 'Courtesans care more for themselves than anyone else.' He smiled and held out a hand as the Jongleurs struck up another dance. 'They may tumble, but they never reel.'

The next few hours were a blur as Leesha danced and laughed with the handsome count. He shared her with the other dancers grudgingly, always keeping close, and his kisses in the carriage as he drove her home were warm and full of passion. His member was stiff and hard in his breeches, and she pressed close, grinding into it with her hips and thighs. She felt herself growing wetter by the moment, and was considering the mechanics of taking him right there in the carriage when they pulled up to her cottage and the coachman hopped down to set the steps and open the door.

Thamos stepped down first, giving Leesha his hand to lean on as she wobbled unsteadily to the ground.

'Head back to the revel,' Thamos said to the coachman. 'I'll walk back.'

'Highness,' the coachman said. 'It is night and these woods are full of Krasians . . .'

'Come back at dawn, then,' Leesha said. 'Just go!'

The coachman shrugged and cracked the reins, heading off down the road.

'Subtle,' Thamos said, grinning as Leesha took him by the arm and practically dragged him inside.

She made no pretence, pulling him right into the bedroom. She lit a dim chemical light, then turned and pushed him hard, so he fell onto his back on the quilts. She smiled and hiked her skirts, crawling atop him, kissing his face and lips and neck. 'And now, Your Highness, I am going to take advantage of you.'

Thamos squirmed, undoing the laces of her dress as he nuzzled his face into her cleavage. 'Usually it's the other way around.'

Leesha smiled. 'Ay, but we do things different in the Hollow. I am going to ride you from now till your coachman returns.' She reached down, unbuckling his belt, then fumbled with the snaps and laces of his breeches. She'd imagined herself having his member in hand in seconds, but she finally had to break eye contact and look at the last knot before she could untie it. She yanked the trousers open at last, but the member she found had lost much of its rigidity.

She took it in hand, stroking gently at first as she kissed him, but he remained soft. She moved higher, pressing his face into her breasts as she pulled harder, and that seemed to help, stiffening him enough for the deed. She kicked off her petticoats and pressed him to her opening, but again he wilted.

'What's the matter?' she asked, taking him back in hand.

'Ahhh. . . . Nothing . . .' Thamos moaned. 'It's just late . . . and the drink . . . and I didn't expect you to be so . . .'

'Forward?' Leesha asked, moving down to spit on him, lubing her stroke. The count groaned as she took his moistened member in her mouth, but still he remained soft.

Night, is it me? she wondered. *Is Ahmann the only man in the world who truly wants me?*

She shook the thought away, moving off the bed.

'Where are you going?' he asked. 'I'll be fine. I just need . . .'

'Sshhh,' Leesha said, slipping her arms from the sleeves of her dress and pushing it down. 'I'll give you what you need.'

He watched her undress in the dim light, and Leesha, glancing down, saw him stiffen again as she bent to step free of her skirts. He had a spear any man would be proud of, and she bit her lip, excited to have it in her. She reached out and gave it a squeeze.

The count gave an animal growl and was on his feet in an instant, bending her over the bed. She went willingly, and cried out in pleasure as he thrust into her from behind. She pushed back at him, grinding against his powerful thrusts as she felt her own pleasure build.

And then, with a grunt, it was over, and he collapsed atop her. Leesha squirmed, trying to get a last bit of friction to push her over the edge, but he had softened again, and slipped free. She wanted to cry, but didn't have the energy. She wished she'd just told the coachman to wait while they had a cup of tea, rather than trapping the count here for the night. She hoped he would be brave enough to leave.

But Thamos pulled off the rest of his clothes and slipped into bed beside her. 'That was incredible,' he murmured as he pressed himself to her back. He pulled the quilts over them and wrapped his thick arms around her, nuzzling her neck contentedly. 'I've wanted you since I first laid eyes on you in Jizell's hospit, but I never dreamed it would be so good.'

And for a moment, Leesha felt her despair fade, feeling safe and warm in the count's arms. Perhaps he hadn't been man enough for her, but she had been more than woman enough for him. There was a strange feeling of pride in that, and she smiled as she fell asleep.

It was still dark when Leesha awoke from a dream of Ahmann, and the nights they had spent in each other's arms. The magic made him a creature of unbridled passion, and he took her frequently in the dead of night, both of them half sleeping with their eyes closed. He would wake her with kisses and caresses while she slowly stroked him. When she was aroused enough to receive him, he would thrust into her and grind his hips until they both cried out. A moment later they would be asleep again, a quick nap before he took her again to celebrate the dawn.

Creator, she missed him. After twenty-eight years of self-denial, she'd had a week of gluttony, and now her body craved his touch. Any touch, really. She knew increased desire was a common sign of pregnancy, but she had not expected it to be more debilitating than the ever-present headaches and nausea.

Behind her, Thamos snored contentedly, his muscular chest hard and hairy against her back. She squirmed against him, grinding her bottom against his crotch. There was a twitching there, and she rolled him onto his back, taking him in her mouth as she had before. This time, he stiffened almost instantly.

Thamos groaned, still half asleep, but then his hand slipped down, caressing her hair, and she knew he was awake. She was astride him in an instant, still slick with his seed and her own arousal. The count moaned and reached up gentle hands, caressing her hips and breasts as she rode him. She kept her eyes shut, picturing Ahmann.

Every once in a while she felt the count twitch and lifted

herself off, bending down to kiss him until his breathing calmed. Then she would resume.

Before long, she felt her own climax building and increased her pace, pinning the count as she had her way. In a moment she was screaming her pleasure, and Thamos held her hips as if for dear life. Pent as she had been, it lasted a long time. When it started to fade, she smiled and clenched tighter, taking a quick steady rhythm, draining the count again.

She kissed him, but they were both panting, and the kiss broke apart with a laugh.

'Incredible,' Thamos said again.

'Ay,' Leesha said, and meant it, though her stomach did not seem to agree, roiling like a soup forgotten on the fire.

She breathed deeply, trying to ride it out, but after a few moments she had to slap a hand over her mouth and run from the room, sloshing up into the privy. It had become something of a daily ritual, and Leesha had almost begun to look forward to it, if only to get it over with so she could start her morning.

Retching always brought a stabbing pain from her headache, and Leesha instinctively reached up to massage her temple. Then she started.

For the first time in months, her headache was gone. Not just receded, but completely gone. She felt her face tighten as her eyes watered, and she let herself weep a moment for the joy of it.

Thamos was back in his breeches and shirt, waiting by the privy room door when she emerged, naked and mortified but feeling strong once more. He smiled, wrapping her in a quilt and giving her a cup of water. 'Night of drinking and dancing affects us all in some way. You don't mention mine and I won't mention yours.'

Leesha nodded, taking the cup and sipping.

'Before he was duke,' Thamos said, 'my brother used to tell me the best cure for a night of drinking is bacon and eggs. I've tested the theory and never found better.'

'I'll fix you some,' Leesha said, grateful for something to do.

'I'd have done it myself . . .' the count began.

Leesha smiled at him. 'But you've never cooked an egg in your life, have you, Your Highness?'

Thamos shrugged apologetically and flashed a smile Leesha couldn't imagine any woman was immune to.

She dipped a mock curtsy. 'Then it will be my pleasure to make Your Highness's breakfast.'

꙰ ꙮ ꙮ ꙮ ꙮ ꙮ ꙮ ꙮ ꙮ ꙮ ꙮ

21

Auras

333 AR Summer
11 Dawns Before New Moon

The party went on for hours after Arlen and Renna emerged, somewhat dishevelled, from the wedding pavilion. He had thought their consummation would be gentle, but his bride had pounced like an animal the moment the flap fell, her aura lit up with lust.

My bride. Renna Tanner. The thought made his head spin as much as their lovemaking. The girl he ran away from home to avoid marrying was the one he was meant for.

Meant for? He snorted. *Spent your whole life believing there's no Creator, no Deliverer, but you and a girl get along, and that's proof of divine plan?*

But much as he wanted to dismiss the thought as ludicrous, he could not.

They stumbled on watery legs back out into the cheering crowd, and Arlen was amazed once more at its aura.

Arlen had thought magic evil once, but it was beyond such definitions, no more evil than wind or rain or lectrics. It pulsed within all living things, defining them inside and out with a wealth of information. Human auras were dimmer and far more complex than those of demons, but there was a great deal of ambient magic here at the centre of Hollow County's greatwards. Without even realizing it, the Hollowers were imprinting that magic with their joy, and it danced happily around them, powerful and infectious.

Arlen had been seeing auras since he had first painted wards of sight around his eyes, but had never understood what the subtle variations of colour, brightness, and texture had meant until his encounter with the coreling prince. For an instant their minds had touched, and he had seen the world as the demons did.

Now even a peripheral glance could tell him much about a person's emotional state, and a full stare fed him a constant stream of information. He knew when people spoke truth to him and when lie, when they were ready to fight and when they would flee. He could see every single emotion a person was feeling at any given time, though he had to guess at the reasons.

He could not see into minds as the coreling princes had . . . yet. But if he concentrated, Arlen could draw a touch of magic through people, imprinting it with their essence, and then absorb it himself, Knowing them more intimately than lover and Herb Gatherer both – every scar, every ache, every feeling. A firespit burn here, a cat scratch there, telling the body's tale.

Sometimes images would flash in his mind – people, places, and things that held strong emotional connections to whomever he was Knowing, but it was up to him to interpret them.

Even plants could yield secrets. Simply inhaling a current passing through a tree, Arlen could peel back the years more clearly than a woodcutter reading rings. When there had been flood, and when drought. When there had been fire, and when deep freeze. The types of demon claws that had gouged its bark. Everything since the nut had cracked, grasped in an instant.

Shamavah was waiting for them as they returned to the party, along with Rojer, Kendall, and his new wives.

Rojer's aura was particularly interesting. When the Jongleur was playing, be it his fiddle or the part in a drama, a mask fell over his aura that was impossible for Arlen to read.

At other times, though, his young friend was an open book. Images floated around him, some dim, others distinct, all connected to Rojer with complex webs of emotion.

Arlen could make out himself and Renna, as well as Amanvah, Sikvah, and Leesha. Arlen could see Rojer had doubts about Renna and the marriage, but he'd made his own questionable choices in that regard, and felt no right to preach. The deed was done, and as Arlen's friend, Rojer was going to support him.

He put a hand on the Jongleur's shoulder. 'Stand by you, too, Rojer. Honest word. Nothing about Renna lessens what I owe you.'

Rojer blinked. 'How did you know what I was . . .'

There was a flare in Amanvah's aura as she focused on him. She was quick, that one, catching her husband's meaning before he even finished speaking.

For an instant, he saw images floating around her, most prominently her parents. Amanvah walked deep in their shadow. Hovering between their images was a book.

'You are thinking it is said in the Evejah that only the Deliverer can read the hearts of men,' Arlen guessed.

Shock rippled along Amanvah's aura, but then the young *dama'ting* went . . . serene, the surface of her emotions buried under the gentle rhythm of her breath. She stared at him with no less intensity, but his ability to read her vanished.

'It is said,' Amanvah agreed. 'But you are not him.'

He glanced at Sikvah, surprised to note that her mind had the same sharp discipline as Amanvah's. She was more than she seemed. Perhaps it was something to do with her white veil.

But while Rojer's wives hid their auras, they could not mask the magic of the items they carried. Bound and warded bones in Amanvah's and Sikvah's chokers made it seem like their throats were ablaze. Arlen scanned the wards, similar to the ones on Rojer's fiddle. He had seen the amplifying effect onstage. Useful magic.

Other jewellery shone with similar fire. The *hora* pouch at Amanvah's waist veritably throbbed with it, and even Shamavah wore a few bits of demon bone among her rings and bracelets, though he could only guess at the effects.

'You don't trust me,' Arlen said.

'Is there any reason why we should?' Amanvah asked.

Arlen concentrated, drawing a touch of magic through the young women, Knowing them.

'No, but I trust you, Amanvah vah Ahmann.' He nodded to Sikvah. 'You and your sister-wife both. I can see that you are no ally of Nie, and your intentions toward my friend are true.'

'Ay?' Rojer asked.

'Don't get too excited,' Arlen told him. 'They may follow the letter of your commands, but they won't hesitate to disobey the spirit if they think it best for you.'

Amanvah did not seem perturbed by the comment. 'Our honoured husband sometimes requires . . . guidance.'

Arlen chuckled. 'Fair and true.'

'Ay!' Rojer shouted.

Arlen smirked. 'I don't think I'm the Deliverer, Amanvah. Don't think your da is, either. Don't believe the Deliverer exists at all, save perhaps as a symbol all may aspire to.'

'An unbeliever, rather than a heretic?' Amanvah asked. 'Is that better?'

Arlen bowed. 'That is for you to decide, Princess.'

The corners of Amanvah's eyes crinkled. 'A decision for another day. Thank you for honouring us by allowing us to share in your celebration.'

Shamavah stepped up then. She held the same writing tablet Arlen had seen her with a hundred times, bringing back a rush of warm memories of Abban's pavilions in the Great Bazaar.

Arlen could see images in her aura, connected to her in ledger lines of black and red, calculating debts paid and debts owed. Amanvah had sent her as a peace offering, and Shamavah was happy for the chance to ingratiate herself with Amanvah and Arlen both. She would do whatever was necessary to make tonight perfect, no matter whom she had to bribe or shout at, but it was a loan that would one day be called to account.

Arlen smiled. 'You are so much like your husband, it makes my heart ache to see my friend Abban again.'

Shamavah bowed. 'The son of Jeph is too kind.' She gave no outward sign, but her aura was truly touched at the words.

And they were honest. Arlen missed his *khaffit* merchant friend deeply, but Abban had proven many times that while he could occasionally be trusted, he could never be *trusted*. He lied when needed, but more often there was simply something he wasn't telling you. Usually something important.

Arlen had replayed the events of his last visit to Krasia ten thousand times in his mind, always with a lingering sense of doubt. It was Abban, after all, who procured the map that took Arlen to the ruins of Anoch Sun and the tomb of Kaji, where he had found the warded spear. He had revealed the prize to Abban first, verifying its authenticity. Later that night, Jardir, once Abban's best friend, tried to kill him for it.

And now they were working together. Even if Marick hadn't confirmed it months ago, much of the Krasian conquest had Abban's stamp on it. This was better than the alternative, as Abban was never so brutal or wasteful as Jardir. After the initial crushing of Fort Rizon, huge swathes of the southland were conquered with houses and fields and daughters left intact, keeping the trade routes open, if under *dama* rule and Evejan law. That was Abban whispering mercy in Jardir's ear, if only for profit's sake.

Whose side are you on, Abban? he wondered. *Do you not know your friend tried to murder me? Simply accept it? Or was it your idea all along?*

He sighed. Did it even matter? There was no point wasting

thought on it now. Soon, he would confront both men and learn the truth. But first, they had to survive new moon.

The line of well-wishers resumed the moment they returned to the party. The next to come before them was an older woman, leading a middle-aged man along beside her. His white clouded eyes staring off at nothing. There was something familiar about them, and Arlen saw in the woman's aura that she had met him before, and felt she owed him a debt.

'Lorry Shepherd, Mr and Mrs Bales,' the woman said with a stiff bow. 'This is my son, Ken. We have nothing to give but our respects and our thanks, but hope you'll accept them. Corelings took the rest of our family on the road while we fled the Krasians. Would have taken me and Kenny, too, if you hadn't come.' She patted the man's arm. 'Things ent been easy, but the Hollow opened its heart to us when you brought our caravan in, and we ent been cold or hungry, even though Kenny can't work. We're grateful for that.'

'Whole Hollow deserves the credit for that,' Arlen said. 'And you, for being so strong when times were tough.'

He looked at Ken Shepherd, standing silently by his mother's side. The man's aura was one of quiet shame, hating himself for his dependence on his aging mother, and for his inability to help his family. But she leaned on him a bit in her dotage, and in that there was a spark of pride. 'You always been blind?'

Ken nodded. 'Ay, since before I can remember.'

''Twas a fever took his eyes, while he was still in swaddling,' Lorry said.

Arlen drew a breath of magic through him, Knowing Ken's eyes and finding the source of disharmony. He reached out instinctively, drawing a touch of power from the greatward as he traced wards with a finger along the man's forehead and around his eyes.

There were gasps as the clouds left Ken's eyes and they became a vibrant hazel, widening as he sputtered, swinging his head this way and that. His aura flared brightly with joy for an instant, then shifted to disorientation and a crushing fear. Finally he squeezed his eyes shut tight, putting his hands over them as his entire body shook.

Arlen put a steadying hand on his shoulder. 'It'll get a bit easier every day, Ken Shepherd. Honest word. Know exactly what you're going through.'

Soon after the hubbub over the Shepherds moved off, a lone *kha'Sharum* arrived. He did not hesitate in his approach, but Arlen could see fear in his aura. Fear and shame. He caught Amanvah's sharp intake of breath, too low for anyone else to hear, and her aura flashed anger a moment before returning to *dama'ting* calm.

The warrior knelt before Arlen, pressing his forehead to the cobbles. Arlen didn't need to Know the man to understand what he was feeling. He'd spent enough time with *Sharum* to know when he was being insulted, and not by the poor *kha'Sharum* forced to deliver it.

No doubt Drillmaster Kaval thought it a masterful political statement to send a *khaffit* warrior to make obeisance and present the first gift to Heaven. It was a passive insult that conveniently kept the so-called Spears of the Deliverer – men who had all helped Jardir pull Arlen down and rob him of the Spear of Kaji – far away from him.

But the sight of a *khaffit* warrior was no insult to Arlen. How many times had he seen *khaffit* mistreated in Krasia, denied any rights or social mobility? It had been thus since the Return, but within a few short years of his reign, Jardir had changed that. Was this more whisperings from Abban – a quick way to gain warriors – or was his traitorous *ajin'pal* growing a conscience?

The kneeling warrior set a pair of wood demon horns at Arlen and Renna's feet. Arlen could see the magic slowly leaching from the item to feed the greatward's power.

'Jaddah.' Arlen drew the symbol for the first pillar of Heaven in the air. Amanvah looked at him in surprise, but he ignored her, smiling at the warrior.

'Jaddah,' the warrior agreed. His eyes flicked to Amanvah, and his fear intensified.

'Rise and stand tall,' Arlen said in Krasian. When the man did, Arlen bowed. 'Have no fear, brother. Kaval may not see the irony of sending a *khaffit* to deliver an insult he fears to bring in person, but it is not lost on me. The *kha'Sharum* bring honour to the *dal'Sharum*, not the other way around.'

The warrior bowed deeply, and the shift in his aura was beautiful to behold, shame becoming pride and fear becoming elation. 'Thank you, Par'chin.' He bowed again to Renna, and last to Amanvah, then turned and ran back into the night.

Six pillars to come.

'I will discipline Kaval,' Amanvah said when the warrior was gone. 'Please understand his insult is not mine.'

'Spoke honest word,' Arlen said. 'Ran with *Sharum* in the night, but never had much patience for ones apt to start a blood feud over every slight. Kaval only insults himself.'

Amanvah tilted her head at him, and her aura gave off a sense of respect, though her eyes said nothing. He gave a shallow nod in return.

A moment later Wonda Cutter arrived, laying out the long curved horn of a wind demon, still with its dorsal wing membrane attached. 'Woulda been first, but these things are harder to carve than they are to kill.'

Arlen smiled. Her aura was one of fierce pride, but with a touch of fear. He probed deeper, Knowing her. She was going to ask him for something. Something selfish that she was afraid he might not be able to – or worse, might not want to – give.

'Blessings upon you, Wonda Cutter,' Amanvah said, 'first of the *Sharum'ting*.'

Sharum'ting? Arlen was startled. Jardir was giving rights to women now, as well? Would the wonders ever cease?

'Proud of you, Wonda,' Arlen said, raising his voice so others could hear. 'Being the first woman warrior in Krasia is no small deed. There's ever a thing I can do for you, you just name it.'

Wonda smiled, and relief washed over her aura. 'They say you gave Ken Shepherd his eyes back.'

Arlen nodded. 'Ay.'

Wonda had cut her hair to fall over the side of her face the demon had clawed, but she brushed it back, revealing deep puckered lines. Her voice dropped low. 'Can you take away my scars?'

Arlen hesitated. He could do it in an instant, but looking into Wonda's aura, he wasn't sure he should. He drew a ward in the air to keep his reply for her alone.

'I can.' Her eyes lit up and her aura surged in both elation and fear. 'But come new moon, what are you going to be worried about, Wonda Cutter? Your neighbours, or your face?'

Shame filled her aura, and Arlen gestured to his own face, covered in hundreds of tattoos. 'Scars can protect us, Wonda. Remind us what's really important.'

The girl nodded, and he took her shoulders, squeezing. He had to tilt his head up to look in her eyes. 'You think on it. After new moon, you still want this, all you have to do is ask.'

Her aura shifted to a more neutral colour and texture, but a slow swirl began within as she considered his words.

'I suppose this means you're not likely to accept the demon of the desert's proposal, then?' Thamos asked, chewing on the last of his bacon.

Leesha smiled at him. Her own appetite had returned, and she was feeling strong for the first time in weeks. 'It's unlikely.'

'Mother says you can be trusted to do what's best for Hollow County,' Thamos said, 'but that I shouldn't mistake that for following my commands.'

Leesha laughed, rising to clear the plates. 'The Duchess Mum has the right of that.'

'You're a lot like her,' Thamos said.

Leesha cocked a hip at him. 'Not too much like her, I hope, or else last night was something I don't want to think on. I know you Royals like to keep your bloodlines pure.'

Thamos laughed. 'Not that much, though I'll have you know my mother was a great beauty in her day.'

'Of that, I have no doubt,' Leesha said.

'As for bloodlines . . .' Thamos shrugged. 'Ours was a minor house a century ago. My grandfather was the first of us to sit the ivy throne, and it was more money than blood that put him there.'

He stood swiftly, sweeping her into his arms. 'You're the closest thing the Hollow has to royalty in any event. Have you ever thought of what you might accomplish as countess?'

Leesha snorted, gently pushing the count back to arm's length. 'Your Highness has a reputation for bedding every young thing that winks at him. Am I supposed to believe you'll stay true?'

Thamos smiled, and kissed her. 'For you, I might be willing to try.'

'If any of us are still around next week, I'll think on it,' Leesha promised, giving him a peck on the lips in return and pulling away to resume her cleaning. She didn't doubt the offer was sincere, but it was more politics than affection. A union between them would cement Thamos' control of the Hollow, and Rhinebeck's control of his duchy, and Araine knew it.

Would that be such a bad thing? She honestly didn't know.

'Is it true you also encountered one of these mind demons Mr Bales speaks of?' Thamos asked.

Leesha nodded. She went to her writing desk, taking an envelope sealed with wax and pressed with her sigil, a mortar and pestle. She handed it to the count. 'For your mother.'

Thamos raised an eyebrow. 'My brother, you mean.'

Leesha raised a brow in return. 'Must we play that game, even alone and intimate?'

'It's not a game,' Thamos said. 'Rhinebeck is duke, and he is paranoid and proud. If you disrespect him openly, there will be consequences.'

Leesha nodded. 'Ay, but he will get his report from you, and I have no doubt you can get a message to Araine—'

'Her Grace,' Thamos corrected.

'. . . Her Grace,' Leesha allowed, 'without interception. You said yourself that Herb Gatherers were still her purview. There is no disrespect here.'

Thamos frowned, but he took the letter.

'I'll be honest, Highness,' Leesha said. 'I don't know how far I can trust you, either inside my bed or out. Are you here because you care, or because you want to consolidate your hold on Hollow County?'

Thamos smiled. 'Why, both, of course. Cutter's Hollow was always part of Angiers, and depended on the throne for many things, including the Messenger road that kept you connected to the rest of the world. It was a minor hamlet not long ago, but oaths of fealty are not things you can just break when you come into power. Would you have expected the throne to just let you go if you discovered gold or coal on your lands?'

Leesha shook her head. 'Of course not.'

'These wards Mr Bales brought you are no different,' Thamos said. 'And what have we done that is so terrible? Have we not brought food and seed, livestock and warm clothing to your people in their hour of need, as you asked? Helped build them homes and construct the greatwards you helped design? My keep may look imposing, mistress, but it is meant to hold against the Krasians, not to terrorize the people under my protection.'

Leesha nodded. 'For all the good it will do. In two years, the Krasians will have more warriors than there are men, women, and children in Angiers. Even now, they could crush the Hollow in a day if it was their wish, though they would have to leave Everam's Bounty weak and enemies in Lakton at their back to do it. But once the Hollow was theirs, we could do little to take it back, and they would have Lakton caught like a tooth between pliers.'

Thamos shook his head. 'The Krasians will never take Lakton unless the desert rats suddenly become sailors. The Laktonians have port hamlets scattered over hundreds of miles of shoreline to dock for supplies. No force in the world could guard them all, and the crannogs and swamp demons would take a heavy toll if they tried. The Laktonians can turn their ships on a klat, and rain arrows on Docktown or the shores, but the dock-masters are cowards, and will see no gain in taking the fight any farther than the shoreline. A Laktonian off his ship is like a grounded wind demon. No match for anyone.'

'I agree,' Leesha said. 'I've been telling the Laktonians in the hamlets to flee to the Hollow.'

Thamos' eyes narrowed. 'Already acting the countess? You had no right to extend such invitation. We are already at capacity.'

'Nonsense,' Leesha said. 'Our only chance to resist the Krasian advance is to grow as quickly as possible. We must fill the Hollow.' She sighed. 'If there's a Hollow left to fill, once the moon has waned.'

Thamos took her hands, leaning in close. 'We don't need to be at odds, Leesha Paper. I will let every louse-ridden peasant from here to the Krasian desert camp on my doorstep if you'll give me the answers I need.'

'Answers?' Leesha asked, though she knew full well what he meant.

Thamos nodded. 'How many warriors do the Krasians have, and where are they stationed? What did you learn of the mind demons that has you so terrified? Can we trust Mr Bales to not waste lives as he combats them? Will you endorse my rule?'

The sun was beginning to rise, and both of them perked up at the sound of the count's coach approaching. She sighed. 'I'll consider your questions, Highness, and have answers for you soon.'

Thamos stood with military precision, dipping into a tight bow. The sudden formality would have seemed cold, but his eyes never left hers, and he had a mischievous grin splitting his handsome bearded face. 'Dinner, then. Tonight.'

Leesha smiled. 'Your reputation as a hunter is not unwarranted, it seems.'

Thamos winked at her. 'I'll send my coachman at gloaming.'

It was nearly sunrise when the receiving line dwindled, and many of the Hollowers were still dancing. The Cutters and *Sharum* had returned infused with magical energy, leaving a pile of demon bones as tall as a man in the centre of the Corelings' Graveyard and breathing new life into the celebration.

Arlen drew a deep breath and went to the Jongleur's sound shell. He sprang lightly onstage without the need of steps, though the platform was six feet high. The performers ceased their playing and gave him the floor. The crowd cheered, and Arlen held his hand out to Renna. She, too, leapt onstage effortlessly, and he wrapped an arm around her.

'Know it sounds crazy,' Renna said, 'but swear I can see the love these people have for you like a halo around 'em. Ent never seen anything so beautiful.'

'For *us*,' Arlen corrected, giving her a squeeze. 'And ay, it's like looking at the sunrise.'

'Can't last, can it?' Renna said. 'Not with what's coming.'

Love you, Renna Tanner. Arlen shook his head. 'Gonna be a bloody honeymoon.'

Renna leaned her head on his shoulder. 'Glad we got to dance first.'

'Ay,' Arlen agreed, giving one last squeeze before letting go to raise his hands and pat the air. The crowd quieted, though it didn't really matter. Arlen sketched a couple of sound wards in the air and his voice carried far and clear.

'Want to thank everyone for this amazing night,' Arlen called. 'Me and Renna din't tell anyone our plans, yet the Hollow threw us the best party any couple could hope for.' There was a roar with that, people cheering and stamping their feet.

The sky was lightening now, stinging and burning Arlen's skin. He was no stranger to pain at dawn, but now he knew how to pull the power away from the surface of his skin, shielding it from the light and preserving as much as he could hold.

Still, the sun burned the excess that clung to his wards, making them feel etched in flame. There had been a time – not so long ago – when he took the pain to mean he was being rejected by the sun. But now he understood the truth, and gloried in it.

Beside him, Renna gasped.

Pain teaches, Par'chin, Jardir had once told him, *and so we give it freely. Pleasure teaches nothing, and so must be earned.*

Arlen took her hand. 'Pain's the price of walking in the sun, Ren. Earn it.' She nodded, breathing deeply. The warriors felt the sun's effect as well, but with no wards on their flesh or ichor in their blood, the magic burned off them quickly. They paced a bit, scratching at their exposed flesh as if they had a rash. Sparks flew here and there as spots of demon ichor on their thick leathers ignited with flashes and pops. One Cutter who had been well doused in the stuff had his leathers actually catch fire. Arlen was about to go to him when the man picked up a half-empty cask of ale and dumped it over himself. Around him, folk jeered.

'Next time, save the ale and we'll just piss on you!' one Cutter cried. Laughter.

'Hollow's been good to us,' Arlen went on, 'but now it's time

I was alone with my wife.' Renna squeezed his hand at the word, and a thrill ran through him. 'And time we were all back to our business. A night's dancing did us a world of good, but new moon's ten dawns away, and there's work to be done. Demons are gonna be out in force, and Hollow County needs to be prepared to stomp them right back down to the Core where they belong.'

He pointed to the great mound of demon horns just as the sunlight struck it. The pile burst into a bonfire so bright it hurt to look at, and the Cutters roared, lifting their axes. Even the *Sharum* gave a shout, thrusting fists in the air.

With that sound, Arlen knew the demon princes were right to be afraid. But he had seen, too, what the Core could bring to bear. When he thought on it too much, it was he that feared.

Renna touched him. 'You okay?'

Arlen placed his hand over hers. 'Fine, Ren. I'm fine.'

'Everything has been delivered,' Shamavah said as she escorted them back to their rooms at Smitt's tavern. She opened the door to show their marriage gifts placed neatly around their room. The roses had been cut properly and arranged in the ancient painted pot, the fresh food laid out in buffet. Other treasures were placed atop dressers and nightstands.

Arlen had lived in the Hollow more than a year now, getting to know the Cutters well as he trained them to defend themselves against demons. He knew how prized the possessions arrayed around the room were. But he had seen, too, the fierce pride in the auras of the givers. The sincere gratitude and love. The . . . faith.

It was the last that struck him the most. These people would do anything he asked of them, not out of worship, but out of trust. He had proven himself to them, fighting by their sides, and they honestly believed he would never let them down.

And I won't, he silently promised. *Demons take the Hollow at new moon, it'll be because I died trying to stop them.*

Shamavah went to the roses, holding up a string around the pot with a slip of paper attached. 'Each is tagged with the name of the giver. I will consult with Ernal Paper and have the appropriate letters of appreciation drawn up for your signatures.'

Renna stiffened, and her scent changed. It was primitive compared with reading auras, but even in daylight, Arlen's enhanced senses gave him a never-ending stream of information about everything around him. He could smell her fear like dung on a boot.

He felt a pang of sympathy, not needing to see an image to know the cause. Like most folk from Tibbet's Brook, Renna couldn't read or write.

Arlen turned from Shamavah, speaking so softly only Renna, her hearing as enhanced as his own, could hear. 'Don't worry, Ren. Teach you to write your name before then, and have you reading soon enough.'

Renna's eyes flicked to him and she smiled, her scent giving off gratitude and love. 'Oughta do somethin' nice for Gared, too. For standing for us.'

'Ay,' Arlen said.

'I would be honoured to select a gift for the baron,' Shamavah said.

Arlen shook his head. 'Got this one myself, thanks.'

Shamavah bowed. 'The necklace the count gave you is very beautiful,' she told Renna. 'Are you certain you wish to part with it?'

Here it comes, Arlen thought.

Renna went to the mirror, admiring the necklace as she stroked the jewels with the tips of her fingers. Arlen could smell the pleasure it gave her, hear her quiet sigh.

It was a last caress. Renna nodded and removed the necklace. 'Ent right to flaunt something like this when so many are wanting.'

'Do not underestimate the inspiration people may draw from a leader bedecked in finery,' Shamavah said. 'But if that is truly your most generous wish, I would be happy to purchase it. I can pay you in coin or, if you prefer, food and livestock delivered directly to those in need.'

Renna looked up at her, and Arlen was shocked when her scent told him she actually believed the woman was being kind. 'You'd do that for us?'

Ent her fault, he told himself. *Same as readin'. If folk in the Brook could haggle, Hog wouldn't own over half the town.*

Shamavah smiled, whisking a hand as if it was nothing. 'It is no trouble. The necklace is a pretty trinket, one I should have little trouble selling to some wealthy *Damaji* as a gift for one of his wives.'

Arlen looked away as he rolled his eyes. 'No trouble,' he murmured for Renna's ears alone, 'and an opportunity for the Krasians to establish trading contacts throughout Hollow County on an errand using our good name.'

He could smell Renna's disbelief as she regarded Shamavah, followed quickly by disappointment. She pretended to examine the necklace once more as she murmured back, keeping the exchange for their ears alone. 'Should I not sell it?'

'Sell, but demand coin,' Arlen whispered. 'Payment on delivery.'

Renna turned, smiling widely for Shamavah. 'Appreciate the help. Coin on delivery will be fine.'

Shamavah nodded as if she had expected no other answer. 'May I hold the piece?' Renna handed it to her and she examined it closely, putting a lens in her eye as she held the gems to the light.

'Now she'll find flaws and try to haggle you down,' Arlen murmured. 'Whatever she says, tell her she's crazy and threaten to sell to Smitt. She'll double her offer. Ask for five times that.'

'Honest word?' Renna breathed through her smile. 'Don't want to insult her.'

'You won't,' Arlen murmured. 'Krasians don't respect a person who can't haggle. Settle for half as much.'

Renna grunted and waited for Shamavah to finish her inspection.

'More pretty than anything.' Abban's wife put just the right hint of disappointment in her tone. 'The diamonds are clouded and there is a flaw along the edge of the emerald. The gold isn't as pure as we have in Krasia. But perhaps the novelty of having once been the possession of a greenland count will help fetch a buyer. I'll give you a hundred draki for it.'

Renna barked a laugh, though the sum was likely meaningless to her. 'Think you need your lens fixed. Ent a thing wrong with those gems, and that gold is pure as snow. You don't want to pay what it's worth, I'm sure Smitt . . .'

Shamavah laughed, and she bowed. 'I underestimated the *Jiwah Ka* of the Par'chin. You have a sharp eye. Two hundred draki.'

Renna shook her head. 'Thousand.'

Shamavah gasped in perfect indignation. 'I could buy three such necklaces for that. Three hundred, and not a klat more.'

'Five, or I sell to Smitt,' Renna said, her voice cool.

Shamavah regarded her, and Arlen didn't need extra senses to know she was considering a last press. At last she bowed. 'I can deny the new *Jiwah Ka* nothing on her wedding day. Five hundred.'

''Preciate it,' Renna said. 'That'll put livestock in a lot of yards and clothes on a lot of backs.'

'You haggle well,' Shamavah said. She turned to Arlen, and the corners of her eyes crinkled, her scent amused. 'Soon, you will no longer need the Par'chin to advise you.'

'All right, Wonda, I've waited long enough,' Leesha said. 'Come on out.'

'Don't wanna,' Wonda said.

'Wonda Cutter,' Leesha warned, 'if you're not out here in—'
She gasped as Wonda stepped into the room in the clothes from
Duchess Araine.

'Oh, my,' she said.

'Look stupid, don't I?' Wonda said bitterly. 'Knew it.'

'Not at all,' Leesha said. 'You look magnificent. Once you're
seen about town and folk hear this comes from the Duchess
Mum's own dressmaker, every woman in the Hollow is going
to want a set.'

And it was true. Much as Leesha hated to admit it, the royal
dressmaker had outdone herself, crafting an outfit as modest
and practical as any a male soldier might wear, yet with a
distinctly feminine style.

The blouse was dark green silk with embroidered ivy and
wards in thread-of-gold to add texture to her flat front. The
sleeves were loose from shoulder to elbow, but laced tight along
her forearms to keep from catching on a bowstring and to slip
easily into her wooden bracers. Over the blouse was a thick
vest of brown leather, padded on the inside and buttoned snug.
It was meant to serve as a buffer between blouse and breastplate, but the vest's fine and stylish cut made it equally suitable
when she was unarmoured.

From her waist to her knees, the pantaloons of fine brown
wool brought to mind the divided skirts many of the fighting
women of the Hollow favoured – loose enough to appear a
dress if the woman was standing still. In battle, Wonda would
wear an over-skirt of flexible goldwood slats, designed to retain
freedom of movement and speed while offering the protection
of powerful wards.

The pantaloon legs tapered quickly from the knee, coming
to a lace buttoned cuff that slid easily into the soft doeskin knee
boots that cushioned her wooden greaves and shoes. With those
shoes, Wonda could withstand the full force of a wood demon's
bite on one foot while kicking its skull in with the other.

Under her arm Wonda carried her open-faced helm of polished wood, carved with more ivy scrollwork wards. If her boots didn't bash in the demon's skull, Wonda could just as easily do it with her head. It would be simple for Leesha to add a mind ward and wards of sight around the eyes.

'What about the doublet?' Leesha asked.

'Gave those away, like the count said,' Wonda said.

'You didn't keep one for yourself?' Leesha asked.

Wonda shook her head. 'Don't work for the Duchess Mum, so I don't feel right wearing her crest. You give me a doublet with a mortar and pestle, I'll wear it. If not, this is enough.' She took her warded cloak off its peg by the door, throwing it over her shoulders.

Leesha blinked. She pretended to fetch her teacup for the chance to subtly dab her eyes. 'I'll have the additional wards for your armour ready by new moon. Your bow as well, if you'll let it out of your sight for ten seconds.'

Wonda looked at the weapon where it leaned unstrung against the wall by the door. 'Don't see what you need to do with the bow. Painted Man made it himself.'

'I'm not going to change a single ward,' Leesha said. 'I'm just going to slip a sliver of demon bone into the grip.'

Wonda made a face. 'Why?'

'Because while Arlen can charge the bow's wards with his hands, you cannot,' Leesha said. 'The bone will keep the wards active all the time. Even unwarded arrows will bite at demons when launched from it.'

Wonda's eyebrow lifted. 'Ay? Like the sound of that—' Suddenly she tensed, moving instantly for the window, a hand on her knife. She relaxed once she had a look.

'Just Darsy.' She looked back at Leesha. 'Sure I don't look stupid?'

Leesha ignored her. 'Open the door, please, while I put the kettle back on.'

A moment later Darsy walked into the room, wringing her

hands. 'Something you need to know, Leesha, and you ent gonna like it.'

Leesha sighed. 'Good afternoon to you too, Darsy.'

When Darsy just stood there, kneading her hands like tough dough, Leesha rolled her fingers. 'Out with it, then, if it's got you in such a twist.'

Darsy nodded. 'Count's coachman came back to the Corelings' Graveyard after dropping you off last night and had a mug or six of ale. Told a few folk there was no point in heading off to bed, as you told him to come back and pick up the count at dawn.'

'Creator,' Leesha said. 'How many is a few?'

Darsy shrugged. 'Folk talk, Leesh. You know that better'n anyone. And even the new ones in town know your name. You'd have to go ten miles to find someone who hasn't heard by now.'

'What business is it of anyone's who Mistress Leesha spends the night with?' Wonda demanded.

'No one's,' Darsy agreed, 'but try convincing anyone of that.'

Leesha slipped a hand to her belly, stroking. *Do it quick*, Elona had said. *Do it public.*

She gave Darsy a dramatic sigh. 'Just ignore the talk, so long as it's kept out of the hospit. It wouldn't be the Hollow without folk gossiping over my love life.'

Darsy snorted. 'Least you have one.'

'Ay,' Wonda agreed.

Darsy looked at the girl as if noticing her for the first time. 'Love the outfit. You get that down south?'

Wonda shook her head. 'Duchess Araine sent it. Had tea with her last spring. Guess she liked me.'

Arlen looked down at Renna, peaceful as she drifted into her customary afternoon nap. He kissed her temple. 'Back before you wake, love.' She gave a contented whimper and gripped at his arm, a smile on her face. He snuggled in close a moment, then pulled free. Exhausted, he would have loved to collapse beside her, but there was no time for resting. He Drew on the magic in his blood, strengthening himself, and moved out the door and down the steps, quickly leaving the inn behind. Folk pointed as he passed, but he was moving too fast for any to intercept.

Arlen liked to think there was nothing under the sun that could frighten him any more, but he felt his serenity fading with every step he drew closer to Leesha's cottage. Of everyone in the Hollow, Leesha's aura was the hardest for him to read. On the surface, she was as serene as a *dama'ting*, but just below, she was a rage of conflicting emotions. It was one of the reasons he had been so drawn to her in the first place. He often felt the same.

Never had it been worse than last night, when she presented the flowered wreath to Renna. It had been an incredibly kind gesture – one that had mollified Ren considerably – but Arlen knew the struggle beneath the surface. With anyone else, he would have thought nothing of Drawing a touch of magic through her and Knowing her feelings fully, but with Leesha it seemed a violation. It was one thing to Know people in order to heal them or help them, to lead or to inspire. It was another to root around in the soul of a woman he wasn't married to that he might glean her feelings about him.

Arlen wanted to explain himself to her, but how could he? Objectively, Leesha Paper was everything a man could want in a woman. Beautiful, brilliant, kind, rich, selfless. But when the time came, it wasn't enough. He was too far gone down a dark path, and felt he didn't deserve her. He'd needed a woman to pull him from that path, but it hadn't been her. That was something no old lover wanted to hear. No more than he wanted to hear about how Jardir had bedded her.

An image flashed in his mind of the two of them entwined, and he grimaced.

Get past it, he told himself. *Leesha made her choices, and I made mine. Don't change what's coming, or how little time we have left.*

The door to her cottage was ajar, and he heard the women's voices long before he made the porch. It wasn't his intention to spy, but his ears did not ask permission, catching every word.

Leesha slept with Thamos? The notion seemed ludicrous, but Leesha was making no effort to deny it, so it must be true.

He shook his head. *Don't matter. Nothing matters other than new moon.*

He was barefoot, but clomped all the same as he went up the porch steps, announcing his presence before he reached the doorway. He knocked loudly, waiting for permission to enter.

Darsy, Wonda, and Leesha all stared at him, frozen. Darsy and Wonda had a whiff of fear, but Leesha's scent was as hard to decipher as her aura. There was something different about it since her return, something he could not make out. The urge to Know her took him again, and he was thankful for the sunlight streaming into the cottage, banishing magic.

The air in Leesha's cottage was filled as always with myriad scents – spices, herbs, growing plants and dried ones, damp soil and fresh food. Bacon, most of all, hung deliciously over the room. But none of that could mask the scent of sex coming from her bedroom, or the sour tang of vomit in the air.

Guess it's true, he thought, trying not to clench a fist. Leesha was free to do as she pleased, but Thamos had a reputation with women that wasn't terribly positive. If he were to hurt her, or her reputation, Arlen would break that handsome nose of his.

He took a deep breath. *That's just the magic talking.* He tried hard to believe it.

'Morning, ladies,' he said, putting a cheerful smile on his face. 'Visit was cut short last night.' He looked to Leesha. 'Mind if we talk a spell?'

Leesha blinked, then shook her head. 'Of course not. Walk with me in the gardens? They've gone untended too long.'

Arlen nodded, and Leesha took a basket of gardening tools and led the way out into the yard. As they walked into the garden maze, he caught a last exchange between Darsy and Wonda, still back in the cottage.

'What I wouldn't give to be a bee buzzing in the garden right now,' Darsy said.

'They got enough people buzzing about them right now, Darsy Cutter,' Wonda said. 'Best not be hearing talk about them walking in the garden alone, next time I'm in town.'

'You threatening me, girl?' Darsy demanded, her voice rising with her short temper.

'Ay,' Wonda replied quietly. 'And you'd best take heed.'

Arlen smiled to himself. If anyone else had said those words, Darsy would have made them eat them. But even Darsy wasn't fool enough to swing a fist at Wonda Cutter.

Leesha stopped by the hogroot patch, pulling out a weeding tool. 'I swear, Darsy should have been a woodcutter. She's far better at killing plants than growing them.'

Arlen nodded. 'She's also as much a gossip as any in town. Wonda just cowed her into keeping quiet about our stroll.'

Leesha smelled of amusement. 'Love that girl.' She began to dig. 'Guess it wouldn't do for your new bride to know you were here.'

'I told her where I was going,' Arlen said. 'Not interested in starting my marriage with lies.'

'Came on sudden,' Leesha said.

Arlen shrugged. 'Strange night.'

'Ay,' Leesha agreed.

'Sorry about how I acted with you,' Arlen said. 'Didn't have a right to get mad like I did.'

'You did,' Leesha said. Arlen looked at her in surprise, and she held up her spade, coated with rich, fresh soil that smelled of life. 'I'm not apologizing for anything I've done, or saying

I'd act differently if I had it to do over. But if what you say about Ahmann is true, then you had right to be as mad as the Core. I'm sorry for that. I never meant to hurt you.'

'It's true,' Arlen said.

'I know,' Leesha said. 'Can't say I approve of your choices sometimes, but you're as honest a man as I've ever met.' She shrugged. 'For what little that's worth.'

'So we're both sorry, but not sorry,' Arlen said. 'Where do we go from here?'

'To business, of course,' Leesha said. 'Waning is ten dawns away. Do you have a plan?'

Arlen frowned. *Waning.* The Krasian name for it. For some reason, that rankled.

'Have a lot of little plans,' Arlen said. 'Don't know what the demons will do, so it's a fool's choice to make a big one.'

'Agreed,' Leesha said. 'They're smart. Maybe smarter than us.'

'Ay, maybe,' Arlen said, 'but they look down on us, and don't understand our ways half as well as they think. Gut tells me they'll try to overwhelm us right away. Come with a host to make a mountain quake, kill me and Jardir, scatter our armies, and leave the rest of the world cowed.'

Leesha shuddered. 'Do you think they can do that?'

Arlen shrugged. 'Maybe.' He held up a finger. 'But if they fail, folk'll take heart and rally. We'll be stronger in six months than we are now.'

'So we hit back with everything we have,' Leesha said.

Arlen nodded. 'And they won't be ready for half of what I can do.'

Leesha toured the town later in the day, meeting with old friends and patients, asking after their health. It was as Darsy said. Arlen had cleared the hospit of even the most minor injuries and sicknesses, putting all the Hollowers back to work when they were needed most.

The Gatherers kept busy, though, recruiting every man and woman with skill with a needle to make headbands with mind wards and embroider crude but serviceable versions of the Cloaks of Unsight.

She met with the town council, though they were mostly symbolic now, with little real power. Thamos had appointed magistrates and tax collectors who would now report to Gared, of all people.

She shook her head. Gared Cutter, Baron of Cutter's Hollow, capital of Hollow County. That would take more than a little getting used to.

The rest of the town seemed puffed with pride about the appointment. The Hollow had never had a lord, and they quickly forgot Gared the town bully from just a few short years back. He had been popular as a child, handsome and strong as an ox; promised to Leesha Paper, whose father spun paper into gold. But after their split, his reputation had been as ruined as hers, for Bruna made him publicly recant his lies about bedding her.

Without a bride or the esteem of the town, Gared had turned to his strength to gain respect, with mixed success. No one was fool enough to cross him, but they gave him a wide berth all the same.

All that changed with the Battle of Cutter's Hollow. Gared had just lost his father, and all agreed Steave had been a bad influence on the boy from the start. Steave's affair with Elona was common knowledge. But Gared had emerged from the battle a hero, and had put his life at risk every night since, keeping the town safe. It had been easy to forget the old him. Many of the Cutters had found their calling thus, and all the town had come together, forgiving one another's failings in their need to survive the night.

Leesha couldn't even say Gared would be a poor lord. He

had the count to keep him from abusing his power, and seemed content to delegate responsibility and keep his focus on leading the Cutters. If Arlen was right, and the people needed real heroes to look to, Gared fitted the description perfectly.

But again the image of him and her mother flashed in her mind, and she shook her head, trying to clear it.

It seemed nothing could banish the sight.

As promised, Thamos' carriage came for her at gloaming. Leesha was in the hospit, and many saw her climb in. Folk leaned in to whisper to one another, and Leesha could only imagine what they were saying. Was it scorn, or were they hoping for another grand wedding in the near future?

Knowing the Hollow, probably a little of both. Leesha resigned herself to it and sat back in the plush carriage. It would only get worse when her belly began to swell, and better people think the child Thamos' for the nonce.

The count's new keep was impressive, she had to admit. Only a skeleton of what it would become if the corelings and Krasians didn't tear it down first, but already it was a powerful defensive position, built on high ground with a temporary palisade of sharpened stakes to protect the workers who dug the foundation and hauled stone for a more permanent wall.

Leesha was met in the courtyard by Lord Arther, who escorted her through the yard, past pavilions set to house workers, servants, and men-at-arms. The keep at its centre was a skeletal maze, but Arther guided her to the small livable section that housed Thamos' personal quarters, which would probably become guest quarters once the count's proper rooms were appointed.

Nevertheless, the dining room was richly furnished, as befitted a prince of Angiers. Thamos waited at the head of the long table, conferring with Captain Gamon, but the moment

Leesha arrived both men rose and the captain bowed deeply. 'A pleasure to see you again, Mistress Paper. Please excuse me.' Gamon was out the door as soon as Leesha nodded.

Thamos himself pulled out her chair, and then sat himself as a servant filled their wineglasses. He dismissed the woman with a wave, and she scurried from the room.

'Alone at last,' Thamos said. 'I've been thinking of you all day.'

'You and the whole town,' Leesha said. 'Your coachman told tales to half the Hollow after dropping us off last night.'

The count raised an eyebrow. 'Shall I have his tongue cut out?'

Leesha's eyes bulged, and Thamos broke out laughing. 'A jest, only!' He patted the air to placate her. 'Though he should be punished.'

'What did you have in mind?' Leesha asked.

'A week of digging refuse pits without pay should make him think twice,' Thamos said. 'I can't have loose tongues in my servants.' He winked. 'At least not when it doesn't suit my purpose.'

'And this doesn't suit your purpose?' Leesha asked. 'You wouldn't be parading me through town in your coach and dangling your title if you didn't think marrying me would bring you advantage in the Hollow.'

'Courting you properly brings me advantage,' Thamos agreed. 'Bedding you like a tavern wench does not.' He shook his head. 'I can already hear what my mother is going to say when she finds out.'

'I see no reason why she needs to know,' Leesha said.

Thamos chuckled. 'Don't fool yourself. My mother has more spies in the Hollow than you can count.'

'So what do we do about it?' Leesha asked.

Thamos held up his glass. 'You accept the position as Royal Gatherer, and we work together to benefit Hollow County. In the meantime, I will invite you to dinners, send you flowers, and shower you with expensive gifts while entertaining you with witty conversation and playful banter. After that . . . we'll see.'

'And are you expecting these dinners to end in your bedchamber?' Leesha asked.

Thamos smiled. 'I will remind you, Miss Paper, that it was *you* who took advantage of *me* last night.'

Leesha clinked her glass with his. 'So it was.'

Gared was overseeing the Cutters' muster in the Corelings' Graveyard when Arlen found him.

'Evening, Baron,' he said.

Gared looked at him, embarrassment in his aura. 'Don't feel right, you callin' me that, sir.'

'General?' Arlen asked, smiling.

'Night, I think that's worse,' Gared said.

'No better than you callin' me sir,' Arlen said. 'Think you got half a decade on me. So how about we drop the formalities? I'll call you Gared and you call me Arlen.'

The embarrassment turned to actual fear. Gared started to shake his head, but Arlen put a hand on his shoulder. 'You've got demons on one side and corelings on the other, Gar. Either I'm just folk and ent too good to be called my proper name, or I'm the ripping Deliverer and you got to do as I say.'

Gared rubbed the back of his neck. 'Guess when you put it that way, ent got a choice.'

'Arlen,' Arlen said.

'Arlen,' Gared repeated.

Arlen slapped his shoulder. 'Didn't burn your tongue, did it? Walk with me a spell. Got something to show you.'

Gared nodded, and they set off to the private spot where Renna waited with Rockslide. She kept a firm hold on the stallion's thick braided leather reins, though he seemed to have stopped struggling, at last. It had taken a long time, and several broken reins, before

Rockslide came to accept that Renna, who was a tenth his mass, was strong enough to hold him immobile.

Gared stopped short at the sight of the magnificent animal, letting out a low whistle. 'He's even bigger'n Twilight Dancer.'

'Rockslide is Dancer's sire,' Arlen said. 'Only horse I ever saw built on your scale, Gared Cutter, and I don't think there's anyone else strong enough to break him. Cutters managed to get him into a saddle, but none of them has been able to keep the seat.'

'Don't let Arlen scare you,' Renna said, handing Gared the reins. 'Rocky's sweet as can be. Just gotta understand him.'

'Ay?' Gared asked. He reached out to stroke the horse's neck, but Rockslide turned a glare his way, and he thought better of it.

'Ay,' Renna said. 'Rocky's been locked behind the wards for years, but he was meant to run free in the night.'

'Know what that's like,' Gared said.

Renna nodded. 'Don't put him behind walls or tolerate him acting the fool and he'll friend you. And with the wards I cut into his hooves, he'll kick in the skull of any demon so much as looks at you funny.'

'Like the sound of that.' Gared met Rockslide's eyes. The horse tried to pull back, but though Gared was not as strong as Renna, he was still the strongest man Arlen had ever met. His thick arm bunched and the reins creaked, but Rockslide's head did not move as Gared laid a hand on his neck. After a moment, the stallion relaxed again.

'Don't deserve this,' Gared said.

'Ent for you to decide what folk give you,' Arlen said. 'You earned that horse ten times over.'

'Din't just mean the horse,' Gared said. 'All of it. Count has men making me a coat of arms. Me! Gared rippin' Cutter.' He shook his head. 'Feels like I'm about to be caught in a lie and sent back to choppin' trees. Need you to tell me what you want me to do.'

'Want you to man up and think for yourself,' Arlen said. 'Like it or not, you're Baron of Cutter's Hollow now. Your job is to look out for the people under you first, and be the count's man second. He asks you to do something you don't think is right, you follow your conscience.'

'Don't want all that responsibility,' Gared said. 'Ent clever or anything, and my conscience gets me into trouble, oft as not.'

'Don't need to be clever to know right from wrong,' Arlen said, 'and I know all about being saddled with responsibilities you don't want. But life ent fair, Gared Cutter. Won't always be someone around to tell you what to do.'

22

New Moon

333 AR Autumn
First Night of New Moon

The new moon left the cave mouth dark as pitch. Barely more than a fissure, it gaped like an open wound from a rocky outcropping on a forgotten hill. The space within narrowed tightly but never truly ended, leading to an endless maze of cracks and tunnels, some cramped and others opening into huge caverns, all the way down to the core of the world. Here, even starlight failed to give faint glow, and there was true darkness.

From out of that darkness came something darker still, a corruption beyond the absence of light. It flowed like ink, coating the cave floor in oily blackness and spilling out into the night. There along the hill, forms rose from the stain, growing tall as they branched out, solidifying into a stand of six trees that stood around the cave mouth like teeth.

A great stalagmite formed at the centre of the cave, coalescing into an enormous mimic demon. Row upon row of teeth formed along its massive jaws, and its limbs ended in great talons. The rest of its body, sharp in some places and smooth in others, flowed like the coils of a snake, never truly settling.

The coreling studied the area intently, then slithered to take up position at the rear of the cave. There it kept watch as the Royal Consort took form.

He was slight, and hunched as if weighed by the massive head atop his small and slender body. His horns were vestigial, and pulsed like the smooth bumps and ridges flowing up the charcoal skin of his cranium. His nails and teeth were sharp, but more like needles compared with the massive rending instruments of the mimic.

Not that the consort had need of such things. The bodies and senses of his mimics were mere extensions of his own. He saw through their eyes and killed with their claws, tasted the surface air through their nostrils. It was cold and bland, almost devoid of magic, burned clean each cycle by the hated day star. At court, the air was hot – thick and heavy with the magic radiating from the Core, every breath delicious and brimming with power.

Instinctively, the demon Drew magic from the fissure, a wellspring of power leading all the way to the source. He filled himself with it, suffused with power, then moved to the cave mouth. He squinted in the dim starlight, feeling a slight drain of power, like a soft breeze stealing the barest touch of heat.

The cave was high in the rocky hills, and afforded a wide view of the surface. To the southwest and northeast, humans were swarming, their breeding grounds overflowing as they relished their newfound strength. Even many miles away, the consort could sense the magic they were collecting. It took the barest effort to take over the rudimentary consciousness of wind drones in the areas, collecting more information.

The results were impressive. It usually took humans millennia to build back this kind of strength, especially with the drones culling them for sport. All this, in barely a turning.

He had thought the initial reports – culled from the less-than-trustworthy memories of drones – nothing more than an anomaly, and sent two minor princelings to deal with the matter. Their reports had been disturbing. Humans in three of the local breeding grounds had regained both the fighting wards and spirit, two things thought crushed beyond repair. With their drones strengthening, human minds were beginning to form. The Queen had no desire to make humans extinct – what would her minds feed upon? – but neither could this insurgence be tolerated.

But the princelings, eager for the favour of consort and Queen, had assured him they would have little trouble killing the minds and scattering their armies before their corruption could spread to the other breeding grounds. Their last report had them moving to strike.

And then, nothing.

The entire mind court had waited on their return, but there was only silence, and the growing realization of the unthinkable. That they failed was obvious, but that alone was not disgrace enough to prevent their return. Not when the Core could restore their power and replenish their drones, allowing them to return even stronger. The answer was far more ominous.

They had not simply failed, they had been destroyed.

The princelings had been young – weak by the standards of their brethren – but still cunning and cautious, in full control of their magic where the humans played with it like hatchlings drawing their first wards. How could they have been so utterly defeated?

The Queen had raged when the truth became clear. Every prince, from the weakest to the strongest, was a potential mate and precious to her, especially now. Her fury, and the incoherence with which she expressed it, made clear what his brethren had known for some time – she was close to laying, and soon the entire court would tear itself asunder as the princes fought for the right to imprint upon her egg sac.

The consort hated the surface, and hated more having to come here now. He should be at court, attending the Queen and keeping his rivals at bay, not up here tending stock that had forgotten it was food. But the Queen had demanded he go himself, and though her mind was confused this far in her cycle, it was still powerful enough to compel any demon fool enough to refuse her – if she did not kill them with a casual stroke of her claws. She owned him utterly, and he hated her for it.

He reached out, searching for the minds of the other coreling princes that had risen on the moonless night, many miles distant. Three to the north and three south; the consort had persuaded the Queen to send his greatest rivals to the surface with him to do his bidding as he put down the rebellion.

It was a risk. The farther the princes were from the Queen, the less her power over them. With every hour that passed, they would have more freedom to disobey her commands – and those of her consort. The fighting would make them stronger and more experienced, and amid the battle they might even take the opportunity to strike at one another. Feasting on the mind of a rival could double a prince's power, perhaps even enough for one to grow bold enough to strike at him. They could even strike in unison. Few things could make the more powerful coreling princes work together, much less conspire to kill one of their own, but unseating a consort when a mating was near was one of them. The consort was stronger than any of them, but he was not stronger than *all* of them.

But for all the risks, it was better to remove them from court entirely. The Queen was bloated with eggs, and at any time she could croon her laying, sending them all into a frenzy to be the first to her side.

It was for this reason the consort had chosen the cave to direct the battle from. With the most direct path to the Core for a thousand miles, he could Draw powerfully enough to repel any assault, and march prisoners back down for its personal larder. If it came, he would hear the Queen's call before the others on the surface, and be able to return to court faster.

He still would not be the first to her side, but the Queen would not choose instantly, and the consort had fought off challenges before. He was old, older than almost all the others combined, and the magic in his veins older still. He had fed on many minds, first his father, uncles, and brothers, then his sons and grandsons as subsequent matings came and went. He had cunning to match his raw power, and thousands of years of experience to draw upon.

He closed his eyes, cranium throbbing as he touched the minds of his generals. They were even less pleased than he, cut off from the Core's magic – limited to what they could store within themselves and draw from vents and their subordinates. Enough to be a match for almost anything on the surface, but not without becoming vulnerable to their brethren. All were wary as they linked their surface thoughts with the consort.

He transmitted the senses of his wind drone spies, and immediately reports from the others began to flood his mind, feeding the results of their own drones' reconnaissance. Battlegrounds were quickly chosen and preparations under way.

The consort withdrew from their minds, letting his generals conduct the details. A steady stream of information poured in as their efforts went on. The very air hummed with it.

Again he focused on the land in front of him, peering out from his guarded cave. How many centuries had passed since he last felt the need to visit the surface? He breathed in its stink with his own nostrils, and with it came a scent that moistened his teeth.

Humans.

It took only a moment for the consort to pinpoint them, not even needing the use of drones. The small village, far from the travelled paths, had hidden itself well from the bloodshed that came with any unification, but though its wards of protection were strong, there were no mind wards. He was able to slip into the consciousness of the villagers as easily as a mimic might take their shape.

With a pulse of command, every male, female, and juvenile in the village stopped whatever it was doing and quietly gathered as much food and water as they could carry, then walked out beyond the protection of the village's wards, joining the others as they silently followed the demon's call.

The path they followed was thick with drones, drawn to the consort's presence like magic to a ward, but the humans marched unmolested through the thick forest and up the high hill. Soon they stood gathered before the cave mouth, staring blankly.

It was a simple matter to single out their leader, though this one was no mind. Unresistant, he stumbled towards his doom. One of the mimics grabbed him, growing a curved claw to sever the human's neck, letting the rest of the body fall. It came forward, peeling open the skull to present it to its master.

The consort slipped his delicate talons into the skull, scooping out the sweet meat and shovelling it into his mouth. The meat was tough, veined with the meaningless needs and wants of its kind, traits long since bred from the consort's personal larder. He had forgotten how different surface stock could taste, and savoured every thought and emotion of the man's lifetime as he licked the sticky fluid from his teeth.

He looked to the other humans, over two hundred of them, and felt a rush of pleasure. What would his brethren at court pay for a taste of the surface?

His cranium pulsed as he impressed his will deeper into the minds of the humans, imparting upon them precise instructions. One by one, they shouldered their burdens and began squeezing into the fissure at the back of the cave. As they passed, he imparted a touch of his scent upon them so that no creature, demon or otherwise, would dare molest them on their long march down to the Core.

It was late in the afternoon, the last day before new moon, as Leesha watched Araine's royal armourer go about Wonda's final fitting.

Leesha had spent many sleepless nights working on it, adding to the already powerful forbidding wards of strength, speed, and misdirection. If she stood still, coreling eyes would slide off her the way men's eyes slid off a woman's face when her dress was cut low. The suit would Draw upon ambient magic as well as that of corelings that attacked her, and the slivers of demon bone she had worked into the lacquer would act as batteries when those other sources were lacking.

She had powered Wonda's bow in the same way, as well as Gared's gauntlets, his axe and machete. Whatever her feelings for the man, Gared would be in the thick of the fighting tonight, and she had no misconceptions of whose side she was on in the coming conflict. He would be able to crush diamonds in his fists, and his already formidable weapons would bite as never before.

But for all these wardings, she had used only the bones of common wood demons. The desiccated arm and stub of horn from the mind demon she kept safe, save for the tiny claws – little more than a pampered noblewoman's fingernail – that she used to power the wards in their helms. No coreling prince would slip into their minds as had been done to her. She shuddered at the memory.

'Truly breathtaking,' Thamos said, coming into the fitting room. 'My Wooden Soldiers will gnash their teeth in envy.'

Wonda blushed, dropping her eyes as she always did at the sight of the handsome count. Wonda was never far from Leesha's side, and was privy to her every secret, including the nights she spent with the count. But more than that, Wonda was a girl unused to the kind of male attention that Thamos lavished on every woman in his presence, regardless of age or beauty.

Makes you feel like you're the only one in the room, Leesha thought, looking at him and suppressing a shy smile herself.

'Thanks, Yur Highness.' Wonda attempted to bow, but the armourer pulled hard on her stays.

'Keep still,' he grunted.

Wonda blushed deeper, but Thamos pretended not to notice. 'I am told to expect our mistress to be even bolder than Darsy Cutter in the night.'

'I'll keep her safe,' Wonda promised.

'Of that I have no doubt.' Thamos smiled, but Leesha saw him tighten his lips. He did indeed have doubts, and had argued them long and hard with Leesha in private. His eyes flicked to a private alcove, and she moved off to speak with him alone.

'I wish you would reconsider,' he said. 'Stay by my side in the battle. My Wooden Soldiers . . .'

'Would form a ring around me five men thick, and keep me from my business,' Leesha said. 'They, and you, need their attention on the demons, not on protecting me.' She smiled. 'Wonda and I have been at this a lot longer than you.'

Thamos' face soured, but he could not disagree. 'It's not just the demons I worry about. My spies report that since our . . . since the wedding night, many of the Krasians have been grumbling about you and making threats.'

'That reminds me,' Leesha said. 'The *Sharum* will have their weapons returned when they arrive at muster tonight.'

'What?!' Thamos sputtered. 'Did you not hear what I just—'

'It is irrelevant,' Leesha said. 'We need every able-bodied warrior ready tonight, and the *Sharum* have already proven they can kill with or without their weapons. Their religion forbids they attack anyone during Waning. Only demons need fear them. After the moon begins to wax once more, they will surrender them again.'

'I forbid it,' Thamos said.

Leesha smiled. 'It is already done, Highness. None of the Hollowers will support you if you try to disarm them again now.'

Thamos shook his head, laughing helplessly. 'You are an impossible woman, Leesha Paper.'

'Are you sure you wouldn't prefer one of the insipid ladies at court as your countess?' Leesha asked.

Thamos' predatory grin returned. 'Not for an instant.'

Rojer watched as Hary Roller held his conductor's wand aloft, holding the final note. The Jongleurs and apprentices had been practising the *Song of Waning* almost nonstop ever since they recovered from Arlen and Renna's wedding. If Rojer's performance at the celebration hadn't been impetus enough, then his demonstration out beyond the greatwards the following night surely was.

Most of the players weren't ready yet. Hary had proven a fine teacher, learning the song quickly and working tirelessly to pass it on, but only the most skilled of the Jongleurs had been able to master the more complex arrangements in the time given them.

They had tested their abilities last night with mixed results. Many of the Jongleurs could affect the demons much as Rojer once had – mesmerizing them; driving them to dance or follow him, to flee or attack. They could even walk unmolested in the night, so long as they kept the underlying tune.

But they could not improvise, nor could they actually hurt the demons in the way he, Amanvah, and Sikvah could.

Some of that power was the sheer volume that Rojer's trio could produce with their *hora* magic, but Rojer could hear in the other Jongleurs' music that however loud it might grow, a demon would recover instantly the moment the sound stopped. Only Kendall seemed to have anything approaching the knack, and even she still had a long way to go.

Hary closed a fist and the players stopped in perfect sync, then fell into disarray. Some began talking to their fellows, or tuning instruments, or packing them in cases. Hary came over to where Rojer was standing. 'Sound great, don't they?'

Rojer nodded. 'Good enough for less than two weeks' practice. Just pray it's enough.'

Hary grunted. 'Word of advice, if you want to be a teacher, Rojer. A pat on the back encourages more than a frowning nod.'

Not according to Arrick, Rojer thought, but he put a smile on his face and waved at the players as they rested. 'Well done, all! Have a stretch. It's going to be a long night.'

He turned back to Hary. 'Sorry. Everyone is on edge today.'

'Is this "Waning" really so bad?' Hary asked. 'Been through many a new moon without thinking twice. Even spent a couple on the road, back when I was making my name in the hamlets.'

Rojer shrugged. 'Might be a big production for an empty house,' he admitted. 'Night, I hope so. But if what Leesha and the Painted Man say is true and those smart demons they killed have family that's going to come looking for them tonight, we're going to need every bit of help we can get.' He tugged at the hood of his warded cloak. Leesha had stitched mind wards into the hem, but he had drawn one on his forehead with Jongleur's paint regardless, and the other Jongleurs had followed suit.

'This song of yours is that and more,' Hary assured. 'You act disappointed because we're not shattering rock demons with it, but already we can protect ourselves and others, not to mention give the fighters a winning edge.'

Rojer shook his head, though the smile for the players' benefit never left his face. 'An edge perhaps, but not a winning one. No music is going to keep the demons fazed once someone hits one of them with an axe.'

'Still,' Hary said, 'can't believe you just gave the song out for nothing.'

'What was I supposed to do?' Rojer asked. 'Hold it ransom while my friends die?'

Hary shook his head. 'Of course not. But the count offered you a job as herald, and that's no small thing. Lot of men would kill for that offer.'

Men have, Rojer thought, glancing at Hary. The Jongleurs in Angiers knew how to mind their manners when Royals were about, and were happy to take commissions when offered, but talk in the guild hall was seldom loyal to the ivy throne. Rhinebeck was generally reviled for his laws and taxes. 'Being royal herald didn't work out too well for my master, if you recall.'

'It wasn't Arrick that kept the duke from getting his pecker wet by sleeping in the bed of his favourite doxy,' Hary reminded. 'That's apt to put a fire in any man, much less a Royal. You're lucky you didn't get the sticking meant for her.'

Rojer kept his mask in place. He wasn't surprised Hary knew the details of Arrick's fall from grace. Jongleurs were notorious gossips, especially when it came to one another.

'You could have haggled like your man Gared, even if you didn't want the herald job,' Hary went on. 'He got a barony just by asking. A barony! Duchy is on the rise, boy, you mark my words. And Hollow County's going to be its centre. Don't want to be late to the casting call.'

'Ay,' Rojer said, 'but what's Angiers ever done for me? Rhinebeck had one swelling go to waste, and threw my master away like garbage. Left us a performance away from starving on the street. Who's to say he or this new count won't do the same to Gared, or me, when the fighting's done?'

'Got no more love of the duke than you,' Hary said, 'but you're young, and maybe you didn't know your master as well as you'd like to think. I knew him long before you were born, and Arrick Sweetsong was never a man to care a whit for anyone other than himself. The drink made him sloppy, and his pride in his position made him quick to turn up his nose at anyone who had nothing to offer. Duke was looking for an excuse to break his contract long before you got caught in the brothel.'

Rojer opened his mouth, ready to angrily defend his master, but the words caught in his throat. He knew Arrick's failings well.

'To be honest,' Hary said, 'none of us could ever understand why he kept taking care of you.'

Rojer chuckled. 'It wasn't all dancing and song when the crowd broke.'

Hary nodded. 'Ay, I'm sure he was a right coreling when he was in his cups, but he stood by you, even when it would have been better for his career to let you go. Remember when Tom Fiddle offered to take you on?'

'Arrick broke his nose,' Rojer said. He shook his head. 'Didn't want to go with Tom, anyway. Says he searches his apprentices' pockets to make sure they're not hiding klats, but everyone knows he's just going for a grope.'

Hary nodded again. 'Ay, but Tom had connections. That punch cost Arrick a lot of work. Like the one you gave Jasin Goldentone when he laughed that your master was dead.'

'You heard about that?' Rojer asked, his mask slipping in his shock.

Hary laughed. 'Hear? Boy, it was the talk of the guild hall for months! You might not be Arrick's blood, but in some ways you're the spitting image.'

'Don't know if I should take that as a compliment or an insult,' Rojer said. Punching Jasin had got his guild sponsor, Master Jaycob, killed, and had left Rojer in Leesha's hospit, beaten till he could taste death's breath on his lips. She had pulled him back, but at the time, and several times since, he wished she had just let him go.

Hary shrugged. 'Not sure how I meant it.' He winked. 'If he was in your motley right now, Arrick would be pushing for his own county.'

'Why settle?' Rojer asked. 'I'm married to the daughter of the demon of the desert, and best friends with the ripping Deliverer. My firstborn should be king.'

Hary stared at him for a moment, trying to determine if he was serious. At last, he began to laugh, and Rojer joined him. It felt good to laugh in the face of death, and both men gave it free rein, howling till their sides hurt.

When it was over, Rojer sighed. 'Let's focus on keeping

everyone alive for the next few nights. If we can do that, there's twenty-seven more days to worry about how the Royals should reward me.'

Renna watched as Arlen moved for the Jongleurs' sound shell. It had been days since he had slept, but he stubbornly refused her attempts to convince him of the necessity. Even today, when he needed to be at his best.

'Ent resting while there's work to be done,' he told her, and she knew from his tone that he had his back up. Arlen Bales could set his heels as deep as any mule.

But there had been work aplenty, and now, with barely an hour to dusk and thanks in no small part to him, it was all done – or as done as it was going to be. The net of greatwards was weak in places, but it was active and linked, each ward distributing power to the others. No coreling, even a mind demon, could set foot in Hollow County, or fly less than a mile above it.

A hush went through the crowd as Arlen took centre stage. It wasn't everyone in Hollow County – most were already at their posts, protecting workers who would be piling fortifications to strengthen the weaker sections of the greatwards right up to sunset and beyond. But the leaders were all there, waiting on Arlen's final words.

Cutters, seasoned and raw, stood at attention. Most were the thick-armed men that grew so abundantly in the Hollow, but there were many with features that spoke of faraway places. There were also hundreds of women, many clad in tapered pantaloons and vests similar to the one Wonda wore beneath her armour. Most carried bows and stroked the fletching of their warded arrows the way they might caress a lover. All wore bandannas painted with mind wards.

Backs straight, the Wooden Soldiers sat mounted on sleek

coursers. Their long spears had been fitted with special grips to allow them to be used as lances. Shorter stabbing spears hung from harnesses in easy reach. Count Thamos, resplendent in his enamelled armour, towered over them atop his heavy destrier, its barding warded glass over fitted wood.

Kaval's *Sharum*, armed once more with spear and shield, stood in a neat square. Renna watched them, half expecting trouble, but they seemed the most disciplined of all.

A knot of Herb Gatherers, marked by their pocketed aprons, surrounded Leesha to one side, and the Jongleurs stood by Rojer and Hary Roller to the other. Even Inquisitor Hayes and his acolytes waited in silence to hear his words.

'We done good work this month, getting ready for the demons.' Even without magic, Arlen's voice carried far and clear. There was clapping and cheering, and Arlen waited for it to die down before going on, his face grim. 'But I ent gonna lie to you folk. Demons know we're getting strong, and they're going to rise in numbers like you never dreamed tonight, determined to stomp us back down into the mud. Worse, they're gonna fight smart – attack where we're weakest and they can do the most damage. All of you,' he looked pointedly at the Krasians, 'are gonna see fightin' tonight like you never saw before.' His eyes scanned the crowd, seeming to meet everyone at once. 'And you can't count on me to save you tonight.'

There was a murmur of shock at that, and Arlen let it sink in a moment before going on. 'We can kill all the demons we want, but so long as their minds are out there, it's slappin' at raindrops. I'm huntin' mind demons tonight, and ent always gonna have time for the little fights.'

His voice hardened, and his eyes flashed with intensity. 'But if there's anyone in all the world I trust can take care of themselves, it's the folk of Hollow County. Can I count on you to do that?'

The crowd erupted in a roar, holding aloft their weapons. 'Ent gonna let you down!'

'Don't you worry about us, we'll still be cuttin' wood demon when you get back!'

Arlen held up a fist, and they fell silent again, though the energy was thick in the air. 'Had the honour of standing with a lot of you in this very place, shedding blood and more than our share of coreling ichor right on the cobbles beneath your feet. Lost some good people, and still more came out with wounds they carry to this day. But we gave better'n we got, beat those demons down and watched them burn when the sun rose.' He looked back to the Krasians. 'In Krasia, that makes this sacred ground, and it makes us all family.'

There were nods and grunts of agreement from the crowd, though none dared speak, hanging on Arlen's words. 'For more than three hundred years, we been waiting for a Deliverer to come and save us from the demons. And while we waited, we forgot that we, each and every one of us, was strong. Strong enough that together, ent nothing can stop us. But the Deliverers of old didn't do it alone. They get the credit, ay, but they wouldn't have had a chance without the thousands, nay, millions, of good folk like you at their sides.

'So you stand up for you and yours tonight. You stand proud, and come Waxing, when Hollow County's still standing tall, someone asks who the Deliverer is? You can give honest word when you say "Ay, that's me."'

The crowd cheered again, shouting, 'Deliverers!' again and again. The Krasians did not join the chant, but they clattered their spears against their shields to add to the cacophony, and seemed mollified by the words – a careful dance that avoided any claims that Arlen was the Deliverer, or that Jardir was not. Now was not the time for division.

Arlen let the energy flow through the crowd, driving away their fears, then held up his hands, patting the air until there was silence once more. 'Don't know where the attacks will come. The outer boroughs, I expect, but it's hard to say. That's why we're staging here. Cutter's Hollow is the centre of the net, and we'll be able to move swift to support the folk that need it. Demons will be on the rise soon, but the minds won't come till later, when the dark is long and full. For now, keep your weapons ready and look to your commanders. Be ready for a run.'

With that, he hopped lightly down from the stage to join Renna.

'Hunting mind demons?' Renna asked.

'Much as I can,' Arlen said. 'Same goes for you as the Cutters, Ren. Can't hold back tonight. Ent leaving you behind 'cause I think you ent got what it takes, but come night I'm gonna have to go where I'm needed, and fast. Maybe faster'n you can keep up.'

The words grated on Renna, a reminder of the warning Arlen had given her when they first left Tibbet's Brook. *You either keep up, or I'm dropping you at the next town we come to.* Harsh words, but Renna had worked hard and sacrificed much to keep pace. It still wasn't enough. Arlen could dematerialize and slip into the greatward, travelling to anywhere in Hollow County in the time it took to take a deep breath and let it out again.

'Could if you'd teach me the trick,' Renna said.

Arlen shook his head. 'This ent like embracing pain or knowing how to twist a demon into a throw. Took me years of absorbing magic and eatin' demon meat before I could even dissipate, and months from there to learn to do it at will and pull myself back together. And that's just learning to tread water. This is swimming in current so strong it can sweep you along like a twig.'

Renna frowned. 'Can't say I like the sound of that.'

Arlen shrugged and smiled. 'Can't say I do, either. But I'll do what needs to be done to keep the Hollow safe. Need to know you will, too. Cutters are strong, but with me out of the picture, you're the strongest one in the Hollow. Without you to shore the line, they may break. No running off on your own tonight. They need you.'

'Think I don't know that?' Renna snapped. 'Hollowers been good to me. Good in ways I never knew folk could be. Die before I let 'em down.'

Arlen touched her face. 'That's the woman I promised. Just,' he kissed her, 'don't forget to breathe.'

She stuck a finger in his chest. 'And you don't forget that you belong up here,' she pointed to the cobbles, 'and not down there taking on every demon in the world. You leave us, I'm coming down after you and dragging you back by the stones.' She reached between his legs and squeezed tight for emphasis.

Arlen let out a sound that was half squeak and half laughter.

'Honest word,' he said, his voice tightened to a squeak, and Renna laughed.

Easier than expected, Arlen thought as Renna released him. He could smell the emotions warring within her, heightened by the magic. For the last week, she'd kept better control of her temper than since she first tasted the magic on the road from Tibbet's Brook, months ago.

His mam might have said, 'Married life suits her', but it had as much to do with the revelation that he knew all along that she was eating demon flesh. He felt lighter himself after letting go the weight of that lie. He kept silent at first out of respect, thinking she would tell him and was just waiting for the right chance. But as the days and weeks passed, he realized that wasn't it at all.

It became a test to see if she ever admitted it without being caught. A test of her judgement, and her love. A test of how much he could trust her. Renna had a lifetime of bad decisions behind her. She was supposed to be starting fresh, but day by day she built on a lie.

It was only now, having confronted and forgiven her, that he understood how stubborn he had been. Too proud to reach out to someone that needed him until she proved . . . what? Arlen's past was hardly without bad decisions, and he had never hesitated to keep his own counsel. What right did he have to judge her for doing the same?

'What?' Renna asked, and Arlen realized he'd been staring at her.

'Nothing,' he said, putting a hand to her cheek and moving in to kiss her deeply. 'Think maybe married life just suits me.' He smiled, and her scent filled with love.

He turned away quickly, wanting to hold that sight and scent in his mind. Even if he'd trusted himself not to spoil it, there was no more time.

He moved over to where Evin Cutter, Yon Gray, and a pair of Wooden Soldiers stood with the horses. Shadow paced nearby, and the horses, even Evin's own, shifted nervously. Only Rockslide, Twilight Dancer, and Promise held their ground, watching the giant wolfhound the way a dog might watch a cat. Even a nightwolf was no match for an Angierian mustang.

Gared and Captain Gamon joined him, mounting up at his nod. Arlen was used to towering above everyone when mounted on Twilight Dancer, but now Gared loomed over even him. The baron and the giant stallion still regarded each other warily, but in battle they were a terror to behold. Arlen had seen in their auras how people looked up to Gared, trusted him, and whatever else he might see in the baron, Arlen did not think he would let them down in the days to come.

Leesha, Rojer, and the count came soon after, followed by Rojer's wives and their silent bodyguard. They would wait in the graveyard with the others as scouting parties like Arlen's patrolled the border, waiting to see where they would be needed.

Arlen could tell Thamos grated at that, and he smiled. The count was flawed as any man, but he had been a good leader to the Hollow. The prince was a skilled warrior when his courage was roused, but he would be more trouble than he was worth as a scout. There would be battle enough for him if a charge of his heavy horse was required.

'Good luck,' Leesha said. As hard as she was for him to read, he could see in Leesha, too, a fierce desire to come with them. She was unafraid, and thought herself better suited than most to assess the situation at the border. She was right, but her skills at healing were worth far more this night. He was ready to argue with her – for all the good it would do. When Leesha Paper decided to do a thing, all the Core couldn't stop her.

But the argument never came. Whatever her heart wanted, Leesha knew she was of better use readying the hospit and waiting to see where the fighting was thickest.

Rojer stepped up next. 'Still sure you don't need me to come along?' His voice had the same steel he used when playing the part of Marko Rover, the legendary fearless traveller. It sounded to all involved that this had been an ongoing argument between them over the last week, though in truth this was the first time they had spoken of it.

Arlen met Rojer's eyes and shrugged, giving no sign that he saw the show for what it was. 'Come if you want, but there ent much point. No telling which patrol will find something. Best you stay here and wait for the signal. Expect there'll be plenty to keep us all busy soon enough.'

The signal was some of Leesha's best flamework, given to each of the patrols. Rockets that would shriek and put a bright streak in the night sky, leading the reserves to where they were needed. The rockets were specially coloured and marked to dictate the size of the threat and if there were wounded in need.

But then Rojer surprised him. 'No, I'll come. Dancer's carried the both of us before.'

Amanvah put her hand on his shoulder. 'Husband . . .'

'The *jiwah* will be silent!' Rojer kept his back to the women, but turned his head halfway, addressing them in periphery in the manner Krasian men often did to remind women of their place. Arlen blinked, shocked at how quickly the Jongleur had assimilated their culture. 'You will both wait here with the others while I join the patrol.'

Disciplined though they were, the women could not hide the flare of indignation in their scents at being spoken to like common *dal'ting*. Rojer's scent said he knew he would pay for the words, but he was still just reciting lines.

Amanvah turned to Enkido, her fingers a blur. Arlen knew something of Krasian hand codes from his time in the Maze, but this was much more complex. Where *Sharum* used a few quick commands, Amanvah seemed to be having a whole conversation. The big eunuch occasionally gave the sign for *nie*, attempting to refuse, but Amanvah was insistent. At last, the eunuch bowed and walked over to Rojer. He knelt and put his head to the ground, then stood, the act of a warrior swearing his life to protect his *kai'Sharum*.

But Rojer shook his head. 'The Damajah tasked you with protecting her blood, Enkido. You will stay with my wives.'

'Kaval, then,' Amanvah said through gritted teeth.

Rojer laughed, but it, too, was a calculated thing. 'After he tried to kill me? Not a chance. I can take care of myself. Besides,' he held up his fiddle, 'if I get into trouble, you'll know.'

Arlen had noted the connection before, like a sparkling thread in the air connecting the fiddle's chinrest to one of Amanvah's earrings. Once the sun set, she would hear whatever was spoken near Rojer, and apparently he knew it. Interesting.

Arlen leapt astride Twilight Dancer and held down a hand. Rojer took it, and he easily lifted the Jongleur up behind him.

Amanvah stepped forward, holding out a mask made from coloured silk stitched to match the shifting tones of his motley. There were mind wards embroidered into the silk, as well as those for wardsight.

'It was to be a Waning gift,' Amanvah said, 'to help keep our honoured husband safe. Wear it always.' Her scent was honest. Whatever motivations the Krasian women might have – and

Arlen knew they had many – there could be no doubt they loved him.

As Rojer tied on the silk mask, his Jongleur's mask slipped. 'Was I supposed to get you something?'

Amanvah shook her head. 'Wives give Waning gifts to their husband. His gift is to come home alive, honour and spear intact.'

Arlen could smell Rojer's fear, but his Jongleur's mask was back in place. He laughed, grabbing at his crotch. 'Ay, I'll keep it safe.'

Amanvah was not amused. She sniffed and turned on her heel, storming off with Sikvah and Enkido in tow. Rojer stared after them. Arlen turned Twilight Dancer sharply, whipping his eyes away as he led the group down the road.

'You can apologize when you get back,' he said, too low for the others to hear. 'Ent nothing gonna hurt you with two Bales and Gared Cutter beside you.'

Rojer glanced at Gared, and something passed between them. Gared smelled angry and Rojer ashamed.

Wonderful, Arlen thought, and kicked Twilight Dancer's flanks, leading the group to the border at a gallop.

'Why here?' Renna asked, as they rode into the borough of Newhaven.

Less than a month ago, Arlen and Renna had found the Cutters clearing this land of demons. Now the newest district of Hollow County held some twelve hundred settlers, most of them Rizonans who had gone north past the Hollow when they first fled the Krasians, hoping for succour in Angiers. They had found no welcome there – the city already choked with refugees and refusing entry to more.

When Prince Thamos rode south to take control of the Hollow, followed by hundreds of soldiers, carts laden with supplies, and herds of livestock, hundreds had packed up and followed. Some even left the crowded city and hamlets, hoping for a better life in the Hollow.

'I was going to attack the Hollow, this is where I'd do it,' Arlen said.

There were a few partially constructed homes, but the men and women of Newhaven had focused most of their labour building streets, walls, and fences to form its greatward – the last in the net surrounding Hollow County. Each greatward was a forbidding independent of the others, but when they linked their power was shared, allowing those boroughs under direct assault to Draw from those that were still safe, particularly the powerful greatward of Cutter's Hollow, nestled protectively at the centre of the net.

The greatward had only come alive the past night. The Haveners cheered when the first demons tested it and were thrown back, folk dancing in the glowing streets.

Arlen knew it was a fragile thing. The greatward of Cutter's Hollow was formed by cobbled streets, poured crete, thick stands of ancient trees, large buildings, and a diverted stream that formed a small lake. Newhaven's greatward was formed by roads of packed soil, thick bushes, wooden fences, and freshly planted farmland. Partial buildings, walls of piled stone, dirt ramparts, and a few old stands of trees added strength to the ward, but it would be scant protection if the demons set fires to burn the wood away and hurled a few heavy stones at key structures. Even a small force of corelings led by a mind could penetrate the greatward and come pouring into the streets of Newhaven.

'Maybe they know it,' Renna said. 'Maybe they're counting on you being here while they strike the opposite side of the county.'

Arlen shrugged. 'Won't lie and say I'm not thinking the same, but what else can we do? Got scouts all over the county with flamework. They put up a signal and I can be there before the rockets burn out. Till then . . .'

'We guard the weak spot,' Gared said.

Arlen looked at the Haveners, many of them too young or too old to be much help in pitched battle, nonetheless standing with spears and hastily warded shields, ready to defend their new home. Others were ready in bucket lines to douse fires, and even as the sun set, the strongest men continued to bend their backs in the dirt, every shovelful they added to the ramparts strengthening the greatward.

There was a hush as the sun finally dipped beneath the horizon, sending a sweeping blanket of darkness over the land. The streets of Newhaven began to glow softly as the greatward began to Draw upon the power venting from the Core. It was easy enough to see in town, but the gloom crept right up to the border.

'The corespawn could be rising right in front of us and we'd never know,' Gamon said.

Gared shook his head. 'They ent. Leesha warded up my helmet special to see in the dark. Can't make heads or hinds of most of what I see, but demons glow like torches. They were there, I'd see 'em.' Rojer nodded, his new mask telling him much the same.

'Takes getting used to,' Renna said, 'but you're right. Ent no demons close by.'

'Maybe they ent comin' this month,' Evin ventured, but just then Shadow let out a low growl, and Arlen could see the fear creep into the auras of his companions. All save Renna, whose aura became eager – hungry.

'They're out there,' she said, 'but not close. Can smell 'em.'

'They are weakest during the rising,' Captain Gamon said. 'It makes sense for them to rise out of range of our bows.'

Arlen nodded, though it gave him no comfort. He took a deep breath, Drawing a touch of magic from beyond his field of vision, tasting it. There were indeed demons massing in the distance. More than he had ever sensed in one place, but still less than expected.

A moment later the sounds of splintered trees and torn soil began to sound for all to hear. 'They're coming!' someone shouted. The Haveners grew fearful, gripping their weapons and peering vainly into the darkness. Some lost their nerve entirely, fleeing for their homes and locking the doors . . . for all the good it would do.

'Deserting traitors!' Gamon growled. 'I should . . .'

'You should close your mouth and keep your eyes in front,' Arlen said. 'Fighting's your job. These are just scared folk. Won't help anyone to turn on our own with demons at the wards.'

The captain managed to keep his outward composure, but his aura showed outrage at being scolded by a commoner he – and many of the count's most trusted advisors – believed was a threat to his master's rule. Arlen had no desire to stoke that fire, but needed to make sure Gamon – and his men – knew their place. The captain's aura said he would do his duty and obey. For now, that was enough.

'Should we send out the signal?' the captain asked.

Arlen shook his head. 'Not yet. Could be a trick.'

The cacophony grew louder, becoming an ever-present background roar, much like the inside of a noisy tavern. It went on for some time, but still no demons approached. Rojer, Gared, and Renna leaned forward, straining their wardsight, but even Arlen could see no sign of their glow.

Are they using magic to mask their approach?

'Wish they'd just attack and have done.' The sound had grown so loud Rojer had to shout to be heard.

'Just trying to rattle us,' Gared said.

'It's working,' Rojer said.

'Keep calm.' Arlen drew a ward so the words were clear without being shouted. The others relaxed slightly at his tone. He wished it was as simple to ease the writhing in his own gut.

His nostrils flared, catching an acrid scent. Moments later, smoke began to drift from the woods, choking the defenders and fogging their vision as it reflected a growing orange light from within the trees. Even Arlen's wardsight became muddled and blurry.

'Tryin' to smoke us out?' Gared coughed.

'More likely cover for an attack,' Gamon said.

Arlen said nothing as he Drew again, sensing a small number of flame demons approaching through the smoke, gleefully setting everything in their path alight.

Normally, wood demons would keep the flame demons in check, killing any that entered the forest. Under the influence of a mind, though, wood drones would instantly yield their territory, leaving the flame demons to create a blaze that could kill half the Hollow without the demons having to lift a talon.

Firespit could not penetrate the greatward, and there were firebreaks along the border against the non-magical fires it kindled in the heavily wooded area, but no warding could protect the Haveners from choking to death on the smoke.

'Gared's right.' Arlen searched the sky, but there were no other signs of smoke. 'They're doing it here, because the wind's right.

'Ready bows!' Arlen cried. The Haveners quickly complied. After living off the land for so long, most of the Hollowers could shoot, and many were skilled hunters. So many, in fact, that there hadn't been enough warded arrows to go around. The smiths used moulds now, but could still only make them so quickly. In the end, each archer had been given a mere three warded arrowheads. Some had copied the symbols onto the heads of the rest of the arrows in their quivers, but the Hollowers' warding skills varied widely. Arlen expected less than half of them would even work, and those that did at less than half strength.

Every shot had to count.

Yon, Evin, and the Wooden Soldiers dismounted, stringing their bows as well. They carried full warded quivers, with more arrows on their mounts. All were expert shots, but even their skill was useless in the smoke and darkness.

Arlen sketched wards of sound, making his voice carry all along the border. 'Asking folk to trust me. Need to kill the flame demons out there before they choke us to death.'

He paused. 'And that means stepping off the greatward and into the smoke. Everyone make sure your mind wards are in place, and your best arrows nocked.'

'No ripping way!' one man cried. Most of the Haveners echoed his sentiment. Their collective aura flared with fear.

Surprisingly, it was Gared who stepped in. 'Din't have no greatward in the Battle of Cutter's Hollow!' the giant Cutter boomed. 'We start hidin' behind them now, Hollow's already lost. You want to fight for your homes, it means steppin' out into the naked night! Otherwise, go hide in yur beds and wait to get et!'

Arlen smiled as the fear in the crowd's aura began a shift to determination. He looked to Gared, filled with fanatical trust in Arlen. 'Thank you, General. Couldn't have said it better myself.' Gared's aura . . . blushed.

'Need you to lead them out, Gar,' he said. 'I've a card up my sleeve, but ironically, I need to be standing on the greatward to play it.'

'I-what-ically?' Gared asked. Then he shook his head, the confusion in his aura vanishing. 'Dun't matter. You say march into the Core, I'll do it double-time.'

He clapped a hand on Gared's shoulder. 'The flame demons are still a ways off in the woods. Need to get in close and take them by surprise. Ent got time nor arrows to waste.'

Gared coughed. 'Bows ent gonna be much good in all that smoke. How are we supposed to see what we're shootin'?'

Arlen slipped down from his own saddle, feeling the thrum of the greatward beneath his bare feet. 'When you're in place I'll show you your targets. Make sure no one fires till I give the word.'

Gared nodded, leading the rest of the scouts and the best archers of Newhaven out into the gloom. They hadn't gone far before, one by one, they vanished into the smoke.

Arlen breathed deeply and Drew more power than he had ever dared, pulling on the Hollow's entire wardnet. He felt his insides burning with the power, and knew he could not contain it long without being consumed.

'Brace yourselves,' he told the Hollowers, his voice carrying to every ear. Then he lifted two fingers and wrote wards of heat and air, giving shape to the energy as he released it. A huge blast of wind sprang forth, sweeping the smoke away and huffing out the flames like born-day candles.

He felt dizzy as the magic swept through his body and left, but there was no time to waste. He Drew on the greatward again, this time drawing wards to cast brilliant white light into the air, momentarily turning night into day. There, revealed in the light, were the flame demons, eyes and mouths glowing as they stood frozen, frightened by the sudden glare.

This time when the magic left him, Arlen staggered. Renna was there in an instant, grabbing one of his arms. A moment later Rojer caught the other.

Arlen let them steady him, Drawing a touch more power to send his voice carrying to the archers.

'Fire.'

23

Trap

333 AR Autumn
First Night of New Moon

Rojer heard the collective hum of bowstrings and the cries of the flame demons as the Hollowers exterminated them.

Rojer was still getting used to the wardsight his mask imparted, but a moment earlier he had seen Arlen glowing as bright as the sun. Now he was dim. Dimmer even than normal folk.

'Back to the greatward,' Arlen commanded after a moment. 'Now.' The light he conjured began to fail, and he slumped further, suddenly putting his full weight on Renna and Rojer. Rojer stumbled, but Renna tugged them both back upright as effortlessly as she might a small child. Quick as a cat, Rojer had his feet back under him.

He glanced up and saw the first of the Haveners returning, a triumphant look on their faces.

'Pull yourself together,' he said through his teeth. 'I don't know what that did to you, but these people need to see you on your feet.'

'Don't you tell him . . .!' Renna began, but Arlen cut her off.

'No, he's right,' Arlen said. 'I just need a moment to . . .' The luminescent mist at his feet began to rush into him, restoring his glow. He stood again, pulling free of their support. 'There.'

The Haveners took their positions around the border once more, and Gared and the rest of the scouting party returned to where Arlen, Renna, and Rojer stood, oblivious to his moment of weakness. In the distance, the crashing sound of falling trees and ground-shaking rumble of torn stone continued unabated.

'What in the Core are they doing?' Gared shouted above the din.

'It's a trap,' Rojer said. 'Trying to lure us out farther.'

Arlen shook his head. 'Why make so much noise if it's a trap? They're doing something. Bet my stones on it.'

'What do we do?' Gared asked.

'*We* aren't going to do anything,' Arlen said. '*I* am going out to have a look.'

Renna shook her head. '*We* are going for a look.'

Arlen looked at her, and she shot him a hard glare in return. 'Arlen Bales, don't you think for one second I'm letting you go out there alone.'

'Sure as spit ent asking anyone else to,' Arlen said. 'Drones can't hurt me, Ren. I'll be fine.'

'That mimic demon hurt you,' Renna said. 'And the mind did worse.'

'Ay, but now I know how to hurt 'em right back,' Arlen said.

'You hurt *one* of them,' Renna reminded him, 'and only after I snuck up in your warded cloak and stabbed it in the back. Who knows how many are out there tonight?'

'Maybe it's not a trap for us,' Rojer said. 'I think maybe it's a trap for you.'

Arlen looked at him blankly.

'He's right,' Renna said. 'Second you step off the greatward, you'll stand out like a lantern in the dark. They'll be on you in an instant.'

Rojer bit his lip. *Don't say it, don't say it, don't say it.*

'I'll go,' he said, and cursed himself. Everyone looked at him in surprise, and Rojer couldn't blame them. He was not known for his bravery, but there was no other way. He was proud of the power he had brought back to the world with the *Song of Waning*, but after seeing what Arlen had just done, there was no doubt which of them was more expendable.

Arlen shook his head. 'Don't know your power will even work on a mind demon. Can get a cat to chase a bit of reflected light all afternoon, and drones ent much smarter, but you don't try that trick on people.'

Rojer shrugged. 'Even people can be blinded when you shine a light in their eyes. And didn't I just hear Renna say Leesha's cloak fooled it?' He grabbed the hem of his warded motley cloak, turning a spin to let it spread out.

'Rojer, I can't let you—' Arlen began.

'No, I can't let *you*,' Rojer said. 'I may not be able to put out forest fires with a wave of my hand, but I can do this.'

'*We* can do this,' Gared said, coming over to stand beside him. 'Goin' with you. Cloak Darsy made me ent as fine as yurs, but it ent ever failed me.'

'That's because you rarely ever use it.' Rojer shook his head. 'Your place is with your troops, *General*.'

Gared spat at his feet. 'You may be a right little prick some-times, Rojer, but I'll be corespawned before I let you go out there alone.'

Rojer felt his throat tighten, but swallowed the feeling behind his Jongleur's mask. He wanted to argue further, but in truth he felt safer with Gared than he'd ever admit.

'Coming too,' Renna said, pulling her own Cloak of Unsight from the bag slung over Promise's harness and throwing it around her shoulders.

'Ren.' Arlen's voice was pleading as he caught her arm.

She turned and locked stares with him. 'Said it yourself. You can't fret the small stuff. You've got mind demons to hunt, and I need to protect folk when you can't.'

He stared at her, and she put a gentle hand on his cheek. 'I'll be careful, and bring them back alive.' At last he nodded, then swept her into a hug, kissing her deeply.

'Ay!' Gared said. 'Spare us the newlywed display!'

Leesha eyed Amanvah as she and Sikvah lounged on a silk couch in Thamos' tent, their silent guardian standing over them protectively.

The count had erected the pavilion at the edge of the Corelings' Graveyard to wait for reports and direct his forces. As usual, he had furnished the tent with all the trappings of his royal station and wealth. Inside, the walls hung with lavish tapestries, and the rugs were thick fur, soft as a kitten. The furniture was heavy polished wood, ornate, with gold inlays and filigree. And, of course, he had brought a throne.

But with those trappings of royalty came the responsibilities of etiquette. Amanvah and Sikvah might be enemies, but they were princesses in their own right, blood of the Krasian leader. Their station demanded nothing less than proper royal treatment, including access to Thamos' tent and his every courtesy. The boy set to serve them was of noble birth, and he scurried to and fro in terror as Sikvah snapped orders at him and cursed his slowness. Amanvah knelt silently beside her, head cocked to one side.

Listening to Rojer.

The thought galled Leesha. Amanvah had tried to murder her, yet still Rojer trusted her with everything that was happening, while Leesha and Thamos were left in the dark. Wives or no, Leesha had been with him every day for almost two years. How could he trust them more than her?

I should have warded Gared's helmet the same way and not told him, she thought, and immediately felt a pang of guilt. What right did she have to invade even Gared's privacy that way?

No. She shook her head. *That's the* dama'ting *way. I'd sooner become Elona than take up their methods.*

But Creator, how she wished she could hear what was happening!

Suddenly Amanvah hissed and began speaking quickly in Krasian, many of the words curses. She spoke far too quickly for Leesha to follow, but the anger in her tone was clear, with no *dama'ting* artifice. Sikvah looked at her in shock as Amanvah got to her feet, pacing back and forth as the string of epithets continued.

Leesha could bear it no longer. 'What is it? What's happened?'

Amanvah looked at her for a moment, considering her words. 'My honoured husband is brave, but a fool.'

'We all have a little of each in us, at times,' Leesha said.

Amanvah nodded, drawing a steadying breath as her *dama'ting* calm returned. 'It is *inevera.*'

'Is he all right?' Leesha said.

Amanvah whisked a hand. 'For now. He has volunteered to go into the night.'

'Why?' Leesha asked. That didn't sound like the Rojer she knew.

'They apparently believe the demons will sense the Par'chin's power if he leaves the greatward,' Amanvah said. 'And so the Par'chin has sent my honoured husband, the oaf Gared, and his own *Jiwah Ka* out into the night to do his scouting.' One of Amanvah's eyebrows curled, but with her veil in place Leesha could not tell what the gesture signified. 'His very name means bravery, but he commands others to leave the greatward when he fears to do so himself. He is a coward after all.'

'And what does that make me, waiting here in the centre?' Thamos demanded. All eyes turned to the count, and Leesha could see the tension in his face. Leesha remembered how he had been abed that first night, and the tales Darsy had told of the count's fear of demons, and how his need to conquer that fear led to erratic acts of bravery. He was terrified of being labelled a coward and losing the respect of his people. 'A leader must be free to direct his forces.'

Amanvah snorted, sparing him a dismissive glance. 'My holy father does not sit on his throne after the sun sets, and he is the greatest leader the world has ever seen. You are *chin*, and your cowardice is expected, but the Par'chin was said to be different.'

Thamos looked enraged, what little temper was left to him quickly evaporating. In a moment, he would begin shouting, and it would go poorly for everyone.

Leesha stepped between them, locking stares with Amanvah. 'With respect, Amanvah, I have seen your honoured father send men, even his own sons, far into the night to do his scouting. I know you worry for your husband, but Rojer has gone into the night hundreds of times. He'll be all right.'

'How can you claim to know what even the dice will not say?' Amanvah asked.

'I can't,' Leesha admitted. 'But I have faith.'

Amanvah blinked, then nodded. 'It is *inevera*.' She breathed to calm herself, moving back to her corner of the tent and kneeling once again in meditation as she listened.

Rojer held his fiddle and bow in his good left hand as they stepped out into the naked night, trusting in the cloaks to protect them. His right hand he kept free. Even with just three fingers, he could flick a warded knife into it and throw in seconds.

'I'll lead,' Renna said. 'Used to seeing in the dark.' Neither Rojer nor Gared cared to argue. He was still adjusting to the mask Amanvah had given him. He could see well enough that he wasn't apt to run into anything or miss a passing demon, but the swirls of coloured magic clinging to everything were distracting and confusing, making him feel as unsure as if in a thick morning fog.

As Renna moved ahead, right at the edge of their wardsight, Rojer turned to Gared. 'You're right I took you for granted. For what it's worth, I'm sorry. Sometimes I get so caught up in my own drama I forget I'm not the only one in the play.'

Gared grunted. 'It's a fallen tree. No point climbing it.'

Rojer turned to face him. 'I know, I just—'

'We're out in the naked night, Rojer,' Gared cut in, 'and I feel like I'm caught inside a ripping rainbow cloud. Ent mad at you any more. Now eyes in front.'

Rojer nodded, turning his gaze this way and that, but as he did, something unclenched inside him. *One less thing to fret over. Now all I need to worry about is being eaten by demons.*

The walk was agonizingly slow. Leesha's Cloaks of Unsight had never failed, but needed to be wrapped close around the wearer, and they could not move too quickly. Rojer and Renna were more practised, setting the pace for Gared.

Just beyond the tree line they began to see signs of the flame demons' play: blackened trunks and scorched ground that had once been the fertile forest bed. Their boots and the hems of their cloaks became black with ash.

Ahead, the sounds of ongoing destruction were like nothing Rojer had ever heard. Instinct screamed at him to turn and run in the other direction, but he steeled himself and kept putting one foot in front of the other as they picked their way through the trees.

They did not have to go far. The woods ended abruptly, violently, in a place of utter devastation. All the thundersticks Leesha had ever made could not have done a fraction of the damage. The ground was blackened and blasted, with great piles of loose soil next to huge gaping holes where whole trees and heavy stones had been torn free.

There was something repellent about the place. A wrongness Rojer could sense in every fibre of his body. They did not belong here.

Field demons, sleek and low to the ground, prowled the area, climbing atop the piles and sniffing the air. Above, wind demons circled.

Renna drifted back to them. 'Too many places for demons to hide. We stay close from here on.'

Rojer and Gared nodded, the three of them moving deeper into the destruction. Huge piles of stones stood twenty feet high, as did stacks of trees. Rojer looked at one of the stone piles, then back the way they had come. 'How far do you think a rock demon could throw one of those?'

Gared considered the pile, then he, too, glanced back. 'A big one? Too far for my liking.'

'They're stockpiling,' Rojer said. 'We should go back and—'

'Not yet,' Renna interrupted. 'If that's all they're doing, where are all the rock and wood demons?'

Rojer swallowed the lump in his throat, knowing she was right. They kept on, skirting around the piles of wood and rock that might soon be hurtling at Newhaven. At last, they peeked around a giant mound of dirt and saw the demons at work.

The land had been cleared, and huge trenches were being dug by wood and rock demons, as well as some other breeds Rojer could not recognize. The trenches were twenty feet wide and over ten deep, but the demons swept the dirt away with their great claws as if it were nothing more than dry leaves. When they came to a large stone, it was torn free of the ground and carried to one of the many piles.

'What are they doing?' Gared asked, looking at the seemingly random series of trenches. 'Building a defensive perimeter? That don't sound like demons.'

'These are smart demons,' Renna reminded him. 'There's a mind, or more than one, nearby directing them.'

'Still don't make sense,' Gared said. 'Demons flee with the sun. What's the point of taking and holding ground?'

Rojer looked, his eyes running over the precise shapes forming in the ground, and felt his face go cold, suddenly putting a name to the feeling of repulsion he had been feeling steadily increase as they approached.

'They're building a greatward.'

Gared and Renna both snapped their gazes at him, and Rojer felt a sudden pressure in his bladder. *Creator, I'm about to piss myself.*

Wordlessly, he ran back around the great pile of dirt, throwing open his cloak and yanking the drawstrings of his motley trousers. He barely had his member in hand before the stream came pouring out.

'Ahhh,' he gasped, but his relief was short-lived as a low growl sounded a few feet away. Rojer looked up and saw a field demon tamping its feet to spring.

He fell back with a cry as it launched itself at him, getting tangled in his still-undone trousers and landing heavily on his back. He fumbled, trying to free a knife, but could not flick his arm properly from the prone position.

But then Gared was there, roaring as he swung his heavy axe with two hands. Warded by Arlen himself, the blade split the demon's head from the tip of its snout to the base of its neck, covering Rojer in a spray of ichor.

The demon still kicked as Gared bore it to the ground, tearing at his cloak in its death throes. Rojer was up in an instant, retying his trousers and readying his fiddle and bow just as a reap of field demons appeared, surrounding them. Renna had her long, sharp knife in hand and was growling like a demon herself. She looked hungry for the fight, though they had little hope against so many.

This one's nuttier than Arlen, Rojer thought, *and that's saying something.*

'No one move,' he said, putting bow to string. He played a few sharp notes to surprise the demons and drive them back, then wove in a melody to mesmerize them before he caused the distraction that would allow them to disappear.

But the demons were not mesmerized. They had leapt back

from his first shrieking notes, but it didn't last. One darted in to snap at Renna, but a quick slash of her knife drove it back. They began to circle hungrily, growling and clawing at the soil, searching for an opening.

Uh-oh, Rojer thought.

'We can't stay here,' Renna said. 'If they're under the control of a mind, half the Core will be on us in a minute.'

Rojer glanced at Gared's torn cloak, and his own, covered in coreling ichor. There was no escape there, and fighting was madness. He gritted his teeth and deepened the melody, adding layer after layer of complexity. There was a telltale drooping in the demons' eyelids, but still they circled.

'I need a distraction,' Rojer said. 'Renna, your cloak is intact. Can you draw them off for a moment?'

'Ay,' Renna said, 'but they won't all follow me.'

'I can make them,' Rojer said.

'Spit on that plan,' Gared said. 'I ent running and letting you . . .' But before he could finish the sentence, Renna leapt at the ring, tackling one of the field demons and stabbing it repeatedly as they rolled across the ground. She sprang to her feet unharmed, while the demon laboured for breath on the ground. Already it was healing.

'Run!' Rojer called to her, and she did, dashing barefoot to one of the piles of rocks, leaping nimbly from stone to stone until she made the top.

Rojer changed his music accordingly. *She's getting away*, it said, *chase her! There are plenty to take the others!*

With that command, the demons all leapt after Renna, claws scrabbling on the hard stone as they climbed after her. A few paused, looking back with something that went beyond their normal instinct, but the distraction had done its job as Rojer herded Gared to another spot and laid down layer after layer of confusion. He brought more and more of the enchanted fiddle to bear, increasing the volume until the music thrummed in the air, making himself and Gared impossible to pinpoint.

Renna waited atop the pile of stones as long as she could, delivering warded kicks that sent demons flying off the pile with explosions of magic. They landed hard, but quickly rolled back to their feet, shaking off the blows and attempting to regain their wits.

When she saw them safe, Renna crouched and sprang, leaping an amazing thirty feet to land atop one of the massive dirt mounds the rock demons had created with their digging. She sank slightly into the loose soil on impact, but seemed none the worse for wear.

But before she could cloak herself once more, a wind demon gave a shriek, plummeting out of the sky at her. Renna turned to face it, tensed and ready, but the demon did something Rojer had never seen. It threw open its wings against the dive, pulling up short, and spat a bolt of lightning at her.

The night lit up with the blinding flash. Rojer snapped his eyes shut, but not fast enough to prevent himself from being dizzied. He struggled to keep playing as bright flashes of colour danced across the inside of his eyelids. When he opened them again, he saw Renna lying on the ground, having fallen more than a dozen feet. There was smoke drifting from her, and the air smelled of burned flesh and ozone. Amazingly, she was struggling to her feet, growing steadier as she did. Her glow was still bright to his warded eyes, and he imagined she was healing in the same way demons had.

Got to learn that trick, he thought.

Two field demons pounced on Renna before she could recover fully. Gared gave a roar, charging to her aid. Once he was more than a few feet from Rojer and his fiddle, the demons took note of him, but not in time to avoid his first deadly swings. Axe in one hand and machete in the other, he batted the demons away from the fallen woman, leaving deep gashes in their scaled flesh. He was standing protectively over her in an instant, carving out room for her to get her feet under her.

Already the demons Gared had struck were back on their

feet, healing quickly, much as Renna had. More came running, but these kept safely out of the range of Gared and Renna's weapons. More and more field demons arrived, the reap encircling the two. Soon the entire area swarmed with them, a mass of writhing, scaled flesh, glowing bright with magic.

But even with these overwhelming odds, the demons did not attack. They kept in constant motion, forcing Gared and Renna to stand back-to-back, weapons at the ready, waiting for an assault that never came.

Trapped.

But trapped for what? Rojer looked around. Winged demons circled overhead, but did not seem inclined to dive. The rock and wood demons continued to dig, oblivious.

Something worse is coming. Rojer had all too good an idea what that might be.

He considered. Even with the *hora* magic amplifying his music, he was not sure he could drive off so many demons, but even if he could manage it despite their increased resistance tonight, the fleeing corelings would trample right over his friends in the process.

He took a deep, calming breath, thankful he had ordered his wives to stay behind.

'Amanvah,' he said into the chinrest of his fiddle. 'I know I haven't been the best husband, but never once have I regretted taking you and Sikvah to wife. You have honoured me as wives should, and helped show me my own worth. If I don't make it back, remember me when you sing.'

She could not reply, but perhaps that was just as well. Rojer dropped the melody that made him invisible and began a new one, his enchanted fiddle carrying the tune to every coreling ear.

Here I am, the music told them. *Weak and defenceless. And you are so very, very hungry.*

For a moment, nothing happened; then suddenly every coreling face snapped his way. Hundreds of black eyes fixed on him.

Whatever influence the mind demon had over the drones, they could not deny their nature. They shrieked and leapt his way, long claws extended and teeth snapping the air.

Rojer turned and ran, faster than he ever had in his life. All the while he kept playing, calling the demons after him.

Arlen stood still as stone, watching the woods. He tried to Draw, but the ambient magic was faint, and the current flowed away from him, pulled by some unseen force. His Knowings yielded nothing.

They seemed to have been gone an eternity, but in truth he knew it was only minutes. His sharp ears caught the roaring of demons over the background noise and he tensed, but the sound was followed quickly by Rojer's music. He waited.

Long as that music's playing, they're safe, he thought. *But if it stops . . .*

There was a great flash in the cloudless sky. Arlen knew the signature of a lightning demon when he saw it. Even in the places they ranged most people thought the rare demons just a tampweed tale, and Arlen had never seen one in Angiers. Local Warders didn't even bother including lightning wards in their circles.

The minds can summon any breed, he realized, and felt their chances of survival dip still further. How would the Cutters fare against the blunt, butting heads of clay demons, or the coldspit of snow demons that could shatter steel? The acid muck of swamp demons? Those whose shields and armour Arlen or Leesha had warded personally would have some protection, but he knew all too well how poorly common warded armour withstood the talons and spit of those rare breeds.

But Gared and Renna had the right wards, and Rojer was still playing . . .

In fact, the music was getting louder, the sound rapidly

approaching, accompanied by the roaring of what seemed a thousand corelings. He saw Rojer appear from the woods, running as fast as his legs could carry him. His aura was one of pure terror, held in tight check by the rhythm of his playing. An instant later Arlen saw why as a seemingly endless stream of field demons raced out of the trees after him.

They put on speed when they reached open ground, but Rojer stopped short before they could overtake him, changing his tune to the harsh, jarring sounds Arlen had heard him use so many times before. Amplified by the fiddle's magic, the sound struck the reap like a physical blow, scattering the demons in a wave around him.

Arlen dematerialized, and for the split second he was in the between-state, he felt the thrumming of mind demons' power in the air, and knew Renna had been right. He might meet the will of one of them in that state, but two or more could well prove his undoing.

But there was no time for the coreling princes to attack him as he re-formed an instant later at Rojer's side and the mind wards around his shaved head reactivated. Arlen picked up the Jongleur like a toddler and leapt, clearing the distance back to the greatward in two great bounds.

'Where are the others?' he demanded, but before Rojer could answer, there was a cry, and Arlen looked up to see Renna, covered in demon ichor and glowing bright with magic, leaping through the swarm of field demons, Gared Cutter slung over her shoulder like a sack of flour.

Renna landed on a field demon's back with a flash of magic, and when she leapt away, the demon did not rise again. Arlen rushed out again, drawing field wards in the air as he cleared a path for them. After a moment they crossed, Renna leaping onto the open way as Arlen got behind her to cover their retreat. He caught the nearest field demon by its hind leg and used it as a club to bash away its fellows. The demon's flailing claws cut into their scales like no mortal weapon could.

The smell of ichor was thick in the air, and Arlen had to suppress a wave of hunger such as he had not felt in years. He wanted to bite down on the demon sizzling in his warded grasp, tearing through its armour to taste the soft meat beneath.

He shook his head violently, resisting the base instinct long enough to hurl the demon into the reap and run back to the greatward where Renna was gently laying Gared on the ground. The giant Cutter's aura was flat. He was alive but unconscious.

'What happened?' Arlen asked.

'Just a knock to the head,' Renna said, easing Gared's helmet off. 'He saved my life.'

'Or delayed you dying,' Rojer said. Arlen turned to him and saw the Jongleur's mask had slipped, the terror that still coloured his aura evident in his expression. 'The demons are building a greatward of their own.'

So that was why the ambient magic had been drawn away. 'Corespawn me for a fool!' Arlen shouted. He let his atoms slide apart and leapt skyward, floating at the upper edge of the greatward's protection as he looked out over the land. As Rojer had said, there, barely a mile away, glowed a greatward unlike any symbol Arlen had ever seen. It wasn't anywhere near the size of one of the Hollow's greatwards, but already the demon ward was active.

Out of the corner of his eye, Arlen saw something more and turned, his horror growing. Flickering lines of connection were forming as the demon greatward linked to another off to the southeast, near New Rizon. He turned a full circle and saw demons digging a third, off to the southwest by the fledgling borough of Lakdale. This demon ward was incomplete, but already it was beginning to Draw. It would link with the others in only minutes.

Even Arlen's new senses could not pierce the veil of the demon wards – magic flowed in, but not back out. And yet he could feel the three coreling princes, perched like spiders at the centre of a web. And all the while, the rock and wood demons continued to dig, strengthening the wards and making them increasingly permanent.

Arlen dropped back down, landing easily beside Renna and Rojer. 'Not just one. There's three of the ripping things, each with a mind at its centre.'

'Creator,' Rojer muttered.

'Need to tell the count,' Arlen said.

Renna nodded. 'I'll get the horses.'

Arlen shook his head. 'Too slow.'

Renna looked at him, worry on her face. 'Floating and healing the sick is bad enough. You do this . . .'

'Can't be helped, Ren,' Arlen said. 'The rest of you ride hard back to the graveyard. Maybe we'll have something resembling a plan by then.' With that, he dissipated.

Immediately Arlen felt the pull of the greatward. Like blood pumping through a heart, all the power of the wardnet flowed to and from the keyward of Cutter's Hollow. Instead of drawing on that power, he allowed himself to fall into its stream, instantly materializing at the centre of the Corelings' Graveyard.

It happened in the blink of an eye, easy for anyone to miss, but with the crowds gathered in the graveyard, there were still many who saw, and Arlen could hear their shouts of surprise flowing through the rest of the assembly.

Thamos paced the tent like a caged nightwolf. Every so often, his eyes flicked to the throne and his scowl deepened, looking like he might kick it over in a rage. If Amanvah and her entourage had not been present, he likely would have. The *dama'ting*'s harsh words had cut him deeply. She had retreated to her couch and been silent since, but the damage was done.

Leesha laid a hand on the count's arm, feeling the tension he was holding even through his armour. He turned to her and she reached out, tracing the line of fresh enamel on his breastplate where it had been repaired. 'No one in the Hollow thinks you a coward,' she said, her voice too low for the others to hear. 'The scars on your armour tell how you have stood between them and the naked night. I don't like waiting here any more than you do, but there will be work for us both soon enough.'

Thamos nodded. 'It is just those women. They are . . .'

'Simply impossible, I know,' Leesha said. 'But they were right about one thing.'

'Eh?' Thamos asked.

'The throne was too much to bring,' Leesha said. 'It says you think you're better than folk, but that's not the man they need.'

'Is that why they so love your Painted Man?' Thamos asked, a trace of bitterness in his voice.

Leesha smiled. 'That, and he can kick a hole through a rock demon.'

Thamos laughed. 'Ay, I should learn that trick.'

For a moment, there was warmth between them, but then Amanvah spoke again, and Leesha's blood ran cold.

'The *alagai* are building a greatward of their own.'

'Night, are you certain?' Leesha asked.

Thamos strode over to the table with his great map of the Hollow. 'What kind of ward?' he demanded. 'How big? Where?'

Amanvah shrugged, her head cocked as she continued to listen. 'I only know what I've heard.' She paused. 'I am not certain my honoured husband and his companions can see any more from their vantage.'

Inquisitor Hayes drew a ward in the air, mouthing prayers. Part of Leesha wanted to join him, but she had learned long ago that the Creator did not intervene on His children's behalf. If they were to be saved, they would have to save themselves.

Amanvah gasped and gave a shriek. Everyone tensed, waiting for more news, but the *dama'ting* said nothing. There was real fear in her eyes, and Leesha was reminded again that for all her training, she was still little more than a girl. Sikvah, normally the more emotionally demonstrative of the two, was strangely calm. She laid a hand on her sister-wife's shoulder, offering silent strength.

After a few moments, Amanvah let out a breath. 'He was attacked, but he is playing now.' The pride was evident in her voice. 'Even on Waning, the *alagai* cannot resist my honoured husband so long as he plays.'

Sikvah nodded. 'Everam speaks to him.'

But then Amanvah fell to her knees. 'No,' she whispered. 'No, no, no. Please, husband, do not . . .'

She did not finish the sentence. Sikvah dropped to her knees behind her sister-wife, gentling her shoulders. Amanvah's face was blank and she said nothing, but Leesha could imagine what was going through her mind.

Leesha pulled at her skirts as she got to her knees in front of Amanvah. She reached out, taking Amanvah's soft hands in her own and squeezing, trying to lend strength as Sikvah did.

'Amanvah,' she said, not bothering to hide the desperation in her voice, 'please tell me what's happened. Is Rojer . . .?'

'Not yet,' Amanvah said. 'He is still playing, but he is no longer driving back the *alagai*. He is calling them to him, that his companions may live.'

There was a patter, and a spot appeared on the perfect white silk on her lap. Sikvah slipped a tiny bottle from somewhere in her black robes and reached out, catching Amanvah's tears as they fell. 'His honour knows no bounds, and Everam will seat him in His great hall on the sixth pillar of Heaven,' she said. Amanvah nodded, weeping all the harder.

This went on for several minutes, but then Amanvah's eyes lit up and she straightened. 'He fights again! All Nie's forces at his heel, and he stands to face them!'

Sikvah swiftly stoppered the now full bottle and produced another, ready to catch more tears if they fell. 'Can even he—'

'Of course he can!' Amanvah snapped, her strength returned.

'He is Rojer, son of Jessum, disciple of Arrick of the sweetest song and son-in-law to Shar'Dama Ka.' She paused, clenching a fist. 'But the *alagai* will be the least of his worries when I see him again.'

'Honest word,' Leesha agreed.

'The Par'chin is with him now,' Amanvah said a moment later. 'He is . . .' She furrowed her brow. 'The *alagai*, they . . .'

Just then there was a shout, and all eyes turned to see Arlen suddenly standing in the centre of the graveyard. Even Leesha, who understood something of Arlen's powers, gaped. He had been miles away in Newhaven just a moment before.

But there could be no doubt he was here now as his voice boomed like thunder. 'Mount and stand ready! We ride into the night in minutes!'

He turned, striding purposefully towards the count's tent, and the crowd parted around him, some whispering in awe, others shouting.

'He just appeared like a demon!' one woman cried.

Inquisitor Hayes blocked his path as Arlen reached the tent. 'How is this possible?' he demanded. 'The Canon states we must not take the corelings' methods as our . . .'

Arlen reached out, brushing the Inquisitor aside like a child, never slowing. 'Ent got time to argue scripture now, Tender.'

Hayes looked outraged, and Child Franq moved to block Arlen's path, but Thamos banged a gauntleted fist on the table. 'Holy Men out! See that our fighters have the Creator's blessing!' The Inquisitor and his entourage looked at him, but the count met their eyes with a hard look, and they moved quickly to comply.

'What's happened?' Thamos asked as Arlen came over to where he stood by the map. Arlen did not immediately answer, considering the map a moment before taking a brush and dipping it in the bowl of ink, expertly drawing thick wards over areas that had once been virgin woodland.

'The mind demons have built greatwards, here, here, and here,'

Arlen said, pointing to New Rizon, Newhaven, and Lakdale. 'Already they are activating.' He lightened pressure on the brush to draw the thinner lines of connection. When he was done, the great wardnet of Hollow County was a circle within the triangle of the mind demons' wards. 'The net will only get stronger as the rock demons continue to dig, cutting off the Hollow and draining power from our wardnet.'

The wards were elegant, and Leesha knew at a glance that they were powerful. There was a slight similarity in their shape to wards she had seen when Inevera trapped her in Jardir's palace.

'They're human wards,' she guessed. 'We will no more be able to set foot across their lines than they can ours.'

Thamos shook his head. 'That only creates an impasse. There must be more to their plan.'

Arlen nodded. 'They are stockpiling every boulder and tree trunk as they clear the wards. Soon the rock demons will begin throwing, and it won't be long before they destroy enough to break the circuit and short out our net.'

'Circuit?' Thamos asked.

'The link that joins our greatwards,' Leesha supplied. 'It needs to form a closed shape to operate at full power.'

Arlen nodded. 'They do that, we'll have demons in the streets of the outer boroughs, and the rock demons will be able to move in close enough to heave boulders anywhere in Hollow County.'

'Creator,' Thamos said. 'But if these demon wards repel us the way ours do them, how can we destroy them?'

'We can't,' Arlen said. 'Not tonight, or even during the daylight hours if we make it till tomorrow.'

'We could set fire to the woods.' Thamos' face was grim. He knew the cost, but he would do it if necessary.

This is why we keep the secrets of fire from men, she heard Bruna say. *They would curse the world and think they're saving it.*

Arlen shook his head. 'Wouldn't work. The wards are more

than just the shape of cleared-out trees, Highness. We're dealing with trenches dug by rock demons. Twenty feet wide and ten feet deep. Takes a lot to fill in a trench like that, even with thousands of strong backs and an endless supply of flamework, neither of which we'll have by morning.'

'We don't need to destroy the wards,' Amanvah said, coming over. 'Only mar them.'

Leesha looked at her, then nodded. 'The fangs.'

'Ay,' Arlen said.

'What are the fangs?' Thamos demanded. Leesha could hear the desperation in his voice. He wanted to take command as he would in any other instance, but he was out of his depth.

Leesha took a scrap of paper and the brush Arlen had used, quickly drawing a ward. She pointed to two small, curved teardrop shapes next to the main symbol. 'These are the fangs. Almost every ward has them hidden somewhere in its design. They are the place where the ward Draws magic – without them, it will quickly burn out.'

She looked at Arlen. 'You take your clothes with you.'

'Eh?' Arlen asked. Thamos turned to regard Leesha curiously as well.

'When you turn to mist and move as the corelings do,' Leesha said. 'You take your clothes with you. Can you take more?'

'Ay,' Arlen said, 'but nothing heavy, and nothing alive. Breaking things down is easy enough. Putting them back together properly is harder.'

'Can you carry a crate of thundersticks?' Leesha asked.

Arlen considered. 'For a short hop, perhaps, if I have time to study their pattern.' Arlen smiled, a faraway look in his eyes. 'Won't be easy, but easier than hauling one up a frozen mountain.'

Leesha cocked her head. 'What's that?'

Arlen waved the thought away. 'Long story.'

Leesha made a mental note to ask about it later and pressed on. 'Can you materialize out beyond the greatward?'

Arlen shrugged. 'Can, but it's easy to get lost. Simple to skate along the greatward because I know its every twist and turn. Out beyond, I'll need to go deeper into the Ala, and then find a path of magic leading back up to the surface closer to where I want to be. Might need to hop once or thrice to triangulate, but I know the woods well.'

'How is this possible?' Amanvah asked. 'Even my father does not have such powers.'

Arlen ignored her. 'If I knock out the fangs of the centre ward, their net will fail, but expect I'll only have a moment to do it before they sense me. Need a distraction.'

Thamos straightened at that. 'Then you shall have one.' He pointed to the greatward the minds were building near New Rizon. The second oldest of the Hollow's boroughs, it was also the most populous. 'New Rizon has the most open ground, where our horses and archers can inflict maximum damage. If we attack there . . .'

'You ent thinkin' straight,' Renna said as Arlen headed for the tent, well away from the troops and horses, where the crates of Leesha's thundersticks were stacked. The foot soldiers had already begun a march to the east while the horses were readied.

Behind them, Rojer's wives berated his recklessness, shifting back and forth between their heavily accented Thesan and rapid-fire Krasian. Arlen smiled. It was probably for the best Rojer could not understand most of what they were saying. The Jongleur wasn't known for his temper, but he could be as stubborn and cutting as any when his back was up.

'Straight or not, it's the only plan we've got, Ren,' Arlen said. 'Hollow will be destroyed, we don't get this done.' He drew a deep breath. 'Maybe even if we do. But I ent the type to lie down and wait for the end.'

Renna shook her head. 'Me either. Not any more, at least. But do you have to go alone?'

Arlen nodded. 'Need to be quick. All goes to plan, I should be gone and back in an instant. Time you hear the blast, I should be back on the greatward, covering your retreat.'

'Should,' Renna said, not sounding convinced. Her aura was petulant, but resolved.

'Don't like you fighting without me any better,' Arlen said. 'But you seen what the count is like in a fight. Reckless. Hollow needs him right now. Trustin' you to bring him back alive.'

Renna nodded. 'Will. Swear by the sun.'

Arlen saw magic respond to her natural strength, flowing into her and brightening her aura. She had never looked so beautiful. He took her in his arms, kissing her deeply. 'Love you, Renna Bales.'

Renna smiled, and even her beauty from a moment ago was eclipsed. 'Love you, Arlen Bales.'

She turned and went to join the others. A moment later, a horn sounded and they galloped off. Arlen concentrated, pulling magic through one of the crates, Knowing its contents down to the tiniest particle. The materials were surprisingly simple, and he was confident that when the time came he would be able to reassemble them.

He turned back, taking in the graveyard, now almost empty. Leesha had moved her Gatherers to form a temporary hospit in near the fighting, and Rojer's wives had gone with him to add their power to the attack.

They're all going to die, you don't time this right, his father's voice said in his head. *Should have kept 'em safe behind the wards.*

Arlen gritted his teeth. Would that voice ever go away? Even now, having seen his da stand and spear a demon before his very eyes, the voice of Jeph Bales continued to counsel cowardice as wisdom in his head.

But the voice was right that the timing would be key. Arlen

could sense the troops readying for their charge and knew he must wait long enough for them to draw the mind demons' attention, but not enough for them to get fully involved. From their greatward net, they could launch a devastating counter-offensive if they felt their loss of drones was becoming too costly.

Time to be seen, he thought, and dropped into the greatward, instantly materializing behind the mustered Cutters and Wooden Soldiers. He leapt into the air, continuing upward unaffected by gravity until he reached the desired height and stopped there, taking in Hollower and demon both. He cast bright light into the night sky, startling the demons and signalling the attack.

Thamos had insisted on leading the charge. His aura had said it had something to do with Rojer's wives, but the cause was irrelevant. No words would sway the count, so Arlen wasted none trying.

To one side of the count galloped Captain Gamon, and to the other, Gared Cutter. Gared had never been the most proficient rider, but he'd apparently taken training among the Krasians, and managed to keep his seat even as Rockslide trampled corelings, the magic in his hooves making him wild with power. Gared, too, was drinking in the magic, laying about him with his huge axe. With a single swing, he took the head from a field demon that would have taken the count's horse out from under him.

Slightly off to the side, Renna paced them easily on Promise. The horse would still not be saddled, but Renna had got the mare to consent to a few warded harnesses to let her keep her seat and add some protection to the wards painted on the horse's dappled coat.

The cavalry skewered or trampled dozens of field demons, killing few but leaving all dazed and unprepared for the foot soldiers who swept in behind, led by Dug and Merrem Butcher. The pair earned their name as they cut corelings apart with the same practised ease they sectioned a pig.

But then the lightning demons came down, strafing the

battlefield with uniform precision, and Arlen knew the nearby mind demon had taken control.

An instant later he was back in the graveyard, performing a second Knowing on the crate to hold in his mind as he carried it down into the greatward, then deeper still, into the crust of the Ala.

All around, paths opened to his senses. Many led to the surface, while others tempted to take him farther down towards the Core, where all the magic in the world flowed from.

He ignored them, focusing on those heading upward. None were truly straight, but some reached the surface quickly, while others drifted for miles before making their way to the open air. He tasted these, sensing where they led. It was easy in the between-state – sending tendrils of himself out to explore while he stayed in one place – but there were thousands of intersecting paths, a maze one could get lost in for a lifetime and more.

Despite the confusion, the demon wards were easy to find after a few moments of concentration. The keyword of their net drew power like a whirlpool, starting at the fangs. He let the current pull him along, and was surprised at its power. For a moment he feared being sucked into it fully, his entire being devoured by the demon warding's power. He gathered his will and pulled back just in time, finding the closest outlet to the surface and solidifying. Once on the surface he again felt the mind's presence for an instant, but then his protective wards re-formed and his mind was cut off. He hoped it was too brief for them to notice him in turn. He pulled his personal magic as deep within himself as possible, and drew wards of confusion in the air around him to mask his presence.

He approached the greatward, feeling its power of repulsion. His part-demon nature allowed him to get closer than a normal human might, but he was still kept a good twenty yards from its border. Within, he could see the rock and wood demons working tirelessly to deepen and strengthen the lines. Other corelings patrolled the area.

He placed the crate as close to the fangs as he could, then put a foot on it and shoved hard enough to carry it much of the remaining distance without detonating. He might have thrown it, but he was getting stronger all the time, and didn't trust his aim. If he overshot, or the crate fell into a trench and didn't detonate on impact, it would all be for nothing.

The crate skidded to a stop perhaps ten feet from the edge. *Close enough.* Arlen raised a hand to draw a heat ward.

But then there was a roar, and he turned to see dozens of field demons charging his way. Arlen frowned. Despite his efforts to mask his presence, he obviously could not evade detection fully this close to the demons' centre of power. The local mind might not have been able to pinpoint him, but it sensed enough to make it worth sending a reap to sweep the area. Whether they saw him or not, there was nowhere to hide on the open ground.

As the first talons reached him, Arlen dematerialized, meaning to let them pass, re-form, and set off the thundersticks before it was too late.

But in the instant he entered the between-state, the local mind was on him.

He felt the pressure of the demon's will, but Arlen had faced this struggle for dominance before. He gathered his will and struck back, only to run into an impenetrable wall.

The greatward.

Too late, Arlen realized his mistake. The ward was more than just a physical defence and a source of power. It also protected the coreling prince's mind from unwanted intrusion much as Arlen's own mind wards did for him.

He threw himself at the barrier again and again, suddenly understanding for the first time in his life precisely how One Arm and the other demons that had tried to claw through Arlen's Messenger circles over the years must have felt. Angry. Frustrated. Desperate.

Vulnerable.

In that moment of first despair, the demon struck back at him, reaching beyond the wards with no real exposure to himself, like Wonda Cutter standing at the edge of the greatward picking off corelings with her bow.

The coreling prince batted his defences aside effortlessly, seizing control of Arlen's mind and teaching him how arrogant he had been to think himself a fair match for one of these creatures.

Renna was right. He'd been lucky in the last contest, and even so the demon would have defeated him if not for her. For all he'd learned, he was still a novice at a form of combat the mind demons trained to all their lives.

Arlen pulled all his strength and will together, trying desperately to solidify. If he could do that, his mind wards would activate, and he would only have a few hundred corelings between him and the safety of the Hollow's wardnet.

Only.

But the mind demon kept his atoms dispersed. Arlen found a path to the Core and tried to flee out of range, but that, too, was in vain. The demon held him fast, forcibly draining the excess magic from him. Even as mist, Arlen discovered he could know pain, and if he'd had voice, he would have screamed as the power was sucked out of him.

He thought the demon meant to kill him then and there, but it relented just before the last of his energy was depleted, leaving him weak as if he had lost too much blood, helpless as he heard the demon in his mind.

A fool, to leave his centre of power and confront us, the coreling thought to the others of its kind.

He must have thought his drones would distract us in their futile assault, another replied.

Fool, the third agreed. Arlen could sense their mental presence drawing closer, adding their own power to the already overwhelming press of his original assailant.

Must get free. He struggled again. *Others don't stand a chance without me.*

626

He fears for his drones! The thought brought amusement from the three minds. *How did one such as this defeat one of our brethren?*

We shall soon Know. The thought was punctuated by a hunger greater than anything Arlen had ever felt. Knowledge and experience were power to these creatures, and all of them were eager for the feast as they laid open his mind, reading through his thoughts the way Arlen might thumb through a history book.

They walked through his memories, forcing him to relive every powerful experience and sipping his emotions in his moments of deepest pain, weakness and degradation, savouring them like fine Angierian brandy.

Suddenly he was ten years old again, lying on the ground with his arms covering his head as Cobie Fisher literally kicked the piss out of him. Cobie, Gart, and Willum Fisher had taken it in turns kicking him for talking to Willum's sister Aly, who was twelve. Arlen had secretly shined on her, thinking her kinder than the Fisher boys who regularly tormented him.

But Aly had proven him wrong that day, laughing right along with the others as Arlen gripped his piss-soaked overalls and ran off in tears.

The mind demons held on to that moment, vibrations of pleasure resonating in the air. *There is no sweeter taste than humiliation*, one thought.

I enjoy rage, another thought, as they watched Arlen take his violent revenge a few weeks later. *It is so . . . primitive.*

Arlen felt derision from the demon that held him. *Enraging a human is as easy as making a flame drone burn. It is their nature. A more refined taste is anguish.*

Suddenly Arlen was eleven, watching again as his father stood frozen behind the porch wards while his mother and Marea were torn to pieces. He tried to scream, but he had neither mouth nor lungs in the between-state.

He felt the demons feeding on his pain, but there was nothing he could do to stop their invasion of his memories.

Like children with a bag of honey nuts at the Jongleur's show, they forced him to relive the night Mery broke with him, riding his shoulders as he wandered the streets of Fort Miln alone at night, raindrops mixing with the tears on his face.

Instead of kicks, the demons tormented him with every secret shame of his life, every failure, every mistake or loss of control. Some were memories that had haunted him all his life, others all but forgotten until the corelings lifted them out of his mind to examine like trinkets in the bazaar.

He was back in Abban's guest pavilions, trying desperately to pull up his trousers after one of Abban's unwed daughters 'accidentally' walked in on him masturbating. She offered coyly to help, and Arlen did not know what terrified him more, giving his Krasian friend – who had likely orchestrated the event – an excuse to claim offence and force him to take her to wife, or the thought of her laughing at his lack of experience. His erection had vanished in an instant, but in some ways that only made things worse.

He is given a chance to mate and fails, a demon thought, and Arlen's shame doubled, feeding the demons further.

They continued to dissect his mind, reaching the point when he and Abban stole the map to the lost city of Anoch Sun from Sharik Hora. The mind demons drank deeply of his guilt over the theft, surprising even Arlen with its depth and intensity. He had rationalized the crime at the time, but it never sat well with him, especially because the crime had led to his finding the Spear of Kaji and starting the world down a road it might not be ready for.

Suddenly the coreling princes became deadly serious, delving deeper into his memories, sifting every sight and sound and smell as he examined the map and made his trek through the desert. When he opened the sarcophagus of Kaji, finding the spear, they hissed in his mind.

We must see the place razed, the local mind thought. *There may be other secrets locked there.*

Agreed, thought the others.

The more they chattered among themselves, seemingly oblivious – or uncaring – of the fact Arlen could hear them, the
more the demons became three distinct entities in his mind.
The one at the centre of the net who held him prone was older,
stronger, having earned his place in the keyward. The others
were not subordinates precisely, but they deferred like young
men to a greybeard.

Demon manners, Arlen thought, forgetting the pain for an
instant.

The local mind demon sensed his amusement and increased
the pressure again, jarring Arlen out of lucidity and back to
unembraceable agony as they clawed deeper into his mind,
consuming Jardir's betrayal in the Maze.

*If this one's memories are true, the unifier in the south may
not yet understand the full power of the artefacts*, the local
mind thought.

There was assent. *With the unifiers dead, the rest of the
stock can be contained. We can leave the cursed surface and
return to the mind court triumphant.*

Only to have the consort claim the victory as his own, the
eldest mind thought.

*We should kill this one as soon as we are done Knowing
him*, the youngest ventured, *before the consort can feed on his
memories*. Arlen could sense the treason in the thought, and
for a moment all were silent.

*With the Queen about to lay, we must offer the consort no
advantage*, the eldest agreed.

They resumed stripping his memories like tearing pages
from a book. There was understanding when Arlen relived
the night he tattooed himself, followed by shock and disbelief
when, a few weeks later, he began to eat the flesh of demons.

*He is unlike the other unifiers. He steals our power for his
own.*

By accident only, the eldest thought. *The secret will die with
him.*

They continued to stride through his mind, and again there was a vibration of amusement as they witnessed Arlen's time in the mud with Leesha. *Again this one fails at mating!*

There was less amusement as they watched the Battle of Cutter's Hollow, but neither was there great concern. The coreling princes were taking the humans' measure and finding them wanting.

But they hissed as they watched Arlen and Renna kill the mind that had come for them last new moon. He felt their rage, and – for just an instant – fear as they watched him scatter the defeated mind's essence by casting it off a path to the Core.

But the feeling was short-lived. The demons resumed their cold search, watching the events of the last few weeks.

The female knows the secret to power, the local mind thought. *She must be killed as well.*

Arlen, who had thought his own will broken, suddenly felt the strength to resist again. He struggled against the overwhelming press, not seeming to shift it at all, but it was enough for the mind demons to take note.

He cares about her. There was surprise and amusement at the thought.

His anguish upon her death will be exquisite.

A fitting punishment for the trouble he has caused among the stock.

They probed.

His thoughts say she is out in the night even now . . .

For a moment the pressure eased as their thoughts turned out through the senses of their drones, searching for a sign of a woman with warded flesh, glowing bright with stolen magic.

Renna! Arlen focused all his strength in that instant, not trying to break free, but only to solidify the barest fingertip. The mind that held him kept him from re-forming enough to render his painted wards, but he managed just enough to draw one in the air. He had only a slight spark of power to give, but a spark was all that was required as the crate of thundersticks detonated.

The night sky lit up in a flash of intense heat. Roaring filled the air and the ground shook as trenches collapsed onto the demons digging them. The wave of pressure splintered trees and crumpled field demons like wads of paper.

Trapped by the will of his captors, Arlen was caught in the blast, though it could not harm him in his ethereal state. He tried to ignore the distraction, waiting for what seemed an eternity, but a moment later the link among the demons shattered along with their wardnet.

In that instant of shock, Arlen broke free of the mind that held him and fled down the nearest path. He felt the pull of the Hollow's wardnet and in an eyeblink was there, Drawing magic like a drowning man breaking the surface would gasp air. Strength washed over him, driving away the pain and despair, but Arlen wasted no time enjoying it. Immediately he leapt skyward, seeking his former captor.

The mind demon, still reeling in shock from the loss of its greatward, was easily spotted by his power – a beacon in the night. His brothers had never left their own greatwards and remained safe, but deferential though they might have been to the elder mind when the odds were in their favour, Arlen knew the demons would not risk themselves to help him. Altruism was as alien a concept to them as love.

The elder mind demon's mimic, in the form of a gigantic field demon, was loping towards its master at incredible speed, but wasn't there to protect it yet. Arlen Drew hard on the Hollow wardnet, tracing heat and impact wards to send a huge blast of magic at the coreling prince. It had none of the subtlety of their assault upon him, but subtlety was not needed here.

The demon saw the attack coming and dematerialized with the speed of thought, but the magic travelled faster than thought and he was still mostly solid when the blast struck, killing both mimic and mind.

As before, the death scream of the mind demon sent psychic waves through the air more potent than any crate of thundersticks. Drones for more than a mile in every direction dropped dead from the shock of it, and even Arlen put his hands to his head to try to massage out the pain.

The other minds must have felt it, too, for the demons fighting the Hollowers, while not killed, fell into disarray. Arlen looked at his people and realized the price of his arrogance. In the minutes he had been trapped, the organized drones had taken a heavy toll.

Boulders and tree trunks lay scattered about the field amid the broken bodies of dozens of men and horses. There was no sign of Captain Gamon, and Thamos, his armour spattered with ichor, had lost his horse and was fighting spear and shield against a rock demon. Promise ran free, trampling field demons into the ground as Renna fought at his side.

Gared had kept his seat, but Rockslide now had Dug Butcher slung unconscious across his back as well. The Hollowers had killed their share, but the Core could spew an endless stream, whereas every human life was precious and irreplaceable if they hoped to win.

The sight of the dead and wounded filled Arlen with anger and he Drew again, ignoring the burning in his skin as he sent a blast of power into a knot of field demons, clearing a path back to safety.

'Retreat,' he called, sending his voice far and wide. 'Keep your heads, but move back to the greatward quick as you can. Work's done for now.'

Twice more he drew wards of heat and impact, incinerating groups of demons to help his people back to safety. He used the same wards Leesha used to pull moisture from the air to water her garden to drown a pack of flame demons that tried to give chase. They fell to the ground, steaming and writhing as they gurgled water, glowing eyes going dark.

When the Hollowers were safe, Arlen turned to the

stockpiles of boulders and trees the corelings had built, pulling more and more power as he began destroying them.

He Drew so hard, the entire wardnet began to flicker and dim. Arlen's throat and nose were on fire like he had eaten a handful of Krasian firepeppers. His muscles ached and his fingernails grew hot. His eyes were dry and stung when he blinked.

But there were stockpiles still, so he pulled yet more, until suddenly everything went black, and he felt himself falling.

Forgot to breathe again, he thought just before he hit the ground.

24

Attrition

333 AR Autumn
Second Night of New Moon

*L*eesha was in the temporary hospit in New Rizon when the flashes of light began. She was desperately trying to stitch a man's chest back together, but twice needed to stop work and lean over him, shielding the wound with her own body as explosions shook the building and dust clattered from the rafters. Outside, people were cheering and screaming in equal measure.

'What in the Core is going on out there?' she demanded.

'I'll find out, mistress.' Wonda grabbed her bow, glad to have something to do.

She returned a few minutes later. 'Mistress, you need to come quick.'

Leesha could not spare her even a glance, her fingers slick with blood as she tried to stem a bleeding artery. 'I'm a little busy at the moment, Wonda. What's happened?'

'You need to come now,' Wonda said. The urgency in her tone made Leesha glance up at last. Wonda's face was pale with fear. 'Deliverer's down.'

Everyone looked up at that. 'Impossible!' a woman shouted as others began to wail.

Leesha looked back at the open wound, her work far from

complete. 'I can't just . . .' she began, but then Amanvah laid a hand over hers.

'Go,' the *dama'ting* said. 'I will take care of this.'

Leesha looked at her. 'Are you—'

'I have been treating injured *Sharum* since I was seven years old, mistress,' Amanvah cut her off. 'Go.'

Leesha nodded, grabbing a cloth to wipe her hands before lifting her skirts to run after Wonda.

'Tell me what you know,' she said as they went.

'Folk say he appeared in the sky,' Wonda said, 'hurling fire and lightning like the Creator himself to cover the retreat. But then the greatward dimmed, and he fell.' She choked on the last words, and wiped at her face with an arm. Leesha had never seen the giant young woman cry, and the sight did more to bring home the severity of what had happened than anything she could have said. She picked up her pace, arriving breathless at the crowd that had gathered.

'Move aside for Mistress Leesha!' Wonda shouted, but she didn't wait for them to comply, grabbing people and shoving them aside to clear the path.

In the centre of the ring, Renna knelt by Arlen's twisted body, lying still on the cobbles. Blood was pooling around his head. Gared and several Cutters stood by keeping the onlookers back, and they quickly opened a way to admit Leesha.

'Don't you die on me, Arlen Bales!' Renna shouted at him, clutching one of his hands, but Arlen gave no response.

'He's alive,' Leesha said as she found his pulse, weak and erratic. His skull was bashed in where it had struck the cobbles, and Leesha could feel the fractures spiderwebbing out from the spot. Jagged bones jutted from his skin. He had a broken shoulder and collar, shattered ribs, pelvis . . .

But the bleeding had stopped. 'Night,' Leesha breathed. 'He's healing already.'

Renna looked at her. 'Ent that a good thing?'

'Not if he heals all twisted,' Leesha said. 'We need to get him on an operating table. Gared! Can you lift him? Carefully!'

Gared moved to comply, but Renna effortlessly shoved him aside, lifting Arlen as tenderly as a babe in swaddling. 'Everything's gonna be sunny,' she promised as tears streamed down her face.

For the next hour, Leesha, Darsy, and Renna pulled, twisted, and splinted Arlen back into his proper shape. Twice, Darsy had to rebreak bones that had healed incorrectly. Through it all, Arlen remained unconscious, which would have been for the best, if not for the head trauma.

Gared stuck his head in when the sun finally crested the sky. 'He gonna be all right?'

Leesha wiped the sweat from her brow and shrugged. 'We've done all we can. He's alive and healing fast, we'll just have to wait till he wakes up on his own.'

But who will we find when he does? she wondered silently. His skull had been cracked like an egg, and though the fractures had melted away before her eyes, there was no telling if the fall had done damage even magic could not heal.

A Gatherer needs to know how to deliver hard news, Bruna had taught, *but she also needs to know when.* Telling the others, even Renna, that Arlen might have permanent brain damage would set a panic through the Hollow that they couldn't afford.

Gared nodded and left. Thamos came in soon after. He was spattered with ichor, his thick hair matted with sweat and the enamel shattered in more than one part of his armour, but he seemed hale enough. Leesha felt a slight relief at that, holding on to that good news as she asked for the bad.

'How many dead?' she asked.

Thamos shook his head. 'Hundreds confirmed already, but there are over a thousand unaccounted for. We're only just starting to gather the remains of bodies left out in the night and take stock of those here in the hospit. I thought Captain Gamon dead until I saw him here in plaster.'

Leesha nodded. 'He was knocked from his seat, but his armour caught on the saddle, and his horse dragged him all the way back to the greatward. His hip is broken, and he has a concussion.'

'Will he walk again?' Thamos asked.

Leesha shrugged. 'If I have anything to say he will, but we haven't been doing our best work, Highness. Keeping folk alive has been the priority.' She made no mention of the demon bones she had depleted to save Gamon's life. She cared deeply for the count, and believed he had his people's best interests at heart, but the knowledge that she could heal with magic wasn't something she was ready to share just yet. Of those working in the makeshift hospit, only she and Amanvah knew the art. There wasn't nearly enough *hora* to save everyone, and she had no idea how some might take to the idea of being healed with coreling magic.

Thamos moved close to her, putting his strong hands on her shoulders to squeeze. For a moment she let herself lean on him, suddenly realizing how very tired she was.

'You should rest,' Thamos said.

Leesha shook herself, pulling away from his tempting embrace. 'There are people who need my help, Highness. If you think I'm going to let them wait so I can sit and rub my feet, you don't know me at all. Please go and leave me to my work.'

But the count stood his ground. 'We have men scouting the demon wards and mapping their stockpiles of ammunition, but we're going to need flamework to destroy them before the sun sets and it begins again.'

Leesha nodded. 'Tell Darsy Cutter what you need, and she'll see it done, but consult the Warders on where to place it. There's a limit to the flamework, and we can't afford to waste a single thunderstick.'

The count nodded. She turned to go back to her patients, but he caught her arm. When she looked at him, he pulled her close, kissing her deeply.

'Out in the night, I feared I would never get to do that again,' he whispered.

Leesha smiled. 'Take two, then.'

Renna stayed by Arlen's side through the night and into the next day, waiting for him to stir. His wounds had closed, but there was no sign that he was coming around.

Don't you leave me, Arlen Bales, she thought. *Can't do this without you.*

She managed a few hours of sleep after sunrise, curled protectively at Arlen's side. She woke with a start to the sound of an explosion in the distance. She was on her feet instantly, ready to fight, but there was still sunlight streaming in through the tent flap of the healing pavilion. She glanced down at Arlen, but he hadn't moved at all.

'The count's men are marring the greatwards and destroying stockpiles,' Leesha said, catching Renna's eye for a moment before resuming her rounds, checking on the most seriously wounded patients and giving instructions to other Gatherers.

She smelled of exhaustion, but you wouldn't see it looking at her. Renna, still flush with power from the night's fighting, felt strong and alert. Leesha had no such advantage, but still she worked. At the far side of the tent, Amanvah and Sikvah ministered as tirelessly to the injured *Sharum*.

And what have I done? Slept. Renna looked down at Arlen, running a hand down his cheek. 'Keep restin', love.' She kissed him. 'I'll make sure you still have a place to wake up to.'

Folk came to her the moment she left the pavilion, asking after Arlen. She told them he was all right, only sleeping to gather his strength, and moved on to see what she could do to throw in. More explosions echoed in the distance, but there was little she could do to assist there.

She went instead to the weakest points of Newhaven's

greatward, looking to strengthen them as she could. She spent the rest of the day ploughing, digging, and hauling giant stones. The demons were going to break through the net. She knew that from the beginning, but every moment they spent trying was one they could not spend killing the Hollowers.

Leesha watched as Thamos paced behind the map table. Like her, he had not rested throughout the day, and his eyes were dark and sunken in his handsome face. Arther stood near his lord, a contrast in his stillness.

They were back in the count's pavilion in the Corelings' Graveyard, having just overseen the transfer of wounded from Newhaven to the hospit in Cutter's Hollow. Leesha had been so proud of the building when it was first raised, but now, with wounded overflowing, it seemed woefully inadequate. If the Hollow survived, she would need to expand.

With Captain Gamon wounded, Thamos had once again assumed direct control of the Wooden Soldiers. He had called this last meeting as sunlight faded to go over plans for the coming night. Gared, Wonda, and the Butchers were there, along with Renna, Rojer, Amanvah, Sikvah, and Enkido. Even Drillmaster Kaval had been allowed in, though Thamos' guards had disarmed him and eyed him warily. Inquisitor Hayes and Child Franq clutched Canons, eyes closed as they mouthed silent prayers.

Leesha looked back to the count and, for an instant, wished he was Ahmann. She wondered, not for the first time, what was happening to the south in Everam's Bounty. Were they under similar assault? Likely they were, but Leesha did not feel as worried for the Krasians as she did for the Hollow.

It wasn't fair to Thamos, but she could not help but compare him with her Krasian lover. Whatever atrocities Jardir had committed in the name of his Holy War against demonkind, the man exuded confidence and inspired it in others. Thamos was a good man and strong, but he exuded doubt and it was palpable in the room.

It was Amanvah who asked the question on everyone's mind. 'Where is the Par'chin?'

'Sleeping,' Leesha said.

Amanvah gave her a coldly appraising look. 'The sun is soon to set. Should we not wake him?'

Leesha shook her head. 'He took a terrible blow to the head. Shaking and shouting isn't going to rouse him before he's ready, or do him any good even if it could.'

Thamos stopped pacing. 'He bought us this day, and we've made the most of it. It's up to us to hold the Hollow until he wakes, if he ever does.'

'He will,' Renna cut in. 'When the sun sets he'll get his strength back.'

'Like a demon,' Child Franq said.

Renna was across the room in an instant, her face a feral snarl. Franq stumbled backward, tripping over a stool and landing on his backside. 'Say that again,' she dared.

Franq quickly regained his feet. He was taller than Renna, but she seemed the larger of the two, moving forward as he shrank back. Leesha took a steadying breath, feeling her head begin to throb again. Fighting among themselves would serve no one but the corelings, but she, too, wanted to punch the Holy Man, and had no energy to break them apart.

Surprisingly, it was the Inquisitor who ended the confrontation, putting a firm hand on Franq's shoulder. 'The Child will be silent.'

Franq looked at his master in disbelief, but the Tender's eyes were hard. 'His Highness is correct. However he did it, Mr Bales saved us all last night. If he broke the Creator's law to do so, let Him judge that in the afterlife. It is for us to be thankful and strive to see another dawn.'

Renna looked at him and nodded. 'Ent my husband, but I'll do what I can to see it so.'

Thamos looked at her. 'Can you . . . ah . . .' He made
a sweeping gesture, drawing a clumsy ward in the air.

Renna shook her head. 'Don't think so, but I can tear a
demon's arm off and shove it down its throat.'

Gared chuckled. 'Seen her do it.'

Leesha felt her head throb again, wondering if it would be
enough.

Renna stood with the Haveners when night fell. She knew her
presence lent them strength and was glad of it, but wished that
there was someone to lend strength to her. Arlen was still
unconscious, and Thamos had split his forces to guard the
weakest points of the Hollow's net, unable to focus on any one
place. Leesha had insisted on keeping her hospit at the centre
of the Hollow, where it would be safest. Teams of Gatherer's
apprentices and volunteers stood ready with carts to move
wounded.

General Gared and the Cutters guarded New Rizon, where
the eastern mind demon had built its ward, and Thamos and
the bulk of his Wooden Soldiers waited by the border of Lakdale
to the west. The other boroughs had their own militias standing
ready with spear and bow, but there was no way of knowing
precisely where the demons would strike.

Renna had been given command of Newhaven, with Rojer
and the Krasians to bolster the Haveners, who had taken heavy
losses the night before. The rest of the Jongleurs had been split
between the boroughs to help as they could.

She shifted her feet, wondering if she was in the wrong
place. She had felt the mind demon at the centre die, and the
coreling ashes in the area confirmed that its death had taken
all the local demons with it, but the minds had made the
borough the centre of their assault for a reason. Newhaven
still had the weakest wardnet of any borough, too much of

it made from trees and structures that could be easily smashed by a rock demon with even moderate aim. Those not fit to fight had already been evacuated, but they had to hold the ground as long as possible. If Newhaven fell, it would bring the demons in striking range of Cutter's Hollow.

'It's going to be all right,' Rojer said, as if reading her mind.

Renna looked at him and his wives. They were clad in bright colours like a Jongleur's troupe, the women's veils cut short to reveal their full lips, that their voices might carry unimpeded. It was strange that revealing something every other woman Renna had ever known bared without a thought should seem so scandalous, but somehow it did. The Krasian men seemed to feel it even more strongly than her. *Sharum* kept glancing at the women, distracted. Kaval caught one warrior looking and struck him hard with the shaft of his spear, shouting something in Krasian.

'How's that?' she asked. Rojer masked his feelings well, but she could smell his fear.

The red-haired Jongleur shrugged and gave her a smile. 'Either we win and show the world that the demons can't pull us down no matter how hard they try, or we die and someone writes a song about how we stood strong to the end so a hundred years from now, folk remember and take heart in our bravery.'

'Rather live,' Renna said, as the cries of demons began to sound in the night. The greatward was coming to life beneath her feet, a huge pool of strength she did not fully understand. Could she tap it as Arlen had? Would it be enough even if she could? She thought again of her husband, lying still as death in his hospit bed.

There was a rustling in the thin line of trees across the clearing, and she embraced her fear and worry, straightening. As she did, she felt power rush into her, making her strong. Her mouth watered. If they were going to die, let them die fighting.

'Bows at the ready,' she called, and the Haveners raised their weapons. The Krasians were not shooters, but each held three spears, two for throwing and a third for close fighting.

'That's our cue,' Rojer said, stepping forward and raising his fiddle, beginning to play. Amanvah and Sikvah raised their voices to join him, touching the demon bone chokers at their throats.

The music carried far on the currents of magic, growing louder and more complex, weaving a spell in the air that pushed at the demons as strongly as a wardnet. Renna knew they were out there – could see their glow shining in the trees – but they seemed unable to approach so long as the trio continued to play. After several minutes, the pounding in her heart began to slow.

But then a boulder arched high into the air over the trees.

'Look out!' Renna cried. Enkido was already pulling Amanvah out of the way, and Renna grabbed Rojer and Sikvah like children, leaping aside. The gigantic stone hit just as they landed, knocking her from her feet and showering them with bits of rubble. They coughed from the dust, unharmed, but the damage had been done.

The moment the music stopped, the woods exploded with demons. Field demons came in reaps, with flame demons at their heels. Others, their scales a glittering white, followed. Renna had never seen the like, but knew snow demons from Arlen's stories.

Someone screamed, and the Haveners let loose a volley of their precious warded arrows. Their aim was erratic and the targets in fast motion, but the sheer number of demons meant many were struck. Some few of these fell, but most ran on.

'Don't shoot, you fools!' Renna screamed. 'The greatward is still active!'

Indeed, the corelings came up against the ward and were thrown back with a bright flare of magic. Renna wondered at the point of the charge until a falling stone fell on the head of an archer, killing her instantly. She looked up and saw a wind demon bank and fly off even as more came, hauling large stones in their hind talons.

'Shoot the windies!' she cried. The Haveners lifted their bows to comply, but their fear was palpable, shaking hands that needed to be steady. Even with the light of the greatward, the night sky was dark, and they could not see the demons glowing as Renna did. A few wind demons dropped from the sky, crashing into the wardnet and sliding off like birds flying into a thick pane of glass, but most of the arrows vanished harmlessly into the blackness.

'Rock and wood!' Kaval shouted, and Renna turned, cursing. At the tree line, the huge demons were massing, carrying heavy stones and sections of tree trunk in their talons.

Renna froze, unsure, but Kaval smoothly took command. 'Archers!' he cried. 'Target the rock demons! Ignore all else! We will deal with the wood!'

Some of the Haveners looked to Renna, and she gritted her teeth. She should have seen the diversion for what it was, and now she had foolishly wasted much of their ammunition. She hated to admit it, but she was out of her depth. Kaval, calm and ready to lead, had trained a lifetime for this. 'Do as he says!'

The Haveners loosed again, this time at targets even a novice could not miss. As they did, the *Sharum* ran forward, coming to a stop right at the edge of the wardnet and using the momentum of their sprints to aid their throws. The light spears flew far, piercing the hearts of wood demons and knocking them down. The demons shrieked, trying to clutch at the weapons, but the defensive wards along the shafts prevented them from drawing them out, even as the offensive wards continued to suck magic from the corelings, turning it into killing energy they pumped back into the wounds.

The Haveners were having less success. Their strongest arrows wasted, the crude ones stuck from the rock demons like pins in a cushion. The demons shrieked, but it seemed more in annoyance than distress. They cocked their arms back, launching their heavy missiles.

Everyone scattered, but the defenders were not the demons' targets. One stone struck a wooden fence that formed part of the greatward, knocking it to splinters. Another blasted through a section of embankment. Flame demons spat fire on some of the stones, and while the flames winked out when they crossed the wardnet, the rocks remained superheated. One smashed through the doors of a barn, and smoke and flame soon began to stream forth.

And still more demons came on. Stone and wood demons carried ammunition for the larger rocks, whose range and power were incomparable. Even when a few of the rock demons finally succumbed to the dozens of arrows sticking from their armour and fell to the ground, they were swiftly replaced.

Rojer raised his fiddle again, but before he could begin to form a melody, a wood demon threw a log the size of a beer barrel at him and his wives. He managed to roll out of the way, and Amanvah and Sikvah dropped to the ground, dirtying their fine coloured silks but saving their lives. The three of them ran for cover as other demons launched projectiles their way.

They know, Renna realized. *The minds can see through the eyes of their drones.*

The thought filled her with anger, and she felt the greatward respond. She pulled at that strength, feeling it flood her with power, but it was power laced with pain, as if she had been dropped into a cauldron of boiling water. Unable to bear it for long, she drew a heat ward in the air at the offending demons and watched in satisfaction as three wood demons burst into flames and collapsed into ashes.

But then Renna felt her legs give way, barely catching herself with her hands before her face hit the ground. She gasped for breath and her throat felt scalded, eyes dry and burning. The strength that had flooded her a moment earlier had vanished, leaving her muscles weak and watery.

This what Arlen feels? she wondered. *How does he stand it?*

She forced herself to her feet, pulling at the greatward again, but this time it did not respond. She felt the power pulsing beneath her, strong as ever, but whatever connection she had found in her anger was gone now.

Yet looking at the chaos around her, she knew she had to do something. The Krasians were out of throwing spears, and the Haveners were now firing crude arrows that splintered against the rock demons' hard carapaces as often as they stuck. The barn fire was under control as folk threw buckets of water on the blaze, but flame demons were heating more stones, and soon the fires would be too numerous to contain. Wind demons rained smaller stones from the sky, and the other demons were massing, waiting for the wards to fail.

She reached for her belt, feeling the reassuring grip of her father's knife. *Ent no easy way to plough a field*, Harl used to say. *Nothing for it but to bend your back and get it done.*

The magic responded to her resolve, filling her with strength once more as she gave a cry and ran out into the night. Behind her she heard Kaval shout, followed by the sound of the *Sharum* locking shields and charging out after her.

And then it was a blur of tooth and claw and the hard metal of her knife as she dodged around the lesser demons, slashing and kicking, never slowing. Demon ichor arced into the air as she slashed the paw from a field demon, and kicked a flame demon in the throat just as it was about to spit at her, causing it to choke on its own fire. She heard the clatter of talons on shields and the spark of magic, the wet sound of spears piercing coreling scales and the screams of men pierced by coreling jaws.

And then she was at the first rock demon, stomping on the flame demon that was heating its stone. She used the flamer's back as a springboard, leaping high to plunge her knife into a gap in the armour plates of the demon's neck.

Even her father's long blade was not enough to cut the throat of a rock demon, but Renna used the grip to swing herself around behind the behemoth, whipping her brook stone necklace about its throat and pulling tight with all her weight. The warded stones flared to life, pressing inward using the coreling's own strength against it. After a few moments, the head popped free with a flare of magic and a shower of ichor. Renna hit the ground in a crouch, seeking her next target.

Only to find her targets seeking her. The eyes of every demon in the field had turned to lock on her, like a thousand cats staring at a single mouse.

Rojer looked on in amazement as Renna drew a ward in the air, and the demons that had tried to kill him exploded into flames, shrieking as they fell to the ground, blackened and smoking. From the look on her face, she was as surprised as he was.

Hope came alive in him for an instant, remembering the power Arlen had wielded the night before. But then he saw the young woman stagger, and heard Arlen speak in his head. *Ent no such thing as a Deliverer, Rojer. Folk want to be saved, they're gonna have to learn to save themselves.*

Renna seemed to realize it, too, giving up on the magic and charging into the night, cutting a path through the chaos much as Arlen had in the Battle of Cutter's Hollow, taking down a rock demon while he still gaped from behind the embankment where he and his wives had taken cover.

Kaval led his warriors in Renna's wake, and for once Rojer was thankful for the presence of the brutal drillmaster and *Sharum*. Where the Haveners mostly shook with fear and indecision, the Krasians moved as a tight unit, shields locked together, protecting their brothers. They thrust their spears as one, mowing down field demons like hay before the scythe.

It seemed the battle might turn if they could take out the rock demons, but then something terrifying happened. The demons all locked gazes on Renna, ignoring every other target to charge her. Even the rock demons dropped their missiles, leaping for the girl with their giant talons leading.

Renna lasted a few seconds, literally running across the backs of field demons with the grace of a dancing master. A snow demon spat at her, but she dodged aside and the coldspit struck the leg of a rock demon instead. The spot turned white with rime, and she gave a well-placed kick that shattered the demon's leg. It fell into the press, adding to the chaos.

But then a wood demon hurled a section of trunk at her, clipping her with enough force to throw her several yards before she struck the ground. Renna put her hands under her, struggling to rise, but the opening was all the demons needed. Their teeth and claws found little purchase as her blackstem wards flared, but here and there they found gaps and dug in. She bled freely, and soon her wards would be marred and useless.

Kaval cried out and the *Sharum* made a valiant effort to save her, but one of the demons before them reared up, its body elongating to tower over them as it grew a long, horned tentacle that it used to slash over the tops of their shields. The warriors wore metal helms under their turbans, fine warded steel, but the demon slashed through them like fruit, killing several of the warriors instantly.

Kaval gave a shrill whistle and the *Sharum* broke formation and reassembled in a new configuration, surrounding the demon, which could only be the mimic Arlen and Leesha spoke of. It was a tactic Rojer had seen before. They would wait for the demon to strike, those in front locking shields defensively while those behind struck.

But the mimic demon was like nothing they had ever faced. It twisted impossibly as they tried to get behind it, and when that was not enough it grew eyes all around its head and additional tentacles until it faced every warrior at once. Tentacles snatched up fallen warriors by their legs and swung them like clubs to knock others aside. Even when the *Sharum* were lucky enough to strike a blow, their spears seemed to pass through with a puff of smoke, leaving the demon unharmed when they withdrew. Arrows rained in on the creature, but they, too, fell to the ground having done no harm.

Again and again, *Sharum* fell to the mimic's return blows, but they came on fearlessly. This was the sort of death Krasian warriors prayed for, though Rojer could not understand the notion. Kaval leapt forward, and the demon knocked the shield from his grasp. The drillmaster seemed unfazed, spinning his spear faster than Rojer could see as he parried tentacles, buying his warriors time to strike.

But then the demon's maw grew several times its size, and it bit Drillmaster Kaval in half, swallowing his head and torso before his legs and abdomen even knew to fall.

The sight shocked Rojer from his daze, and he saw Renna still struggling, caught in the grip of several wood demons attempting to carry her off.

They want her alive, he realized.

He was playing before he knew it, stepping out of cover and moving for the fray. He was dimly aware of Amanvah, Sikvah, and Enkido following him as he headed for the edge of the wardnet, but he ignored them, ignored everything but the music as he stepped out into the naked night. He made no effort to mask his presence. Quite the contrary, he drew the attention of every demon in earshot, causing them to lock in on him much as they had on Renna a few moments earlier.

Freeze, he told them. *Prey approaches. Be ready to pounce.*

They did, talons tearing at the soil as they tamped down powerful limbs, preparing to spring. Even the demons trying to steal away with Renna stopped in their tracks, as he had intended.

Only the mimic demon was unaffected, leaping out of the ring of *Sharum* and charging at him like a nightmare come to life.

Rojer allowed himself a smile, and filled the night with pain, the lure of his magic turning to harsh discordance that had the demons shrieking and clawing at their own heads. Even the mimic felt it, pulling up short with a bone-chilling cry.

Amanvah and Sikvah added their voices to his power, the three of them reaching new heights of union in their disharmony, *hora* magic making the screeching sounds pierce the night for miles. Lesser demons fled the sound, but Rojer and his wives circled the mimic, building on its pain. Rojer experimented, learning more of what hurt the creature the longer he played.

The demon writhed in pain, tentacles pressing against its head as it melted and shifted, becoming a roaring rock demon, and then a howling wood. A shrieking wind demon and even a screaming human man. Again and again it changed form, but Rojer and his wives changed their sounds to match, giving no respite. The shifts became erratic, the mimic's flesh bubbling and sloughing off into a growing puddle of goo at its feet.

Got you now, you son of the Core. Rojer's smile was grim as he pressed in for the kill.

But when he did, the demon seemed to perk up, slightly. It looked at him with what almost seemed a smile as its ears melted away entirely, leaving only smooth scales along its skull.

Rojer had no time to dodge as it swept a tentacle at him, but there was a shout and Enkido hurled himself between them, taking the blow meant for him. Sikvah shrieked as the eunuch was disembowelled, but he managed to throw his spear even as he leapt. It stuck from the demon, flaring brightly with magic, but Rojer knew it would not be enough to kill the beast, and his music now held no power over it.

The mimic reared again, and Rojer's bow slipped from the strings as he dived into a roll, barely dodging the lash of its tentacle. The demon drew back to swing at him again, and Rojer flinched, knowing he could not dodge aside in time.

The appendage whipped forward, but instead of the sharp horns along its length, Rojer was struck by a spray of ichor from the severed limb. He looked and saw Renna standing there, ichor-stained knife in hand. She dropped the length of tentacle to the dirt where it melted into slime as she leapt forward, blade leading.

The demon turned to meet her charge, but this time Amanvah stepped forward, reaching into the *hora* pouch at her waist. She pulled forth a blackened lump of demon bone, pointing it at the mimic as her fingers manipulated the wards carved into its surface.

A blast of magic leapt from the bone like lightning, striking the mimic and lifting it clear off the ground. Renna was on it in an instant, stabbing and cutting. Amanvah swept the dust of the crumbled bone from her hands and reached into her pouch again, pulling forth a handful of demon talons. She threw these, and they shot forth like crank bow bolts, lodging deep in the mimic's body. It twisted and shrieked, unfocused as Renna threw it to the ground, sawing at its neck. The remaining *Sharum*, led by Coliv, joined the fray, stabbing and shouting, blocking flailing tentacles with their shields as they kept the creature from gathering its wits once more.

Out of the corner of his warded eyes, Rojer saw the bright glow of demons, no longer held back by his music, beginning to return. He put his fiddle back to work, trying to drive them away, but a field demon had caught sight of Sikvah, who knelt over the still body of Enkido, weeping. It launched itself at her, faster than any creature alive, and Rojer knew he could not turn it in time.

But Sikvah saw the coreling coming. Her thin veil was soaked with tears, and she tore it away with one hand as she touched the choker at her throat with the other. The shriek she let loose at the creature was so piercing that human and demon alike were forced to cover their ears. The field demon stumbled mid-lope, tumbling end-over-end to lie dead at her feet.

The Haveners had joined Renna and the *Sharum* now, all piling on the mimic demon, giving it no time to melt away until Renna finally succeeded in separating its head from its body. She held it high for all to see, and there was a ragged cheer.

'Enough!' Rojer shouted. 'Back to the wardnet! I can't hold them back forever!'

Two *Sharum* had to pull Sikvah away from Enkido's body as they ran back to safety. Rojer, still playing, breathed a moment's relief.

Until he saw the rockets leaving red streaks across the night sky, signalling that demons had breached the wards and were on the streets of New Rizon.

25

Lost Circle

333 AR Autumn
Third Night of New Moon

'*Oot!* They come!' Coliv called down.

An acrobat himself, Rojer knew a thing or two about balance, but even he was amazed at the ease with which the Krevakh Watcher had planted his twelve-foot-tall ladder on open ground and run straight up to the top rung without using his hands, standing motionless for long minutes as he scanned the horizon.

The two men were alone in the town square of New Rizon, amid the ruins that only a day ago had been a thriving town. Now it was a rotting corpse, almost every structure around the cobbled square smashed by hurled stones or blackened by fire. It was eerily silent.

They had spent the day piling wreckage to restore the greatward, but none had any illusions it would hold for more than a few minutes. They had prevented demons from rising directly in the town, but the corelings had begun dismantling the protection as soon as they solidified, and the Hollowers did not have the strength to prevent it.

And so they waited, Jongleur and Watcher, in the small portable circle Rojer had used all his life. No one liked the plan, least of all Rojer, though it had been his idea. When Amanvah had seen he would not be deterred she insisted that Coliv accompany him, though Rojer thought it would likely mean two deaths instead of one. Still, he could not deny a touch of comfort at the presence of the warrior.

The man tried to kill Arlen, Rojer reminded himself, but he could not bring himself to feel anger over it. Coliv had assumed command of the few remaining *Sharum*, and they followed Rojer and his wives everywhere. He had lost count of how many times the Watcher had saved his life the night before.

Rojer lifted his fiddle as the sounds of the demons reached his ears. They would need to come through New Rizon to strike at Cutter's Hollow, and with most of the town destroyed, the easiest path was through the town square.

It was simple to use that fact to enhance his call. *Come this way!* his music told the corelings. *It is quicker! It is easier! There is prey!*

And indeed there was. Him.

The demons responded. Dozens at first, striking at his wards with flashes of magic. The number quickly swelled to hundreds, then thousands. They filled the square, and still his call went out, drawing them to him. Soon he and Coliv were lost in a sea of teeth and scales, unable to see anything else.

Corelings crawled over one another, fighting among themselves for the privilege of attacking his wards. But the worn portable circle had been well made, and it turned their attacks back on them, the field only growing stronger as more and more of them fed it with their magic.

But then the inevitable happened. The swirling mass of corelings parted to allow wood demons to advance, these carrying giant clubs made from the trunks of trees. It would be a simple matter for them to smash Rojer and Coliv to pulp and knock his circle out of alignment.

But Coliv was ready, producing a twisted ram's horn, hollowed and polished. He put the horn to his lips and blew a long note.

At the sound, shutters slammed open around the square, archers appearing in the windows and atop the roofs of the ruined buildings. They did not hesitate, opening fire into the mass of corelings. The demons were packed so tightly it was impossible to miss, but a few of the most skilled marksmen were sure to put down the wood demons threatening Rojer. He saw one of Wonda's unmistakable shafts appear in one of the demons' eyes just before it fell.

Demons charged the doorways to the buildings, but they were doused in spray pumped from barrels on the floors above. A moment later torches followed, igniting the liquid demonfire and setting them ablaze.

Another horn sounded. 'Now,' Coliv said, never one to waste words. He set his ladder and climbed quickly, taking a weighted line and throwing it to a third-floor window.

Rojer stopped playing, shoving his fiddle into the bag of marvels slung over his shoulder. He ran up the ladder almost as nimbly as Coliv, grabbing onto the Watcher as he leapt. Men in the window pulled at the line as they tucked their legs and swung, feeling the puff of air as snatching talons just missed them.

They slammed into the blackened wall of the building, smashing some of the weakened wood, but Coliv was already climbing to the window, hauling Rojer who clung to his shoulders.

They escaped just in time as Count Thamos and Gared led a charge of heavy horse into the press. Rojer looked sadly at the spot where they had once stood, now trampled by hundreds of steel-shod hooves.

'Gonna miss that circle,' he said.

Renna paced back and forth, hating that she was forced to wait while battle was met. But as they had with Arlen, the demons knew her on sight now, and abandoned all other pursuits when she was beyond the wards.

The Hollowers were in full rout when they returned, running hard before a swarm of corelings. At least a third of the archers who had stationed themselves in the square did not return. Thamos' cavalry appeared to have fared even worse, with many horses carrying two, and still hundreds missing. They gave cover to the footmen, but the horsemen, too, were fleeing, their spears mostly gone as they laid about with warded axe and hammer. Coliv had Rojer slung over his shoulder as he ran.

They flowed around Renna as she stood alone at the border, breathing deeply as she felt the magic pooled at her feet. When they were clear, she Drew.

Ignoring the lesser demons, Renna focused on the rocks, drawing heat and impact wards, targeting the gaps in their stony carapaces. She blasted shoulders and knees, less concerned with killing the demons than with crippling them and preventing them from hurling their deadly projectiles.

She lasted longer tonight, but quickly reached her limit, feeling dizzy as the magic burned at her from the inside.

Still the demons came on. She fell to one knee, bracing herself with a hand on the cobbles, and Drew again.

Leesha could feel her muscles knotting tighter the closer the sounds of battle came to the hospit of Cutter's Hollow. There were too many wounded to move, and where would they move them if the Corelings' Graveyard fell?

For now, the greatward was secure. Shaped by wide cobbled streets, thick low walls, and huge swathes of land, the ward would require hours of bombardment to weaken sufficiently for demons to gain access – and even then, there were wards on the hospit and other safe zones. It was unlikely the demons could destroy it all in a night.

But they don't need to, she reminded herself. *They just need to do more damage than we can repair in a month. Then as soon as the moon wanes again, they'll come finish the job.*

Outside she heard the explosions as the last of her flamework was used, and boulders fell like rain. Every crash was a stab of pain in her eye. The headaches had returned with a vengeance with the new moon, but there was nothing for it but to endure. She could not afford to take the strong drugs needed to counter them, and neither she nor Thamos was in any state to attempt the alternative solution.

Leesha was not used to feeling so helpless. She wanted desperately to be outside, helping in some way, but what could she hope to do? Her Gatherer's art was already in play, the Cutters using the last of her flamework, acid, and sleeping draughts. She could risk herself helping wounded on the field, but to what end? They poured into her hospit at a steady rate, more than enough to fill the hands of all the Gatherers and apprentices.

She looked around the main hall, beds and the floor between filled with moans of pain, white bandages and red splotches. The most stable had been sent to the Holy House in Tender Hayes' care, but the hospit was still at capacity.

Leesha caught Amanvah's eye, and the young *dama'ting* nodded. Leesha knew she was no happier to be trapped inside, but her fighting *hora* had been depleted battling the mimic, and she and Sikvah were needed here. The Krasians healed differently than she had been taught, but Leesha could not deny their skill at treating battle wounds.

There was a shout and the door to the hospit slammed open, admitting Coliv. Leesha could see at a glance from the coloured silk that he was carrying Rojer. The Jongleur's carrot hair was matted red with blood.

Leesha ran to him, but Amanvah got there first, cradling his head to inspect the damage as Coliv laid him down. Sikvah moved to bar the way.

'I don't have time for this demonshit, Sikvah,' Leesha said, moving to shove the younger woman aside.

But Sikvah was faster, grabbing her arm and twisting it. Leesha found herself spun around and propelled away from them, barely managing to quickstep and keep her feet.

'See to the others,' Sikvah said in her heavily accented Thesan. 'We will tend our husband.'

Leesha drew breath to argue, but just then the rest of the wounded reached the hospit, and it was all she and the other women could do to find space for them and triage.

The sounds of battle drew too close for comfort as they worked. The demons were at the border, which meant Renna Tanner was their last real line of defence. Leesha knew the woman would do her best, but it wasn't yet midnight. Could she hold back the entire Core till dawn?

The hospit shook as something huge struck the ground out front.

Apparently not.

'Creator,' Leesha whispered too quietly for the others to hear, 'I know you aid those who aid themselves, but we could really use a miracle.'

She didn't expect an answer, but it came a moment later, as the entire building seemed to rock from side to side. The crash was deafening, and ceiling beams fell into the floor amid a cloud of dust and rubble.

'Arlen!' Leesha cried, for his room was on the second floor. She ran to the steps, putting a cloth over her mouth and nearly choking on the dust in any event.

The second floor was partially collapsed. A boulder had apparently passed clear through, shearing off part of the roof and taking out several walls. Leesha tried not to think of the patients who had been in those rooms, picking her way over the wreckage to the small private room where Arlen lay unconscious.

Her worst fears were realized as she moved through the hole where the door had been. Part of the ceiling was open to the night sky, and the space where the bed had been was a mass of rubble from a collapsed wall.

Leesha backed away from the sight until she struck one of the remaining walls. She slid down to the floor, shaking.

'It's over,' she whispered. 'We're all going to die.'

But then the rubble shifted and began to rise. A fresh cloud of dust filled the room as beams lifted out of the mass and stones fell away. Arlen Bales was in the centre, his wards glowing brightly as he worked his hands under the beams across his knotted shoulders, pressing them up over his head long enough for him to step free.

Leesha stared at him as he approached, looking like a seraph of the Creator Himself. She was normally the first to deny Arlen was Heaven-sent, but even she found herself believing as he reached a glowing hand out to her.

'Deliverer,' she whispered, taking his hand and letting him pull her to her feet. He caught her as she stumbled, and for a moment they held each other close.

Arlen laid a gentle hand on her face. 'Just me, Leesha. Arlen Bales.'

Leesha reached out, touching his face in return. 'Sometimes it's hard to tell.'

'What's happened?' Arlen asked. 'Last I remember I was destroying the demon's ammunition piles . . .'

'That was two days ago,' Leesha said. 'New Rizon is gone. The demons are at the edge of the Corelings' Graveyard. Renna is holding them back.'

Arlen pulled back at the name. 'Renna's out there alone?'

And just like that, he collapsed into smoke, Leesha left holding empty air.

Arlen materialized in the Corelings' Graveyard an instant later, immediately spotting Renna on her elbows and knees. The remaining Wooden Soldiers stood in a half circle around her, their indestructible shields locked together to block her from sight and bombardment as she struggled to rise.

But Arlen could see she would not be able to rise again. Her aura was flickering. She was seconds from passing out.

He was at her side immediately, not bothering to draw wards as he laid a hand on her shoulder. He reached through her into the greatward, feeling its power. The link that connected the net of Hollow County was gone, but the central keyward of Cutter's Hollow was the strongest by far, more power than they could use and live to tell the tale.

He Drew, pulling magic through Renna steadily until her aura was restored and the blackstem wards on her skin began to glow of their own accord.

'Arlen,' she breathed, rising to her feet and throwing her arms around him, kissing him deeply.

Arlen held her face in both hands, meeting her eyes. 'Promised I'd die before I let demons take the Hollow, Ren. You mean it when you said the same?'

Renna nodded. 'Every word.'

Arlen kissed her again. He pulled back, taking her hand in a firm grip. 'Then Draw with me.' The two of them pulled at the greatward, flooding themselves with power.

'Shields open!' Arlen shouted, and the Wooden Soldiers broke apart, giving them a clear view of the enemy. As one, they raised their hands to trace wards in the air.

Leesha wept as dawn came and the sounds of crashing boulders, exploding flamework, and screams of pain fell away. The last notes of the *Song of Waning*, which Rojer's Jongleurs had been playing constantly to keep the enemy at bay, ended as cramped and bleeding fingers finally released their instruments. There was silence for a moment, and then ragged cheering throughout the Hollow.

They had survived.

Some of us, Leesha amended, looking at the shrouded bodies lying all over the Corelings' Graveyard. The battle hadn't ended when Arlen and Renna collapsed. Reinforcements had come from the other boroughs when it was clear the demons were making a full press for the centre of the Hollow and battle had been joined directly. Arlen and Renna had destroyed most of the larger demons by then, and denied ammunition to the rest. It became an open melee, tooth and talon against warded steel, with Gared and Thamos leading assault after assault.

There were so many wounded she had been forced to begin laying them out in the square, and then on the streets. There was death everywhere, but she had neither the time nor the help to move the bodies, and they were left where they lay. Thousands of dead and wounded mixed together. Even those on their feet looked half dead. No one had slept in days.

She looked sadly at the Holy House where they had made their last stand in the Battle of Cutter's Hollow, its roof now caved by several boulder strikes. Perhaps it was well after all that Inquisitor Hayes was building his cathedral to replace it. New Rizon had been nearly levelled, as well as the now ironically named Sweet Succour, but the defences had held in the other boroughs.

Horns and flamework had signalled Thamos and his mounted soldiers through the night, sending them along the border as the demons probed for weak spots and tried to break the greatward. Rojer's Jongleurs drove back the demons and confused them as the Cutters struck, and Coliv and the remaining *Sharum* were found wherever the fighting was thickest.

She went to her office in the hospit to check on Rojer. He lay propped up on her desk, his head wrapped in bandages as Amanvah and Sikvah took it in turns talking to him and asking questions, trying to keep him awake and alert. Amanvah had used the last of her *hora* to close the wound, but he had still taken a heavy blow to the head, and if he passed out, there was still a chance he might not awaken.

'How is he?' she asked.

'He will recover,' Amanvah said. 'The dice tell me Everam still has need of him.'

Leesha nodded. 'He needs us all.'

'My people think the *chin* weak,' Amanvah said, 'but my father spoke of the Hollow tribe's strength. In this, as in all things, he was right. Your people have honoured the Creator this Waning. You will rise stronger than ever.'

Leesha shook her head. 'We can't keep taking losses like this. We'll need to deepen and strengthen our greatwards, and get people off the streets on Waning. Dig basements, tunnels, sewers . . .'

'You must build an Undercity,' Amanvah said.

'Good start,' a voice said behind her, 'but it won't be enough.'

Leesha turned, and her eyes widened. 'Arlen!' she cried, throwing her arms around him before she could help herself. He wrapped his arms around her, squeezing, and for the first time in days, she felt a touch of hope. 'Thank the Creator you're all right. We won't survive another new moon without you.'

Arlen looked at her sadly. 'May have to. I'm why the minds have come. It's all my fault.'

'That's not—' Leesha began.

'Demons were in my head, Leesha,' Arlen cut her off. 'Heard their plans – and worse, they heard mine. Know everything I do, including my plans for Jardir, and for taking the offensive against them. Everything I've been devising, made worthless in an instant.'

He looked up, meeting Amanvah's eyes. 'Need to do something they won't expect.'

26

Sharum'ting

333 AR Summer
14 Dawns Before Waning

'How dare you spin your lies in the court of the Deliverer,' Damaji Qezan of the Jama tribe accused.

'Lies?!' Damaji Ichach of the Khanjin cried, his face growing red. 'You are the one whose tongue drips with false witness. You know full well . . .'

Ichach and Qezan, neither the fittest to begin with, had put on even more weight in recent months. Virtually every Krasian had since they conquered the abundant green lands, but few so grossly.

Ahmann asu Hoshkamin am'Jardir am'Kaji, Shar'Dama Ka and the most powerful man in the world, looked at the squabbling clerics and had to suppress the urge to blood his spear with the both of them. The Jama and Khanjin were ever at each other's throats.

Jardir felt stronger than ever in his life, muscles brimming with energy, yet he had never felt so weary as he did now, watching fat old men argue the latest bit of political nonsense even as the battle lines of Sharak Ka were being drawn.

It wasn't just the Jama and Khanjin. The tribes had been united for years and were wealthy as never before, yet still they found reasons to offend one another, stealing wells and women just to burn rivals. The *Damaji* could have put a stop to it, but the cycle of vengeance on the council of *Damaji* was no better than that among the most incensed tribesmen. These men were *zahven*, and the only thing that truly mattered to them was their standing among one another.

He noticed the *Damaji* looking at him, and realized he'd stopped paying attention. They were awaiting a decree, and he had no idea what for. Some bit of contested land . . .

Jardir looked to Jayan, standing at the foot of his dais. 'Jayan my son, what think you of this great crisis between the Jama and Khanjin?' He made no effort to hide the displeasure in his voice.

Jayan bowed deeply. 'The Jama have a legitimate claim to injury, Father.' Jardir saw Damaji Qezan puff up. 'But so, too, do the Khanjin.' Ichach straightened at that.

Jardir nodded. 'And how would you deal with it in my place?' Both *Damaji* turned in surprise to look at the young Sharum Ka. Traditionally, the Sharum Ka was the servant of the council, not the other way around, and Jayan was only nineteen. With the exception of Ashan, there was not a man on the council under sixty.

Jayan bowed again. 'Both tribes have proven they are unworthy of the land. I would confiscate it for the war effort.'

Of course you would, Jardir thought. Jayan had not been happy with the three million draki he had been given, but Jardir had seen Jayan's clumsy accounting of how he had spent the war tax, and read between the lines. *The only one of my sons to have his own palace, and already it must be grander than any other.*

He looked to Asome, standing beside Damaji Ashan and Dama Asukaji. 'And you, Asome? Do you agree with your brother?'

Asome bowed. 'The land is meaningless, Father, and will not solve the true problem.'

'And what is that, my son?' Jardir asked.

'That Sharak Ka is nigh, yet the *Damaji* continue to waste the Deliverer's time with petty matters even children could settle among themselves.'

There was a burst of chatter among the *Damaji* at this. Jardir thumped his spear on the marble dais. 'Silence!'

The room quieted immediately. Jardir kept his eyes on Asome. 'And your solution to this problem?'

'Let the *Damaji* settle it among themselves.' Asome turned, eyeing the two *Damaji* as his voice grew cold. 'And give Damajis Qezan and Ichach three lashes of the alagai tail each for incentive.' He dropped a hand to the barbed whip he carried on his belt. Every *dama* owned one – a symbol of the new power given when they took the white – but carrying them on one's person had fallen from fashion over the centuries, only to be brought back by Asome. Now more and more *dama* carried the weapons with them at all times.

For a moment, there was utter silence, but then the entire court broke out in angry shouting.

'How dare you, boy?!' Qezan shouted.

'Outrageous!' Ichach growled.

Asome only smiled. 'You see, Damaji? Already you agree on something.' Qezan's and Ichach's faces grew so red, Jardir thought they might burst.

Careful, my son, he thought. *You make powerful enemies.*

Other clerics added outrage to the chorus. No *Damaji* had been whipped in centuries, and certainly not on the orders of a young *dama* not yet eighteen. They had become so secure in their power over the years they believed themselves above the laws that governed other men. Even Ashan, secure in the Deliverer's favour and Asome's uncle, looked at the boy in displeasure.

The *Damaji'ting* only looked on in silence.

'Once again, my brother proves why he is heir to nothing,' Jayan said with a smirk, but Asome did not flinch, his gaze cool. He did not have the look of an heir to nothing.

He has the look of an Andrah, Jardir thought. *As if his appointment is a foregone conclusion.*

Jardir considered. Asome had masterfully cornered him. If he followed Jayan's solution, his second son would lose face, and indeed, the true problem would continue. But if he agreed . . .

Only Damaji Aleverak – once Jardir's bitter enemy and now one of his most trusted advisors – was unperturbed. Aleverak gave Jardir his own share of frustration, but he was a man of honour and courage, a true leader to his people and not just a despot like many of his brethren on the council. He would never behave so foolishly as these men, and if he did, he would strip his robe and bend to receive the lash without losing a grain of dignity. But even Aleverak would not suggest a whipping in open council. Asome's directness was a refreshing change.

Jardir glanced at Aleverak, and the ancient cleric gave a tiny nod, the gesture lost amid the chaos. He, too, carried an alagai tail.

'The Damajah!' came Hasik's call from the door. All the men looked up, their conflict momentarily forgotten at the sight of Inevera.

She does take the breath away, Jardir thought, gazing at his First Wife as his council bowed to her.

Inevera nodded in acceptance of the honour, but made no effort to approach the throne. She caught Jardir's eye and touched her *hora* pouch, then inclined her head slightly towards her pillow chamber. There was no missing the meaning behind the gesture.

Her new *alagai hora* were at last complete.

Jardir felt dizzied by the feelings that raised in him. For twenty-five years he had been a virtual slave to the *alagai hora*, the whole course of his life dictated by their throws. The last fortnight had felt freer than he imagined possible, unburdened by their yoke.

But with that freedom came uncertainty. The dice kept him

captive in their way, but they gave him power, too. In those throws were truths he sorely needed if they were to win the Daylight War and Sharak Ka. The problem was that their truths were filtered through Inevera, and she kept her own counsel on which to share and which to keep.

He looked back at the *Damaji*, still waiting in shocked silence for his response to their petty drama. 'It shall be as both my sons suggest. The contested land will go to Jayan, and Damajis Ichach and Qezan will have the kiss of the alagai tail.'

All the clerics save Ashan and Aleverak opened their mouths to protest, but Jardir raised the Spear of Kaji and the words died on their tongues. 'Damaji Aleverak will administer the punishments here and now.'

He set the spear butt on the dais with a thump that made several clerics flinch. 'Sharak Ka is upon us, Damaji. We have no more time to fight among ourselves. From now on, these matters will be handled within your closed council. Waste my time like this again, and the next whippings will be in the city square for all to see.'

Faces blanched as Jardir descended the seven steps from his dais and strode past them, following Inevera.

Jardir watched the sway of Inevera's hips as she strode into her pillow chamber, mesmerized as always by her beauty. Like his warriors who absorbed demon magic each night in *alagai'sharak*, years of manipulating *alagai hora* had lent his First Wife the air of immortality. She moved with the confidence of a matriarch, yet despite being forty-two and having borne him several children, her curves still had the bounce of a woman on the bright side of thirty.

But only a fool would think her value lay in her beauty. Would he be where he was today without Inevera? Would he have seized power when the opportunity came to him? Would it even have come, or would he be just another illiterate *dal'Sharum* – or worse, a bleached skull in Sharik Hora?

And I love her still, he thought, hating himself for the weakness. There were times he dared dream that she loved him in return, but in his heart he could not trust her. Not since the Andrah.

An image of the two of them entwined flashed in his mind's eye, Inevera beautiful and seductive as ever as she rode the fat old man, manipulating him to her ends much as she did Jardir. What did her cries of pleasure in their marital pillows mean, now that he saw how easily she feigned them?

The Damajah's pillow chamber had been completely remodelled since Ahmann's last visit, when he stole inside with Leesha Paper. It had given them both pleasure to mark Inevera's special place, the lovemaking intense and passionate. If his intent had been to hurt her, it seemed he had succeeded. His *Jiwah Ka* had never spoken of the incident, but there had been a fire in the room the next day, destroying everything down to the stone walls. Officially, an oil lamp had accidentally tipped onto a pillow, but palace rumour had Inevera storming out of the burning room with a flame demon skull in hand. Now any hint of Leesha Paper was expunged.

For some reason, this only made Jardir love her more.

She is the Damajah. Her jealousy is a storm, and she will suffer no woman to stand above her. Did not Kaji ponder in his private diaries the same questions of his *Jiwah Ka*? The holy verses said she vexed him and soothed him in turn, for the Deliverer's First Wife was his *zahven*.

Outside the room, there was a crack, and a cry. Damaji Qezan had forgotten his lessons on embracing pain, it seemed. This refresher was a good one. Aleverak scolded his weakness, and the next blow was borne with only a gasp. The third in silence.

Not bothering to light a lamp, Inevera moved to close the thick curtains that hung beside the room's great windows. As she shrouded them in darkness, Jardir's senses came alive.

The Crown of Kaji had always conveyed wardsight, much as the coins on Inevera's brow, but ever since the fight with the mind demon when the greater powers of his crown came alive, he had begun to see more – auras surrounding people that told him their feelings and gave him insight into their motives. Suddenly the infinite wisdom of Kaji began to make sense. With the crownsight to see the hearts of his people, Jardir could be a greater leader by far.

More, he realized that he could tap into the power of the crown and spear at will. During the day, he could pull power from the ancient artefacts to heal himself, ignore exhaustion, or give himself superhuman strength and speed. It was a powerful advantage, but not without its limitations.

In the darkness, many of those limitations faded away. He was powerful like he never dreamed possible, but, with Waning approaching, he feared in his heart it was still not enough.

Inevera moved to her favoured casting pillow, and Jardir moved to take the one facing as was his habit. Outside, Damaji Ichach's punishment had begun, and the cleric shamed himself by weeping. Jardir turned his attention from it as Inevera drew the curved blade that had cut him countless times over the years.

'What shall I ask first?' she said.

Her aura pulsed on the word *first*, and Jardir knew she had already used the dice for her own purposes. It was not a lie precisely, but it told him much. Inevera had always kept her own plans a mystery while insisting she be privy to his.

Jardir rolled his sleeve and held out his arm. She pressed the sharp point into a vein and tipped a small bowl to catch the flow. When it was full, she pressed her thumb against the vein and reached for her herb pouch.

'There is no need,' Jardir said, pulling a touch of power from the spear resting beside him. He lifted his arm from her grasp, showing that the blood flow had ceased and the wound closed. Inevera eyed the healing in surprise, but he gave her no time to question. 'Let us begin with Abban's plan to assault Docktown on first snow. Those plans must be set in motion soon, if we are to have the advantage of surprise.'

Hatred skittered across Inevera's aura at the mention of Abban. He knew she blamed the *khaffit* for their rift, and did not trust him. She was eager to prove her worth by showing him the errors in the plan and offering better advice in turn.

But these were surface feelings. At her centre she was calm as she reached for the dice, spilling a bit of his blood upon them as she whispered her prayers and shook. As always, the evil glow pulsing between her fingers unsettled him.

Inevera cast the dice down and spent a few moments staring at them, studying the pattern. Jardir studied her in turn, searching her aura for hints of truth behind her coming words. She was not pleased with the results. This much was clear.

'You cannot go back,' she said, staring at the patterns. 'And you cannot afford to stand still. The only way is forward. The *khaffit*'s,' she hissed the word, 'plan will spare many lives.'

'More to stand in Sharak Ka,' Jardir said.

'Or oppose you later,' Inevera noted. It was good advice, but her aura said it was spoken more in bitterness at having to admit Abban was right.

'That is a risk I must take,' Jardir said. 'What else do the dice say? Tell me everything for once, and spare me the dissembling!'

Inevera's aura flashed at him, telling him to step wisely. She wanted to impress him, but her pride was a mountain. He could not bully her as he did the *Damaji*.

'Doom befall the armies of the Deliverer if they should march north with enemies unconquered at their back.' She tilted her head, examining the dice from another angle. 'You cannot take your forces to the Hollow without first taking Lakton, nor Angiers without the Hollow beside you.'

'Of that, at least, I am unconcerned,' Jardir said. 'The Hollow tribe will follow me when called.'

An image of Mistress Leesha hovered ghostlike above Inevera, connected to her by anger, jealousy, and hate. It was a vision he had seen before, but there was genuine doubt beneath this veneer. Inevera did not believe the Hollow as secure as he did. She thought him a fool to be so trusting. 'You will not have the loyalty of the Hollow until you kill the Painted Man. The one they call Deliverer.'

It was clear from her aura that this was her opinion and not that of the dice, but it was sound advice. Leesha loved him, he did not doubt, and was fated to marry him and bring him her tribe, but it would not happen without confronting this false Deliverer and throwing him down.

He nodded. 'Is there anything else?'

Irritation skittered along Inevera's aura, never touching her face or bearing. Her eyes drifted along the dozens of facing symbols, all glowing with varying degrees of brightness, following paths of meaning. He recognized some symbols, but their meaning had ever been beyond him. Sometimes he thought to command the *dama'ting* teach him to read the dice, but knew they would baulk, and Inevera find a way to prevent it. Even the Evejah said it was a woman's art.

Finally, Inevera spoke. 'You must lead your armies if they are to achieve victory in the Daylight War, but do not leave the Skull Throne vacant too long. You have fifty-two sons, and they will all eye it hungrily.'

Jardir frowned. Jayan and Asome coveted the throne, he knew. Perhaps making the boy Andrah was best after all. 'Are any of my sons worthy to sit it in my absence, and willing to stand back up upon my return?'

Inevera cut her own hand, dripping her own blood on the dice in addition to Jardir's as she cast again. She studied the pattern for only a moment before looking up. 'No.'

'No?' Jardir asked. 'Just "no"?'

Inevera shrugged. 'It is not as I would have it, either, husband, but the dice are clear. I have cast the dice for thousands of men, and never found another with your potential.'

There. It was clear in her aura, shining like a beacon through her mask of *dama'ting* serenity.

She was lying. There was another.

Anger filled him. Who was this man, or boy? Why was she protecting him? Did she mean to supplant him if he should prove too difficult to control?

He embraced the feeling as quickly as it came, showing no sign. He was not a manipulator like Inevera or Abban, dissembling with half-truths, omissions, and leading statements, but he was learning to keep his thoughts to himself, giving them no thread to spin, much as he denied opponents energy to turn against him in *sharusahk*. He set aside the concern for later. For now, he had more pressing questions.

'How can I throw back my enemies in the coming Waning?' he asked.

Again Inevera wet the dice with his blood and cast the bones to the floor. She saw something that made her aura become one of sharp concentration, crawling on her knees to study the pattern from all sides. Her gossamer clothing pulled tight, presenting her much as she was in lovemaking, but her growing aura of fear drove such thoughts from his mind. She was seeing something she did not wish to tell him, and was searching for a way out of it. He wanted to shout at her, to demand what she was seeing, but forced himself to remain calm.

At last she looked at him. 'The Deliverer must go into the night alone to hunt the centre of the web, or all will be lost when Alagai Ka and his princelings come. But even if you survive, there will be a heavy price.'

He looked at her, seeing the fear in her aura reach out and clutch at him. She did not want him to risk himself. Was it born of love, or was her replacement simply not ready? There was no way to know. He hated himself for considering the latter, but she had already deceived him more than once.

'Princelings?' he asked instead. 'How many? What web?'

'Seven will rise, one for each layer of Nie's abyss,' Inevera said, 'but only three will strike at Everam's Bounty.'

'"Only", you say.' Jardir shook his head. 'Everam's beard. One nearly proved our undoing.'

'You were not prepared then,' Inevera said.

'It infiltrated the palace, Inevera,' Jardir said. 'Slipped past the work of our finest Warders like it was nothing.'

'We have added protections since,' Inevera said. 'The *alagai* princes will not penetrate our warding so easily now, and I will cast the dice to find the weakest points of our net and bolster them.'

Jardir nodded. 'And this web?'

Inevera shrugged. 'Of that, I can tell you nothing.'

'No attempts to dissuade me from this course?' he asked.

His *Jiwah Ka* shook her head sadly. 'It is *inevera*. Sharak Ka is yours to win, husband.'

Or lose. Inevera did not speak the words, but they were clear in her aura. His success was by no means assured.

'Where will the demons strike hardest?' Jardir asked, his most pressing question. 'Where should I position my forces?'

Inevera cast again, staring for a long time at the result. At last, she sighed. 'I do not know. There are too many variables. I will try again in the coming days.'

'Every day,' Jardir said. 'A hundred times if you must. Nothing is more important.'

Inevera bowed slightly, lifting the dice one last time. 'We will cast now for the coming day.'

Jardir nodded. This was a practice they had done nightly for almost twenty years. Some days, the dice told him nothing – at least, nothing Inevera chose to share – but others they warned of hidden knives and poison, or when to be ready to seize an advantage.

Inevera tipped the last of his blood onto the dice and shook as she said the words Jardir had heard countless times. 'Everam, giver of light and life, I beseech you, give this lowly servant knowledge

673

of what is to come. Tell me of Ahmann, son of Hoshkamin, last scion of the line of Jardir, the seventh son of Kaji.'

She threw, and the dice scattered wide, symbols pulsing in patterns he could not hope to comprehend.

'You will give the *dama'ting* a powerful gift today,' Inevera said.

'Kind of me,' Jardir noted. He saw no deception in his wife, but that did not mean his gift would be a willing one, rather than something duped from him.

Inevera gave no indication she had heard him. 'You will gain warriors tonight, but lose others on the morrow.'

'Gain at night?' Jardir asked. 'Lose during the day? How is this possible?'

'I do not know,' Inevera said, but Jardir could see in her aura that her words were only half true, and had to suppress a flash of anger. What secrets was she hiding? How was he to lead their people to victory when his own wife kept secrets about his warriors?

As they had frequently in recent weeks, his thoughts turned to Leesha Paper. The woman could be vexing in her own ways, but he did not believe she had ever lied to him. He wished she was here by his side, not this . . . tunnel asp.

'Not long after sunrise tomorrow, an unexpected Messenger will bring you ill tidings,' Inevera went on.

'That happens every day,' Jardir said, hardly caring any more.

Inevera shook her head. 'This one has passed through death to see his missive delivered.'

That got Jardir's attention, and he looked up at her as she squinted at the dice. 'His message will bring you pain.'

He saw no deception in her, but as she spoke the words, her aura pulsed. There was nothing in her expression, no outward sign, but to his eyes it was plain as day.

Empathy. Without even knowing the cause, her heart had cried out for him, when she realized he would be hurt. His pain was her pain.

He reached out to her, his anger gone, and gently touched her face. She looked at him, and her aura had never shone so bright.

Whatever else she might feel, wherever her loyalties might lie, she loved him.

Oh, my Jiwah Ka, Jardir thought sadly. *How I have wronged you.*

۞

'The Deliverer is not to be disturbed, *khaffit*!' Jardir heard Hasik's growl even through the covered walls and door of Inevera's pillow chamber. With the crown atop his head, he could hear the wind buffeting the wings of birds high in the sky, and his *ajin'pal* was not a quiet man.

Jardir sat up, waking Inevera in the process. *Abban.*

He looked at Inevera and smiled, trying to convey all the love he felt for her, and knowing it fell short. Inevera's return smile was genuine, and her aura gave back his love with equal fervour.

He kissed her again. 'Duty calls, beloved.'

She nodded, helping him into his raiment before seeing to her own. When they were composed, they left the chamber, returning to the throne room.

It was empty, but it was little surprise after Asome's lesson. Jardir sniffed, smelling the blood of the *Damaji* spattered on the carpet.

He pointed to a few drops. 'Ichach.' He sniffed again and turned, pointing a few feet away. 'Qezan.'

Inevera nodded, taking special cloths from her pouch and carefully blotting up as much of the blood as possible for her spells. If his *Damaji* were to turn on him over this indignity, he wished to know of it. His Jama and Khanjin sons were still in their *nie'dama* bidos, but he would raise them himself if necessary to keep his tribes unified.

He strode up the steps to the Skull Throne, throwing back his warded cloak as he sat. He waited for Inevera to join him on the dais, then clapped his hands loudly. Immediately, Hasik appeared at the door, bowing deeply.

'Show Abban in,' Jardir said. Hasik had a surprised look on his face, but he nodded, and a moment later the fat *khaffit* appeared at the door, bowing as low as his crutch would allow.

'Abban, my friend!' Jardir beckoned the *khaffit*. Inevera shifted beside him, and he did not need to see her aura to know what she was feeling. He had seen Abban's aura, and knew the *khaffit* harboured similar feelings towards his First Wife.

No matter, he thought. *They must learn to abide each other.*

Abban stopped at the base of the dais, but Jardir waved him still closer. 'You may climb three steps,' he smiled, 'one for each of your legs.'

Abban smirked, tapping his crutch against his leg. 'My wives would tell you that meant I could take a fourth step as well.'

To Jardir's surprise, Inevera laughed at this, and Jardir nodded. 'I remember you in your bido, and think your wives flatter you, but the sound of the Damajah's laughter pleases me. You may take the fourth step.' Abban ascended quickly, not questioning his fortune.

'We have consulted on your plan, and find it sound,' Jardir said. 'We will attack Docktown on first snow. Begin the preparations, but say nothing to anyone.'

Abban bowed. 'The longer the secret is kept, the less chance the Laktonians will have to flee. If I had my way, even your generals would know nothing until the time came to signal the attack.'

'It is sound advice,' Inevera agreed.

Jardir nodded. 'But that is not why you come to me today, Abban, and I have not summoned you. What draws you from the centre of your web?'

'My people have made a . . . delicate discovery,' Abban said. For an instant his eyes flicked to Inevera.

Jardir sighed. Was there no trust to be found anywhere in his court? 'Speak.'

Abban bowed again, reaching into a pocket in the fine tan vest he wore over his colourful silk shirt. He withdrew the hand, holding out a lump of silvery metal.

Inevera stiffened, and Jardir, too, recognized it immediately. He was out of the throne in an instant, snatching it from the *khaffit*'s hand. He hadn't held it a moment before Inevera snatched it in turn, holding it to the light, this way and that.

'This is the same metal as the Spear and Crown of Kaji,' she said, voicing all their thoughts.

Abban nodded. 'Our metallurgists have long sought to unlock the secrets of the artefacts of the first Deliverer. Too pale to be gold, but neither were they silver, or platinum. Our best guess had been white gold, an alloy made by adding nickel to pure gold. Jewellers in the bazaar have been using it for centuries.' He smiled. 'Cheaper than gold, it sells for nearly twice the price to fools who think it exotic. This,' he pointed to the lump of metal, 'is electrum.'

'Electrum?' Jardir asked.

'A natural alloy of silver and gold, I am told,' Abban said.

Jardir's eyes narrowed. 'Told by whom?'

Abban turned, clapping loudly as Jardir himself had done before. Immediately Hasik appeared at the door. 'Show in our guest,' Abban called. Hasik glared at him, but when Jardir did not countermand the order, he vanished, escorting a Rizonan man into the room. The man was old, squinting in the light, his face and hands smudged with dirt. He held a hat in his hands.

'Rennick, master of one of Shar'Dama Ka's gold mines,' Abban introduced. Hasik grabbed the man roughly, forcing him to his knees and pressing his forehead to the floor.

'Enough,' Jardir said. 'Hasik. Leave us.' The warrior pursed his lips, but bowed and vanished again.

'You, Master Rennick, approach the dais,' Jardir called. 'Tell us what you know of this metal.'

Rennick approached, wringing the hat in his hands like a laundress. 'It's like I said to Abban, Yur Grace. That there is electrum. Seen it once before, when I was a boy working another mine down south. The signs are in the rock. Vein of silver ran into the gold. It don't happen often, and there ent much of it. Yur mine is safe.'

Safe, Jardir thought, *as if I care a whit for gold.*

'Can you make more of it?' Jardir asked.

The miner shrugged. 'Reckon so, though maybe not as pure. But why? Might fetch a fair price as a novelty, but it ent worth as much as pure gold.'

Jardir nodded, then clapped again, signalling Hasik to remove the man. 'Make sure that man does not speak to anyone,' he told Abban.

'Already done,' Abban said. 'He will be taken right to the forges where my private smiths work, and never seen again. His family will be told he was killed in a cave-in, and compensated handsomely.' Jardir nodded.

'I must take it to my chamber and confirm its power,' Inevera said.

Jardir nodded. 'We will wait.'

Inevera looked at Abban, and Jardir cut her off with a chopping motion of his hand. 'I am not a fool, wife. I see how you and Abban look at each other, circling my throne and marking it with your piss. But I have chosen to trust the two of you, and in this, at least, you must trust each other.'

Inevera drew in her brows, but she nodded, disappearing into her chamber and returning several minutes later.

'What is more precious than gold?' she asked.

Jardir looked to Abban, and both men shrugged.

'It is an ancient question of the *dama'ting* seeking the Damajah's sacred metal,' Inevera said. 'Precious metals conduct magic better than base ones, but even gold cannot transfer without loss.' She held up the lump of electrum. 'At long last, we have found the answer.'

Jardir took the lump, studying it. He lifted it and put his teeth to it, seeing the imprint they left. 'But the crown and spear are harder than the finest steel. No hammer or forge can even scratch them. This metal is soft. It will not even hold an edge.'

'Not now, perhaps,' Inevera said, 'but when charged with magic, it will be indestructible.'

Jardir felt a tingle in his crotch at the word. The thought of making more weapons as powerful as his spear was intoxicating. Suddenly winning Sharak Ka seemed within his grasp. 'Imagine the power my warriors will have . . .'

Abban cleared his throat, interrupting the thought.

'A thousand apologies, Deliverer,' the *khaffit* said when Jardir looked to him, 'but do not put the cart before the camel. As Rennick said, there is but a small vein of the stuff.'

'How small?' Jardir asked. He gave Abban a hard look. 'I will know if you lie to me, Abban.'

Abban shrugged. 'Thirty pounds? Perhaps fifty? Not enough to arm even the Spears of the Deliverer. And, I might add, you might think twice about arming any warrior with such a potent weapon, lest he begin to have delusions of grandeur.' He smiled. 'It's been known to happen.'

Jardir scowled, but Inevera broke in. 'I agree with the *khaffit*.'

Jardir looked at her in surprise. 'Twice in one day? Everam's wonders never cease.'

'Do not grow accustomed to it,' Inevera said drily. 'But in this case, your weaponsmiths are not the ones best suited to make use of this discovery.'

Jardir looked at her a long time, remembering her words in the pillow chamber.

You will give the dama'ting *a powerful gift today.*

He nodded. 'So be it.'

Safe in her Chamber of Shadows, Inevera stared at the lump of electrum in her left hand while slowly rolling her *alagai hora* in her right. She marvelled as thin tendrils of ambient magic wafted towards the electrum and were absorbed, the way a slight draught might pull at smoke. Even without wards the metal Drew, glowing dully in the wardlight.

Dama'ting frequently made jewellery with demon bone cores, but it was forbidden to coat the dice, for the transfer with other precious metals was imperfect, and had been proven to affect foretelling. She looked at her precious dice, restored at last, and smiled. She was already preparing to carve another set as a safeguard, but now she need never fear exposing them to the sun again.

Already she was pondering other applications. *Hora* were destroyed when their power was expended, but coated in electrum, they could be recharged, used again and again, as the Spear of Kaji. Abban had not lied when he said this power was too great to be trusted to common soldiers. Even *dama'ting* would stop at nothing to get more of the metal if they learned its origins. She might gift electrum-coated *hora* to her most trusted followers, but she would need to prepare it all herself. She looked around the chamber, considering how best to vent a forge so deep underground without sacrificing the security of her private Vault.

At last she breathed deeply, clearing her mind, and put the metal away. She cast her bones once more, hoping to glean a few last clues of the night to come, then left the Chamber of Shadows.

She kept her centre, but the wind was strong. For all the precautions she might take, the secret of the metal was already in the hands of the one she trusted least.

As she felt the Vault door lock behind her, she made a slight gesture, and three eunuch Watchers melted out of the shadows to stand before her. These were Enkido's finest protégés, men who did not exist, trained to walk unseen even in crowded day, to stand motionless for hours, to climb sheer walls, and to kill quickly and silently. Tongueless, they could not speak, but they knew well how to listen.

Follow the Shar'Dama Ka's khaffit, Inevera told them with quick gestures of her nimble fingers. *Track his every movement, and report to me everyone he speaks with, everywhere he goes. Infiltrate the fortress he is building, and take stock of the secrets within.*

The men moved their fingers in perfect unison, like mirror images of one another. *We understand, and obey.* They bowed, and vanished as Inevera began the long climb back up to the palace proper.

Even after months, Jardir still marvelled at the lightness of his fighting robes as Inevera helped him prepare for the night's *alagai'sharak*. No longer thick material housing metal plates, he now wore thin silk that could be quickly cast aside to bring his skin, scarred into fighting and protective wards, to bear. He was now safer naked than in the strongest armour.

'I will join you tonight as you walk the naked night,' Inevera said, when the dressing was done.

Jardir looked at her, but the sun had not quite set, and her aura was hidden. 'I do not think that is wise, beloved. *Alagai'sharak* is no . . .'

Inevera hissed, dismissing his words with a wave. 'You will walk the night with Leesha Paper, but not your *Jiwah Ka*?'

In his heart, Jardir knew the anger on her face was only a mask. He would bet his crown that she had planned this conversation well in advance, likely with the aid of her dice. But even so, he could not deny the effectiveness of her scowl.

Perhaps it was because she was right.

The look softened immediately, and Inevera pressed in so close he could feel the warmth and softness of her skin through his silk robes. 'I battled at your side against an *alagai* prince and his bodyguard,' she reminded him. 'What need I fear of common demons when I walk at the side of Shar'Dama Ka?'

'Even common demons must be respected,' he said, though he knew she had already won. 'Forget that for an instant, and even the Damajah can be killed.' He reached out, sliding his hand under the vaporous silks to caress the smooth skin between her breasts, feeling the beat of her heart. 'Chosen of Everam or not, we are but flesh and blood.'

Inevera moved into his caress, snaking her own hands into his robes. 'I will not forget, beloved.' She traced her fingers over the wards she had cut into his chest. 'But do not forget that as you have your protections, I have my own.'

Jardir smiled. 'Of that, I have no doubt.'

They left the palace together, Inevera resting in a palanquin atop a camel and Jardir on his white charger. They were followed by the amazed stares of everyone they passed, but none dared speak a word of protest.

Despite his words, Jardir did not truly fear for his bride. Most of the demons had been cleared from his territory, and the thin remainder served as little more than a training exercise for his men.

Everam's Bounty was built like the head of a sunflower with the city proper as its centre, spreading out into vast petals of farm and pasture. The central city was Jardir's personal territory, and tribe neutral. It consisted of an inner walled district surrounded by a much larger outer city. The petals he had given to the tribes according to their size. The Kaji, Majah, and Mehnding controlled huge territories of individually warded farmland and villages. The smaller tribes were given as much land as they could hold, and to spare. Even so, there were *chin* villages on the outskirts that had yet to fully take the yoke, simply because there were not enough *Sharum* and *dama* to minister them.

Many of Jardir's warriors remained spread over these territories

– both a weakness and a strength. Decentralizing his forces weakened them in some ways, but it made it as difficult for the *alagai* to choose targets as it was for him to guess where they would strike hardest. Each tribe had its own strongholds and was responsible for seeing as many of its people and as much of its produce as possible through the Waning. But all sent Jayan a tithe of their best men to defend the capital.

Jayan was at the training grounds when they arrived, supervising the muster of these elite warriors. His white turban singled him out from a distance, surrounded by his white-veiled *kai'Sharum*. Asome was with him, leading the men in prayer to almighty Everam before the sun set and Nie's abyss opened.

The two men looked up at their approach, and despite their rivalry, Jardir could not deny his pleasure at seeing his eldest sons standing together, leading his forces. As children they had dreamed of being Sharum Ka and Andrah, a dream shared by their father. Already, Jayan had taken his title, and Asome was readying for his.

Jayan bowed deeply, but his disapproval was clear as he eyed his mother, outside after the *dama* had sung the curfew. Asome likely shared his opinion, but the younger man's face was blank, revealing nothing. Jayan had learned well the strategy and fighting skills of the *dama* in Sharik Hora, but their discipline had been a harder lesson. Not for the first time, Jardir wondered at the wisdom of giving him the white turban when he was so young. It was difficult to teach a man discipline when he already sat a throne.

'Your warriors stand ready for inspection, Father,' Jayan said. While not skilled at hiding his feelings, he wasn't fool enough to disrespect his mother by speaking his thoughts aloud. It was not out of respect for his father – though they both knew Jardir would not hesitate to put the boy down should he think himself above the Damajah. Inevera had instilled fear of her own into her sons, and even now they grew chill at the notion of disobedience.

None of your sons is worthy, the dice had said, and in his heart Jardir knew it to be true. With the magic of the crown and spear strengthening him and keeping him young, Jardir might live for centuries, as did Kaji. But he was not fool enough to fail to prepare for his death. If he could not find an heir to take his place as Shar'Dama Ka, perhaps he could leave Jayan the spear and Asome the crown. Again he wondered at the secret Inevera was keeping from him. Who was the other she had seen?

Inevera took in the assembled warriors, and Jardir felt himself swell with pride. In the years since he had taken the white turban of Sharum Ka, he had built them up with blood and sweat from a loose group of shrinking tribal militias to an elite fighting force unified in purpose and growing exponentially in number.

Even the assembled *kha'Sharum* and *chi'Sharum* were marching with precision. He had been amazed at how effective the *khaffit* warriors had proven, and while most greenlanders remained soft and cowardly, many were finding their hearts. The rest would slow the *alagai* long enough for his real warriors to slaughter them, and go to Everam clean of spirit.

He looked to Inevera, but she only shrugged. 'It is as I expected. Let us tour the defences.'

Jardir tried not to feel stung as he turned to Jayan and Asome. 'The inner city is yours tonight, my sons. We will range as the Damajah wills. The Spears of the Deliverer will see to our protection.'

Inevera touched his arm. 'I would feel safer, beloved, with our sons leading our honour guard.'

Jardir looked at her curiously, wishing the sun would set so he could pierce the veil of serenity on her face to find the truth of her intentions. At last he shrugged.

Jayan turned, giving last orders to his *kai'Sharum*. Immediately the units began to break out of the training ground on their way to their posts.

Asome bowed deeply. 'It is our honour to escort our divine

mother.' He called for his horse, a white charger like the one his father rode, save for a black diamond at its forehead. Jayan signalled for his, a black charger with white fetlocks and muzzle. They flanked Jardir and Inevera as they rode, followed in turn by the Spears of the Deliverer on their great black mustang.

As they conducted the tour Jardir lamented – not for the first time – how woefully insecure the greenland city was. The very weaknesses that had allowed his warriors to take 'Fort' Rizon so easily made the coming Waning fill him with dread. In time he would make Everam's Bounty more impregnable than the Desert Spear itself, but for now he was left to work with what the lax Northern barbarians had built.

The inner city was the most defensible area, but also the most obvious target, as it housed the grain silos and Jardir's seat of power. It was also where, lacking a proper Undercity, the women and children of the outer regions would be sent to take refuge. Even the *chin* were to be taken in. The *Damaji* had protested, but Jardir ignored them. It was the duty of men to protect women and children. Even *chin*.

The greenlanders claimed no *alagai* had penetrated the inner city in a century, but Jardir suspected it was because it had never truly been tested. The wardwall was barely taller than most rock demons. His stonemasons and Warders had been adding to it since they took the city, but it was still pathetic compared with the great wardwall of the Desert Spear. Jardir looked at the scorpions and stone slingers lining the newly built crenellations and hoped they would be enough to hold back a more direct assault. He was prepared for fighting in the streets of the main city, but if it came to that, it would mean the battle was going very badly.

The next line of defence was the outer city, several times the size of the inner and protected by a wardwall so low a man could leap over it. This wall had stone wardpillars like the obelisks of Anoch Sun set every twenty feet, casting overlapping protections to strengthen the defensive field.

Pillars throughout the outer city linked with it and one another, maintaining a net to cover the land from above as well, protecting the New Bazaar, orchards, and farmland that the inner city needed to survive.

The territory had been too vast for the *chin* to ward completely, leaving many pockets large enough for demons to rise. These were hunted clean each night, but places where the demons could infiltrate if they rose in numbers. Even with thousands of *chin* conscripts, Jardir did not have enough men to guard them all.

Yet despite these weaknesses, the outer city was surprisingly defensible. A single thrown boulder could take out a wardpillar, but the gap would soon be closed by another, each able to work independent of the others. This created a Maze of sorts, and his men knew well how to fight in a Maze, filling it with lures, pits, and ambush points. *Alagai* attempting to make their way to the inner city's walls would be harried every step of the way.

Darkness fell as they rode, and with it came the welcome glow of crownsight. He felt his senses sharpen even further as his powers came to life, picking out the cries of *alagai* and the clash of spears and shields as the *Sharum* made their ambushes. It seemed a sin that Jardir felt more comfortable at night than in the day, but no thing happened but that Everam willed it. The Shar'Dama Ka needed to be at home in darkness.

He glanced at his sons, and took hope seeing they, too, were pondering the defences. Occasionally they came upon groups of *Sharum* engaged in fighting, but in most cases it was firmly under control, with seasoned warriors using the sparse demons as living lessons to the less experienced. Once they witnessed a more protracted battle, but even that was handled smoothly without need of their interference.

'Have you seen all you wish, my wife?' Jardir asked after they had ridden for more than an hour. He watched her aura carefully, but it was calm and smooth, telling him nothing.

'Almost, husband.' Inevera pointed to a hillock not far off. 'But first, perhaps we could have a greater vantage atop there?'

Jardir nodded, and they set off. It came as no surprise when the sounds of battle reached his ears.

From atop the hill, they saw a reap of field demons in the valley below, circling a pair of slender *dal'Sharum* standing back-to-back. The warriors seemed unharmed, but they were outnumbered more than three to one, and thus unlikely to remain so. On foot, the warriors could not hope to escape. Even Krasian chargers could not outsprint a field demon.

Jardir tensed, ready to gallop to their aid, when Inevera raised a hand. 'Just watch, beloved. We are not meant to interfere.'

All three men looked at Inevera, but she sat serene in her palanquin, her aura calm, though laced with satisfaction. They turned back, watching the battle unfold.

'Who are they?' Jayan wondered. 'What unit are they from? This pocket isn't due to be swept for another hour.'

Just then the largest of the field demons broke the circling ring to leap at one of the warriors who seemed to have dropped his guard. It was a lure, and the warrior whirled the moment the attack came, driving his spear right down its throat. Another demon leapt at the opening, but the warrior's partner had his shield in place to block. He struck a blow of his own, hard in the foreleg joint, that sent the demon skittering back with a yelp.

From the other side of the ring, more attacks came, but the first warrior pulled his ichor-stained spear free and they rotated a quarter turn in perfect precision to put his shield in place.

So impressed was Jardir with the warriors' skill, it took him a moment to realize there had been no flare of magic when the warriors struck. He looked to Inevera. 'Their spears are not warded?'

Inevera shook her head. 'They fight in the old way, as did my honoured husband.'

'Everam's beard,' Jayan said. Even he had never faced an *alagai* without a warded weapon. Asome was silent, but he drew wards in the air, blessing the combatants.

Without combat magic the *Sharum* blows had to be precise, for the demons' armour had few weaknesses, and they healed quickly. The field demons struck like lightning, flashing paws and snapping jaws, sometimes darting in low and others standing on hind legs to strike high. After the first of them fell, its fellows grew more cautious, the quick and agile beasts dodging return blows the moment they began.

But the warriors fought like nothing Jardir had ever seen, working in perfect unison, like a single fighter with two heads and four arms. Again and again the demons were thrown back, until one, struck what seemed a glancing blow by one of the warriors, had its leg collapse under it. The pair had already begun to turn, and the other warrior put the sharp point of his spear into its eye socket and the brain beyond, killing it.

They might have fallen into a more defensive posture then, but instead the warriors exploded into motion, spinning to let a pouncing demon get between them. They stepped together hard, the defensive wards on their shields flaring and crushing the demon between them.

Now outnumbered two to one, the warriors grew more bold, stepping apart and letting the demons surround them.

Fools, Jardir thought. *Why give up the advantage?*

But the warriors had given up nothing. The demons came at them from all sides, but they used their shields to maximum effect, whipping their spears· to parry and harry as they moved, every step in control. A demon charged one headlong while his shield and spear were out wide, but the warrior leaned forward and kicked his foot up behind him like a scorpion to strike over his head. The demon took the blow to the face, knocking it aside. Before it could recover, he was on its fellow, striking a precise blow down its throat for another kill.

The other warrior had finished a demon as well, and fighting one-to-one they dropped their shields, forgoing defence entirely. The demons attacking them went for the bait, snapping their jaws forward, but the warriors, like mirror images of each other, caught the bites on the shafts of their spears, twisting before the wood could shatter and turning the demons' own momentum against them. They swung, slamming the flailing demons together, taking satisfaction at the deep gouges their talons left on one another. They snapped their spears back into position and struck at the wounds, driving into the vulnerable flesh beneath.

They stood breathless, regarding the *alagai* corpses around them. One twitched, but the nearest warrior was quick to finish it off as Inevera kicked her camel and headed down the hill towards them.

Jardir and the others followed, awestruck. When they closed in, the warriors bowed deeply, first to Inevera, and then to Jardir. When they straightened, Jardir's eyes nearly bulged from his head. Their warrior's garb hid much, but their auras could not hide the curves of their bodies.

Women.

'Shar'Dama Ka,' their melodious voices said in unison, 'we come before you to answer your call. We pray these *alagai* are a worthy sacrifice for the first of your *Sharum'ting*.'

'*Sharum . . . ting?*' Jayan said in disbelief.

In response, the women reached up, removing their turbans and veils with the same synchronous precision with which they fought. Jardir held his breath, having already identified them by their auras. Inevera was clever. He could not deny it. But she had struck a hornets' nest this time. Even Asome's calm was broken. 'What in Nie's abyss?!'

'Shanvah?' Shanjat demanded, seeing his daughter, Jardir's niece by his sister Hoshvah, standing before them.

But it was the other woman that caused Asome's aura to

flare so bright with rage that Jardir felt blinded by it even in periphery. Ashia, Ashan's daughter by his eldest sister, Imisandre.

Asome's First Wife.

Dawn was approaching; the stained-glass windows of the throne room beginning to fill with colour. Every ancient rite of *Sharum* naming had been observed. The young women had more than fulfilled the demon killing requirements, standing face-to-face with *alagai* in the naked night and not giving ground. Inevera had cast the bones for them, and – of course – pronounced them worthy. Now all that was left was to wait for sunrise, and his decision.

It was not an easy decision to make. Beyond the far-reaching cultural implications, either choice would directly cost him respect and loyalty from valuable allies and family.

He looked at Inevera, her aura still infuriatingly self-satisfied. She loved him, but that was not the same as being on his side. She seemed almost bored as she lounged on her bed of pillows, but beneath she was intensely focused.

Beside her on his throne, Jardir watched as Asome and Ashia quietly argued in a small alcove at the far end of the room. It took only a little concentration to see through the stone and make out their auras. His sharp ears picked up every word.

'How can you shame me like this?' Asome demanded, his hands shaking. Jardir had made a point of reminding him that he considered striking his sister's daughters as great a crime as striking a *dama'ting*, but Asome's aura showed he was considering it anyway.

'Shame you?' Ashia's aura was flat and even, like that of a warrior who had embraced her fears and let them fall away. 'Husband, you should be proud of me. Shanvah and I are the first Krasian women in history to stand in the night and be baptized in demon ichor. How does this bring anything but honour to your name?'

'Honour?' Asome asked. 'As you parade around unveiled in men's clothes? Where is the honour in every man I meet thinking I cannot control my own wife?'

'I do not wish to be controlled!' Ashia snapped. 'You and my brother may have convinced my father to give me to you, but it was never my desire.'

'Am I unworthy?' Asome asked. 'The Deliverer's second son is not enough for you? Perhaps you wish you had been given to Jayan?'

'I, too, am blood of the Deliverer,' Ashia said, 'and a princess of the Kaji. I do not wish be *given* to anyone!'

Asome shook his head, genuine confusion in his aura. 'Have I not been a good husband? Given you everything you desire? Put a child in you?'

'You and Asukaji have never cared a whit for my desires,' Ashia said. 'You dressed me in silk and bathed me in luxuries, but otherwise haven't given me a thought, save on our wedding night when Asukaji watched and stroked his cock as you put a child in me, and forty weeks later when the two of you ripped my newborn son from my arms.'

'I will give you more children,' Asome said. 'Sons. Daughters . . .' Jardir could see him desperately trying to understand her desires, if only to deter her and save face.

'No,' Ashia said. 'I am not just a womb to carry your children because Asukaji cannot! You and your pillow friend have the son you wanted. Now I will have my own life.'

Asome's aura went red then, and Ashia's showed she knew her husband was about to strike her – was goading him even. She had already planned her parry and return blows.

'Asome!' Jardir boomed. 'Attend me!' Man and wife turned to him, the moment shattered. Asome strode away from his wife without another look.

'Father!' he called. 'You cannot permit this madness to continue!'

'I agree,' Ashan said, standing at the base of the throne with Asukaji. His aura made clear his expectation that Jardir, out of the love and loyalty they shared, would not condemn his foolish daughter to life as a *Sharum*.

'I gave my word, Ashan,' Jardir said. 'I will not be forsworn.'

'The Deliverer is correct, he cannot be forsworn,' Aleverak said. Everyone looked at him in surprise, not believing the conservative *Damaji* would approve.

Jardir would never admit it, but he loved Damaji Aleverak. He did not always agree with the man, but the *Damaji's* honour was greater than that of any man he had ever met. Even after he tore Aleverak's arm off, Jardir had not managed to make the ancient cleric fear him. Aleverak could ever be counted on to argue Jardir's decisions.

Before they were made. Afterwards, however foolish he might think them, Aleverak followed the commands of the Shar'Dama Ka, and would kill any who opposed them. Jardir looked at his aura and felt something akin to what a son felt for a father. The *Damaji* had been his greatest opponent on the path to the Skull Throne, and was now perhaps the only man in the world he could trust fully.

Ashan looked about to reply when Aleverak raised his hand to forestall him. He looked at Jardir, and his aura went cold. 'If the Deliverer sees fit to allow some women to become *Sharum*, then that is how it shall be. But your decree did not negate the duties of a daughter and wife that are prescribed in the Evejah. For did not Kaji himself command their obedience?'

Inevera's aura changed to one of amusement at the thought. Everam knew, she was anything but obedient. Jardir snorted and immediately regretted it as he saw how the sound had offended proud Aleverak.

'Wise words, Damaji,' he said quickly, and relaxed as the man's aura was mollified. 'It is true I can bend my words if I wish.'

'Then bend them!' came a shout from across the room.

Jardir looked up as Hasik belatedly shouted, 'The Holy Mother!'

Kajivah, still in sleep blacks, stormed into the room with his sisters Imisandre and Hoshvah in tow, three auras showing as one in outrage. Next to him, Inevera's aura went cold with fear, all sense of smugness gone.

Interesting, he thought, eyes flicking to his wife and watching the threads of emotion that connected her to Kajivah. *She believes my mother can sway me when even my counsellors cannot.*

Looking back to Kajivah, Jardir couldn't deny his wife was right to worry. His mother had occasionally been vexed with him over the years. He was no stranger to that. But never had he dreamed his divine mother could direct such fury at him.

'This is your fault,' Kajivah said, drawing gasps from around the room. 'This is what comes of refusing your nieces the white.'

Asome nodded. 'It was enough you told the world they were not worthy of Everam's grace. Now you decree they should man a spearwall like common warriors?'

Jardir felt his temper flare. He pulled the edge of his white outer robe, revealing the black beneath. '*I* am a common warrior, my son. As is your elder brother.' He glanced at Jayan's aura, not surprised that the boy did not care what he decided. His eldest son did not want the headache of women warriors, but neither did he consider the issue worth crossing his father over. He was content to stand by and enjoy Asome's suffering.

'There was a time when you begged to be a warrior, as well,' Jardir told Asome. 'I mourn the loss of that boy. His honour was boundless.'

'I have led men in the night,' Asome said. Jardir regretted the insult when he saw how deeply it cut at his son's spirit, but now was not the time to coddle.

'From the rear,' Jardir said. 'You are a master tactician and general, my son, but you have not felt the rancid breath of an *alagai* on your face. If you had, you would have more respect for the spear.'

'Father speaks truly, brother,' Jayan said. His aura made his motivations clear, attempting to appear wise while currying his father's favour and kicking his brother for the pleasure of it.

Jardir cast a displeased glance his way, and saw Jayan's aura shrink. 'Everam bless me if I could meld the two of you together like silver and gold to make a fitting heir.'

'I have always respected the spear, my son,' Kajivah said. 'I raised you to do the same, did I not? Everam knows it was hard without Hoshkamin . . .'

Inevera's aura was so exasperated she might as well be shouting, though only Jardir could sense it. To the rest she was studying her painted nails as if they were more interesting than the events at hand. She knew better than to force Jardir to choose between them publicly.

'But I also taught you to respect women,' Kajivah went on. 'To protect and cherish them. To keep them safe in the night, and provide for them. Now you will make them fight? Will you ask children to take up arms next?'

'If I must, to win Sharak Ka,' Jardir said, and even Kajivah sputtered to a stop at that.

He looked around the room for further thoughts, his eyes lighting on Shanjat. He had known the man since they were children in *sharaj* together, and had fought and bled beside him in the night countless times. The *kai'Sharum*'s aura was conflicted, but Jardir could not glean its meaning without more information.

'And you, Shanjat?' he asked. 'What does your heart tell you? Do you wish to see your daughter take the spear?'

Shanjat knelt before the throne, laying his spear next to him. He put his hands on the marble floor and pressed his forehead to it. 'It is not my place to question your decree, Deliverer. It is also not my place to question Damaji Ashan's feelings regarding his daughter, nor Dama Asome his *Jiwah Ka*.'

He lifted his forehead and fell back on his heels. 'For my part, if you had asked me yesterday, I would have shouted at the thought of women beside me in a spearwall, or trusting one with my back in *sharak*.' He looked at Shanvah, and his aura filled with love. 'But I cannot deny that when I watched those two warriors fight, it was glorious. I can think of none, even Spears of the Deliverer, who could have fought better. When they unveiled and I saw my daughter's face, it was not shock or anger I felt, it was pride.'

Shanvah returned her father's look. Jardir could see in the emotions connecting them that she barely knew the man – ignored by him in favour of her brothers and taken from his household early to train in the Dama'ting Palace. Until now, she had felt little for Shanjat, but with his words, a thread of love went out to him in return.

Jardir nodded, considering.

Inevera cleared her throat. 'Husband, with respect, you have consulted your clerics and counsellors. You have consulted the fathers, you have consulted the mothers. You have consulted the husbands, you have consulted the brothers. You have even consulted the *alagai hora*. You have consulted everyone and everything, save the women themselves.'

Jardir nodded, beckoning the would-be *Sharum'ting* forth. 'My beloved nieces,' he said as they knelt before him, 'know that like Shanjat, your honour is boundless in my eyes. But I cannot deny I fear the idea of you out in the night. If you wished to prove something to me, you have proven it. If you wished to honour me, and your bloodline, you have done so. Nothing more is needed for my esteem, and I would not see you pushed into this life by some,' he glanced at Inevera, 'or fleeing to it from others.' His eyes flicked to Asome. 'And so I ask, is this truly what you want?'

Both women nodded immediately. 'It is, Uncle.'

'Think well on this,' Jardir said. 'Your lives will change forever if you take the spear. You may look upon the *Sharum* and see only the excesses they are allowed, but those excesses come at a heavy price. There is glory in the night, but there is also pain and loss. Blood and sacrifice. You will see horrors to haunt you, awake and asleep.'

The women nodded, but he went on. 'It will be even harder on you than on men. The male *Sharum* will expect you to be weak, and will not wish to heed your commands. You will be challenged, and have to be twice the fighters your male *zahven* are until you have their respect. This will not be easy, and I cannot help you there. If men fear to strike you only because they fear me, they will not respect you.'

Ashia looked up at him. 'I have always known Everam had a different path for me than He did your daughters. Now, having stood in the night, I know. If I shame my husband, then dissolve our union that he may find a worthier *Jiwah Ka*. I was meant to die on *alagai* talons.'

Shanvah nodded, taking Ashia's hand as the morning's first sunbeam came in through the windows. 'On *alagai* talons.'

You will gain warriors in the night, Inevera had said, *but lose others on the morrow*. But what did it mean? Did it mean he would refuse them? Or that his men would rebel at the thought of fighting alongside women?

He shook his head. They said the same thing when he made the *kha'Sharum*. Now those men served him with honour. He would not lose warriors by choice. He'd hated the shameful way his mother was treated when he was a child, with no man to speak for her. He had been terrified that he would die, too, and his sisters be claimed by the local *dama* and sold as *jiwah'Sharum*.

Jardir cast his gaze over the court. 'I do not wish to make women fight, but Sharak Ka is nigh, and I will not turn away those who choose to. Kaji may have forbidden women the spear, but the first Deliverer had an army of millions. I do not, but must fight the same war.' He pointed to the kneeling young women with the Spear of Kaji. 'I name you *kai'Sharum'ting*.'

Kajivah wailed.

'Holy Father,' Asome said. 'If my *jiwah* thinks nothing of

her vows to me, then I ask you divorce us now, as she suggests.'

Ashan looked at Asome sharply. The union between Ashan's daughter and Ahmann's son strengthened the ties between their families, and it would be a loss of face for them to be severed.

'No,' Jardir said. 'You and my niece declared your vows before Everam, and I will not let you go back on them. She remains your *Jiwah Ka*, and you will not deny her time with young Kaji. A son needs his mother.'

'So now my granddaughters go to *alagai'sharak* each night?' Kajivah demanded.

'It need not be so,' Inevera offered.

Kajivah stared at her in shock. 'What do you mean?'

'Many of the *dama* have personal guards, *Sharum* only called to *alagai'sharak* on Wanings,' Inevera said. 'If it pleases my honoured husband, I will take them as such.' Jardir gave her a slight nod, and did not need to see her aura to know the sense of satisfaction had returned to his wife.

'Even on Wanings, it will be a mistake to let them join the front lines,' Asome said. 'They will distract men whose attention needs to be in front of them.'

'My warriors will learn to adapt,' Jardir said, though he knew it was not quite so simple.

Asome nodded. 'Perhaps. But is it a lesson you wish to begin while Alagai Ka stalks the land?'

Jardir pursed his lips. 'No,' he said at last. 'I do not know what is coming with the new moon, and it is not the time to force change.'

Asome smirked at the small victory. 'But that goes for the *dama*, as well,' Jardir said.

Asome's eyes widened just slightly. 'Eh?'

'Everam's Bounty would fall into chaos without the *dama*,' Jardir said. 'And so I will not risk you on Waning until I know what we are facing each month. You may join your mother and wife in the underpalace come the new moon.'

Jayan stifled his laugh, but not enough for it to escape his brother's ears.

Be careful, husband, Inevera thought as she watched Ahmann and Asome face off. *He is still your son, and he has his pride.*

Thankfully, their staring was broken by a commotion at the door. Inevera saw a lone *Sharum* striding into the hall. He looked thin and haggard, his blacks filthy with mud, and he stank. She could smell him from across the room.

The warrior planted his spear and fell to one knee before the Skull Throne. 'Shar'Dama Ka, I bring urgent missive from your first daughter, holy Amanvah.'

Ahmann nodded. 'Ghilan asu Fahkin, is it not? You were sent north to guard Mistress Leesha's caravan. What has happened? Are my daughter and intended safe?'

Intended. The word cut at Inevera, even now.

'Both were safe when I left them, Deliverer,' the warrior said, 'but they appeared to have had a . . . conflict.'

'What kind of conflict?' Ahmann demanded.

Ghilan shook his head. 'I do not know, but I believe the holy daughter's letter will say.' He held up a small scroll, sealed in wax.

Ahmann nodded and motioned for Shanjat to take the letter. Shanjat was Ghilan's *kai*, but still the warrior leapt to his feet, backing away.

'What is the meaning of this?' Ahmann said.

'The holy daughter made me take an oath, Shar'Dama Ka, to put the letter into your hand and no other,' Ghilan said.

Ahmann nodded, motioning the man forward. Ghilan sprinted up the steps, falling to one knee again when he was in reach. He kept his eyes down as he handed Ahmann the letter. His voice was low, so only Ahmann and Inevera could hear. 'I will say this, Deliverer. By her own admission, Mistress Leesha poisoned me to prevent my reaching you.'

'She was bluffing,' Ahmann said.

The young *Sharum* shook his head. 'Your pardon, Deliverer, but she was not. After two days I began to weaken. On the third, I fell from my horse and lay for hours, waiting for death.'

'How did you survive?' Inevera asked.

The *Sharum* bowed to her. 'Night was falling, Damajah, and I thought it better to die on *alagai* talons than lying in the dirt, my strength sapped by a woman's poison.'

Ahmann nodded. 'Your heart is that of a true *Sharum*, Ghilan asu Fahkin. What happened then?'

'I barely had strength to stand,' Ghilan said, 'but I hid myself well and bided my time, waiting for a fool *alagai* to venture too close. After some time, a field demon came by, attempting to track my scent. When it drew up to my hiding place, I struck hard.'

'And grew stronger,' Inevera guessed.

Ghilan nodded. 'The blessings of Everam come to those who kill the creatures of Nie. My horse fled, I hunted for the next two nights before my strength was restored. I apologize for the delay, but I have come as quickly as I was able.'

Ahmann put a hand on the man's shoulder. 'I am proud of you, Ghilan asu Fahkin. Know that your honour is boundless. Go now to the great harem and have the *jiwah'Sharum* bathe you and comfort you into a well-needed sleep.'

The warrior nodded, leaving the room as quickly as he entered. Ahmann opened the letter, read it, and passed it to Inevera.

'Husband, I am sorry,' she said as she scanned the contents, 'but I did warn you.'

'Once again your dice have proven true,' Ahmann said. 'I gained two *Sharum'ting* in the night, and lost the warriors of the Hollow come morning.'

'I take no pleasure in it, beloved,' she said, but it was not entirely true. 'If it is any consolation, you cannot truly lose what you never had.'

Ahmann shook his head sadly. 'It is no consolation, wife.'

Inevera moved the stone covering one of the many hidden nooks in her Chamber of Shadows. There was a small box, warded for cold and powered by a demon bone core. A thin rime of frost covered its surface.

Inevera opened the cloth and removed the stiff bit of silk from within. It was precious, but with her dice restored and Mistress Leesha discredited at last, it was time to finally cast the bones for the Northern witch.

The silk was one of Inevera's many kerchiefs, this one used to daub the blood Leesha had lost during their fight in Inevera's pillow chamber. She carefully cut out the bits of bloodied silk, tossing them into a small bowl of steaming liquid. When blood had been fully leached, she poured the mixture over her dice and shook.

'Almighty Everam,' she prayed, 'give me knowledge of Leesha, daughter of Erny, of the Paper family of the Hollow tribe.' With a final shake, she cast the dice before her.

And gaped.

– She is your *zahven*, and carries a child.—

27

Waning

333 AR Autumn
Waning

'How does it work?' Jardir asked, staring in fascination at the Skull Throne, now sheathed in electrum. She had drawn the thick curtains in the throne room, allowing his crownsight though sunset was still an hour away. He could see the steady stream of power the throne radiated in every direction. Its centre shone hot with concentrated magic, like a miniature sun.

'Your throne now projects a—' Inevera began.

'—warding field,' Jardir finished for her. 'Not even the princes of Nie will be able to approach my seat . . .' He turned, following the path of the magic, looking through the great stone walls as easily as one might look through glass. '. . . for miles.'

It was truly amazing. The Crown of Kaji could repel *alagai* as well. Jardir had mastered its power in recent weeks, learning to extend the protection far beyond his physical reach. No *alagai* could approach within a quarter mile of him, but that he willed it. He could protect an army on the field, but this, this protected the entire inner city and beyond. The demons might strike at his walls, even knock them down, but they would never get past them.

He looked back at Inevera, his mouth curling in a smile. 'I did not ask what it did, beloved. I asked how it worked.'

Inevera's aura flushed with shock, and then disappointment that she would not be able to parade around the marvel she had made, revealing its power to him in teasing bits.

Let her have the moment next time, he chided himself. *With this gift, she has earned it a thousandfold.*

To his surprise, Inevera laughed. Not the bark of derision she threw now and then, but a full laugh, infectious and true. There was no more beautiful sound in all Everam's creation.

'You never cease to amaze me, Ahmann,' Inevera said. 'Every time I begin to question, you remind me you truly are Shar'Dama Ka.'

Jardir might have doubted, but her aura swelled with pride and he knew she meant every word. He reached out, touching her cheek, and watched the shiver it sent through her spirit. 'I understand perfectly . . . Damajah.' He bent and kissed her, feeling himself flush at the passion she was radiating. She might lie to him when she thought it necessary, but Inevera's love for him was true. What more could a man ask in his *Jiwah Ka*?

She took a step back when he broke the kiss, reining her feelings in. He was amazed at her control, watching the hot chaos of her aura quickly become cool, ordered. Now was not the time.

'The skull of an *alagai* prince has been added to your sacred throne, amplifying the wards that have adorned the skulls of martyred Sharum Ka for centuries,' Inevera said. 'We used almost all the electrum to coat it . . .'

'Almost?' Jardir asked, smiling.

Inevera returned the grin, showing him her dice, now safely encased in the bright white metal. 'You have your tools, and now I have mine.' Her aura said she had coated more than just her dice, but he let her have her secrets. She was his Damajah, and it was fitting she wield power of her own.

'I was right to give the metal to you,' Jardir said. 'Abban would have found a clever use for it, no doubt, but would never have thought of something so . . .'

'Altruistic?' Inevera supplied, and he had to laugh.

'Unprofitable,' he agreed.

'I do not trust the *khaffit*, husband,' Inevera said.

'Abban is as loyal to me as you are,' Jardir said.

Inevera shook her head. 'He is loyal to himself first, and you second.'

Jardir nodded. 'The same could be said of you, Bride of Everam.'

'There is a difference in serving the Creator first,' Inevera said.

'Yes,' Jardir agreed. 'And no. No mortal man or woman can truly trust another, beloved. And yet somehow we must find a way, if we are to win Sharak Ka. Waning is upon us. Now is the time to face the dark, not worry about poisoned blades at our backs.'

Inevera opened her mouth to reply, but Jardir touched a finger to her lips. 'You are the Bride of Everam, wife, yet I am the one with faith. Not just in the Creator, but in His children.'

'*Faith never gets the weaving done*, my mother used to say,' Inevera said. 'The Creator helps those who earn it.' Her aura called him a brave fool.

'"The Creator helps",' Jardir repeated. 'Do you think it coincidence we found the sacred metal of Kaji just weeks before the greatest test of my reign? We do not fight Nie alone, even if He does not strike the *alagai* down Himself. And if I am to deliver this world, I must believe that for all our differences, no one, man, woman or child, wishes it to fall to the *alagai*.'

Inevera did not argue further, but her aura remained unconvinced.

'Your mother was a weaver?' he asked, trying to change the subject. 'I assumed she was *dama'ting*.'

Inevera's aura suddenly went wild. There was shock, and fear, and a secret. Enough to fill him with questions, but not enough to answer them. He wondered if this was what reading the *alagai hora* was like for her.

'You never speak of your family,' he pressed, watching closely.

Inevera's aura showed her searching desperately for a way to evade the question and change the subject. She gave off the scent of a cornered animal that would rather flee than fight. But then her chest rose and fell several times in rhythm, and a wave of calm spread over her.

'Most *dama'ting* are the daughters of our order,' she said. 'Some few others are called by the dice in *Hannu Pash*. We cut off all contact with our families when called, and they do not know our fate from the moment we are taken.'

It was fascinating. Every word she said was true, and yet it read on her aura as a lie. 'But you did not.'

Inevera smiled. A practised distraction while she breathed herself into serenity. She was wondering how much he knew, if he had been spying on her. She was carefully choosing words to reveal nothing she did not wish.

Jardir was tiring of the game. '*Jiwah*, you will stop your dissembling.'

His tone was harsh, and he watched as she leapt on it, using the excuse to get angry as a way to avoid the topic. Her brows drew into the thundercloud she had practised to perfection.

He smiled. 'Stop that, too.' He moved to her, taking her in his arms. She stiffened, and there was a token resistance as he pulled her close. 'Do you love me, *jiwah*?'

'Of course, husband,' Inevera said without hesitation.

'And do you trust me?'

There was a spike in her aura, and the slightest delay. 'Yes.' It wasn't a lie, not precisely, but neither was it truth.

'I do not know what secret you hold about your family,' Jardir said. 'But I see that you hold one, and that dishonours me.' Inevera pulled back and tried to speak, but he shook his head. 'When we wed, it was more than a union between us. Your family became mine, and mine yours. Whatever it is, I have a right to know.'

Inevera stared at him a long moment, her aura so chaotic

he could not guess what her response would be. But then it calmed once more. 'My parents are alive and in Everam's Bounty. They are a source both of pride and of shame to me, and I fear for them if our relation is revealed.' She met his eyes and bowed. 'It was wrong of me to keep this secret from you, beloved. For this, I apologize.'

Jardir nodded. 'Accepted, on one condition.'

Inevera raised an eyebrow.

'I want to meet them,' Jardir said.

'I do not think that is wise, husband,' Inevera said. 'They would be in danger . . .'

'I am Shar'Dama Ka,' Jardir said. 'I have hundreds of relatives. You think I cannot protect them?'

'Not without costing them the simple life they enjoy now, far from palace intrigue,' Inevera said.

Jardir laughed. 'You can engineer my nieces into the ranks of *Sharum*, but not plot a way for me to meet your parents away from prying eyes? We both know you can find a way if you wish it.'

Inevera regarded him, still wary. 'And if I do not wish it?'

Jardir shrugged. 'Then I will know I come third in your eyes, and not second after Everam, as you claim.'

The curtains were still drawn as the counsellors entered the throne room. A few oil lamps gave artificial light, preserving Jardir's crownsight as he regarded Jayan and his twelve *Damaji*. At the side of each of the tribal leaders were his second sons, and in Ashan's case his nephew. Save for Asome and Asukaji, both eighteen years old, all were fifteen. Not wholly boys, but not men, either, still in the white bidos of *nie'dama*, a strip of white cloth thrown over one shoulder.

He could see in their auras that the *Damaji* still resented the boys who had displaced their own heirs. Leadership of a tribe was not automatically hereditary as it was in the green lands, but it was functionally so, with the brothers, sons, and nephews of the *Damaji* holding every advantage.

More, he could see the ties that bound the men to him like threads in the air. The common *Sharum* and *dama* might truly believe Jardir divine, but the *Damaji* served out of fear.

If I die this night, he thought, *my sons will be killed the moment it is known.* Jayan might hold his grip on the white turban, perhaps, and Ashan would protect Asukaji and Asome, but the other *Damaji* would not hesitate to slaughter his *nie'dama* sons. Aleverak would not break his oath not to harm Maji, but that oath had a clause they knew well. The ancient *Damaji* would drink poison to allow one of his sons to do the deed.

The *Damaji* talked among themselves, but Jardir thumped his spear once, and they fell silent. 'Waning is upon us, Damaji. Alagai Ka and his princelings will rise tonight to test our people as we have not been since the Return.' He could see doubt in some of the men, and fear in others. Most, however, held the flat control of years of meditation. 'Jayan,' he looked to the boy, seeing in his aura an eager excitement and a hope to prove himself, 'will lead the *Sharum*.'

There was a burst of chatter at that. Jardir thumped his spear again.

'Forgive us, Deliverer,' Damaji Aleverak said. 'Jayan has done well as Sharum Ka, and we offer no disrespect, but is it not the place of Shar'Dama Ka to lead in Sharak Ka?'

Jardir nodded. 'I will stand beside my son for as long as I may, but when the princes of Nie show themselves, I must be free to act.'

'And what will our place be?' Asome asked.

Jardir looked at his son, seeing the seething anger beneath his calm exterior. 'The *dama* will beseech Everam's favour in the coming battle. That is no small thing, my son.' He could see immediately that Asome thought prayer less than nothing with demons at the walls, but hoped he was wise enough not to voice the feeling.

Asome was not so easily deterred. 'Why do *dama* study *sharusahk*, Father?'

'Eh?' Jardir asked.

'Since I took my first steps, I have been practising the *sharukin*,' Asome said. 'I know of none, *dama* or *Sharum*, who can stand against me.'

Jayan snorted. 'You boast because you have never faced a real opponent. You would find the *alagai* more formidable than the empty air you fought in Sharik Hora.'

Asome turned to his elder brother and sneered openly. 'Come at me then, O great killer of *alagai*, and we will see.'

Jayan growled and took a step forward.

'You will do no such thing!' Jardir shouted with a thump of the spear. He had forbidden all of his sons to fight one another, even in sparring, and the wisdom of that decree was never clearer. He could see in their auras that Jayan and Asome would not hesitate to kill each other to clear their own path to the Skull Throne. 'I will not have my sons brawling like *nie'Sharum* in the gruel line!'

Asome turned back to him, bowing. 'As you command, Father, but you have not answered my question. I am forbidden to fight my brother. I am forbidden to fight the *alagai*. You have abolished the title of Andrah, so there is no need to fight the *Damaji* for the throne. Why have I spent every day of my life learning to fight, if I must stand idly by as Alagai Ka walks the land?'

Jardir hesitated. In truth, he could not disagree. Prayer would not help this night. But the *Damaji* and *dama* were not just Holy Men to his people; they were the secular leaders as well. The clerics were masters of *sharusahk*, but with the exception of Ashan they had never personally faced the *alagai*, and would offer little aid in coming battle. When dawn finally came, they would be essential in restoring order.

'There is wisdom in what you say,' Jardir admitted, 'but

Jayan speaks truly that the *alagai* are a foe the *dama* are not prepared for, and you yourself said Waning was not the time to introduce untried forces into *alagai'sharak*.' He deepened his tone and swept his spear across the men in white. 'The *dama* will bestow the blessings of the Creator upon the assembled men, and then go to the underpalace.'

Asome gave no outward sign as he bowed, back straight with dignity, but his aura seethed with rage, even as Jayan's danced in delight. Already Jardir was regretting the decision, but it was done and he could not be forsworn with all Nie's abyss about to rise.

'Go!' He clapped his hands, and the men began to file out. 'Ashan,' he called, and the *Damaji* waited behind as the others left. Jardir descended from the dais to stand beside him, Inevera following a step behind.

Ashan had been at Jardir's side for twenty-five years, steadfast in his support as Jardir climbed the rungs of Krasian society to his place of power. The *Damaji* was married to his eldest sister, and had produced children of shared blood. There was no reason to doubt his devotion, but still Jardir called upon the powers of his crown, not just reading his surface aura, but probing deeply into his very spirit.

He saw in his friend's heart that his trust had not been misplaced. Ashan did not crave power for its own sake, and truly believed, where many other *Damaji* did not, that Jardir was the Deliverer, sent by Everam to remake the world. He was not happy about the fate of Ashia, but he remained fiercely loyal.

'Brother,' he said, putting his hands on Ashan's shoulders. 'If I am killed tonight, you must take the Skull Throne.' Ashan's aura lit up in surprise, though Inevera's remained flat, waiting for him to finish speaking.

'Do not hesitate,' Jardir said. 'Announce your claim as Andrah and have Aleverak taken into custody. Kill the other *Damaji* before they have time to scheme.' He looked hard into Ashan's eyes. 'Before they have time to kill my sons.'

Ashan nodded. 'And then?'

'The Spear of Kaji will go to Jayan,' Jardir said, 'but you will hold the crown and throne until the Damajah declares my successor.'

Ashan's aura went white with shock, followed quickly with derision as he turned to regard Inevera, whose aura was now warm with approval. 'You will deny your firstborn his birthright, and let a woman decide the fate of our people?'

Jardir nodded. 'It was she who picked me, Ashan. We both know Jayan is not yet worthy, and may never be.'

'And what of Asome?' Ashan demanded. 'I love your second son as if he were my own, and we have been grooming him since birth to be Andrah. Why should I take the Skull Throne and not him?'

'I have looked into Asome's heart, brother. He is no more ready than Jayan to rule, and if he sits above his brother, there will be blood on the streets. I have fifty-two sons, but most are still in the bido, or just out of it. It may be years before the worthiest is known.'

He tightened his hands, feeling the bones in Ashan's shoulders grind and strain. The *Damaji*'s aura showed the pain, but he gave no indication of it. 'For the good of our people, you will protect my *Jiwah Ka* and obey her in this, or I will find you in the afterlife, and we will have a reckoning.'

Ashan's aura went cold for a moment, then warmed with determination. 'That will not be necessary, Deliverer. If you should fall, it will be as you command.' He looked up, meeting Jardir's eyes. 'But do not fall . . . brother.'

Jardir laughed and embraced him. 'If I do, I will take Alagai Ka down with me.'

'On *alagai* talons!' the warriors roared, a call that must reach all the way to Heaven.

Jardir looked out over the assembled warriors with pride as Ashan led the *Damaji* in bestowing the blessings of Everam upon them. The sun was setting, and though it would still be some time before the *alagai* dare surface, wisps of magic were beginning to rise in the shadows, and his senses were coming alive.

The trained and blooded *Sharum* radiated confidence and faith, ready to fight and die on *alagai* talons, as was their right and honour. Their belief strengthened him, as did the knowledge that Inevera had secured the inner city. No matter what happened, his people would survive.

He rode with Jayan and the Spears of the Deliverer towards the wall of the outer city where Inevera had predicted the fighting would be thickest. She had been unable to fathom where the demons would strike first, but many futures held a single field littered with dead. Jardir prayed they weren't riding into a trap.

He heard the crack of a whip, and turned to see a long line of *chin* marching for the wall. There were hundreds of them, lightly armed and armoured with warded spears and small shields, but they did not carry the weapons with confidence. All were shackled, connected by long chains threaded through iron loops, and their fear was palpable. These were men marching resignedly to their deaths, terrified of the lonely path. Many would not even have the courage to fight. They would break before the *alagai* like water poured on stone.

Jardir pulled up his white charger, and the others stopped with him. 'Who are those men?'

'*Chin* who have tried to flee the call to *alagai'sharak*, or dishonoured themselves in the night,' Jayan said. 'They are to be tethered like *nie'Sharum*, the chains staked in position. If they will not fight for honour, let them fight for their own lives.'

'Halt!' Jardir cried to the *Sharum* driving the line, and the men immediately stopped. All eyes turned to Jardir as he sprang lightly to his feet upon his horse's back for all to see. He looked to the condemned men.

'Your Tenders have lied to you!' he shouted, drawing on the power of his crown to spread his voice far into the gloaming. 'Since you were infants at your mother's breasts, they have told you the *alagai* are a Plague sent by the Creator to punish the sins of man. They have told you that you deserve this, that you have no choice but to cower and hide and await forgiveness and redemption.'

He scanned the men, letting them see his eyes. 'But Everam loves His children, and would not curse us so. The *alagai* are a Plague, but it is one sent by Nie, the Enemy, and redemption does not come to men who cower and skulk! It comes to those who take up the fight, struggling against the children of Nie on His Ala even as Everam struggles with Her in the heavens.'

A month ago, he might have thought the words pointless with such men, but now he could see into their hearts, and knew they were tired of blaming themselves for the *alagai*, tired of being told that the homes and loved ones they lost were punishments they had brought upon themselves. They wanted to believe, but his people had broken them as badly as the demons, leaving them dispirited. They would give anything to be as men once more.

'You have seen my people fight the *alagai*,' Jardir said. 'You know it can be done. They have training, it is true, but more than that, they have courage. Courage coming not from their spears, but from the knowledge that they fight for more than themselves. They fight for their wives and mothers, their sisters and daughters and infant sons. Their old and infirm.'

He swept his spear over the line of greenlanders. 'You wear chains because my warriors do not believe you care. They believe you will not even fight to save yourselves, so they mean to stake you in the path of the *alagai*.' He pointed back to the wall of the inner city. 'But it is not just *our* women and children behind those walls! I have offered my protection to all who cannot fight, even your greenland women and children. They are crowded and cramped, but so long as we hold the walls, they are safe.'

He could sense a change in the men's hearts, and grasped for it, holding aloft his spear and drawing on its power to make it shine bright with magic. 'I will go into the night to fight for your people! I ask the same of you, but if you do not have the heart, you are no use to me this night.'

He pointed the spear at the centre of the line, its light flaring even brighter, and men pressed to either side in fear, opening a length of chain between them. Jardir drew a ward with the spear's tip, and a bolt of white energy leapt from the weapon, shattering the chain.

'Stand or flee,' he shouted, 'but remember you are men, and not dogs!'

The fear and doubt in the hearts of the men turned to awe, and many of them fell to their knees. Shanjat, astride his black charger next to Jardir, thrust his spear into the air. 'Deliverer!'

The other *Sharum* took up the chant, followed by the kneeling *chin*, and then, a moment later, the rest of them. They thrust their spears skyward with every call, and their voices carried far into the night.

'Those are the voices of men!' Jardir boomed. 'The servants of Nie will hear you, and quail in fear!' He dropped back into his saddle, kicking off for the wall, followed by the Spears of the Deliverer and hundreds of roaring *chin*.

'Everam curse me,' Qeran muttered from atop the compound wall as he watched the *Sharum* march. 'Waning is upon us, and here I stand, useless.'

'Nonsense,' Abban said. 'The Deliverer needs his forges and glasseries guarded, that he may continue to arm his men after Waning. There may yet be fighting here.'

Qeran shook his head. 'You have done well in hiding yourself, *khaffit*. There is no tactical advantage to this place, no reason for the *alagai* to test your walls. And the walls,' he stamped his spear on the rampart, 'are stronger than those of the inner city. The Deliverer's . . . craftsmen are safe.' He made the title seem a foul taste he could not scrape from his tongue.

'You said yourself the men are not ready,' Abban said, 'nor yourself. You have barely had your new leg a fortnight.'

'I said the men were not yet at their full strength,' Qeran said, 'nor me. But my hundred and I are still more fit than nine-tenths of the warriors out there.'

'*Your* hundred?' Abban asked.

Qeran looked at him, and Abban remembered how brutally the man had treated him in *sharaj*. He waited patiently, and savoured the slight nod Qeran gave him. 'Abban's hundred.'

Abban nodded, turning his gaze back to look out from the walls one last time before leaving the drillmaster to command as he limped back to the safety of the underpalace growing beneath the squat building in the centre of his compound.

Inevera found Asome and Asukaji in their private chambers in Ahmann's underpalace. The two were playing with Asome's infant son, Kaji.

'What is it now, Mother?' Asome glared at her as she entered, Ashia at her back. 'Has not humiliation enough been heaped upon me?'

Inevera looked sadly at her son.

– The only thing that exceeds his potential is his ambition – the dice had said when she cast them eighteen years ago, bathed in his birthing blood. It told her he would be powerful, but spoke a warning as well.

'Your wife and I will walk the walls during the battle, my son,' she said. 'I invite you to come with us.'

Asome looked at her as if sensing a trap. 'Hasn't Father ordered his wives and the *dama'ting* into the underpalace as well?'

Inevera shrugged. 'Perhaps, but who will dare stop us?'

'I might,' Asome said.

Inevera nodded. 'Or you might follow me . . . for my own safety. Surely your father would forgive you that.'

Asome turned to Asukaji. 'Just you, my son,' Inevera said.

The two men looked back at her, mistrust in their eyes once more.

'Ahmann has not dissolved your marriage, Asome. At least, not yet. I would walk with my son and daughter-in-law at my side as Alagai Ka walks the night.' She looked to Asukaji and infant Kaji. 'Surely while we are gone, my nephew will protect my grandson as if he were his own.'

Asome darkened a bit at that, but Asukaji laid a hand on his arm. 'It is all right, cousin. Go.' His voice dropped to a whisper, but Inevera, her senses sharpened by magic, heard him. 'I will keep our son until your return.' He kissed Asome with such tenderness that Inevera's heart ached for them both, but Ashia's shifting behind her was a reminder that there was a third side in the triangle.

She looked to her grandson. *And poor Kaji in the middle.*

They walked in silence to the wall of the inner city. Inevera wore opaque robes of white silk, looking much like her *dama'ting* robes of old, but she wore her hood back, and her veil was gossamer. The warded gold coins were warm at her forehead, and she wore considerable jewellery, not all of it decorative. Her robes shimmered with wards of unsight stitched in electrum thread. The wards were Mistress Leesha's, stolen from Ahmann's Cloak of Unsight, but even knowing the Skull Throne would hold the *alagai* from the wall, she could not deny the comfort they gave her in the naked night.

Take her power and make it your own, Manvah had said, and Inevera silently thanked her mother once more for the lesson. She would have been a fool to turn away such magics simply because she despised the source.

But even without the protections of her robes and the Skull Throne, Inevera felt safe so long as Ashia was at her side. Enkido had told Inevera he could not be prouder of the girl's fighting skill if she had been his own daughter.

Born to sharusahk, his nimble hands had said.

Ashia had a short, stabbing spear over her right shoulder, along with a small quiver of arrows. In her left hand, the same arm where she strapped her round shield, she gripped a short bow. The weapons were banded with warded gold and strips of *hora*. The armour beneath her black robes was indestructible warded glass, moulded to accent her feminine figure rather than mask it. Asome's expression was unreadable as he regarded his wife.

The Mehnding *Sharum* guarding the gatehouse began buzzing among themselves as the trio approached. A moment later a *kai'Sharum* appeared, blocking their path with a deep bow. 'Apologies, Damajah, but . . .'

Asome was moving before the man could straighten, taking his chin firmly in hand as he threw. There was an audible snap, and the man hit the ground, dead. 'Does anyone else wish to hinder the Damajah?'

The remaining *Sharum* fell to their knees, pressing foreheads to the cobbled street. After a moment, a red-veiled drillmaster rose with a bow and escorted them up to the wall.

The Mehnding tribe was third largest of the twelve tribes of Krasia, due in no small part to the mastery of war engines and ranged weapons that kept them from the close combat other *Sharum* engaged in. They were more engineers and marksmen than warriors, but they manned the walls of the inner and outer city with the steel-eyed vigilance of trained killers.

Everam's Bounty was built on a hill, with the inner city at its peak. Ahmann's palace was its highest point, but even the low wall of the inner city offered an impressive vantage of the countryside. Wardlight dotted the terrain as the sun set, and mirrored bonfires sprang up to help the *Sharum* see the enemy.

And as feared, the enemy came in force. The Skull Throne protected a large section of ground past the walls, but in the unwarded patches of the outer city, massive rock demons – larger than anything Inevera had ever seen – rose to tower over the warriors assembled to contain them. At their heels clustered field and flame demons, filling the open patches in seething scales and gouts of bright flame.

The Mehnding *kai'Sharum* signalled the attack. Keen-eyed spotters with distance lenses mounted on tripods called calculations to the stinger and sling teams, who adjusted their tensions accordingly and began to fire. Giant stinger spears arced into the air, their powerful warding blasting through even rock demon armour. The sling teams, careful to give no ammunition to the rocks, fired payloads of small warded stones that scattered demons with hundreds of tiny explosions of magic.

They did heavy damage, as did the teams of Mehnding bowmen bolstering the infantry. The *alagai* screamed, and for a moment, men had the advantage.

But then the rocks began to dig, heedless of the smaller demons they brushed aside. Several of them had large stingers jutting from their armour, but none had been brought down. They were quickly underground, safe from missile fire, even as the stinger and sling teams hurried to reload.

The teams had time to fire again, killing dozens of the smaller demons, but then the first rock reappeared holding a sizable boulder. Arrows fell on it like rain, but seemed to hinder it no more than insect bites as it cocked its arm and threw, blasting the stone through the nearest wardpillar, breaking a portion of the net. Immediately the field demons charged the breach, moving with terrifying speed. The *Sharum* locked their shields, but were not fully in position to hold the breach. The demons fell on them, tearing and biting as others circled around, some harrying their flanks and yet more escaping unhindered into the night to stalk the unwary. Firespit scattered off shields, starting blazes that quickly grew on their own.

The rock bent, digging again, as several more of its fellows rose with boulders of their own.

Inevera had never seen fighting on such a scale. The *Sharum* acquitted themselves well, but even she could see the *alagai* acted with unusual cunning, striking in unexpected places and steadily weakening the wardnet of the outer city, slowly working their way up the hill towards the inner walls. They would not enter, but the demons could easily smash the walls and rain destruction on the city. Fires and collapsing buildings could kill as easily as *alagai* talons.

Out in the city, the *Sharum* were fighting for their lives. Rock demons occasionally lobbed stones into clusters of warriors, breaking them apart long enough for the field and flame demons to swarm the openings. Most of the men were armoured, but that meant little against boulders and firespit. Wind demons began to circle in the sky above the wardnet, dropping stones carried in their hind talons. Their aim was less precise than the rocks, but the havoc they created did more damage than the stones themselves.

With the *Sharum* fighting spear-to-claw, the Mehnding on the wall could not risk firing on the demons harrying them, focusing instead on the rocks. Whenever one appeared with a stone, it was hit with several stingers or a sling of warded stones. A few of the giant demons were killed outright, and more missed their marks entirely.

But one mammoth rock managed to get within range of the city gates, carrying a boulder big enough to shatter them wide. It would not allow demons ingress, but it would kill many warriors guarding the gatehouse, and strike fear into the hearts of men who needed to be brave. Stingers stuck from the demon's thick carapace, but it moved with focus, hurling its stone.

'Everam's beard,' Asome breathed.

Inevera ignored the comment, reaching into her robe and producing the slender forearm bone she had taken from the mind demon Ahmann had killed. Dipped in electrum, it shone bright with power to her wardsight. She pointed the item at the stone, her fingers skilfully manipulating the wards etched at the gripping end. She uncovered heat and impact wards, sending the power hurtling at the stone.

The spell looked like a greenland firefly as it flew to its target, but when it struck, there was an explosion that lit the night and heated the faces of the observers, smashing the stone into a cloud of dust.

Amazed eyes turned to Inevera as she next pointed her *hora* wand at the rock demon itself. Again a sizzling speck of light that exploded on impact, throwing down the demon and driving the stingers already embedded in its armour through to the more vulnerable flesh beneath. It landed on its back, chest smoking, and did not rise.

'Mother . . .' Asome began, but his words trailed off as he stared at her. Inevera smiled. It was good to remind her ambitious son that she commanded power he should fear. Ashia and the Mehnding looked no less awestruck, and that, too, was well.

Out on the field, warriors took heart at the display, redoubling their efforts to contain the demons even as reinforcements came.

But there was reaction from the *alagai* as well. A flight of wind demons dived out of the sky, heading directly for Inevera, each carrying a heavy stone in its talons. Ashia had her bow in hand and plucked one from the sky like a fattened goose. The Mehnding bowmen took down others, but not before a number of stones hurtled their way. Inevera felt herself grabbed and thrown to the rampart as one of the battlements exploded right next to her. Rubble fell like rain, but Asome remained atop her, taking the brunt of the impact.

When it was over, half his face was covered in blood, and she could see his arm was broken, twisted at an impossible angle. She reached out for him, but her son rose smoothly to his feet. He took the wrist of his broken arm in his good hand, pulling the limb straight and letting it hang loosely at his side. The pain was no doubt incredible, but Asome kept control, showing no sign of it as he reached down to her, offering his good hand to help her to her feet. 'It is nothing that cannot wait, Mother.' He thrust his chin out beyond the wall. 'You have greater concerns.'

Inevera accepted the hand, but put no weight on it as she sprang to her feet. She looked out in the direction her son had indicated, eyes widening. Fighting was fierce in the outer city, and fiercer still beyond the outer wall, but it was all a distraction.

From her vantage, Inevera could see what Ahmann could not, though even she had been so occupied by the battle she might have missed it until it was too late. Out in the teeming wheat beyond the city, flame demons were burning with precision, forming wards the size of entire fields. Soon the symbols would activate, giving the *alagai* a terrifying advantage.

Asome saw it, too. 'They are truly the agents of Nie, stealing our ability to feed our people and using it to power their dark magics. We have no choice but to burn the rest of the fields to destroy the wardnet.'

'Perhaps,' Inevera said, remembering her prophecy. She looked to Ashia. 'Your uncle must hear of this.'

The *kai'Sharum'ting* did not hesitate, leaping from the wall and redirecting the impact of her landing into a tight roll that threw her right back onto her feet. She sprinted down the hill into the outer city, quickly disappearing into the darkness.

Asome looked at her. 'Bad enough you defy the Deliverer by bringing her out onto the wall, but now you send my *jiwah* out into the naked night? If the *alagai* don't get her, surely Father will kill her for her disobedience.'

'What do you care?' Inevera asked. 'If she dies in the night or is killed for her disobedience, your problems are solved, are they not?'

'I asked for divorce, not her death,' Asome said.

'You will get neither, my son,' Inevera said. 'No demon will touch her, and you do not know your father as well as you think. His first duty is to Sharak Ka. Ashia's information may mean the difference between victory and defeat. He will thank her for her service and forget it until Waning is past, and then offer her a token reprimand, followed by a public honouring. No longer will *Sharum'ting* be confined to the Undercity on Wanings.'

'Your goal all along,' Asome said. There was no bitterness in his tone, but she sensed it nevertheless.

'What is more important to you,' Inevera asked, 'winning Sharak Ka, or keeping your wife beneath your sandal? The heroism of your *jiwah* can boost your power, if you let it. I know you do not feel for her as you do Asukaji, but she is the sister of your lover, the mother of your son, and you made oaths to her before Everam. Those ties bind an honest man as tightly as love.'

Asome looked ready to argue the words, but then deflated, considering. Inevera reached out, touching his good arm. 'A great man does not fear his wife will steal his glory, Asome. He uses her support to reach even higher.'

28

Early Harvest

333 AR Autumn
Waning

The *alagai* massed outside the city walls in a horde that cut fear into even the bravest *Sharum*. Thousands of demons, field and flame, rock and wood. The night sky teemed with wind demons, shrieking as they circled.

One of the rocks stomped over to a tree, its footfalls shaking the very ground. It pulled the thirty-foot trunk out by the roots, effortlessly snapping away the excess branches. Club in hand, it strode towards the nearest wardpost, a full reap of field demons at its flanks. Stinger teams took aim and fired, but even at this range it took many of the giant bolts to bring down a single rock. They would not stop it before the demon smashed the post, and there were dozens of the mammoth demons.

Jardir raised his spear, drawing a heat ward in the air. The tree in the demon's hands exploded in flames, and the creature dropped it in shock.

'Lock shields and advance,' Jardir shouted, using the power of his crown to magically enhance his voice. 'Strike on my command. We will fight our way to the rocks and bring them down!'

A line of interlocked shields formed, their wards glowing with power as they forced the *alagai* back. 'Strike!' Jardir called when the demons were clustered too tightly for a single thrust to miss. The *Sharum* took a unified step back, opening their shields enough to thrust warded weapons into the press. There was a flash of magic and a spray of ichor to accompany each point, but the disciplined warriors did not pause to savour it, snapping their shields closed again, continuing to press forward until Jardir called the next strike. A second line of warriors finished off the demons trampled into the ground by the front line's advance.

Their first real test came when a copse of wood demons approached, carrying huge clubs. While not the massive trees the rocks were carrying, the weapons were larger than men, and the simple wood did what *alagai* talons could not, smashing into the shields of his warriors and scattering them in wide swathes.

Jardir concentrated before the demons could take advantage of the breaches, extending the power of his crown out beyond his warriors and stopping the demons short. He raised his spear and drew heat wards in the air, incinerating the wood demons, and then charged forward, his magic throwing the lesser *alagai* aside until he came up to the nearest rock. He pulled the protective field in tight, letting him get close enough to leap ten feet into the air and thrust the Spear of Kaji into the demon's chest. Magic refilled the spear's well as it pulsed up his arm, suffusing him with energy.

He kicked off from the falling demon, landing in a clear spot twenty feet away. Demons leapt at him from all sides, but their attacks skittered off his warding field, even as he attacked with impunity. Several demons fell to thrusts of his spear, but as many were destroyed by wards he drew in the air. Flame demons shattered as he froze the firespit in their bellies, and wood demons ran about frantically, immolated in flame. Impact wards threw field demons aside by the half dozen.

Still they closed in, their numbers undiminished. Every demon on the field was focused on him now. He extended the crown's power again, driving them back until he could rejoin his men, but that only made him a clearer target as a rock demon threw a heavy boulder his way.

Jardir leapt aside, but was struck even as he landed by another stone dropped from above. He rolled with the impact, keeping hold of his spear and drawing on its magic to heal himself. He was given no respite, as rocks the size of melons began to fall like rain around him.

But as fast as the stones fell, Jardir was faster, dodging them like lazily drifting bubbles of soap. Even as he dodged the barrage from above, the rock and wood demons on the ground continued to hurl whatever they could grasp in their talons at him: rocks, trees, even a few of his own men. Wind demons bounced off his warding field, falling from the sky where his men quickly dispatched them before they could recover and take off again. One wind demon pulled up short just outside the limit of his protection and roared at him, a bolt of lightning leaping from its long toothed beak.

With a thunderous boom, the energy pierced the warding, going right for him, but Jardir could see the power for what it was, and did not fear. He raised his spear crosswise, absorbing the energy. The weapon tingled and burned with the power, but he threw it right back at the creature, blasting it from the sky.

He felt suffused with power, unstoppable, and yet he saw he was being slowly cut off from his men and surrounded. Rock demons were hurling more and larger missiles at him, and sooner or later one would connect.

I have made a target of myself, he realized.

With that thought, he pulled his protective field in close, throwing up his hood and wrapping himself in Leesha's Cloak of Unsight as he quickstepped several yards to the side. To his warriors nothing had changed, but he could see confusion in the auras of the *alagai*. To their senses, he had simply vanished.

Calmly, he walked back to the re-formed lines of the *Sharum* as the warriors took advantage of the demons' confusion, striking hard as the *alagai* vainly searched for sign of him.

'Uncle!' a voice cried, and he saw Ashia running towards him. His niece was wrapped in her *Sharum* blacks, but in the darkness he recognized her aura more clearly than he ever might her face. A field demon leapt at her, but she turned to catch it on her shield, throwing it aside without slowing. A flame demon stopped in her path and hawked firespit, but she sidestepped smoothly as the creature closed its eyes to spew, skewering it.

Next, a pair of wood demons barred her path. Charged now with demon magic, Ashia only increased the speed of her advance, using the edge of her shield to stab at the joints of their long, spindly limbs, keeping them off balance and unable to attack. To an untrained eye, every move was as if practised by rote, but Jardir could see that she was in fact probing, applying *dama'ting sharusahk* as she searched for pressure points. At last she found one in a demon's thigh, collapsing the limb with a relatively gentle blow. Only then did she plunge her spear in for the kill.

She spun to meet the next attack from the other wood demon, slapping it aside with a casual thrust of her shield's edge into its spindly armpit as it lashed its talons at her. The demon stumbled back, and she advanced calmly. Her aura confirmed what he already knew: that she was utterly confident in her ability to kill it at will, and was using the opportunity to learn her enemy better.

No two demons were precisely alike. Each was shaped by its preferred hunting terrain, and Everam's Ala was vast and varied. It took her two blows to find the same pressure point on the next wood demon, but after a moment she collapsed its leg. She filed the information away, finishing the demon quickly and closing the space between herself and Jardir in two great bounds.

Jardir frowned. His pride in his beloved sister Imisandre's daughter was overwhelming. He had commanded she be twice the warrior of her male *zahven*, but she had surpassed them by far, and her own father, as well. Watching the graceful and precise movements of her art, so confident and in control, was like reading a poem.

But for all his pride, her defiance of his will in coming out into the night was unacceptable. No doubt Inevera had a hand in it, but he could not allow even the Damajah to flaunt his decrees so openly. Poor Ashia would be caught in the middle when he was forced to make an example of her.

He grabbed her arm hard when she reached his side, extending his crown's protection just enough to envelop, but hopefully not enough to alert the *alagai* princes who even now sought him through the eyes of their drones. 'Are you begging to have your new blacks stripped from you, girl, to defy my command?'

'Forgive me, Uncle,' Ashia said, falling to one knee and baring her neck. 'The Damajah bade me to inform you that the *alagai* are burning great wards into the crops outside the city, creating a net.'

Jardir felt a chill run down his spine as he looked up, seeing the magic gathering off in the distance and sensing its purpose. The demons were constructing wards to repel men. If they succeeded in creating a circle around Everam's Bounty, they could kill every man, woman, and child within. The Skull Throne was no protection against this.

'Did she tell you anything else?' he asked.

'No,' Ashia said. 'But when my honoured husband told her the only way to stop them would be to burn our harvest, the Damajah suggested there might be alternatives.'

Jardir nodded. How could he forget the words he had pondered day and night since Inevera's foretelling?

– The Deliverer must go into the night alone to hunt the centre of the web, or all will be lost when the Alagai Ka comes—

He looked back at his niece. She had as much as told him that his wife and son also defied his will, but that seemed an insignificant thing now. 'Tell the Damajah I understand, and will follow the path Everam has set before me.' Ashia bowed and turned to go, but he caught her arm once more. 'I am proud of you, niece.'

Ashia's aura, so flat and professional, suddenly blossomed with warmth. Jardir hugged her close, then drew back, meeting her eyes. 'Remember that, when I must punish your defiance.'

The warmth of her aura did not dim in the least as she bowed one last time and turned back into the night. Only then did her detachment return, like a cloak she threw over herself before stepping into battle.

Jardir threw off his robes, stripping down to his white bido to reveal his warded flesh. Beyond that he wore only plain sandals, his crown, and Leesha's cloak. In his hands he carried only the Spear of Kaji.

He looked back at Jayan, spotting his son's aura in the crowd of warriors even more easily than his white turban.

Everam grant you be worthy, my son, he prayed.

There was a whispering on the night wind, and without understanding how he knew, he understood it was the demon princes, speaking to one another with magic rather than simple words. He could not understand what they were saying, but he isolated the nearest of the voices and followed it into the night. Warriors cried out and attempted to go with him, but while a berth appeared in the demons barring Jardir's way as the crown forced them aside, they closed in quickly behind him.

It was not far before he began to see the currents of magic flowing towards the wheat fields. Demons patrolled the area, but they walked by him, oblivious to his presence as he crept through the stalks to the edge of the *alagai* princes' wards. The tall wheat stopped abruptly, and before him the *ala* was scorched clean, glowing with magic.

Jardir marvelled at the precision of the lines. Flame demons could burn almost anything, but their magical fires tended to start very real ones. The fact that the burning went only in one direction, stopping as abruptly as it began, spoke of other magics involved.

He could feel the ward pushing at him. At first approaching had been like walking against a heavy wind, then like striding in deep water. When he reached out to the edge, it felt as solid as a wall of thick glass. Energy skittered along his fingertips, but he embraced the sting, tasting the magic.

Finally understanding the power, he concentrated, and felt the Crown of Kaji warm at his brow. He thrust his hand into the ward, and the magic parted around him like the stalks of wheat he had pushed through to get here.

Still the call on the night wind led him on as he walked openly along the lines of the demons' web. He kept the power tight around himself, seeming no more than a slight ripple in the warding, like a pebble thrown into a rushing river.

He walked for some time before finding his quarry. The mind demon wasn't even looking his way, its attention on the blaze of flame demons burning a path in the wheat. The demon was drawing wards in the air, snuffing the flames along precise lines. Its bodyguard, an amorphous blob of flowing black scales, hot with magic, slithered at its side.

The demon's aura was bright with power, like looking at the sun, and it moved with casual security. And Jardir could see why. Magic was woven around the creature to protect it from prying eyes, but not, it seemed, his crownsight. Trusting in Leesha's cloak, he strode right up to it.

The mimic perked up when he came within striking distance and the mind demon turned to face him, but it was too late. He stabbed hard with the Spear of Kaji, piercing its black heart.

The burst of power was like nothing Jardir had ever dreamed. He had killed powerful demons before, used to the feeling of magic running up the length of the spear, filling its well and pumping into him, making him stronger, faster. It healed his wounds, honed his senses, and polished away the years like rust buffed from steel.

But that feeling was a sip of water compared with the flood that ran through him, threatening to drown him in magic.

The demon prince shrieked in agony, and its pain was reflected in the screams and convulsions of the mimic and every other demon in the area. The demon reached for him, and while the claws at the end of its spindle arms were no longer than a pillow wife's manicured nail, they were sharp as razors.

Jardir growled, sending a blast of the magic suffusing him back through the spear. It shocked through the demon like lightning, rattling it so hard its teeth ground and shattered. Its body began to smoke and stink, and Jardir pulled the spear free, swinging it in a tight slash that took the razor edge right through the slender demon's neck.

The lesser demons collapsed as the mind demon's head struck the *ala*, but the mimic took longer to die, shrieking wildly as its flesh bubbled and shifted, sometimes taking on familiar shapes, and others taking forms only seen in nightmares.

Still awash in power, Jardir pointed at it and drew a ward with the tip of his spear, blasting the creature back to Nie. He could hear bits of gelatinous flesh strike the ground as the smoke cleared.

Jardir stood still in the silence that followed, listening hard, but the calls of the other demon princes were gone.

They had felt their brother's death, and fled the field.

Jardir bent, slinging the *alagai* prince's body over his shoulder. He picked up its conical head with his free hand. With enough electrum, he could double the range of the Skull Throne, or build another to take with him as he conquered the North.

But first, there needed to be an early harvest.

'I do not see the point of this, Father,' Jayan said, when Jardir called his court in the hours before dawn and laid out his plan.

'We should be rebuilding the defences and resting for the coming night, not . . .'

'Be silent and listen well,' Jardir snapped. 'The *alagai* cannot defeat us on the field, and your mother has magicked the central city beyond their reach. The mind demons' plan to build great-wards in the wheat fields has failed, and they will not attempt it again, lest they reveal their locations to me and meet the same fate as their brother.'

'Then we have won,' Jayan said.

'Do not be a fool,' Asome said. 'The *alagai* need not meet our spears or storm our wards to kill us. They have only to burn the fields.'

'And so we must leave them nothing to burn,' Ashan agreed. 'Harvest everything. Even grain not fully fruited.'

'Work for the women, *khaffit*, and *chin* who cowered behind the walls while men stood for them in the night,' Jayan said.

'Work for all of us,' Jardir corrected. 'Even if every man, woman, and child in Everam's Bounty, from the proudest *dama* to the lowliest *chin* cripple, bends their back from sunup to sunset, we will only be able to harvest . . .'

'Twenty-two percent,' Abban supplied.

'. . . twenty-two per cent of the crop before night falls and the fires begin,' Jardir finished. 'It is essential that we have every hand, and that those of us considered above such toil be seen in the fields with the rest.'

Aleverak laid a hand on Jayan's shoulder. 'You did great honour to the white turban last night, son of Ahmann. Take heart in this. Did not Kaji himself begin life as a simple fruit picker?'

Jayan glanced at the hand, and there was a flare of anger in his aura at the perceived condescension. Aleverak had humbled him before, however, and he was wise enough to swallow the emotion.

There, my son, is the beginning of wisdom, Jardir thought.

'Be careful, Deliverer,' Hasik said as they approached a group of *chin* farmers, 'they're armed.'

Jardir studied the huge reaping tools the men held and did not deny they could be effective weapons in the right hands, but he sensed no danger here. The *chin* seemed terrified of him.

'You worry too much, Hasik,' he chided. 'If a *chin* can kill me with a farming tool, what hope have I against Alagai Ka?'

He strode up to the men, and as expected they immediately fell to their knees, clumsily pressing their faces to the dirt in a crude imitation of proper obeisance.

'Rise, brothers,' Jardir said, bowing in return. 'We have work to do, and no time for such formality.' He reached out, taking one of the reaping tools. 'What is this called?'

'Ah, that's a scythe, Y'Grace,' one of the men said. He was past his prime but still strong.

Jardir nodded. He had heard the name. 'Show me how to use it?'

'Yur gonna mow?' the man asked, incredulous.

The man next to him slapped him on the back. 'Do as he says, idiot,' he whispered.

The farmer nodded, taking the tool and demonstrating how to hold it, his muscular arms straight as he twisted to pass the blade close to the ground, mowing a small section of stalks with each pass.

'A good tool, and an efficient stroke,' Jardir said. 'You would have been a great warrior, if you had taken that path.'

The man bowed. 'Thank you, Y'Grace.'

'But it is slow,' Jardir said, taking the tool, 'and our time is short. Please stand aside.' He removed his outer robe, stripped to the waist save for the Crown of Kaji at his brow and the Spear strapped to his back. He held the scythe in reverse, blade behind him as he crouched low and called upon the magic in the items, filling himself with the strength and speed of a hundred men.

He leapt forward, moving along the field at a run as he brought the blade into the stalks. His sandalled feet beat a steady rhythm on the soft tilled *ala*, and in moments he was at the far end, turning for another pass. Cut stalks were still falling as he mowed those beside them.

The sun was still low in the sky when Jardir paused and looked out over the mown field. Inevera had found a basket weaver in the bazaar to deliver a cartload, and she herself led the work of harvesting the wheat, carrying a full basket as she directed women and children like she had been working the fields her entire life.

She was beautiful in the morning light, almost demure in opaque linen pants and a tight vest, maroon trimmed with gold. The *khaffit* and *chin* looked at her with worship in their eyes, and bent their backs all the harder at seeing her toil.

He looked out over the fields, seeing *dama* and *Sharum* working side by side with the lesser castes. It was an inspiring sight, a taste of the unity Kaji dreamed of, the common cause that would allow mankind to throw back the *alagai* and win Sharak Ka.

He prayed it would be enough.

'. . . complete destruction of the Mehnding apple orchards,' Abban said, 'and over two thousand acres of pasture.'

Jardir sat the Skull Throne, stinking of the greasy ash that covered his clothes and smudged his skin. The burns were already healed, but he listened with a heavy heart to Abban's private morning report after the third night of Waning.

His fears proved true the second night as the *alagai* princes, their original plan thwarted and unwilling to attempt it again lest they meet him on the field, moved instead to destroy his people through starvation.

The many rivers and streams throughout his fertile lands had proven natural firebreaks, and he had led warriors to destroy the flame demons and fight fires wherever they might appear, but even his powers were not infinite, and the depredations were devastating. Jardir lost count of the tonnage as Abban read list after list.

Abban turned over the next sheet. 'In the Krevakh lands, there was a loss of . . .'

Jardir felt as if he might burst out of his skin if he had to sit and listen another moment. He stood abruptly, striding down the steps to pace the court floor. 'Just tell me, *khaffit*,' he growled. 'How bad is it?'

Abban shrugged. 'If the loss is done, then your people will survive, Deliverer.' He met Jardir's eyes. 'But if the loss continues, month after month, half the people of Everam's Bounty will lie dead before the winter snows recede, all without the *alagai* raising a claw.'

Jardir put his face in one of his hands.

'You do have two advantages, however,' Abban said.

Jardir looked up at him. 'Advantages?'

'Your people see you as the true son of Everam now,' Abban said. 'Even the *chin* whisper your name with awe, spreading the tales of your efforts to protect them, day and night. Working in the fields alongside them was a masterstroke.'

'I didn't do it to win hearts,' Jardir said.

'It does not matter *why* you did it, my friend,' Abban said. 'With that gesture, and the body of the *alagai* prince to parade before the *Damaji*, they will follow you, Krasian and greenlander alike.'

'Follow me where?' Jardir asked.

'Why, to Lakton,' Abban smiled. 'The fields in the *chin* lands to the east of Everam's Bounty are still ripening.'

The Royal Consort waited in the cave as dawn approached. The dark was still enough to leave the surface stock blind, and the lesser drones could hunt for hours more, but to the coreling prince, used to the utter blackness of the mind court, the sky was brightening at an alarming rate.

He had waited purposely until the last moment to summon the others as the last night of Waning drew to a close. They would be forced to materialize outside the cave, weakening in the light as they approached. The consort had drawn powerful wardings around the cave and the fissure at its rear, focusing the magic venting from the Core and ensuring no other could Draw upon it.

Two of the six minds he had brought with him to the surface were dead – the most powerful, no less, but it was still wise to take every precaution when facing so many of his brethren so far from the Queen's influence.

It was an advantage to be rid of two potential rivals, but not worth drawing the Queen's displeasure this close to a laying. The other four minds seemed heroes by comparison, fighting on even as his plans failed, sapping the enemy's strength. The experience and prestige they gained positioned them well to take the place of his lost rivals.

He Drew hard on the vent as the four approached, holding as much power as he could bear. He made no effort to mask the energy, letting the others see and fear it. His mimics surrounded him, but a simple forbiddance kept the rival mimics outside the cave.

The day star approaches, brother, one of the demons thought.

We should return to court and report to the Queen, another agreed.

The consort hissed. *You will report first to me.*

We have given you our reports, one of the princes sent to the North argued. He was older than the other, and stronger. His will had grown considerably since coming to the surface. He masked his aura well, but the consort could sense his tension.

At a thought, one of his mimics lashed out, wrapping a tentacle around the prince's throat and hauling him in close.

The consort did not change his stance, but he readied his power. If they were to strike in unison, it would be now.

But the others stood frozen. They might hate the consort even more than the day star, but they hated one another as well, and none would risk his own life without assurance of victory.

The consort caressed the knobbed skin of the prince's cranium. *You have given your reports, but have not told all. Did you think me a fool?*

The young mind struggled, no match for the mimic's strength. His cranium pulsed, attempting to seize control of the drone, but the consort's will was second only to that of the Queen herself. The mimic tightened the tentacle around the prince's throat, and his efforts to escape ceased.

What happened the night your brother died? the consort asked.

We captured the unifier, the prince admitted, drawing a hiss from his cohort. The princes sent south tensed at the words, craniums pulsing as they conversed.

Then why is your brother gone while the unifier continues to kill drones and draw humans to serve him? the consort demanded.

We walked his mind to learn of his power, the prince thought, *but he escaped before we could bring him to you.*

A second lie? the consort asked. The prince's lidless eyes widened, but he had no time to protest before the mimic slashed a talon, opening his cranium wide. The consort reached inside, tearing bits of the prince's mind, feeding as the others watched with horror and jealousy mingled in their auras.

As he fed, the memories and will of the prince transferred to him, and he learned in an instant everything they had taken from the unifier's mind. The consort was nearly overwhelmed by the pleasure and power of it. He had feasted on the minds of his brethren numerous times over the millennia, and it never failed to leave him dizzy with strength. Outside, the prince's mimic shrieked and began to lose cohesion.

The consort looked to the other prince that had shared in

the deception. He stood frozen with fear, no doubt wondering if he would share his brother's fate.

Go, the consort ordered, and the prince did not question his fortune, backing quickly out of the cave and fleeing to the Core, taking his mimic with him.

The other two princes stood motionless as the consort digested the memories of their brother. One licked his teeth, looking at the broken cranium.

The consort was shocked to learn that the unifier had stolen much of his power by consuming drones. He had not known it was possible for the surface stock to store Core magic in their bodies and learn to Draw. It seemed as impossible as a rock drone debating philosophy, but there was no denying it.

And now he knew, too, the answer to the question that had drawn them all to the surface in the first place. The fighting wards had been found buried in the sand to the south.

The Northern unifier has stolen a bit of our power, but I have his measure now, he thought to the others. *There is nothing he can do we cannot. We must simply devise the right lure to draw him off his greatwards.*

No mind would be so foolish, one of the princes thought.

This one has foolishness to spare, the consort assured him. *He is not nearly as evolved as he thinks, and he has led us to the source of the uprising.* He sent a mental image of the lost city of the last unifier.

We must go there on the next cycle and grind every last stone to powder, the consort thought. *I will shit on the unifier's corpse myself, for the trouble he caused us.*

The other minds gave their agreement, and the consort met their eyes, letting them see him in the fullness of power.

Open your minds to me, he ordered. It was not something he would dare back in the mind court, but these princes knew well that they would never see the court again if they did not comply, and it was a better fate by far than having their minds consumed.

As one, they lowered their defences, letting the consort sift their memories of the last three nights.

They had been in contact with their brother when the heir appeared, wearing the cursed crown and driving his vicious weapon into the prince's chest.

The consort felt a chill of fear as he relived the memory. The Northerner was powerful, but his power was no more than the weakest of princelings. The heir had done what he feared most and unlocked the full power of the artefacts.

He had become the mind hunter, like the withered corpse out in the desert.

How many of the consort's brethren and ancestors had fallen before that one? The Queen herself had not been alive then, but he was. He had been juvenile and weak, surviving more by luck than cunning, but he remembered well the terror that permeated the air of the mind court.

The consort dismissed the others with a nod, letting them flee the surface before gathering his mimics and riding the currents of the vent back to the Core.

The heir must be killed quickly, before he could set up a dynasty.

29

Eunuch

333 AR Autumn

'I have taken the *alagai* princes' measure,' Ahmann said, 'and found them wanting.' He pointed to the foot of the dais. The curtains of his throne room had been pulled tight and the room lit by oil lamps that he might display the bulbous head of the demon prince, staked there. He had ordered Abban to commission masons to brick the windows permanently.

His counsellors had taken it in turn to stare into the huge bulbous black eyes of their enemy, each hiding his revulsion behind a forced scoff of derision. Abban could not blame them. The demon was not nearly so large or full of teeth and claws as many of its other brethren, but its otherworldly stare was unnerving. Its high conical head, vestigial horns, and almost gentle features were not those of a mindless killer. It was a thinker. A planner.

Not for the first time, Abban thanked Everam that he was a crippled *khaffit* and denied the night.

He adjusted his camel crutch into a more comfortable position as his friend gave the speech the two of them had so carefully prepared. Though he often stood on the dais where he could advise his master, they had agreed that for this decree Abban should remain on the floor, that none should suspect his involvement. Ahmann would get his way regardless, but the clerics would fall into line much more quickly if they thought the plans were coming from the Shar'Dama Ka and not a spineless *khaffit*.

They think me spineless, but I can make them dance like puppets. He kept his eyes respectfully down, but he had learned to see much in periphery watching the clerics as Ahmann spoke.

'But we must not grow complacent,' Ahmann went on. 'The return of the sons of Alagai Ka signals the beginning of Sharak Ka, and Sharak Ka cannot be won until Sharak Sun is brought to a close. The *alagai* cannot break our defences, but they can wear them down, burning fields and killing livestock until we are too weak to fight, even as the greenlanders gird themselves against us. To win both wars, we must continue to expand, bringing the Northern cities one by one under Evejan law, levying their men and confiscating their resources.'

Damaji Aleverak nodded. 'The Daylight War must be won, and we grow soft in Everam's Bounty.'

'Agreed,' Ashan said. Technically he spoke for the council, but all knew he was Ahmann's puppet. Aleverak was the oldest and most venerated of the *Damaji*, the only man who had fought Ahmann for the Skull Throne and lived to speak of it. All treated the ancient cleric with deference, and his words were given enormous weight.

This was why Ahmann, when he met with them privately earlier in the day, ordered Aleverak to speak first, and Ashan second.

Ahmann thumped the butt of his spear on the dais. 'We will attack Lakton in two months.' On cue, Abban furrowed his brow and pursed his lips.

'You frown, *khaffit*,' Ahmann said. 'Do you doubt the wisdom of my plan?'

All eyes turned to Abban, and he pretended to wilt under their glare. No doubt everyone in the room was praying for him to say something foolish that would cost him his favour with the Shar'Dama Ka.

It was, Abban had to admit, a valid concern. He knew full well that should he ever publicly fall from Ahmann's favour, every man in the room – not to mention the Damajah herself – would move immediately to dominate or kill him.

'The Deliverer's wisdom exceeds my own,' Abban said, adding just the right bit of snivelling to his tone. 'But your forces are stretched thin attempting to hold the land you have already taken. The cost—'

'Do not listen to the cowardly words of this pig-eating *khaffit*, Father,' Jayan cut in. 'He spoke against your attack on Everam's Bounty, as well.' The other *Damaji* nodded, muttering their agreement.

Pig-eating khaffit *is redundant, you idiot*, Abban thought. *Khaffit* literally meant 'pig-eater', for the Evejah forbade the eating of pork, and poor *khaffit* could often afford no other meat. Abban's lip twitched imperceptibly as he resisted the urge to smirk. No man in this room had the slightest idea what they were missing. Pigs were such delicious animals, denied to all men simply because Kaji's half brother had poisoned a suckling and set it before the Deliverer three thousand years ago. Kaji's legendary strength had resisted death, but he had – most likely in a moment of pique after spending hours on the commode – declared pig unclean, denying countless generations of fools their sweet, tender meat.

His mouth watered. He would have suckling pig tonight, and then have one of his wives spill his seed in some manner the clerics had seen fit to forbid.

He looked at Jayan, unsurprised at the eager look in the young Sharum Ka's eyes. The boy was little more than an animal, enjoying conquest and plunder too much, and ruling too little. Killing men was far easier than killing *alagai*, and killing soft greenlanders easiest of all. Easy victories to add to his quite lacking list of accomplishments.

He resisted the urge to shake his head. An accident of birth had dropped all the power and opportunity anyone could ever dream of in Jayan's hands, and all he could think of was the size of his palace, and new ways for his toadies to flatter him.

Asome and Asukaji kept their faces blank, but the two men had a language all their own – an elaborate mixture of subtle stances and gestures the lovers had no doubt concocted in the pillows – that allowed them to hold whole conversations without anyone around them knowing.

Abban, after watching them for months, had only deciphered a fraction of the code, but he could guess the current content well enough. There were advantages and disadvantages to being left behind while his father and brother went off to war. Ashan would speak for the council, the *Damaji* ruling in concert with the Damajah in the Deliverer's absence, but while the glory would go to those in the field, there was much Asome could do to increase his own power while they were gone.

'And you, Asome?' Jardir asked.

Asome bowed ever so slightly in his elder brother's direction. 'I agree, Father. The time to strike is now. The *khaffit*'s concerns are not without merit, but they are small things in Everam's great plan. You have lost much of the harvest to the *alagai*, and those losses will mount. Taking more territory will mitigate this.'

Ahmann turned to the other ten *Damaji,* and Abban studied them while their eyes were directed at the throne. The men stood in precise order based on the number of *Sharum* in their tribes, no matter that the difference was negligible in many cases. The line changed slightly every few months.

After Ashan and Aleverak was Enkaji of the Mehnding. The *Damaji* had grown fat over the years, now that the path to the Skull Throne was beyond his reach. Ahmann still bore a grudge after Enkaji's attempt to hide the Crown of Kaji from him, but Abban could not blame the man for that. He wouldn't have just handed the thing over for free, either. Enkaji had survived since by marching in lockstep with Ashan and Aleverak, at least in court.

'The Daylight War is the purview of Shar'Dama Ka,' Enkaji said. 'Who are we to question?' He looked to the men standing next to him, the *Damaji* of the Krevakh and Nanji tribes. The Watcher *Damaji* wore night veils, even in the day, hiding their true identities to all save the leaders of the tribes they served and the Deliverer himself.

As always, the men bowed and said nothing.

Abban barely spared the other *Damaji* a glance. Ever since the lesson Ichach and Qezan had been given, the lesser *Damaji* had become even more obsequious than Enkaji. Only Kevera of the Sharach spoke out, meeting Ahmann's eyes. 'I do not wish to cast aspersions on your wise plan, Deliverer, but it is true my tribe cannot spare men for a new assault and continue to hold what we have taken.'

'Stay behind, then!' Chusen of the Shunjin barked. 'More spoils for the rest of us!' Some of the other *Damaji* chuckled at that, but all of them wilted at the glare Ahmann threw them.

'I am Sharach,' Ahmann said, 'by blood and marriage. I am Shunjin as well, and every tribe between. When you insult one another in my presence, you insult me.'

Asome stroked the handle of his alagai tail, and Damaji Chusen paled. He fell to his knees, pressing his head against the floor. 'I apologize, Deliverer. I meant no disrespect.'

Ahmann nodded. 'That is good. You will leave behind men to guard the Sharach lands in Everam's Bounty as they march to claim more in the land of the lake men.'

Abban wanted to laugh aloud at the stricken look that crossed Chusen's face. Every warrior he left behind would mean less spoils for his tribe, and might mean Damaji Fashin of the Halvas passing him in the order from the Skull Throne. He glanced at Fashin, and saw the *Damaji* smiling openly at the decree, though he was wise enough to say nothing.

Abban's mind began to wander as Ahmann went over the

details of the plan with them – at least, the details they needed to know. The meat of the plan, including the exact timing and location of their strike, would be given when there was no chance for the fools to bungle it.

He eyed the Skull Throne, wondering what the point of covering it in electrum had been. It seemed such an enormous waste.

Abban had given the Damajah the entire mine's electrum as commanded. He'd expected the metal to disappear, put to some secret purpose, or at the least to reappear as a suit of armour for Ahmann. Instead, it had been dumped over his throne, a meaningless show of power.

Or was it? He snuck a glance at the Damajah. The woman was not given to empty displays. There were few who could display better, but it was never meaningless.

It mattered little. Abban had delivered the metal, but he had not been idle in locating more, starting with the mine where Rennick first encountered the alloy – a gold mine marbled with veins of silver that still yielded a fair bit of electrum each year. Abban had bought the mine through an intermediary, and throughout Everam's Bounty his agents were tracking and buying the jewels and coins made from it. Already, he had amassed a considerable amount of the precious metal, using it to replace the retractable blade on his crutch and hammering some into filigree for the weapons and armour of his most trusted *kha'Sharum*.

The audience was soon over. Ahmann was first to leave, followed quickly by Jayan, Asome, and the *Damaji*. Abban turned to follow in their wake.

'Abban,' the Damajah called, and Abban froze. Ahead, Hasik closed the great doors and stood in front of them with his arms crossed, blocking his path.

Abban turned to watch Inevera descend from the Skull Throne's dais, his eyes quickly moving to avoid the hypnotic sway of her hips and lock on her eyes.

You have your own beautiful wives, he reminded himself. *This one displays her wares openly, but the price of looking is too high.*

He bowed. 'Damajah. How may this humble *khaffit* be of service to you?'

Inevera drew close to him. She was too close for Hasik to overhear their words, but at her back was Shanvah. By all accounts the *kai'Sharum'ting* was every bit as deadly as Ahmann's brutal bodyguard.

'Have your metalworkers made any further progress?' Inevera asked. 'The last batch of alloy they sent was worthless.'

Abban shrugged. 'Alloying the metals is simple enough, but finding the right mixture is a slow process. The fires of Ala may have introduced agents we have not anticipated.'

'We need more,' Inevera said.

'I see that,' Abban said. 'Coating a throne requires a great deal of metal. Will you do the steps next?'

'What I do with it is not your concern, *khaffit*,' Inevera said. Her voice was serene, but there was a warning in it nonetheless.

Abban bowed. 'As you say, Damajah. Nor is it my concern what you do with your eunuchs, though I am told by the city guard that three of them were found dead, washed up on the shore of the river.' He smiled at her, and knew immediately he had taken the game too far.

At a gesture from Inevera, Shanvah stepped in. Her punch was little more than a flicker, but pain blossomed in his face and he found himself falling onto his back.

Abban clutched his nose, eyes widening at how quickly his hand was covered in blood. He pulled a kerchief from his vest pocket, but that, too, became saturated. 'The Shar'Dama Ka has said he will kill any man that strikes me.'

'*Sharum'ting* are not men, *khaffit*.' Inevera smiled, her full lips turning up beneath her translucent veil as she swept a hand at the chamber doors. 'But by all means, hobble out and tell

Ahmann that you insulted me and I had Shanvah strike you. Let us see what he will do.'

When Abban did not move, she snatched the kerchief from his hand, holding the blood-drenched cloth before his eyes. 'This is the least of what will happen the next time you are insolent with me.'

Abban swallowed as she and the warrior woman strode into her private pillow chamber. He might not fear the *Damaji*, but Ahmann's First Wife was another matter entirely. His plot to install Leesha Paper as her rival had failed, and now he had made an enemy he would wish on no one.

When the door to the pillow chamber closed behind the women, Hasik honked a laugh. 'Not so bold now, eh, *khaffit*?'

Abban looked at him coldly. 'Open the door, dog, or I will tell Ahmann this bloodied nose came from you.'

Rage blossomed across Hasik's face, soothing the pain in Abban's own. Abban hid his smile as the huge warrior opened the door. Hasik would come soon to collect payment for the indignity, but this time Abban looked forward to it.

My metalworkers have made another attempt at reproducing the sacred metal, Abban wrote to Ahmann later in the day. *Send a strong-backed messenger you trust to retrieve the Damajah's sample at day's end.*

And Ahmann, as he often did, sent Hasik.

Abban's daughter Cielvah was working alone in the front of his pavilion in the New Bazaar when the warrior was spotted coming their way. Curfew was looming and the bazaar nearly empty, most of the pavilions and storefronts closed for the night. Abban watched through a pinhole as Hasik entered the tent. Cielvah was young and beautiful, intelligent with skilled hands. She had a bright future, and Abban loved her dearly. Something Hasik had known when

744

he raped her. It was never about Cielvah. It was about hurting Abban.

The girl gasped when she saw Hasik. She scurried behind the counter and down a short hallway where she disappeared through a canvas flap. Like a cat after a mouse, Hasik followed, leaping nimbly over the counter in pursuit and disappearing through the flap an instant after the girl.

Abban heard a door slam, and counted to ten before following, taking his time with the walk. His leg still pained him even after so many years, and he saw no need to tax it.

Hasik was still struggling when he entered the room, shutting the heavy door behind him. The pavilion abutted a large warehouse, and Hasik had unwittingly stepped inside. Two Sharach *kha'Sharum* had the situation well in hand with their *alagai*-catchers. The hollow poles were twice the length of Hasik's arms, threaded with woven steel cable, the end loops tight around his neck. Hasik grasped one in each fist, trying to keep them from tightening, but it was useless against the skilled Sharach warriors. When he pulled they pushed, and vice versa, all the while tightening the cords. Abban watched in pleasure as Hasik's struggles slowed, and he dropped to his knees, face reddening.

Cielvah came over to him, and Abban put an arm around her. 'Ah, Hasik, how good of you to visit! I trust you remember my daughter Cielvah? You took her virginity last spring. I have promised her a front seat to what I do to you in return.'

Still unmarried, Cielvah did not have a veil to lift as she spat in the *Sharum*'s face. Hasik tried to lunge at her, but the Sharach held him fast, choking him back down to his knees. Abban raised a hand, and another of his *kha'Sharum*, standing invisibly in the shadows, came forward. The Nanji were renowned for their skill at torture, and the small man was no exception. He moved with easy grace, silent as death save for the ring of the sharp, curved blade he drew. Hasik's eyes bulged at the sight, but he was not allowed air to protest.

The small man considered. 'This would be easier if he were on his back.' His voice was low and quiet, barely a whisper. 'And his limbs held tight.'

Abban nodded, clapping his hands loudly. The Sharach twisted their poles, throwing Hasik flat onto his back as the doors opened and a number of black-clad women entered – Abban's wives and daughters. Many wore marriage veils, while others, like Cielvah, had their faces uncovered. More than one of them had fallen prey to Hasik's attentions over the years.

Four of the women carried *alagai*-catchers of their own, and in short order they had looped Hasik's wrists and ankles, pulling tight. The *Sharum* was strong as only a warrior who regularly felt the magical rush of killing *alagai* could be, but the women had numbers and leverage, and he was held fast, even without the Sharach. The two *kha'Sharum* eased tension of their nooses, that all might better enjoy Hasik's screams and frantic, impotent thrashing as the Nanji sliced open his pantaloons.

The women all laughed at the sight of Hasik's limp member as it was revealed. Abban, too, chuckled, knowing the presence of the women multiplied Hasik's pain and humiliation a thousandfold. 'This pathetic thing is what my women fear when you visit my pavilion?'

'Dogs have tiny members as well, Father,' Cielvah said. 'That does not mean I wish to be humped by one.'

Abban nodded. 'My daughter has a point,' he told Hasik. He nodded to the Nanji. 'Cut it off.'

Hasik shrieked, thrashing again, but it did him no good as the women held him fast. 'I am the Deliverer's *ajin'pal*! He will not let you get away with this, *khaffit*!'

'Tell him, Whistler!' Abban laughed using the mocking nickname Hasik had been given after Qeran knocked out one of his teeth for calling Abban a pig-eater's son when they were boys in *sharaj*. 'Tell the whole world a *khaffit* cut your manhood away, and watch as they snigger at your back!'

'I will kill you for this!' Hasik growled.

Abban shook his head. 'I am of more value to the Deliverer than you, Hasik.' He gestured to the three *kha'Sharum*. 'In his wisdom, he has given me warriors to see to my protection.' He smiled. 'And to protect the honour of my women.'

Hasik opened his mouth again, but Abban gestured and the Sharach choked off his words. 'The time for talk is over, old friend. We were taught in *sharaj* to embrace pain. I hope you took the lessons better than I did.'

The Nanji worked quickly, skilled as a *dama'ting* as he wound a tight cord around shaft and sack both, cutting them away and dropping them onto a plate as he inserted a metal tube to drain waste and sewed up the wound with practised efficiency. When he was finished, he lifted the plate. 'How shall I dispose of this, master?'

Abban looked to Cielvah. 'The dogs have not yet been fed today, Father,' she noted.

Abban nodded. 'Take your sisters and see that they have something to chew on.' The girl took the plate and the other women dropped their *alagai*-catchers to follow her out the door, all of them laughing and talking amiably among themselves.

'I will encourage them to be discreet, my friend,' Abban said, 'but you know how women are. Tell a secret to one and soon they all hear of it. Before long, every woman in the bazaar will know to no longer fear Hasik, the man with a woman's slit between his legs.'

He tossed a heavy leather sack at the warrior, eliciting a grunt of pain as it struck his stomach with a clink. 'Take that to the Damajah on your way back to the palace.'

Jardir followed Inevera down the winding stair leading from their private quarters to the underpalace. He had never had need to visit the underpalace – he had not hidden in the night for over a quarter century – and was mildly fascinated as they descended. Wardlight lit their way, but Jardir's crownsight was all he needed. He could see the eunuch Watchers hiding in the shadows as easily as he could in brightest day. Their auras were clean, intensely loyal to his wife. He was glad of this. Her safety was everything.

She led him through twisting tunnels, freshly hewn from the rock, and several more doors, leaving even the eunuch guards behind. At last, they arrived at a small private chamber where a man and a woman sat on pillows, sharing tea.

Inevera pulled the door closed behind them as the couple quickly got to their feet. The woman looked much as any other *dal'ting*, swathed in black robes that hid all but her eyes and hands. The man was in a *khaffit*'s tan and pushed hard on a cane as he rose. His aura ended abruptly halfway down one leg.

Cripple, Jardir noted, not having to ask who they were. Their auras told him everything, but he allowed Inevera the niceties all the same.

'Honoured husband,' she said. 'Please allow me to present my father, Kasaad asu Kasaad am'Damaj am'Kaji, and his *Jiwah Ka*, my mother, Manvah.'

Jardir bowed deeply. 'Mother, Father. It is an honour to meet you at last.'

The couple bowed in return. 'The honour is ours, Deliverer,' Manvah said.

'A mother need not cover her face when alone with her husband and children,' Jardir said. Manvah nodded, removing her hood and veil. Jardir smiled, seeing many of the features he loved in the woman's face. 'I can see where the Damajah gets her legendary beauty.'

Manvah dropped her eyes politely, but she was not truly moved by the words, sincere though they were. Her aura was sharp, focused. He could sense her pride in her daughter, and the respect Inevera gave her in return, but nevertheless there was discomfort in the room. Jardir could see it dancing in the auras of his wife and her parents, a discordant web of anger and fear and shame and love that doubled and redoubled on itself, all of it centring on Kasaad.

He looked at his *khaffit* father-in-law, peering deeper into his aura. The man's body was covered in the telltale scars of a warrior, but the wound at his knee was not from the rending claws or tearing teeth of an *alagai*. It was even – surgical. 'You were once a *Sharum*,' he guessed, 'but you did not lose your leg in battle.' The words caused a spike in the man's aura, yielding another flood of information. 'You lost the black over a crime. The leg was removed as punishment.'

'How did you . . .' Inevera began.

Jardir looked at her, reading the waves of emotion connecting her to her father. 'A crime your wife and daughter long to forgive you for, but dare not.' He looked back to Kasaad. 'What was this unforgivable crime?'

Shock registered in Inevera's and Manvah's auras, but it was worse for Kasaad, who paled in the wardlight, sweat running down the side of his face. He leaned heavily on his cane and lowered himself to his knees with as much dignity as he could manage, then put his hands before him and pressed his forehead into the thick carpet.

'I struck my *dama'ting* daughter and murdered my eldest son for being *push'ting*, Deliverer,' he said. 'I thought myself righteous, defending Kaji's law even as I broke it myself with drink and behaviour that brought far more dishonour to my family than anything my son could ever have done. Soli was a brave *Sharum* who sent many *alagai* back into the abyss. I was a coward who got drunk in the Maze and hid in the lower levels where *alagai* seldom wandered.'

He looked up, his eyes wet with tears, and turned to Inevera. 'My daughter was within her rights to have me killed for my crimes, but she deemed it a greater punishment to let me live with my shame and the loss of the limb I used to strike her.'

Jardir nodded, looking to Inevera and her mother. Manvah's

face was streaked with tears to match her husband's. Inevera's eyes were dry, but pain streaked her aura as clearly as tears would her face. This wound had been open too long.

He looked back to Kasaad. 'Everam's mercy is infinite, Kasaad son of Kasaad. No crime is unforgivable. I can see in your heart you understand and regret your actions, and the loss of your son has punished you more over the years than the loss of your leg and honour combined. You have not strayed since from Everam's path. If you wish it, I will return your blacks to you, and you may die with honour.'

Kasaad looked sadly at his wife and daughter, then shook his head. 'I thought there was shame in being *khaffit*, Deliverer, but in truth I have never been happier, nor seen Everam's path more clearly. I am crippled and cannot serve you in Sharak Ka, so I beg you let me die as *khaffit*, that I might strive to be better in my next life.'

Jardir nodded. 'As you wish. Everam makes the souls of *khaffit* wait outside Heaven until they have gained the wisdom to return to the Ala with a chance to be better men. I will pray for you, but I do not think the Creator will make you wait long when your time comes.'

Kasaad's aura changed then, a weight lifting. The web among the three changed, but it was still without proper harmony for a family in Everam's grace.

He turned to Manvah, peering into her heart as well. 'You have not been as man and wife since the crime, unable to bear the touch of the man who killed your son.'

Manvah's calm, focused aura had gone cold with fear and awe. She, too, got down on her knees and put her head to the floor. 'It is so, Deliverer.'

'Even the wife of a *khaffit* must be a wife,' Jardir said. 'And so you must decide now. Either find forgiveness in your heart, or I will dissolve your marriage.'

Manvah looked at her husband, and Jardir could see she was peeling back the years, remembering the man he had been and comparing it with who he was now. Slowly, tentatively, she reached her hand out. She shivered when it touched Kasaad's hand, and he took it squeezing tightly. 'I do not think that will be necessary, Deliverer.'

'I swear,' Kasaad said, 'with the Deliverer as my witness, that I will be worthy of your touch, wife.'

'You already are, son of Kasaad,' Jardir said. 'I am sorry that the cost of your path to wisdom brought so much pain to you and those around you, but wisdom is no small thing to be bargained for like a basket in the bazaar.'

He looked at the aura the two now shared and nodded, satisfied. He turned to Inevera. 'Your mourning does Soli honour, beloved, but remember that you mourn not for him but for yourself. I regret I could not know him, but if your brother was half the man he is in your heart, he is twice the man Everam asks we be to join Him in Heaven. Likely Soli asu Kasaad am'Damaj am'Kaji has already supped at the Creator's table and been returned to the Ala to aid our people in their time of need.'

He looked back to Kasaad, indicating he rise. The *khaffit* did so, slowly, and then opened his arms. Slowly at first, Inevera drifted towards them, but she closed the last steps in a rush, and they embraced tightly. Manvah threw her arms around them both.

Jardir watched as their auras became one, finally flowing together as a family should.

After a moment, Inevera looked up at him. He could see the love burning in her, but also her question before she could even utter it. 'How did you know?'

To his surprise, it was Manvah who answered, squeezing her daughter's shoulder. 'He is the Deliverer, daughter. Kaji could see into the hearts of men, and he has been born again in Ahmann Jardir. The time for doubt is over.'

Jardir gritted his teeth as he entered his throne room, seeing Kajivah and Hanya waiting with Ashan and Shanjat. He could see the rage and indignation in their auras, and assumed he was in for another lengthy debate on the merits of *Sharum'ting*.

'Everam's balls, is a minute of peace too much to ask?' Inevera muttered as she followed at his back. Jardir chuckled, but then Hanya turned to face him, and he saw her eye.

He was across the room in an eyeblink, cupping her chin firmly but gently as he examined the bruise. It was a dark, angry colour, but nothing compared with the darkness of his own anger.

'Who struck you, sister?' he asked quietly.

Hanya sobbed and did not answer. 'Her worthless husband,' Kajivah said for her. His sister's aura confirmed it. Jardir turned to Shanjat.

'He is already in custody, Deliverer,' Shanjat said. 'We found him in his quarters in the palace. He was lying in a pool of his own piss, drunk on couzi.'

Jardir drew a deep breath, embracing all his rage and letting it fall away as he climbed the steps to the Skull Throne. He did not trust himself in striking distance of the man. 'Bring him before me. Now.'

Inevera squeezed his shoulder briefly in support before taking her place on the pillows beside his throne. He could feel the strength of her support, and drew upon it heavily.

Hasik was dragged into the room like an animal, held fast by two *Sharum* with *alagai*-catchers. His arms were chained to a metal band around his waist, with a spear shaft threaded through his elbows behind his back. His ankles were connected by a short length of chain. A bit kept his teeth open and his tongue pushed back, held in place with a tight leather strap. He was hungover, his aura bright with pain and impotent rage. Beneath that was shame, and fear. He knew what he had done, and what it meant. It was all Jardir could do not to kill him on sight.

'Sister,' he commanded instead. 'Tell me everything that happened.'

Hanya was still sobbing, but with soothing from Kajivah, she managed to draw strength enough to look up and meet her brother's eyes. 'I do not understand it myself, brother. Hasik has been vexed with me before, but he has never drunk couzi, or struck me. But these last few days, he changed. He began sneaking bottles into our chambers, drinking too much and weeping to himself when he thought he was alone. I tried to offer comfort as a wife should, but all my efforts were rebuffed. Then, last night as he slept, I decided to . . . surprise him.' Her aura grew hot with shame.

Jardir regretted forcing her to recount the story in open court, but what was done was done. 'What happened then?'

Hanya's aura was bright with pain and confusion to match her shame. 'His manhood . . . it was gone.'

'Gone?' Jardir asked.

'Cut away,' Hanya said. 'There was only a scar in its place, and a tiny metal tube.' Ashan and Shanjat's auras told him they had already heard this news, but he could see the discomfort the topic gave them still. Everyone in the room shifted uncomfortably, Jardir included. Only Inevera and the *Damaji'ting*, used to cunuch servants, were unperturbed.

Hanya's aura told him the rest, though he could easily have guessed it. 'Hasik woke, saw that you had seen his shame, and struck you.'

Hanya nodded, and Jardir turned back to Hasik. 'Show me.'

The humiliation in Hasik's aura was a scream in the air, but he stood slumped, not resisting as one of the guards pulled down his pantaloons, revealing that he had indeed lost his manhood. Jardir nodded to the guard, and he undid the strap, pulling the bit from Hasik's teeth.

'What happened to you, Hasik?' Jardir demanded.

Hasik did not respond right away, his eyes still on the floor. 'I thought it might grow back.'

'Eh?' Jardir asked.

'If I killed enough *alagai*,' Hasik said. 'If I bathed in their magic, I thought it might grow back.'

Inevera nodded. 'It does not work that way, *Sharum*. What is severed cannot be regrown. You only closed the wound.' Hasik slumped again.

'Who did this to you?' Jardir asked. 'You will still answer for striking my sister, but you are my brother-in-law and one of the Spears of the Deliverer. Any assault upon you is one upon me, as well.'

Hasik looked at him, but his shame and fear were overwhelming, and he did not speak.

'The Deliverer asked you a question, dog!' Ashan barked. Shanjat punched Hasik hard in the face, knocking him to the floor. Still, the giant *Sharum* was silent.

He would rather die than tell me, Jardir realized. Fortunately, for a *Sharum* there were worse fates than death.

'Strip his blacks, and burn them,' Jardir said. 'Cut off the hand he struck my sister with and throw him out in tan. I will dissolve his marriage and he can live out his days a crippled *khaffit*, denied Heaven for all eternity.'

'No, please!' Hasik cried in anguish. 'I have served you loyally! It was Abban! Abban the cursed *khaffit*!' His aura said he was telling the truth, and upon hearing it, Jardir was not surprised that Hasik would have been ashamed to admit it.

Still, it presented him with a difficult problem. He looked to Shanjat. 'Take a dozen men and find the *khaffit*. Bring him to me untouched. If there is so much as a hair out of place before I question him, it will be paid for ten thousandfold.'

Shanjat bowed, leaving quickly. Before long, he returned with Abban in tow. Hasik remained chained and noosed, but he had been allowed the dignity of his clothes once more. When Abban appeared, he recovered something of himself, seeming to slump as he prepared himself to spring. Jardir could see ghostly visions of him leaping at Abban as he planned the strike. If he could break free and kill the *khaffit*, the guards might slay him while he still wore his blacks.

Jardir looked to the men holding the *alagai*-catchers. These were Spears of the Deliverer, and no fools. They were prepared, pulling tight as Hasik sprang and choking him to the ground.

He turned back to regard Abban, probing deeply with his crownsight. The *khaffit* had already guessed the purpose of the summons, but his aura was calm. He was indeed guilty, but expected to talk his way out of this unscathed. Normally, Abban was skilled at masking his emotions, but here his arrogance was without end. He looked at Hasik flatly, but his aura was one of utter disdain and more than a little satisfaction.

'Did you castrate Hasik?' Jardir asked, wasting no time on pleasantries. His anger was only growing. He might be left with no choice but to kill his bodyguard and most favoured advisor both.

'No, Deliverer,' Abban said. It was truth, but not the whole truth.

'Did you order your *kha'Sharum* to do it?' he asked, losing patience.

Abban nodded. 'Yes, Deliverer.'

The men in the room all began angry muttering, but Jardir thumped his spear, and they fell silent. Abban still stood there, calm.

'I gave you those warriors to protect your business and facilitate trade, not to assault my warriors,' Jardir said.

'And so I have,' Abban said. He turned to Hasik, lifting his crutch to point at the chained man. 'That one, frustrated with your decree that I not be harmed, has been taking out his ire in my pavilion. You send him to me frequently as your errand boy, and without fail, he takes the opportunity to steal, or break precious merchandise for the pleasure of it.'

'And for this, you sever his cock?!' Jardir demanded.

Abban shook his head. 'Trinkets and baubles are easily replaced,

Deliverer. My daughter's virginity is not. Nor the honour of my wives.'

'The *khaffit* lies, Deliverer!' Hasik shouted. 'I never . . .!'

Jardir gave a curt gesture, and one of the guards tightened his noose, cutting off his words. 'I am Shar'Dama Ka, Hasik, and can see your heart. The next lie that escapes your lips will cost you your life, your honour, and your place in Heaven.'

Hasik's eyes widened, and his aura went cold.

'Did you rape Abban's daughter, Hasik?' Jardir asked softly.

Hasik was weeping openly now. He did not have the strength to answer, but he nodded. Hanya began sobbing again. Kajivah pulled her daughter in close, catching the tears on her breast while she glared daggers at Hasik.

'And his wives?' Jardir asked. Again, a defeated nod.

'Nevertheless, this cannot be allowed to stand, Deliverer,' Ashan said. 'If *khaffit* – even *kha'Sharum* – can kill *dal*, then all civilization crumbles.'

'Your pardon, Damaji,' Abban said, 'but neither I nor my men have killed anyone.' He gestured to Hasik. 'As you can see, the Deliverer's bodyguard is very much alive and able to continue his part in Sharak Ka.'

Jardir glared at him. 'Why did you not come to me with this?'

Abban bowed as deeply as his crutch would allow. 'The Shar'Dama Ka has more pressing matters than giving constant reprimands to overzealous *Sharum* and *dama* seeking to find loopholes to bully me without breaking your decree.'

Jardir did not miss the change in Shanjat's and Ashan's auras at those words. They, too, were guilty of the crime, if not so unsubtly as Hasik. He would have to deal with them in turn.

But then he looked back at Abban, and wondered. Abban was asking, nay, *demanding*, the right to defend himself. The *khaffit* stared at him calmly, daring him to take the *Sharum*'s side over his. *If you are fool enough to turn on me over this, then my loyalty has been misplaced*, his aura said.

756

Jardir sighed loudly. 'Time and again, I have told men in this very hall that Abban is not to be harmed. He is my property, and any harm that comes to him will be from me alone.

'Every man has the right to stop his daughter's rape, or avenge it if he can. Even *khaffit*. Even *chin*. If Hasik was too weak to defend himself, then he was not worthy of the prize. His cock has gotten him in trouble for the last time. He has sons and daughters to carry on his name, and as the *khaffit* says, he is still fit for *sharak*.'

He looked to Hasik. 'You have paid your due to Abban. The price for striking my sister is divorce, not only from your *Jiwah Ka*, but your other wives as well. I will not have my sister married to half a man. Hanya will keep her sister-wives, all your property and children.' He could see how he was crushing Hasik's spirit, but he did not pity the man. He still remembered what Hasik had done to him, all those years ago in the Maze.

'You,' he pointed his spear at the chained warrior, 'will keep your spear, your shield, and your blacks. You are expelled from the Spears of the Deliverer, but Jayan will find you a new unit to fight for. None here will speak of your injury, and if discovered, you may say it was an *alagai* wound. Continue to win glory in the night, and you may yet see Heaven. Break Everam's law again, with even so much as a cup of couzi, and I will see you cast into Nie's abyss.'

He looked to Ashan and Shanjat. 'I trust the lesson is clear to you, as well?'

Both men looked chastened, and nodded. 'Good,' Jardir said. 'Make sure the other *Sharum* and *dama* know this as well. I will not repeat it.'

Inevera went immediately to her Chamber of Shadows when the audience was over. After the scene with her parents, she had wanted nothing more than to have some time alone with her husband, but it was not to be. The usual mass of courtiers and petitioners were lining up to make their pleas before the Skull Throne, and she had no patience to sit through it all.

She had hoped to save the blood taken from Abban's kerchief for the right moment, but with his power – and boldness – growing, she could no longer afford to wait. She had not known Ahmann had given the *khaffit* warriors of his own, and it explained much. Still, she could not believe any *kha'Sharum* a match for her eunuch Watchers, trained by Enkido himself. They had killed *Damaji*'s wives in their beds while the men slept beside them.

Hasik had deserved his fate, and so, perhaps, had her Watchers, if they had been fool enough to be caught. But still the trend disturbed her. Already, the *khaffit* had tried to supplant her. How long before he attempted to strike at her again?

She had leached the blood from the cloth while it was still fresh, storing it in a sealed vial. She took this now, pouring it over her dice. 'Almighty Everam, give me knowledge of Abban asu Chabin am'Haman am'Kaji. Can he be trusted to serve the Deliverer? Will he continue to strike at me?' She felt the dice grow warm as she shook, and then cast them to the floor, staring at the brightly glowing symbols.

As always, she was prepared to follow their guidance, but she was not prepared for the answer.

– The *khaffit* is loyal to the Deliverer. Your fates are intertwined. Harm to one is the same as harm to the other.—

30

My True Friend

333 AR Autumn

Arlen breathed deeply, unused to feeling so afraid.

'Sure you need to do this?' Renna asked.

Arlen nodded. 'Ent got excuse to put things off any longer. Hollow's recovering, and they know what to expect now. Rojer's Jongleurs are spreading word wide through the duchy, and folk will come from all over when they hear we won. Defences'll be stronger by the next new moon than they were on the last. Equinox is just a fortnight away, new moon ten days after that. I'm gonna do this, need to do it now. Ent got time to ride all the way to Rizon. I'll be careful. Won't let myself be pulled into the Core.'

He turned to Renna before she could reply, seeing in her aura that he had misunderstood the question. 'You weren't asking about me skating so far. You ent sure I should go at all.'

Renna gave him a look that matched the annoyance in her aura perfectly. 'That Jongleur's mind-readin' act of yours is startin' to give folk the shivers.'

'It's not mind reading,' Arlen said.

'Heart reading, then,' Renna said. 'Makes you hard to talk to, way you glance at a body and know everything they're feeling, even better'n they do themselves.'

Arlen laughed. 'Creator, if only it were so.'

Renna looked away, staring up at the stars so he could not see her face – as if that could hide anything from him now. 'Like you're in my head sometimes, way that demon was . . .'

'Ent like that, Ren,' Arlen said, reaching out to put a hand on her shoulder. 'You see the same things I do with your wardsight. Reckon everyone with the sight does. Look close and it can tell you all sorts of things about a body. Just figuring it out myself, and I cheated a bit, stealing some of the language from the mind demon we met when I was in its head. Soon I'll be able to teach it to you, one way or another.'

'Not sure I like the sound of that,' Renna said. 'Love you, Arlen Bales, but my head's my own place. Ent lookin' to share it with anyone.'

Arlen nodded. 'Honest word.'

She looked at him, her aura amused. 'Don't think you've tricked me by changing the subject. You sure this trip is a good idea? This is what you want?'

Arlen shook his head. 'All I ever wanted was to kill demons. Didn't want to war with Krasia. Didn't want Miln making flame-work weapons. Didn't want to be the corespawned Deliverer.'

He sighed, feeling so very, very tired. 'But it seems the world means to make me one, like it or not. All because Ahmann Jardir thinks the Creator speaks to him.'

Renna tilted her head, regarding him. *She's trying to read my aura*, he thought, surprised at how disconcerting it was. He felt a rush as she pulled a wisp of magic through him, Knowing.

'You still love him, even now,' Renna said. 'Like he's your brother.'

Arlen shrugged. 'Never had a friend like that in my life, and I've had a few. He was proud, and casually cruel in the way of *Sharum*. We argued plenty, but there was no one else in the world I wanted to guard my back when night fell.' He shuddered suddenly, feeling goose pimples rise on his skin though the night was not cold. 'At least, until he stabbed me there.'

'And you think throwin' him off a cliff is the answer,' Renna said.

Arlen shrugged again. 'Don't know, Ren, but I can't leave things the way they are. For everyone's sake, we've got to make a change. Got to do something the minds won't expect.'

'Worried about you skatin', too,' Renna admitted.

'Me, too,' Arlen said, taking another deep breath. Renna reached out, taking his chin in her hand and pulling him into a kiss. 'Love you, Arlen Bales.'

He felt some of his tension ease, and smiled. 'Love you, Renna Bales. You keep the Hollow safe while I'm gone.'

Renna nodded. 'And you come back quick.'

'Swear by the sun,' Arlen said, and dissipated.

Immediately Arlen felt the call of the Core, the source of all magic, begging to be explored. Faint fractions of its power drifted up all around him in paths, and he took the nearest of these, making sure to keep his sense of direction even as he passed through layers of soil and stone. He sensed a path heading southwest before breaking to the surface, and took it, skating along as quick as a beam of light.

He materialized a moment later on the surface and looked about to get his bearings. He knew the place, perhaps a dozen miles from the Hollow.

Not enough, he thought. *Need to go deeper.*

Again he slipped beneath the surface, this time dropping so far down that the call of the Core became more than just a seductive song. It filled his senses, bright and beautiful, pulling at him like flame drew a moth. A tendril of his being began to drift that way, wanting just a taste of its infinite power. It would be so simple to just . . .

No! He had no head to shake, but he pulled his incorporeal form together and quickly sought another path to the surface, riding the current southwest.

He materialized a moment later under a cloudless sky, and quickly realized he had overshot his target. He did not know precisely where he was, but he knew well the cold clay flats of the Krasian desert at night.

He turned a circle, tasting the magic on the wind until he knew where he was. Less than a day's ride from the weapons cache he had left outside Anoch Sun. He made a note of the path. Visiting the lost city again before the minds could destroy it on the next new moon was important, but not his goal this night. Again he dropped down a path, this time skating northeast.

It took several more hops to finally get within sight of Rizon. Arlen might have kept at it, inching closer, but each time the Core dangled its lure, and like a cat confronted with a string, he could not resist it forever. He began to run instead, his bare feet eating up the miles. Once, a reap of field demons spotted him and gave chase, but even they could not match him now. The demons fell farther and farther behind, eventually breaking off in search of easier prey.

He bypassed most of the villages and guard stations until he came to an isolated sentry booth, warded to protect the *Sharum* runner within. He slowed, letting the man hear him coming.

The warrior stepped out of his booth, spear and shield at the ready. His aura and stance said he was ready to face a demon, but both relaxed when he spotted Arlen's human silhouette. At least until he saw that Arlen carried neither spear nor shield.

'Who goes—' he began, but then Arlen was on him, slipping around his guard with ease and getting behind him with his forearm across the man's throat in a *sharusahk* hold. He squeezed gently, careful not to crush, until the man fell limp in his hands.

Inside the booth, Arlen saw a mat for sleeping, food stores and cooking utensils, and other necessaries. Likely this warrior slept most of the days and kept watch at night, ready to carry word if one of the outlying villages needed reinforcements.

When the *dal'Sharum* woke a few minutes later, he was stripped to his bido with his arms and legs tied tightly behind him. The rope was looped around his neck so that too much struggling would cut off his air. He groaned through the gag in his teeth, and Arlen, dressed in the man's blacks with his night veil in place, looked down at him.

'Apologies, honoured warrior,' he said in flawless Krasian, bowing. 'It is not my intent to shame you, but I have need of your robes and equipment. I will return tomorrow night to free you and give them back. Inevera, no one will know of your defeat.'

The warrior growled and struggled, but there was nothing he could do. Arlen bowed once more and raced back into the night. There were still miles to go before he reached the capital.

The low wall of the outer city had been strengthened and fortified since Arlen's last visit to Rizon, and mounted *Sharum* patrolled its length, but it was too vast to guard completely. He found a clear section and bounded over the wall easily.

Dawn was not far off by the time he reached the wall of the inner city, but enough darkness remained for him to see the warding field that now protected the area as surely as one of the Hollow's greatwards. He studied the energy with fascination. What was the source?

'There's Warders, and then there's Krasian Warders,' his old master Cob had said. 'None better in all the Free Cities.'

Arlen shook his head, leaving the puzzle for another day. As the sky continued to lighten, he headed for the bazaar, slumping slightly like a *Sharum* worn from a night's patrols. His nose

763

keener than a hunting hound's, it was simple to find an apothecary. He stole into the empty tent, stealing ladies' face paint and powder to hide his warded skin and pale complexion. He took the coin purse from his stolen robes and left a few draki on the counter before slipping back into the street. Other *Sharum* were filtering in from their patrols, and he kept his night veil loose around his chin, low enough not to draw attention or cause offence to the other warriors in the light, while still hiding his painted skin as much as possible. He needn't have bothered. The warriors saw only his blacks, nodded, and moved on their way.

For all that he was prepared, it shook him to hear the familiar sound of *dama* singing the end to curfew ringing out over the streets of Fort Rizon. Arlen looked up, seeing the newly built minarets rising above the wall of the inner city, surrounding what had been the great Holy House of Rizon. He wondered if the Krasians had already begun to decorate it with the bones of the fallen.

He watched as the city around him woke and came to greet the day. The Krasians came first, women and *khaffit* opening their kiosks and pavilions for a day's business. Soon after, when most of the returning *Sharum* had found their beds, the *chin* began to appear, opening their businesses as customers, Rizonan and Krasian alike, began to clog the narrow streets.

Soon, it began to feel achingly familiar, even as his sense of discomfort grew. The shouts of vendors, filled with exaggerations and outright lies, the noise and stink of livestock mixing with the smells of cooking food, meat and spices that made his mouth water as vendors displayed everything a buyer could want, and many they did not even know existed.

He had loved the Great Bazaar of Krasia, and it seemed a lifetime since he had wandered its maze of streets.

But you're not in *Krasia*, he reminded himself, seeing the differences, now that he had absorbed the familiar. Here, a group of *dal'ting* were followed by Rizonan men who carried their purchases like slaves. There, a pair of Rizonan women walked in the hot sun with their heads and faces wrapped in coloured veils. Everywhere, vendors called their wares in their native languages, but also in broken Thesan or Krasian, and buyers did the same. Already, a pidgin was forming, melding words from both languages with gestures, much like the trade language Northern Messengers used when visiting the Desert Spear. Arlen understood it instinctively.

A *dama* walked slowly by, watching the activity. An *alagai* tail hung from his belt in easy reach. Vendors and shoppers alike gave him nervous looks and a wide berth, but Arlen was in black, and simply gave a nod the *dama* returned casually before returning to his inspection. Arlen had no doubt that the whip would soon be put to use, if for nothing other than a warning to others.

This ent how it's supposed to be.

Abban did not need to look up when the *dal'Sharum* entered his office. Only one of his men wore black, and Abban did not need to raise his eyes past ankle level to know when his drillmaster darkened his door – something that had never happened in the bazaar. Qeran despised the place.

'You were not invited, warrior,' he said, dipping his electrum pen into the inkwell and continuing to write in his ledger.

The *Sharum* said nothing, pulling the door closed behind him. Abban saw the feet of his two *kha'Sharum* Watchers appear at his back. They moved with utter silence on the soft carpet, one holding a short metal club, and the other the handles of a garrotte. As they moved to strike, Abban finally allowed his eyes to rise. He did so love to see his investments pay off.

The Watchers were from different tribes, one Nanji and the other Krevakh. Anywhere else in the world, the two men could not have been in the same room as each other without shedding blood.

765

But tribe meant nothing to Abban's hundred. He was their tribe. He wondered sometimes if, three thousand years after Ahmann's reign, the Haman tribe might endure. Had not Nanji and Krevakh been men once, serving at the side of Kaji?

He snorted. Haman? If Ahmann was truly the Deliverer, it should be the Abban tribe. That had a nice sound to it.

The men struck as one body, the first swinging his club at the meat of the newcomer's thigh, a blow meant for maximum pain and surprise, but minimum damage. While the *Sharum* recoiled, the other would move in, catching him from behind with the garrotte and allowing his partner open access to attack. Abban had seen them do the dance several times now, and never tired of it.

But the *dal'Sharum* surprised him, moving as if he had known the men were there all along. He was baiting them, Abban realized as the stranger slipped his leg away from the club and threw his head back just in time to avoid the garrotte. He came back up fast with a punch the Krevakh barely parried in time and a kick that the Nanji managed to turn aside with his wire, though he failed to catch the ankle as it retracted.

The *dal'Sharum* had a chance to slip the shield onto his arm, but he didn't bother, leaving it slung over his back. He twirled his spear like a *dama*'s whip staff, parrying a club blow from the Krevakh, then spinning to strike the Nanji in the kidney. It came back and caught the Krevakh across the face before the Nanji finally caught it in his loop. He pulled, trying to yank the weapon from the man's grasp, but the *Sharum* thrust at the same time, breaking the Nanji's hold and slamming the butt of the spear hard into the centre of his chest.

As the Nanji dropped, the warrior turned to face the Krevakh fully. The *kha'Sharum* regarded him coolly, but pressed the hidden button on his club that extended a sharp, poisoned blade. The *dal'Sharum* attacked, but the Krevakh parried it smoothly and came in hard.

A moment later he was lying on the floor, gasping for air.

It happened so fast that it took a moment for Abban's eyes to catch up to his mind. The warrior had sidestepped the blow and put an elbow in the Watcher's throat.

Abban hesitated. He had not thought it possible that any single man could defeat his Watchers, much less a common *dal'Sharum*. Thankfully, he was prepared to handle far more than a single man. He reached under his desk for the hidden bell rope that would bring a dozen *kha'Sharum* rushing into the room.

'Please don't do that,' the newcomer warned, pointing at Abban with his spear. His voice was a rasp, but it had a familiar ring to it. 'The more people you send running in, the more likely someone will get seriously hurt.' He gave Abban a look so intense the *khaffit* had to suppress a shudder. 'And I assure you, it won't be me.'

Abban swallowed deeply, but he nodded, slowly lifting his hands into the air. 'Who are you? What do you want?'

'Abban, my true friend,' the man said, dropping the rasp from his voice. 'Do you not recognize your favourite fool? This is not the first time you've seen me in a *Sharum*'s blacks.'

Abban felt his blood turn to ice. 'Par'chin?'

The man gave a slight nod. One of the Watchers let out a slight groan, struggling to put a knee under himself. The other was climbing shakily to his feet.

'Out, both of you,' Abban snapped. 'Your salaries will be docked for incompetence. Wait outside and make sure my friend and I are not disturbed.'

As the men stumbled out the door, the Par'chin closed it behind them. He turned, removing his turban and veil. Beneath, his head was shaved clean, covered in hundreds of tattooed wards. Abban drew in a breath, covering his shock with a booming laugh and his customary greeting. 'By Everam, it is good to see you, son of Jeph!'

'You don't seem surprised.' The Par'chin looked disappointed.

Abban came around his desk as fast as his crutch would allow, slapping the Par'chin on the back. 'Mistress Leesha hinted that you were alive, son of Jeph,' Abban said. 'I knew then this "Painted Man" could be no other. Would you like some couzi?' He moved to the delicate porcelain couzi set on his desk. The drink was still illegal in Everam's Bounty, but Abban displayed it on his desk openly now. After what had happened to Hasik, who would dare say a word? He poured two cups, holding one out to the Par'chin.

'Not poisoned, is it?' the Par'chin asked, taking the cup.

It was a fair question. One of the delicate porcelain bottles in Abban's set was indeed poisoned, a drug Abban took the antidote to daily. Still, he put a hurt look on his face. 'You wound me, my friend! Why would I wish to harm you?'

The Par'chin shrugged. 'Been in the bazaar long enough to get caught up. Word is you and Jardir are suddenly pillow friends again. Makes me wonder if you always were, and your public bickering was just a Jongleur's show. Makes me wonder if you tricked me into retrieving the spear so your friend could steal it.'

'I warned you,' Abban said. 'You cannot claim I did not, Par'chin. Did I not say to you that I would deal in no Sunian artefacts? Warned you what my people would do if you so much as profaned the holy city with your footsteps, much less stole its treasures?'

'Yet you gave me the map,' Arlen said.

'You *asked* for it, Par'chin,' Abban pointed out. 'To be honest, I thought the holy city was a myth, and that you would never find it. But I owed you a debt, and I paid it.'

He paused. 'Now that I think of it, Par'chin, it is you who have not paid. "A mule load of Bahavan pottery" you promised. Is this why you have come? To pay your debt to me at last?'

The Par'chin laughed, and Abban was struck with how much he had missed the sound. They clicked cups and drank, Abban immediately refilling them for another round. They took their time about it, quietly enjoying each other's presence after so long. It was not until they tasted cinnamon that they moved to business.

'Why are you here, Par'chin?' Abban said. 'You must know Ahmann will kill you if he finds you, and his senses are sharp.'

The Par'chin waved dismissively. 'I will be long gone before he can catch my scent.' He met Abban's eyes. 'Will you tell him of this meeting?'

Abban shrugged. 'I do not see the profit in keeping silent, and I will not lie to my master.'

The Par'chin nodded. 'Nor would I ask you to. In truth, I want you to give him a message from me.' From inside his robes, he pulled a small, rolled paper, tied with a simple string. When Abban took the paper, he smiled. 'I saved you the trouble of breaking the seal and forging a new one. Jardir will know my script.'

Abban chuckled, untying the string. The Par'chin's handwriting was as florid and beautiful as ever, but the contents of the letter made his stomach sink. He looked at his true friend and shook his head.

'You do not understand what he has become, Par'chin,' he said. 'You are no match for him. This one time I beg you. Run far and never return. Run, and I swear by Everam's beard I will say nothing of this meeting to Ahmann.'

But the Par'chin only smiled. 'He couldn't kill me in the Maze, and then I was only a pale shadow of what I am now. You'd best start looking for a new master.'

'That pleases me no more than the thought of him killing you,' Abban said. 'Is there no other way?'

The son of Jeph shook his head. 'Ala is too small for us two.'

31

Alive

333 AR Autumn

'Shar'Dama Ka, the *khaffit* is here to speak with you.'

Jardir nodded, dismissing the guard as Abban limped into his map room. The *khaffit* wove unsteadily towards one of the soft chairs. He stumbled, but managed to guide his fall into the seat. He gave a sigh of relief.

Jardir's nose knew the cause even before he could look into his friend's aura. 'Nie's black heart, you dare come before me drunk on couzi?'

Abban looked at him flatly. 'The Par'chin is alive, Ahmann.'

The words, and the truth he could see behind them, cut off all other thoughts. Jardir shook his head slowly, turning away while he embraced his feelings.

'I had suspected,' he admitted. 'Months ago when we first heard of this "Painted Man".'

Abban nodded. 'We all did.'

'But I told myself it was ridiculous. We left him for dead in the dunes.' He looked back at Abban. 'How did he survive? Did he shelter in one of the *khaffit* villages?'

'I did not ask,' Abban said. 'What does it matter? It was *inevera*.'

Jardir conceded the point with a wave. 'What did he want?'

Abban produced a simple roll of parchment, tied with rough cord. 'He asked me to give you this.'

Jardir took the paper, slipping off the string and reading quickly.

Greetings, Ahmann asu Hoshkamin am'Jardir am'Kaji, in this year of our Creator, 333 AR—

I testify before Everam that you, my ajin'pal, have broken faith and robbed me on the sacred ground of the Maze, in the night when all men are brothers.

In accordance with Evejan law, I demand you meet me in Domin Sharum, an hour before dusk on the autumnal equinox, when Everam and Nie are in balance.

As the aggrieved, the location will be a place of my choosing. You will be given its location one week in advance, and allowed to arrive first, ensuring there is no trap. We will each bring seven witnesses, no more and no less, to honour the seven pillars of Heaven. We will settle our differences as men, and let Everam judge.

The alternative is for our men to meet in the field, shedding red blood in the day instead of black ichor at night. I hope you will see there is no honour in this.

I await your response,
Arlen asu Jeph am'Bales am'Brook

Jardir shook his head. *Domin Sharum.* Literally it meant 'two warriors', referring to trial by single combat as prescribed in the Evejah, based on the rules agreed upon by Kaji and his treacherous half brother before they fought to the death.

'Autumnal equinox,' Abban said. 'One month to the day before we invade Lakton. It's as if he knew.'

Jardir smiled wanly. 'My *ajin'pal* is no fool, and knows our traditions well. But though he speaks of Everam and Heaven, he does not believe their truth in his heart.' He shook his head. 'The "aggrieved", he calls himself. As if taking back what he stole from my ancestor's grave was common robbery.'

The question had gnawed at him for years. 'Was it?'

Abban shrugged. 'Who can say? I've done worse to men; even lied to the Par'chin for my own profit. But for all that, I was fond of him. He was very true. When I was around him, I felt . . .'

'How?' Jardir asked. They had both known the man well, but in very different ways.

'Like I once did around you, when we were boys in *sharaj*,' Abban said. 'That he would stand in an instant between me and any harm, as he did when you called us before the Spear Throne so many years ago. He made me feel safe.'

Jardir nodded. The way they had known him was not so different after all. 'And now?'

Abban's aura became unreadable and he sighed, taking a small clay bottle from his vest and pulling the stopper.

'Do not . . .' Jardir began.

Abban cut him off with a roll of his eyes. 'The blood of thousands pools at your feet, Ahmann. Are you truly about to lecture me about drinking couzi like I'm a drunken *Sharum* in the Maze?'

Jardir frowned, but he did not protest further as Abban took a thoughtful pull, his eyes distant. The *khaffit* looked back at him, holding the bottle out. 'Drink with me, Ahmann. Just this once. These are things best discussed with lips of cinnamon.'

Jardir shook his head. 'Kaji forbids—'

Abban threw back his head and laughed. 'He forbade it because his men were slaughtered in Rusk by a force they outnumbered five to one after spending the night before celebrating a battle that had not yet been won! It was a decree meant for uneducated sheep with weapons, not two men sharing a cup during the day at the centre of their stronghold.'

Jardir looked at Abban sadly. He could see in the man's aura that he not only did not understand, he thought Jardir the fool in this exchange. 'This, my friend, is why you are *khaffit*.'

'Why?' Abban asked. 'Because I do not treat every single utterance of Kaji as the direct word of Everam? You are Shar'Dama Ka now, Ahmann, and I've known you a long time. You are a brilliant man, but you have said and done many a stupid and naïve thing over the years.'

Such words might have got him killed in open court, but Ahmann could see his friend spoke from his heart, and could not fault him for that. 'I make no claims to divine infallibility, Abban, mine or Kaji's. You are *khaffit* because you are unable to see that the reasons for Kaji's decree do not matter. What matters is your obedience and submission. Your sacrifice.'

He pointed to the cup. 'Everam will not damn me to Nie's abyss if I drink that, Abban, nor Kaji's spirit grow restless. But remembering the lesson of the defeat at Rusk is well worth the sacrifice of couzi, just as remembering the betrayal of Kaji's half brother is worth the taste of pig, no matter how succulent you claim it to be.'

Abban looked at him a moment, shrugged, and drank again. 'The Par'chin is the man I knew, and he is not. I never felt for a moment he would harm me, or let harm come to me, but he was nonetheless . . . unsettling.'

'The rumours are true?' Jardir asked. 'He has warded his flesh with ink?'

Abban nodded. 'Much as you have with scars.'

Jardir shook his head. 'My wards are made of my own flesh. I have not profaned the temple of my body with—'

'Please,' Abban said, holding up a hand to cut him off while rubbing his other hand against his temple. 'My head hurts enough already.

'The Par'chin did not spare his face, as you did,' Abban continued, 'but he was never handsome as you. I suppose even the Damajah has a limit to how much she will . . . sacrifice.'

Jardir felt his jaw tighten. 'I have been most tolerant of you today, Abban, but there is a limit.'

Abban's aura went cold, and he bowed as much as he could without rising. 'I apologize, my friend. I meant no dishonour to you or your *Jiwah Ka*.'

Jardir nodded, whisking a hand to dismiss the matter. 'You once told me that if one of us were the Deliverer, it was the Par'chin. Do you still think it so?'

'I do not know that there is such a thing as a Deliverer at all.' Abban drank again. 'But I have looked into the eyes of thousands of hagglers, and in all my years met only two men I judged to be true. One of them was the Par'chin, and the other, Ahmann, was you.

'Ten years ago, our people were splintered. Weak. Unable to control even our own city. Great warriors, perhaps, but fools, also. Spending and spending, but never turning a profit. Our numbers were dwindling, women had no rights to speak of, and *khaffit* were beneath contempt.' He held up his couzi cup. 'Drinking couzi could get you executed.

'You might have stolen the throne, but you brought wisdom to it. United our people and made them strong again. Fed the hungry. Gave women and *khaffit* paths to glory. Our people owe you a great debt. Would the Par'chin have done as well? Who can say?'

Jardir frowned. 'So what would honourless Abban do? Is there profit in my fighting the Par'chin?'

'What does it matter?' Abban asked. 'You and I both know you are going to accept his challenge.'

Jardir nodded. 'It is *inevera*. But I would hear your counsel all the same.'

Abban sighed. 'I wish the Par'chin had never made this challenge. I wish he had taken my advice and run to the ends of Ala and beyond. But I saw in his eyes he means to fight you, *Domin Sharum* or no. If that is so, you are better off with a private battle over one held before all with untold thousands of bystanders ready to join the slaughter.'

'This is why we have *Domin Sharum*,' Jardir said. 'For when wishes come to naught. I will go, and I will fight the Par'chin with all I have, and he me. One of us will walk away, and upon his shoulders rest the fate of humanity. Let Everam decide who it shall be.'

Jardir looked at Inevera as she lay waiting for him in their bedroom. They had not spent a night apart since they had reconciled, weeks ago. His other wives clamoured for his attention, but Inevera's power over them was absolute, and none dared come to his pillow chamber uninvited.

Jardir could see the love and passion radiating from his wife, and steeled himself for what was to come. He could only hope she would forgive him.

'The Par'chin is alive,' he said, blurting the words and letting them hang in the air much as the *khaffit* had done.

Inevera straightened in an instant, her aura losing its warmth and invitation as she stared at him. 'Impossible. You told me you put your spear between his eyes and left his body on the dunes.'

Jardir nodded. 'That was all true, but it was the butt of the spear. He was alive when we dumped him on the dunes.'

'He was *what*?!' Inevera shouted so loudly Jardir wondered if even her sound-blocking *hora* magic could keep it from echoing throughout the palace. The anger in her aura was terrifying to behold, like looking over the edge of Nie's abyss.

'I told you I would not murder my friend,' Jardir said. 'I took the spear as you said, but had mercy on the Par'chin, leaving him alive to face the coming night on his feet that he might die a warrior's death on *alagai* talons.'

'Mercy?' Inevera was incredulous. 'The dice made clear you will not take your place until he is dead. How many thousands of lives will we pay for that "mercy"?'

'Take my place?' Jardir asked. The words tickled something

in his memory, and he probed deeper with his crownsight. 'Of course. The Par'chin.'

'Eh?' Inevera asked.

'You lied to me when you said I was the only man with the potential to be the Deliverer. I had thought you hiding an heir, but it was the Par'chin, wasn't it? Did the dice command I kill him at all, or was that simply you?'

She did not need to open her mouth for him to see it was so.

'No matter,' he said. 'He is alive, and has challenged me to *Domin Sharum*. I have already accepted.'

'Have you gone mad?' Inevera demanded. 'You accepted without even letting me cast the dice?'

'To the abyss with your dice!' Jardir snapped. 'It is *inevera*. Either I am the Deliverer, or I am not. The *alagai hora* are no different from Abban's tallies, tools for educated guessing.'

Inevera hissed, and he could see he had gone too far. She might lie to him about their meanings, but in her heart the dice were the voice of Everam.

'And perhaps they were right,' he conceded. 'Perhaps the Par'chin *is* the Shar'Dama Ka. The *Sharum* in the Maze followed him without question when he first brandished the Spear of Kaji. A spear he bled and risked his life for. A spear he used to kill the most powerful demon Krasia had ever known, one that had brought short the lives of thousands of *dal'Sharum*. It was he that found the holy city of Kaji, not me.'

'You are Kaji's heir,' Inevera said.

Jardir shrugged. 'Kaji took Northern wives when he conquered the green lands. I have seen his blood run true in places like Deliverer's Hollow. After three thousand years, the son of Jeph could be as much Kaji's heir as I. Perhaps my part in Everam's great plan is simply to bring the unified armies of Krasia to him, and then die.'

Inevera leapt from the bed, wrapping him in her arms. 'No. I refuse to believe it.' And she did. He could see her will preventing the very idea from taking hold. 'It is you,' she said. 'It must be you.'

Jardir put his arms around her, nodding. 'I think so, too. But I need to be *sure*. Can you understand that, my *Jiwah Ka*? It must be true, or the blood at my feet is for nothing.'

32

Domin Sharum

333 AR Autumn

'Tell me again how you know this isn't a trap?' Thamos asked as they left the contingent of Cutters and Wooden Soldiers behind to ride up the steep rock face. Behind the count rode Leesha and Wonda, followed by Rojer and Amanvah, with Gared bringing up the rear. Renna rode at Arlen's right, the count, his left.

'Your own scouts have confirmed there are only eight people up there, one a woman and one an old man,' Arlen said.

'There could be others in hiding,' Thamos said. 'The scouts also say they have a full company of men camped a mile to the south.'

Arlen pointed to the cliff face they approached. There was only one narrow path up the sheer slope, the rock bare and cold. 'Where do you think these others might be hidden, Highness? Will they drop on us from the clouds?'

Thamos frowned, and Arlen realized he was costing the man too much face before Leesha, Gared, and the others. If this continued, he would become an increasing hindrance, if only to show his own strength.

'I know Ahmann Jardir, Highness,' Arlen said. 'He would sooner throw himself off that cliff than violate *Domin Sharum*.'

'This is the same man stabbed you in the back, ay?' Renna asked.

'Figuratively,' Arlen said, sparing her an annoyed glance. She grinned in the face of it, and he wanted to laugh. 'In truth, he had the stones to look me in the eye.'

'Makes it so much better,' Renna muttered.

Arlen could see Thamos remained unconvinced. He sighed, lowering his voice. 'You don't need to risk yourself, Highness. There is still time for you to turn back and send Arther or Inquisitor Hayes in your stead.'

He of course wanted no such thing, but the challenge to the count's courage worked where other tactics failed. Thamos straightened in his saddle, his aura becoming steady and confident once more.

'We should all turn back,' Leesha said. 'This whole ritual is barbaric. A bunch of meaningless rules to give the illusion of civility to murder.'

'Ent murder when the other man sees it coming and means to kill you, too,' Arlen said. 'And the rules have meaning. Seven witnesses, so all those affected by the outcome can see the truth of it. A remote location difficult to stage an ambush. A fight right before dusk, when all men set aside their differences and become brothers, to force peace on the witnesses when it is done.'

'None of which makes it civilized,' Leesha said.

'Would you rather thousands die on the field?' Arlen asked. 'So long as men eat and shit and grow old and die . . .'

'. . . we will never truly be civilized,' Leesha finished, surprising him. 'Don't quote philosophers at me when you're about to force your friends and family to watch you two try and kill each other.'

'You don't have to come, either,' Arlen said. 'Send Darsy Cutter if you ent got the stomach for it.'

'Oh, shut it,' Leesha snapped.

Jardir watched as the greenlanders ascended the slope. As Inevera foretold, they brought Leesha Paper, his daughter, and his new son-in-law with them, as well as the greenland prince who had laid claim to the Hollow Tribe. This was well. It would make things easier when the Par'chin was cast down, and despite Amanvah's letter, he could not deny a flash of pleasure at the sight of Leesha after six weeks apart.

He looked at the man leading the greenlanders, and despite the changes to his appearance, Jardir knew his *ajin'pal* instantly. The way he sat a horse, his carriage and careful gaze. He, too, had always felt safe at the greenlander's side, always knew where he stood in the man's esteem.

Oh, my brother, Jardir thought sadly. *Truly Everam is testing me, if I must kill you twice.*

The greenlanders dismounted and tethered their horses on the opposite side of the cliff from the Krasian mounts. Jardir and his seven stood to meet them, their backs to the yawning drop.

'It has been too long, Par'chin,' he said when the greenlanders came forward. He could not see into the Par'chin's heart in sunlight, but Jardir could sense the power in his *ajin'pal*, contained by the will of a *sharusahk* master. The son of Jeph carried a fine warded spear, but it was plain wood and steel, with none of the innate power of the Spear of Kaji. 'You look well.'

'No thanks to you,' the Par'chin said, 'and a thousand years is too soon to have to look at your face again.' He spat at Jardir's feet, and there was tension in Jardir's entourage at the insult.

He threw an arm out to stay them, and met the eyes of Jayan, the most volatile of the group. 'You are here as witnesses, not participants.'

He turned back to the Par'chin, pointedly ignoring the spittle on his boot. 'You remember my *Jiwah Ka*, of course, and Abban, Damaji Ashan, and Shanjat. These,' he gestured at the others, 'are Damaji Aleverak of the Majah, and my sons Jayan and Asome.'

The Par'chin nodded. He turned to the woman to his right, whose sparse clothing revealed enough flesh to make even Inevera look demure. She was covered in painted wards as he was. Her eyes were wild, with none of the Par'chin's control. She looked at him with open hatred. 'My wife, Renna Bales, and His Highness Count Thamos of Hollow County, brother to Duke Rhinebeck of Fort Angiers. I believe you know the others.'

Jardir nodded. 'Before we begin, I would speak with my intended privately, to assure myself of her good treatment.'

'And I, my daughter,' Inevera put in. Jardir cast an irritated eye at her, but she ignored him.

'Intended?' Thamos asked. The look he gave Leesha made Jardir's eyes narrow.

Leesha came forward without waiting for anyone's permission, and Amanvah followed a moment later. Jardir took Leesha aside. When they were far enough that their voices would not be overheard, he moved to embrace her. 'Intended, how I have missed your touch . . .'

Leesha pulled back, stepping to the side and evading his arms. 'What is this?' he demanded. 'We shared more than a simple embrace the last time we were alone.'

Leesha nodded. 'But we are not alone, and this is not the time, Ahmann. I won't have you marking me like a dog. I have already refused your proposal.'

Jardir smiled. 'Thus far.'

'No, not thus far,' Leesha snapped. 'I lay with you in the pillows, yes, but I am not your property, and I will never wed you. Not if you divorce all your wives and return to the Desert Spear, nor if you kill all the dukes of the Free Cities and name yourself king of Thesa. Never.'

'And this is why you betrayed me?' Jardir asked. 'The warrior you poisoned made it to me alive with Amanvah's letter. I know what you were doing on the road.'

Leesha's anger seemed to lessen at that. He had expected her to become defensive, but instead she let out a relieved breath. 'Oh, thank the Creator,' she whispered.

'This pleases you?' he asked, confused.

'I don't have a *dama'ting*'s stomach for poisons,' Leesha said. 'And I betray no one by warning my people about the truth of your intentions.

'Speaking of poisons and betrayal,' she went on, 'did your daughter's letter mention how she herself tried to poison me with blackleaf while we were in the Palace of Mirrors? Or that your wife had me kidnapped and beaten the night after we first made love?'

Jardir could feel his face grow slack at the words. He reached out, taking her hand that he might sense her aura even in the light. He hoped to find proof of the lie, but he sensed beyond doubt that she spoke truth. Anger filled him, but then he sensed something else as well, and his rage was forgotten.

'You carry a child!'

Leesha's eyes widened. 'What? I most certainly do not.' Jardir did not need to probe these words. The lie was as clear in her eyes as it was in her aura. She was as aware as he of the new life that pulsed in harmony with her own.

Jardir grabbed her arm, squeezing so tightly she flinched in pain as he dragged her into the shadow of the cliff wall. 'Do not lie to me. Is it that pathetic greenland . . .' He looked closer in the shade, examining the life within her. 'No, the child is mine. It is mine and you sully it by cavorting with this *chin* princeling. Did you mean to hide this from me? Do you think I will let this man, or any man, keep me from claiming what is mine? I will feed his balls to the dogs. I will—'

'You will do nothing.' Leesha yanked her arm away, holding the other protectively over her belly. 'This child isn't yours, Ahmann! *I* am not yours! We are human beings and do not *belong* to anyone. This is where you fail time and again, and why my people will never bow willingly to you. You cannot own people.'

'You parse words like a *khaffit* to deny what you know is just,' Jardir said. 'Would you deny the child the chance to know its father?'

Leesha laughed, the sound harsh and biting. Her aura coloured with disdain, and it stung to see it directed at him. 'You have over seventy children, Ahmann, and you barter them like casks of ale. How many of them do you truly know?'

Jardir hesitated, and Leesha's aura flushed with victory. She gave him a mocking smile. 'Tell me the name days of all of them, and I will be your wife, here and now.'

Jardir gritted his teeth, flexing his fingers to keep them from curling into a fist.

So that's why she smelled different. Arlen growled low in his throat as he watched Jardir and Leesha, his sharp ears catching every word. He cursed himself. He would have seen it long ago had he Known her like he did everyone else.

Should have told me, he thought. *Never would have brought her if I'd known. Probably why she didn't. Word of this gets out, it could ruin everything.* Not for the first time, he wondered whose side that woman was on.

'Thought you said there wern't nothing left 'tween you and Leesha Paper,' Renna said, snapping him from his musing.

Arlen glanced at her, and then back at Leesha and Jardir. He tensed as Jardir grabbed her arm. 'Don't mean I want to see her playing kissy with a man who did his best to murder me.'

Renna grunted. 'Nothin' in the plan says you can't stomp him a bit 'fore you finish things.'

'Mean to,' Arlen said, stepping forward. 'Had your moment, Jardir! Hour's come to answer for your crimes!'

Jardir released Leesha's arm. 'We will speak more of this, after.'

'Only if you win, Ahmann,' Leesha said. The words cut him deeply, but he embraced the feeling and pushed it aside, turning to stride over to where the Par'chin waited at the centre of the cliff. The sun still bathed the area, and would until it fully set. His crownsight winked out as he left the shadow of the cliff.

The witnesses gathered around in a semicircle with the cliff wall at their backs. The challenge was simple. They would fight within the ring until one of them surrendered, or went over the cliff. They were allowed only spears and *sharusahk*, and both men stood with arms raised as Shanjat patted the son of Jeph's simple clothing for hidden weapons, and Gared did the same for him.

'No disrespect,' the giant greenlander said as he went about the business.

'You have nothing but honour in my eyes, son of Steave,' Jardir replied.

His sharp ears caught Shanjat's words to the son of Jeph. 'You should be thankful for the mercy my master showed you, Par'chin.'

'And you should be thankful I don't blame a man's dogs for who he tells them to bite,' the Par'chin said.

Shanjat sneered. 'The Shar'Dama Ka will finish what he started that night, Par'chin. You cannot hope to stand against him.'

'Then why are you hiding a knife in your sleeve?' the Par'chin demanded. 'Use it, if you dare.'

The warrior tensed, and Jardir knew the Par'chin spoke truly. 'Shanjat!' he shouted, stealing the moment before his brother-in-law could shame him. 'Attend me!'

When the *Sharum* seconds retreated, Jardir and the Par'chin bowed, both at a precise angle and duration, giving neither man greater or lesser face before Everam.

'I have come as you demanded, son of Jeph,' Jardir said.

'Speak your accusations for all assembled and almighty Everam, from whom all justice flows, to hear.'

'The spear you hold is not yours,' the Par'chin said. 'I risked my own life to bring it back to the world, and brought it first to you, my brother in *sharak*, to share its power. But sharing its secrets was not enough for you. The moment you realized its power was true, you conspired to steal it from me, ambushing me at night on the holy floor of the Maze. Your men beat me, and you took the spear, then cast me into a demon pit to die.'

There were murmurs from both sides at this, but Jardir ignored them, letting the Par'chin continue. He had carried these burdens too long in secret. *Let us have it out, and have it done.*

'When I killed the sand demon and climbed from the pit, I told you you would need to kill me yourself,' the Par'chin said. 'But you chose instead to knock me out and leave me on the dunes to die. You should have known then this was coming.'

Jardir nodded. 'You speak truly, Par'chin. I deny none of these actions, but I do deny the crime. One cannot steal one's own property from the thief that took it.'

The Par'chin laughed. '*Your* property? I found it hundreds of miles from you, in a place no one had been to in three thousand years!'

'Kaji was my ancestor,' Jardir said.

The son of Jeph snorted. 'Your stories are true, he had thousands of children, spread across the land. Got descendants in every sheep-sticking hamlet from here to the mountains of Miln.'

'But it is we of Krasia who have kept to his word and tradition, Par'chin,' Jardir said. 'The holy city of Anoch Sun is sacred. You violated it and stole its treasures.'

'You attack living cities, yet try to murder me for a crime against a dead one?' the Par'chin demanded. He narrowed his eyes. 'Where did you get that crown, my old friend? How much of the holy city did you have to violate to find it?'

Jardir felt his face grow cold, for of course, his army had

ransacked the city during their exodus from the desert. But there was no way the Par'chin could know that . . .

But the son of Jeph smiled, as if he could read Jardir's mind. 'I've been back there, my friend, and seen how you left things. I treated your "sacred city" with far more reverence than you did, and brought its secrets to you in peace and brotherhood. Even offered to take you back there myself. What has your visit brought the world? Rape, pillage, and murder.'

'Order,' Jardir said. 'Unity. I have made Krasia whole again, and soon the known world.'

The Par'chin shook his head. 'Once you're gone, your tribes will be back to slaughtering one another over a bucket of water. Gettin' rid of you is my last piece of business before I take the fight down to the Core itself.'

Jardir smiled, readying his spear. 'Whatever on Ala makes you think you can kill me, Par'chin?'

The Par'chin, too, gave a smile and lifted his spear. Whatever else he was, the son of Jeph was *Sharum* to his core, his soul at peace and ready for the lonely path.

I will sup with you again at Everam's table, my true friend, Jardir thought as he leapt to attack.

Jardir's attack was fast. Faster than Arlen had thought possible in daylight. But even so, Arlen was faster, the magic humming just beneath the surface of his skin, giving him strength and speed his foe could never match. He parried the thrust, smoothly following through into a return strike. He would strike with the shaft of his weapon at first, stealing face from Jardir before he finished the fight for real.

But Jardir surprised him, spinning his weapon inhumanly fast to parry the attack. They struck again and again, each move blending into the next. Both men gave and took ground, but when they broke apart, neither held advantage. There was grudging respect in Jardir's eyes, and Arlen, too, knew he had been arrogant.

He's drawing on the spear to give him strength in the day, Arlen realized.

'You fight even better than I remember, Par'chin,' Jardir complimented with a slight bow, his aura unreadable in the light of the setting sun. 'Again I underestimate you.'

Arlen smiled. 'You always say that.'

'This time is the last,' Jardir said. 'I will not hold back any longer.'

And he did not. The First Warrior Priest of Krasia attacked again, and it was all Arlen could do to keep up. He was faster, barely, but Jardir had martial skills that even Arlen could not match. He managed to keep the point of Jardir's spear at bay, but the butt and shaft began connecting, blows aided by impact wards and Jardir's own enhanced strength.

But while he could not use his magic out in the sunlight, beneath the protective layer of his skin Arlen had free rein. His bones were stronger than warded glass, his muscles and tendons spring steel. The blows buffeted him, but none did serious damage, and the little they did was healed instantly.

Still, he was not dominating as expected. In fact, to the eyes of all around him, he was losing.

'It is still my hope you will surrender, Par'chin,' Jardir said. 'Admit your crime and submit to me. My mercy is boundless, and I would still have you at my side in Sharak Ka.'

'You don't know the meaning of mercy,' Arlen said. 'If you truly cared about the First War, you would stop this meaningless grandstanding. Don't you understand? We are *drawing* the mind demons. They don't fear armies. They fear other minds, and will keep coming till we're dead. In the meantime, all our peoples suffer for it.'

'This is why we must unify now,' Jardir said.

Arlen gritted his teeth and came back in, his anger redoubled. Their weapons were a blur as they leapt, twisted, and tumbled, clashing together and throwing each other back. Jardir came in with a blurring series of thrusts and spins of his weapon, and Arlen parried them all, realizing at the last moment they were all a feint as Jardir kicked high at his spear shaft, his sandalled foot blasting through the warded wood like a cornstalk.

Arlen stumbled back, keeping both his feet and the broken halves of the weapon, but in that instant his guard slipped slightly, and Jardir thrust. The Spear of Kaji sank into his abdomen, and Arlen screamed.

It wasn't the cut. Arlen had been stabbed before, and it was a pain he could ignore in the heat of battle. This was something far more. The wards on the speartip activated, burning at the wound as they Drew his magic, sharpening the blade and adding to the impact. The shock ran through his whole body, an agony beyond comparison, like having his very soul sucked away.

Jardir's own eyes bulged as he felt the drain, and in that instant he, too, dropped his guard. Arlen struck him hard across the face with the butt end of his sundered spear, sending his foe stumbling away and breaking the killing Draw.

Arlen dropped one of the spear halves to clutch at the wound, his hand coming away bright with blood. There were cries of anguish and triumph from the bystanders, but he ignored them, desperately trying to focus his remaining strength to heal the wound. It continued to burn, unable to heal fully, but the flow of blood slowed as it crusted.

That's gonna scar, Arlen knew.

He glanced at the setting sun, wishing it would sink faster. He gave up all hope of humiliating his foe, focused now on simply surviving the next three-quarters of an hour.

Jardir hit the ground hard, but rolled right to his feet, more stunned than harmed. His cheekbone and jaw had fractured with the blow, but he had been so suffused with power when the Par'chin struck, the damage healed almost instantly.

He looked at the Par'chin, and Abban's words came back to him. *He is the man I remember, and he is not.*

Indeed, the Par'chin had a whole new fighting style now, a blend of *sharusahk* and something else entirely. He was even faster and stronger than Jardir, but more than that, he fought as if accustomed to the advantage, while Jardir was still learning to apply it fully.

But it was only a matter of time until he could analyse the style and bring his rival down. He thought he had done so on the last pass, but he had been unprepared for the way the Spear of Kaji came alive with the thrust, as charged with magic as when he had thrust it into the *alagai* prince.

Was the Par'chin an agent of Nie? It seemed impossible. Unthinkable. But what other explanation could there be?

He Drew hard on the magic filling the spear, attacking with renewed fury.

Arlen dodged and leapt, ducked and twisted, doing everything in his power to avoid the deadly speartip. Giving up all thought of offence made it easier, but it was a sign of desperation that all assembled could see. Jardir was the better fighter, and tireless, now using Arlen's own strength against him. He dominated the battle, and everyone around them held their breath, waiting for the killing blow.

But then the sun slipped below the horizon at last, and the rules changed. He could see Jardir's crown and spear glowing fiercely, but he Drew on the ambient magic rising all around them, and felt his own strength returning as well.

The next time Jardir thrust, the Spear of Kaji passed through him as if Jardir had stabbed a cloud of smoke. It still burned at him, wards brightening as they pulled at his magic, but it was worth the pain as Arlen stepped into the blow, punching Jardir hard in the throat. He solidified fully with his arm hooked around the shaft of the Spear of Kaji and ducked with a twist, pulling the powerful weapon from Jardir's grasp and flipping him onto his back.

Jardir kicked back up to his feet in an instant, whirling to face the Par'chin, his mind racing as he tried to make sense of what had just happened.

'You may have gained the spear for a moment, Par'chin, but you will not keep it,' he promised.

'Keep it?' the Par'chin asked, looking at the weapon with disdain. 'Don't even want it any more. World's better off without it.' Then he did the unthinkable.

He turned and threw the Spear of Kaji over the edge of the cliff.

Jayan cried out, breaking ranks to run down the mountain path in search of it. The Par'chin turned, drawing heat and impact wards in the air that blasted the cliff face, sending a shower of stones to block his path.

'No one leaves until this is finished!' he thundered.

'Very well, servant of Nie,' Jardir said. 'Let us finish it.' He concentrated, extending the protective field of his crown as he charged, meaning to use its power to drive the son of Jeph over the edge into the abyss where he belonged.

But the magic of the crown, which he had thought could repel all *alagai*, had no effect on the Par'chin, and they grappled instead. Jardir took an immediate advantage, working into a strong hold, but again the Par'chin collapsed into smoke, escaping to re-form an instant later, landing heavy blows.

'I am no servant of Nie,' the Par'chin said, 'simply because I have learned to use stolen magic more effectively than you and your bone-throwing *dama'ting*.'

Jardir snarled as he got his feet under him and came back in, blocking the lightning-fast kicks and punches as he returned his own probing strikes. Some of these the Par'chin parried, and others he avoided by dematerializing.

It seemed an impossible advantage, but there was a reason why Jardir had never lost a battle in his adult life. He memorized the patterns of the Par'chin's shifts, and the next time he solidified, expecting an easy return strike, Jardir was ready, dodging aside and punching him hard in the stomach. He followed it with a knee to the throat as the man doubled over, and slammed his open palms into his ears, making his head ring and his thoughts scatter.

'It seems you cannot use your magic at all when your mind is reeling,' Jardir said, head-butting the Par'chin in the nose. Blood spattered his face, but Jardir pressed the attack, putting his hands around the greenlander's throat.

Steel fingers clasped his own throat as the Par'chin surged back at him. 'Don't need it,' he said, pushing Jardir back a few steps and leaping, pitching them both off the cliff after the spear.

'World's better off without us, too,' he said as they fell.

Arlen felt cold wind on his face, clearing his thoughts as he and Jardir continued to grapple, twisting to try to dominate even as the wind howled in their ears.

Jardir proved the more skilled in the struggle, managing to put himself on top as ground rushed to meet them. It seemed pointless – the fall would kill them both, whoever was on top, but Arlen could see in his aura that Jardir didn't care. Arlen would die a split second before him, and that would be enough.

Arlen stopped struggling, embracing the fall. Jardir's aura lit with victory, but then Arlen dematerialized, and Jardir struck the ground with a bone-shattering crunch.

Krasian Dictionary

Abban am'Haman am'Kaji: Wealthy *khaffit* merchant, friend to both Jardir and Arlen, crippled during his warrior training.

Acha: Exclamation meaning 'heads up!'

Ahmanjah: Book Jardir is penning about his life. It will be to him what the Evejah was to Kaji.

Ahmann asu Hoshkamin am'Jardir am'Kaji: Ahmann, son of Hoshkamin, of the line of Jardir, of the tribe Kaji. Leader of all Krasia. Believed by many to be the Deliverer. See also: Shar'Dama Ka.

Ajin'pal (blood brother): Name for the bond that forms on a boy's first night fighting in the Maze, when he is tethered to a *dal'Sharum* warrior to keep him from running when the demons first come at them. An *ajin'pal* is considered a blood relative thereafter.

Ala: (1) The perfect world created by Everam, corrupted by Nie. (2) Dirt, soil, clay, etc.

Alagai: The Krasian word for corelings (demons). Direct translation is 'plague of Ala'.

Alagai hora: Demon bones used by *dama'ting* to create magic items, such as the warded dice they use to tell the future. *Alagai hora* burst into flame if exposed to sunlight.

Alagai Ka: Ancient Krasian name for the consort to Alagai'ting Ka, the Mother of All Demons. Alagai Ka and his sons were said to be the most powerful of the demon lords, generals, and captains of Nie's forces.

Alagai'sharak: Holy War against demonkind.

Alagai tail: A whip consisting of three strips of braided leather ending in sharp barbs meant to cut deeply into a victim's flesh. Used by *dama* as an instrument of punishment.

Alagai'ting Ka: The Mother of All Demons, the demon queen of Krasian myth.

Aleverak: Damaji of the Majah tribe in Krasia.

Amadeveram: Damaji of the Kaji tribe in Krasia before Jardir comes to power.

Amanvah: Jardir's first daughter by Inevera, Amanvah is *dama'ting* in her own right. Offered to Rojer as a bride along with her cousin Sikvah.

Andrah: Krasian secular and religious dictator.

Anjha: One of the lesser tribes of Krasia.

Anoch Sun: Lost city that was once the seat of power for Kaji, the Shar'Dama Ka. It is believed to have been claimed by the sands; no one has seen or heard of the city in centuries. People and artefacts called Sunian.

Asavi: Dama'ting of the Kaji tribe. Former rival of Inevera as *nie'dama'ting*. Lover of Melan.

Ashan: Son of Dama Khevat and closest friend of Jardir's during his training in Sharik Hora, Ashan is *Damaji* of the Kaji tribe and part of Jardir's inner circle. Married to Jardir's eldest sister, Imisandre. Father of Asukaji and Ashia.

Ashia: Jardir's *Sharum'ting* niece. Daughter of Ashan and Imisandre. Married to Asome.

Asome: Jardir's second son by Inevera. *Dama.* Known as the 'heir to nothing'. Married to Ashia.

Asu: 'Son', or 'son of'. Used as a prefix in formal names, as in Ahmann asu Hoshkamin am'Jardir am'Kaji.

Asukaji: Ashan's eldest son by Jardir's sister Imisandre. *Dama.* Name literally means 'son of Kaji'.

Baden: Rich and powerful *dama* of the Kaji tribe. *Push'ting.* Known to possess several items of *hora* magic.

Bazaar, Great: The largest merchant area in Krasia, located right inside the main gates. It is run entirely by women and *khaffit.*

Belina: Jardir's *dama'ting* wife from the Majah tribe.

Bido: Loincloth, most commonly the white *nie'Sharum* cloth boys are given after they are taken from their mothers and stripped of their tans.

Cashiv: Push'ting kai'Sharum in personal service to Dama Baden. Lover of Soli.

Chin: Outsider/infidel. This word is also considered an insult, meaning that a person is a coward.

Chusen: Damaji of the Shunjin tribe.

Cielvah: Daughter of Abban. Raped by Hasik.

Coliv: Krevakh Watcher assigned to Jardir's unit as *kai'Sharum.* Sent to guard Leesha on her return to the Hollow.

Couzi: A harsh, illegal Krasian liquor flavoured with cinnamon. Because of its potency, it is served in tiny cups meant to be taken in one swallow.

Dal: Prefix meaning 'honoured'.

Dal'Sharum: The Krasian warrior caste, which includes the vast majority of the men. *Dal'Sharum* are broken into tribes controlled by the *Damaji,* and smaller units answerable to a *dama* and a *kai'Sharum. Dal'Sharum* dress in black robes with a black turban and night veil. All are trained in hand-to-hand combat (*sharusahk*), as well as spear fighting and shield formations.

Dal'ting: Fertile married women, or older women who have given birth.

Dama: A Krasian Holy Man. *Dama* are both religious and secular leaders. They wear white robes and carry no weapons. All *dama* are masters of *sharusahk,* the Krasian hand-to-hand martial art.

Damajah: Singular title for the First Wife of the Shar'Dama Ka.

Damaji: The twelve *Damaji* are the religious and secular leaders of their individual tribes, and serve the Andrah as ministers and advisors.

Damaji'ting: The tribal leaders of the *dama'ting*, and the most powerful women in Krasia.

Dama'ting: Krasian Holy Women who also serve as healers and midwives. *Dama'ting* hold the secrets of *hora* magic, including the power to foretell the future, and are held in fear and awe. Harming a *dama'ting* in any way is punishable by death.

Daylight War, the: Also known as Sharak Sun. Ancient war during which Kaji conquered the known world, uniting them for Sharak Ka.

Desert Spear, the: The Krasians' term for their city. Known in the North as Fort Krasia.

Drillmasters: Elite warriors who train *nie'Sharum*. Drillmasters wear standard *dal'Sharum* blacks, but their night veils are red.

Enkaji: Damaji of the powerful Mehnding tribe.

Enkido: Eunuch servant and *sharusahk* instructor of the Kaji *dama'ting*. Made personal bodyguard to Amanvah.

Evejah, the: The holy book of Everam, written by Kaji, the first Deliverer, some thirty-five hundred years past. The Evejah is separated into sections called Dunes. Each *dama* pens a copy of the Evejah in his own blood during his clerical training.

Evejan: Name of the Krasian religion, 'those who follow the Evejah'.

Evejan law: The militant religious law the Krasians impose on *chin*, meant to force nonbelievers to follow the Evejah under threat rather than belief.

Everalia: Jardir's third Kaji wife.

Everam: The Creator.

Everam's Bounty: After Fort Rizon was taken with its vast

farmland in 333 AR, the city-state was renamed Everam's Bounty to honour the Creator. It is the Krasian foothold in the green lands.

Fahki: Dal'Sharum son of Abban. Raised to hate his *khaffit* father.

Fashin: Damaji of the Halvas tribe.

Gai: Plague.

Greenlander: One from the green lands.

Green lands: Krasian name for Thesa (the lands north of the Krasian desert).

Halvan: Friend of Jardir and Ashan during Jardir's training in Sharik Hora. Dama Halvan is advisor to Damaji Ashan.

Hannu Pash: Literally 'life's path', this represents the period of a boy's life after he has been taken from his mother but before his caste (*dal'Sharum, dama,* or *khaffit*) is set. It is a period of intense and brutal physical training, along with religious indoctrination.

Hanya: Jardir's youngest sister, four years younger than he. Married to Hasik, mother to Sikvah.

Hasik: Nie'Sharum boy who insults and bullies Jardir. Called Whistler because his missing tooth causes his *s*'s to whistle. Later becomes one of the Spears of the Deliverer and Jardir's bodyguard.

Horn of Sharak: Ceremonial horn blown to begin and end *alagai'sharak.*

Hoshkamin: Father of Ahmann Jardir; deceased.

Hoshvah: Jardir's middle sister, three years younger than he. Married to Shanjat. Mother of Shanvah.

Ichach: Damaji of the Khanjin tribe.

Imisandre: Jardir's eldest sister, one year younger than he. Married to Ashan. Mother of Asukaji and Ashia.

Inevera: (1) Jardir's powerful *dama'ting* First Wife. Kaji tribe. Also known as the Damajah. (2) Krasian word meaning 'Everam's will' or 'Everam willing'.

Jama: Lesser Krasian tribe. Enemies of the Khanjin.

Jardir: The seventh son of Kaji, the Deliverer. Once a great house, the line of Jardir lasted more than three thousand years, slowly dwindling in number and glory until its last son, Ahmann Jardir, restored the line to glory.

Jayan: Jardir's first *Sharum* son by Inevera. Later appointed Sharum Ka.

Jiwah: Wife.

Jiwah Ka: First wife. The *Jiwah Ka* is the first and most honoured of a Krasian man's wives. She has veto power over subsequent marriages, and can command the lesser wives.

Jiwah Sen: Lesser wives, subservient to a man's *Jiwah Ka*.

Jiwah'Sharum: Literally 'wives of warriors', these are women purchased for the great harem of the *Sharum* during their fertile years. It is considered a great honour to serve. All warriors have access to their tribe's *jiwah'Sharum*, and are expected to keep them continually pregnant, adding warriors to the tribe.

Jurim: *Dal'Sharum* who trained with Jardir. Kaji tribe. Later one of the Spears of the Deliverer.

Kad': Prefix meaning 'of'.

Kai'Sharum: Krasian military captains, the *kai'Sharum* receive special training in Sharik Hora and lead individual units in *alagai'sharak*. The number of *kai'Sharum* in a tribe depends on its number of warriors. Some tribes have many, some just one. *Kai'Sharum* wear *dal'Sharum* blacks, but their night veils are white.

Kaji: The name of the original Deliverer and patriarch of the Kaji tribe, also known as Shar'Dama Ka, the Spear of Everam, and various other titles. Kaji united the known world in war against demons some thirty-five hundred years past. His seat of power was the lost city of Anoch Sun, but he also founded Fort Krasia.

Kaji had three artefacts for which he was famous: (1) The Spear of Kaji – the metal spear he used to slay *alagai* by the thousand. (2) The Crown of Kaji – bejewelled and moulded in the shape of powerful wards. (3) The Cloak of

Kaji – a cloak that made him invisible to demons, so he could walk freely in the night.

Kaji'sharaj: Training barracks for boys of the Kaji tribe.

Kajivah: Mother of Ahmann Jardir and his three sisters, Imisandre, Hoshvah, and Hanya. Widow of Hoshkamin Jardir. Once considered cursed for bearing three daughters in a row.

Kasaad: Inevera's father. Crippled *khaffit*. Former *Sharum*.

Kaval: Gavram asu Chenin am'Kaval am'Kaji. Drillmaster of the Kaji tribe. One of Jardir's *dal'Sharum* instructors during his *Hannu Pash*.

Kenevah: *Damaji'ting* of the Kaji tribe during Inevera's *dama'ting* training.

Kevera: *Damaji* of the Sharach tribe.

Khaffit: A man who takes up a craft instead of becoming a Holy Man or warrior. Lowest male station in Krasian society. Expelled from *Hannu Pash*, *khaffit* are forced to dress in the tan clothes of children and shave their cheeks as a sign that they are not men.

Khaffit'sharaj: Training camps set up by each tribe for the *kha'Sharum*.

Khanjin: Lesser Krasian tribe. Enemies of the Jama.

Kha'Sharum: Able-bodied *khaffit* Jardir has made into low-skill infantry. *Kha'Sharum* wear tan robes, turbans, and night veils to show their *khaffit* status.

Kha'ting: Non-*dama'ting* blood relatives of Jardir. *Kha'ting* are given special training, and are considered blood of the Deliverer. As with *dama'ting*, the punishment for striking a *kha'ting* is death or the loss of the striking limb.

Khevat: Kaji *dama* who trains Jardir in his youth. Father of Ashan.

Lonely road: Krasian term for death. All warriors must walk the lonely road to Heaven, with temptations on the path to test their spirit and ensure only the worthy make it to stand before Everam to be judged. Spirits who venture off the path are lost.

Loremaster: Dama who have dedicated themselves to the study of ancient texts. Researchers and career academicians, they stay out of politics for the most part, teaching *nie'dama* their basic lessons.

Maji: Jardir's second Majah son, a *nie'dama* who will have to fight Aleverak's heir for the Majah *Damaji* throne.

Manvah: Mother of Inevera. Wife of Kasaad. Successful basket weaver.

Mehnding tribe: The largest and most powerful tribe after the Majah, the Mehnding devote themselves wholly to the art of ranged weapons. They build the catapults, slings, and scorpions used in *sharak*, quarry and haul the stones for ammunition, make the scorpion bolts, etc.

Melan: *Dama'ting* daughter of Qeva. Granddaughter of Kenevah. Former rival of Inevera. Lover of Asavi.

Nie: (1) The name of the Uncreator, feminine opposite to Everam, and the goddess of night and demonkind. (2) Nothing, none, void, no, not.

Nie'dama: *Nie'Sharum* selected for *dama* training.

Nie'dama'ting: Krasian girl who is in *dama'ting* training but is too young to take her veil. *Nie'dama'ting* are given great respect by men and women alike, unlike *nie'Sharum*, who are less than *khaffit* until they complete the *Hannu Pash*.

Nie Ka: Literally 'first of none', a term for the head boy of a *nie'Sharum* class, who commands the other boys as lieutenant to the *dal'Sharum* drillmasters.

Nie's Abyss: Also known as the Core. The seven-layered underworld where *alagai* hide from the sun. Each layer is populated with a different breed of demon.

Nie'Sharum: Literally 'not warriors', name for boys who have gone to the training grounds to be judged and set on the path to *dal'Sharum*, *dama*, or *khaffit*.

Nie'ting: Barren women. The lowest rank in Krasian society.

Night veil: Veil worn by *dal'Sharum* during *alagai'sharak* to hide their identities, showing that all men are equal allies in the night.

Omara: Abban's widowed Kaji mother, considered cursed for bearing several daughters in a row, until the birth of Abban, her youngest.

Oot: *Dal'Sharum* signal for 'beware' or 'demon approaching'.

Par'chin: 'Brave outsider'; singular title for Arlen Bales.

Pig-eater: Krasian insult meaning *khaffit*. Only *khaffit* eat pig, as it is considered unclean.

Push'ting: Literally 'false woman', Krasian insult for homosexual men who shun women altogether. Homosexuality is tolerated in Krasia only so long as the men also impregnate women and add to their tribe.

Qasha: Jardir's Sharach *dama'ting* wife.

Qeran: One of Jardir's Kaji *dal'Sharum* drillmasters during his *Hannu Pash*. Later crippled, he is taken in by Abban to train his *kha'Sharum* hundred.

Qezan: Damaji of the Jama tribe.

Savas: Jardir's Mehnding *dama* son.

Scorpion: A Krasian ballista, the scorpion is a giant crossbow using springs instead of a bowstring. It shoots thick spears with heavy heads (stingers) and can kill sand and wind demons outright at a thousand feet, even without wards.

Shamavah: Abban's *Jiwah Ka*. She speaks fluent Thesan and is assigned to oversee Abban's operations in Hollow County.

Shanjat: Kaji *kai'Sharum* who trained with Jardir. Leader of the Spears of the Deliverer and wed to Jardir's middle sister, Hoshvah. Father of Shanvah.

Shanvah: *Sharum'ting* niece of Jardir. Daughter of Shanjat and Hoshvah.

Sharach: The smallest tribe in Krasia, with fewer than two dozen warriors at one point. They were rescued from extinction by Jardir.

Sharaj: Barrack for young boys in *Hannu Pash*, much like a military boarding school. The *sharaj* are located around the training grounds, and there is one for each tribe. The name of the tribe is a prefix, followed by an apostrophe, so the *sharaj* for the Kaji tribe is known as the Kaji'sharaj. Plural is *sharaji*.

Sharak Ka: Literally 'the First War', the great war against demon-kind the Deliverer will begin upon completion of Sharak Sun.

Sharak Sun: Literally 'the Daylight War', during which Kaji conquered the known world, uniting it in Sharak Ka. It is believed that Jardir must do the same if he is to win Sharak Ka.

Shar'Dama Ka: Literally 'First Warrior Cleric', this is the Krasian term for the Deliverer, who will come to free mankind from the *alagai*.

Sharik Hora: Literally 'heroes' bones', the name for the great temple in Krasia made out of the bones of fallen warriors. Having their bones lacquered and added to the temple is the highest honour that warriors can attain.

Sharukin: Literally 'warrior poses', practised series of movements for *sharusahk*.

Sharum: Warrior. The *Sharum* dress in robes often inlaid with fired clay plates as armour.

Sharum Ka: Literally 'First Warrior', a title in Krasia for the secular leader of *alagai'sharak*. The Sharum Ka is appointed by the Andrah, and the *kai'Sharum* of all tribes answer to him and him only from dusk until dawn. The Sharum Ka has his own palace and sits on the Spear Throne. He wears *dal'Sharum* blacks, but his turban and night veil are white.

Sharum'ting: Female warrior. Wonda Cutter is the first recognized by Evejans.

Sharusahk: The Krasian art of unarmed combat. There are various schools of *sharusahk* depending on caste and tribe, but all consist of brutal, efficient moves designed to stun, cripple, and kill.

Shevali: Friend of Jardir and Ashan during Jardir's training in Sharik Hora, Dama Shevali is advisor to Damaji Ashan.

Shusten: Dal'Sharum son of Abban. Raised to hate his *khaffit* father.

Sikvah: Hasik's daughter by Jardir's sister Hanya, and Amanvah's personal servant. Offered to Rojer as a second bride.

Soli: Dal'Sharum brother of Inevera. *Push'ting.* Lover of Cashiv.

Spears of the Deliverer: The elite personal bodyguard to Ahmann Jardir, made up mostly of the *Sharum* from his old Maze unit.

Spear Throne: The throne of the Sharum Ka, made from the spears of previous Sharum Kas.

Stinger: The ammunition for the scorpion ballistae. Stingers are giant spears with heavy iron heads that can punch through sand demon armour on a parabolic shot.

Sunian: Artefacts from the city of Anoch Sun. Also the name of its people.

Thalaja: Jardir's second Kaji wife.

'Ting: Suffix meaning 'woman'.

Tribes: Anjha, Bajin, Jama, Kaji, Khanjin, Majah, Sharach, Krevakh, Nanji, Shunjin, Mehnding, Halvas. The prefix *am'* is used to denote both family and tribe, as in Ahmann asu Hoshkamin am'Jardir am'Kaji.

Umshala: One of Jardir's *dama'ting* wives.

Undercity: Huge honeycomb of warded caverns beneath Fort Krasia where women, children, and *khaffit* are locked at night to keep them safe from corelings while the men fight.

Vah: Literally 'daughter' or 'daughter of'. Used as a suffix when a girl is named after her mother or father, as in Amanvah, or as a prefix in a full name, as in Amanvah vah Ahmann am'Jardir am'Kaji.

Waning: (1) Three-day monthly religious observance for Evejans occurring on the days before, of, and after the new moon. Attendance at Sharik Hora is mandatory, and families spend the days together, even pulling sons out of *sharaj.* Demons are supposedly stronger these nights, when it is said Alagai Ka walks the surface. (2) The three nights each month when it is dark enough for mind demons to rise to the surface.

Watchers: Watchers are the *dal'Sharum* of the Krevakh and Nanji tribes. Trained in special weapons and tactics, they serve as scouts, spies, and assassins. Each Watcher carries an iron-shod ladder about twelve feet long and a short stabbing spear. The ladders are light, flexible, and strong. They have interconnecting ends (male/top, female/bottom), and so many ladders can be joined together. Watchers are so proficient they can run straight up a ladder without bracing it and balance at the top.

Zahven: Ancient Krasian word meaning 'rival', 'nemesis', or 'peer'.